HISTORIC

HOUSTON STREETS

*Includes streets in Brazoria, Galveston, Montgomery,
Ft. Bend, Waller, Harris and Liberty Counties*

bright sky press
HOUSTON, TEXAS

2365 Rice Boulevard, Suite 202,
Houston, Texas 77005
www.brightskypress.com

10 9 8 7 6 5 4 3 2 1

Library of Congress Cataloging-in-Publication Data on file with publisher.

Creative Direction by Ellen Cregan
Design by Marla Garcia
Printed in Canada

Includes streets in Brazoria, Galveston, Montgomery, Ft. Bend, Waller, Harris and Liberty Counties

The Stories Behind the Names

A definitive tale about our community's people, politics and power, courage and sacrifice, heroes and scoundrels, humor and tragedy, myths and legends—all told on the streets you drive every day.

by Marks Hinton
2nd Edition

OTHER WORKS BY MARKS HINTON

Tanglewood Tales: A History Series

The Catalyst: Historic Series

Afton Village Streets: A History

Inside Sacred Spaces with Aaron Howard

The Great Houston History Quiz with Aaron Howard

Paved in History: The Colorful Stories Behind Houston's Historic Streets

And Death Came from the Sea:
In the Catastrophic Wake of Hurricane Ike

One Ocean and Seven Seas: A Grand Voyage

A Modern Tour of the Spanish Main:
Exploring the Isthmus of Panama and Cartagena

Visitors Guide to the Beer Can House:
An Annotated History of the Environment's Creation and Guided Tour

WORKS IN PROGRESS

The Short Stories of Marks Hinton

Houston's Historic Cemeteries: Tales from Beyond the Crypt

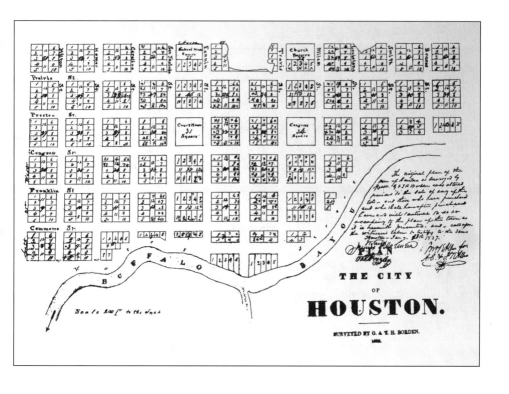

The First Map of Houston – 1836
Houston Metropolitan Research Center

BRIGHT SKY PRESS

DEDICATION

This book is dedicated to my wife Barbara,
my best friend, strongest supporter, travel companion
and the most wonderful woman I have ever known

and

to the memory of my parents, C. Marks Hinton Sr. and
Mocco Dunn Hinton
whose unyielding belief in education
made me the man I am today

and

in memory of George W. Donehoo, Jr
(1935 – 2009)

PREFACE

I wrote *Historic Houston Streets: The Stories Behind the Names* for three reasons. First, no one in the 174 years since Houston was founded had produced such a book. I felt the information discovered during the nine years of research I conducted would be of interest to the citizens of Houston. I received a letter from Mayor Bill White following the first printing thanking me for my efforts. He said "we will put it to good use." Second, while considerable historical information existed there was no central place that one could go to easily get an answer on "Who is this street named for?" This book answers many but not all of those questions about the highways and byways of our area. Today it is available in 38 Houston libraries and 8 Harris County libraries, as well as the Houston Metropolitan Research Center's Texas Room at the main library downtown. Librarians tell me they are constantly taking calls from people who want to know who their street is named for. For the answer they turn to *Historic Houston Streets: The Stories Behind the Names*. Citizens must be interested in the subject judging by the number of invitations I receive to address historical societies, civic clubs, senior citizen groups, church gatherings and professional societies to mention a few. My talk at the Houston Heritage Society still holds the record for attendance at almost three times the average turnout for their monthly lecture series. And lastly, I wrote it for my own pleasure. Houston area streets have always been an unending source of fascination to me. I sincerely enjoyed looking through old books, maps, newspapers and anything else I thought might yield another answer. In addition I was able to interview a large number of Houstonians who were willing to share any information about streets with me. Despite publishing this second edition I will never stop gathering information about our areas streets and will continue to publish new discoveries on my web site, archivaltexas.com.

I truly believe that after over nine years of researching this subject I have succeeded in amassing in one book a huge amount of information about not only Houston streets but hundreds in cities, towns and rural areas of Harris, Galveston, Brazoria, Montgomery, Waller, Liberty and Ft. Bend counties. My goal is to make sure this book remains the seminal source of information on our streets and roads for the next 174 years.

Marks Hinton
The Street Whisperer
Houston, Texas

ACKNOWLEDGEMENTS

Jessie Anderson – black historian

Thomas Anderson – attorney-at-law

Thu Nhi Barrus – opera expert

Vivian Bennett – my second biggest supporter

August C. Bering III – multigenerational Houstonian

Trevia Wooster Beverly – Texas historian

Kelly Blakley – Gandalf of Graphics

Lou Carvelli – CBI Corporation

Katherine Center – Heights resident

Betty Trapp Chapman – Houston historian

Sherrie Chisholm – Norhill Historic District

Karla Cisneros – Spring resident

Daughters of the Republic of Texas

Carl Detering Jr. – multigenerational Houstonian

Deborah Detering – multigenerational Houstonian

Gay Donehoo – editing assistant

George Donehoo – main man & research sidekick

Susan Smith Dorsey – Texas General Land Office

Joel Draut – Houston Metropolitan Research Center, Archives

Ivon Dupont – Heights resident

Lynn Edmundson – Historic Houston

Christine Farrier – Old West End Association

Kirk Ferris – Houston historian

Jan Gibson – Westmoreland Preservation Alliance

Dora Guerra – Daughters of the Republic of Texas Library

Virginia Hancock – Houston historian

Mary Lou Henry – Vernon Henry & Associates

Nancy Hernandez – Houston Chronicle

Barbara Bennett Hinton – chief editor and publisher of 1st Edition

C. Marks Hinton Sr. – old time Houstonian

Mocco Dunn Hinton – old time Houstonian

Dorothy Knox Houghton – Houston historian

Houston Heritage Society

Will Howard – manager, Texas Room, Houston Public Library

Vivian Seals Hubbard – Houston historian

Flossie Huckabee – Heights resident

Lee McClellan – River Oaks Property Owners Association

Leslie Mickellis – George's Diner

Mary Catherine Farrington Miller – author

Syd Moen – Historic Houston

Terri Mote – Bellaire Library

Tracy Murley – Texas Medical Center

Randy Pace – Historical Preservation Officer, City of Houston

Patricia Smith Prather – Houston historian

Imogene Pulleine – LaPorte resident

Mary Ramos – Texas Almanac

John Raia – Senior Planner-Planning & Development, City of Houston

Tim Rice – thoroughbred-racing expert

Yvonne Robertson, Houston historian

Sister Wilfred Shorten – Sisters of Charity of the Incarnate Word

Staff at Texas Room (Ellen, Nina, Mirasol & Doug) – No request was too much

Harvey Strain – black historian

Mike Stude – multigenerational Houstonian

Courtney Key Tardy – Greater Houston Preservation Alliance

Paul Teten – Texas historian

Texas General Land Office and Texas Veterans Land Board

Texas State Library and Archives Commission

Bart Truxillo – architectural preservationist

Jerry Wood – Deputy Assistant Director-Planning & Development-City of Houston

A. J. FOYT: A Houston native, Foyt was the first racecar driver to win four Indianapolis 500s (1961, 1964, 1967, 1977). He also won the Daytona 500 and the 24-hours of Le Mans. [1]

A. P. GEORGE RANCH: Albert P. George (1873-1955) and his wife Mamie (1877-1971) owned a large ranch in Fort Bend that they inherited from her family. In addition to raising cattle, oil and gas was discovered in 1923 and again in 1931 dramatically increasing their net worth. In 1945 the Georges established the George Foundation for "...religious, charitable and/or education purposes... for the use and benefit of the people of Fort Bend County." Over the years these philanthropists gave grants to establish the Polly Ryan Memorial Hospital, George Memorial Library, George Observatory, George Ranch Historical Park and many other projects in the Richmond/Rosenberg area. [2]

ABBOTT: Newton C. – Born in New York in the 1850s, Abbott came to Houston in 1900 and opened his law practice. He gave some of his westside land to the city for the construction of a school. Consequently the street and the school were named for him. The school no longer exists but the building had a short reincarnation as a hamburger stand in the early 1980s. [3]

ABERCROMBIE: The Abercrombies were significant landowners in Houston. However, they made their fortune in the oilfield equipment business. James "Jim" Smithers Abercrombie invented the blowout preventer to keep an oil well under control when large pockets of high-pressure gas were hit while drilling. He partnered with Harry Cameron to found Cameron Iron Works, a company that became a world leader in the manufacture of oil well equipment. [4]

ACADEMY: Developers of West University Place chose to name many of the streets in their addition for famous colleges and universities in keeping with the neighborhood's proximity to Rice University (nee Institute). Since academy is defined as "a secondary or college preparatory school, especially a private one," it only makes sense that it is located in this community with its focus on higher learning. [5]

ACADIA: See sidebar *Laissez les bon temps roulez* (Let the good times roll), page 188.

ADAGIO: See sidebar **It's Music to My Ears,** page 218.

ADAMS: John – Based on the historical evidence of accomplishments during his term as President of the United States, it would seem this street is named for John and not his son John Quincy. A revolutionary hero, signatory of the Declaration of Independence and George Washington's Vice President, John Adams became the 2nd President of the United States (1789-1801). He was the first President to live in the White House. [6]

ADDICKS LEVEE: Addicks Reservoir is on South Mayde Creek in western Harris County. This rolled earthen levee is 61,166 feet long, 121 feet high and covers 129 square miles. It was built by the U. S. Army Corps of Engineers in 1948 to provide flood control for Buffalo Bayou and the San Jacinto River. (See **Addicks** and **Mayde Creek.**) [7]

ADDICKS-HOWELL: T. E. Howell was a principal landowner of a village on the Harris/Fort Bend County lines named Howellville. It was a stop on the Texas & New Orleans Railroad. Except for the street named for Mr. Howell, Howellville has passed into history. [8]

ADDICKS-SATSUMA: (See **Dairy Ashford.**)

ADDICKS: Henry J. – "Neither snow nor rain nor heat nor gloom of night stayed this courier from the swift completion of his appointed rounds" and as a result Mr. Addicks was honored by several roads in west Houston bearing his name including **Addicks-Clodine, Addicks-Fairbanks** and **Addicks-Howell.** He was the first postman in Addicks, Texas, a village named for him in 1884. Prior to that date, the town was known as Bear Creek (named for the nearby waterway), Bear Hill and Letitia. [9]

ADDISON: Joseph – Often in an attempt to make a neighborhood appear more intellectual than those around it, a real estate developer will name the streets for well-known authors, poets and playwrights. This practice caught on in our fair city many years ago. Addison was an Englishman who wrote poems, prose and essays. These works were often published in *The Tatler*, a magazine he founded. [10]

ADKINS: Elbert E., Sr. – He came to Houston in the early 1900s from Ripley, Ohio. His wife, Grace Noble, was the granddaughter of Houston Mayor I. C. Lord (1875-6). Adkins established a very successful real estate development and insurance business. (See **Noble.**) [11]

AFFIRMED: Winner of the 1978 Kentucky Derby and the last Triple Crown (Derby, Preakness and Belmont) winner. His battles with rival Alydar were the stuff of racing legend. While Affirmed defeated Alydar for the Crown, each race was closer than the previous one. [12]

AFTON: See sidebar **All Things English,** page 175.

AFTONSHIRE: See sidebar **All Things English,** page 175.

AGASSI ACE: Andre Agassi was an American tennis professional. An early phenom, he gained a reputation of not being able to win the big matches. He eventually proved his critics wrong by capturing major titles at Wimbledon (1992), the U.S. Open (1994 and 1999), the Australian Open (1995 and 2001) and the French Open (1999). He is one of only a few tennis players to have won each Grand Slam tournament. [13]

AIRFIELD: This short street leads to Williams Airfield, a private airstrip in southern Montgomery County. [14]

AIRHART: This Baytown street is named for a family of early settlers. [15]

AIRLINE: On a 1930 Houston city map North Main appears to dead end at Airline, a street that goes north on the map straight as an arrow. Near the outskirts of town Airline became U.S. Highway 75, the main route to Dallas before the construction of Interstate 45. The story is that the street was named because this was the route an airline would fly to go directly to Dallas. [16]

AIRLINE: This unique neighborhood, Polly Ranch Estates, southeast of Friendswood, has its own airstrip. In 1953 Raymond Kliesing developed this area prior to earning his pilot's license. He also created a park with an island he called Monkey Island. It received its name when his brother, Donald, was given a monkey as a pet. Donald thought his pet needed female companionship so he acquired another monkey from a local pet shop. It was not long before the island was teeming with their offspring. Unfortunately the monkeys were wiped out in a huge flood in the 1970s. [17]

AIRPORT: This boulevard is the main thoroughfare fronting William P. Hobby Airport from which it derives its name. One of Houston's longer streets it runs from the Gulf Freeway on the east into Fort Bend County on the west. (See photograph on page 12.) [18]

ALADDIN: He was the boy hero of *Arabian Nights* who possessed a magic lamp that contained two genies. When he rubbed the lamp they would appear and do his bidding.

ALAMO: This street is named for the most recognizable site in the state of Texas. It was originally named San Antonio de Padua Mission and then changed to San Antonio de Valero Mission in 1718. The cornerstone of the building we see today in

» **AIRPORT: Houston architect Joseph Finger designed this terminal in 1940**

San Antonio was laid in 1744. The mission's purpose was to Christianize and educate the local Indians. It was abandoned in 1793. Ten years later it was occupied by a troop of Mexican soldiers. It was at this time that it became known as the Alamo, most likely resulting from its location near a grove of cottonwood (*alamo* in Spanish) trees. Of course, it is remembered for the famous 13 day siege that occurred here during the Texas Revolution. (See **Travis, Crockett** and **James Bowie.**)

ALBANS: See sidebar **Southampton's English Streets,** page 255.

ALDEN BRIDGE: This street is named for the Louisiana hometown of Woodlands Operating Company president, Roger Galatas. [19]

ALDERNEY: See sidebar **All Things English,** page 175.

ALDERON WOODS: Susan Vreeland-Wendt, marketing director of the Woodlands Operating Company, names the streets in that neighborhood. Although this one is misspelled (it should be Alderaan) it recalls the home planet of Princess Leia from the movie *Star Wars*. Obi-Wan Kenobi and Luke Skywalker hire Han Solo in the famous scene in the Mos Eisley Cantina to fly them to Alderaan. She named **Millennium Forest** for the Millennium Falcon, a modified Corellian freighter, flown by Han Solo and his first mate, Chewbacca. [20]

ALDINE: This small village on Houston's north side was a station on the International-Great Northern Railroad beginning in the 1890s. The place and the streets were named after a family who owned a farm in the area. Today Aldine is usually connected with another name such as **Aldine-Mail, Aldine-Bender, Aldine-Westfield,** etc. [21]

ALEXANDER: C. Q. "Kid" – He was the mayor of Goose Creek before it was annexed by Baytown. [22]

ALEXANDER: Robert – This early Baytown citizen was a well-known Methodist missionary in the 1840s. He founded what is today known as the Cedar Bayou United Methodist Church. This sanctuary was originally called Alexander Chapel. [23]

ALGOA: This is a small village in northern Galveston County. It was founded in 1880 along the Gulf, Colorado & Santa Fe railroad line. Up until 1957 Algoa was mainly an agricultural community raising figs, pears, oranges and strawberries. Then oil was discovered nearby and Milwhite Mud Company, a manufacturer of drilling fluids became a major employer. [24]

ALIEF-CLODINE: The earliest settlers of the town of Dairy were John S. and Alief Ozelda Magee. Mrs. Magee's first application for a post office was rejected because of possible confusion with another Texas town so the citizens decided to honor her by changing the name to Alief. In the early days she operated the post office out of the front room of her home. **Clodine,** in Fort Bend County, was a station on the San Antonio & Aransas Pass Railroad. It was named for a railroad employee named Clodine King. [25, 26]

ALLEGRO: See sidebar **It's Music to My Ears,** page 218.

» ALIEF O. MAGEE: Tombstone

» ALLEN PARKWAY: Looking east on Allen Parkway when it was still known as Buffalo Drive

» ALLEN PARKWAY: Portrait of Houston co-founder, John Kirby Allen

THE BELLAIRE TREE STREET NAMES

William W. Baldwin, the developer of Bellaire and Westmoreland Farms, was a man with a plan. It was no small plan either. His goal was to turn a treeless prairie southwest of Houston into "the future garden spot of the South." He actively marketed his landscape plans and was soon talking with editors of magazines interested in gardening. He enlisted three important partners to help pull off this grandiose scheme. Frank L. Dormant was a civil engineer who worked for the City of Houston from 1902 to 1905. Edward Teas was the owner of Teas Nursery Company. He was hired to handle the planting of the greenery. Sid J. Hare was a landscape architect with the Kansas City firm of Hare & Hare. In order to convey the impression that Bellaire was a garden city, Hare decided to name many of the streets after trees. According to *Perspective,* for some unknown reason, Hare's street names were not used but other tree names were substituted. For example, Hare's Olive became Chestnut and Evergreen became Beech. Never-the-less Bellaire still has a number of streets named for trees and shrubs. They are as follows: **Pin Oak, Elm, Palmetto, Beech, Locust, Spruce, Cedar, Live Oak, Acacia, Laurel, Magnolia, Willow, Oleander, Birch, Pine, Holly, Mimosa, Maple, Aspen, Jessamine, Palm, Azalea, Huisache, Wisteria, Fern, Linden** and **Mulberry.** And finally **Holt,** an archaic Middle English word meaning a wood or grove. [1]

ALLEN PARKWAY: Our city's *laissez faire* attitude has been part of our warp and woof from the beginning. In 1836 two New York real estate speculators, John Kirby Allen and his brother Augustus Chapman Allen, bought half a league of land on Buffalo Bayou, just north of the town of Harrisburg. As the Bayou was deep enough for navigation, they laid out a town and named it after General Sam Houston. The rest is history and an interesting story it is. John died of disease just two years after the city's founding. Augustus lived until 1864 when he passed away from pneumonia. This beautiful parkway was called Buffalo Drive until its name was changed in 1961 to honor Houston's Founding Fathers. (See photographs on page 13.) [27]

ALLEN STREET: There are two possible sources for this street. The most likely is Henry R. Allen, the brother of city founders John and Augustus Allen. He was an early landowner in the Sixth Ward where parts of this street are located. Allen was also a city alderman, helped organize the first Chamber of Commerce in 1840 and strongly backed the creation of a deep-water port in Houston. Next is Augustus C. Allen, a co-founder of Houston and the owner of a large tract of land north of where this street is located. The street first appeared on a city map in 1839. [28]

ALLEN: N. A. – Most likely this street is named for a well respected and long time black educator in Needville. In 1960 the elementary school was also given this person's name. [29]

ALLISON: One of the two firms that developed Pearland was the Allison-Richey Suburban Garden Company. Why Allison got a street named for him in what was called "an agricultural Eden" and Richey did not remains a mystery. [30]

ALLSTON: Early investors in Houston Heights lived in this Boston suburb. It was named for Washington Allston, an artist from Cambridge, Massachusetts. One of his paintings, "Fields West of Boston" is of Allston. Originally a livestock and railroad town, today it is home for Harvard, M.I.T., Boston College and Boston University. Notable citizens include New York City Mayor Michael Bloomberg and members of the rock band Aerosmith. [31]

ALMEDA SCHOOL: This road leads to Almeda Elementary School. (See **Almeda-Genoa.**) [32]

ALMEDA-GENOA: This road runs between the southwestern Harris County towns of Almeda, named by Dr. Willis King for his daughter, to the town of Genoa (named for the Italian city by its founder J. H. Burnett). It ran along the Galveston, Houston & Henderson Railroad line. [33, 34]

ALTAIR: See sidebar **Starry Night,** page 111.

ALTIC: Russell — See sidebar **Houston Streets Named for Men Killed During World War I,** page 22. [35]

ALUMNI: Located on the campus of Rice University this street near the football stadium recalls the graduates of this outstanding institution of higher learning. [36]

ALVIN-SUGAR LAND: In 1876 Alvin Morgan founded the town of Alvin as a station on the Houston Tap & Brazoria Railroad. Sugar Land is named for the sugar cane fields and sugar mill located there. Up until the mid-1940s the Imperial Sugar Company operated the world's largest sugar refinery here. [37, 38]

ALYDAR: This thoroughbred may be the best racehorse to ever place second. In 1977 as a two-year-old colt Alydar began what was to become a legendary rivalry with Affirmed. These two horses captivated the racing public with their head to head duels for two years. For the fading Calumet Farms, the once mythic Kentucky thoroughbred stable, Alydar was a final burst of glory. Despite losing each Triple Crown race in 1978 to Affirmed, Alydar's "never quit" resoluteness earned him a place in racing lore. (See **Affirmed.**) [39]

ALYSHEBA: This 1987 Kentucky Derby winner turned in one of the greatest racing performances of all time. Coming down the stretch Alysheba caught the rear hooves of race leader Bet Twice. He stumbled and it looked as if horse and jockey, Chris McCarron, were about to go head over heels. But somehow Alysheba regained his balance, took up the chase again and nipped Bet Twice at the wire to win by 3/4 of a length. Those who saw the race called McCarron's ride the greatest of the 20th century. [40]

AMC: This short street leads to the AMC 20 Cineplex at Katy Mills. [41]

AMERICAN PETROLEUM: This early Texas oil company is credited with finding the massive Goose Creek Oilfield near Baytown. On August 23, 1916 drilling contractor Charles Mitchell hit pay dirt at 2,017 feet. That well came in at 10,000 barrels per day. Over its productive lifetime this field produced 140,644,377 barrels of crude oil. (See **Galliard** and **Goose Creek.**) [42]

AMHERST: This street is named for a liberal arts college founded in 1821 in the small Massachusetts town of the same name. [43]

ANACORTES: It is possible that this street is named for Anacortes, Washington where both Texaco and Shell Oil (both firms with close ties to Houston) constructed refineries in the 1950s. [44]

ANCHOR: Now a virtual ghost town, Anchor, was a thriving community from the 1850s until the 1920s when three rail lines passed it. First known as Fruitland, Jacob Whistler changed the name in 1895 to recall his hometown of Anchor, Illinois. It was a trading center for the many Brazoria County farmers who raised corn and cotton in the area. One of the more unusual businesses here was a large plant for processing frog legs. [45]

ANCLA: See sidebar **Learn a Foreign Language on Your Morning Walk,** page 125.

ANDANTE: See sidebar **It's Music to My Ears,** page 218.

ANDRAU: Evert Willem Karel – This World War II veteran served in the U.S. Army Air Corps where he developed his affinity for flying. Born of Dutch parents in Sumatra, Indonesia, his family immigrated to California prior to the Japanese capture of Indonesia in the early 1940s. He joined Shell Oil Company as a geologist and moved to Houston following the close of the War. Andrau was nicknamed the "Flying Dutchman" as he used a private plane to visit many remote oil well locations. Andrau Airport was built on a rice farm he owned out Westheimer Road in 1946. He was killed in a plane crash in 1951 but his airfield continued to operate for another 47 years. It was sold to real estate developers in 1998 and is now a planned community. [46]

ANDREWS: John – Andrews came from Virginia in the late 1830s and settled in Houston. He was president of the Buffalo Bayou Company, a maritime services firm. He bought 10 acres of land in Freedman's Town where this street is today. Active in local politics Andrews served as mayor in 1841-42. In return for granting the city the right of way to put a street through his property, the street was named for him in about 1890. [47]

ANDRUS: This is an old Fort Bend County family. William Andrus was among the first of Stephen F. Austin's colonists. His son, Walter Andrus, was born here in 1830. They were farmers and cattlemen. [48]

ANGLETON: This Brazoria County community was founded in 1890 by Lewis R. Bryan Sr. and Faustino Kiber. It was named for the wife of the general manager of the Velasco Terminal Railroad that passed through Angleton. Confederate general Albert Sidney Johnson's plantation, China Grove, was very near here. One odd and little known fact about this community is the last legal hanging in Texas took place here on August 31, 1923. (See **China Grove.**) [49]

ANITA: She was one of the daughters of Samuel K. McIlhenny, a wealthy merchant in early Houston. Anita, her sister **Rosalie** and their mother Eva made the fatal mistake of going to the family's beach house in Galveston on the weekend of September 8, 1900. That was when the most devastating hurricane in history ripped into Galveston Island killing more than 7,000 persons, the three women among them. Their bodies were miraculously recovered and returned to Houston for burial in the family plot in Glenwood Cemetery. The streets Anita and Rosalie, just south of McIlhenny Street, first appear on the 1900 Houston map. They were cut between Tuam and Elgin that year. These streets were named in honor of these sisters, victims of the Great Storm of 1900. (See **McIlhenny.**) [50]

» **ANITA: Anita Mary McIlhenny's tombstone in Glenwood Cemetery**

ANNAPOLIS: Founded in 1845 the United States Naval Academy is located in Annapolis MD. The nickname of this military college is "Annapolis." [51]

ANNUNCIATION: Under law there is a separation of church and state; but, Planning & Development may not disallow a street name unless it is repetitious, so developers are free to use religious references on their plats. This street is named for the Angel

Gabriel's announcement to the Virgin Mary that Jesus was conceived in the womb of Mary and he is the Son of God. In a possible fit of religious fervor the developer named the street just to the south **Guadalupe,** as in the Virgin of. [52]

ANTHA: Elbert Adkins, Sr. – He was the developer of Tidwell Timbers Addition and named this street after his daughter. The next street to the north of Antha is **Rietta,** his second daughter. [53]

ANTIETAM: On September 17, 1862 the bloodiest battle of the War Between the States occurred. On that morning General Robert E. Lee and 35,000 Confederate soldiers squared off against General George B. McClellan and his 95,000 Union troops. By sundown 4,808 men were dead, the most people ever to die in a battle on American soil. This place will always be remembered as "Bloody Antietam." [54]

ANZIO: In January 1944 Allied troops landed at this Italian beach town to divert German forces away from Cassino. Because of the success of the attack here troops were able to the capture Rome in June of that year. Anzio also happens to be the birthplace of Roman emperors Nero and Caligula. [55]

APOLLO: See sidebar **Space City U.S.A. or "Houston the Eagle Has Landed",** page 106.

APPALOOSA: The developer of Saratoga Ranch Addition chose an equine theme for the streets. Appaloosa is a North American saddle horse noted for its spotted rump. **Palomino** is an Arabian horse with a golden or tan coat and a white or cream colored mane and tail. **Bay** is a reddish-brown horse with a black tail and mane. **Sorrel** horses have a brownish orange to light brown coat. **Pinto,** also called a Paint horse, has patchy markings of white with other darker colors. [56]

APPIAN WAY: This is the most famous of the Roman roads. Begun in 312 B.C. it extended more than 350 miles and was the main highway to Greece. It had connecting roads to Naples and Rome's seaport. [57]

APPOMATTOX: This is a small town in south central Virginia where Robert E. Lee surrendered to Ulysses S. Grant at the courthouse on April 9, 1865, thus ending the Civil War. [58]

ARCHER: This street recalls a ghost town that was located east of Old River. The settlement existed in the 1830s but was eventually absorbed by the community of Old River-Winfree, Texas. [59]

ARCHIBALD BLAIR: Williamsburg Colony Addition has many streets related to that historic Virginia community. Born in Edinburgh, Scotland in 1665 he immigrated to Williamsburg in 1690 following graduation from medical school. He was one of the first doctors in the colony. He died in 1733. [60]

OUR CITY'S BIRTH CERTIFICATE

Before we had our first map or our first street name we had to be declared a city. That happened on December 22, 1836.

━━━━━ ∞ ━━━━━

Laws of the Republic of Texas

AN ACT

Locating the Seat of Justice for County of Harrisburg, and other purposes.

Sec. 1. Be it enacted, by the senate and house of representatives of the republic of Texas, in congress assembled, That the seat of justice for the county of Harrisburg be, and the same is hereby established at the town of Houston. Sec. 6. And be it further enacted, That the Island of Galveston, shall for the future be included within the limits of the county of Harrisburg, and be, and compose a part of said county.

IRA INGRAM
Speaker of the House of Representatives
RICHARD ELLIS
President pro tem. of the Senate
Approved, Dec. 22, 1836
SAM HOUSTON

ARDENNES: Also known as the "Battle of the Bulge," this audacious German attack on the Western front caught Allied forces by surprise in mid-December of 1944. It was the Nazis last offensive thrust and was the greatest pitched battle ever fought by American soldiers before or since. More than one million military personnel were involved in this gargantuan conflict. In this Allied victory the German Air Force was destroyed with the loss of more than 300 pilots. [61]

ARLINGTON: Houston Heights developer O. M. Carter named this street for Arlington Mills, a large cotton mill in Lawrence, Massachusetts. (See **Lawrence.**) [62]

ARMOUR: One of the earliest industrial ventures on the newly opened Houston Ship

Channel in 1914 was the Armour Fertilizer Works. Due to the confluence of railroads, shipping lines and chemical plants, phosphate was readily available to be used in the production of fertilizer. This company is also remembered for the publication of *Armour's Farmers Almanac* in the 1920s and 1930s. [63]

ARNOLD: Because of its location between Browning and Marlowe, both famous English authors, it is most likely that this street is named for Matthew Arnold, an English poet and literary critic. He is remembered for two volumes of his poetry, *Narrative and Elegiac Poems* (1869) and *Dramatic And Lyric Poems* (1869). There is an outside chance, however, since he is the least well-known of any writer for whom a West University Place street is named that the street might recall A. V. Arnold, vice president of Preston R. Plumb's Realty Servicing Corporation. It was not unusual for developers in that neighborhood to name streets for themselves. (See **Plumb** and **Jarrard.**) [64]

> ## THE BELLAIRE STREETS NAMED FOR WOMEN
>
> Mary Catherine Farrington Miller verified this story for me. When developer Jim West went to file his plat for this section of Bellaire he did not have all of the street names filled in, a requirement for a plat to be accepted by the city. Not wanting to waste any more time he whipped out his pen and began furiously filling in the blank spaces on his map. He first named a street after himself. Then began to list the names of the wives of his partners and all of the women who worked in his office. This solved the problem and today we have streets in Bellaire remembering **Jim West, Dorothy, Darsey, Mildred, Cynthia, Jane, Effie, Valerie, Betty, Lula, Edith, Bess** and **Vivian.** However, prior to developing the property, West sold it to William Farrington, who would also create Tanglewood. He asked West the provenance of the female street names and was told the story. Farrington found the story amusing and left well enough alone even though he could have re-plated the neighborhood and given the streets new names. [2]

ARNOT: See sidebar **Texas Heroes' Names for Houston Streets Urged in 72 Proposed Changes,** page 96.

ARROYO: See sidebar **Learn a Foreign Language on Your Morning Walk,** page 125.

ARTESIAN: In the late 1880s Houston's water supply was questionable. The city could not afford to build a water system so a private company dammed Buffalo Bayou and was selling water from the reservoir. Unfortunately it was not potable. However, in the early 1890s, it was discovered that Houston was sitting on a huge supply of pure artesian water. This street is named for the early well drilled by Houston Water Works on the banks of the bayou. Old maps produced by the Sanford Insurance Company clearly show the location of the well, suction pipes, water pumps and water pipes. (See photograph on page 21.) [65]

ARTHUR: William – Arthur came to Texas in 1850 from Kentucky. He was a farmer and fought for the Confederacy in the War Between the States. In 1894 his son, Hugh,

» ARTESIAN: The original Waterworks, now the site of the Downtown Aquarium

acquired a small Baytown cemetery where his father is buried. What makes this story interesting is the Arthur-Hale Cemetery is now inside the boundaries of the Exxon Mobil Refinery, the largest refinery in the United States and to my knowledge the only refinery in America with a cemetery. Six Texas pioneers are interred here in this 28'x28' plot. Exxon Mobil and its predecessor, Humble Oil & Refining Company, have maintained the graveyard since 1919. [66]

ASHBEL: Born in Connecticut in 1805, Ashbel Smith is one of Texas' renaissance men. He arrived in Texas just after the Revolution in 1837. Smith held a medical degree from Yale and was appointed Surgeon General of the Texas Army. Also a great statesman, he served as Secretary of State of the Republic of Texas and was *charge d'affaires* to Great Britain, France, Belgium and Spain. Following Texas' admission into the Union, Smith was elected to several terms in the State Legislature. He was a veteran of the Mexican War and the War Between the States. Smith was

» ASHBEL: Old Red at University of Texas Medical Branch Galveston

elected the first president of the Board of Regents of the University of Texas. It was due to his diligent efforts that the University's medical branch was built in Galveston. Architect Nicholas Clayton's beautiful building on that campus is named in his honor. Most people now know it by its nickname "Old Red." [67]

HOUSTON STREETS NAMED FOR MEN KILLED DURING WORLD WAR I

With the exception of the Civil War, the First World War was probably the most horrific event in American history up to that time. Hundreds of thousands of young American servicemen and women marched off to fight the "War to End All Wars" and many came home in a pine box. We were a much smaller city in 1920. People knew their neighbors and felt the grief at the lost son or daughter in the conflict of 1914-18. The combination of great angst and a desire to honor those that gave their lives in defense of their country prompted City Council to name a number of streets for those fallen heroes. Today many of those names are engraved on a brass plaque mounted on a large stone memorial behind the Heritage Society Museum at 1100 Bagby. Those persons with street names in their honor include: Russell **Altic** (U. S. Army – died of disease), Max **Autry** (U. S. Army – lost aboard ship), John L. **Banks** (U. S. Army – killed in action) or William W. **Banks** (U.S. Army – killed in action), Earl **Barkdull** (U.S. Army – killed in action), S. L. **Barnes** (U.S. Army – killed in action), H. B. **Bartlett** (U.S. Army – killed in action), Cecil G. **Bethea** (U.S. Army – killed in action), George H. **Bissonnet** (U. S. Army Air Corps – died in an aviation accident), Thomas R. **Brailsford** (U. S. Navy – unknown cause of death), Felix H. **Briley** (U.S. Army – killed in action), Captain John R. **Burkett** (U.S. Army – killed in action), Frank P. **Burkhart** (U. S. Marines – died of disease), Hugo O. **Byrne** (U.S. Army – died of wounds), Sergeant Henry R. **Canfield** (U. S. Army – died by accident), Joseph B. **Caylor** (U. S. Marines – killed in action), W. E. **Chandler** (U. S. Army – died of disease), William B. **Cowart** (Aviator – missing in action), Samuel L. **D'Amico** (U. S. Army – died of disease), Thomas **Dismuke** (U. S. Navy – killed in action), Justin **Dorbandt** (U. S. Army – died of disease), Herbert D. **Dunlavy** (U.S. Marines – killed in action), Lieutenant Karl L. **Elliott** (U. S. Army – died of disease), M. D. **Everton** (U. S. Army – killed in a Houston riot), August J. **Fashion** (U. S. Army – died of wounds), Lewis **Floyd** (U. S. Marines – died of disease), Captain R. M. **Gibson** (U. S. Army – died of disease), Lee G. **Glogler** (U. S. Army – died of disease), Alphonse **Gonzales** (U. S. Army – missing in action), Sergeant Thomas **Green** (U. S. Army – died of wounds), Lawrence **Halpern** (U. S. Navy – lost at sea), John P. **Hawkins** (U. S. Army – died of disease), Earl **Hicks** (U. S. Army – died of disease) or Thomas B. **Hicks** (U. S. Army – died of wounds), Fred **Hopkins** (U.S. Army – killed in action), Lawrence C. **Jensen** (U. S. Marines – killed in action), Ralph A. **Johnson** (U. S. Army – died on shipboard), William J. **Jones** (U. S. Army – died of disease), Colin M. **Lemke** (U. S. Army – died of disease), Andrew **McCall** (U.S. Army – killed in action), Allen J. **McDonald** (U. S. Army – died of disease), Lieutenant John McK. **McIntosh** (U.S. Army – killed in action), Dr. H. Lee **McNeil** (U. S. Army – died of disease), Chester A. **Meek** (U.S. Army – killed in action), Charles E. **Miller** (U.S. Army – killed in action) or James E. **Miller** (U.S. Army – killed in action), Ollie **Mills** (U.S. Army – killed in action), Lieutenant Frank M. **Moore** (Aviator – killed in action) or Thomas W. **Moore** (U. S. Army – died by accident), Roscoe W. **Morris** (U. S. Navy – died by accident), Dominick **Naplava** (U. S. Army – killed in action), Robert E. **Nettleton** (U. S. Army – died of disease), Claud **Nicholson** (U.S. Army – killed in action), Sam L. **Norvic** (Aviator – died by accident), W. M. **O'Reilly** (U.S. Marines – killed in action), Charles H. **Patterson** (U. S. Marines – died of wounds), Sergeant R. C. **Pecore** (U. S. Army – died of disease), Nathan L. **Pizner** (U. S. Marines – killed in action), Sergeant T. H. **Quinn** (U. S. Army – died of disease), Sergeant Charles E. **Russell** (U. S. Army – died of disease), William L. **Sanders** (U. S. Army – died of disease), Herman **Sauer** (information not available), Marion **Schuler** (U. S. Army – died of wounds), Claud C. **Simmons** (U. S. Army – died of disease) or William L. **Simmons** (U.S. Army – killed in action), Sergeant Drue **Singleton** (U. S. Army – died of disease), Oscar **Snover** (U. S. Army – died of disease), James M. **Stedman** (U. S. Army – died of disease), James L. **Styers** (U. S. Army – died of disease), Harry **Taggart** (U. S. Navy – lost at sea), Ray **Teetshorn** (Aviator – died of disease), William **Truett** (U. S. Army – died of disease), Robert E. **Tuck** (U. S. Army – died of disease), Charles **Vick** (U. S. Army – killed in action), Leland J. **Wagner** (U. S. Army – killed in action), Terrell T. **Waugh** (U. S. Marines – killed in action) Sergeant

CONTINUED ON THE NEXT PAGE

HOUSTON STREETS NAMED FOR MEN KILLED DURING WORLD WAR I, *continuation*

Joseph C. **Weber** (U. S. Marines – died of disease), Charles H. **Westcott** (U. S. Army – died of disease), Milton J. **Winkler** (U. S. Army – killed in action), Charles H. **Wood** (U. S. Army – killed in action) or Thomas W. **Wood** (U. S. Army – killed in action). [3]

These streets are also named for service men that died but there are no additional details about them: **Blossom, Butler, Collier, Kaiser** and **Lane.** This last information came from *1930 City Guide & Map* (Texas Map & Blue Print Co., 1930.)

ASHLAND: As Houston Heights co-founders Oscar M. Carter and Daniel D. Cooley were officers (president and cashier, respectively) of the First National Bank of Ashland, Nebraska before moving to the Houston area, it is likely this street is to remember that town. In addition D. D. Cooley was married in Ashland. [68]

ASHTEX: See sidebar **Howdy Tex,** page 263.

ASTON: See sidebar **Fairbanks Could Have Its Own Concours d' Elegance and Road Rally,** page 140.

ATASCOCITA: This road is most likely a misspelling of *Atascosito,* the Spanish name for a military trail laid out in the mid-1700s. It extended from the settlement and fort of Atascosito on the Trinity River through northern Harris County to Refugio and Goliad in South Texas. Eventually ranchers used it for driving cattle from Texas to New Orleans. It is probably the oldest street in the Houston area. [69]

AUBURN: A land grant college in the eastern Alabama town of the same name, it was founded in 1859. The name was changed to Auburn University in 1960. [70]

AUDEN: One of the developers of West University Place and Southside Place was Austin & Haden. This street is a contraction of the two partners' surnames, W. D. Haden and D. T. Austin. [71]

AUDUBON: See sidebar *Laissez les bon temps roulez* (Let the good times roll), page 188.

AUGUSTA: Augusta Bering was an early resident of Houston. Born here in 1860, she died in 1901. She was August Bering's niece. This street is located just west of Bering Drive in southwest Houston. (See **Bering.**) [72]

AUGUSTA: Just northeast of Golfcrest County Club this street recalls arguably the most beautiful golf links in America. The Augusta National Golf Course was designed by famed golfer Robert Trent Jones, the only person to win golf's grand slam (National Open, National Amateur, British Open and British Amateur) in the same year (1930). He founded the Masters tournament in Augusta, Georgia in 1934. [73]

HOUSTON STREETS WITH THE BEST ARCHITECTURE

Houston has been blessed over the past over the past 174 years to have had buildings and homes designed by some of finest architects in America as well as around the world. Do your self a favor and acquire a copy of Stephen Fox book, *Houston Architectural Guide*, the seminal source of architecturally significant structures in our fair city, and go for a Sunday drive on the following streets and roads for a truly awe inspiring experience. Below is a small sample of what I consider the finest examples with the street, structure, architect and date.

⊛ Bagby – City Hall – Joseph Finger - 1939
⊛ McKinney – Julia Ideson Building – William Ward Watkin - 1926
⊛ Sam Houston Park – A time capsule of Houston's architecture - 1899
⊛ Louisiana – Wells Fargo Bank Plaza – Skidmore, Owens & Merrill - 1983; Bank of America Center – Johnson/Burgee - 1983; Pennzoil Place – Johnson/Burgee - 1976; Jones Hall – Caudill Rowlett Scott - 1966
⊛ Milam – El Paso Energy Building - Skidmore, Owens & Merrill - 1963
⊛ Texas – Alley Theater – MacKie & Kamrath - 1969; Annunciation Catholic Church – Nicholas Clayton - 1871
⊛ Smith – Tranquility Park – Tapley Associates -1979; Kirby Mansion – James Bailey - 1926
⊛ Main – JPMorgan Chase Bank building – Alfred C. Finn – 1929; Sweeny, Coombs & Fredericks Building – George Dickey - 1889; Rice University Campus – Various – 1912 to today; Wortham Fountain – John Burgee - 1993
⊛ Travis – Niels Esperson Building – John Eberson - 1927: Houston Cotton Exchange & Board of Trade – Eugene Heiner - 1884
⊛ Congress – La Carafe – Unknown - 1861
⊛ West Clay – Tribeca Lofts – Joseph Finger - 1936
⊛ Caroline – Light Guard Armory – Alfred C. Finn - 1925; Houston Holocaust Museum – Ralph Appelbaum & Associates - 1996
⊛ Isabella – Isabella Courts – W. D. Bordeaux - 1929
⊛ Montrose – University of St. Thomas Administration Building – Sanguinet, Staata & Barnes\ - 1912; Contemporary Arts Museum – Gunnar Birkerts & Associates - 1972
⊛ Courtland Place – the Entire Street – Briscoe, Warren & Wetmore, Finn, etc - 1911-21
⊛ Westmoreland – Private Homes - Cook & Co., Wilmer Waldo -1905-7
⊛ Sul Ross – Rothko Chapel – Howard Barnstone – 1971; Menil Collection – Renzo Piano - 1987
⊛ Yupon - Byzantine Fresco Chapel Museum – Francois de Menil - 4011
⊛ Remington & Longfellow Lanes – Entire Streets – John F. Staub, Brisco & Dixon etc. - 1920-38
⊛ River Oaks – Entire Neighborhood – Various - 1923 to current
⊛ Fannin – St. Luke's Medical Tower – Cesar Pelli - 1991
⊛ North & South Boulevards – Entire Streets – Briscoe, Staub, Watkin, etc. - 1924-30
⊛ Tynebrook – Private Home - Bruce Goff - 1960
⊛ Tall Oaks – Private Home – Frank Lloyd Wright - 1954

» **AUSTIN: A portrait of Stephen F. Austin, Father of Texas Independence**

AUSTIN: John – Brazoria was established in 1828 when this gentleman laid out the plat for this now historic Texas town. Austin said he chose the name "for the single reason that I know of none like it in the world." [74]

AUSTIN: Stephen Fuller – He is the Father of Texas. There are volumes detailing his great accomplishments. Just prior to his untimely death at the age of 43 in 1836 he wrote, "The prosperity of Texas has been the object of my labors, the idol of my existence--it has assumed the character of a religion for the guidance of my thoughts and actions, for fifteen years." Why don't we have men and women of character like Austin in political office today? On the original map of Houston (1836) this street was called Homer for the Greek poet who authored the *Iliad* and the *Odyssey*. The name was changed in 1839. (See map page 5.) [75]

AUTRY: Max – See sidebar **Houston Streets Named for Men Killed During World War I,** page 22.

AVALON: According to Arthurian legend this is the island where the mortally wounded King Arthur was taken for burial. Some stories say Glastonbury is actually the Isle of Avalon. (See **Glastonbury.**) [76]

AVENIDA DE LAS AMERICAS: Great pressure was placed on the Planning & Development Department as well as City Council to give a Houston street this name to honor our neighbors to the south. The consuls from every Central and South American country in Houston wanted Post Oak Boulevard, the principal thoroughfare in the Galleria, changed to Avenida de las Americas. However, a compromise was reached and the new street in front of the George R. Brown Convention Center was so christened. [77]

AVENUE H: During the 1940s the Fort Bend County Fairgrounds were on this street. During World War II the U. S. military took over the property and turned it into a prisoner-of-war camp. Approximately 250 captured German soldiers were held here. The locals called the facility "Camp Fritz." Prisoners worked on farms in the area until the war ended and they were repatriated. [78]

AVONDALE: Houston historian Betty Chapman says this Montrose area street was named as the result of a citywide contest. Originally known as "Meyer's Pasture" for its owner, Joseph E. Meyer, the 31-acres was sold to the Greater Houston Improvement

Co. in 1907 for the princely sum of $105,000. Over 600 nominations were received, hoping to claim the $25 prize. Avondale was selected because of its Shakespearian connection and that it was "beautiful, musical, historical and appealed to culture, refinement and intelligence." William Shakespeare lived in Stratford-on-Avon, England. The street to the north is **Stratford.** To the south the street was called **Hathaway,** for Shakespeare's wife, Anne. However, its name was changed years ago when it was connected to Westheimer. [79]

AWTY SCHOOL: This short road leads to the Awty International School of Houston. It is one of the city's better preparatory schools. [80]

B

B. F. TERRY: Benjamin Franklin Terry's mother moved to Texas in 1834 from their home in Kentucky via Mississippi. Orphaned at a young age he was raised on the family plantation in Brazoria County. At 20 he took control of the business. In 1851 Terry won the contract to construct the first railroad in Texas: the Buffalo Bayou, Brazos & Colorado.

» **B. F. TERRY: Grave Marker in Glenwood Cemetery**

The following year he purchased the Oakland sugar plantation nearby and added considerably to his already sizable net worth. In 1861 Terry and Thomas Lubbock were named aides to General James Longstreet of the Confederate Army. Soon the Confederate War Department granted the men the authority to organize a cavalry unit, Terry's Texas Rangers. They fought with valor at the first Battle of Manassas. Terry was killed in the Battle of Woodsonville. He was praised in the Texas state senate by Governor Frank Lubbock who said "no braver man ever lived-no truer patriot ever died." [1]

B. J. LEWIS: This street is named for a black pastor who lived in the Acres Homes area. His ministry was at the Progressive Missionary Baptist Church which he founded. [2]

B. P. AMOCO: This corporation can trace its roots to 1866 when Charles Lockhart began shipping and storing crude and refined oil products. Today it is one of the world's largest energy companies and consists of Amoco, ARCO, British Petroleum and Burmah Castrol. The company explores for oil and gas, operates refineries and petrochemical plants and produces solar power. [3]

BACCHUS: He was the Roman god of wine. In Greek mythology his name is Dionysus. [4]

BACE: The Bace family purchased a farm on the south side of Katy Road that originally belonged to the Beinhorns. J. D. Bace was a land developer. (See **Beinhorn.**) [5]

BACLIFF: Once solely a weekend resort, it was originally called Clifton-by-the-Sea. In the 1960s the name was changed to Bacliff, a combination of its location on Galveston Bay and the old name of Clifton. [6]

BAGBY: Thomas M. – Born in Virginia in 1814 he moved to Houston in 1837. Bagby was a commission merchant and prosperous cotton factor. He was a Freemason and member of the Presbyterian Church. Bagby was a founder of the Library and the Julia Ideson Building stands on the site of his residence. The Houston Public Library grew out of the Houston Lyceum that he chartered March 20, 1848. Bagby was also interested in horticulture, especially roses. One of the most famous rosebushes, a Lady Banksia, was trained across the entire length of Bagby's front porch and was known for its profuse output of blossoms. He was one of the founders of the First National Bank in 1866, the city's first bank with a national charter. It failed and was taken over by B.A Shepherd in 1867. (See **Shepherd.**) [7]

BAILEY: James Briton "Brit" – He was born in North Carolina in 1779. He fought in the War of 1812. Bailey arrived in Texas in about 1818 and settled near the Brazos River. He named the place Bailey's Prairie. He fought in two battles that preceded the Texas Revolution – Jones Creek (1824) and Velasco (1832). Bailey was known for his eccentric behavior. His will stated he should be buried standing up, facing west, with his rifle at his side and a whiskey jug between his feet. He did not live to see Texas win her independence as he died in a cholera epidemic in 1832. Legend says at night Bailey's ghost called "Bailey's Light" wanders the prairie lands here in search of more whiskey. [8]

BAILEY: James – A number of Fourth Ward streets are named for early Houston mayors and I believe this is the case here as well. Bailey was mayor in 1846, the year that Texas was admitted to the Union. Among the major public works projects during his administration were drainage systems to help reduce the perennial threat of yellow fever. [9]

BAIRD: C. L. – When Katy, Texas incorporated in 1945, this gentleman was elected the city's first mayor. [10]

BAKER: Basil – Born in Virginia in 1804, he moved to the area near where Decker's Prairie is today. [11]

BAKER: Hance – An early Baytown pioneer, Baker's home was used in 1844 to organize the first Methodist church in the area. Originally called Alexander Chapel after a well-known minister, it is now known as Cedar Bayou United Methodist Church. Baker allowed the congregation to use his home for services until they built a small log church building in 1847. (See **Alexander.**) [12]

BAKER: Mosley – This Alabaman came to Texas in 1834 to join the fight for independence. He was a landowner in Fort Bend County. During the Revolution Captain Mosley's heroic stand at San Felipe caused the Mexican army to retreat down river to cross the Brazos. He fought and was wounded at the Battle of San Jacinto. He served in the Congress of the Republic of Texas in 1838-9. He died of yellow fever in 1848. [13]

BAKER: Orestes J. – Born in Alabama this black librarian earned degrees at Morehouse College (A. B.), Hampton Library School (B. L. S.) and Columbia University (M. L. S.). In 1931 he was made head librarian at Prairie View A & M University, a position he would hold until his retirement. In addition Baker was Administrative Assistant to the University's President from 1946-1966 as well as President of Prairie View Employees Credit Union for 18 years. [14]

» **BAKER: Street sign on Prairie View A&M campus**

BAKER: The Baker family settled this area east of Katy, Texas in the 1800s. Anna Baker was the first female school bus driver for the Katy ISD. In 2006 her grandson, Craig, caused quite a stir when a group of Moslems bought property next door to his stone cutting business to build a mosque and demanded he move the operation elsewhere. He declined the offer and exercising his rights as a rural landowner announced construction a pig racing track. More than 100 people showed up for the first day of racing. The whole flap finally died down. [15]

BAKER: William R. – Research strongly indicates this street was named for Houston's mayor from 1880 to 1886. He later owned an interest in the *Houston Post* and was president of City Bank of Houston. Baker was the developer of the Sixth Ward. He was also president of the Houston & Texas Central Railroad. [17]

BALDWIN: Horace Rice – Baldwin's sister Charlotte was the wife of Houston founder Augustus Allen. They were children of a wealthy New York doctor. Horace came to Houston in the 1830s to join his sister. He was a talented man and within a few years he was elected mayor in 1844. Baldwin was a nephew of William Marsh Rice. (See **Rice**.) [18]

BALL: George – Born in New York in 1817, he moved to Galveston in 1839 and opened a dry goods store. He learned the banking business as a director of Commercial & Agricultural Bank, the first incorporated bank in Texas. With that knowledge he opened his own bank, Ball, Hutchens & Company, in 1854. Ball was a generous philanthropist contributing to charities, hospitals and schools. Ball High School is also named for him. [19]

BALTHASAR: He is one of the three Wise Men from the East who are mentioned as bringing gifts to the newborn Jesus in the New Testament. It is curious that we have no streets named for the other two - Gaspar and Melchior. [20]

BALTIMORE & OHIO: Started in 1828, this railroad ran from Baltimore, Maryland to its terminus on the Ohio River at Wheeling, West Virginia. [21]

BAMMEL: Charles - A small north Harris County community and road remember this Houstonian of German descent who opened a general store, Bammel & Kuehnle Merchandise, in 1915. He was later named postmaster of Westfield, a station on the International-Great Western Railroad. (See **Westfield Village.**) [22]

BANBURY: See sidebar **All Things English,** page 175.

BANKER: (See **Stavinoha.**)

BANKS: John L. or William W. – See sidebar **Houston Streets Named for Men Killed During World War I,** page 22.

BANKS: See sidebar **Southampton's English Streets,** page 255.

BARBARA: This West University Place lane is named for Barbara Page, an investor in the Pemberton Company. Her husband, Dr. J. H. Page, was also a shareholder in that real estate development firm. (See **Pemberton.**) [23]

BARBARELLA: Jane Fonda played this leading character in the 1968 science-fiction movie of the same name.

BARBERS HILL: This road recalls the first settler of the area near Mont Belvieu, Amos Barber. A rancher, he built his house on the high ground in the area called the "Hill" in 1849. The town of Barbers Hill sprang up near the ranch. In 1890 the name of the city was changed to Mont Belvieu, French for "Mount Beautiful View," to avoid confusion by postal authorities with other Texas towns. [24]

BARBOURS CUT: In 1928 Captain Clyde A. Barbour purchased 1,435 acres in Morgan's Point with hopes of building a marine terminal to compete with the Port of Houston. He succeeded in dredging a canal he called Barbour's Cut. Unfortunately his timing was poor and the Great Depression ended his dream. Beginning in 1985 a terminal was built here that is one of the largest, most modern container shipping facilities along

---

POLITICIANS, STREETS AND MAYORAL ELECTIONS

In his 11 terms as Houston's mayor the "Old Grey Fox," Oscar Holcombe, acquired a number of political enemies. According to the *Houston Chronicle* the mud slinging between the pro and anti-Holcombe forces became particularly ugly during the 1952 campaign. Councilman Louie Welch announced during his campaign for the City's top job that "When elected I will not build boulevards on the prairie that start nowhere and go nowhere and serve only the needs of a real estate promoter." The leader of the anti-Holcombe crowd, former City attorney Lewis Cutrer, pointed out that Welch had backed Holcombe on 54 votes in a 20 month period to extend South Park Boulevard, Belfort Boulevard and Wayside Drive. Candidate Welch's memory was Clintonesque in his inability to recall these votes. Cutrer's response was classic: "Personally I don't feel that his plea of ignorance on these 54 occasions is a very sound platform on which to base a campaign for mayor." [4]

the Gulf of Mexico. Its official name is the Fentress Bracewell Barbours Cut Container Terminal. Bracewell served as chairman of the Port Commission for 15 years. [25]

BAREK: This family was among the first settlers in Guy. (See **Old Guy.**) [26]

BARKDULL: Earl – See sidebar **Houston Streets Named for Men Killed During World War I,** page 22.

BARKER: Barker, as in **Barker-Cypress,** derives its name from the town of Barker in western Harris County. In 1895 the Missouri, Kansas and Texas Railroad sent Ed Barker here to lay tracks for the extension of the railroad. [27]

BARNES: S. L. – See sidebar **Houston Streets Named for Men Killed During World War I,** page 22.

BARNETT: Thomas & Virginia – These early pioneers settled in what would become Richmond/Rosenberg. He was *alcalde* (mayor) of Austin (1827-9), *ayuntamento* (important civic official) of San Felipe (1833) and a signatory of the Texas Declaration of Independence (1836). [28]

BARNSTON: Henry – Born in Dover, England in 1868, Barnston received his rabbinical diploma in London and his Ph.D. at Heidelberg. He came to America in 1900 after answering an advertisement from a Reform Congregation, Beth Israel, in Houston that was seeking a rabbi. He accepted the pulpit upon arrival and presided over the congregation until his death in 1949. Rabbi Barnston was very active in civic affairs and was a founding member of the Museum of Fine Arts and the Houston Symphony. [29]

BARRETT STATION: The small town of Barrett is located off U. S. 90 in eastern Harris County. This black community sprang up during Reconstruction. Founded by a former slave named Harrison Barrett, by 1889 he had become the largest freed slave landowner in the county. This thriving community had many homes, a sawmill, gristmill and coffee mill. Barrett donated land for the Shiloh Baptist Church and School. [30]

BARRETT: C. E. – In 1904 this Humble, Texas resident discovered oil at Moonshine Hill. A year later he hit the mother lode with a well named No. 2 Beaty that flowed 8,500 barrels per day. The boom was on. In 1905 the population of Humble grew from 700 to 20,000 and the oilfield produced 15,594,932 barrels of "black gold." The Humble Field became the greatest salt dome discovery in history eventually surpassing the legendary Spindletop Field near Beaumont. (See **Moonshine Hill, Spindletop** and **Humble.**) [31]

BARROW: Benjamin – He was an early settler in the Spring Cypress area. [32]

BARTLETT: H. B. – See sidebar **Houston Streets Named for Men Killed During World War I,** page 22. [33]

BARTLETT: See sidebar **Southampton's English Streets,** page 255.

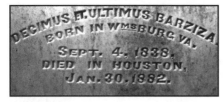

» **BARZIZA: Decimus et Ultimus - Tombstone in Glenwood Cemetery**

BARZIZA: Decimus et Ultimus – This Houstonian has the most unusual name of any person for whom a city street is named. "Decimus et Ultimus" means tenth and last in Latin. This gentleman was the tenth and last child of Phillip Ignatius and Cecelia Amanda Barziza. He was a Captain in Hood's Texas Brigade and saw action at Gettysburg. Barziza was wounded in the attack on Little Round Top on July 2, 1863 and was taken prisoner. After a year in a Union prisoner of war camp he escaped to Canada. He settled in Houston and opened a law practice. Barziza was an author (*The Adventures of a Prisoner of War and Life* and *Scenes in Federal Prisons*), politician (representative to the Texas Legislature) and businessman (founded the state's first trust company, Houston Land & Trust). [34]

BASS PRO: This short drive leads to the Bass Pro Shop Outdoor World in the Katy Mills Mall. This gigantic (138,000 square foot or 3.2 acre) sporting goods store offers fishing, hunting, camping, boating, golf and outdoor gear. It is a mind boggling display of equipment and kitschy woodsy ambience. [35]

BASS: Frederick S – This veteran of the War Between the States commanded Company E, 1st Texas Infantry, Hood's Texas Brigade for a time during the Battle of the Wilderness (May 4-8, 1864). Despite being outnumbered 120,000 to 64,000 the Confederates forced General Ulysses S. Grant to withdraw after suffering 17,666 casualties. [36]

BASSETT: Clement Newton, Jr. – Born in Richmond, Virginia in 1842, he moved to Fort Bend County and became a very successful merchant, rancher and farmer. Bassett was county sheriff during the Jaybird-Woodpecker War (1888-90), a political feud between two factions vying for control of the county. He later served a four year term as county tax collector. A religious man, Bassett was a founder of the first Baptist church in Richmond. [37]

BASTOGNE: This small Belgian town was a critical defensive point for the Allies during the Battle of the Bulge in WW II. (See **Ardennes.**) [38]

BASTROP: Baron Felipe Enrique Neri de – While not much of this European adventurers' provenance is known, it does appear he settled in San Antonio by 1806 where he operated a freight company. He achieved great influence and became an *alcalde* (mayor) in Bexar. History remembers the Baron as the man whose authority allowed Moses Austin to acquire the land grant for Anglo-Americans to move into Texas and who assisted Stephen F. Austin in establishing the Republic of Texas. [39]

BATAAN: This street is named for a peninsula in the Philippines. It was defended against the Japanese by U.S. troops under the command of General Jonathan Wainwright until they were forced to surrender on April 9, 1942. The 70-mile forced march to a POW camp became known as the "Bataan Death March" as more than 100,000 American prisoners, out of a force of 600,000, died from torture or starvation. [40]

BATES: William B. – Bates was a trustee of the M.D. Anderson Foundation and a principal force in the founding of the Texas Medical Center. Known by the honorary title of Colonel Bates, conferred on him by Texas Governor Dan Moody, this bright young attorney became an early partner in the law firm of Fulbright, Crooker & Freeman. His name was soon added to the moniker. [41]

BATTERSON: Isaac – An early resident of Harris County, Batterson lived on Buffalo Bayou near the town of Clinton. Today he is thought of as the first resident of Galena Park. The Texas army crossed his land to reach the battleground at San Jacinto. In 1837 he was elected Justice of the Peace. During his term he worked on the committee to build the first Harris County courthouse (at a cost of $3,800) as well as the city's first jail ($4,750). (See **Clinton** and **Galena**.) [42]

BATTLE: Mills M. – This early settler received a land grant in 1827-8 where Fort Bend County is today. Mills was one of Stephen F. Austin's Old 300. He was elected clerk of the county in 1858. [43]

BATTLEGROUND: Today this road leads to San Jacinto State Park, the home of the San Jacinto Monument and the berth of the Battleship Texas. However at 3:30 PM on Thursday, April 21, 1836 the scene was very different from the tranquil green space you see today. It was here on that fateful afternoon that in an 18-minute battle, General Sam Houston's army defeated General Santa Anna and Texas won her independence. [44]

» **BATTLEGROUND: Santa Anna surrendered under this mossy oak tree after his defeat at the Battle of San Jacinto**

BAUER: Siegesmund – This road is named for Bauer, a German immigrant from Wiesenbad, who arrived in Houston's Spring Branch area in 1847. Like many of his neighbors he was a farmer. Bauer also was a founder of St. Peter's Evangelical Lutheran Church; a congregation that still exists today. He died in a yellow fever epidemic in 1854. [45]

BAUER: The Bauers were among the many Germans who immigrated to Texas in the 1800s and settled on land northwest of Houston. Early arrivals, including Heinrich Bauer (1826-1895) and Anna Bauer (1826-1896), are buried in the historic Roberts Cemetery. (See **Roberts Cemetery.**) [46]

BAY OAKS: (See **Shoreacres.**)

BAY: (See **Appaloosa.**)

BAYBROOK MALL & BAYBROOK SQUARE: These two gigantic shopping malls face each other on opposite's sides of I-45 between Webster and Friendswood. [47]

BAYER: Both this street and the nearby park are named for Arthur Bayer, a resident of the Spring area. [48]

BAYLAND: This beautiful tree-lined avenue was named for Bayland Orphans Home that was located in this Woodland Heights neighborhood from 1887 until it burned down in 1914. The orphanage was originally on Galveston Bay, thus the genesis of the name. [49]

BAYLOR: Founded in Independence, Texas in 1845 as a Baptist university, the campus was moved to Waco in 1886. Its famous medical school was opened in 1900 in Dallas and moved to Houston in 1943. The University was named for District Judge R. E. B. Baylor, one of the founders. [50]

BAYPORT: This boulevard leads to one of the largest petrochemical complexes (the Bayport Industrial Complex) in our region. It is the site of the world's largest styrene plant. Produced from a combination of benzene and ethylene, styrene is used in the manufacture of a wide variety of polystyrene products. [51]

BAYRIDGE: In 1893 twelve prominent Houston families purchased 40 acres of land in the town of Morgan's Point to develop a summer resort community. They called themselves the Bay Ridge Park Association. Long narrow lots were platted and allotted to the families by drawing numbers. Texas Governor Ross Sterling built the most palatial home. It was modeled after the White House. It still exists and is listed on the National Register of Historic Places. [52]

BAYS CHAPEL: The Thomas Bay family arrived from Tennessee with a group of settlers in this part of Montgomery in the 1851. They constructed a log building called Bays Chapel Church and School. The church had eight members including the Bay, Harrison and Williamson families. [53]

HOUSTON STREETS THAT HAVE CHANGED NAMES

Over the years, since the first map of our city was drawn up in 1836, Houston has seen literally hundreds of streets change names. There are many reasons for this including laws that prevent more than one street with the same name (this makes postal deliveries in the same town possible), citizens requesting changes, streets renamed to honor famous or heroic persons, major streets being extended and connecting with lesser thoroughfares, etc. If the reader wants a more complete list of current and former street names there is a fairly comprehensive list I have compiled in the Texas Room of the Houston Public Library at 500 McKinney downtown. For the purposes of this book I have elected to only show the most important street name changes that have occurred over the last 174 years. [5]

CURRENT NAME	ORIGINAL NAME
Austin	Homer
Bagby	Calhoun
Bastrop	Broadway
Bissonnet	County Poor Farm Road
Canal	German
Caroline	Carolina
Cavalcade	Newton
Cullen	St. Bernard
Dowling	East Broadway
Dunlavy	High
Elysian	Panola
Fairview	Minnesota
Hardy	Tyler
Hutchins	West Broadway
LaBranch	Milton
Lawndale	Cut Off Road
Lockwood	Orriene
Lyons	Odin
McGowen	Murry
Montrose	Lincoln
North Durham	Nashua
North Main	Montgomery
North Shepherd	Brunner
Riesner	Young
St. Joseph's Parkway	Calhoun
Shepherd	Shepherd's Dam
South McGregor	Savannah
Tulane	Portland
Waugh	Euclid
Welch	Nebraska
West Dallas	San Felipe
Westheimer	Hathaway
University	Amerman

BAYTOWN: Named for its location fronting on Burnet, Scott, Mitchell, Black Duck, Tabbs and Galveston Bays, this industrial city east of Houston comes to its name legitimately. Principally an industrial town, Baytown is home to numerous refineries and chemical plants. The area was first settled by Nathaniel Lynch in about 1822. (See **Lynchburg.**)[54]

BEACH: Isaac Conroe established this community when he opened a saw mill here in the late 1800s. It was located along the Gulf, Colorado & Santa Fe Railroad line. For unknown reasons he named it Beach. When the timber boom played out the town disappeared. (See **Conroe-Hufsmith.**)[55]

BEAR CREEK: This creek rises near Wolf Hill in northwest Harris County and flows for 18 miles to its mouth on Buffalo Bayou near Addicks Reservoir. (See **Addicks Levee.**)[56]

BEAR-RAM: Alief ISD has two high schools, Elsik and Hastings, that are located next to each other on this road. Hastings mascot is the bear. Elsik students are known as the rams. At the end of each football season these sister schools play a friendly rivalry game in the shared Crump Stadium.[57]

» **SAMUEL DAMON: Tombstone and historic marker in Damon Cemetery**

BEASLEY-DAMON: This road connects these two Fort Bend County towns. Beasley was laid out along the Galveston, Harrisburg & San Antonio Railway by Cecil A. Beasley, a Richmond banker, in the mid-1890s. He originally called it Dyer for Miss Isabel Dyer whom he later married. However, when it came time to establish a post office it was discovered that another Texas town was already called Dyer so he changed the name. Damon was founded in 1831 by Samuel Damon, an early Texas pioneer. He established his farm on a large geological mound called a salt dome that rises dramatically above the surrounding flat coastal plains. By 1918 sulfur was discovered under the dome and it was also used to quarry limestone. As a result the Galveston, Harrisburg & San Antonio Railway laid a 21 mile spur to Damon to ship these products to Richmond.[58]

BEASLEY-TAVENER: This Fort Bend County town was established along the Texas & New Orleans Railroad line in 1890. It is named for an area pioneer, Charley Tavener. (See **Beasley-Damon.**)[59]

BEAU GESTE: From the French meaning "magnanimous gesture," this is Percival Christopher Wren's novel about the three Geste brothers. Combining mystery, loyalty, a missing blue sapphire, the French Foreign Legion, an abusive sergeant and a battle against marauding tribesmen, the author created a marvelous story and a very enjoyable read.[60]

BEAUCHAMP: Thomas D. – An early settler in Harris County, he owned 50 acres north of town that possessed artesian springs. He would haul water to Houstonians who hated the taste of Buffalo Bayou water. The springs became known as Beauchamp's Springs and a Confederate camp was established near them during the War Between the States. In April 1838 a new jail and courthouse were completed in downtown Houston and officials were determined that citizens show respect for these institutions. District Judge A. B. Shelby assessed fines to violators of the court's dignity including one of $500 to Beauchamp for contempt. (See **Artesian.**) [61]

BEAUJOLAIS: This hilly Rhone region of France is famous for its fresh, light-bodied red wine. [62]

BEAUMONT: This highway leads to the county seat of Jefferson County. Beaumont was named either for James Beaumont, Chief Justice of Calhoun County, or for a hill southeast of town called *Beau Mont* in French, meaning beautiful mountain. The area was first settled in 1825 with the town being laid out in 1837. In 1901 one of the world's greatest oilfields was discovered in nearby Spindletop. (See **Spindletop.**) [63]

BEAUREGARD: Pierre Gustave Toutant – This Louisiana native graduated from West Point in 1838. He served in the Mexican War where he was twice wounded. During the War Between the States General Beauregard fought at Manassas, Shiloh, Corinth, Charleston and Petersburg. Despite his diminutive size, his soldiers called him "Napoleon in Gray" and "the Great Creole." Following the War he was named president of the New Orleans, Jackson & Great Northern Railroad, was adjutant general of Louisiana, manager of the Louisiana lottery and commissioner of public works for the City of New Orleans. [64]

BECKENDORF: This German family was a landholder around Bear Creek in west Houston. In 1945 the Beckendorfs and 40 other families were forced to move due to the construction of the Barker Reservoir, a flood control project in the watershed of Buffalo Bayou. They resettled near Tomball where family members are buried in the Beckendorf Cemetery. [65]

BECKER LINE: Boris Becker was the youngest tennis player, at only 17, to capture the men's title at Wimbledon. This young German won Wimbledon three times (1985, 1986, 1989), the Australian Open twice (1991, 1996) and the U. S. Open once (1989). [66]

BEDFORD FORREST: Nathan – He is arguably the best general Robert E. Lee had during the War Between the States. Despite a lack of any formal education, this self-educated man is considered by experts to have been a military genius. Forrest was a brilliant cavalry tactician. He saw action at Chickamauga, Fort Pillow, Blue Cross Roads, Nashville and Selma. His most remarkable feat was the capture of an entire Union cavalry brigade at Rome, Georgia. Forrest was named president of the Selma, Marion & Memphis Railroad following the War. [67]

BEEBE: Howard Ward – This gentleman was instrumental in the incorporation of Bunker Hill Village in the Memorial area. Beebe was named the village city's historian in 1991 due to his encyclopedic knowledge of the area. He was the founder and president of the Houston-based investment firm of Beebe & Lavalle. [68]

BEECHCRAFT: In 1932 Walter H. and Olive Ann Beech founded the Beechcraft Aircraft Corporation. Since producing the first model called the 17, Beechcraft has introduced the Twin Beech, trainers for fighter pilots during World War II, the Baron and the King Air. In 1980 the Company was acquired by the Raytheon Corporation. [69]

BEINHORN: William E. – This Memorial area street was named for a German immigrant who arrived in Houston in 1853 and acquired substantial land holdings in the area. [70]

BELKNAP COURT: Charles – Most likely this Sugar Land street recalls this early Texas pioneer and one of Stephen F. Austin's Old 300 colonists. He was awarded a land grant in Fort Bend County in 1827. The 1826 census lists Belknap as a farmer and cattle rancher. After his death in 1829 his acreage was sold at public auction. [71]

BELKNAP: Sugar Land Industries owned Belknap Real Estate Development Company that was used to oversee their real property activities. Belknap developed Imperial Estates, Brookside, Belknap, Alkire Lake, Horseshoe Lake and Venetian Estates in the Sugar Land area. [72]

BELL OAKS: This Bellville street recalls the town's founder Thomas Bell. He was one of Stephen F. Austin's Old 300. Bell arrived in Texas in 1822 and settled in this area in 1838. [73]

BELL: Peter H. – Bell came to Texas to fight for independence. He saw action at San Jacinto. He joined the Texas Rangers in 1840 and fought with them in the Mexican War of 1845. Elected Governor, he served two terms (1849 and 1851). Bell resigned to fill the unexpired term of a U.S. Congressman. He fought in and survived the War Between the States and died at the ripe old age of 86. [74]

BELLAIRE: In 1908 a Burlington Railroad executive named William W. Baldwin purchased 9,449 acres southwest of Houston and named it Westmoreland Farms. He called the town at its center Bellaire. The name was thought to come from a marketing brochure that stated "The town is Bellaire (fine air), for Westmoreland Farms is fanned day and night by the cooling breezes of the Gulf of Mexico." A 1910 advertisement describes the Boulevard as "a fine double road of white shell" and "Houston's most popular driveway." However, it is more likely Baldwin named it for Bellaire, OH, a town served by his Chicago, Burlington & Quincy Railroad. (See **Westmoreland.**) [75,76]

BELLE: See sidebar **Gone With the Wind Too Far,** page 303.

BELLINGRATH: See sidebar the **Antebellum Streets of River Plantation,** page 122.

BELLMEADE: It is possible that this street is a misspelling of the name of the famous

Belle Meade Country Club in Nashville, Tennessee, since so many other streets in River Oaks are named for exclusive golf clubs. Donald Ross designed the beautiful old moss covered anti-bellum style club's golf course in 1901. [77]

BELLOWS: George F. and Ann – On June 9, 2000 he was honored with a street in the Texas Medical Center. He joined the board of Texas Children's Hospital in 1967 and the TMC board in 1976. A tireless volunteer and benefactor, Bellows and his wife Ann presided over much of the growth of both of these organizations for more than a quarter of a century. [78]

» **BELL'S LANDING: Historical marker in East Columbia**

BELL'S LANDING: Josiah Hughes Bell came to Texas with Stephen F. Austin in 1821. He was Austin's second in command in the colony. He settled in what is today Brazoria County in 1824. Bell was a planter and built a plantation on the banks of the Brazos River. By 1829 Bell established a community nearby. First it was named Marion, then Bell's Landing, Columbia and finally East Columbia. This landing became a very important port and trade center for the young Republic of Texas. Today the entire town of East Columbia is on the National Register of Historic Places and well worth a visit. [79]

BELMONT: Located in Belmont, New York, this thoroughbred racetrack is the home of the final race constituting the Triple Crown. The first leg is the Kentucky Derby, followed by the Preakness. Belmont opened in 1905. Five years later 150,000 people came to the track to see the Wright Brothers put on an international aerial tournament. [80]

BELMONT: See sidebar **Tennis or Golf, Anyone?,** page 348.

BEN HUR: Lew Wallace wrote this biblical novel in 1880. It tells the story of Judah Ben Hur who is wrongly accused of a crime, enslaved by his Roman masters and achieves redemption in one of the most famous chariot races of all time. It was made into a movie in 1926 and again in 1959. [81]

BEN TAUB: He was a financier, philanthropist and World War I hero. Taub was instrumental in creating the University of Houston, contributing 35 acres of land in 1936 for its main campus. Concerned for the health of the poor, he was chairman of the original Jefferson Davis Hospital and was a driving force in the construction of the facility on Allen Parkway (demolished 1999). Taub was responsible for saving DePelchin Faith Home (now DePelchin Children's Center) and amassing funds for construction of its campus on Sandman. Ben Taub General Hospital is named in his honor. [82]

BENDER: Members of this family were early landowners in the Humble, Texas area. Bender Street as well as Bender Square remembers these pioneers. Charles

HOUSTON STREETS WITH HUMOROUS NAMES

According to the City's Planning & Development Department there are very few rules about naming streets. Basically as long as there is not another street with the name proposed on a developers plat or on a street that is going to have a name change, then a street can be called whatever the namer chooses. Department employees cannot ask the developer why he chose the street names he plans to use. As a result we can get some unusual monikers for our highways and byways. Over the years the Houston real estate development community has exhibited a great deal of humor when it came to christening our streets. From studying the numerous maps at Planning & Development as well as reading the index of the Key Map of Houston. We have chosen some streets just for their funny names. They are: **Animal Cracker, Attaway, Betty Boop, Bittersweet, Boorstown, Bourgeois, Broken Glass, Carpet Bagger, Catbird, Chew, Chipshot, Clay Pigeon, Concrete, Crackerneck, Cry Baby, Easy, Ding-an-Sich, Far Fetch, Flintstone, Four Sixes, Generic, Glassblower, Go Man Go, Good Intention, Hades Ferry, Hardscrabble, Hazard, Hog Heaven, Hound Dog, Ice Palace, Igloo, Jaberwalky, Jury Rig, Kangaroo Court, King's Ransom, Kissing Camel, Lazy, Mellow Brew, Memory Lane, Mexican John, Moe's Place, Monkeyfist, Neon, North by Northwest, Okay, Old Token, Parcel Three, Proswimmer, Psuedo, Quark, Ram's Bottom, Red-an-Gold, Restaurant Row, Rustler's Way, Salty Dog, Sissy, Smokey the Bear, Snake Canyon, Sotired, Sweet Surrender, Tater Tot, Teddy Bear, Temperance, The Alley, Thirsty Fish, Trailer Park, Ubetcha, Wages, Wasp, West by Northwest, Whistling Dixie, Wicked Wicket, Wildoats, X Can** and **Yellow Jacket.** [6]

Bender owned a sawmill near Spring, Texas. He was known as the "Lumber Baron of Humble." [83]

BENFER: In 1845 a group of German immigrants settled along the banks of Cypress Creek near where Klein is located today. They were farmers and raised cotton, potatoes and corn among other crops. They sold their produce in Houston, a two-day trip by wagon in those days. The Benfer family was one of these pioneer settlers. Henry Benfer was a founding member of the Trinity Lutheran Church in Klein. A number of family members are buried in the church cemetery. [84]

BERING: August and Conrad – These two brothers emigrated from Kassel, Germany in 1842. They were on their way from Galveston to Fredericksburg when their oxen died in the Houston area. Cabinetmakers by trade, they set up shop here and went to work. Their business eventually expanded into lumber and hardware. That company still operates today under the ownership of the Bering family. The brothers began acquiring acreage west of the city and eventually owned about 2,000 acres of what is now Tanglewood and Briargrove. [85]

BERNARDO DE GALVEZ: This Spaniard was born in 1746. He chose a career in the military and was honored for his distinguished service to the royal crown. Galvez visited the New World for the first time in the 1760s. His assignment was to defeat raiding Apaches that were attacking Spanish outposts. By 1777 he was appointed Governor of Louisiana. He strongly supported the Americans during the Revolutionary War. He dispatched Jose de Evia, a surveyor and map maker, to chart the Texas coast. Evia named the largest bay Galvez in honor of his patron. However, Galvez died before he ever saw that body of water. Later the name was changed to Galveston. [86]

BERRY: James – This Kentucky gentleman came to Texas to fight for independence in 1836. He was a lieutenant at the Battle of San Jacinto. In 1840 Berry acquired some acreage in northern Harris County where this road is located. He entered politics and held the office of justice of the peace and treasurer of the county from 1845 until 1858. Berry Elementary School is also named for him. [46]

BERTNER: Dr. E. William – The Texas Medical Center has honored a number of important people associated with this complex with street names. This New York City physician was convinced to come to Houston by the wealthy tycoon Jesse H. Jones. His work at Johns Hopkins Medical School in Baltimore resulted in him becoming one of the nation's experts on cancer. So his association with the M.D. Anderson Hospital was only natural. In 1946 he was named the first president of the TMC. [87]

BERZIN: (See **Bhandara.**)

BETHEA: Cecil G. – See sidebar **Houston Streets Named for Men Killed During World War I,** page 22. [88]

BETHJE: Bertha – She was the wife of Anton Brunner who developed the Brunner Addition just east of Memorial Park. North Shepherd was once named Brunner. He was a German immigrant who was orphaned almost as soon as he arrived in Houston with his parents. Brunner went on to make his fortune in the shoe business and invested his profits in real estate. [89]

BETTY BOOP: She is a cartoon character introduced in 1931. Betty was a strip (no pun intended) for adults. In two of her early cartoons, "You're Driving Me Crazy" and "Silly Scandals" her blouse kept falling down reveling her buxom chest in a lacy French bra. In 1933 the Hays Code of censorship for cartoons went into effect and Betty was morphed into a less vampish character. [90]

» **BETTY BOOP: A cartoon character street sign**

BEUTEL: Louis – He was a large landowner in the Spring Valley area. Beutel married the daughter of pioneer settler Wilhelm Rummel. His property was part of the Osborne Survey that consisted of tracts of land given by Sam Houston to soldiers who served in the Army of the Republic of Texas. (See **Rummel.**) [91]

BEVERLY: (See **Marjorie, Bintliff** and **Sharpstown.**)

BEXAR: The presidio or mission fortress called San Antonio de Bexar and the town of San Fernando de Bexar were the original names for the area where San Antonio is today. [92]

BFI WHISPERING PINES LANDFILL ROAD: Named by the waste management company, Browning-Ferris Industries, this name is subtle corporate humor to lessen the impact of its ultimate destination - a huge garbage dump! [93]

BHANDARA: Fred – This real estate developer named most of the streets in Heritage Park West near Katy in 1994. **Zubin** and **Berzin** are his sons. **Jessica** and **Zareen** are his daughters. **Bradley** Luedecke is his godson and son of his business partner. **Kenny** Luedecke is also the son of his partner. **Kyla** Flueckiger is the daughter of another business associate. [94]

BIG LEAGUE DREAMS: This parkway leads to a sports complex of the same name in League City. The baseball parks here are scaled down versions of major league fields such as Fenway Park (Boston), Polo Grounds (New York) and Wrigley Field (Chicago). [95]

BIGELOW: Charles – He served as Houston's fourth mayor in 1840-41. In that era railroad companies were the high technology businesses. Houston was awarded the charter for one of four rail lines to be built in the Republic of Texas. The Houston & Brazos Railroad Company was authorized to lay track from the city to the river. To celebrate this great event citizens, politicians, educators and preachers turned out. They walked the first nine miles of the proposed line where Mayor Bigelow broke ground for the construction. [96]

BINGLE: Charles Henry – He was an early resident of the Spring Valley area. [97]

BINTLIFF: David C. – Real estate developer Frank Sharp named this street for his friend David Bintliff. He was a well-known oilman, rancher and investor in the Houston area. (See **Sharpstown.**) [98]

BINZ: Jacob – A Chicago native, Binz built Houston's first "skyscraper" in 1895. A Renaissance-and-Romanesque-style structure at 513-19 Main Street, it cost $60,000. The Binz Building was the first in Houston to be built out of concrete, stone and steel. While the structure was six stories high plus a basement, architects said the foundation and superstruc-

» BINZ: The Binz Building on Main Street

ture could have supported a 20-story building. When it was opened, people came from miles around to ride its elevators to the top floor and admire the view of the surrounding countryside. The building was demolished in 1950. [99]

BIRDIE: See sidebar **A Neighborhood for Linksters,** page 318.

BIRDSALL: The Hogg family and their friends, Judge and Mrs. Frederick C. Proctor, hired Birdsall P. Briscoe and John F. Staub as associate architects to design their respective homes, Bayou Bend and Dogwood, which were next door to one another and shared a common driveway onto Lazy Lane. The architects divided the work between themselves: Staub designing Bayou Bend and Briscoe designing Dogwood. A plaque on the wall facing the Diana Garden at Bayou Bend memorializes this collaboration. [100]

BISSONNET: George Herman – This Houston native was a pilot in the U. S. Army Air Corps (predecessor to the U. S. Air Force) during World War I who, records indicate, was killed in a plane crash while training in Florida. The street has had three other names: County Poor Farm Road because it led to the Harris County Poor Farm, Richmond Road as it was the principal artery to the Fort Bend County seat of Richmond and 11th Street (on the early planning map of Southampton Place). [101]

BLACK GOLD: Located among a complex of petroleum services companies this name is slang for "oil." [102]

BLACKBEARD: See sidebar **Pirates of the Caribbean,** page 280.

BLACKSHEAR: William Newton and Hanna Elizabeth – Originally from Trinity County, the Blackshears arrived in the Willow Creek area in 1862 where they operated a general store. He became the first postmaster of Klein, Texas. (See **Klein.)** [103]

BLAHA: This short lane recalls another family of European immigrants who settled west of Houston in the 1800s. Some of the Blahas are buried in the Roberts Cemetery that is located just northeast of this street. (See **Roberts Cemetery.)** [104]

BLAIR: John – This Tennessee native came to Texas to fight for independence under the command of Colonel James Bowie. He died at the fall of the Alamo in 1836 at the age of 33. [105]

BLANDFORD: See sidebar **All Things English,** page 175.

BLIMP BASE: The Hitchcock Naval Air Station was a World War II base for lighter-than-air craft better known as blimps. In 1942 the U. S. Navy acquired 3,000 acres of land northwest of Galveston and erected a $10 million hanger that would hold six giant blimps. It was 1,000 feet long, 300 feet wide and over 200 feet in height. The base was to protect shipping along the Texas coast from Nazi submarine attacks.

Following the war the facility was used for storage of equipment and later rice. When the Navy declared the property surplus in 1950, Houston oilman John Mecom bought it. He planned to develop it as a resort called Flamingo Isle. That never happened. The hanger, clearly visible to traffic on the Gulf Freeway, was seriously damaged in Hurricane Carla in 1961 and was torn down the following year. (See **Mecom.**) [106]

» **FLAMINGO ISLE: A Galveston county resort that was never built**

BLODGETT: According to John Raia, senior planner in the City's Planning & Development Division and a veteran of more than half a century of working with developers naming streets, he believes this street recalls the surname of Henry MacGregor's mother-in-law. (See **MacGregor.**) [107]

BLOUNT: Stephen William – He signed the Texas Declaration of Independence, fought in the Texas Revolution in Captain William D. Ratcliff's Company, was the county clerk of San Augustine County as well as its postmaster and served as fiscal agent for the Confederate States of America. [108]

BLUE RIDGE: Located near Missouri City this is the name of a geological formation where oil and gas were discovered in 1919 and a salt mine soon after. The *Texas Coaster* reported "Richmond was an excited town on Monday morning when news spread that a gusher had come in on the Blue Ridge Oilfield." The discovery allowed nearby Missouri City to become the first town in Fort Bend County to use natural gas. [109]

» **BLUEWATER HIGHWAY: Destruction caused by hurricane Ike in 2008**

BLUE: See sidebar **Neighborhoods with Interesting Stories,** page 104.

BLUEWATER HIGHWAY: Also known as County Road 257, this 16 mile stretch of road runs along the Texas coast from Surfside to San Luis Pass at Galveston Island. Much of the way drivers have an unimpeded view of the blue waters of the Gulf. The highway lost two miles of surface and experienced serious damage to another six miles when Hurricane Ike made landfall in 2008. Fortunately, it has been repaired so the almost 400,000 users can once again enjoy this beautiful drive. (See photograph on page 44.) [110]

BOBCAT: (See **Cougar.**)

BOBCAT: High schools in our area love to name streets near their athletic facilities for the team mascot. In this case it is Hempstead High who are the Bobcats. [111]

BOBVILLE: This road remembers another of the many ghost towns of Montgomery County. Bobville was on the Central & Montgomery Railway and the Atchison, Topeka & Santa Fe Railroad lines. An employee of the A, T & SF named the depot in 1878 and a town was established in 1887. By 1990 Bobville had disappeared off highway maps. [112]

BOGIE: The denizens of this west Houston development have a passion for golf and flying. They own a golf course and airstrip. Bogie is a links score that is one over par for the hole. You would think the developer would have called it birdie (one under par) or eagle (two better than par.) [113]

BOGS: Fritz William – In 1872 he was sent here by his family in Germany to avoid conscription in the army. At that time there were many wars raging in Europe. He bought 500 acres near Huffsmith on Spring Creek, an area that became the "swimming hole of Tomball" for the next 40 years. He operated a saw mill and a cotton gin on his land. It was not unusual for German families to send a son to America in the late 1800s. Mike Stude told me his great-grandfather (who developed Studewood) immigrated to the Houston area after his 11 brothers were killed fighting in European wars. [114]

BOHEME: French for "Bohemian," this tragic four act opera by Giacomo Puccini was first preformed in Turin, Italy in 1896. It is the story about the love lives and personal relationships of four young men and two young women that we would likely call "hippies" today. [115]

BOLD RULER: After a disappointing fourth place finish in the 1957 Kentucky Derby, Bold Ruler went on to win the Preakness and was named Horse of the Year for his record of 11 wins in 16 starts. He sired the greatest thoroughbred of all modern times, Secretariat. (See **Secretariat.**) [116]

BOLING: Located in Fort Bend County this community which was originally called Floyd's Lane was established in 1900 when the New York, Texas & Mexican Railway was constructed through here. Robert E. Vineyard who surveyed the town renamed it Bolling for his daughter Mary Bolling Vineyard. However, the post office altered the spelling to Boling. In 1925 oil, gas and sulfur were discovered at the Boling Dome and the little village became a boomtown overnight. A subdivision established at that time named its streets for oil companies operating there including **Sinclair, Gulf, Magnolia, Sun, Texas** and **Humble.** [117]

» **BOLING MURAL: Artwork telling the history of Boling, Texas**

BOLIVAR: Simon – Known as "The Liberator," this South American hero was born in Caracas, Venezuela in 1783. His life was dedicated to the independence of Spanish colonies on that continent. Between 1810 and 1830 he succeeded in gaining freedom for the people of Venezuela, Colombia, Ecuador, Peru and Panama. In addition he founded the Republic of Bolivia that is named for this statesman. Closer to home Boliver Peninsula and Port Bolivar on the Texas Gulf Coast also recall this important man. (See **Boyt.**) [118]

» **BOLIVAR LIGHTHOUSE: Historic 1872 Structure on Boliver Peninsula**

BOLSOVER: See **Southampton's English Streets,** page 255.

BONAPARTE: Napoleon – One of the greatest military geniuses of all time, he is most remembered for the battle he lost, Waterloo, than the hundreds he won. He named himself Emperor of the French Empire in 1804. Bonaparte was forced to abdicate in 1814. He spent the rest of his life in exile on Elba and later St. Helena. [119]

BONHAM: James Butler – This South Carolinian became one of the most revered of Texas heroes. Bonham came to Texas in 1835 to help fight in the Revolution. He arrived at the Alamo with Jim Bowie on January 19, 1836. He died at the Siege of the Alamo on March 19, 1836 while manning one of the mission's cannons. The town of Bonham was named in his honor also. [120]

BONNARD: Pierre – This French painter was born in Fontenay-aux-Roses. His father insisted he become a lawyer but after practicing for a short time he enrolled in art classes and decided to become an artist. He is known for his complex compositions and intense use of color. His friend, Henri de Toulouse-Lautrec, arranged for Bonnard to show his works at the *Societe des Artistes Independants* in 1891. [121]

BOONE: Sylvester – This gentleman arrived in Alief, Texas in 1908. Boone along with A. J. Martin and S. A. Brasfield were responsible for establishing an independent school district here. In 1910 the first school opened. The Boone clan has lived in the area for almost a century. Boone Park and Boone Elementary School also are named in their honor. In June 2006 the Alief Old Timers Group hosted a reunion presided over by 104-year old Mora Boone who moved to Alief in 1921 to marry James L. Boone Sr. (See **Alief-Clodine.**) [122]

» BOOT HILL: Lester Moore's Tombstone

» BOOTH SCHOOL: Ruins of 1912 Structure

BOOT HILL: The Wild West is still alive in this subdivision called Stagecoach Farms in Montgomery County. The original Boot Hill was the cemetery in Dodge City, Kansas where outlaws and gunfighters were buried with their boots on. The most famous Boot Hill is in Tombstone, Arizona. A grave marker there has one of the all-time great epitaphs: "Here lies Lester Moore, Four slugs from a 44, No Les, No More." Other colorful street names in this neighborhood are **Stagecoach, Cimarron, Westward Ho, Tomahawk** and **Broken Spoke.** [123]

BOOTH: This site was originally part of the league of land Stephen F. Austin granted to

Henry Jones in the early 1830s. The town was founded by Freeman Irby Booth in the 1890s. Booth was a wealthy resident, who operated a general store, lumber yard, cotton gin, hotel, bank and a cane syrup mill here. The syrup, Open Kettle Pure Ribbon Cane brand, won awards for its excellent taste. He had the first telephone line in the county strung from his home in Richmond to the store in Booth. Booth owned Fort Bend County's first automobile (1907). In 1912 he erected Booth Public School. Its architecture is based on the famous San Jose Mission in San Antonio. (See photograph on page 47.) (See **Jones, Henry.**) [124]

BOOTH: W. R. – He lead a group of settlers to this Brazoria County area in 1857. They were farmers and ranchers who settled along the banks of Chocolate Bayou. (See **Chocolate Bayou** and **Manvel.**) [125]

BORA BORA: See sidebar **Bali Hai May Call You,** page 322.

BORDEN: Paschal Paolo – He was born in New York in 1806 and came to Texas in 1839 to fight for independence from Mexico. Borden settled in the area where Stafford is today. He saw action during the Siege of Bexar and the Battle of San Jacinto. [43]

BORDERS: Edgar – This is an example of sometimes it's better not to have a street named after you. In 1927 a sawmill in Humble closed down. This put a number of people, many of whom were black, out of work. Borders opened a new mill, hired many of the workers and gave them some shacks to live in. He was forced to close his operation in 1941 and Borders sold or rented the land near the mill to his ex-employees. Borders died in 1963. By the time Houston annexed what became known as Bordersville in 1965 it was one of the most destitute neighborhoods in the city. [126]

BORDLEY: Developer William Farrington's wife Bernice, affectionately known as "Birdie," named this street for a branch of her family, according to her daughter. [127]

BORG BREAKPOINT: Swedish born Bjorn Borg accomplished one of the greatest feats in modern tennis history. He won five consecutive men's singles championships at the All-England matches at Wimbledon between 1976 and 1980. On his way to victory in 1976 he did not lose a set. Borg also won the French Open championship six times between 1974 and 1981. Breakpoint is a tennis term indicating the server has lost his advantage and is in danger of losing his service game. [128]

BORGESTEDT CEMETERY: The family settled in the area along Cypress Creek. Many are buried in this graveyard off Huffmeister Road. Johann Peter Borgestedt was born in 1826 and died in 1891. Descendents interred here include Peter (born 1867), Benjamin, Bernice, Anna and Alma. The cemetery is still in use with the latest burial I noted dated 2005. [102]

BOUDREAUX: In the late 1830s French settlers began arriving in the Willow Creek area south of what is today Tomball, Texas. Louisiana Cajuns including the Boudreaux family joined them. Prior to construction of the Catholic Church, services were held in the Boudreaux home. [129]

BOUNDARY: Although the story behind Boundary may be more urban legend than fact, several Houston historians and street naming experts agree that it could be true. It seems an early city map showed this street as the last one to the north when the map was drawn, thus marking the city limit or boundary. [130]

BOURGEOIS: Since this French word means typically middle class we question why a developer would christen a street with this name. However, in the neighborhood where it is located it represents truth in advertising. [131]

BOWLING GREEN: Bowling Green State University in the Ohio town of the same name was founded in 1914, became a college in 1929 and was chartered as a university in 1935. [132]

BOY: See sidebar **Neighborhoods with Interesting Stories,** page 104.

BOYCE: Albert Gallatin – A veteran of the War Between the States, he was wounded at the Battle of Chickamauga in September 1863. He was a rancher and became the general manager of the famous XIT Ranch. A strict Methodist, he rode moral herd over the ranch hands, forbidding them to wear six-guns, to drink alcohol or gamble. Later in life he founded Midway Bank and Trust of Dalhart where he was president until he was shot to death. It seems Boyce's son Al ran off with the wife of John B. Sneed. Sneed didn't take this lightly, so he killed the senior Boyce. Tried and acquitted, Sneed then hunted Al Boyce Jr. down and murdered him in Amarillo. [133]

BOYS COUNTRY: In the early 1960s T. A. "Tom" Robinson donated 10 acres of land near Hockley to establish this unique home for at risk boys. Later Girls Country was added. Today the campus is nearly 200 acres with over 20 buildings. The facility has been home to more than 1,200 children from the greater Houston area. [134]

BOYT: E. W. – This gentleman purchased the historic Bolivar Lighthouse on the west end of the Bolivar Peninsula in 1947 when the U. S. Government declared the property surplus. It was built in 1872 out of brick, sheathed in cast-iron plates that were riveted together. Standing 117 feet high, it has survived every hurricane to strike the Texas coast over the last 138 years and served as a place of refuge in most of those storms. The lighthouse was retired in 1933 when it was replaced by the South Jetty Light. (See **Bolivar.**) [135]

BRADFORD: This family was one of the two major landowners in Kemah, Texas in the late 1890s. Early on, the city was called Shell Siding because the Southern Pacific Railroad established a station there to haul oyster shells for construction materials. The Bradfords sold the shell to the railway for $0.75 per car. There was a shell reef in front of the Bradford home that extended hundreds of feet into Galveston Bay and was 20 to 30 feet thick in some locations. (See **Kemah** and **Kipp.**) [136]

BRADLEY: (See **Bhandara.**)

BRADY: John Thomas – This Houston pioneer was a substantial landowner with holdings between Houston and Harrisburg. In addition, he was an attorney, owned a brick-manufacturing kiln and was a founder of Bayland Orphans Home. An early advocate of making the Port of Houston accessible to ocean going traffic Brady attended the "Deep Water Meeting" in Galveston on January 6, 1890. Following the gathering, he led a contingent of businessmen up Buffalo Bayou, docking at Magnolia Park, land he had given to the city. Brady led a tour of his property, proudly pointing out the park's 3,750 blooming magnolia trees. His colleagues must have been impressed for soon the Houston Belt & Magnolia Park Railway was incorporated. It ran from Brady's land to Constitution Bend on the Channel. Partly through Brady's efforts, President Benjamin Harrison signed the Rivers and Harbors Bill that led to substantial Port improvements. Brady Island on the Ship Channel is also named for this Houstonian. [137]

BRAEBURN: Braeburn Country Club is one of the oldest in Houston, being founded in 1926. The 150 acre property has a 6,808 yard, par 72 golf course originally designed by John Bredemus. From 1936 until 1941 the golf professional here was the great Jimmy Demaret. During his tenure many of his Hollywood friends, including Bob Hope and Bing Crosby, could be seen playing a round. [138]

BRAESWOOD: Braes is the Scottish word for hillside. [139]

BRAHMAN: In the western themed neighborhood of Southfork near Pearland a number of streets recall cattle breeds including this one. They originated in India. Due to centuries of inadequate food supplies, insects, parasites, diseases and extremely tropical weather the breed developed an ability to survive under very adverse conditions. They were shipped to the U. S. in 1849 and soon arrived in Texas where conditions were somewhat similar to those of India. The beast is easily recognized by the large hump over the shoulders and neck. [15]

BRAHMS: See sidebar **It's Music to My Ears,** page 218.

BRANARD: George A – The Branard family lived on this Montrose area street. Mr. Branard was a plumber for the city of Houston. [140]

BRANDT: (See **Koch.**)

BRANDT: Gustavus – Located in the James Bute Addition, this street is named for a gentleman who was a manager of the James Bute Paint Company. [141]

BRANIFF: T. E. – Bordering the south end of Hobby Airport this street is named for the founder of the now departed Braniff Airways.

BRASHEAR: Isaac or Sam H. – There are two excellent possibilities here. **Isaac** Brashear was a surveyor whose name appears on the 1890 map where this street is first mentioned. It was commonplace at that time for surveyors to name a street for themselves in an area they were mapping. **Sam H.** was what we would call today an environmentally in-touch mayor of Houston. He is best remembered for his strong position on acquiring land for green spaces. During his term (1898-1900) Sam Houston Park and Brashear Park (no longer on the city plats) were purchased. He could have been well enough known in 1890 to be honored with a street. [142]

BRAUTIGAM: Christoph and Martha Peter – These German immigrants settled near Tomball in the 1850s. They were cattlemen and ranchers. Their descendants operated a very successful grocery store in the area named Brautigam & Froelich. [143]

BRAXTON BRAGG: See sidebar the **Antebellum Streets of River Plantation,** page 122.

BRAXTON: Warner – This freed slave was one of the first black men to purchase land in Texas. William E. Kendle, the wealthiest man in Fort Bend County, knew the emancipated slaves would need somewhere to live. So, in 1867 he purchased thousands of acres of land where Kendleton (named for Kendle in 1884) is today and sold 100 acre plots to them for $0.50-$1.50 per acre. (See **Powell Point School** and **Gin.**) [144]

BRAY: James – This gentleman was one of the area's first Anglo settlers. He was a surveyor who worked for the Mexican government before Texas independence. In the 1820s he lived near the mouth of the bayou that now bears his name. (See **Bray's Bayou.**) [145]

BRAY'S BAYOU: Rising just north of Clodine in northern Fort Bend County, Bray's Bayou flows 14 miles to its mouth on Buffalo Bayou. (See **Bray.**) [146]

BRAZOS: Named for the longest river in Texas at 840 miles, its full name in Spanish is *Brazos de Dios* or Arms of God. Most historical accounts credit Francisco Vazquez de Coronado for naming the river when his men, almost dying of thirst in the Llano Estacado, were led to the headwaters by a band of Indians. [147]

BRAZOSPORT: This is a 214-acre urbanized industrial and port development near the mouth of the Brazos River south of Freeport. In was built in 1947. The name was taken from 18th century nautical charts. Today it services the marine, sulfur and chemical industries that dominate the area. [148]

BREMOND: Paul – A New Yorker who came to Texas in the 1840s, he had a successful general merchandise business. He wanted to build a railroad connecting Houston to North Texas. Bremond said he got the idea from a ghost. In 1856 he took over the Galveston & Red River Railroad and changed the name to the Houston & Central Texas Railway. After the Civil War he became interested in narrow gage railroads and started the Houston, East & West Texas Railway to build such a line from Houston to

Laredo and Texarkana. He died in 1885 before the project got off the ground. [149]

BRENTWOOD: Developers of River Oaks named many streets in that exclusive neighborhood for well-known country clubs around America or famous golf links in Scotland. It is likely this street was named after the New York club of the same name that was founded in 1900. [150]

BRIAR HOLLOW: This lane was laid out paralleling the Texas & New Orleans railroad tracks and the Harris Count Flood Control Ditch in the 1940s. It went north from San Felipe, made a sharp left, a sharp right and ended in a cul-de-sac. On a Sunday the developer took his wife for a drive to see his latest project. A large gully or hollow ran through the property (still visible today). She mentioned the large number of briar bushes lining the estuary, inspiring the husband to name the street Briar Hollow. In 1971 the section paralleling the tracks was renamed East Briar Hollow and the east-west portion was renamed South Briar Hollow. Your author has lived on Briar Hollow Lane for many years. [151]

BRIEFWAY: Developer B. F. Sturman called this street Briefway because it is only three blocks long. (See **Southway.**) [152]

BRIG-O-DOON: This is another example of the lack of spelling ability on the part of our real estate developers. Famous American lyricist Alan Jay Lerner wrote the musical play *Brigadoon* in 1947. It became a film seven years later. It is the fanciful tale of a Scottish village that went to sleep in 1754 and only awakens for one day each century thereafter. [153]

BRILEY: Felix H. - See sidebar **Houston Streets Named for Men Killed During World War I,** page 22.

BRILL: This family emigrated from Germany and settled in the Klein, Texas area. In the mid-1870s they, along with a number of other people, organized the Trinity Lutheran Church. Johannes Brill, his wife, Anna Schafer, and their daughter, Emilie arrived here in 1873. [154]

BRINGHURST: George Hunter – This veteran of the Texas Revolution arrived in Houston in 1836. Captured at Goliad he was a prisoner of war until after the Battle of San Jacinto. Following the war he became a surveyor for Harris County and was eventually elected Wharf Master when the Port of Houston was still at the foot of Main Street. [155]

BRITTMORE: Brit Moore was a dairy farmer in the area now called Denver Harbor. As urbanization closed in on his operation Moore sold it and moved west. He purchased a tract of land off Katy Road, cut a street through it and called it Brittmore. However he did not return to farming but chose real estate development, opening a "Red Flag" subdivision. (See sidebar **"Red Flag" Subdivisions** on page 81.) [156]

BRITTON: Whitney – This New York native came to Texas in the early 1830s to fight in the Texas Revolution. He owned 300 acres near what is Baytown today. Britton died in 1841. [157]

BROADMOOR: See sidebar **Tennis or Golf, Anyone?**, page 348.

BROADMOOR: The Broadmoor Corporation developed this neighborhood and thoroughfare off Telephone Road. [158]

BROM BONES: Abraham "Brom" Bones is the town rowdy in Sleepy Hollow. He is competing with Ichabod Crane for the hand of the farmer's daughter, Katrina. The story leads the reader to believe that Bones dressed up as the Headless Horseman and ran Crane out of town. (See **Washington Irving, Crane, Sleepy Hollow** and **Tarrytown.**) [159]

BROOKSHIRE-FULSHEAR: Captain Nathan Brookshire received a land grant here from Stephen F. Austin in 1835. He was a member of Austin's fifth colony. The town became a booming agricultural area when the Missouri, Kansas & Texas Railroad arrived allowing farmers to easily transport their crops to market. Since 1900 rice has been a major crop in Brookshire. (See **Katy-Fulshear.**) [160]

BROOKSIDE VILLAGE: This community sprang up on the banks of Clear Creek in north central Brazoria County in the 1930s. It was once served by the Atchison, Topeka & Santa Fe Railroad. Today the population is about 2,000. [157]

BROOKSIDE: This road leads to Brookside Village, a residential community that sits south of Houston on the Harris and Brazoria County lines. It was once a stop on the Atchison, Topeka & Santa Fe Railroad. Maps show this village as early as 1936 but it did not incorporate until 1959. [161]

BROWN: Jonel Leonard – This black gentleman was Chairman of the Department of Economics, Social Sciences and Geography at Prairie View A & M University from 1944 until 1969. Brown earned his degrees at Morehouse College (A. B.) and University of Wisconsin (A. M.) and (Ph.D.) He authored books including *Money and Banking* (1957) and *Principals of Economics* (1959). He earned many honors during his long career including a Distinguished Service Award from Prairie View. [162]

» **BROWN: Street sign on the Prairie View A&M campus**

BROWN: This Providence, R.I. university was chartered in 1764 as Rhode Island College. It was renamed in 1804 for philanthropist Nicholas Brown. [163]

BROWNE: John T. – This Fifth Ward resident was elected mayor of Houston (1892-96). His residence was one block off Lyons Avenue at Odin and Gregg. One of his civic projects was to pave Lyons with bricks. He succeeded in the task but had the paving halted when it went one block past his intersection, leaving the rest unpaved. [164]

BROWNING: Robert – This famous English poet was the husband of another great poet, Elizabeth Barrett Browning. His masterpiece, *The Ring and the Book,* is a four-volume murder mystery. [165]

BROWNWOOD: This upscale Baytown neighborhood and street are named for Edwin Rice Brown Sr. who purchased the property from Quincy Adams Wooster's heirs. (See **Wooster.**) [166]

BRUSHY CREEK: This Waller County road is named for this watercourse. It runs 10 miles and empties into Spring Creek. The name is derived from the abundance of elm, hackberry, loblolly pine and short leaf pine trees that line its banks. On February 13, 1687 the French explorer Rene La Salle crossed this creek on his way to the Trinity River. [167]

BRUTUS: Marcus Junius – This Roman, along with Cassius and other conspirators, assassinated Julius Caesar on the Ides of March 44 B.C. He and Cassius fled Rome and took up arms against Marc Anthony who defeated them at the Battle of Philippi in 42 B.C. Brutus committed suicide after the battle. (See **Cassius, Caesar** and **Marc Anthony**) [168]

BRYAN BEACH: This Gulf of Mexico coastal village is named for James Perry Bryan, a landowner in Brazoria County in the 1880s. Today it is principally a State Recreation Area used by beachgoers and fishermen. [169]

BRYAN: John L. – This gentleman practiced dentistry in the Baytown area in the 1850s when he charged $1 to extract a tooth. He was a founder of Texas Methodist Church. [170]

BRYAN: Louis R. Sr. (See **Angleton.**)

BRYAN: See sidebar **Brazoria County's Old Plantation Streets and Roads,** page 258.

BRYN MAR: Bryn Mar College, located in the small Pennsylvania town of the same name, is credited with introducing "historic gothic" architecture to the U.S. The campus is modeled after Oxford and Cambridge in the U.K. [171]

BUCCANEER: See sidebar **Pirates of the Caribbean,** page 280.

BUCKINGHAM: Located in a neighborhood with English street names, it is most likely named for Buckingham Palace in London. Built as a house in 1705 for John Sheffield, the duke of Buckingham, it was converted into a palace in the 1820's. Since that time it has been the principal residence of the reigning English monarch. Today it draws huge crowds of tourists to witness the pomp and circumstance of the changing of the guard. [104]

BUCKNER: B. P. – He was mayor of Houston in 1847-1848. Buckner served two terms during a financially difficult time for the city. Our treasury was broke and creditors were owed $1,300. However he was popular enough to be re-elected and have a street named for him. [172]

BUDDE CEMETERY: This road leads to the historic old Budde family cemetery, also known as the Budde-Holzwarth cemetery. Among the early pioneer families buried here are the Lemms, Mittelstaedts, Haudes, Holzwarths and Tautenhahns. [173]

BUETEL: Louis and Mary – This couple arrived in the Spring Valley area in the 1840s from Germany. Their property was near where Campbell and Westview intersect today. [174]

BUFFALO RUN: This road runs in front of Thurgood Marshall High School in Missouri City. Their mascot is the buffalo. [175]

BUFFALO SPEEDWAY: Urban legend says there was an automobile racetrack located south of where St. John's School is on the corner of Westheimer and Buffalo Speedway that has long ceased to exist, as have the stock car racetracks at Arrowhead Park on Old Spanish Trail and at Playland Park on South Main. However, this is not true. The street earned its name when a mile long strip of concrete was laid where Buffalo Speedway is today. It seems every boy with a hot rod wanted to see how fast he could go on this smooth, straight strip, thus the name. [176]

BUFORD: See sidebar **Texas Heroes' Names for Houston Streets Urged in 72 Proposed Changes,** page 96.

BULL RUN: This is a small stream in northeast Virginia where two battles in the War Between the States occurred. On July 21, 1861 the Battle of Bull Run, or Manassas as Southerners call it, occurred. It was the first major engagement of the Civil War and was a victory for the Confederate States of America. The second battle, also a win for the Confederacy, took place on August 29, 1862. [177]

BUNKER HILL: There are two possibilities for this street. First, there was a landowner in the area in the 1840s named Isaac Bunker. Second, another story says that prior to WW I this road was called Bunker, again possibly for the early settler. Later the name was changed to Bunker Hill to honor the June 17, 1775 battle between the British and the American Colonists during the War of Independence. [178]

BURGUNDY: See sidebar **Laissez les bon temps roulez** (Let the good times roll), page 188.

BURKETT: John Robbins – Since many Houstonians killed during World War I had streets named in their honor in the 1920s it's possible this one is named for a U. S. Army captain killed in France on September 18, 1918. He was the only attorney from our city who perished in the Great War. He was remembered with a tribute by the Harris County Bar Association that stated "A gallant knight without fear and without reproach." Burkett Street first appears on the city map in 1924. [179]

BURKHARDT: Take a look at a map of northwest Harris County to see how many family and church cemeteries are located there. Most of these were started by German immigrants who settled here and built Lutheran churches and dug burying grounds. The Burkhardt family arrived in the late 1800s and members are buried in the Siedel (Rosewood) cemetery including William Burkhardt (1837-1915). (See **Siedel Cemetery.**) [16]

BURLINGTON: The developer of the Westmoreland Addition, W. W. Baldwin, named this street for his hometown of Burlington, Iowa. [180]

BURLINGTON: This Montgomery County street recalls the Burlington Railroad. Started in 1849, over the next 150 years the line bought more than 390 other rail lines including such famous names as Great Northern, Frisco and Santa Fe. Today it is known as the Burlington Northern Santa Fe Railroad. (See **Santa Fe.**) [181]

BURMA: This is one of many streets in Houston's South Park Addition relating to World War II. This one most likely recalls the Burma Road, a lifeline used to transport military supplies, gasoline and other war materials to China. However, in May 1942 the Japanese Army seized the road cutting off the supply line. In order to continue re-supplying the Chinese Army cargo planes began flying materials over the Himalayas. Needless to say, this was a very dangerous operation with very high incidents of accidents. Called "flying the Burma Hump," it was successful airlifting over 650,000 tons of war materials. It was the largest air bridge in the world until the 1949 Berlin airlift. Such legendary military figures as Generals Orde Wingate and Joseph Stillwell, Lord Mountbatten and Merrill's Marauders saw action there. [182]

BURNET: David Gouverneur – Burnet, a lawyer, came to Texas in 1826. He was President of the Republic of Texas in the difficult period following independence. Burnet opposed succession. Elected to the U. S. Senate in 1866, he was not allowed to be sworn in because Texas was a slave state. Burnet County was named for him following his death. Burnet Elementary School on Canal Street also honors this early Texan. [183]

BURNET: Hannah Este – This early Baytown resident was the wife of David G. Burnet. Born in Morriston, N. J. in 1800 she died in 1858. Baytown honored her with this street. (See **Burnet.**) [184]

BURNETT: John H. – This gentleman, who helped in drawing the plan for our neighboring community of Pasadena in 1893, once owned more than 3,000 acres that comprise the town today. [185]

BURNING TREE: This hilly Bethesda, Maryland golf club was founded in 1924. It has been a favorite course of American Presidents because of its proximity to the White House. Its signature 16th hole is a 412-yard par four. Linksters must clear an elevated fairway and negotiate a small, well-bunkered green to score well here. Exclusively a men's club, ladies are not allowed on the course. [186]

BURRELL'S CHAPEL: Located on Bailey's Prairie in Brazoria County this road leads to this small chapel. It was built in 1900 and is named for the first pastor Reverend Burrell. (See **Bailey**.) [187]

BURTON CEMETERY: This far west Harris County road leads to the Burton-Mathis-Canon cemetery. At first this burying ground was solely used by the Burton and Mathis families. Some of the older tombstones here are W. T. (1833-1910) and Judge J. (1882-1947) Mathis. It appears that the Canon name was added much later as the Canon Funeral Home of Waller, Texas became associated with this property. (See **Mathis**) [35]

BUTE: James – This son of a Scottish immigrant inherited the family business, Bute Paint Company, that still exists. In addition he was a landowner whose holdings included the area today near the street known as Westmoreland. He was very interested in gardening and became the first treasurer of the Texas Horticultural Society. [188]

BUTLER: George W. – He settled in the Houston area in 1873. His land was located at the confluence of Clear Creek and Chigger Creek in northern Galveston County. The town was called Butler's Ranch or Clear Creek until it was renamed League City in 1893. (See **League**.) [189]

BUTTERFIELD: The Butterfield Overland Mail was a stagecoach line that ran from St. Louis to Memphis, across Texas to El Paso, through New Mexico, on to Tucson and Fort Yuma in Arizona, turned north at San Diego and ended in San Francisco. It commenced service on September 15, 1858. The line was created to speed up mail service from the East coast to California. Travel time for a letter from St. Louis to San Francisco was less than 25 days. Maritime delivery of mail either around Cape Horn or through the Caribbean, across Panama on horseback and by ship to San Francisco took considerably longer. The line was named for its founder John Butterfield of Utica, New York. [190]

NOW THAT'S A SPICY MEATBALL

If Julia Childs, Marcella Hazen or Diana Kennedy were to move to our area I suspect they would gravitate to a small suburb of Baytown named Preston Place. The reason – the culinary street names. In this little neighborhood we find **Caraway, Thyme, Tarragon, Cinnamon, Cilantro, Ginger** and **Taro**. And just in case someone burns a finger on a hot skillet you could treat the blister with **Aloe**. [7]

BUTTERFLY: Along with other operatic related street names in this Memorial neighborhood, this lane honors the two-act Italian opera by Puccini, "Madam Butterfly." It premiered in Milan in 1904. It is the story of a beautiful Japanese heroine who is deserted by an American naval officer. This opera contains a musical error in that the samisen is a lute-like stringed instrument that is plucked with the fingers and not a gong as Puccini made it. [191]

BYRNE: Hugo O. – See sidebar **Houston Streets Named for Men Killed During World War I,** page 22.

BYRON: George Gordon Noel – This troubled soul, considered one of England's greatest poets and satirists, made great contributions to the literature of the Romantic Era. His downfall was the result of his prodigious sexual appetite. Byron's outcast status caused him to leave Britain in a self-imposed exile. Late in life while living with his mistress in Venice he became involved in the cause to gain Greek independence. He died of a fever in 1819. [192]

C

C.E. KING: This gentleman was a large landowner in Harris County. He developed Southpark following World War II. Many of the streets in this neighborhood are named for famous battles of that conflict and their histories are detailed elsewhere in this book. These starter homes could be bought for $50 per month in the 1950s. King said his goal was to build houses "young people may buy and be proud of." Old timers may recall the twin screen King Center Drive-In. Once located near where Loop 610 South and M. L. King intersect, it has been closed for years. The theater became infamous in it final days. With the popularity of drive-in theaters waning in the late 1960s and early 1970s, economic considerations forced operators to adopt drastic measures to keep the gates open. The King Center began showing pornographic films that evening commuters on the Loop could not help noticing. But even the likes of *Deep Throat* and *Debbie Does Dallas* couldn't save the King. [1]

CABELL: William Louis – A graduate of West Point he resigned his commission in 1861 to fight for the South in the War Between the States. He was a brigadier general in the Army of the Potomac. Cabell saw action in more than 30 battles. He was wounded at Hatcher's Creek in 1862 and captured at Mine Creek in 1864. Following the War he graduated from law school and moved to Dallas. He was elected mayor of that city in 1874 and served several terms until 1883. [2]

CADENZA: See sidebar **It's Music to My Ears,** page 218.

CADUCEUS: It is only appropriate that a city like Galveston with its long association with the University of Texas Medical Branch would have a street named for this insignia symbolizing a physician. The symbol is a staff with two entwined serpents and two wings. The caduceus dates back to 1577. [3]

CAELIN: Woodlands resident Joel Deretchin named this street for his grand daughter. Nearby **Colewood** is named for his grandson, Cole. [4]

HOUSTON'S GERMANIC HERITAGE

Germans and people of Germanic decent have been an important part of Texas history for 250 years. Prior to arriving in Houston, records show German traders visited other parts of Texas in the 1750s. Germans were associated with the Louisiana Purchase (1804), the Long Expedition (1821) and the Texas Revolution (1835-36). Beginning in 1831 German immigrants began to arrive in small numbers in Texas. By 1845 this trickle was a flood. Most of them settled in Houston, Galveston and the Brazos and Colorado River Valleys. The combination of difficult economic conditions at home, plentiful job opportunities, better wages and an abundance of inexpensive but fertile farmland were the reasons so many Germans came to the Lone Star State. The first record of Germans in Houston appears in 1842. A large number lived in the Second Ward. So many in fact that that area was called Germantown and Canal Street was on the city maps as German Street. Much of our Germanic heritage is contained in our cemeteries. Washington Cemetery was known as the German Society Cemetery from its founding in 1887 until the name was changed due to anti-war sentiment during WW I in 1918. Three smaller cemeteries in west Houston (Hillendahl, St. Peter's United Church and Vollmer) were also the burial grounds of many people of German descent. A number of streets in the Spring Branch and Memorial Villages area memorialize many of the German settler families. These would include: **Bauer, Beinhorn, Beutel, Conrad Sauer, Hedwig, Hillendahl, Moritz, Neuns, Ojeman, Pech, Pifer, Riedel, Rummel, Schroeder** and **Witte.** [8]

CAESAR: Caius Julius – He is the most famous Roman of all. A brilliant orator, author and military man he eventually parlayed that prowess into becoming Emperor of Rome. Unfortunately, Caesar abused his powers and was assassinated on the Ides of March (March 15, 44 B.C.) by a group of Roman senators lead by Cassius and Brutus, prompting his last words "Et tu Brute?" He is little remembered for one of his greatest accomplishments: reforming the calendar. The Julian calendar was used until the 16th century when it was slightly modified and called the Gregorian calendar. (See **Brutus, Cassius** and **Marc Anthony.**) [5]

CAGE: Benjamin F. – In Houston's younger days it was not unusual to honor veterans of the Battle of San Jacinto with a street name. Such is the case with Mr. Cage who came to Texas in 1832. He fought under the command of Captain William H. Patton. It is believed that Indians killed him in 1838 near San Antonio. [6]

CAJON: See sidebar **Learn a Foreign Language on Your Morning Walk,** page 125.

CALAIS: In May 1940 after the Germans captured this French port city as well as the harbor town of Boulogne, the only avenue of retreat for the British forces facing annihilation was through Dunkirk. (See **Dunkirk.**) [7]

CALHOUN: John Caldwell – Here is another example of Houston showing its appreciation of South Carolina for that state's support of the annexation of Texas. This gentleman, along with South Carolina Senator W. C. Preston, was a strong supporter of statehood for Texas. Calhoun County in south Texas is named for him also. (See **Preston.**) [8]

CALHOUN: This Richmond street was originally called Railroad because it paralleled the train tracks. An old map at the George Memorial Library there shows the following businesses in a two block area of that street: Blue Light Tavern, Horse Saloon, Manuel's Bar, Sunset Saloon, Cinder Club, Dally Saloon, Emil and John Joseph Saloon, Jackson's Bar & Café, Gooden's Bar, C. F. Austin's Exchange Saloon, Spells Liquor Store and Three Brothers Saloon. The latter business was forced to close when the brothers married hard shell Baptist wives who strongly disapproved of imbibing spirits, wine and beer. [9]

CAMBRIDGE: This is one of the oldest English speaking universities in the world dating from the 12th century. Located in Cambridge, England it predates Oxford University by almost a century. Today it has 31 colleges. [10]

CAMELOT: This is the site of King Arthur's Court in Arthurian legend.

CAMP STRAKE: This is one of the largest and most attended Boy Scout camps in America. It is named for Houston oilman George Strake, a philanthropist who donated generously to the Scouts during his lifetime. Over 80,000 Cub and Boy Scouts visit Camp Strake annually at no cost to them. (See **Strake.**) [11]

CAMP WALLACE: This was a training center for antiaircraft units near Hitchcock during World War II. It was built in 1941. It is named for Colonel Elmer J. Wallace who was killed in the Battle of Meuse-Argonne in the First World War in 1918. Camp Wallace became a naval training center in 1944 and was closed and sold in 1946. (See **Hitchcock.**) [12]

CAMPBELL: John W. – He was a lawyer and judge who owned property near the intersection of where Campbell and Katy Road intersect today in Houston. Campbell was originally from Louisiana. [13]

CANADA DRY: In the 1950s the Houston distributor of this once popular club soda and soft drink was located on this street that intersects the Gulf Freeway. [15]

CANAL: Briscoe Irrigation Company developed a network of canals to provide Brazos River water for irrigation and industrial use in Fort Bend, Brazoria and Galveston Counties. In the 1930s the system was sold to American Rice Growers Association. They dug the American Canal which taps water from Oyster Creek. In 1967 the canals were taken over by the Brazos River Authority. This system still is a major component of the watershed management in this area. [16]

CANAL: Prior to 1918 this Houston thoroughfare was called German Street. The name was changed because of the anti-German sentiment caused by WW I. Although none of the early city maps I studied showed any canal in the area, its proximity to the Houston Ship Channel and other maritime themed streets such as Navigation, may have influenced its name. (See sidebar **Houston's Germanic Heritage** page 60.) [17]

CANDLEWOOD: (See **Chimney Rock.**) [18]

CANEY: Texas is home to more than 30 streams named Caney Creek. They are so called because of the cane-like vegetation along their banks. This one, in Montgomery County, runs about 50 miles, eventually flowing into the San Jacinto River near Lake Houston. The area was first settled in the 1830s. The town of New Caney rose on its banks in 1860. One of our state's more interestingly named towns, Cut and Shoot, is on this waterway. (See **Roy Harris.**) [19]

CANFIELD: Henry R. – See sidebar **Houston Streets Named for Men Killed During World War I,** page 22.

CANGELOSI: Frank & Carlo – These brothers established a general store and cotton gin in Stafford in the early 1900s. (See **Stafford.**) [20]

CANNONADE: This thoroughbred horse won the centennial running of the Kentucky Derby in 1974. The race was uneventful and he cruised to a 2 ¼-length victory. The fifth place finisher in this race, Little Current, went on to win the Preakness and the Belmont. [21]

CANONERO: Winning the 1971 Kentucky Derby was the easiest thing this thorough-bred did in May of that year. He was air freighted with a load of chickens from

» **CAPITOL: Sketch of the first capitol of Texas**

Venezuela to Miami where he spent several days in quarantine. With no workouts he was placed in a horse trailer and driven 1,000 miles to Churchill Downs in Louisville, Kentucky, site of the Derby. He trailed the field before coming on strong, recording a 3 ¾-length victory. Canonero proved his upset at Churchill was not luck when he posted a win in the second leg of the Triple Crown at the Preakness. In that run he led gate to wire. Unfortunately, he lost to Pass Catcher in the rubber match of the Triple Crown at Belmont. [22]

CANTATA: See sidebar **It's Music to My Ears,** page 218.

CAPELLA: See sidebar **Starry Night,** page 111.

CAPITOL: It was named to remind us that Houston was the second capitol of the Republic of Texas. We held this prestigious title from 1837 to 1839 when the government was moved to Austin. The actual Capitol Building was located on the northwest corner of Main and Texas where the Rice Loft condominiums are today. Named the Capitol Hotel by the Allen Brothers who owned the structure, it was purchased by William Marsh Rice. Following his murder it was renamed in his honor. (See **Rice.**) (See photograph of the first capitol at West Columbia on page 62.) [23]

CAPROCK CANYON: See sidebar **The Most Scenic Spots in Texas,** page 310.

CAPTAIN BLIGHT: See sidebar **Pirates of the Caribbean,** page 280.

CAPTAIN HOOK: See sidebar **Pirates of the Caribbean,** page 280.

CARBON BLACK: The U. S. Government owned a carbon black plant in Sweeny that they sold to Phillips Petroleum in 1942. Carbon black is a by-product of the incomplete combustion of natural gas or petroleum. It is used to reinforce rubber as well as in inks, paints and polishes.

CARDWELL: Bedford C. – This street as well as Cardwell Estates may be named for this 1950s real estate developer. [24]

CARNARVON: George Edward Stanhope – Its location in the Sherwood Forest addition leads me to believe this street is named for the British archeologist who was the patron of Howard Carter, the man who found the tomb of King Tutankhamen on November 4, 1922. Carnarvon died from an infection he contracted shortly after opening the sarcophagus, prompting the legend of the mummy's curse. [25]

CARNEGIE: This university was founded in Pittsburgh, Pennsylvania by industrialist and philanthropist, Andrew Carnegie, in 1900. It began as a technical school. Carnegie's vision was to open a vocational training school for the sons and daughters of working-class Pittsburghers. [26]

CAROLINE: On some of the earliest street maps of Houston this street is named Carolina. South Carolina and one of its two U.S. Senators, W. C. Preston, strongly backed Texas annexation when this was not a popular cause in Washington D. C. because of fear of starting a war with Mexico. In return for this support city fathers honored that state with a major downtown thoroughfare. Somewhere along the way a transcription error changed the name to Caroline. In a way this is a shame because we have streets named for 48 of the 50 states. Only South Carolina and Maine are omitted. (See **Preston** and **Calhoun.**) [27]

CARPETBAGGER: Feelings about the War Between the States do not die easily, especially in the South. Thus the name of this street in western Harris County near Fairfield. A carpetbagger is a Northerner who came to the South after the conflict and became active in Republican politics and profited from the disordered conditions during the Reconstruction Era. Today the word represents any opportunistic or exploitive outsider. [28]

CARRELL: W. A. – He owned property northeast of Tomball. Carrell sold three acres of land to the city for its first hospital in 1944. (See **Hospital.**) [29]

» CARTER: Houston Heights founder O. M. Carter

CARTER: Oscar M. – He was a self-made millionaire from Nebraska who brought his utopian vision for a 20th century town to Houston. He created the Omaha and South Texas Land Company that purchased 1,756 acres on the highest point in the area northwest of downtown. Calling it Houston Heights, the corporation invested $500,000 in infrastructure including utilities, parks, schools, landscaping, streets and alleys. [30]

CARTWRIGHT: Jessie H. – He arrived in Texas in 1825 from Mississippi. In 1828 Stephen F. Austin awarded Cartwright a league of land where Missouri City is today. He farmed and ranched on his Cartwright Plantation. Santa Anna and the Mexican Army crossed his property in pursuit of their fateful meeting with Sam Houston at the Battle of San Jacinto in 1836. During the Republic of Texas he served in the Congress in 1836-7. He died in 1878. [31]

» CARVER: George Washington Carver

CARVER: George Washington – This neighborhood (Carverdale) and street honor one of America's most outstanding African-Americans. His expertise was agriculture. He was head of the Agriculture Department and director of Agricultural Research at Tuskegee Institute. He devoted his life and work to improving the lot of poor southern farmers. In 1940 he endowed the George Washington Carver Foundation to perpetuate his research. He was the recipient of numerous honors and awards. In 1953 the Alabama plantation where he was born of slave parents was named a national monument. [32]

CASCADA: See sidebar **Learn a Foreign Language on Your Morning Walk,** page 125.

CASEY: Mike – He founded a brickyard in the Baytown area in 1869 that produced 600,000 bricks yearly. Casey died in 1871. His family closed the business and moved away. In the 1880s the brickyard was reopened to take advantage of the building boom going on in Galveston. Once again the yard fell on hard times and the site was sold to the City of Baytown for a garbage dump. [33]

CASH: R. M. – In Katy, Texas a neighborhood named Heritage Meadows contains the names of the men who platted the city in 1895. Cash was one of these founders. [34]

CASSANDRA: In Greek mythology Apollo gives Cassandra the ability to predict the future. In return Apollo wants Cassandra to be his lover. When she refuses he makes sure that no one believes her prophesies. [35]

CASSIUS: Caius Longinus – This Roman was involved in the conspiracy to assassinate Julius Caesar on March 15, 44 B.C. In his stirring " Friends, Romans, countrymen lend me your ears" speech, Marc Anthony enraged the citizens, forcing Cassius to flee to Syria. He was pursued by Anthony and Octavian who engaged him in battle at Philippi. Mistakenly believing he lost the skirmish, Cassius committed suicide. (See **Caesar, Marc Anthony** and **Brutus.**) [36]

CASTLE HARBOUR: See sidebar **Tennis or Golf, Anyone?,** page 348.

CASTOR: In Greek and Roman mythology Castor along with his twin brother Pollux were children of Zeus and Leda. They were revered by sailors and were said to appear during storms as St. Elmo's fire, a visible electric discharge that can appear on a ship's mast in foul weather. [37]

CASTOR: See sidebar **Starry Night,** page 111.

CAT SPRING: In 1834 a group of Germans from Oldenburg and Westphalia, lead by Ludwig Anton Siegmund von Roeder and Robert Kleberg, settled in this area of western Austin County. They were joining another Oldenburg citizen who arrived three years earlier and wrote enthusiastically about this area of Texas. The name came from von Roeder's son who killed a puma near one of the springs here. [38]

CATFEET COURT: Located in the Woodlands this street name was inspired by Carl Sandberg's short poem. "The fog comes on little cat feet. It sits looking over the harbor and city on silent haunches and then moves on." [39]

CAT'S CRADLE: Also in the Woodlands, Susan Vreeland-Wendt was inspired by Harry

Chapin's *Cat's in the Cradle* off of his 1974 hit album *Verities & Balderdash* when she named this street. [40]

CAYLOR: Joseph B. – See sidebar **Houston Streets Named for Men Killed During World War I,** page 22.

CEDAR BAYOU: This drive is named for the bayou of the same name. That estuary meanders 46 miles through Liberty County, emptying into Trinity Bay southeast of Baytown. Early settlers named it because of the great abundance of cedar trees that lined its banks. [41]

CEDAR CREEK: Tanglewood developer William Farrington named this street for a small Texas town where his wife's family had lived for over 100 years and had founded the Baptist church there. [42]

CEDAR CREEK: This Waller County village was named for the nearby creek of the same name by Henry Kloecker in the 1880s. (See **Kloecker.**) [43]

CEDAR GROVE CEMETERY: This burying ground is all that remains of the small Brazoria County town of the same name. Cedar Grove was established in 1886 where the Dance family's Cedar Brake Plantation once stood. [44]

CEDAR GROVE: Lying east of Houston near the Harris/Chambers county line is this two-block long street. It recalls the small village of the same name. Cedar Grove was on most Texas maps up until the late 1930s. [45]

CEMETERY: (See **Zion Lutheran Cemetery.**)

CENTENARY: Founded in 1825, and affiliated with the United Methodist Church, Centenary College is the oldest chartered liberal arts college west of the Mississippi River. Located in Shreveport, Louisiana, this college's name came from the desire to remember the 100th anniversary of John Wesley's founding of the Methodist Societies in England. [46]

CENTER WAY: The streets of Lake Jackson were laid out to provide easy access to the

---

HOUSTON STREETS NAMED FOR OTHER TEXAS TOWNS

Developers of Denver Harbor and Houston Harbor, just northwest of the Houston Ship Channel, elected to name streets after towns where newcomers had moved from in order to become residents of our fair city. From north to south these streets are named: **Gainesville, Longview, Texarkana, Eagle Pass, Victoria, Corpus Christi, Brownsville, Laredo, Hillsboro, Waxahachie, Brownwood, Greenville, Bonham, Dennison, Amarillo, Abilene, El Paso, San Angelo, Gonzales, Corsicana** and **Palestine.** [9]

STREETS NAMED FOR PATRON SAINTS

Although we do have separation of church and state in America there is no law preventing developers for naming streets for Saints. As a result we might be considered a quite religious community by outsiders who notice how many of our highways and byways are named for these holy souls and whom or what they protect. Some examples include: **St. Agnes**-young girls; **St. Alban**-converts; **St. Andrew**-fishermen and Scotland; **St. Anne** & **Santa Anna**-housewives, miners and childless women; **San Antonio**-shipwrecks and lost articles; **San Augustine**-brewers, theologians and eye sores; **St. Benedict**-farmers, spelunkers and gall stones; **St. Cecilia**-music and musicians; **St. Christopher** & **San Cristobal**-travelers and safe journeys; **St. Clare** & **Santa Clara**-embroiderers, TV and eye disorders; **St. Claude**-toy makers; **San Clemente**-stoneworkers and sick kids; **St. Cloud**-nail makers; **St. Francis**-Italy, merchants and animals; **San Gabriel**-broadcasters, clergy and telephones; **St. George**-England, soldiers and boy scouts; **St. Helena**-difficult marriages and divorced people; **St. Ives**-England; **St. John**-poison sufferers; **St. Joseph** & **San Jose**-fathers, joiners and Russia; **St. Jude**-lost, desperate or hopeless causes; **St. Lawrence**-the poor; **St. Louis** & **San Luis**-masons and sculptors; **St. Lucia**-authors and eye diseases; **St. Mark** & **San Marco**-Venice, notaries and lawyers; **St. Martin** & **San Martin**-vintners, tailors and innkeepers; **St. Mary** & **Santa Maria**-Spain; **St. Michael**-security forces, bankers and grocers; **Santa Monica**-difficult marriages, victims of adultery and victims of unfaithfulness; **St. Patrick** & **San Patrico**-Ireland and engineers; **St. Paul** & **San Pablo**-Rome and public relations; **St. Peter** & **San Pedro**-Rome and foot problems; **San Ramon**-lawyers and medical records librarians; **St. Regis**-lace makers and social workers; **Santa Rita**-forgotten causes and sickness; **San Sebastian**-athletes, police and archers; **St. Simon**-curriers and saw men; **Santa Theresa**-bodily ills and headaches and **San Vicente**-charities and prisoners. [10]

center of town. "Drives" go around the outskirts and handle through traffic. "Ways" lead to the city center. Thus the name of this street. **Circle Way** circles the business district. (See **This Way** and **That Way**.) [47]

CENTURION: A military title during the Roman Empire, this officer commanded a troop of 100 legionaries. [48]

CESAR CHAVEZ: Born during the Great Depression and raised in migrant farm labor camps in California, he experienced first hand the plight of American and Mexican farm workers. He was driven by this experience to form the National Farm Workers Association to unionize the pickers. He fought bitterly but successfully with California grape, lettuce and citrus farmers for better pay and improved working conditions for the members. [49]

CESSNA: Clyde Cessna was an aviation pioneer. In 1927 he unveiled a monoplane with a full cantilever wing (one without supporting struts or braces) that forever changed the way aircraft were designed. Since then the Cessna Aircraft Company of Wichita, Kansas has produced multi-engine aircraft, gliders for use during World War II as well a turbo-prop airplanes and business jets. [50]

CHAFFIN: James A. – This gentleman is another veteran of the Battle of San Jacinto.

He had only been in the state a short time, arriving in 1835, when he enlisted in the Texas Army. He fought in the company of Captain William Kimbro. After the war he moved to San Augustine where he operated a saloon. [51]

CHAGALL: Marc – This Russian born artist is best remembered for his works about Jewish life and folklore. Although he spent most of his life in France, his works are on display around the world. His dreamlike, fantasy style and use of bright colors make his paintings distinctive. [52]

CHALLENGER SEVEN: On January 28, 1986, America's space program suffered one of its most tragic disasters. That morning the Space Shuttle Challenger Seven exploded shortly after takeoff, killing the crew of seven astronauts. These heroic Americans are honored by this Jacinto City street. [53]

CHALMETTE: See sidebar *Laissez les bon temps roulez* (Let the good times roll), page 188.

CHANCELLORSVILLE: This was the site of the South's most costly victory in the War Between the States. Although General Lee's 53,000 rebels routed General Hooker's 120,000 federals, Thomas "Stonewall" Jackson, one of the Confederates' greatest military geniuses, was seriously wounded by a South Carolina regiment that accidentally fired on him on the night of May 2, 1863. The next morning surgeons were forced to amputate Jackson's arm in an attempt to save his life. However, he died on May 10 at a farmhouse in Fairfield, Virginia and was taken to Lexington for burial. A strange twist of events caused his arm to not make that trip. Jackson's chaplain, Reverend B. Tucker Lacy, found the arm at the field hospital and took it to his brother's plantation, Elmwood, where it was buried in the family cemetery. Today

» **CHANCELLORSVILLE: Tombstone of Stonewall Jackson's arm**

it lies in peace under a tombstone with the epitaph "Arm of Stonewall Jackson - May 3, 1863," buried seven days before its owner expired. [54]

CHANDLER: W. E. – See sidebar **Houston Streets Named for Men Killed During World War I,** page 22.

CHANEY COURT & CHANEY LANE: These two streets are named for Chaney Junction, a stop on the Galveston, Harrisburg & San Antonio Railroad that operated in the 1880s and early 1900s. [55]

CHANNEL CITY: In the 1920s this road led to Channel, Texas, a small community on the

Houston Ship Channel. Today docks owned by Tenneco, Georgia Pacific and Ethyl are on the site. Channel was also known as Houston Terminals, not the most charming name for a residential neighborhood. [56]

CHANNELVIEW: Both the street and this Houston refinery suburb are named because of the location on the north side of the Houston Ship Channel. When founded at the turn of the 20th century the town was perched on the banks of Buffalo Bayou and the nascent shipping channel there. [57]

CHANTILLY: In 1947 real estate developer Frank Sharp began construction of the Oak Forest Addition in Houston. Many of the houses were sold to returning veterans of WWII for $8,000-$10,000, one of whom was Harold P. Hill. He was hired by Sharp as an office manager. This street was named for Hill's wife's silver pattern. It is produced by Gorham, a company that began in Germany in 1813. Chantilly was first made in 1895 and became the most popular sterling silverware pattern of the 20th century. (See **Nina Lee** and **Frank Sharp**.) [58]

CHARING CROSS: This is a neighborhood in London where the grieving Edward I erected the last of 12 crosses marking the locations where his wife Eleanor of Castile's funeral procession camped between Nottinghamshire and London in 1290. [59]

CHARLES E. SELECMAN: He was chairman of the board, president and chief executive officer of Input/Output, a seismic acquisition imaging technology company for land and marine oil and gas exploration headquartered in Stafford. [60]

CHARPIOT: In the 1800s this family settled in north Harris County where this street is located. Fifteen members of the family were buried in Teeter Cemetery, north of Bush Intercontinental Airport. The most beautiful tombstone in that burying ground is that of Rebecca Jane Charpiot (1835-1896). She was the wife of Severin Charpiot. (See **Teeter Cemetery**.) [61]

CHARRO: In Mexico they use this word to describe a cowboy or cowboy associated objects such as *frijoles ala charro* or cowboy beans. [62]

CHARTRES: When this street first appeared on a Houston city map in 1839 it was spelled Chartre and then Charter. Its current name appeared on the 1866 map. The best guess as to the provenance of this street is that A. Girard, most probably a Frenchman, could have been from the French town of Chartres (although the town name was misspelled on the 1839 map) or it honors the beautiful Chartres Cathedral. Girard may not have been around by the time the map was printed to call attention to the error. Read about Girard Street to see possibly why he was nowhere to be found. (See **Girard**.) [63]

CHATTANOOGA: A Civil War battle took place at Chattanooga, Tennessee on November 24-27, 1863. The Confederate Army of the West was dug in on Lookout

Mountain when the Union forces attacked. Because of the thick ground fog this skirmish earned the nickname of "The Battle Above the Clouds." Northerners chalked up one in the win column here. [64]

CHAUCER: Geoffrey – He was one of the first great English poets. His writings did much to establish English as a literary language. Chaucer's most famous work is *The Canterbury Tales.* [65]

CHEMICAL: So named as it leads to the manufacturing facilities of Dixie Chemical and Carpenter Chemical in the Bayport Industrial Complex. (See **Bayport.**) [66]

CHENANGO PLANTATION: This antebellum plantation was named for a town in New York. It was originally part of William Smith's 1,300 acre land grant. Later 3,000 additional acres were added to it when land belonging to Richardson and Joshua Abbot were merged into Chenango. The property passed through many hands until it was acquired by the Texas Department of Corrections who made it into the Ramsey Prison Farm near Angleton. [67]

CHENEVERT: This street appears on the second map of Houston drawn in 1839. The map was produced by A. Girard, most likely a Frenchman who immigrated to Texas prior to the Texas Revolution in 1836. He probably named the street for the thick forest that existed in the Houston area then. In French *chene* means oak and *veret* is green. (See **Girard.**) [68]

CHENNAULT: Clare Lee – A fighter pilot through and through, Chennault fought in WW I. He went to China in 1937 to assist Chiang Kai-shek in building an air defense against the Japanese invaders. He founded the famed American volunteer force, the Flying Tigers, in 1941. In 1942 Chennault was named commander of the U. S. air operations in China. [69]

CHERRYHURST: The addition and street of the same name are on property that was owned by D. B. and H.H. Cherry in 1906. The 45-acre neighborhood was platted on the city map in 1908. Mirabeau B. Lamar, the second President of the Republic of Texas, once owned this acreage. His home was rumored to have been near the intersection of Commonwealth and Hyde Park. The neighborhood was principally developed by Edward Lillo Crane Sr. beginning in 1921 following his purchase of the land from the Cherrys. (See **Edloe.**) [70]

CHEVRON OIL FIELD: This Fort Bend road recalls a historic oil company. Chevron traces its roots to an 1879 oil discovery north of Los Angeles. The firm was then named Standard Oil Co. of California. The moniker was changed to Chevron when they acquired Gulf Oil Corporation in 1984. In 2001 the company merged with Texaco and purchased Unocal Corporation in 2005. Today it is one of the world's largest integrated energy firms. [71]

CHEVY CHASE: This street is named for the famous Chevy Chase Club in the Maryland town of the same name in Houston's River Oaks. The Club was incorporated in 1895. Its famous golf course dates back to 1910. [72]

CHICAGO BRIDGE-IRON: It is named for the Chicago Bridge & Iron Company, a 136-year old construction firm. Today CB & I is best known for manufacturing bulk liquid terminals, storage terminals and process vessels. [73]

CHICKAMAUGA: A Civil War battle occurred here in Georgia on September 19 and 20, 1863. On these days the Confederates were victorious with General Bragg forcing Union General Rosecrans to retire to Chattanooga. [74]

CHICORA WOOD: See sidebar the **Antebellum Streets of River Plantation,** page 122.

CHILTON: George W. – Chilton fought with John C. "Jack" Hays' Texas Rangers in the Mexican-American War in 1846-48. He was a member of the Texas State Legislature and later a colonel in the Confederate Army. Following the War Between the States he was elected a U.S. Representative. However, it was payback time for the Union and the Reconstructionists in Congress denied the Texans their House seats. [75]

CHIMNEY ROCK: The Farringtons, developers of the posh southwest Houston neighborhood of Tanglewood, named this street as well as **Huckleberry, Sugar Hill, Lynbrook, Candlewood** and **Russet** as "picturesque regional identifications." [76]

CHINA GROVE: Albert Sidney Johnson was born in Kentucky in 1803. Shortly after graduating from the U. S. Military Academy he fought in the Black Hawk War. In 1836 he moved to Texas and enlisted in the Texas Army where he earned the rank of brigadier general. Two years later he was appointed Secretary of War for the Republic of Texas. He settled in Brazoria County and developed China Grove Plantation. Johnson fought in the Mexican War (1846-8). Jefferson Davis appointed him a general in the Confederate Army. He saw action at Nashville, Tennessee, Corinth Mississippi and was killed at the Battle of Shiloh on August 6, 1862. [77]

"PARENTS OFFERED NAMES FOR CHILDREN FROM CITY STREET "SURPLUS" LISTS"

This unusual headline appeared in the *Houston Chronicle.* In the 1930s Houston had numerous streets with duplicate names. This problem made mail delivery extremely difficult. In various sections of the city there were numerical streets, alphabetical streets, streets named for ladies, streets honoring historical figures, etc. This often meant the postman would have to take a letter to as many as five different houses on streets with the same names in different parts of the city to finally make delivery to the correct person. To solve this dilemma the Engineering Department assigned two engineers, Jack Tooke and Jack Graham, to rename the duplicate thoroughfares. They selected 241 street names, a number that well exceeded the number actually needed. So it was decided "Proud parents who find it difficult to select an appropriate name for their new arrivals might do well to confer with Tooke and Graham." "We have a lot of names left over, too" said Tooke. "They'd fit children, dogs, cats, streets or anything." It is not known if any of our indecisive citizens availed themselves of this generous offer. [11]

» CHINQUAPIN SCHOOL: Bob and Maxine Moore

CHINQUAPIN SCHOOL: Robert and Maxine Moore founded this college preparatory academy in 1969. Its mission is to provide intelligent but low-income children an opportunity to receive a first class education. The first class consisted of 16 students. Today enrollment tops 120. Your author had the pleasure of knowing Bob and Maxine well. I was lucky enough to study English at St. John's School while Bob taught there during his 19-year tenure. They named the school after Chinquapin Creek near their summer home in Palestine, Texas as well as for the chinquapin oak tree. Bob and Maxine passed away in 1999.

CHISHOLM TRAIL: This famous cattle drive trail was named for Jesse Chisholm. In the 1860s and 1870s millions of longhorn cattle were herded from as far south as the Rio Grand, through Texas to Wichita, Kansas. [78]

CHISUM: See sidebar **Texas Heroes' Names for Houston Streets Urged in 72 Proposed Changes,** page 96.

CHOATE: Moses L. – This gentleman settled in the La Porte area in 1822 and is thought to be, along with William Pettus, the city's first citizens. Choate was a sizable landowner in east Texas. He platted a town there called Springfield in 1839. When Polk County was created the politicians wanted the county seat closer to the geographic center of the county. The site they wanted happened to be near Springfield. Choate gave them 100 acres for the new county seat provided they would name it Livingston after his hometown in Tennessee. [79]

CHOCOLATE BAYOU: This bayou rises north of Manvel and flows 30 miles to its mouth on Chocolate Bay. It was the eastern boundary of Stephen F. Austin's first colony. The ghost town of Chocolate Bayou was located nearby on the Austin-Perry land grant. It came into being in the early 1900s. Emily Perry, Austin's sister, ran a plantation here known as Peach Point. She raised cotton and sugar cane. [80]

CHOKE CANYON: See sidebar **The Most Scenic Spots in Texas,** page 310.

CHOPIN: Frederic Francois – He was a Polish composer who wrote primarily piano solos. [81]

CHORALE: See sidebar **It's Music to My Ears,** page 218.

CHRIESMAN: Horatio – This Virginian who was born in 1792, arrived in Texas in 1821 to lead Stephen F. Austin's corps of surveyors. He settled in Fort Bend County.

Chriesman is a member of the Old 300. [82]

CHRISTOPHER WREN: He was unquestionably England's greatest architect. Wren was chosen as the man to oversee the rebuilding of London following the Great Fire of 1666. His strong suit was places of worship. He designed 52 of them including his masterpiece, St. Paul's Cathedral. [83]

CHURCHILL DOWNS: This thoroughbred racehorse track is the home of the "most exciting two minutes in sports" – the Kentucky Derby. It opened in 1875 and since that time 135 Derbies have been run here, with the winners passing into horse racing history. With its famous twin white spires that are copyrighted, this Louisville, Kentucky track is among the most architecturally appealing racecourses in the world. If you are ever given the opportunity, don't fail to be trackside on the first Saturday in May for the "Run for the Roses." It is the thrill of a lifetime. [84]

CINCO RANCH: This 7,500 acre planned community is located in Katy. Its master plan offers single-family, custom, estate and low-maintenance housing. [85]

CINDERELLA: She was the fairy tale maiden who escaped a life of oppression under her stepmother and stepsisters to marry a prince and live happily ever after.

CIRCLE WAY: (See **Center Way.**)

CITATION: The 1948 Triple Crown winner, this thoroughbred won at distances ranging from five furlongs to two miles. His trainer once said, "He could catch any horse he could see." He had one of the greatest seasons any three-year-old horse ever had winning 15 straight races after the Derby and posting a record of 19 wins in 20 starts in 1948. (See **Triple Crown.**) [86]

CITY CLUB: Located in Greenway Plaza, Houston City Club is a private business, tennis and athletic facility. Founded in 1979 the club has 10 indoor, climate-controlled tennis courts, exercise facilities, indoor running track, racquetball courts and locker rooms. It also offers food and beverage service as well as meeting rooms. [87]

CLAIBORNE: See sidebar *Laissez les bon temps roulez* (Let the good times roll), page 188.

CLAREMONT: This is another River Oaks street with the moniker of a famous American country club. This Oakland, California golf club was founded in 1904. The course was designed by architect Jim Smith. "Slammin" Sammy Sneed won the U. S. Open here in 1937. [88]

CLARION: See sidebar **It's Music to My Ears,** page 218.

CLARK: W. Floyd – Located in the village of Spring Valley, it is possible this street is named for one of that municipality's first aldermen. He was sworn into office on June 30, 1955. [89]

CLAY: Clarence and Rebecca – A west Houston road, it is named after this brother and sister who were residents of the Memorial area. [90]

CLAY: Henry – This downtown Houston street was named for a Kentucky politician who, during his distinguished career in the U.S. Congress (both as a Congressman and a Senator) was considered a friend of Texas. Clay opposed the Transcontinental Treaty of 1819 with Spain that would have given up America's claim over Texas. He later was a supporter of Texas annexation. Clay was a major factor in the Compromise of 1850 that wiped out the state's debt and adjusted the boundary with New Mexico in Texas' favor. [91]

CLEAR CREEK: This League City street is named for one of the longest creeks in our area. The watercourse headwaters are in northeast Fort Bend County. The creek runs 41 miles east, forming the border between Harris, Brazoria and Galveston counties before reaching its mouth in Galveston Bay. [92]

CLEAR LAKE CITY: This boulevard leads to a real estate development named for a large coastal body of brackish water called Clear Lake. Originally part of the 30,000-acre James West Ranch, the land was sold to Humble Oil & Refining Company (now Exxon Mobil) in 1938. In 1961 the National Aeronautics & Space Administration purchased 1,000 acres from Humble to build the Manned Spacecraft Center. To house all of the rocket scientists and their families, Humble partnered with Del E. Webb Corporation to build a residential development nearby. Clear Lake City formally opened on September 15, 1963. [93]

CLEAR LAKE: This lake separates Harris County from Galveston County and connects Clear Creek to Galveston Bay. A considerable amount of recreational activity occurs here including boating, sailing, water skiing, etc. (See **Clear Creek.**) [94]

CLEAVER: A. G. – Born in Nacogdoches he came to Prairie View A & M University in 1907 to study agriculture. Impressed with his talent the school hired this black educator in 1925 to head up the Industrial Education Department which he ran for the next 32 years. Early on during Cleaver's tenure his salary was only $100 per month. To make ends meet he raised hogs, cows and owned over 700 chickens. [95]

CLEMONS SWITCH: Known now as Clemons it was founded as a switch on the Texas Western Railroad, a narrow gauge line that passed through here. It is named for Martin Key Clemons who operated a general store and was the postmaster from 1885 until 1888. The town was the home of Edwin A. Waller for whom Waller County is named. Today it is a small rural community with a few scattered dwellings. (See **Waller.**) [96]

CLEMSON: This land grant South Carolina college opened in 1893 in a town of the same name. It is well thought of for its agricultural courses. [97]

CLEVELAND: Eddie – He was mayor of Pelly, Texas prior to its annexation by Baytown. [98]

CLEVELAND: Settlers began arriving in this area in 1836 when the Texas General Land Office offered acreage in exchange for military service. Father Peter La Cour built a church and convent here in 1854. The town formed in 1878 after Charles Lander Cleveland donated 64 acres of land to the Houston, East & West Texas Railway and asked the station here be named for him. Since its founding Cleveland's economy has been driven by oil and gas discoveries, farming, ranching and the mining of sand and gravel. [99, 100]

CLEVELAND: William D. – Evidence indicates this Third Ward street is named for an influential alderman during Mayor William R. Baker's term (1880-1884). He was known for his financial acumen and was closely involved with the city treasury, bondholders as well as local and out of state bankers. From 1884 until 1891 he was president of the Cotton Exchange. As a cotton merchant he founded Cleveland Compress Company in 1895. Captain Cleveland was a founder, director and first president of Houston's Young Men's Christian Association (YMCA). [101]

CLIFTON: (See **Bacliff**.)

CLINTON: No, it's not named for William Jefferson Clinton, the 42nd President of the United States. In 1874 the Morgan Steamship Line and the Port of Galveston had a falling out over wharf fees. Ship owner Charles Morgan, who founded the port of Morgan City, Louisiana, dredged a channel up Buffalo Bayou from Morgan's Point to Simms Bayou. There he constructed a turning basin and named the new town Clinton. The docks opened in 1876 with rail lines to the major railroads in the area. Now he not only didn't have to pay a red cent to Galveston but also could charge hefty fees to other ship owners that wanted to use his channel and docks. [102]

CLODINE: (See **Alief-Clodine**.)

CLOVERLEAF: Both this street and the small town of the same name began life as a station on the Beaumont, Sour Lake & Western Railroad. It has appeared on county highway maps since 1936. [103]

CLUTE-ANGLETON: One of Brazoria County's first plantations (1824) was located near the future site of Clute. Called Evergreen, it was owned by Alexander Calvit, one of Austin's Old 300, and Jared E. Groce. John Herndon bought it and named the plantation for himself. When Soloman J. Clute established a town nearby he named it for his family. (See **Angleton**.) [104]

COCHET: Henri – This French tennis player was ranked No. 1 in the world in 1926-30. He won five French Championships in singles and three in doubles, Wimbledon singles and doubles twice and the U. S. Championship singles once. Oddly enough, he is the only male player in tennis history who failed to defend all eight of his singles titles. [105]

COCHRAN: Owen L. – In the 1850s he was Houston's postmaster. Cochran opened an insurance agency in 1856, the first in Texas. By the time the firm was 100 years old in 1956 it was the oldest existing business in Houston. He married one of Benjamin A. Shepherd's daughters and was an officer and director of Shepherd's First National Bank. This civic-minded Houstonian gave almost 1,000 books to the Lyceum (predecessor to the Houston Public Library) in 1876. (See **Shepherd.**) [106]

COCHRAN'S CROSSING: Prior to the development of The Woodlands, where this street is located, the Grogan-Cochran Lumber Company owned this property. [107]

COLDSTREAM: See sidebar **All Things English,** page 175.

COLEMAN: John D. – This Houstonian was a civic leader and active in politics in the city's Third Ward. Governor Dolph Briscoe appointed Dr. Coleman to the Board of Regents at Texas A & M University. His son, Garnet F. Coleman, was a Texas State Representative from District 147 that includes the Third Ward. [108]

COLERIDGE: Samuel Taylor – An English poet and philosopher, he is famous for his *Rime of the Ancient Mariner.* It is a tale of the sea that revolves around the killing of an albatross, considered a mariner's good luck charm. It is a story of adventure, fright, fall from grace and penance. [109]

COLEWOOD: (See **Caelin.**)

COLISEUM: Emperor Vespasian started this Flavian amphitheater in the Forum in Rome in 79 B.C. His son, Emperor Titus, completed it five years later. This huge oval arena had seating for over 45,000 spectators and was the site of the gladiatorial contests. It was the inspiration for our Astrodome. Impresario Roy Hofheinz had visited it on a trip to Rome and sold his partners on the idea of a domed stadium. The Coliseum had a removable canvas roof. [110]

COLLINSWORTH: James – Research leads me to believe this street is named for this early Texas politician. The Republic of Texas' Constitution prohibited a president from serving consecutive terms. So in 1838 Sam Houston could not stand for re-election. Houston's opponents and critics backed Mirabeau B. Lamar as the second president. He faced two other

» **COLLINSWORTH: Historical marker on James Collinsworth's grave in Founders' Cemetery**

candidates, Peter W. Grayson and James Collinsworth. Before the election Grayson committed suicide and Collinsworth drowned in Galveston Bay. So Lamar, as the only living candidate, won in a walk. [111]

COLONY: (See **Iowa School.**)

COLORADO: The Old Sixth Ward remembers three of Texas' most important rivers. The Colorado flows about 600 miles from its headwaters in Dawson County to its mouth at Matagorda Bay. The word *colorado* in Spanish means "red," a misnomer since the waters of this river are very clear. The **Sabine** courses 360 miles to reach the Gulf of Mexico and represents the border between Texas and Louisiana. The name comes from the Spanish word meaning "cypress" due to the abundance of those trees that line its banks. The **Trinity** is one of the longest rivers that has its entire course within Texas. It was named *La Santisima Trinidad* in 1690 by the Spanish explorer Alonso de Leon. In 1716 the anglicized name was adopted. [112]

COLQUITT: Oscar Branch – This long time Texas politician held numerous appointed and elected offices in his lifetime. Among those positions were state senator, revenue agent, railroad commissioner, governor (1910-15) and member of the Reconstruction Finance Corporation. In addition he was a newspaper publisher and oilman. Colquitt was one of the honored speakers at the dedicatory ceremonies at the opening of Rice Institute (now Rice University) in 1912. [113]

COLUMBARIUM: The owners of Garden Park Cemetery in Tomball named this street. A columbarium is a sepulchral building containing many small niches for cinerary urns. The term is derived from the Latin word *columba* or dove and its resemblance to a dovecote. [114]

COLUMBIA BLUE: The Houston Oilers may have fled town for Nashville, Tennessee but this Missouri City street recalls the team's uniform colors that were red, white and Columbia blue.

COLUMBIA MEMORIAL: This NASA area highway remembers the tragic crash of the space shuttle Columbia on February 1, 2003. A few minutes before 8 AM as the spacecraft was descending for a landing in Florida residents of East Texas heard a series of explosions overhead. As they looked up they saw the shuttle being ripped apart as it headed toward Earth at 12,000 MPH. Unfortunately, the mission was doomed just 82 seconds after lift off. At that time a small piece of insulating foam broke lose from the orbiter's external fuel tank and slammed into the left wing. When the craft re-entered the atmosphere, the 5,000 degree air temperature penetrated the damaged wing and melted critical support structures. All seven astronauts perished in the crash. [115]

COLUMBIA: Located in the Houston Heights, it is named for Columbia University in New York City. [116]

COLUMBUS: This Austin County road runs from Sealy to Columbus in Colorado County. The town was settled in 1821 by members of Stephen F. Austin's Old 300. It was first called Beeson's Ferry or Beeson's Ford. In 1835 a former resident of Columbus, Ohio suggested renaming it for his hometown. By 1837 it was know for its bars, gambling houses and horse race track. As time passed the economy was driven by tobacco production, cottonseed oil, cattle ranching as well as sand and gravel mining.

COMMERCE: In an effort to promote the new city of Houston as an important place to do business, the Allen Brothers elected to name the first major street fronting on Buffalo Bayou Commerce. With its proximity to the steamboat docks, warehouses and merchant stores this street was a public relations gimmick to inflate our status as a bustling business community. [117]

COMMUNITY COLLEGE: At the end of this street is Houston Community College's Northwest Campus. HCC is the 4th largest community college system in America. Founded in 1971, over 1.3 million students have studied here. More than 70 curriculums annually are offered to the 55,000 members of the student body. [118]

COMPAQ CENTER: Compaq Computer was founded in 1982 by three former Texas Instruments employees who each invested $1,000 to develop a portable personal computer capable of running all of the software being developed for the IBM PC. Compaq went on to become one of the great success stories of the technology industry. This wide boulevard leads to the company's headquarters. Compaq was acquired by Hewlett-Packard in 2002. [119]

CONCERT: Located in Hermann Park this street leads to the Miller Outdoor Theater where many concerts are held. This 7.5 acre site hosts more than 250,000 people an-

» **CONCERT: Miller Theater in Hermann Park**

nually to free performances. The theater is named for Jesse W. Miller who willed the property to the city in 1919. The theater was constructed in 1921 (William Ward Watkin was the architect) and was dedicated in 1923. In 1968 the original theater was replaced with the one we see today. (See photograph on page 78). [120]

CONCERTO: See sidebar **It's Music to My Ears,** page 218.

CONCORDIA: The German immigrants who settled in the Bellville area started a singing society and named it *Concordia Gesangverein.* [121]

CONCRETE: This street was named in the 1920's. It leads to the Texas Portland Cement Plant on the Houston Ship Channel. [122]

CONGRESS: On November 30, 1836 the legislature of the Republic of Texas voted Houston as the seat of government. On the earliest map of the city (1836) it was clear that the Allen Brothers intended this street to be for government buildings. Two prominent features were Congress Square (between Travis and Milam) and Court House Square (between San Jacinto and Fannin). The Harris County Court House is still at this latter location. The State government was moved to Austin in 1837. Today Market Square is where those august legislative bodies were in the old days. [123]

THE FAKE STREETS OF HOUSTON

A Key Map is a cartographer's as well as a taxi driver's dream. No better map of the city of Houston exists. The user can pinpoint with incredible accuracy the location of streets, subdivisions, cemeteries, schools, hospitals, public buildings, parks and post offices just to name a few places. Started over 50 years ago by James M. Rau this company has flourished over the years. In 2010 they published the 51st edition of this map book. Because of the tremendous amount of proprietary data that these maps display the company takes its copyright protection very seriously. On the maps first page in bold letters is the statement, "It is the intent of the publisher to enforce these provisions in federal court." Over the years those who have infringed on Key Maps' rights have been prosecuted to the fullest extent of the law. The Company developed a clever way of detecting piracy – the fake street. An interesting game for the industrial strength Houston streetophile is to take the official city map and compare it to the Key Map and find these fake streets. Management and the cartographers display a keen sense of humor as well as a bit of disdain for the plagiarists in naming these non-existent streets, lanes and boulevards. In the 2010 edition try to physically locate **Fake, Lawsuit, Pistol Whipper, Inkahoots** and **D+** to name a few. They don't exist except in the crafty minds of Key Maps' cartographers. But just try putting one or more of them on your purloined map and see how long it takes to be contacted by the *Federales.* Enjoy yourself trying to identify other fake streets. [12]

C-D

CONNORS ACE: Jimmy Connors was one of America's greatest tennis players. He was ranked number one in the world from 1974 until 1978. He won five U. S. Opens, two Wimbledon titles and one Australian Open championship. He was the dominant player of the time winning 98 matches at the U. S. Open and 84 at Wimbledon. In his career Connors won 109 singles titles. [124]

CONRAD SAUER: Many immigrants from Germany settled west of Houston in the area we know today as Spring Branch. Land was plentiful, productive and inexpensive. Water was abundant from the region's many streams. This gentleman was one of the early German farmers in Houston. Sauer operated a dairy as well. For a time he worked as a maintenance man paving and repairing area streets. He was born in 1843 and died in 1876. His grave is in Vollmer Cemetery. [125]

» **CONROE-HUFSMITH: Issac Conroe's tombstone in Glenwood Cemetery**

CONROE-HUFSMITH: In 1881 Isaac Conroe established a sawmill where this road is today. At that time it was near the International-Great Northern Railroad line. In 1884 a railroad officer suggested the name Conroe Switch in honor of Mr. Conroe. About 10 years later it was shortened to Conroe. It was principally an agricultural and timber center until oil was discovered southeast of town in 1931. Conroe suffered greatly during the Great Depression but the oil strike changed that. The school district became one of the wealthiest in the state and for a period of time Conroe had more millionaires per capita than any city in the U.S. As a boy your author lived on the Conroe Texas Company lease where my father was a petroleum engineer. (See **Hufsmith.**) [126]

CONROE-PORTER: Also known as FM 1314, this highway connects these two towns. Porter (early on known as Porters) was founded in the late 1800s. It was a lumber and livestock town. A famous resident was astronaut Robert L. Crippen who piloted the space shuttle Colombia in 1981. (See **Conroe-Hufsmith.**) [127]

CONSTELLATION: This street is named for one of America's classic aircraft, the Lockheed "Super G" Constellation. This four-engine propeller plane had a range of 5,400 miles and a top speed of 328 mph. The last model rolled off the line in 1959. [128]

CONTI: On the city map of 1882 several streets in this 2nd Ward neighborhood were named in conjunction with Louisiana. Conti is a street in the Big Easy's French Quarter. The street to Conti's north was once called New Orleans Avenue. **Opelousas,** named for the Louisiana hometown of Jim Bowie, is also in the neighborhood. [129]

CONVAIR: This aircraft was one of the most popular commercial airplanes in the 1950s and 1960s. There were four models of this two-engine piston driven aircraft. [130]

COOK: John D. – This gentleman was a cotton farmer in the Alief, Texas area. Born two years after the War Between the States he lived to be 87 years old and is buried in the historic Alief Cemetery. [131]

COOLIDGE: Calvin – He was our 30th President, serving from 1923 until 1929. A conservative Republican he cut taxes, reduced Federal spending and lowered the national debt. [132]

COPANO BAY: See sidebar **The Most Scenic Spots in Texas,** page 310.

COPPAGE: H. – This gentleman fought with Walker's Texas Division during the War Between the States. He was a lieutenant in the 16th Cavalry in command of Company A. [133]

COPPERAS COVE: See sidebar **The Most Scenic Spots in Texas,** page 310.

COPRA: See sidebar **Bali Hai May Call You,** page 322.

CORBINDALE: Ira Corbin was an early resident of Memorial. He operated one of the earliest gas stations in the area for many years. [134]

"RED FLAG" SUBDIVISIONS

Developers have had the upper hand in shaping Houston since the Allen Brothers first platted the city in 1836. But their unprincipled behavior never was more egregious than with the creation of the "red flag" communities. Beginning in the 1960s land speculators would buy blocks of inexpensive land on the edge of town and lay out a "subdivision" with cheap lots along dirt roads marked with little red flags. The neighborhoods were totally void of municipal services such as paved streets, curbs, gutters, sewer lines, etc. By the 1980s 26 of these communities were located in Houston. An example of one is Magnolia Point. Situated on the north shore of Lake Houston, this suburb was "red flagged" in 1965 and still lacked any services as late as 1984. Is it just coincidence that one of the principal streets here is named Cheatham? [13]

CORDELL BRICK: This lane leads to the Cordell Brick Company. I believe it was originally named the Lighthouse Brick Works. The owner Henry R. Lighthouse manufactured many of the bricks used in commercial buildings and homes in the 6th Ward, including his own two-story Colonial Revival house. Later the name was changed to the Andy Cordell Brick Company. Years ago brick producers imprinted their company names in the product. Keep an eye open in historic areas of the city for Cordell bricks. [135]

CORDES: Roy – He was mayor of Sugar Land from 1973 until 1981. Being mayor was not a full time job so he operated a dry cleaning plant there. [136]

CORNELL: This land grant university opened in Ithaca, NY in 1868. It is named for Ezra Cornell who donated the land and endowed the school. [137]

CORNISH: J. R. – This street is named for an assistant surgeon in the 13th Texas Cavalry Dismounted. He fought with Walker's Texas Division during the War Between the States. [138]

CORONADO: Francisco Vasquez de – This Spanish explorer is best remembered for his failed quest to find the "Seven Cities of Cibola" and the riches of "El Dorado." In 1540 he set out from Mexico to discover these rumored cities of gold. Two years of difficult trekking turned up nothing but dirt-poor Indian villages. Dispirited, the remnants of his expedition returned empty handed. He retired in Mexico City in 1544 where he died ten years later a broken man. [139]

CORTLANDT: Houston Heights developers Oscar Carter and Daniel Cooley named this street for a town of the same name located in their home state of Nebraska. [140]

CORVETTE: America's quintessential sports car debuted in 1953. That first year each Corvette was hand built and all were white with red interiors. The developer who named this north central Harris County street must have had a sense of humor. The next street over is Isetta, probably the least sporty car ever made. (See **Isetta.**)

COSSEY: Kohrville, Texas was a small black community in northwest Harris County founded by freed slaves from Alabama in the 1870s. It was named for Paul Kohrmann, the village postman in the 1880s. Today little remains of this town except the Kohrville Cemetery. Members of the Cossey family are interred here. This street is located just south of the burying ground. [141]

COTTONWOOD CHURCH & COTTONWOOD SCHOOL: Located on Cottonwood Creek in Fort Bend County. This area was promoted by the Waddill brothers as an excellent place to farm corn, broom corn and cotton. The brothers erected a white framed wooden church and a brick school house. [31]

COTTONWOOD SCHOOL: (See **Cottonwood Church.**)

COUGAR PLACE: Located on the campus of the University of Houston next to Robertson Stadium, this street is named for the ever popular mascot, the cougar. For years the school brought a live cougar named Shasta to football games and other events. This beautiful beast lived in a zoo-like cage on campus when she was not giving command performances. A more politically correct world ended Shasta's stardom and she was retired. [142]

COUGAR: Abutting Cy-Fair Stadium, this short street is named for the mascot of Cypress-Creek High School. The two connecting streets, **Bobcat** and **Falcon,** are the mascots of Cypress-Fairbanks High School and Jersey Village High School, respectively. [143]

COUNTRY CLUB GREEN: At the end of this tree lined lane sits the Tomball Country Club. Opened in 1948 the club only had a 9-hole golf course. In 2001 9 more holes were added resulting in a 6,275 yard, par 71 links. [144]

COUNTRY CLUB: C. E. King developed Houston Country Club Place in 1941. At that time the venerable old Houston Country Club (now Gus Wortham Park Golf Course) was located just across Wayside from this neighborhood. Graced with brick cottages and ranch-style homes, some rather grand arches once marked its entry, similar to those at the entrance to Villa de Matel. However, only one remains today. (See **C. E. King.**) [145]

C-D

COUNTRY CLUB: This street leads to Golfcrest Country Club. Earl Gammage Sr., a real estate developer opened this golf course in 1927. In 1932 Golfcrest became one of the country's first clubs to experiment with night golf. Flood lights illuminated nine holes but the novelty soon wore off and night golf was discontinued. The very popular four-ball tournament, one of the most popular in Houston, began in 1951 as a pro-am event. (See **Golfcrest.**) [146]

COUNTY LINE: This is the closest road to the Waller-Montgomery county line. [147]

» **COURTLANDT PLACE: The neighborhood's east gate**

COURTLANDT PLACE: The area was originally part of the Obedience Smith land grant. In 1908 it was sold to the Courtlandt Improvement Company. The developers modeled the street after an exclusive area in St. Louis, Missouri. This block-long street with its beautiful esplanade was one of the city's first areas with deed restrictions. These rules prohibited any commercial establishments. Between 1911 and 1921 the homes here were designed by Houston's finest architects including Birdsall P. Briscoe, Alfred C. Finn (who also designed the San Jacinto Monument), Sanguinet & Staats and Warren & Wetmore. (See **Birdsall.**) [148]

COW CREEK: This estuary rises a mile north of Damon and runs 12 miles to its mouth on the Brazos River near the Ramsey Prison Farm. (See **Beasley-Damon.**) [149]

COX: Charles – (See **Splendora.**)

CRANE: Ichabod – He is the lean and extremely superstitious schoolmaster in Washington Irving's *The Legend of Sleepy Hollow*. After attending a party one evening where he was wooing the farmer's daughter, Katrina, he is pursued by the Headless Horseman. This specter is supposedly a Hessian trooper whose head was shot off by a stray cannonball. Nightly he rides the roads near Sleepy Hollow in quest of his head. Crane is so frightened by this sight that he flees town. (See **Washington Irving, Sleepy Hollow, Brom Bones** and **Tarrytown.**) [150]

CRAWFORD: Joseph Tucker – He was an agent of the British government who was sent to evaluate the situation in the newly born Republic of Texas in 1837. While the English were not interested in making Texas a colony they were trying to find a way to halt American expansion westward. This international attention was one of the major factors in the United States annexing Texas in 1845. [151]

CRAZY HORSE: This Oglala Sioux chief is remembered for his victory at the Battle of Little Bighorn. Also called "Custer's Last Stand," Crazy Horse inflicted the worst defeat of the Indian Wars on the American frontier army. It took the Sioux less than an hour to kill Lieutenant-Colonel George Armstrong Custer and all 211 of his men. (See **Custer** and **Sitting Bull.**) [152]

CRESCENDO: See sidebar **It's Music to My Ears,** page 218.

» CROCKETT: Davy Crockett: Battle of the Alamo hero

CROCKETT: Davy – He sits in the highest pantheon of Texas heroes. Jane Bowers immortalizes him in her 1959 song, *Remember the Alamo*, with the lines "Young Davy Crockett stood smiling and laughing, the challenge fierce in his eye/For Texas and freedom a man bold and willing to die." Prior to coming to Texas he served as a U.S. Congressman from his native Tennessee. Teddy Roosevelt characterized Crockett as "distinctly, intensely American stock." [153]

CROSBY-DAYTON: In eastern Harris County there are a number of roads with dual names involving Crosby such as **Crosby-Cedar Bayou** and **Crosby-Barbers Hill.** In this case the Crosby is for the small town of Crosby, Texas. It was named for G. J. Crosby, a railroad construction foreman. Charles Karcher opened the town's first business, a general store, in 1865. Dayton, in Liberty County, a small town three miles west of Liberty (named for *Santisima Trinidad de la Libertad*) was first called West Liberty. By 1854 it was known as Day's Town for a landowner there named I. C. Day. Over the next few years the name was Days Station and Dayton Station. It officially became known as Dayton in the mid 1880s. [154]

CROSBY: This 4th Ward street is named for the Crosby family who were early land-owners in the area. [155]

CROW: W. D. – Now a part of Baytown, in 1892 this gentleman and his partner, Q. A. Wooster, laid out the town of Wooster. (See **Wooster.**) [156]

CROWN: In 1917 the Crown Oil & Refining Company (now Crown Central Petroleum) was almost bankrupt when they hit "black gold" with "Well Number 3" near the Pasadena city limit. This strike saved the young firm. In 1920 the company constructed a refinery on the Houston Ship Channel just east of where the entrance of the Washburn Tunnel is located today. This Pasadena street leads to a facility on that same site that refines 100,000 barrels of crude oil a day. [157]

CRUSADER WAY: In 1960 Father Michael F. Kennelly received permission from the Catholic Church to establish a college preparatory school for boys in Houston. Strake Jesuit opened its doors to the freshman class in 1961. Today it is one of our city's finest schools. Their mascot is the "Fighting Crusader." [158]

CRUSE: Aubrey – Prior to the formation of the Pasadena Police Department in 1937, law and order in our neighboring city was maintained by city marshals. This gentleman was Pasadena's second marshal. [159]

» **CRYSTAL BEACH: Hurricane Ike devastated this town in 2008**

CRYSTAL BEACH: Originally called Patton and then Patton Beach its current name was made official in the early 1940s. The seven mile community runs through the middle section of Bolivar Peninsula. Crystal Beach suffered catastrophic destruction during Hurricane Ike in 2008 when a 20-foot storm surge rolled over the peninsula destroying 80% of the buildings. [160]

CULBERSON: Charles Allen – This Texas politician started his career as attorney general. He was elected governor in 1894 and re-elected in 1896. Nicknamed the "veto governor" he once vetoed a general appropriations bill that he thought had too much "pork" in it. Culberson called the Texas Legislature to a special session in 1895 to pass a bill prohibiting the Corbett-Fitzsimmons heavyweight-boxing match in the state. In 1898 he was elected to the U.S. Senate where he served for 24 years. (See **Roy Bean.**) [161]

CULLEN: Hugh Roy – Here is one of the larger than life Houstonians that we love to brag about. He earned a phenomenal fortune in cotton, real estate and oil despite his lack of a formal education. He had a reputation for finding huge pools of oil where others drilled dry holes. But the real story is what Cullen did with his money. During his lifetime he gave away $175,000,000 to charitable and educational institutions, created the Cullen Foundation and established the University of Houston among many great deeds. When once asked about his generous donations Cullen was quoted in the *Houston Chronicle* as saying "It's just as easy to give away $2 million as two bits." In one four day period he gave four Houston hospitals more than a million dollars each. Now that's philanthropy Houston style! [162]

» CULLEN: Hugh Roy Cullen

CUMMINS: See sidebar **Texas Heroes' Names for Houston Streets Urged in 72 Proposed Changes,** page 96.

CUNEY: Norris Wright – Son of a white plantation owner and a black slave, Cuney settled in Galveston in the late 1860s. He was a remarkable man. Cuney became an attorney, Inspector of Customs at Galveston, elected alderman in 1883 (the first black Galvestonian to hold this office), Collector of Customs, operated a stevedore business and served as Grand Master of the Negro Masons of Texas. Cuney Street leads to Cuney Homes, the first black housing project in Houston (1940). Cuney, Texas, a small town southwest of Tyler is also named for him. [163]

CUNNINGHAM CREEK: This stream is named for Colonel E. H. Cunningham a veteran of the War Between the States who was wounded four times during that conflict while fighting for the Confederacy. After the War he bought the Sugarland Plantation from W. J. Kyle and Benjamin F. Terry. He purchased other acreage in the area forming one of the largest plantations in Texas. Cunningham invested more than $1 million to construct a sugar refinery on the property. Like other owners in the area he leased convicts from the State of Texas to work his sugar cane fields. (See **Kyle** and **Terry**) [164]

CURTIN: Henry M. – A number of streets in Houston are named for political figures—mayors, congressmen, etc. This gentleman was a prominent citizen as well as the Harris County tax assessor. Evidence leads me to believe this east side street remembers this man. [165]

CUSHING: Edward Hopkins – This pioneer Houstonian was the publisher of the *Houston Telegram,* the city's earliest newspaper. Cushing bought it from Gail Borden in 1856 and operated it for the next 10 years. During the War Between the States he faced two serious problems for a newspaperman. One was how to gather accurate news without mail service (suspended during the War) or telegraph lines (often cut by marauding troops). He solved this dilemma by setting up his own pony express. Two, he faced a severe shortage of newsprint. He used any paper he could find, so often, the newspaper was different colors every day. Cushing sometimes used wallpaper, just printing the news on the reverse side. He obviously succeeded in solving his problems and printed much accurate history of the War. In fact, Jefferson Davis, President of the Confederate States of America, used Cushing files when writing his version of the conflict. [166]

» CUSHING: "Bohemia," the home of Edward Cushing

» GAIL BORDEN: Early Houston newspaper publisher

CUSTER: George Armstrong – Custer was a brilliant and heroic Union cavalry officer who distinguished himself in the Civil War and the campaign against the Cheyenne. However his ego overwhelmed his tactical skills and cost him and many men their lives. At what came to be called the Battle of Little Bighorn (1876), Custer, underestimating the strength of the Sioux, divided his troop into three columns and attacked Chief Crazy Horse. It was a fatal mistake and the troopers were slaughtered. (See **Crazy Horse** and **Sitting Bull**) [167]

CYMBAL: See sidebar **It's Music to My Ears,** page 218.

CYPRESS CHURCH: German immigrants began settling here in the 1840s. This street led to one of the early Lutheran churches in the area. [168]

CYPRESS CREEK: Rising where Snake and Mound Creeks meet southeast of Waller, this estuary runs 49 miles to its mouth at Spring Creek. Stephen F. Austin made his first land grant on Cypress Creek to John Callihan in 1835. In the 1840s and 1850s this area was a popular place with German immigrants because of its fertile soil and abundance of fresh water. [169]

CYPRESS GARDENS: For 65 years this Winter Haven, Florida theme park hosted the finest water ski extravaganza in the world. Over the years it expanded to add a botanical garden, alligator habitat and an ice skating show. Unfortunately, the arrival of mega-theme parks like Disney World resulted in it and other smaller entertainment venues' demise. Cypress Gardens closed in April 2003. [170]

CYPRESS-ROSEHILL: This road leads from Cypress, west of Houston, to the small rural community of Rosehill to the north. German immigrants settled Cypress in the 1840s. Its name is derived from a nearby stream, Cypress Creek, the banks of which were lined with cypress trees. In 1904 while drilling for oil here a wildcatter accidentally hit a hot artesian well. It wasn't long before entrepreneurs opened the Houston Hotwell Sanitarium and Hotel. Houstonians flocked to the spa to soak in its supposedly "healing waters." P. W. Rose settled Rosehill in the early 1830s but until 1892 it was called Spring Creek. He was chosen for the first grand jury of Harrisburg County (the name was shortened to Harris in 1839). German immigrants found the area excellent farm country. In 1852 they founded Salem Lutheran Church, one of the oldest Lutheran congregations in Texas. (See **Cypress Creek.**) [171]

D

D. S. BAILEY: For over 30 years beginning in the 1960s this black pastor founded and served the congregation of Galilee Baptist Church in Acres Homes. [1]

DA VINCI: See sidebar **Buon Giorno, Let's Visit Italia,** page 268.

DACUS: Over the years many communities came and went in Montgomery County including this one. In 1687 the French explorer, Le Salle, passed through here and recorded about 40 Indian huts. White settlement began in 1823 with a man named Francis Wheeler. Later the village was named for J. B. Dacus, also an early arrival. [2]

DAGG CEMETERY: This small family cemetery is located in southwest Harris County. Family members buried here include Garret W. Dagg Sr. (1856-1922), Elizabeth Dagg (1866-1928), Garrett W. Dagg Jr. (1890-1942) and Lee M. Dagg (1885-1905). Other families interred here include Perrys and Woods. Coincidently, there is a dead end road sign on this street. (See **Dagg.**) [3]

DAGG: Garrett W. Sr. – This man settled in the area near Pearland in the late 1800s. The Dagg Family Cemetery is located nearby. (See **Dagg Cemetery.**) [4]

DAIRY-ASHFORD: In 1894 surveyors named the town we call Alief today Dairy or Dairy Station as it was located on the San Antonio & Aransas Pass Railroad line. Residents nicknamed the day train the "Dinky" and the night train the "Davy Crockett." When the U. S. Post Office denied an application under the name Dairy the town changed its name to Alief honoring the first postmistress, Alief Ozelda Magee. Ashford, also known as Satsuma or Thompson Switch, was located near Cypress on the Houston & Texas Central Railroad. J. T. Thompson platted the town and called it Satsuma because of the orange groves in the area. It was later changed to Ashford. (See **Alief-Clodine**) [5,6]

DAMON GIN: The old cotton gin in Damon was on this road. (See **Beasley-Damon.**) [7]

HOUSTON'S BEST STREET INTERSECTIONS

Never let it be said that real estate developers in Houston lack a sense of humor. While some of these intersections and parallel streets might have just been put together accidentally I can't help believe most were intentional. Here are some examples: [14]

- **Sears & Roebuck** – old line retailer
- **Bell & Telephone** – the phone company
- **Preston & Smith** - a Texas governor
- **Thomas & Jefferson** – our third President
- **Corvette & Isetta** – high horsepower vs. no horsepower
- **Longneck & Lite** – have a cold one
- **Six Pack & Strohs** – a little free advertising
- **Plantation, Tara & Rhett** – Gone with the Wind Too Far
- **Scarlett & O'Hara** – ditto
- **Affirmed & Alydar** – greatest thoroughbred rivals
- **Girl Scout, Campfire, Boy Scout & Webelos** – all-American
- **Discipline & Patience** – good virtues
- **Currency & Dividend** – financial responsibility
- **Perception, Edification, Insight & Enlightenment** – good streets for a guru
- **Fearless, Courageous, Bravery & Victorious** – early Texas virtues
- **Sigma, Kappa, Gamma & Epsilon** – fraternity row
- **Faith, Grace & Hope** – an intersection for optimists
- **Stonewall & Jackson** – the South's great martyred general
- **Miracle & Gospel Way** – hallelujah
- **Gulf Stream & Jet Stream** – rapid water and air currents
- **Edinburgh & Castle** – that city's most famous site
- **Aztec & Inca** – two great pre-Columbian civilizations
- **Madrigal & Minstrel** – olde English music
- **Black Gold & Oil Center** – it's a gusher
- **Metairie & Ponchartrain** – laissez les bon temps roulez
- **Mutiny & Bounty** – Captain Bligh vs. Fletcher Christian
- **Pitcairn & Mutineer** – the resting place of HMS Bounty
- **Okra, Tomato, Carrot, Turnip & Squash** – vegetarian's delight
- **Old Masters & Rembrandt** – very artsy
- **Packard, Reo & Kaiser** – defunct automobile manufacturers
- **Parsley, Sage & Rosemary** – all we need is a little thyme
- **Dallas & Southfork** – where is J. R.
- **Macbeth & Banquo** – tragic Scottish King and the ghost
- **Romeo & Juliet** – "...wherefore art thou"
- **Varsity, Faculty & Graduate** – cap and gown stuff
- **Winkin, Blinkin & Nod** – snuggled in the arms of Morpheus
- **Sunshine, Moonlight & Raindrops** – the Weather Channel
- **Spring, Summer, Autumn & Fall** – a season for everyone

DAMON QUARRY: Located on the flanks of the Damon Mound this quarry has been supplying limestone to the surrounding area since 1918. (See **Beasley-Damon.**) [8]

DANBURY: This community sprang up along the Missouri Pacific Railroad line in Brazoria County in 1905-6. There are two stories about how it was named. One says the men building the line named it for D. J. "Dan" Moller, a popular rancher in the area, who entertained the crews at night with music and tall tales. The other attributes the name to Daniel T. Miller, another resident. [9]

DANDRIDGE: See sidebar **America the Beautiful,** page 176.

DANVILLE: Another Montgomery ghost town, it was named by Samuel and Joseph Lindley in 1830 for their hometown in Illinois. By 1838 it was a bustling community. Danville threw a barbeque for Sam Houston in 1858. The town's demise began in 1870 when the railroad line was laid through nearby Willis. By 1920 even the Catholic Church had been abandoned. [10]

DARRINGTON: This street is the main entrance to the Texas Department of Corrections Darrington Unit in Brazoria County. The 6,770 acre prison farm is a medium security level facility established in 1917. It can house up to 1,610 male prisoners. Much of the food for the Texas prison system is produced here including field crops, cattle, pigs and eggs. Horses and guard dogs are also raised here for prison use. [11]

DARST: Abraham – He came to Texas from Missouri in the early 1820s and settled at Damon Mound. Darst received a league of land from Stephen F. Austin and was a member of the Old 300. Edward and R. B. Darst fought at the Battle of San Jacinto. W. H. Darst was a member of Terry's Texas Rangers during the War Between the States and later, Sheriff of Fort Bend County. A number of members of the Darst family are buried in the historic cemetery on top of Damon Mound. (See **Beasley-Damon.**) [12]

» **ABRAHAM DARST: Historic marker on his grave in Damon**

DARST: Emory – This early Fort Bend County pioneer was born in 1814. He is a direct descendent of Daniel Boone. His daughter, Lorena Darst Damon had the famous Damon Salt Dome named in her honor. In 1908 his grandson built the historic Darst-Yoder house in Richmond. (See **Beasley-Damon.**) [13]

DARTMOUTH: A university in Hanover, NH, this institution of higher education was chartered in 1769 by King George III and is named after the Earl of Dartmouth. [14]

DAVID MEMORIAL: (See **David Vetter.**)

DAVID VETTER: This young boy was born in Shenandoah, near The Woodlands, in 1971. Unfortunately, he was diagnosed prior to his birth with a rare genetic disease known as severe combined immune deficiency syndrome (SCIDS). Less than 10 seconds after being removed from his mother's womb David was placed in a plastic germ-free environment that would be his home for the rest of his life. He was dubbed "the boy in the plastic bubble" by the media. He lived in this environment at Texas Children's Hospital until 1981 when he was discharged to a plastic bubble at his home. He died of cancer at age 12. David Elementary School was named for him in 1990. [15]

DAVIS: J.O. – This Pasadena street is named for the civil engineer who laid out the city. [16]

DAVIS: League City was once the site of Davis Auxiliary Army Airfield #3. In 1942 near what is now the intersection of Marina Bay Drive and FM 518, this field was used to support flight training at nearby Ellington Air Force Base. It was one of several of these auxiliary airfields around Houston during World War II. It was closed in 1946 but the runways were still visible in 1976. However, all traces of the base disappeared over the next 20 years as South Shore Harbor was developed. [17]

DAVIS: William Kenchen – This Rosenberg street may be named for this early Texan. He was a member of the Mier Expedition, a failed raid on the Mexican town of Mier Cuidad in 1842. Davis is buried in the Morton Cemetery here. His son, John H. Pickens Davis, was a leader of the Jaybirds during the Jaybird-Woodpecker War, a political struggle that took place in Richmond in 1888. He was a rancher, banker and built the historic Davis Bank and Trust in Richmond. (See **Morton.**) [18]

» W.K. DAVIS: William Kenchen tombstone

DAVIS MOUNTAINS: See sidebar **The Most Scenic Spots in Texas,** page 310.

DAVY JONES: As the third largest port in the United States, Houston has many streets with marine related names. Davy Jones is the nickname for the devil/saint/god of the seas. Davy Jones Locker is an idiom for the resting place of drowned sailors at the bottom of the sea. [19]

DAWN HILL: See sidebar **Tennis or Golf, Anyone?,** page 348.

DAY: This Montrose area street is named for the Day family who lived on it. [20]

DAYTON: (See **Crosby-Dayton.**)

DE CHAUMES: Michael – He was an architect who built the third Harris County courthouse. As it was not yet finished when the War Between the States erupted in 1861, the Confederate army assumed control of the structure and used it for a guard house, cartridge factory and officers quarters. [21]

DE CHIRICO: Giorgio – This Greek-Italian surrealist was born in 1888. He is most remembered for the haunting mood of the paintings of his "metaphysical period" (1909-1919). Among his greatest works are *Enigma of the Oracle, Enigma of an Afternoon* and *The Red Tower.*

DE GAULLE: Charles Andre Joseph Marie – A French general during WW II he organized the Free French Forces to oppose German occupation. From 1959 to 1969 he was the first President of the Fifth Republic in France. [22]

DE GEORGE: Michael – Real estate developers in our city have historically named streets for themselves and/or family members. This man was an Italian immigrant who arrived in Houston in about 1890. He started as a fruit and vegetable cart operator. De George invested his profits in real estate and may have named this Norhill area street. He operated a grocery store where Hobby Center is today and built the De George Hotel that has recently been turned into housing for veterans. His son Gaspar M. De George built the Auditorium Hotel (now the Lancaster.) [23]

DE ZAVALA: Manuel Lorenzo Justiniano – Born in Merida, Mexico in 1789, he became a young liberal firebrand and was imprisoned by the Mexican government. He was constantly persecuted by the *Federales* and finally came to Texas in 1835. He was an active participant in the Texas Revolution. Following the Battle of San Jacinto, his home on Buffalo Bayou was used as a hospital for the wounded. He also owned land on Old River. He died in 1837. In 1858 the State named Zavala County in his honor. (See **Old River.**) [24]

DEAF SMITH: Although deaf from birth, this handicap did not stop Erastus Smith from becoming one of the heroes of the Texas Revolution. He fought valiantly at the Battles of Concepcion, Grass Fight and San Jacinto. Upon hearing of the fall of the Alamo, General Sam Houston sent Smith to obtain the details. He returned with Mrs. Almaron Dickenson and her baby daughter, the only survivors of the Battle of the Alamo. [25]

DEBORAH: Early Houston resident, landowner and building supply impresario Herman E. Detering named this East End street for his granddaughter, Deborah Detering, in the early 1940s. In high school at St. John's in 1959 your author's chemistry lab partner was Miss Detering. (See **Detering** and **Eberhard.**) [26]

DECKER PRAIRIE: This road in northwest Harris County recalls Isaac Decker, a County Commissioner of the short-lived Spring Creek County in the early 1840s. He was a Canadian immigrant who arrived in the area in 1834 to claim a land grant along Spring Creek. He operated a tannery. [27]

DECKER: Thomas – One of the major thoroughfares in Baytown is named for this Harris County Commissioner. [28]

HOUSTON STREETS WITH AGGRESSIVE NAMES

Maybe it's just our Old West mentality but developers love to christen our streets with names that glorify our "don't mess with Texas or Houston" attitude. Again a search of various maps produced the following street names with aggressive personalities. They are: **Ambush, Armory, Arsenal, Battle, Buck Knife, Cannon Ball, Cannon Fire, Donnybrook, Gunpowder, Long Barrel, Marksman, Musket, Point Blank, Powder Keg, Powderhorn, Rifle Gap, Rifleman** and **Ruffian.** [15]

DEEPWATER: Once a small community between Pasadena and Deer Park, Deepwater was named because of its location on the Houston Ship Channel. In the late 1890s the town was a stop on the Galveston, Houston & Northern Railroad. The town was platted by Colonel J. H. Burnett who also founded Genoa, Texas and platted Pasadena. (See **Burnett.**) [29]

DEFEE: W. E. – He was a land developer in Baytown. (See **Jack** and **Wright.**) [30]

DEKE SLAYTON: Chosen as one of the first U. S. astronauts in April 1959, Donald K. "Deke" Slayton was the only one of the seven not to fly a Mercury mission after a heart condition was discovered. However, 16 years later he was given a clean bill of health and flew with the Apollo Soyuz Test Project in July 1975. [31]

DEL MONTE: Dating from 1897, the Del Monte Golf Course in Monterey, California is the oldest golf links west of the Mississippi. [32]

DELANEY: John and Nancy – This couple owned a dairy farm where this street is located today near the intersection of I-45 and Loop 610 North. [33]

DEMONTROND: The DeMontrond family has owned automobile dealerships in Houston for over 50 years. George DeMontrond opened a Buick dealership on the corner of Westheimer and Kirby in the 1950s. When that property became too valuable for a car lot, DeMontrond, like most dealers, moved operations to the suburbs. Today they sell Buick, Volkswagen, Volvo, Kia and Suzuki from their new location on the I-45 North. [34]

DEMOSS: James – This early Houstonian leased approximately 9,700 acres of ranch land where Bellaire is today. Although he resided in the city of Houston he would ride out to the ranch to work. The DeMoss home was located just west of Peggy Point Park at the intersection of Richmond and Main. Bellaire developer W. W. Baldwin purchased 9,449 acres that DeMoss leased to begin the development of Westmoreland Farms, later named Bellaire. (See **Bellaire.**) [35]

DENMAN: Leroy Gilbert – He was appointed an associate judge of the Texas Supreme Court by Governor James S. Hogg in 1894. He remained on the bench until 1899.

Sources say Denman was not known for his legal acumen but was a great speaker. During his tenure he handed down 146 opinions that were known for their "brevity, simplicity and accuracy." [36]

DENNIS: E. L. – It is likely that this street honors a man who was a founder and one of the first directors of Houston's Young Men's Christian Association (YMCA). [37]

DEPELCHIN: Kezia Payne – The DePelchin family arrived in Galveston in 1837. By 1839 Kezia was an orphan as both of her parents died in a yellow fever epidemic. During the Civil War she was a nurse in Houston. In 1888 DePelchin was chosen the first woman matron of Bayland Orphans Home for Boys. She founded the city's first day care center in 1892 and a year later chartered Faith Home, a facility that still exists today as DePelchin Children's Center. [38]

» DEPELCHIN: Kezia Payne DePelchin

DEPOT: Brookshire was a stop on the Missouri, Kansas & Texas Railroad (now Union Pacific). This street ran in front of the train station or depot, although the building is now a memory. [39]

DESERT AIRE: See sidebar **Tennis or Golf, Anyone?,** page 348.

DESOTA: Wedged between LaSalle and Coronado streets we have another example of the often-demonstrated poor spelling abilities of area developers. Mission Estates Addition in Friendswood is full of names of early explorers. However, this gentleman's correct name is Hernando de Soto. Born in Spain in about 1496, he sailed to the New World in 1519 to explore the coasts of Guatemala and Yucatan. In 1532 he joined Francisco Pizarro in conquering the Incas. Hearing tales of great treasure in Florida he arrived there in 1538. Unfortunately, a four-year search proved fruitless and he died in 1542. [40]

DETERING: Herman Eberhard – He was an early Houston merchant and landowner. He founded the Detering Company, a building material supply firm that is still in operation today. Detering wanted to develop some property he owned east of Memorial Park. According to his grandson and current president of the family operation, Carl, the bureaucrats were slow in installing the utilities. To accelerate the process Mr. Detering decided to name a number of the streets in the addition for Harris County commissioners. That was all it took. (See **Eberhard.**) [41]

DEVON: See sidebar **All Things English,** page 175.

DEWALT: Thomas Walters – He arrived from Virginia in the mid-1850s and established a large plantation in Fort Bend County on Oyster Creek where he grew sugar cane.

In addition Dewalt was a lawyer and justice of the peace. The Dewalt Cemetery has been in operation since 1850 and is still in use. Many individuals from old Richmond families are interred here including Dewalt, Roane, Martin and Robinson. [42]

DIABLO: See sidebar **Learn a Foreign Language on Your Morning Walk,** page 125.

DIAMOND HEAD: See sidebar **Bali Hai May Call You,** page 322.

DIAMONDHEAD: Located in the small residential neighborhood of Newport east of Lake Houston, this road is named for the developer of that area, Diamondhead Corporation, known for their resort projects around the country. [43]

DICK SCOBEE: Viet Nam war hero (Distinguished Flying Cross and the Air Medal) and test pilot, NASA chose him for astronaut training in January 1978. An experienced spacecraft commander, he died tragically, along with six other astronauts, in the

"TEXAS HEROES' NAMES FOR HOUSTON STREETS URGED IN 72 PROPOSED CHANGES"

This headline appeared in the May 8, 1929 edition of the *Houston Chronicle*. Two city engineers, Jack Graham and C. E. "Jack " Tooke, recommended that City Council change the names of 72 duplicate streets to honor heroes of the Battle of San Jacinto, The War Between the States, Texas statesmen and local citizens. Searching such records as the *1890 Texas Census Index of Civil War Veterans* and *The Campaign of Walker's Texas Division* by J.P. Blessington I was able to verify a number of these individuals did exist. However, there were 16 men that I could not locate in the search of the database available to me. The other 56 are included in the main text. Not wanting to omit information on the history of our street names I assume Messers. Graham and Tooke had correct information that has disappeared since 1929. Therefore below is a listing of the 16 "missing" recommended street names as they were given to Council. [16]

- **Arnot** – fought at Battle of San Jacinto
- **Buford** – colonel commanding a Texas regiment in the Civil War
- **Cummins** – a city employee in 1929
- **Chisum** – fought in the 2nd Regiment of the Texas Partisan Rangers
- **Doney** – fought with Walker's Texas Division in the War Between the States
- **Eddington** – member of Walker's Texas Division in the Civil War
- **Flowers** - member of Walker's Texas Division in the Civil War
- **Gwinn** - member of Walker's Texas Division in the Civil War
- **Karnes** – a captain in the Texas Revolutionary Army
- **Kelton** – a surgeon in the Texas Navy
- **Mellus** – a lieutenant in the Texas Navy
- **Pickens** – Inspector General of Holtclaw's Brigade of the Confederate Army
- **Rains** – an attorney in early Texas
- **Stratton** – fought with the 2nd Regiment of the Texas Partisan Rangers
- **Wingate** – killed in the Goliad Massacre

explosion of the orbiter Challenger on January 28, 1986. His memory is preserved at the Model Airplane Facility in George Bush Park. (See **Challenger Seven.**) [44]

DICKEY PLACE: William M. Dickey owned a farm near where River Oaks is today. When that area was being developed in 1923-4 he sold a portion of his land for the construction of River Oaks Elementary School. He then developed Avalon and Dickey Place nearby as well as the Avalon Center at the corner of Westheimer and Kirby. [45]

DICKINSON: John – The street, the town and the bayou are named after this early pioneer. He was given a land grant for this area in 1824. In the 1850s Dickinson became a stop on the Galveston, Houston & Henderson Railroad. In the early 1900s the Galveston & Houston Electric Railway made regular stops there. [46]

DIEPPE: On August 19, 1942 Canadian troops attacked the German coastal defenses at Dieppe, a French city on the English Channel. The battle was a debacle for the allies physically, with the Canadians sustaining huge casualties. However, tactically it answered questions about the strength of the Nazi defenses and the problems an invading force would face in the future. [47]

DING-AN-SICH: This oddly named Liberty County drive is German for "a thing in itself." It is a notion in the philosophy of Immanuel Kant. A "thing-in-itself" is an object as it would appear to us if we did not have to approach it under the conditions of space and time. For more information on this obscure subject see his classic works *Critique of Pure Reason* (1781) and *Critique of Practical Reason* (1788), in which he put forward a system of ethics based on the categorical imperative. [48]

MAYOR OSCAR HOLCOMBE'S REVENGE

Years ago a *Houston Press* (a newspaper from 1911 to 1964) reporter named Tom Abernathy succeeded in aggravating Mayor Holcombe. Not one to take this lying down the Mayor decided to level the playing field with Mr. Abernathy. Contacting the head of the Public Works Department, Holcombe indicated he wanted to name a street after Abernathy – but not just any street. Director J. M. Nagle instructed Chief City Draftsman Keating that the Mayor wanted the worst street in the city renamed for the reporter. So Keating recommended Oates as the candidate for renaming. It was a short, muddy, unimportant, Fifth Ward lane that abutted the San Antonio & Aransas Pass Railroad tracks. Then the Mayor issued a press release stating he was naming a street for "a *Houston Press* reporter." Abernathy's initial reaction was a combination of excitement and confusion due to his adversarial relationship with Holcombe. He was quoted in his own paper as saying "I was excited and a bit flattered when I first saw the list and noted my name proposed for one of the streets." Further investigation "promptly deflated my ego" according to Abernathy. So the "Grey Fox" as the mayor was known, proved again how he got his nickname when the *Press* headline stated "Press Reporter Not Greatly Flattered When He Finally Finds Street That Was Named For Him." Although this story remains, Abernathy Street no longer exists. [17]

DINNER CREEK: This 4-mile long estuary rises a mile north of Settlers Village and empties into Langham Creek in northwest Harris County. (See **Settlers Village.**) [49]

DISMUKE: Thomas – See sidebar **Houston Streets Named for Men Killed During World War I,** page 22.

DIVOT: When a piece of turf on a golf course is torn out as a ball is being struck, it is called a divot. For more on the odd street names of the Sky Lakes subdivision, see **Bogie.**

DOBBIN-HUFSMITH: What would become west Montgomery County was first visited by the French explorer LaSalle in 1687. Americans settled in the area in 1831. In 1880 the Navasota & Montgomery Railroad opened a station here called Bobbin. In 1909 the name was changed to Dobbin. (See **Hufsmith.**) [50]

DOERRE: This family owned land in the area near Klein, Texas where this street is located. A number of these early settlers are interred in the Trinity Lutheran Cemetery. (See **Klein Cemetery.**) [4]

DOLIVER: Because of his daughter Mary Catherine's fascination with Hawthorne's *Tanglewood Tales*, developer William Farrington planned to name all of the streets in his new project for people and places in the novel. Except for the title street however, Doliver was the only other name he liked in the book. [51]

DONERAIL: The naming of this street proves that the winner of the Kentucky Derby achieves immortality. Donerail won the Run for the Roses in 1913 by 1/2 a length. This high-strung thoroughbred refused to stand still while the blanket of roses was placed over his head, a winner's circle tradition. Jockey Roscoe Goose dismounted, removed the saddle and climbed back on. No one knows why, but this seemed to satisfy Donerail and he was photographed with Goose and the roses on his bareback. He never won another major race. [52]

DONEY: A. G. V. – This man was a surgeon in the 11th Texas Volunteer Infantry during the Civil War. He was in Walker's Texas Division. [53]

DONEY: See sidebar **Texas Heroes' Names for Houston Streets Urged in 72 Proposed Changes,** page 96.

DONIGAN: Paul – This gentleman was a prominent doctor in Brookshire. Donigan was born in Turkey. His former home is now the Waller County Museum. [54]

DONNA BELL: Real estate developer Frank Sharp named this Oak Forest Addition street for his secretary's daughter. (See **Frank Sharp.**) [55]

DONOVAN: James G. – This gentleman was the city attorney for Houston Heights from its incorporation until Houston annexed it in 1918. His daughter was financier Marcella Perry (see **Marcella**). [56]

DOOLITTLE: James H. – He became famous as the U. S. Army Air Corps general who led the air raid on Tokyo on April 14, 1942. Leaving from the aircraft carrier *Hornet*, this daring raid gave American morale a needed boost following the sneak attack on Pearl Harbor by the Japanese on December 7, 1941. [57]

DORAL: This Miami, Florida golf club and spa is the home of five championship links including the famed "Blue Monster."

DOUBLETREE PLAZA: This short street fronts on the 313-room Doubletree Hotel at Houston Intercontinental Airport. [58]

DOW: C. Milby – This Deer Park street and park of the same name remember this gentleman who donated the land for a park in 1958. [59]

DOW: Dow Chemical Company was incorporated in 1897 by Herbert H. Dow to produce bleach. Along the way the product line expanded to include chlorine, ethylene, anti-knock gasoline, polystyrene, Saran Wrap, measles vaccine, Ziploc bags and compact discs to mention a few. The company has a large presence in the Ship Channel town of Deer Park. [60]

DOWDELL: In the U. S. Census of 1850 there was a 55-year-old Virginian living in north Harris County where this road is located by the name of Edward R. Dowdle. It is possible the street is named for him. It was not uncommon in those days for people to have their names misspelled or later alter the spelling. Examples in the area include Kurkendale to Kuykendall, Thaisz to Theis or Struck to Strack. [61]

DOWLING: Richard W. "Dick" – Dowling was born in Tuam, Galway County, Ireland in 1838 and immigrated to America. He was a saloonkeeper in a Houston bar named The Finish. It was known for a drink called "kiss me quick and go." He volunteered for the Confederate army and became a hero by defeating a Union effort to invade Texas at the Battle of Sabine Pass. Returning to Houston, Dowling opened a bar called The Bank of Bacchus Saloon. He died of yellow

» **DOWLING: Dick Dowling statue when it was in Market Square**

fever in 1867 and is buried in St. Vincent's Cemetery on **Navigation.** The Ancient Order of Hibernians commissioned Frank Teich to sculpt a statue of him that originally stood in Market Square. Moved several times over the years, it has been in Hermann Park since 1958. Dressed proudly in his Confederate uniform he now guards the concrete lined concourse of Brays Bayou but is often missing his sword. It has been stolen five times since the statue was completed in 1905. Historically the Hibernians gave the statue a bath every St. Patrick's Day. (See **Sabine** and **Tuam.**) [62]

DOWNS: (See **Epsom.**)

DR. JOHN E. CODWELL: He was one of Houston's greatest black educators. HISD valued his skills so highly they waived the retirement age policy so he could continue his service for another decade. Among the positions he held were coach, assistant principal and principal at Phyllis Wheatley Senior High School and principal of Jack Yates Senior High School. (See **Wheatley.**) [63]

DRAKE: Founded in 1881 in Des Moines, Iowa this university is named for a major financial contributor, General Francis Marion Drake. He was a Civil War general, Iowa governor, attorney, banker and railroad man. Drake consistently ranks academically as one of the top schools in the Midwest. Since 1910 it has been the home of the Drake Relays, one of the greatest track and field meets held in America. [64]

DRISCOLL: Years ago the Driscoll family owned a large dairy farm where Montrose and this street are today. The vintage family farmhouse was razed in 2004 to make way for a townhouse complex. One of our city's grisliest murders took place at 1815 Driscoll on June 20, 1965, Father's Day. Three days later Houston homicide detectives discovered the neatly butchered bodies of Fred and Edwina Rogers in the icebox of the home. The crime has never been solved but their mysterious son, Charles, remains the chief suspect. No one has seen him for more than 40 years. Learn more about this heinous crime by reading *The Ice Box Murders* by Hugh and Martha Gardenier. [59]

DRY BAYOU: This estuary rises northwest of Angleton where its source was dammed up to form Harris Reservoir. It runs 14 miles to join Middle Bayou before emptying into the Brazos River near Brazoria. (See **Harris Reservoir.**) [65]

DRYDEN: John – He was a 17th century English poet and dramatist. But it was his essays on literary criticism that made him famous. His best-known work in this field, *A Defense of an Essay of Dramatique Poesie,* was written in 1668. To make a neighborhood seem full of intellectuals, who better to name a street after than John Dryden? [66]

DUESSEN: Alexander – He was a petroleum engineer who donated a 309-acre site on Lake Houston to Harris County in 1956. Subsequently the land was converted into a public park named for him. [67]

DUKE: James Buchanan – Duke, an industrialist and philanthropist, founded Duke

» HONORARY STREET MARKER: At
Hood's studio home at 819 Highland

University in 1924 in Durham, North
Carolina. His final consuming interest
was building the university. As Duke
lay dying, one of his last recorded
statements was "Don't bother me,
nurse. Today, I am laying out the university grounds." [68]

DULLES: John Foster – Diplomat,
civil servant and U. S. senator, this
gentleman is best remembered as
the Secretary of State during the
Eisenhower administration. As chief
architect of American foreign policy
during the early years of the Cold
War, Dulles believed peace could
only be maintained by threats of
"massive retaliation" against any
Communist aggression. Dulles High
school in the Fort Bend ISD is also
named in his honor. [69]

DUMONT: This was the original name
of South Houston from 1907 until
its incorporation in 1913. (See **South
Houston.**) [70]

DUNCAN: Hartford – This FM 1960-
area road is the surname of an early
settler in the area. Descendants of
the man still live there. [71]

DUNKIRK: A seaport in France on the
English Channel, it was the scene of

HONORARY STREET MARKERS

Unless you are a real estate developer, your
best friend is a developer, you are an employee of Vernon Henry & Associates or you have
strong ties to city government, it is difficult
to name a street. It is even a greater challenge
to change the name of an existing street.
Both of these processes involve applications,
lengthy reviews and approvals. However,
City Council is willing to consider "honorary
street markers" in certain cases. An excellent example of this is the marker honoring
world famous Houston artist **Dorothy Hood.**
She lived and worked at 819 Highlands in the
Houston Heights. Her studio was a Mecca for
established as well as "starving" artists. Hood
was born in 1919 in Bryan, Texas and attended
the Rhode Island School of Design and the
Art Students League in New York City. In the
1940s she met many famous artists, poets
and composers from Latin America including
the Mexican muralist Jose Clemente Orozco
and conductor Valasco Maidana who became her husband. They moved to Houston
in 1962. Her career as an artist took off. Hood
had works shown in the Museum of Fine Art
Houston, Contemporary Arts Museum of
Houston, Museum of Modern Art in New
York and the National Gallery in Washington,
D. C. Her neighbors loved her and following
her death in October 2000 they initiated
the plan to have Highland Street renamed in
her honor. The Planning and Development
Department suggested an "honorary street
marker' would be much easier to get. The
marker was placed in front of her home/stu-
dio in February 2001.

Standards for Honorary Street Markers are as
follows: 1) A request must be made to Planning
and Development listing the individual's contribution to society; 2) Requests must be approved by City Council; 3) Honorary markers
are only for local streets; 4) They are limited
to one block and 5) Use of proper names is
only allowed if the honoree is deceased.

C-D

Thursday, July 4, 1918

CENTRAL HIGH MOURNS PASSING OF DEAD MARINE

HERBERT DUNLAVY

In Flanders Fields the poppies
Between the crosses, row on
That mark our place and in th
The larks still bravely sing
Scarce heard amidst the gun
low.

We are the dead.
Short days ago we lived, felt
saw sunset glow,
Loved and were loved, and no
lie
In Flanders Fields.

Take up our quarrel with the fo
To you from failing hands we t
the torch;
Be yours to hold it high;
If ye break faith with us who
We shall not sleep, though po
grow
In Flanders Fields.

Dunlavy First Local Athlete to Die; Settegast, Litterest, Brown, Scott, Mitchell and Others in Action.

"* * * That other generations might possess—
From shame and menace free in years to come—
A richer heritage of happiness,
He marched to that heroic martyrdom.
Esteeming less the forfeit that he paid
Than undishonored that his flag might float
Over the towers of liberty, he made
His breast the bulwark and his blood the moat."

So the inspired American legionary, Alan Seeger, wrote before a deadly cross-fire from German machine guns claimed him in a charge on Belloy-en-Santerre in July, 1916. So thought Herbert Dunlavy, just two years later, as, heeding an officer's call, he "carried on" with his unit of marines in another sector of France.

It has not been established yet what kind of a weapon or missile took the life of the former Houston High boy and amateur ball player, the first athlete from Houston to "Go West." Quite possibly letters from comrades will bring more of the details.

Two years ago this month young Dunlavy was a prominent figure in the City and the Sunday baseball leagues of Houston. Earlier in 1916 he was leader of the Houston Central High nine. In football he played equally as brilliant a game. Physical fitness gained on the field and diamond qualified him for the Marine Corps and after a period of intensive training on the Atlantic seaboard he went overseas.

◊ ◊ ◊

First Athlete to Go.

Though there are scores of Houston lads abroad who were prominent in sports during their school and college days, Dunlavy is the first to pay the supreme price. With the Rainbow Division is Marion Settegast, also of Central High. He is wearing a lieutenant's bar now. Now so very far removed from "Betty" may be Penny Thornton, Joe Litterest, Ed Brown, Tom Scott, Sidney

Mitchell and a dozen others, each of whom won a reputation in local football circles.

It may be that Dunlavy was sweeping forward in the first wave of an attack when he received the fatal wound. It may be that a shell burst caused the mortal injury. In its measure of condolence to his mother, the war department does not go into detail. "Killed in action" practically sums up the intelligence sent to Houston over the wire. Today is Fourth of July in France as well as in this republic. Possibly friends of Dunlavy have already started exacting a great toll from the enemy for their comrade's life. A prophetic chord was sounded by Alan Seegar in his wartime poem of 1916 written in France just before his last charge. In it he seemed to sense his final resting place amid the "sunny chalk field of Champagne." Closing, he wrote:

"Under the little crosses where they rise
The soldier rests. Now round him undismayed
The cannon thunders, and at night he lies
At peace beneath the eternal fusillade."

» DUNLAVY: U.S. Marine Herbert Dunlavy's obituary

about 1000 ships evacuating approximately 300,000 trapped English and Allied troops from its beachfront between May 27 and June 4, 1940 as the German forces were advancing. English civilians manned many of the boats. The RAF offered air cover for the operation. It ranks among the most tremendous feats of naval history. [72]

DUNLAVY: Herbert D. – This U. S. Marine was killed in action in WW I. He was the first Houstonian casualty of that war. This hero single-handedly captured the crew of a German machine gun nest on June 6, 1918. For this action he was awarded the Distinguished

Service Cross. Unfortunately on June 7 Dunlavy was resting in a trench when he was killed by the force of an artillery shell that exploded near him. In 1921 he was honored by his church, Christ Church Cathedral, along with five other servicemen who lost their lives in the conflict, with a special war memorial. (See obituary page 102.) [73]

DUNMAN: Joseph – An early resident of Humble, Texas, this gentleman holds the honor of being the first documented burial in the Humble Cemetery. [74]

DUNSTAN: See **Southampton's English Streets,** page 255.

DURANZO: See sidebar **Brazoria County's Old Plantation Streets and Roads,** page 258.

DURHAM: Mylie E. – This gentleman was a general practitioner in the Houston Heights for many years. He was a founder of Heights Hospital. Long-time Heights resident Flossie Huckabee said Dr. Durham passed away on his birthday while enjoying a round of golf. [75]

DUVAL: John Crittenden – He came to Texas to fight for independence from Mexico. Duval was captured with Fannin but managed to escape before the Palm Sunday massacre at Goliad. He fought in the War Between the States but did not believe in secession. He took up writing at age 48 and was called "the First Texas Man of Letters" by J. Frank Dobie. He wrote of his fantastic escape at Goliad as well as his adventures with Bigfoot Wallace. [76]

DWIGHT: (See **Eisenhower.**)

DYER MOORE RANCH: John Matthew Moore was born in Brazoria in 1862. Following his graduation from Texas A & M, he worked on the family's farm. In 1883 he married Lottie Dyer and became manager of her land and cattle operations. He served four terms in the U. S. Congress and was instrumental in getting funds appropriated for construction of the Houston Ship Channel. [77]

DYER: C.C. or J. E. – C. C. Dyer was a judge in Fort Bend County. His son, J. E., was born at Stafford's Point in 1832. He was a rancher, merchant (J. E. Dyer Dry Goods Store) and banker. In addition he was county treasurer from 1852 until 1859. J. E. fought for the Confederates in the War Between the States. [78]

D'AMICO: Samuel L. – See sidebar **Houston Streets Named for Men Killed During World War I,** page 22.

NEIGHBORHOODS WITH INTERESTING STORIES

⊛ **Westhaven Estates.** This west side neighborhood only has two streets, **Potomac** (named for the river that runs into Chesapeake Bay near Washington, D. C.) and **Nantucket** (the Massachusetts island and one time whaling port and now posh resort). Today Westhaven is chock-a-block with pricey town homes with median values approximating $300,000. However, it comes from more rural beginnings. In the 1950s Italian truck farmers were forced to move their gardens west from Post Oak due to construction of Loop 610 West. They built modest farmhouses on these two streets with construction materials supplied from Bering Hardware (see **Bering**). Residents grew much of the city's fresh produce. Only a few of these charming little cottages remain. Neither street had curbs or gutters. Rainwater was carried away in large bar ditches. Developer/builder William Carl got the streets repaved and began putting up town homes in the 1970s starting the neighborhood on its road to gentrification.

⊛ **Home Owned Estates.** Located near the Houston Ship Channel, this area initially served as residences for the thousands of workers employed by the businesses serving the maritime industries. The neighborhood sprang up following World War II. Old time residents say the name came from the fact that prior to the War few people owned their own home in the area. It was a marketing ploy used by developers according to Maxine Cunningham, an original owner. Signs said "Come to your Home Owned Estate." Many of the streets here are named for towns where early residents may have lived prior to moving to the Houston area. It is an odd geographic mixture including **Louisville, Indianapolis, Joliet, Peoria, Mobile, Rochester, Sacramento, Utica, Duluth, Boise** and **Topeka.**

⊛ **Magnolia Point.** In the 1950s as Houston began to boom, real estate developers began gobbling up large chunks of cheap suburban property. To call attention to these future communities, developers would place red flags on the property to mark the boundaries of the lots. Most of these developments were totally lacking in improvements such as paved streets, curbs, gutters, streetlights, water and sewer lines and sidewalks. Local pundits took to calling these schemes "Red Flag" subdivisions. Magnolia Park was just one of many of these neighborhoods. When it was annexed by Houston in 1984, it was still lacking most of these amenities.

⊛ **Stagecoach.** This Montgomery County development was started in 1958. Previously it had been a farm owned by W. L. Swinley. And prior to that it was a station on a 19th century stagecoach route. In keeping with the western theme of the neighborhood, the developers named the streets **Tomahawk, Surrey, Boot Hill, Cimarron, Wagon Wheel, Broken Spoke, Indian Springs, Westward Ho, Old Coach, Silver Spur** and of course, **Stagecoach.**

⊛ **University Oaks.** Ben Taub and I. G. Strauss developed this neighborhood between Wheeler, Cullen, N. MacGregor and Calhoun in 1939. Naturally the street names relate to academia including **University Oaks, Graduate, Faculty** and **Varsity.**

⊛ **Frenchtown.** In 1922 a group of Louisiana Creoles, persons of a mix of African and French or Spanish blood, arrived in Houston. They brought with them their culture, customs, food and music. These Creoles were joined by a second wave that arrived following a severe Mississippi River flood in 1927. This neighborhood on our city's north side is bounded by **Collinsworth** on the north, **Russell** on the east, **Liberty** on the south and **Des Chaumes** to the west. Over the years the Creole influence has been diluted but it is still possible to enjoy some marvelous Cajun cuisine and dance to some rocking Zydeco music in Frenchtown.

⊛ **Venetian Estates.** In the 1950s the Imperial Sugar Company, the major land owner in Sugar Land, Texas, decided to dredge Oyster Creek and create a waterfront district that would attract homebuyers. Canals were dug. The area was named Venetian Estates, as the waterways recalled those of the beautiful Italian city of Venice. Carrying the theme further, all the streets in the development have an Italian connection: **Gondola, Salerno, Venice, San Marino, Santa Maria, Piedmont, Tuscany, Sorrento, St. Marks, Capri** and **Lombardy.**

⊛ **East Houston.** The principally African-American neighborhood has three inexplicably named streets in a row. **Little, Boy, Blue.** Is this real estate developer humor? [18]

E

EAGLETON: Barrett Station is a black community off U. S. 90 that sprang up during Reconstruction. The Eagleton family are landowners in this small town. (See **Barrett Station.**) [1]

EARLINE: Located just to the north of Laura Koppe, this street is named for Earline Trone. [2]

EAST BAY: This body of water is the southeast extension of Galveston Bay lying along Chambers County between Bolivar Peninsula and the mainland. It is 20 miles long and 5 miles wide. [3]

EAST SAN JACINTO: The east fork of the San Jacinto River flows 69 miles from Dodge, Texas to where it joins the west fork at Lake Houston. This river was the eastern boundary of Stephen F. Austin's colony where settlement began in the 1820s. In 1844 Sam Houston built a plantation home, Raven Hill, on the upper east fork bank. [4]

EASTEX FREEWAY: When freeway construction began in the 1940s and 50s city officials decided to involve the populous in naming these concrete monsters. A young Houston lass won a contest to name the Gulf Freeway. This superhighway was also named as the result of a contest held in 1953 as it became the main road to East Texas. (See **Gulf Freeway.**) [5]

EASTGATE: Leading to the tiny Liberty County town of the same name, this community was established in 1911. The name is due to the town's location at the east gate of the Beaumont, Sour Lake & Western Railroad's yard. That line operated from 1903 until 1956. Today the Union Pacific Railroad owns the tracks. [6]

EASY JET: We love our horses in Houston and this street recalls another one. He became a legend in quarter horse racing circles. As a two year old he was loaded into the starting gate a staggering 26 times and won 22 of those races. For his effort he was named World Champion Running Quarter Horse. A year later he won the title of World Champion Racing American Quarter Horse. Easy Jet retired with a record of 27 wins, 7 places, 2 shows and 2 out of the money in his 38 race career. [7]

EASY: If we have streets in Houston that are misnamed, this is a leading candidate for the title. Located in a depressed neighborhood northwest of downtown, Easy was christened by the area's developer as a marketing ploy to draw potential buyers. He saw the name on a street in an Ohio town and liked it. One resident told a *Houston Chronicle* reporter, "I don't like the name. It ought to be called 'Hard Knocks.'" [8]

EBERHARD: This street is the middle name of Herman Detering, an early landowner and merchant in the city. He owned property in the 4th Ward and since he had already named a street using his surname he elected to use his middle name on this lane. (See **Detering**.) [9]

EDDINGTON: See sidebar **Texas Heroes' Names for Houston Streets Urged in 72 Proposed Changes,** page 96.

EDLOE: Real estate developer Edward Lillo Crain Sr. named this street for his son, Edward Jr. It is from a contraction of the first two letters of Edward plus the first and last letters of Lillo with an "e" added on the end. Running south to north, Edloe dead

---

SPACE CITY U.S.A. OR "HOUSTON THE EAGLE HAS LANDED"

It is no wonder that as important as Houston has been to the Space Program that the area near NASA would have a number of streets recalling space age verbiage. **Saturn** recalls the rocket series that eventually culminated in the Saturn V, the largest launch vehicle ever built at 363-feet in height and capable of generating 7.7 million pounds of thrust on take off, propelling our astronauts to the Moon. **Skywalker** remembers the many space walks astronauts took while conducting research. **Moon Rock** is for the lunar rocks returned to NASA by the Apollo astronauts that landed on the surface of our nearest planetary neighbor. **Thor** was initially an intermediate range ballistic missile. It was later modified to be a first stage launch vehicle for space craft. **Gemini** was the space capsule employed by NASA between the Mercury and Apollo programs. Ten manned and two unmanned missions were launched in 1965-66. Ed White made the first space walk during Gemini V. **Mercury** was America's first manned space craft. Our first heroic astronauts Alan Shepard, Virgil "Gus" Grissom, John Glenn, Scott Carpenter, Walter "Wally" Schirra and Gordon Cooper hurled their bodies into the great void in these tiny (6' by 6') capsules. **Titan** was the U. S. first intercontinental ballistic missile. It was later modified for use by NASA. Between 1959 and 2005 about 170 of these behemoths were launched from Cape Canaveral. The **Apollo** program (1963-1972) was designed to send American astronauts to the Moon and return them safely. Six missions (Apollo 11, 12, 14, 15, 16 and 17) did land on the lunar surface. Apollo 13 experienced a frightening malfunction but returned to Earth safely. Later a terrific motion picture was made about this almost disaster. **Hercules** is a solid rocket motor propellant. [19]

ends into Westheimer. If you extended the street north into River Oaks it would run into Mr. Crain's front door in the 3600 block of Chevy Chase. Mr. Crain, who developed Garden Oaks, Southside Place, Riverside Terrace, Cherryhurst and Pineview, is buried in Glenwood Cemetery. [10]

EDMUNDSON: W. L. – He came to Houston from Galveston in 1900. Edmundson became a very successful real estate developer with such projects as Edmundson's Addition (bordered by Leeland, Scott, Miller and Hutchins) as well as Avalon Place near River Oaks. He eventually became the world's largest hay dealer. He is credited with inventing the cotton compress during WW I. [11]

EDNA: Located in the Park Place Addition, this two block street is named for Edna Davis, the wife of American General Insurance Company vice president, Bob Davis. [12]

EDWARD TEACH: See sidebar **Pirates of the Caribbean,** page 280.

EGBERT: James D. – A printer from New York City, Egbert came to Texas in 1836. He fought at the Battle of San Jacinto in Captain George M. Casey's Company of Regulars. Egbert held the rank of corporal. [13]

EGGLING: Henry – All of this area in west Harris County was originally part of the George survey. In 1859 this gentleman bought 480 acres from Patrick George and Darius Gregg who had acquired the land in 1838 from a gentleman named Toliver. [14]

EGYPT: An Englishman, George Bell Madeley, settled in this area of Montgomery County in the 1840s. He raised corn, cotton, fruits, cattle, owned a grist mill and a vineyard. Other farmers bought corn from Madeley and they named the town for the biblical story of Jacob's family going to Egypt to buy corn from their brother during a famine. [15]

EICHWURZEL: Sam – Located just east of the intersection of I-45 and Loop 610 near the banks of White Oak Bayou, this man was a land owner here in the 1890s. Other residents of the area were the Sharman family for which **Sharman** street is named. Members of both families are buried in the cemetery on Enid. [16]

LET'S GO TO A TRACK AND FIELD MEET

The developers of Walden on Lake Houston must be like your author – a fanatic about track and field – because they named most of the streets in the beautiful lakeside community for that sport. If you like jogging or racing this is your kind of place. Lace up the Nikes and go for a run on **Relay, Cross Country, Runners, Sprinters, Joggers, Olympic, Pacesetter, Baton Pass, Mile Run** and **Sebastian** (most likely for Sebastian Coe, two-time Olympic gold medal winner in the 1,500 meters and record holder in the one mile run). If you prefer the field events check out **Discus** and **Vaulted.** Finally for the truly gifted have a go at **Decathlon.** [20]

EISENHOWER: Dwight David – This street is named after the Supreme Commander of the Allied Forces in Europe during WW II and later the 34th President of the United States. This native Texan was born in Denison. [17]

EL CAMINO REAL: Meaning "The Royal Highway" in Spanish, this 530 mile road from San Diego to Sonoma, California linked the 21 Franciscan missions built in that state between 1769 and 1823. Each mission was one day's ride on horseback from the next. [18]

EL CID: A Spanish soldier whose real name was Rodrigo Diaz de Vivar became a national hero after capturing Valencia in 1049. His exploits are recorded in the epic tale entitled *The Song of El Cid.* [19]

EL MATADOR: See sidebar **Learn a Foreign Language on Your Morning Walk,** page 125.

ELDRIDGE: William Thomas – A jack of many trades, Eldridge was a marshal, hotelier, land developer and railroad man before moving to Sugar Land, Texas where he joined with the Kempner family of Galveston in buying the Cunningham Sugar Refinery. This 20,000 acre plantation was renamed Imperial Sugar Company with Eldridge as the manager. It remains a very successful business operation today. (See **Howell-Sugarland, Imperial** and **Kempner.**) [20]

ELEVATOR: Located at the Port of Houston, this street leads to a huge complex of grain storage elevators and the Elevator Storage Railroad Yard. [21]

» **ELEVATOR: Early photograph of grain elevators along the Houston Ship Channel**

ELGIN: Robert Morris – He arrived in Texas in 1842. Elgin came to Houston and lived at 1402 Texas at Austin in a home built in 1870. It was demolished in about 1928. He was a partner in a stationery and printing company called Dealy, Cochran & Elgin. The city of Elgin is also named for him and his family. Elgin is buried in Glenwood Cemetery. [22]

ELISSA: This restored 19th century iron-hulled, three-masted sailing barque is owned by the Galveston Historical Foundation. She was launched on the Clyde River in Aberdeen, Scotland in 1877. The Elissa is 162 feet in length, 28 feet at her beam, gross capacity is 430 tons and she carries 19 sails. During her more than 100 years of service she passed through many owners, sailed the seven seas and did visit Galveston in 1883 and 1886. The Foundation purchased the Elissa in 1974. The ship underwent a complete restoration and now is visited by close to 100,000 tourists anually at her berth at Galveston's Fisherman's Wharf. [23]

» **ELISSA: Docked at Galveston's Fisherman's Wharf**

ELLA LEE: The River Oaks urban legend claims Miss Ima Hogg named this lane for one of her best friends. Lee was the maiden name of developer Hugh Potter's wife. [24]

ELLA: This lady was the wife of one of Houston real estate developer Edward Lillo Crane Sr.'s partners. This thoroughfare was named in her honor. [25]

MY HOW THINGS HAVE CHANGED OR
WEST UNIVERSITY PLACE GETS STOP SIGNS

By the early 1930s West University Place had become quite a bustling bedroom community. As a result the City Commissioners ordered six stop signs to aid in traffic control. Two were placed at the intersection of **Wake Forest** and **Rice**, two at **Belmont** and **University** and the remaining two at **Buffalo Speedway** and **University**. [21]

ELLINGTON PARK: This street recalls a historic airfield north of Friendswood. Ellington Field was built in 1917 on 1,280 acres of coastal prairie land. It was named for Eric L. Ellington who died in a plane crash in San Diego, California in 1913. Its purpose was pilot and bombardier training. Following World War I it was mothballed until 1941 when once again it was opened to train servicemen. Following World War II Ellington trained air reservists, air guardsmen and Navy and Marine pilots. It is the field where Air Force One lands when the President of the United States visits the Houston area. [26, 27]

ELLIOTT: Karl L. – See sidebar **Houston Streets Named for Men Killed During World War I,** page 22.

ELLIS: Littleberry Ambrose – This gentleman was a plantation owner in the area near where Sugar Land is today. He was a business partner of Colonel E. H. Cunningham. (See **Cunningham.**) [28]

ELMORA: Edward Lillo Crain Sr. was a real estate developer in the city during the 1920s and 30s. He named a number of streets in Southside Place. Crain named this one block street for his secretary of many years. (See **Edloe.**) [29]

ELMTEX: See sidebar **Howdy Tex,** page 263.

ELSBURY: The Elsbury family lived on this Montrose area street. [30]

ELVIS: It's named for the "King," who else?

ELYSIAN: In Greek mythology the Elysian Fields were the abode of the blessed after death. [31]

EMILY MORGAN: Better known as the "Yellow Rose of Texas," she was born a mulatto slave. Captured by Santa Anna at Morgan's Point on Buffalo Bayou, Morgan learned of *El General's* attack plan on the Texans. She sent another slave to warn Sam Houston and then distracted Santa Anna with her feminine charms. With his interest focused on the Rose rather than the Battle at San Jacinto, the Texans won their independence in 18 minutes. Morgan was granted freedom for her heroic efforts. [32]

EMMET O. HUTTO: He was born in Bertram, Texas in 1918. After attending the University of Texas he joined the Army Air Force during World War II. Hutto flew 38 missions over Nazi targets in Europe and North Africa. He was awarded the Distinguished Flying Cross and a citation for bravery. Hutto was a successful businessman in Baytown operating a real estate office, hotel and restaurant. He also served on the Baytown City Council. [33]

EMNORA: It is possible that this Spring Valley street is named for two members of the Bauer family. The "Em" comes from Emily with Nora added on. [34]

EMORY: The Methodist Church founded this southern university in 1836. It was named for John Emory, a popular bishop who had been killed in 1835 in a carriage accident. It is located in Atlanta, Georgia. [35]

ENDEAVOUR: This British Royal Navy research vessel was under the command of Captain James Cook. In April 1770 she became the first ship to reach the east coast of Australia. Cook landed at what he named Botany Bay. While sailing up the Australian coast the Endeavour ran aground on the Great Barrier Reef. She limped into the Dutch East Indies for repair. Sailing on around the Cape of Good Hope, she returned to England after a three year expedition. This Seabrook street recalls this historic vessel. [36]

ENGELKE: This pioneer German family were landowners in the 2nd Ward, east of downtown. There were so many immigrants from Germany that Canal Street was originally named German Street and the area was called Germantown. (See sidebar titled **Houston's Germanic Heritage,** page 60.) [37]

ENGLEWOOD: Leading to the large railroad yard of the same name, both derive their names from the Southern Pacific Rail Road's Englewood Yard in Chicago. [38]

ENNIS: Cornelius – His was another typical early Houston success story. Ennis owned a general store, shipped the first cotton out of Galveston to New England, was mayor in 1856-57, was a founder of the Great Northern Railroad, built the Houston & Texas Central Railroad, was a successful blockade-runner during the War Between the States and chaired the building committee that erected the Galveston Daily News building. Ennis is buried in Glenwood Cemetery. [39]

STARRY NIGHT

If you visit North Star Estates in Tomball you can take a celestial tour of the major stars in our heavens. **Altair** is the 15th brightest star in the sky. Located a mere 45 light-years from Earth is **Capella,** the 6th brightest star in the night sky. **Castor** is one of the two major stars in the constellation Gemini. **Orion** is one of the most visible constellations in the Houston area. Named for the mythological Greek hunter it is easily spotted by finding his belt and sword. **Polaris,** also known as the North Star, is the last star in the handle of the Little Dipper. **Pollux** is the other main star in Gemini. **Rigel** is a blue-white supergiant in the Orion constellation. Located 600 light-years from the Sun it is 25,000 times more luminous. **Spica,** one of the 15 brightest stars in the sky, is in the constellation of Virgo. [22]

ENSEMBLE: See sidebar **It's Music to My Ears,** page 218.

EPSOM DOWNS: This famous English racecourse is where the 12th Earl of Derby in 1780 held the famous horserace named after himself, prompting the use of the word derby to describe a race for three-year old horses. [40]

EPSOM: On Thanksgiving Day 1933 Houston's first pari-mutuel horse race track opened. It was named Epsom Downs, in honor of the famous English racecourse. The Texas Breeders and Racing Association owned the track. Built at a cost of $650,000, an enormous sum of money during the Great Depression, it would hold 52,000 spectators. Epsom closed in 1937 when the Texas Legislature outlawed pari-mutuel wagering but the street lives on in its memory. This Eastex/Jensen neighborhood also has a **Downs** Street. (See **Epson Downs.**) [41]

ESPERANZA: A tobacco farmer named William Spiller named this town. In Spanish it means hope. His rationale was to hope this optimistic name would help his ailing tobacco business. Unfortunately the idea failed and Esperanza disappeared, leaving only this lonely road. [42]

ETHYL: This industrial thoroughfare leads to the Ethyl Corporation Industrial District docks on the Houston Ship Channel. In 1921 Ethyl discovered a combination of chemicals that when added to gasoline reduced engine "knocks." After that, motorists could buy "regular" or the higher test "ethyl" gasoline. Some readers may remember when all gas stations were full service and an attendant would ask the driver if he wanted to fill up with "regular or ethyl." Today Ethyl Corporation develops and produces additives for fuels and lubricants on a worldwide basis. [43]

ETON: One of the most prestigious private boys schools in England, it was founded by King Henry VI in 1441. [44]

EULE: William – One of the best rice farming regions in Texas is the area around Katy. This gentleman was responsible for the introduction of rice cultivation there in 1901.

DO YOU HAVE TO OWN AN EXPENSIVE IMPORT CAR TO LIVE HERE?

We all know Houstonians are crazy about their automobiles. Just look how much time we spend and fun we have showing them off on our freeways. But there are two area neighborhoods where you cannot only own a fancy sports car but also live on a street named after it. In northwest Harris County near George Bush Intercontinental Airport you can live on **Ferrari** (Italian), **De Lorean** (American), **Boxster** (German), **Volvo** (Swedish), **Porsche** (German), **Mercedes Benz** (German), **Rolls Royce** (English) or **Lexus** (Japanese). If these models do not suit your taste go down to Pearland to see **Morris** (English), **Lotus** (English), **Avanti** (American), **Bentley** (English), **Duesenberg** (American) **Berlinetta** (Italian) or **Leyland** (English). [23]

Hunters owe a debt of gratitude to Mr. Eule. The world-class duck and goose hunting in the Katy region is partially due to the massive amounts of land there devoted to rice farming. [45]

EUREKA: In 1872 a large cotton factory, Eureka Mills, was located here. There was even a small town named Eureka Mills, Texas that existed for seven years. Today the area is a major train yard for the Union Pacific Railroad. [46]

EVA: Real estate developer Herbert Tatar named this South Pasadena Villas street for his wife. [47]

EVANS: Reda Bland – This black woman was born in Goliad in 1913. She earned her bachelors (1943) and masters (1945) degrees at Prairie View A & M University. She joined the staff there and taught mathematics from 1945 to 1952. Evans was named Dean of Women in 1946 and served in that capacity until her retirement in 1983. As Dean she was responsible for seven residence halls, each containing 150 girls. [48]

» EVANS: Black educator at Prairie View A & M

EVANS: W. L. – This gentleman developed Riverview on Houston's southeast side. The neighborhood was located east of Telephone Road and south of Braes Bayou where this street is today. I believe he named the street for himself. [49]

EVERETT: See sidebar **Tennis or Golf, Anyone?,** page 348.

EVERGREEN: In 1847 Ashbel Smith purchased Evergreen Plantation from Mosley Baker for $5,000. Located in Baytown near the mouth of Cedar Bayou on Galveston Bay, all that remain of this historic site are the Evergreen Plantation Cemetery and this street named in honor of that ranch. In 1915 the famous Goose Creek Oilfield was discovered on land that was formerly the plantation. (See **Ashbel** and **Goose Creek.**) [50]

EVERTON: M. D. – See sidebar **Houston Streets Named for Men Killed During World War I,** page 22.

EWELL: Richard Stoddert – This Confederate general saw as much action as almost any officer in the War Between the States. He led his troops in the Battles of Crosskeys (1862), Seven Days (1862), Cedar Mountain (1862), Richmond (1862), Manassas II (1862), Winchester (1863), Gettysburg (1863), Wilderness (1864) and Spotsylvania (1864). He was shot at Groveton, Virginia in 1862 and lost a leg. However, Ewell was undeterred by this mishap. Following his recovery he would be hoisted upon his horse and strapped to the saddle so he could lead his men. Tough guy! [18]

EWING: Presley K. – This prominent Houston attorney was president of the Texas

Bar Association in 1899 and was elected Chief Justice of the Texas Supreme Court in 1903. Ewing was a factor in the social scene and served as King Nottoc in the 1904 No-tsu-oH Carnival. (Nottoc is cotton spelled backwards and No-tsu-oH is Houston reversed.) He was not the only famous person in his family. His wife Nell was inducted into the Texas Women's Hall of Fame for her civic activities. [51]

EXCALIBUR: This is the name of the famous sword that the Lady of the Lake gave to King Arthur.

» **EXXON: Street sign near Conroe**

EXXON: This gigantic energy company traces it roots back to the late 19th century. It was once part of John D. Rockefeller's Standard Oil Trust that the Supreme Court broke apart into 34 different firms in 1911. Today the company has worldwide operations including: oil and gas exploration, refining, chemicals, petrochemicals, etc. [52]

EZZARD CHARLES: He held the World Heavyweight Boxing Championship for less than a year between 1950 and 1951. His only claim to fame was out-pointing an aging Joe Louis, who returned to the ring from retirement as the undefeated champ. Charles was knocked out in the 7th round of his 1951 fight with Jersey Joe Walcott and was never a contender again. Why did we ever name a street in North Houston after him? [53]

HONORING NATIVE AMERICANS IN BAYTOWN

Developers of Meadow Lake in Baytown used an Indian theme to name their streets. Tribes remembered here are **Apache, Shoshone, Seminole, Cherokee, Shawnee, Huron, Mohawk, Arapaho, Erie, Osage, Cheyenne, Chippewa, Kiowa, Pawnee, Choctaw, Caddo, Sioux, Wichita, Mohave, Makah, Mohegan, Chetco, Omaha** and **Taino.** Streets related to the theme include **Broken Arrow, Beaver Bend, Sundance, Seneca, Mesa, Pocahontas, Hiawatha** and **Bighorn.** [24]

F

FACTORY OUTLET: City officials in Hempstead named this street for the VF Corporation's huge mall of outlet stores that are a major contributor to city revenue. The outlet opened in 1970. [1]

FACULTY: See sidebar **Neighborhoods with Interesting Street Names,** page 104.

FAIRBANKS: This road as well as **Fairbanks-North Houston** and **Fairbanks-White Oak** are all named after the small town of Fairbanks on U.S. 290 just west of Houston. Founded in 1893 as a stop on the Texas & New Orleans Railroad, the area was originally called Gum Island for all the gum trees that grew along White Oak Bayou that runs nearby. When a settler name Fairbanks founded the town he named it for himself. [2]

FAIRCHILDS-LONG POINT: Long Point was named by early settlers for a point of timber that extended a considerable distance into the coastal prairie lands. A sulfur dome and an oilfield were discovered in 1836 near this tiny Fort Bend County town. (See **Fairchilds.**) [3]

FAIRCHILDS: In 1840 Philo Fairchilds built a home in Fort Bend County. By 1890 the area had attracted a number of immigrant farmers from Germany. In 1896 a colony of 50 northern Mennonite families established residence in Fairchilds. A malaria epidemic and the Great Storm of 1900 eventually drove them away. Since that time it has remained a small rural community. [4]

FAIRGROUNDS: The Brazoria County Fairgrounds in Angleton are located on this road. [5]

FAIRVIEW: This street is named for the Fairview Addition through which it passes. Most likely the name came from the fact that, from this street, residents in the 1870s would have had a clear view of the State Fairgrounds, located south of what is today the Pierce Elevated. A Southern Pacific Railroad station named Fairview was located in the middle of the neighborhood. In the 1920s the Houston & Fairview Street Railway ran down the avenue. [6]

FAIRWAY: See sidebar **Tennis or Golf, Anyone?,** page 348.

» **FANNIN: A portrait of James Walker Fannin, Jr.**

FALCON: (See **Cougar.**)

FANNIN: James Walker, Jr. – He was born in 1804 in Georgia. Fannin attended the U. S. Military Academy in West Point, New York. He moved his family to Texas in 1834 and immediately became an agitator for Texas Independence. Fannin fought at the Battle of Gonzales, Battle of Conception and Siege of Bexar. He was captured by Santa Anna and taken to Goliad where he was executed in what we call the "Goliad Massacre." This Tomball street remembers this Texas hero as does Fannin County and the town of Fannin. (See **Goliad** and **Bexar.**) [7]

FARBER: Jerome H. – Located in Southside Place, Farber recalls a director of the Houston Chamber of Commerce in the early 1900s. [8]

FARISH: William Stamps – He was born in Mississippi in 1881. His granduncle was Confederate States of America president Jefferson Davis. Farish earned a law degree but soon fell under the spell of the oil business and moved to Beaumont to drill in the Spindletop oilfield. In 1917 he and others organized Humble Oil & Refining Company (now Exxon Mobil). Farish eventually was named chairman and president of Standard Oil Company of New Jersey. He was a great aficionado of polo and stabled his ponies where this Memorial area lane is located. (See **Spindletop.**) [9]

FARM & RANCH: This Bear Creek Park road leads to the Farm & Ranch Club, an organization that promotes agriculture and ranching in the area. Founded in 1947, the club awards scholarships as well as makes their facilities available to youth groups including Boy and Girl Scouts, 4-H, FFA and FHA. [10]

FARRAGUT: David Glasgow – An American admiral, he saw action in the War of 1812, the Mexican War and the Civil War. Although a Southerner by birth he opposed secession and fought for the Union. His most famous encounter was the capture of Mobile Bay, Alabama in August 1864 effectively ending the Confederates' ability to run the Northern naval blockade. He is remembered for his famous quote during that battle "Damn the torpedoes full speed ahead!" [11]

FARRINGTON: This gentleman was a real estate developer in La Porte, Texas. He built the first 100 homes in the Fairmont Park addition where this boulevard is located. Fairmont Parkway, a word play on his last name, forms the southern border of the neighborhood. [12]

FASHION: August J. – See sidebar **Houston Streets Named for Men Killed During World War I,** page 22.

FAULKEY GULLY: Located in northwest Harris County, this street is named for the watercourse of the same name located near it. Faulkey Gully runs six miles from its headwaters and empties into Cypress Creek. It traverses an area where the coastal plain begins to yield to woodlands. Following the War Between the States, freed slaves settled along this gully that was known as "the Bottoms" at that time. [13]

FAUNA: This street is all that remains of a small town that sat alongside the Texas & New Orleans Railroad line. By the 1960s all that was visible was an abandoned depot, now long gone. [14]

FAUST: This legendary 16th century German magician and charlatan sold his soul to the devil, Mephistopheles, in return for knowledge and pleasure. In Christopher Marlow's *Dr. Faustus* he is depicted as a talented man who is doomed to failure by his own limitations. He receives better treatment at the pen of Johann Goethe. In *Faust* his failings are forgiven in the end as he is portrayed as striving for good. [15]

FAYLE: William R. – This Englishman arrived in the Baytown area in 1859. He was a merchant and operated a brickyard. Fayle was a founder of Texas Methodist Church. [16]

FEAGAN: Richard H. – This man served in the U. S. Navy in WW I. He died from disease as did many American servicemen during the Great War. [17]

HOUSTON STREETS ASSOCIATED WITH CEMETERIES

Cemeteries, burial grounds, boot hill, places of eternal rest, marble orchards, memorial gardens or whatever else we call these sites, they allow us to identify where those who proceeded us through this veil of tears have been laid to rest. In Houston we have numerous streets, roads and lanes that lead to our public, private, churchyard and military cemeteries. In the city you can find our ancestors buried at the end of roads called: **Budde Cemetery, Burton Cemetery, Fritsche Cemetery, Kidd Cemetery, Klein Cemetery, Knigge Cemetery, Lutheran Cemetery, Macedonia Cemetery, Mueller Cemetery, Old Cemetery, Roberts Cemetery, Sanders Cemetery, Siedel Cemetery, Tetter Cemetery, Tomball Cemetery** and **White Cemetery.** [25]

FENN: The Fenn family arrived in Texas in 1833. John Rutherford Fenn settled in Fort Bend County on land fronting the Brazos River. He engaged in farming and ranching. Francis Marion Oatis Fenn attended Roanoke College in Virginia and studied law at the University of Virginia. He developed a liking for politics while in school. In 1886 he supported former Houston mayor Alexander McGowan for County Treasurer, a post he would hold for the rest of his life. The following year he backed the successful election of D. C. Smith for mayor of Richmond. [18]

FENSKE: German families began settling the area along Little Cypress Creek in the 1840's. A town sprang up called Cypress City. However, it was really little more than several general stores, a post office and a saloon. The Fenske family arrived with the second wave of German settlers who came to the area. [19]

FERN: E. A. "Squatty" Lyons was a Harris County commissioner for decades beginning in the 1940s. For ages his wife, Fern, asked Squatty to name a street after her. He resisted for years but finally relented and named a short street that was about to be redistricted into another precinct on the south side of Darrell Tully Stadium for her. When she saw the street she said, "...he picked something just like me: short and something he hoped he wouldn't have to maintain for very long." [20]

FERRY: Named for the Galveston Island Ferry, ferries have been part of the Texas transportation system since the 19th century. In 1929 the first regularly scheduled ferry service between Galveston and Bolivar Peninsula was instituted. Today TxDOT operates five free ferries daily that are capable of transporting 70 vehicles and 500 passengers per trip. The 2.7 mile voyage takes about 18 minutes. The greatest number of passengers carried in a day was 43,472 on July 3, 1994. The record for vehicles was set July 4, 1993 with 12,733. [21]

» FERRY: Known as the Boliver Ferry, docked in Galveston

FIELD STORE: In 1872 Andrew Field and his son, Druey Holland Field opened this general store 10 miles northeast of Hempstead. By 1874 a small community with the name Field Store had risen here. When cotton gins were established in nearby Myrtle Grove and Joseph the population of Field Store began declining. Today it only exists on maps as this road. [22]

FIELDS: W. I. – He was born in Kentucky in 1834. Fields visited Texas several times before deciding to make it his home. After the War Between the States he moved to Houston and worked as a cotton trader. Later he drove a heard of cattle from Houston to Kansas City. Fields moved to Fort Bend County and became one of the largest planters in the area. His home was near Sartartia where he lived for 35 years. He also served a four year term as county commissioner. (See **Sartartia.**) [23]

FIGARO: A dramatic character in the opera Barber of Seville, he is remembered as a daring and clever rogue involved in all forms of intrigue. [24]

FINNIGAN: John D. – This early Houston pioneer was a hide and leather merchant. Finnigan once owned the Nichols-Rice-Cherry house that is now property of the Harris County Heritage Society and is on display in Sam Houston Park. He paid $2,500 for the property in 1886. In 1894 he decided to sell and requested sealed bids. The only one he received was from a starving artist. Emma Richardson Cherry and her husband offered $25. Since there was no reserve set, the house and furnishings were theirs. Finnigan's daughter, Annette, was a suffragist and art patron. She helped establish the State Woman Suffrage Association and served as its president in 1904-1906. She gave the city 18 acres of land on the northeast side to be used as a recreation area principally for the area's black citizens. Finnigan Park is named in her honor. [25]

» **FINNIGAN:** Annette Finnigan on graduation day

FIRST COLONY: When Sugar Land Industries decided to liquidate its assets in 1972, Houston real estate developer, Gerald Hines (builder of The Galleria), offered $43 million for 7,500 acres of prime land in Fort Bend County owned by them. At the time it was one of the largest land deals ever done in Texas. Hinds began construction on this huge master planned community in 1976. [26]

FISHER: Jeremiah – Born in 1819 Fisher and his family owned a farm on Trinity Bay. He was instrumental in founding the early Methodist church in the Baytown area. [27]

FITZGERALD: Susan Ann Hodges – She was the wife of Amos Barber. Fitzgerald was her maiden name. They were the first settlers in the area around Mont Belvieu. (See **Barbers Hill.**) [28]

FIVE IRON: See sidebar **A Neighborhood for Linksters,** page 318.

FLAHERTY: Pat – See **Salt Grass Trail**

FLETCHER CHRISTIAN: See sidebar **Pirates of the Caribbean,** page 280.

FLEWELLEN: The Katy-Flewellen road once connected these two farming communities. Flewellen was originally part of Stephen F. Austin's colony. The site of this virtual ghost town is located off of FM 1093 (Westheimer Road in eastern Fort Bend County) at Spring Green Road on the way to Fulshear, Texas. It was named for an early resident of the area. [29]

FLORA: This lady is the wife of real estate developer William. W. Baldwin. (See **Bellaire.**) [30]

FLORENCE: William A. Wilson developed Woodland Heights on Houston's near north side. He named this street and **Helen** for his daughters. [31]

FLORES BAYOU: This watercourse rises north of Angleton and flows 12 miles southeast to its mouth on Austin Bayou. About midway there is a dam that created Bieri Lakes. [32]

FLOWERS: See sidebar **Texas Heroes' Names for Houston Streets Urged in 72 Proposed Changes,** page 96.

FLOYD: Lewis – See sidebar **Houston Streets Named for Men Killed During World War I,** page 22.

FONDREN: The Fondren family made their fortune in oil but is remembered for their philanthropy. Patriarch Walter William Fondren (1877-1939) was an orphan who worked on farms and in sawmills until his mid-teens. He came to Texas in 1897 to work in the oil business. He had a nose for finding large oilfields. In 1911 he, along with several partners, founded Humble Oil & Refining Company (Exxon Mobile today) and the rest is history. Because of his lack of a formal education, Fondren gave a fortune to universities for libraries and scholarships so others would be able to earn a degree. [33]

FOOTBALL: As far as I can tell this is the only area street named for a sport. It leads to Turner Stadium on the campus of Humble 9th Grade School. [34]

FOOTE: Albert Horton Jr. – This man was one of Wharton's most famous residents which leads me to believe this street is named for him. Foote was a playwright

» **FONDREN:** Fondren family gravesite in Forest Park Lawndale Cemetery

and Academy Award winning screenwriter for his work on the 1962 film *To Kill a Mockingbird* and 1983's *Tender Mercies*. He won a Pulitzer Prize in 1995 for his play *The Young Man from Atlanta*. Foote was named for his ancestor Albert Horton, Texas first lieutenant governor. (See **Horton.**) [35]

FOOTE: Henry Stuart – This early Texas traveler sailed into Galveston Bay and up Buffalo Bayou in 1840. He wrote a book about his adventures in which he makes one of the very few references to buffalos in the area. He claims to have seen a large herd on the shores of the Bay. But you must remember the artists who painted scenes of early Houston included mountains in the background. So take this sighting with a grain of salt. He goes on to mention huge flocks of white birds (probably ibis and egrets), pelicans, eagles, ricebirds, flamingos (most likely roseate spoonbills) and cranes. [36]

FORDHAM: This New York City university was founded as a Jesuit college in 1841. [37]

FORRESTAL: James Vincent. – He was a high-ranking official in President Franklin D. Roosevelt's administration during WW II. Named Undersecretary of the Navy in 1940, Forrestal was elevated to Naval Secretary in 1944. He served in that position for three years. He was made the first Secretary of Defense in 1947, a position he held until his death in 1949. [38]

FORT BEND: In 1822 colonists from Stephen F. Austin's Old 300 built a blockhouse on a wide bend in the Brazos River for protection against Indian raids. The small settlement here was absorbed into Richmond, Texas in 1838 after that town was named the county seat. [39]

FORT CROCKETT: Named for Alamo hero Davy Crockett, this was a military base on Galveston Island used for coastal artillery training and harbor defense. Founded in 1897 little remains today. One of its 10-inch gun emplacements (minus the artillery) is

ANTEBELLUM STREETS OF RIVER PLANTATION

River Plantation is a lovely wooded neighborhood that sits along the banks of the San Jacinto River in southern Montgomery County. Many of the streets here recall the halcyon days of the Old South. **Bellingrath** is named for the 65-acre garden in Mobile, Alabama created by Walter Bellingrath and his wife. It was opened in 1932-4. The garden is abloom with camellias in winter, azaleas in spring, roses in summer and chrysanthemums in fall. **Braxton Brag** was a Confederate general. After graduating from West Point he fought in the Seminole and Mexican Wars. Bragg saw action at some of the bloodiest battles of the War Between the States including Shiloh, Murfreesboro, Chattanooga and Chickamauga. Fort Bragg in North Carolina is named in his honor. **Chicora Wood** is a South Carolina plantation. It was built in 1809. Today the property is listed on the National Register of Historic Places. **Jubal Early** was also a Confederate general. He was born in Virginia in 1816. Like Bragg, he was a West Point graduate who saw action in the Seminole and Mexican Wars before commanding in the War Between the States. Early fought at Williamsburg, First and Second Manassas, Fredericksburg and Waynesboro. When he died in 1894 it was said "Virginia holds the dust of many a faithful son, but not one whom loved her more, who fought for her better or would have died for her more willingly." **Old Hickory** is the nickname of Andrew Jackson, 7th President of the United States. During his distinguished military career he fought the British several times including the decisive Battle of New Orleans in 1812. Jackson was elected President in 1828 and again in 1832. He is remembered also for his policy of Jacksonian Democracy. **Petersburg** was where one of the longest battles of the War Between the States took place. Union troops attacked on June 15, 1864 but were repelled. Then the North laid siege to the town. That tactic was employed until April 1865. **Rapidan** is the largest tributary of the Rappahannock River of north-central Virginia. Numerous battles were fought here during the War Between the States (Ely's Ford, Chancellorsville, Brandy Station and The Wilderness). Its name is a combination of "rapids" and Queen Anne of England. **Stone Mountain** is a 1,686 foot granite dome near a town of the same name in Georgia. It is known for its geology and the enormous bas-relief on its north face. The carved surface is three acres, making it the world's largest bas-relief. It features Confederate President Jefferson Davis and Generals Robert E. Lee and Thomas "Stonewall" Jackson along with their horses Blackjack, Traveler and Little Sorrel. **Stonewall Jackson** was one of the Confederacy's greatest military heroes. His first name was Thomas. Jackson earned his nickname at the first Battle of Bull Run when General Barnard Bee stated "he stood there like a stonewall" in the face of withering fire from Union troops. Jackson fought valiantly during the Valley Campaign as well as at Antietam and Fredericksburg. He was killed by friendly fire at Chancellorsville while riding into his camp at night. (See **Chancellorsville**.) [26]

visible on the San Luis Hotel property. German prisoners-of-war were incarcerated here during World War II. Following that conflict Fort Crocket was used as a military recreational area. The government declared the property surplus in 1955 and began selling it. (See **Crockett.**) [40]

FORT DAVIS: Established in 1854, this was the first military outpost between San Antonio and El Paso. Located deep in Apache and Comanche territory it was constructed to protect travelers from raiding bands of Indians. Following the War Between the States Fort Davis became the home of the famous African-American military regiments known as the "Buffalo Soldiers." [41]

FORT SETTLEMENT: The settlement of Fort Bend County began in the early 1820s as part of the colonization of Texas. In November 1821 Stephen F. Austin and a band of colonists sailed from New Orleans to the mouth of the Brazos River. A scouting party proceeded upriver 90 miles to an impressive bend. They landed here and erected a two-room cabin that they named Fort Settlement. Others later called it Fort Bend, a name that stuck. [42]

FORT SUMTER: This is where the War Between the States began. Confederate troops shelled the fort for 36 hours beginning April 12, 1861. Realizing the indefensibility of their position, the Union troops retreated. [43]

FORTINBERRY: C. I. – He was a mayor of Goose Creek, Texas before it was absorbed by Baytown. (See **Goose Creek.**) [44]

FORUM: This archeological site is among the most famous of the Roman Empire. Located in the Eternal City of Rome between the Capitoline and Palatine hills it contained temples, shops, courts, sporting arenas, etc. As the city grew other forums were developed in the area. [45]

FOSTER SCHOOL: In 1822 John and Randolph Foster, members of Stephen F. Austin's Old 300, were granted 12,000 acres of land in southwest Fort Bend County. They were ranchers and farmers. They grew cotton, rice and sugar cane. The Fosters erected a school on their plantation. [46]

FOSTER: Cora Bacon – Mrs. Foster, a land speculator, and Charles Munger, a retired banker from Kansas, were early backers of the city of Pasadena, Texas. As it was typical for developers of towns to name a street for themselves, it is likely this one remembers her. [47]

FOSTER: John – He was one of Stephen F. Austin's Old 300 who moved from Mississippi to Texas in 1822. Foster received a land grant from Austin in Fort Bend County in 1824. While visiting Mississippi in 1837 he passed away. [48]

FOSTER: The Foster-Epps Company of Fort Worth was granted the right to sell lots in the newly developed town of Tomball in 1907. It is a mystery why Epps did not merit recognition with a street. [49]

FOSTORIA: The Foster Lumber Company named this company town. The company store sold employees clothing, groceries, furniture or anything else they needed. Workers were paid with company issued script that had no value except at the store. By 1925 over 1,500 people were employed by Foster Lumber. In 1941 the sawmill produced 20 million board feet of lumber, making it one of the largest sellers of southern pine in America. The plant closed in 1957 and the town ceased to exist. [50]

FOUR SIXES: Samuel Burk Burnett established this brand (6666) and ranch near the present day site of Wichita Falls in the early 1870s. He eventually moved the headquarters to King County where is remains today. This 280,000 acre spread was used for Marlboro cigarette commercials in the 1960s with ranch hands playing the role of the "Marlboro Man." [51]

FOURNACE: J. J. – This gentleman was a long-time resident of Bellaire. When Texaco established a large research center on Gulfton in Bellaire, management did not like the fact that their address contained the name of a major competitor, Gulf Oil. They went to city council and had the name of this stretch of Gulfton changed to honor Fournace. [52]

FRANCIS DRAKE: See sidebar **Pirates of the Caribbean,** page 280.

FRANKLIN: Benjamin Cromwell – He arrived in Texas in 1835. Franklin actively supported the Texas Revolution and fought at the Battle of San Jacinto. Thomas Rusk, Secretary of War, sent Franklin to Galveston to inform President David Burnet of the victory at San Jacinto. In December 1836 the Republic of Texas established four district courts. He was the first person in the new Republic given a judicial position. Harrisburg was District 2 with Franklin as a district judge. He was not re-elected in 1838 and was fined $20 for sitting on the bar in the new courthouse. Franklin died in 1873 and is buried in Galveston. Franklin was the first street in the city to be paved. It was covered in asphalt in 1897. [53]

FRANZ: One of the main streets of Katy is named for this family who began growing rice in the area in the early 1900s. David Peter Franz was a watchmaker in town. [54]

FRASER: Neale – He was known as a great tennis doubles player. Fraser won men's doubles championships in Australia (3), France (3), Wimbledon (2) and U. S. (3). He also won the singles championships at Wimbledon in 1960 and the U. S. in 1959-60. [55]

FRASIER: This Freeland Addition street was named for Wilson and Samuel Fraser, land developers in Houston Heights. For unknown reasons it was originally named Fraser, then changed to Frazier and finally renamed Frasier even though the old curb tiles spell it Fraser. For years the street signs at each end had a different spelling. (See **Granberry** and **Reserve.**) [56]

FREDERICKSBURG: One of the largest battles of the War Between the States took place December 13, 1862. Here General Robert E. Lee's 80,000 troops defeated Union General Ambrose Burnside's 150,000 men. However, Lee was so undermanned that he had to allow Burnside to retreat and thus failed to capitalize on the victory. [57]

FREEMAN: In 1897 the Freeman family moved to Katy from Missouri. Most likely they were rice farmers. [58]

FREEMAN: John H. – Without the efforts of this Houston attorney we would not have the world-class medical center our city possesses today. In 1924 four bright lawyers started the firm of Fulbright, Crooker and Freeman. Monroe D. Anderson was one of their clients. In 1936 Freeman was elected a trustee of the M. D. Anderson Foundation. The Texas government voted in 1941 to approve a Texas State Cancer Hospital to be administered by the University of Texas Board of Regents. Through the work of Freeman and others the Regents decided to locate the hospital in Houston. From this medical acorn the mighty Texas Medical Center grew. [59]

LEARN A FOREIGN LANGUAGE ON YOUR MORNING WALK

Residents of Saddle Creek Farm, a neighborhood on Lake Houston, can exercise their minds as well as their bodies by studying their street signs. All of them are in Spanish. Words to be learned include: **Arroyo** (ravine), **Tesoro** (treasure), **Cascada** (waterfall), **Diablo** (devil), **Lente** (lens), **Pino** (pine tree), **El Matador** (bullfighter), **Cajon** (box), **Ancla** (anchor), **Mariachi** (musician), **Vera Cruz** (coastal city), **Nogalus** (possibly a misspelling of nogal or walnut), and **Piñata** (a hanging container of sweets usually broken with a stick at a party). [27]

FREEPORT: The Freeport Sulfur Company founded this as a company town in 1929. It is located at the site of the world's largest sulfur discovery. However, that yellow mineral is no longer mined here. In 1939 Dow Chemical Corporation began erecting what would become one of the nation's largest chemical plants. Freeport is also home to one of the largest shrimping fleets in the Gulf of Mexico. [60]

FRESNO: An early resident named this Fort Bend highway and town after Fresno, California. The area was agricultural. Because of the many plantations in Fresno the main crop was cotton. [61]

FRIAR TUCK: A man of the cloth, Tuck was a member of the legendary English hero/ outlaw Robin Hood's band of "merry men" who were known for robbing from the rich and giving to the poor.

FRIENDSWOOD: In the late 1890s a group of Quakers, also known as the Society of Friends, purchased 1,500 acres of land near the Harris and Galveston County lines. This wooded area was to be home to this religious sect for more than 60 years. Many were farmers and the area produced many fruits and vegetables, rice and livestock. [62]

FRIES: This family lived in the Memorial village of Spring Valley. They owned several plant nurseries in the area. [63]

FRITSCHE CEMETERY: There are more than 20 small cemeteries in northwest Harris County that contain the remains of some of this area's early German immigrant families. The odd fact about this burial ground is that there are no tombstones marking graves of members of the Fritsche family although some of them are interred in nearby Roberts Cemetery. Of course it is possible that the burials may have been unmarked or the markers were lost, stolen or damaged over the years. Other early residents buried here include members of the Schiel, Wolters, and Nuemeyer families. (See **Schiel** and **Roberts Cemetery.**) [64]

FROST RANCH: In the 1940s Milo Frost purchased 4,500 acres of land from the State of Texas near Highway 6 and FM 1092. He established the Frost Brahman Ranch. Later he was elected president of the American Brahman Breeders Association. Much of the master planned community of First Colony is on former ranch land. (See **First Colony.**) [65]

FRYDEK: In the early 1820s Czech settlers named this town for the Moravian city of Frydek-Mistek. These farmers were members of one of Stephen F. Austin's early colonies. [66]

FUEL STORAGE: This road leads to where jet aviation fuel is stored at George Bush Intercontinental Airport. [67]

FULTON: William – A steamboat captain, he arrived in Houston in the 1840s from Pittsburgh, Pennsylvania. He became a very successful cotton merchant and built a beautiful home at 1507 Rusk in 1859. The house was demolished in 1920. [68]

FURLONG: A distance of 1/8 of a mile, it is the unit of measure for horse races that are less than one mile long. These sprints are usually five or six furlongs in length. [69]

G

GAILLARD: John I. – In 1903 this Baytown landowner noticed natural gas bubbles rising to the surface of Goose Creek near where it empties into Galveston Bay. Gaillard leased his property to several petroleum companies over the next few years but none found oil or gas. However, on August 23, 1916 leaseholder American Petroleum Company hit the jackpot. A gusher flowed 10,000 barrels per day and the Goose Creek oil rush was on. By 1918 the field was producing 8.9 million barrels of black gold annually. (See **Goose Creek** and **American Petroleum.**) [1]

GALAHAD: The son of Sir Lancelot and Elaine, he was considered the purest of the Arthurian Knights of the Roundtable. Because of the mystical power of the Holy Grail it could only be revealed to a pure Knight. Galahad was sent on a quest to find it. [2]

GALENA: Located on the Houston Ship Channel, the city of Galena Park was originally named Clinton, Texas by Isaac Batterson. The Galena Signal Oil Company of Texas owned the first refinery in Clinton. The city's name was changed to Galena Park in 1935 when residents made application for a post office and the name Clinton was already taken by another Texas town. (See **Clinton** and **Batterson.**) [3]

GALLANT FOX: This legendary thoroughbred was the second racehorse to win the Kentucky Derby, Preakness and Belmont, thus prompting the naming of that feat as winning the Triple Crown. His jockey, Earl Sande, one of the top riders of his day, retired after winning the Derby in 1923 (on Zev) and 1925 (on Flying Ebony). Lured back into the irons by owner William Woodward for a swansong, Sande accomplished the feat in 1930 on Gallant Fox. (See **Triple Crown.**) [4]

GALVESTON: This highway was once the main road to the beach town to our south before the opening of the Gulf Freeway. That city is named for Bernardo de Galvez, a Mexican viceroy who never set foot on the island. Galveston claims many firsts for Texas including the first: telegraph, private bank, jewelry store, national bank, electric

» GALVESTON: Aftermath of the Great Storm of 1900

lights, nursing school, brewery, medical college and golf course. The city has one of the state's more colorful histories. There are tales of cannibals, pirates, vicious storms, gambling and prostitution to mention a few. For more information read Gary Cartwright's *Galveston: A History of the Island.* [5]

GAMMAGE: T. E. – Golfcrest, where this street is located, was a T. E. Gammage & Co. development. [6]

GANGES: This holiest of Hindu rivers begins its sacred journey high in the Himalayas and travels 1,500 miles through India to the Bay of Bengal.

GARCIA: Macario – On November 22, 1944 near Grosshau, Germany, a wounded Staff Sergeant Garcia single-handedly captured two German machine-gun nests killing six of the enemy and capturing four others. For his extraordinary act of bravery he was awarded the Congressional Medal of Honor by President Harry S. Truman on August 23, 1945. Garcia also earned a Purple Heart, Bronze Star and Combat Infantryman's Badge. The Government of Mexico gave him its highest honor, the *Merito Militar*. Killed in a car accident in 1972, he is buried in the ring of honor in the Houston National Cemetery here. (See **Veterans-Memorial**.) [7]

» GARCIA: Tombstone in Houston National Cemetery

GARDEN OAKS: Edward Lillo Crane Sr. developed this area in 1937. Crane loved gardens and gave this neighborhood, with its oversized lots, its name. This area was just outside the city limits when Crane acquired it. Garden Oaks quickly became a popular place to live. By 1941, Crane had platted 1,150 lots on this 750 acres and built almost 700 homes. (See **Edloe** and **Jardine.**) [8]

GARNET: This block-long Southside Place street is named for the birthstone of real estate developer Edward L. Crain Sr. [9]

GARNER PARK: See sidebar **The Most Scenic Spots in Texas,** page 310.

GARROTT: John F. – This man and his family lived in the James Bute Addition in the Montrose area. He was the general manager of the James Bute Paint Company. [10]

GARROW: John Wanroy – He was a very successful cotton broker. The Garrows lived in posh Courtlandt Place. Their Italian renaissance home is a Texas Historic Landmark. The architect was Birdsall P. Briscoe. (See **Birdsall** and **Courtland Place.**) [11]

GASTON: Hudson – Katy-Gaston Road was a connector between the farming communities of the same names. Gaston, also known as White's Switch, was located on FM 1093 (the far west extension of Westheimer Road). The town was established in 1888 near the site of Hudson Gaston's plantation. For a while it was a switching station on the San Antonio & Aransas Pass Railroad. [12]

GATLING: Richard Jordan – He was a prolific American inventor best known for developing the rapid-fire machine gun. Capable of firing 350 shots per minute this weapon would change the face of warfare forever. Few remember his other successes such as machines for sowing rice, cotton and other grains and a screw propeller for steamboats. [13]

GAUGUIN: Paul – This French stockbroker turned Post-Impressionist painter is famous for his ultimate dropout. During a trip to Martinique he conceived a plan to flee his responsibilities in Paris and move to the South Seas. Selling all his paintings and possessions he sailed to Tahiti in 1891. He returned to his native France once but quickly found life in the Parisian capitol was not for him. Returning to the South Pacific Gauguin turned out some of his most famous work. He moved to the Marquesas in 1901 where he died in poverty two years later. [14]

GAZIN: Henry J. – As this Denver Harbor street is located in a neighborhood with streets named for a mens-and-boys-wear store, a grocer, a department store, two five and dimes and two theaters, why not a pharmacy? He operated Gazin Drug Store at 516 Main Street in the Rice Hotel for many years beginning in the 1940s until the 1960s. His pharmacy was located in the premier hotel in the city and at the corner of Main and Texas Streets, the center of city life at that time. [15]

GEARS: John – This German immigrant owned a farm north of town where this road is located. Following his death his heirs continued the operation. [16]

GEMINI: See sidebar **Space City U.S.A. or "Houston the Eagle Has Landed",** page 106.

GENE CAMPBELL: Owner of a concrete plant and a real estate developer, he donated 60 acres of land to Montgomery County for a park. This road and Gene Campbell Sports Park honor this man. A life size statue of him stands in the park. [17]

GEORGE ALTVATER: He is credited with establishing the hugely successful Barbours Cut Container Terminal on the Houston Ship Channel. Altvater arrived in Houston in 1959 and was named Director of Trade Development for the Port of Houston. He retired in 1979 having served as the Port's Executive Director for the previous eight years. [18]

GEORGE BUSH: George Herbert Walker Bush was the 41st President of the United States serving from 1988-1992. He was born in Milton, Massachusetts in 1924. On his 18th birthday he enlisted in the armed services becoming the youngest pilot in the Navy when he earned his wings. He flew 58 missions during WW II, was shot down in the Pacific and won the Distinguished Service Cross for bravery. Bush served two terms as a U. S. Congressman from Texas. Subsequently he was Ambassador to the United Nations, Director of the CIA and Vice President of the United States during the Reagan Administration. [19]

GEORGETOWN: This street is named for Georgetown University. It is in a suburb of Washington D. C. and was founded in 1789. [20]

GERONIMO: This Chiricahua Apache chief was a fearsome fighter during the Indian Wars of 1867-8. Eventually captured, he died in Fort Sill, Oklahoma in 1909. [21]

GESSNER: August – This German immigrant arrived in the United States in 1886. A Spanish-American War veteran, he built a monument to Teddy Roosevelt and the Rough Riders in Puerto Rico. He arrived in Houston and opened A. Gessner Cabinet Works. Gessner became friends with longtime Harris County Commissioner E. A. "Squatty" Lyons who named the street for his friend. [22]

GETTYSBURG: This is a small town in Pennsylvania where the most famous battle of the Civil War occurred. Here between July 1-3, 1863, Union General George G. Meade faced off against General Robert E. Lee's Army of Northern Virginia. The carnage was staggering with the North reporting 23,000 casualties and the Rebels 25,000. Both commanders were criticized for their tactics - Lee for using unseasoned commanders and authorizing the disastrous Pickett's Charge and Meade for not pursuing Lee's retreating army when the battle was over. [23]

GIBSON: J. A. or John T. – The former was a Mississippi native who moved to Texas as a boy. His son, John T., was born in Fort Bend County in 1878. John was elected county tax assessor in 1902. [24]

GIBSON: R. M. – See sidebar **Houston Streets Named for Men Killed During World War I,** page 22.

GIFFORD HILL: The Gifford-Hill Pipe Company was formed in 1931. It manufactured concrete pipe for sewer and culvert construction. Today it operates 12 plants in Arizona, Oklahoma, Louisiana and Texas (including the one for whom this street is named). It is now owned by Hanson Pipe & Products, the largest producer of concrete pipe and precast in North America. [25]

GILLETTE: H. F. – This gentleman was a schoolteacher who founded the college preparatory school, the Houston Academy, at Main Street and Preston Avenue. The school charged $2 per month for liberal arts classes and $3 monthly for math, geography and foreign languages. Gillette was also a reverend and a founder of Bayland Orphans Home for Boys. (See **Bayland.**) [26]

GILLETTE: Located in the Fourth Ward, this neighborhood, Castania Addition, was developed by Frederick & Gillette. [19]

GIN: No dear reader, this Kendleton street is not named for Bombay Sapphire or Plymouth gin. It leads to the historic cotton gin in that community. (See **Braxton.**) [27]

GIRARD: Auguste – In 1839 public officials hired him to produce a new map of Houston. Of French descent he was born in 1805. He had no formal education. Girard came to Texas from Alabama in 1838 and joined the Texas Army with the rank of "colonel of engineers" but only served for 13 days. Printed on this map is the statement, "City of Houston and Vicinity Drawn and Partly Surveyed by A. Girard, Late Chief Engineer of the Texas Army, January, 1839." In addition to doing the survey, Girard named a street north of Buffalo Bayou for himself and another for his wife Susan. The plot thickens when you try to find out more about Mr. Girard. It seems that a man who was Chief Engineer of the Texas Army would appear in our historical records. But he does not. The only mention of him in *The Handbook of Texas* quotes the 1839 map. I have not found him in any other book. There is no record of him at the City of Houston Preservation Office, Houston Heritage Society, Daughters of the Republic of Texas, Historic Houston, Government Land Office, Texas State Historical Association, Texas General Land Office, Texas Veterans Land Board, Texas Army Muster Rolls or Texas Army Service Records. And finally, according to historian and map expert Kirk Ferris the numbering system for the blocks on the 1839 map are all wrong, indicating Mr. Girard knew nothing about surveying. It is likely that Girard made up the title in order to be hired and then drew a very poor map. He began speculating in real estate but the 1839 price crash and a yellow fever epidemic sent him packing back to Alabama. (See **Chartres** and **Chenevert.**) (See photograph on page 132.) [28]

GIRL SCOUT: Located in Lake Houston State Park the land where this road is was once

G-H

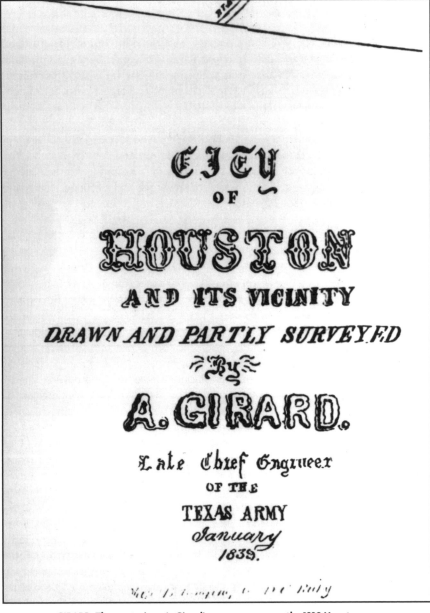

» GIRARD: The mysterious A. Girard's name appears on the 1839 Houston map.

owned by the San Jacinto Girl Scout Council and had been the home of the Peach Creek Girl Scout Camp since 1955. The Council sold the 202 acres to the State of Texas for park land in 1990. (See **Peach Creek.**) [6]

GLADYS YOAKUM: The music for our state song, *Texas, Our Texas,* was written by an Englishman, William J. Marsh, while he was living in Fort Worth. He partnered with native Texan Gladys Yoakum (later Wright) who wrote the words. They submitted their entry to a statewide contest sponsored by the Texas Legislature in 1929 and won. [29]

GLASTONBURY: A beautiful town in southwest England, Glastonbury is known for its two major legends. The first is that King Arthur is buried at Glastonbury Abbey. The other says that St. Joseph of Arimathea founded the first Christian church there on Wearyall Hill. (See **King Arthur, Lancelot, Merlin** and **Guinevere.**) [30]

GLEN CHEEK: Located in front of the Tin Hall, a honky-tonk and reception hall founded in 1889 in Cypress, is Glen Cheek Road. It was named in memory of a longtime Precinct 5 Constable who died of cancer in 2007. (See **Tin Hall.**) [31]

GLENEAGLES: The famous James Braid designed this superb Scottish golf links in 1919. After playing his first round here, American golf professional Lee Trevino, a man known for his wit as well as his golf game, said "if Heaven is as good as this, I sure hope they have some tee times left." [32]

GLENHAVEN: Glenn Herbert McCarthy was born in Beaumont, Texas on Christmas Day 1907. He began working in the oilfields near town at the age of eight years earning $0.50 a day. McCarthy enrolled at Rice Institute (now University) but soon dropped out to start his own oil company. He hit major fields 38 times between 1932 and 1942. His wealth, estimated at $200 million in 1949, came from 400 producing oil and gas wells. He pur-

» **GLENN HERBERT McCARTHY: Tombstone in Glenwood Cemetery**

chased a tract of land south of downtown and in 1949 McCarthy invested $21 million building the Shamrock Hotel. He spent over $1 million on its lavish opening, dubbed "Houston's biggest party." In spite of his assets the "King of the Wildcatters" found himself more than $50 million in debt in 1952. However, a federal loan bailed him out for the time being. By 1955 he lost control of the Shamrock, selling it to the Hilton chain. Two years later he opened the exclusive Cork Club in downtown. (Your author was invited to the grand opening.) McCarthy was a notorious drinker who introduced his own label, *Wildcatter,* bourbon. He was the inspiration for the character Jett Rink in Edna Ferber's novel, *Giant.* (See **Shamrock.**) [33]

G–H

GLYCOL: It is only right that this dihydric alcohol named street leads into the massive Dow Chemical Company complex in Lake Jackson. The formula is (CH2)n(OH)2. The most important glycol is ethylene glycol used to manufacture antifreeze, Dacron and explosives. [34]

GO-MAN-GO: This street honors one of the greatest American quarter horses. Foaled in 1953 he was later named World Champion Racing American Quarter Horse three times. He set track records, world records and retired to be one of the greatest sires in quarter horse racing history. (See **Easy Jet.**) [35]

GOEDECKE: This is another German immigrant family who settled in the Spring, Texas area in the late 1800s. Five family members (Dora, George, George Jr., Katie and Sophie) are buried in the nearby Budde Cemetery. (See **Budde Cemetery.**) [36]

GOLDEN CHORD: See sidebar **It's Music to My Ears,** page 218.

GOLDEN SPIKE: On May 10, 1869 at Promontory, Utah the rail lines of the Union Pacific and the Central Pacific joined creating the world's first transcontinental railroad. This tremendous engineering feat was celebrated by the driving of a golden spike. [37]

GOLDENROD: This Pasadena street recalls a residential development there called Golden Acres, Texas. The name came from a marketing slogan used by the developers – "a golden opportunity." Golden Acres Elementary School is a part of Pasadena ISD. [38]

GOLFCREST: (See **Country Club.**)

GOLIAD: Founded in 1749 this city is one of the oldest of the Spanish colonial municipalities in Texas. Colonizer Jose de Escandon erected the historic Espiritu Santo mission here. In 1836 James Walker Fannin was in charge of the garrison stationed in Goliad. General Sam Houston ordered him to evacuate as the Mexican army was bearing down on the presidio. Nonetheless, Fannin and 500 retreating Texians were capture by Santa Anna. They were returned to Goliad where they were executed. This tragedy became known as the "Goliad Massacre." At the Battle of San Jacinto the battle cry of the Texians was "Remember the Alamo! Remember Goliad!" (See **Fannin** and **Texian.**) [39, 40]

GONZALES: Alphonse – See sidebar **Houston Streets Named for Men Killed During World War I,** page 22.

GOODE: Commercial artist turned bar-b-q, seafood and Mexican restaurant impresario Jim Goode and his wife Kate have been extremely generous over the years to West University

» **GOODE: West University street sign**

Elementary School. They raised funds via auctions prompting the principal to annually name a small street north of the school for the couple. When the Goodes made a particularly important contribution to the school library the street was permanently named Goode. [41]

GOODNIGHT TRAIL: Charles Goodnight was a Texas Ranger, Indian scout, cattle rancher and Civil War veteran. He and his partner, Oliver Loving, founded one of the most famous cattle drive trails in the Old West. The original Goodnight Trail was an extension of the Goodnight-Loving Trail. It ran from Young County, Texas to the Pecos River, then over to Fort Sumner, New Mexico and finally up to Goodnight's ranch at Trinidad, Colorado. [42]

GOODSON: James – The town of Hufsmith was founded as a station stop on the International-Great Northern Railroad in 1872. It is likely this north Harris county loop is named for that town's first blacksmith. [43]

GOODYEAR: This street is named for the Goodyear Tire & Rubber Chemical plant that is located on it. [44]

GOOSE CREEK: This Baytown street is named for a creek of the same name that flows into Galveston Bay near Hog Island. Oil was discovered at Goose Creek in 1915, creating a boomtown the locals called Old Town. It was wiped out in an oil well explosion. Immediately the survivors started New Town near by. The name Goose Creek was adopted in 1916. (See **Gaillard** and **American Petroleum.**) [45]

» **GOOSE CREEK: Wooden derricks in Goose Creek Oil Field**

GORE: Arthur William Charles Wentworth – This English tennis star won gold in the men's indoor singles and doubles at the 1908 London Olympic Games. He was also Wimbledon singles champion in 1901, 1908 and 1909 and doubles champ in 1909. [46]

GOSHEN: Located on the banks of the West Fork of the San Jacinto River in Montgomery County this tiny town was named for the biblical Land of Goshen. It was in the eastern part of the Nile River delta and was inhabited by Israelites from the time of Jacob until the Exodus. [47]

GOSTIC: Like other streets in our area this one is misspelled. Gabriel "Gabe" Gostick was an Englishman who arrived in Houston in 1839. He quickly purchased 600 acres of land where the Houston Heights is today. Shortly after Gostick was beaten to death in his own yard. The crime remains unsolved. Rumors at the time said someone was outraged that he was able to buy this parcel from Houston founders John and Augustus Allen when the brothers were forced to sell it to pay off debts. [48]

GOULD: Robert Simonton – This Alabama attorney supported secession and assembled Gould's Battalion for the Confederates. He was a major in Walker's Texas Division. During the War he saw action at Mansfield and Pleasant Hill, Louisiana. Gould was wounded at Jenkins' Ferry, Arkansas. He came to Texas in 1870. Elected to the Texas Supreme Court, he served there from 1876 until 1882. He became one of the first law professors at the University of Texas in 1883 and taught there until his death in 1904. [49]

GRADUATE: See sidebar **Neighborhoods with Interesting Street Names,** page 104.

GRAF NET: Steffi Graf was one of the world's best female tennis players. At 19 this German professional won the Grand Slam (tennis' four major tournaments) and an Olympic gold medal. In her career she claimed victory in 22 Grand Slam events winning Wimbledon (7), French Open (6), U. S. Open (5) and Australian Open (4). She retired in 1999 with 107 singles titles to her credit. [50]

GRANBERRY: In 1904 oil was discovered near Humble, Texas. The Granberry Oil Company was one of the early participants in this famous oil play. (See **Humble** and **Moonshine Hill.**) [51]

GRANBERRY: Prentiss M. – This gentleman was one of the partners that platted the Freeland Addition, a small neighborhood on the eastern edge of Houston Heights in 1920. Born in Mississippi in 1856, Granberry arrived in Houston in 1900. He worked for William Marsh Rice as a ranch foreman and manager of Rice's Houston Brick Works. He made his fortune on oil wells in the Spindletop Field. The Granberry family lived at 241 Heights Boulevard. (See **Spindletop, Frasier** and **Reserve.**) [52]

GRANGERLAND: Now a bedroom community for Houston and Conroe, Grangerland was once a booming oil town. Until discovery of the huge Conroe Field by the Texas Company in 1931, this area was mainly a cotton and lumber producer. In order to house the oilfield

» GRANGERLAND: Old Texas Company filling station sign

hands and their families Don D. Granger constructed a camp with 32 houses, thus prompting the name. [53]

GRANT: George W. – In 1841 he bought a significant amount of land from Mirabeau B. Lamar, who owned a large farm where Montrose is today. From this sale several developments were platted including Hyde Park Addition. It is very likely that he named this street for himself. [54]

GRAY: Peter – He was a Harrisburg judge and founding member of the Houston Library. Chief Justice Oran Roberts named Gray the "very best district judge upon the Texas bench." Another judge fined him for sitting on a courtroom table ($20) and smoking in court ($20) in 1838. A year later he was named district attorney. He was an organizer of the law firm Gray, Botts & Baker, predecessor to today's Baker & Botts. Gray founded and captained the Civil War Texas Grays, was General John B. Magruder's aide at the 1863 New Year's Day Battle of Galveston and was elected to the House of the Confederate Congress. He developed tuberculosis in 1873. In 1874 Gray was appointed to the Texas Supreme Court but only served two months due to his failing health. He died October 3, 1874 at the age of 54. Chief Justice Roberts said he was "a man who ought to be remembered." [55]

GREEN: Thomas – See sidebar **Houston Streets Named for Men Killed During World War I,** page 22.

GREENSPOINT: This area is a 12-square mile district on the north side of Houston. It achieved notoriety in the 1980s because of its high crime rate. The Greenspoint Shopping Mall was dubbed "Gunspoint Mall" by local wags. To my knowledge it is the only shopping center in American that was forced to post snipers on the roof for a period of time to deter the criminal element. [56]

GREEN'S BAYOU: This northeast-side thoroughfare is named for the 42-mile bayou that runs from northwest Harris County near Jersey Village to where it joins Buffalo Bayou just north of Pasadena. During the 1970s it was so polluted that it was declared a public health hazard. [57]

GREGG: Darius – Born in Kentucky, Gregg came to Texas around 1827 and was granted a league of land by Stephen F. Austin. He fought in the Texas Revolution seeing action at the Siege of Bexar and the Grass Fight. He was a land developer and surveyor in the Fifth Ward. His name still appears on the 1900 Houston map, among others, as a major property owner. Surveyors in early Houston like Gregg often named streets after themselves. The Reverend Toby Gregg, a former slave freed by Darius Gregg following the War Between the States, founded Mount Vernon United Methodist Church, the oldest religious organization in the Fifth Ward. [58]

G–H

GRETEL: (See **Hansel.**)

GRIMES: Alfred C. – This Georgia born Texas hero was killed at the Alamo. He was only 19 years old. Grimes was a member of Captain John H. Forsyth's cavalry company. His father signed the Texas Declaration of Independence on March 2, 1836 while the Battle of the Alamo raged. The younger Grimes would be massacred four days later by General Santa Anna's Mexican army. [59]

GRISSOM: Virgil Ivan "Gus" – One of America's first space heroes, this brave astronaut died in a tragic fire in an Apollo capsule at Cape Kennedy on January 27, 1967. Grissom was among the first group of test pilots to become America's astronauts in 1959. He was the pilot for the Mercury-Redstone 4, commander of Gemini 3 and was named flight commander of the first Apollo flight prior to his death. [60]

GROESCHKE: Louis and Charlotte – This west side road was named for this German couple who operated a farm in the area in the 1850s. [61]

GROGAN'S MILL: This Woodlands street recalls a sawmill owned by the Grogan-Cochran Lumber Company that had a lumber camp south of Magnolia, Texas in the early 1920s. At one time the company operated 25 sawmills in Texas, with three of those in Montgomery County. (See **Cochran's Crossing.**) [62]

GRUNWALD: Fred – This man owned a ranch and farm near the town of Beasley. (See **Beasley-Damon.**) [63]

GUADALCANNAL: This is one of several street names in Houston that is misspelled. The correct name is Guadalcanal, the largest of the Solomon Islands in the South Pacific. It was the site of a decisive WW II battle when Allied troops recaptured it from the Japanese in 1943. It was the first time the American forces launched a large-scale maritime invasion of a Japanese-held island. [64]

GUADALUPE VICTORIA: Located in San Felipe, this street recalls the original name of Victoria, Texas. It was founded in 1824 and named for the first president of the Republic of Mexico by Martin de Leon. The town became a stock-raising center and a shipping point. Guadalupe Victoria was a major contributor of volunteers, supplies and weapons to the Texans during the War of Independence. [65]

GUADALUPE: The developer named this street for the Virgin of Guadalupe, the patron saint of Mexico. (See **Annunciation.**)

GUINEVERE: She was the wife of King Arthur in the Arthurian legends. Her tragic affair with Sir Lancelot presaged the downfall of Arthur's kingdom. Guinevere retired to a convent.

GULF FREEWAY: Referred to as a "concrete engineering marvel - the longest toll-free superhighway in the nation constructed since WW II," this expressway was 16 years in planning and another 6 to build. However, many believe it has never been finished based upon the continual construction that has taken place over the last half century. W. J. Van London, engineering manager of Houston Urban Expressways, designed and supervised construction of the freeway. The original cost was $28,643,521. Initially called the "Superhighway," the city held a contest to rename it and in December 1952 Miss Sara Yancey won $100 for her choice of Gulf Freeway. It officially opened August 2, 1952. [66]

GULF STATES POWER PLANT: This utility was founded in Beaumont in the early 1900s. Gulf States generates and transmits electric power. In 1992 the company was merged into New Orleans' based Entergy Corporation. This short road leads to the GSU Lewis Creek Power Station #1 near Conroe. [67]

GULF TERMINAL: Located on Houston's industrial east side, this short street was created to offer frontage to trucking companies seeking terminal space to store and ship goods. [68]

GULF: The city of Baytown is proud of its roots as a major center for oil refining. One neighborhood there honors some of the old-line oil refiners such as Gulf Oil, Humble Oil & Refining and Superior Oil. Gulf Oil was born with the discovery of oil at Spindletop, near Beaumont, in 1901. The company is best remembered for its orange disc logo as well as "Gulfpride Motor Oil." (See **Spindletop**.) [69]

GUM GULLY: Located 1.5 miles east of Lake Houston, this street is named for the gully of the same name. This short watercourse only runs 2.5 miles from its headwaters to its mouth on Jackson Bayou. (See **Jackson Bayou.**) [70]

GUNRANGE: This short League City street leads to the Clear Creek Gun Range so exercise caution when driving by. [71]

GWINN: See sidebar **Texas Heroes' Names for Houston Streets Urged in 72 Proposed Changes,** page 96.

FAIRBANKS COULD HAVE ITS OWN *CONCOURS D' ELEGANCE* AND ROAD RALLY

Fairbanks is a pleasant little neighborhood north of Hempstead Highway. The developer was clearly a fan of exotic antique automobiles because he named the streets here for some of the more interesting vehicles. When automobile collectors get together to show off their prize wheels it is often called a *Concours d' Elegance*. The event usually includes a road rally when the owners drive these beautiful machines around the countryside. So here you could display and drive the following vehicles:

Henry J. Kaiser and Joseph W. Frazer formed Kaiser-Frazer Corporation in 1945 to produce automobiles. Brands included **Kaiser,** Henry J., Frazer, Willys and Jeep.

Packard was a luxury automobile manufactured by the Packard Motor Car Company of South Bend, Indiana. Founded by James W. and William D. Packard and George L. Weiss in 1899, this company introduced many new innovations including the modern steering wheel and the 12-cylinder engine.

Aston Martin is a British manufacturer of luxury sports cars founded in 1913. It takes its name from a founder, Lionel Martin, and the Aston Hill speed climb race. Today this vehicle is best associated with Agent 007, James Bond.

George Singer founded a bicycle company in England in 1875. By 1905 he was producing an automobile called the **Singer.** This brand disappeared in 1970.

When Ransom E. Olds left the Olds Motor Works he formed a new auto manufacturing company called REO Motor Car Company. The name came from his initials and he called his automobile a **REO.**

Stanley Motor Carriage Company was founded in 1897 by Francis and Freelan Stanley. Their most innovative auto hit the market in 1902 and was sold until 1924. It was driven by a steam engine and was called the Stanley Steamer. During their peak years this vehicle outsold every gasoline powered car in the market.

Sprite was produced by Austin Healey, an English manufacturer. Starting in 1958 this economical roadster known as "Bug Eyes" due to its oversized headlights, used the catchy marketing phrase "a chap can keep his bike in the shed." Eventually it was rebadged as the MG Midget. Production ceased in 1980.

Premier Motor Manufacturing Company produced a luxury car called the **Premier** at their factory in Indianapolis, Indiana. It was manufactured from 1903 until the 1920s. A model from 1903 is on display at the Indianapolis 500 Speedway Museum.

Tony Vandervell owned a Formula One racing team in the 1950s. He invented and patented Thinwall Bearings. When he engineered his own race car in 1954 he called it the **Vanwall,** a combination of his name and the bearing. [28]

H.M.C.: (See **M.A.S.**) [1]

HADLEY: Thomas B. J. – This early Houstonian was a Harris County judge, chief justice of the county in 1863-64 and very active in civic affairs. He is remembered for his hard work on the Committee for Annexation of Texas along with other Houstonians honored with street names including Thomas M. Bagby, William Marsh Rice and Francis R. Lubbock. He was a founding member of the First Baptist Church of Houston in 1841. As an interesting side note his wife was named Piety and his sister-in-law was Obedience. The Hadley farm was located near where Montrose is today. In the 1870s the Texas State Fair was held on a portion of the land that the family sold to the Fair Association. (See **Fairview.**) [2]

HALLMARK: This road leads to one of the city's more upscale retirement communities of the same name. [3]

HALL'S BAYOU: This bayou is named for Jacob Hall who was a sizable landowner along its banks. Its source is northeast of Angleton. Hall's Bayou runs 18 miles, passing through Hall's Lake and the Narrows before emptying into Chocolate Bayou. [4]

HALPERN: Lawrence – See sidebar **Houston Streets Named for Men Killed During World War I,** page 22.

HALSEY: William Frederick "Bull" Jr. – He was Commander of the Pacific theater in World War II. Although he saw much action during the War as commander of an aircraft carrier fleet, Halsey is most remembered for the crippling blow he delivered to the Japanese Navy at the battle of Leyte Gulf on October 23-26, 1944. His brilliant tactics in this, possibly the most complex naval battle of the Pacific War, resulted in the Japanese losing three battleships, four aircraft carriers, ten cruisers and nine destroyers – 300,000 tons of shipping. At the same time Halsey kept his losses to just 37,000 tons. [5]

HAMILTON: James – This former governor of South Carolina was a big supporter of Texas in its early years lending the state $200,000 in gold to finance operations. He was given scrip for land as collateral but it had little value back then. Unfortunately for 20 years Texas refused to repay him. Finally the powers that were agreed to meet with Hamilton and discuss an "adjustment." He sailed from New Orleans for Galveston. However his ship was rammed by another boat in the Gulf and was sinking. He gave his life vest to a woman and her child. In the end not only did he never see a cent of his money, he drowned in the accident. [6]

HAMLET: He was the Danish prince in William Shakespeare's play of the same name.

HAMPTON: Wade – He was the prototypical aristocratic southerner in antebellum South Carolina. Hampton fought for the Confederates at Manassas, Seven Pines and Gettysburg. He was severely wounded at the latter two engagements. After the War he was first elected governor of South Carolina and later U. S. Senator. [7]

HANCOCK: See sidebar **America the Beautiful,** page 176.

HANSEL: This young boy and his sister Gretel are characters in *Grimm's Fairy Tales.* They are abandoned in a forest by their poor parents, leave a trail of bread crumbs, come upon a house of cake and sugar owned by a witch and barely escape her clutches to find their way home.

HANSFORD: John M. – It is likely this street was named after a judge who served the Republic of Texas and met a tragic and violent end. After the Louisiana Purchase, America and Spain could not agree on a borderline so an area called the Neutral Ground was created. This area drew a violent criminal element that eventually provoked the Regulator-Moderator War. Hansford's efforts to clean up this mess infuriated some Regulators who captured the Judge's home and gunned him down. [8]

HARBORSIDE: Until recently this was known as Port Industrial as it did pass through the more industrial sections of the Port of Galveston. Since the city fathers have been working hard to make Galveston a major tourist destination, have attracted cruise ships and cleaned up the waterfront, a name change was in order. [9]

HARDING: Warren G. – This 29th President of the United States died in office after serving a little more than two years of his term. His reputation suffered from one of the most scandal plagued administrations (mainly the Tea Pot Dome) prior to the arrival of William Jefferson Clinton to the White House. In addition, his philandering did not enhance his place in history. [10]

HARGRAVE: North of downtown and east of the Tomball Parkway is where the Hargrave and Hilton families purchased land in the 1860s. Their family cemetery is located in a grove of trees near here. [11]

HARLEM: The area where this Fort Bend County road is located was the Harlem Prison Farm from 1885 until the 1950's when the name was changed to Jester State Prison Farm. It was the second prison farm owned by the State of Texas. In 1913 twelve black inmates were locked in a tiny enclosure 9'x7'x6'. Eight suffocated and the guards were charged with negligent homicide. They were not convicted but were reprimanded for "bad judgment." (See **Prison.**) [12]

HAROLD: J. W. Link, developer of Montrose, named this street for his son Harold Link. (See **Montrose.**) [13]

HARPERS FERRY: A picturesque town in eastern West Virginia, it is famous for abolitionist John Brown and 21 followers' raid on the arsenal there on October 16, 1859. The next morning a company of U.S. Marines under the command of then Colonel Robert E. Lee recaptured the armory, killing 10 of Brown's men and wounding Brown. For his trouble Brown was hanged on December 2, 1859. [14]

HARRIS COUNTY: This road is named for our county. Harris County is bounded on the north and west by Waller County, the north by Montgomery County, on the east by Liberty and Chambers Counties, on the south by Galveston and Brazoria Counties and the west by Fort Bend County. Almost 75% of its 1,778 square mile area is covered by Houston and 30 smaller communities. It averages 55-feet above sea level, has average rainfall of 48.19 inches and a mean temperature of 69.1 degrees. [15]

HARRIS RESERVOIR: Named for William Harris, who settled in what is now Brazoria County in 1824, it is an off-channel project between the Brazos River and Oyster Creek. The reservoir is owned by Dow Chemical Company and is used as an industrial water supply for plants in the Freeport area. (See **Dry Bayou.**) [16]

HARRIS: Robert Locke or Robert Dudley – Robert was the first doctor in Fort Bend County. His son, Robert Dudley Harris, became the first doctor in Fulshear. (See **Katy-Fulshear.**) [17]

HARRIS: William Plunkett – This New York native moved to Texas in 1830 and developed a plantation at Red Bluff on Galveston Bay near where this Seabrook street is today. Harris operated a steamboat line and volunteered his boat *Cayuga* for service during the Texas Revolution. In the 12-day period between April 15 and 26, 1836 the *Cayuga* served as the temporary capitol of the interim Texas government. His brother was John Richardson Harris for whom Harris County is named. (See stock certificate on next page showing William P. Harris' partial ownership of Harrisburg.) [18]

HARRISBURG: John Richardson Harris established the town of Harrisburg in 1825. He named it after himself as well as after Harrisburg Pennsylvania, a city founded by his great grandfather. General Antonio Lopez de Santa Anna burned the town on April 16, 1836, five days before his fateful encounter with Sam Houston at the Battle of San Jacinto. In 1847 Harrisburg became the first railroad terminal in Texas with the

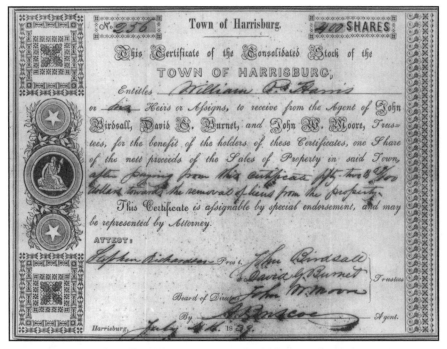

» HARRISBURG: A stock certificate representing ownership in the town of Harrisburg

creation of the Buffalo Bayou, Brazos & Colorado Railroad Company. Houston annexed the town in December 1926. [19]

HARRISON: Benjamin – The 23rd President of the United States, not unlike George W. Bush, the 43rd to hold that office, won the electoral college tally but lost the popular vote to Grover Cleveland in 1889. Republicans reluctantly nominated Harrison to run for a second term despite his flagging popularity. He lost to Cleveland in the rematch in 1893. [20]

HARTLAND: See sidebar **All Things English,** page 175.

HARTMAN: Fred – He was one of our quintessential newspaper editors. Hartman was chairman of Southern Newspapers Inc., publisher of the *Baytown Sun.* He held the title of editor from 1950 until 1974. He would peddle his bicycle to the Houston Ship Channel and ride the ferry across to his office. He was a great friend of former Houston Mayor Bob Lanier (who delivered the *Sun* as a boy). It was through Lanier's influence that the bridge spanning the ship channel was named for Hartman. The fact this bridge took three years longer to construct and was over budget by $27 million does not take away from its visual beauty. The 1,250-foot span (the longest in the State) is held 178 feet above the Houston Ship Channel by two 440-foot diamond shaped towers that hold up the steel cables of this suspension bridge. With eight lanes of traffic and generous shoulders, it is the widest cable-stayed bridge in the world. [21]

HARVARD: This street is named after Harvard University, the nation's oldest bastion of higher learning. Founded in 1636, it is located in Cambridge, Massachusetts. My favorite story about Harvard tells of a Russian delegation visiting the campus just after the Russian Revolution in 1919. When they saw the huge library the visitors asked the dean, who was acting as their guide, "How has America, such a young country, managed to amass such a great volume of knowledge?" In response the dean said, "It's because the freshmen bring so much knowledge and the seniors take so little away." [22]

HARVEY: (See **Whiting.**)

HASKELL: Charles Ready – This brave Tennessee volunteer came to Texas to fight in the Revolution. He saw action at the Battle of Coleto but was killed in the Goliad Massacre. Haskell County is also named in his honor. [23]

HASTINGS FIELD: This oil field was discovered by Stanolind Oil & Gas Company (later to become Amoco) on December 23, 1934. It is located 18 miles south of Houston. Two days after Stanolind announced its discovery well lease prices here jumped from $1 per acre to $5,000 per acre. Although production has diminished over the years it still produces oil today. (See **Hastings-Friendswood** and **Stanolin.**) [13]

HASTINGS-FRIENDSWOOD: Now swallowed up by Angleton, Hastings was a small community on the Atchison, Topeka & Santa Fe Railroad. It was named for a pioneer family who lived in the area. (See **Hastings Field.**) [24]

HAUDE: Most of the early settlers in the Klein, Texas area were German Lutherans. In 1874 these pioneers founded Trinity Lutheran Church. The Haude family was among these settlers and church members. A number of Haudes are buried in the old Budde Cemetery off of Louetta Road and I-45 North. (See **Budde Cemetery.**) [25]

HAWKINS: John P. – See sidebar **Houston Streets Named for Men Killed During World War I,** page 22.

HAWTHORNE: Nathaniel – He was one of America's greatest novelists. In a very short period he published his two best-known works – *The Scarlet Letter* (1850) and *The House of Seven Gables* (1851). [26]

HAZARD: See **Southampton's English Streets,** page 255.

HEDWIG: In return for allowing the city to put a road through his property, Henry Schroeder had this street named for a relative, Hedwig Jankowski Schroeder, who came to Houston in 1906 from Germany. Located in Hedwig Village, an affluent neighborhood in the Memorial area, most of the acreage here was originally part of the John D. Taylor and Isaac Bunker leagues. (See **Bunker Hill** and **Taylorcrest.**) [27]

HEGAR: Louis – In 1847 a German immigrant named Otto Hegar purchased some land in Waller County where this road is located. By 1887 his son, Oscar George Hegar, had settled in the area and was operating a general store. In 1899 he became postmaster of this rural farming community. Louis Hegar was a very successful rancher in the area. He would drive his herd north in the spring along the Salt Grass Trail and bring them back to the ranch for winter foraging. Many of the early area residents are buried in the Macedonia Methodist Cemetery located between Hegar and Macedonia School Roads. (See **Springer Cemetery.**) [28, 29]

HEGAR: Otto – The Hegar family were German immigrants who settled on land northwest of Waller, Texas in 1847. By 1887 a town known as Hegar or Springer existed. Oscar George Hegar, Otto's son, had opened a general store and post office by 1899. Family members are buried in the nearby Roberts Cemetery including Wm. Hegar (1826-1895). (See **Roberts Cemetery.**) [30]

» HEIGHTS: Heights Boulevard with trolley

HEIGHTS: Houston Heights was incorporated in 1891. It was named because of it's proximity to Houston and the fact that the elevation was over 70 feet above sea level, 23 feet more altitude than downtown Houston. Heights Boulevard was modeled after Commonwealth Avenue in Boston. The City annexed this historic neighborhood in 1918. [31]

HEINER: Eugene T. – He was Houston's most famous architect of the late 19th century. Heiner's specialty was designing courthouses (Galveston, Hallettsville), jails (Galveston, Harris and Tarrant counties) and prisons (Texas State Penitentiary at Huntsville). Among his educational offerings were buildings on the Texas A & M campus. Heiner is most re-

EUGENE T. HEINER,

ARCHITECT AND SUPERINTENDENT.

Office 57½ Main (3d Floor) Corner Preston Street, Houston, Texas.

HOUSTON REFERENCES:
Charles S. House's Residence,
T. W. Porter's Residence,
George J. H. Blake's Residence.

HOUSTON REFERENCES:
W. D. Cleveland's Building,
Sweeney & Coomb's Building,
Henry Brasher's Building.

Wm. D. Cleveland's Building, Houston, Texas.

HOUSTON REFERENCES:

L. M. & T. W. JONES' BUILDINGS,   L. M. RICH'S BUILDING,

E. P. HILL'S BUILDING,   HOUSTON COTTON EXCHANGE.

PLANS, ESTIMATES AND SUPERINTENDENCE FURNISHED

For Every Description of Building, Public or Private.

STATE REFERENCES:
TRINITY COUNTY COURTHOUSE,
POLK COUNTY COURTHOUSE,
HENDERSON COUNTY JAIL, ATHENS,
SMITH CO. JAIL AND COURTHOUSE,
TARRANT CO. JAIL, FT. WORTH, TEXAS.

STATE REFERENCES:
KAUFFMAN & RUNGE'S BUILDING, GALVESTON,
LEON & H. BLUM'S BUILDING, GALVESTON,
LAMPASAS SPRINGS CO'S HOTEL, LAMPASAS,
HARRIS COUNTY JAIL, HOUSTON, TEXAS.
GALVESTON COUNTY JAIL AND COURTHOUSE.

Kauffman & Runge's Building, Galveston, Texas.

LARGE & DIFFICULT BUILDING CONSTRUCTION A SPECIALTY.

Correspondence Solicited.   Specifications Furnished.

G-H

» HEINER: An 1881 advertisement for architect Eugene T. Heiner

membered for his magnificent High Victorian style Cotton Exchange & Board of Trade building (1884) on Houston's Market Square. Other commercial successes included the Sweeney & Coombs building (1880), Henry Brashear building (1882) and the Houston Ice & Brewing Company plant (1893). He loved to employ stucco, color, texture and cast iron in his edifices. In addition, in 1891 Heiner was a founder and the first secretary of the Houston Business League, a commercial association of leading citizens. One of Heiner's advertisements is on the previous page. (See **Kincheloe.**) [32]

HELEN: See **Florence.**

HEMPHILL: John – This lawyer and Indian fighter arrived in Texas in 1838. By 1842 Hemphill was Chief Justice of the Supreme Court of the Republic of Texas. He took over Sam Houston's U.S. Senate seat in 1859. He strongly supported secession and, during the Civil War, served in the Provisional Confederate Congress. Sixth Ward developer William Baker named this street for Hemphill after the Chief Justice ruled in favor of Baker's son in a case in 1856. (See **Henderson.**) [33, 34]

HEMPHILL: R. "Bob" B. – For opening one of the first automobile dealerships in Baytown in 1939, he was honored with this street. [35]

HEMPSTEAD: This highway leads to the town of Hempstead, Texas, once a station on the Houston & Texas Central Railroad. Dr. Richard R. Peebles and James W. McDade founded it in 1856. Peebles named the town in honor of his brother-in-law, Dr. G. S. B. Hempstead, who was a native of Portsmouth, Ohio. In the early 1900s Hempstead earned the dubious nickname of "Six-Shooter Junction" because of the contentious nature of the various political groups that lived there. [36]

HENDERSON: J. W. – Sixth Ward developer William Baker named this street after this attorney who won a case for Baker's son before the Texas Supreme Court in 1856. (See **Hemphill.**) [37]

HENKE: Henry – In the late 1880s this German immigrant was a prosperous wholesale and retail grocer and liquor distributor. Old line Houstonians will remember the grocery chain of Henke & Pillot that operated for many years until being sold to Kroger. His first place of business was Henke's New Orleans Store, an emporium on Congress Street, opened in 1872. Business boomed and he soon needed facilities to serve out of town clients so he opened Henke's Wagon Yard nearby that functioned as a camping ground for these customers. [38]

» **HENKE: Mausoleum in Glenwood Cemetery**

HENRY MORGAN: See sidebar **Pirates of the Caribbean,** page 280.

HENRY SHREVE: This gentleman played an important role in the development of steamboats. His designs proved to be more technologically advanced that those of the more famous Robert Fulton. Captain Henry Miller Shreve, commanding a battalion of U. S. Army Corps of Engineers, cleared a 180-mile long raft of debris that clogged the Red River. The project took five years (1833-1838). This feat allowed the 1,600 mile river to remain navigable until 1914 when it began silting up. It was not dredged due to the rising use of railroads to move goods. In 1836 a town at the junction of the Red River and the Texas Trail was named Shreve Town in his honor. Three years later it was renamed Shreveport (Louisiana). [39]

HENRY: John – This was a prominent citizen of Aldine who operated a poultry breeding business in the early 1900s. [40]

HERCULES: See sidebar **Space City U.S.A. or "Houston the Eagle Has Landed",** page 106.

HEREFORD: In a pastoral neighborhood just south of Pearland a number of the streets are named for famous breeds of cattle. This breed was developed in Herefordshire, England 250 years ago. It arrived in the U. S. in 1817 when Henry Clay of Kentucky imported a herd. It is mainly raised for beef. [41]

HERMANN MUSEUM: The Houston Museum of Natural History is on this street. Attendance totals over 2 million visitors annually (second to only the American Museum of Natural History amongst non-Smithsonian museums). Founded in 1909, much of the

» HERMANN: George H. Hermann's funeral procession passes through downtown Houston

» **HERMANN: George - tombstone in Glenwood Cemetery**

collection was acquired between 1914 and 1930. The building we see today was erected in 1969. Outstanding permanent exhibits include: Cullen Hall of Gems & Minerals, Lester and Sue Smith Gem Vault, Weiss Energy Hall, Cockrell Butterfly Center, Burke Baker Planetarium and Wortham IMAX.

HERMANN: George H. – He was a man destined to become one of Houston's greatest philanthropists. Hermann was born August 6, 1843 in a log cabin where the City Hall reflection pool is today. He came from humble beginnings. His parents arrived here in 1838 with $5 and three kids. Mrs. Hermann pawned her jewelry so they could open a bakery. George's first job was as a stock keeper for Governor Lubbock's Simms Bayou ranch. Active in the Civil War, he served with distinction in Company A of the 26th Cavalry. Hermann took up cattle ranching in 1872. He made his fortune on livestock, land and oil. In 1885, as Houston's importance as a world port increased, he traveled by train to New York City and caught a steamship to Europe. This tour was possibly the only big indulgence he allowed himself in his long and frugal life. When the Board of Park Commissioners was formed in 1910, Hermann was one of its founding members. Later that year Hermann gave the land where he was born to the city for a park. One condition of the gift was that anyone who was drunk could sleep it off in the park without being arrested. The reason: Hermann did not want to constantly bail out his employees, thus wasting time and money when they could be working. On May 30, 1914 he gave the city 278 acres of beautifully wooded land that became Hermann Park. He died October 21, 1914. Hermann Park officially opened July 4, 1915. As Hermann never married, his estate, valued a $2.5 million, was willed to a foundation to build and operate a hospital. Hermann Hospital, constructed at a cost of $1 million, commenced operations July 1, 1925. He is buried in Glenwood Cemetery beside his parents and two bachelor brothers. [42]

HERNDON: John H. – He was a wealthy real estate developer in the Richmond/Rosenberg area. [43]

HERRIDGE: The neighborhood where this street is located was called Oak Ridge in the 1930s. It was developed by Herridge & Company. [44]

HEWITT: Thurman – This gentleman was real estate developer Frank Sharp's in-house home architect. (See **Frank Sharp.**) [45]

HIALEAH: This street is named for the beautifully landscaped Hialeah Park and Race Course in Florida. This visually stunning horse race track is famous for its large flock of flamingos. [46]

HICKOK: James Butler – Best known as Wild Bill Hickok, he was born in Illinois in 1837. He moved west to become a stagecoach driver. Hickok became famous as a skilled driver, marksman and gunfighter (carrying two Colt 1851 Navy revolvers), scout, lawman and professional gambler. It was in this latter profession that Hickok met his maker. While playing poker in a Deadwood, South Dakota saloon Jack McCall shot him several times in the back. At the time Hickok was holding two pairs – aces and eights. Ever sense, poker players have called this a "dead man's hand." [47]

HICKORYTEX: See sidebar **Howdy Tex,** page 263.

HICKS: A. – This gentleman was the first real estate agent in Tomball. He and his brother, Howard, owned Homeseekers Land & Loan Company. He later became manager of Tomball Townsite Company. William Malone, a major land owner in the area, owned that firm. (See **Malone** and **Tomball.**)

HICKS: Earl or Thomas B. – See sidebar **Houston Streets Named for Men Killed During World War I,** page 22.

HIDALGO: Padre Miguel Hidalgo y Costilla was the father of Mexican Independence. This Roman Catholic priest was born in the state of Guanajuato in 1753. Prior to the revolution Hidalgo was not only a humanitarian but an entrepreneur as well. He started a night school for artists, operated a pottery plant, a tannery, vineyard, olive grove, carpenter shop, smithy and wool weaving looms. In addition he raised silkworms. On September 15, 1810 he called for the overthrow of the Spaniards from his pulpit and began leading a rag-tag army toward Mexico City. Successful early on, Hidalgo was betrayed by a traitor. Spanish authorities executed him before a firing squad on July 30, 1811. However, his courageous efforts did lead to the independence of Mexico. [48]

» **HIDALGO: Miguel Hidalgo, father of Mexican Independence**

HIGGINS: The Higgins Oil Company was one of the early wildcatters in the Moonshine Hill section of the famous Humble oilfield, located in the town of the same name. (See **Humble** and **Moonshine Hill.**) [49]

HIGHLAND BAYOU: From its source south of La Marque this bayou travels 12 miles southeast and empties into Jones and West Bays. At its mouth is a brackish water marsh. [50]

HIGHLAND: (See **Highland Bayou** and **Hitchcock.**)

HIGHLAND: Studemont was developed by Varner Realty Company in conjunction with Mike and Will Hogg (who later joined forces with Hugh Potter to develop River Oaks). Executives at Varner named the streets in the subdivision. Miss Dorothy Witt, a resident of Studemont since 1929 (the streets were not even paved when she moved there), believes Highland was named because of its elevation above Buffalo Bayou. [51]

HIGHLANDS WOODS: Located on the east bank of the San Jacinto River, it was named because the east bank was higher than the west. The town of Highlands was a station on the Beaumont, Sour Lake & Western Railroad. For a time the community was also know as Elena. [52]

HIGHLIFE: Houston Distributing Company's property abuts this road. They are the local distributor of Miller High Life Beer. [53]

HILDEBRANDT: John – In the 1870s this gentleman owned a sawmill in the area of north Houston where this road is today. The land where Hildebrandt Intermediate School is located was originally farmland owned by the family. A descendant, Paul Hildebrandt, was a founder of the Farmer's Market on Airline Drive. [54]

HILLENDAHL: Heinrich – The first of the Hillendahl family arrived from Hanover, Germany in 1851. Heinrich bought 80 acres in the Spring Branch area for $2 an acre. By 1896 Spring Branch was called Hillendahl, Texas. He was one of the founders of St. Peter's Evangelical Lutheran Church. He is buried along with other family members in a small cemetery in the parking lot of an auto repair shop on Long Point and Pech. [55]

HILSHIRE GROVE: This street is in Hilshire, one of the six incorporated Memorial Villages. A local landowner, Frank Bruess, named the Village for an English country estate. [30]

HINKLE'S FERRY-CHURCHILL: Churchill Bridge is a small Brazoria County community located on the banks of the San Bernard River. It was named for Andrew S. Churchill who arrived here in 1836 and built a ferry landing. In 1875 postmaster Lewis T. Bennett bought the ferry and 200 acres of land from Churchill. Bennett changed the name to Bennett's Ferry. When the Bennett family sold the land the place was renamed Churchill Place and later Churchill Bridge when the ferry was retired and replaced by a highway bridge. (See **Hinkle's Ferry.**) [56]

HINKLE'S FERRY: A small town was located here near the San Bernard River ferry crossing on FM 2611 southwest of Brazoria. The place and the ferry were named for J. V. Hinkle who owned a general store and was also the town's postmaster in 1884. Your author recalls using this little ferry in the 1950s and 60s to reach our family compound on Caney Creek. If memory serves me correctly it only carried two or four cars per crossing. (See **Old Caney** and **San Bernard.**) [57]

HINTON: W. H. – Dr. Hinton was named first president of Houston Baptist College in 1962. The school opened in September of 1963 with a freshman class of 193 students. He remained very active with this institution of higher learning until his retirement as University Chancellor in 1991. There is no indication that your author and Dr. Hinton are related. [58]

» **HINTON: Entrance to Houston Baptist College**

HIRAM CLARKE: Hiram O. Clarke was an executive vice president of Houston Lighting & Power (now Reliant Energy). In addition he was chairman of the committee to build the San Jacinto Monument as well as vice president of the Chamber of Commerce for more than 20 years. Clarke also headed the drive that secured funds to build the Downtown YMCA. This street and the power station on it are named for him. [59]

HIRSCH: John – An immigrant from Germany, he settled in the Tomball area in 1856. [60]

HIRSCH: William – This German immigrant settled in Tomball in the 1800s as did hundreds of other families who fled the wars of Europe at that time for a better life in the New World. William Hirsch owned the Hirsch Cotton Gin and was a founder and director of the town's first bank, First State Bank of Tomball. Some of the family members are buried in Siedel (Rosehill) Cemetery. (See **Siedel Cemetery.**) [61]

HITCHCOCK: Jonas Butler bought a league of land here in Galveston County in 1848, naming it Highland as it was on the banks of Highland Bayou. About 1873 it was re-named for Lent M. Hitchcock when his widow, Emily, donated a 450-foot wide tract of land to the Atchison, Topeka & Santa Fe Railroad for a depot if they would name the town after her late husband. (See **Camp Wallace** and **Highland Bayou.**) [62]

HOAD DEUCE: Lew Hoad was an Australian tennis professional and two-time Wimbledon champion (1956, 1957). Going into the 1956 U.S. Open he had posted victories at the Australian and French Opens as well as Wimbledon and was seeking the Grand Slam of tennis by winning all four majors. However, he lost the final in four sets to Ken Rosewall. Deuce is a tennis term for each player in the match having the same number of points. [63]

HOBBY: This Fort Bend County road recalls a ghost town from the 1920s. Between 1919 and 1925 a salt mine opened and oil was discovered nearby. Hobby became a boom-town full of gambling houses and saloons. The name was later changed to Blue Ridge. The town disappeared when the land was sold to the Texas prison system in 1936. [64]

HOCKLEY: The town of Hockley lies northwest of Houston on U.S. 290. The **Bauer-Hockley** road recalls George Washington Hockley who established the town in 1835. This was one of many towns served by the Houston & Texas Central Railroad. It is possible that Bauer was named for one of the early European immigrants who came to Texas in the mid-1800s and settled in this area. [65]

HODGE'S BEND: Alexander Hodge was born in 1760. He fought in the American Revolution under the command of "Swamp Fox" Francis Marion's South Carolina Brigade. He arrived in Texas in 1825 as a member of Austin's Old 300 families. He named his 1828 land grant Hodge's Bend. Two of his sons fought in the Texas Revolution. [66]

HOFFMAN ESTATE: This street in the Tomball area, most likely remembers Charles F. Hoffman who opened the city's first general store. He may have also owned a sawmill in nearby Rosehill. [67]

HOFFMAN: This Kansas gentleman was one of the early investors in the development of Pasadena. Alvida Munger named this street in his honor. [68]

HOGAN: James B. Jr. and Thomas M. - These brothers came to Texas in 1836 to help the fledgling Republic gain her independence. Both fought with Sam Houston at the Battle of San Jacinto. Following the revolution, James opened the first blacksmith shop in Houston on Main Street. He was elected sheriff of Harris County in 1850 and served in that position until 1854. Thomas won election to that post in 1854 and held it for the next two years. He is remembered for pursuing a murderer named Hyde to Louisiana where Hogan arrested him. Upon their return to Houston, Hyde was publicly executed in the first legal hanging in the city's history in 1854. Retiring from public life, the men opened Hogan's New Hotel on Market Square. Both are buried in Founders Memorial Park on W. Dallas. [69]

HOGAN'S ALLEY: Ben Hogan was one of America's greatest golf pros in the 1940s and 50s. Born in Dublin, Texas (the only place on the planet where you can still buy Dr. Pepper made from the original recipe at the local bottling plant) in 1912 Hogan began his professional career in 1937. Winning the P. G. A. Tournament in 1946 and 1948, he was in an almost career ending car wreck in 1949. Hogan made an amazing recovery and comeback, going on to win four U. S. Opens, two Masters and one British Open. [70]

HOLCOMBE: Oscar – Holcombe is one of Houston's legendary politicians. First elected mayor in 1921 he would be re-elected 11 times. In 1922 the Ku Klux Klan controlled many county offices. The Klan asked Holcombe to fire three city administrators who were Catholic. He refused and the KKK set out to defeat him in the most outrageous campaign in the city's history. In their newspaper the KKK claimed Holcombe was a drunk and a gambler. Actually he was a member in good standing of the First Baptist Church and had no known vices. Slandered by a rumor that he shot craps at a New Year's party, Holcombe challenged the Klan to prove it. He asked the Baptist Ministers Association to try him on the charges. The Klan produced two witnesses

» HOLCOMBE: Mayor Oscar Holcombe

who claimed they peeked over the transom and saw the Mayor but he produced six attendees who swore Holcombe was not there. He won acquittal and a second term. Early in his career he became known as the "Gray Fox" for his political showmanship, cunning and premature silver hair. Holcombe was a good businessman and became very wealthy through investments in lumber, home building, gas stations, apartments, oil and a turkey farm. He combined the power of city manager and mayor giving mayors of Houston more power than those in other American cities. Under his administrations the Harris County Navigation District and the Houston Independent School District were created. Once while the mayor was out of town the city council changed the name of the street on which he lived from Marlborough to Holcombe and it remains so today. [71]

HOLDERRIETH: All we know about this gentleman is that he was Fritz Bogs' partner in a cotton gin in the Tomball area. (See **Bogs.**) [72]

HOLIDAY: This Galveston street is a double entendre. Many people enjoy taking a holiday in the sun in this beach town. However, the street also led to a large Holiday Inn here that no longer exists. [73]

HOLLY HALL: Located near the Astrodome, this street leads to a retirement community of the same name. [74]

» HOLMAN: Mayor James S. Holman

HOLMAN: James S. – He was elected district court clerk of the County of Harrisburg in early 1837. The City of Houston was incorporated a few months later and Chief Justice Andrew Briscoe called an election. Holman was elected the first mayor in a tight contest, collecting 12 votes to Francis Lubbock's 11 and Thomas W. Ward's 10. After this cliffhanger there were no reports of hanging chads, lawsuits, lawyers, Supreme Court intervention or sore losers. [75]

HOLMES: H. H. – I believe this road located south of south loop 610 West is named for this land developer. In 1912 Holmes purchased acreage here and named it Sunnyside. He marketed the development to blacks. Holmes platted lots and built homes that could be purchased for as little as $10 down and $10 a month. The first black woman in Texas to earn a private pilot's license lived here. [76]

HOLMES: I. R. – (See **La Porte** and **Lee.**)

HOLY ROOD: The story behind this Memorial area street is very interesting. The old English word "rood" means "cross." So this street is named for the holy cross Jesus was crucified upon. One of the earliest poems in the English language, possibly written by Cynewulf in the 8th century, is titled "The Dream of the Rood." The plot tells of the crucifixion from the viewpoint of the cross. It is forced to be the instrument of Christ's death. The cross suffers nail wounds, spear shafts and insults as did Jesus to fulfill God's will. [61]

HOLY SEE: Also known as the State of Vatican City, this monarchical-sacerdotal state has the Pope as its chief executive officer. Established from former Papal States and given special status in Italy, it was granted independence in February 1929. This 44 square kilometer land-locked enclave is the world's smallest state. For all the power it wields the Holy See has no pastureland, crops, arable land, woodlands, industry or military forces. [77]

HOLZWARTH: Many immigrants from Germany settled in the Spring, Texas area during the mid to late 19th century. A number of them are buried in the Budde Cemetery there including seven members of the Holzwarth family: Amelia, Charles, Christian, Katharina, Rosa, Matilda and William. (See **Budde Cemetery.**) [78]

HOMCO: Located in an industrial area on Houston's east side this street is named for a manufacturing company that was once located on it. Houston Oilfield Materials Company was usually shortened to a combination of initials taken from the first letter of each word plus two from Company. [79]

HOMER: Contrary to what some of our school children might think this street is not honoring Homer Simpson of the Fox television show, *The Simpsons*. It is named for the 8th century B.C. classical Greek poet, author of the *Odyssey* and the *Iliad*. [80]

HONEA-EGYPT: (See **Lake Conroe** and **Egypt.**)

HOOVER: Herbert C. - This highly intelligent individual was the 31st President of the U.S. (1929-33). Unfortunately the stock market crash of October 1929 and the resulting Great Depression were blamed on him. Unable to do anything about the dire economic climate Hoover was crushed in the 1932 election by Franklin D. Roosevelt. [81]

HOPFE: One of many German immigrant families to arrive in our county in the 1800s, the Hopfes were landowners in the area near Tomball, Texas. Many of them are buried in Roberts Cemetery. (See **Roberts Cemetery.**) [44]

HOPKINS: Fred – See sidebar **Houston Streets Named for Men Killed During World War I,** page 22.

HORACE MANN: It is only appropriate that a street named for this American educator runs beside Lamar Consolidated High School in Rosenberg. Mann's primary education was sparse but he was allowed to attend Brown University and was valedictorian of his class. He also earned a law degree. In 1837 he was hired as secretary of the newly created Massachusetts State Board of Education. He succeeded in improving teaching methods, raised salaries for teachers, upgraded schoolroom equipment and taught the practicality of coeducation. [82]

HORTON: Albert. – He was the first lieutenant governor of Texas and an early resident of Wharton. [83]

HORTON: The Hortons were early settlers of Guy. They operated a farm there. (See **Old Guy.**) [84]

HOSKINS: T. A. – He was a surveyor who practiced his trade near where Spring Valley is today in western Harris County. He did a survey here in 1846 and it is possible Hoskins street recalls this early Texan. [85]

HOSKIN'S MOUND: One of many salt domes along the Texas coast, the Freeport Company discovered oil and sulfur here while drilling the flanks of the formation in 1922. [86]

HOSPITAL: This short Tomball street led to the site of the city's first hospital. This 16-bed facility cost $120,000 and opened in 1948. It closed in 1976 when a new hospital was constructed nearby. (See **Carrell.**) [87]

HOSPITAL: This street passes in front of the Angleton-Danbury General Hospital. This facility opened in 1969 and serves the citizens of Brazoria County. [88]

HOUSE HAHL: Pronounced "house haul," this western Harris County road was the area's thoroughfare with the fewest obstructions. As a result when a house was moved in this area this was the path taken. I can't help thinking this story is apocryphal but my source swears to its validity. [89]

HOUSE: Joseph – Many of Stephen F. Austin's second wave of colonists settled along the cool, spring-fed waters of Spring Creek in northwestern Harris County. In 1831 this gentleman was given a one-league land grant on that watercourse just north of where the town of Tomball is located today. [90]

HOUSMAN: Louis M. – This Spring Branch family donated land for a school. Today Housman Elementary School is located on this street. [91]

HOUSTON CHRONICLE: Years ago the Houston Chronicle Publishing Company purchased a large tract of land on the west side of town with the idea of moving the newspaper's production facility there. Management named the principal boulevard into the property for the paper. The story of the *Chronicle's* founding is classic Houston lore. A cub reporter for the *Houston Post* was sent to Spindletop to cover the discovery of this giant oilfield in 1901. Marcellus E. Foster knew he was witnessing something huge and had a chance to get in on the ground floor. He invested his $30 weekly salary in a well. Two weeks later he sold his interest for $5,000. Returning to Houston he quit the *Post* and started the *Chronicle*. If nothing else Houstonians have always been entrepreneurial. [92]

» **HOUSTON CHRONICLE:**
Founder and publisher Marcellus E. Foster

HOUSTON NATIONAL: The Houston National Golf Club, a 27 hole public golf links, is at the end of this northwest Harris County road. [76]

HOUSTON: Samuel – One of the most famous Texans of all time, Sam Houston was a frontiersman, politician, war hero, liberator of Texas, first president of the Republic of Texas, U.S. Senator and Governor of Texas.

HOUSTONIAN: No, this short street is not named for all of us. Rather it leads into the posh Houstonian Hotel, Club and Spa in the Galleria area. Some of Houston's wealthiest families' homes were on this property in the 1950s and 60s before the Houstonian was constructed in this beautifully wooded glen. [93]

» **HOUSTON: Sam Houston monument in Hemann Park**

HOWE: Milton G. – This gentleman came to Texas in 1859 from Massachusetts. He was a captain in the Confederate Army and devised the firing plan for Dick Dowling's victory at the Battle of Sabine Pass in 1863. In civilian life he worked for the Houston & Texas Central Railroad. Howe was active in civic affairs and was elected a City of Houston alderman. (See **Dowling**.) [94]

HOWELL-SUGAR LAND: This area was granted to Samuel M. Williams in 1828. He raised sugar on his plantation. By 1858 the town of Sugar Land was well established. Between 1906-8 Isaac H. Kempner and William T. Eldridge had purchased most of the land in the area and created a company town for their Imperial Sugar Company. Additional labor was acquired from the nearby state prison farms. Needless to say the convicts were not crazy about working all day in the hot sun chopping cane and referred to the area as "Hell hole on the Brazos." Urbanization occurred and the last sugar cane crop raised in Fort Bend County was in 1928. (See **Addicks-Howell** and **Eldridge**.) [95]

HUCKLEBERRY: (See **Chimney Rock**.) [96]

HUDSON CIRCLE & HUDSON PLACE: From the 1920s until the 1950s the area where these streets are located were way past the Houston city limit. In 1925 a local furniture store owner, E. A. Hudson, gave approximately 100 acres of this heavily wooded land to the Sam Houston Area Council of Boy Scouts. They in turn named the property Camp Hudson and used it for scouting activities and campouts. Urban sprawl eventually surrounded Camp Hudson so the Scouts sold the property in 1973 for development. [74]

HUECO TANKS: This historic state site is east of El Paso and is famous for its archeology. The three massive granite hills that rise 450 feet above the desert floor are known for their prehistoric Indian rock art. *Hueco* is the Spanish word for "hollows" that are located in the hills. Folsom projectile points found here indicate human inhabitation occurred here more that 10,000 years ago.

HUFFMAN: Roads emanating from this small east Harris County town are most likely honoring David Huffman who first settled in the region in 1839. The town later became a stop on the Beaumont, Sour Lake & Western Railroad. **Huffman-New Caney** road leads to the town of New Caney. It was originally called Presswood for early pioneers Austin and Sarah Presswood, who were cattle ranchers in the area in the 1860s. Postmaster James B. Robinson named it New Caney when the name Caney was already taken. The **Huffman-Cleveland** highway leads to the east Texas town of Cleveland. This community was founded in 1878 when Charles Lander Cleveland deeded 64 acres to the Houston, East & West Texas Railway who named the station after him. The **Huffman-Eastgate** road ran from Huffman to the small Liberty County town of Eastgate. It was named for its location at the east gate of the Beaumont, Sour Lake & Western Railroad yard. [97]

HUFFMEISTER: Members of this family were farmers in the Cypress, Texas area as early as the 1840s. In the 1980s the powers that be decided to honor some of the early German immigrants to the area with street names. [98]

HUFSMITH: Frank – He emigrated from Prussia, Germany as a young boy. Hufsmith arrived in Texas in 1887. The International-Great Northern Railroad employed him as the general superintendent. The I-GNRR Company owned a small railroad station that was located in the Tomball area. It was named in his honor in 1902 because of "his labor and dedication" to the rail line. [99]

HUGGINS: Joe – He was an early resident of Baytown. [100]

HUGGINS: John and/or E. M. – John moved to Fulshear in the 1850s from North Carolina. Huggins was a horse trainer and jockey at Churchill Fulshear's stables. In 1901

G–H

he trained the first American horse to win the English Derby. E.M. was a rancher in Fulshear in the 1800s. (See **Katy-Fulshear.**) [101]

» HUGHES: Hughes family grave site in Glenwood Cemetery

HUGHES: Howard Robard – Born in Missouri in 1869, he intended to become a lawyer. However, when the Spindletop field was discovered near Beaumont he recognized the opportunity to establish himself in the oil drilling business. He and his partner, Walter B. Sharp attempted to drill some wells near Pierce Junction and Goose Creek, Texas but found the rock extremely hard and impenetrable. Hughes took some time off and developed the rock bit, a specially designed cone-shaped bit with tough steel teeth that could penetrate these hard formations. In addition it drilled 10 times faster than any previous technology. In 1909 the men organized the Sharp-Hughes Tool Company to manufacture the bit. It was the basis of the Hughes family fortune. He had one son, Howard R. Hughes Jr., the flamboyant aviator, playboy, movie director and investor. The plant, now called Baker-Hughes, is located nearby. (See **Sharp.**) [102]

HUMBLE PLACE: This street and neighborhood recall Humble Oil & Refining Company (now Exxon Mobil). This oilfield theme carries to other streets. **Roughneck** is a member of a drilling crew. **Rotary** drilling is a method of making a hole that relies on the continuous circular motion of a bit to break rock at the bottom of the hole. Oil **Derrick** is a stationary tower capable of supporting hundreds of tons of oilfield drilling equipment over the bore hole. It is named for Thomas Derrick, an English hangman, who developed the gallows in Elizabethan times. [103]

HUMBLE: Roads such as **Humble-Westfield** are named for the small Harris County town located approximately 20 miles north of Houston. It was named for its founder, Pleasant Smith Humble, a ferryboat operator, merchant, lumberman and justice of the peace. According to the *Handbook of Texas*, Humble was called "Rabbit" in 1876 because train passengers would shoot long-eared hares when the train stopped at this station on its route between Houston and Beaumont. The Humble Oil & Refining Company (now Exxon Mobil) took its name from this town following a gigantic oil discovery here in 1905. [104]

» HUMBLE: Humble Oil tanker truck

HUMBLE: This Baytown street recalls the Humble Oil & Refining Company. The firm was organized in 1911 by some of Texas' most famous oilmen including W. W. Fondren, Ross S. Sterling, W. S. Farish and R. L. Blaffer. The company did have a small refinery in Humble, Texas early on. Humble was the largest domestic producer of oil during World War II. (See **Fondren, Ross Sterling** and **Humble.**), [105]

HUNTER: Johnson – This doctor was one of the earliest settlers in the Baytown area, arriving from Missouri in 1822. In addition Hunter traded with Indians, farmed, ranched and surveyed. In 1829 he sold his land known as Hunter's Point and disappeared into the mists of history. [35]

HUNTER'S CREEK: This Memorial area village and street recall the days when this place was a hunter's paradise. Early residents hunted a variety of wild game and birds before the village became "gentrified." [106]

HUNTINGTON: River Oaks Corporation vice president Herbert A. Kip named this street after his wife's Pennsylvania hometown. [107]

HURTGEN FORREST: Located near Aachen, the first German town to be captured by the Allies in WW II, these woods were the site of a major battle during November-December 1944. [108]

HUTCHENS: The 200-acre Hutchens Research and Experimental Farm is part of the Wharton Junior College Campus. [109]

HUTCHESON: Joseph Chappell – A native of Virginia, this attorney moved to Houston in 1874. He was elected to Congress in 1892 and served until 1897. Among his accomplishments while in Washington D. C. was to seek federal funding for a deep water port in Houston. The Hutchesons lived in a beautiful home on the corner of McKinney and LaBranch. [110]

HUTCHINGS: John Henry – Born in North Carolina in 1822, he arrived in Galveston in 1845. Two years later he formed a partnership with John Sealy. In 1854 they joined George Ball to found the banking firm of Ball, Hutchings & Company (later Hutchings-Sealy National Bank). Hutchings was a Galveston alderman (1859-60) who worked to have a bridge built connecting the Island to the Mainland. During the War Between the States he served as a judge in the Confederate States court system. Following the conflict he was named president of the Galveston Wharf Company. He also invested in insurance, manufacturing, railroads and cotton oil firms. [111]

HUTCHINS: William J. – He moved to Texas in 1838 from Florida. He was initially involved in banking and merchandise but became most active in railroading. He was a founder of the Buffalo Bayou, Brazos & Colorado Railroad and bought the Houston & Texas Central Railroad. He was elected an alderman in Houston and was mayor in 1861. [112]

HYDE PARK: This Montrose Addition street is named after the famous London, England park where King Henry VIII hunted deer and wild boars after its creation in 1536. [113]

HYDRO-55: This oddly named little industrial boulevard is named for the tank farm and fueling station located on it that is owned by Palm Petroleum. [114]

IGLOO: Houston is a strange place to find a street with this name until you realize it is not named for the Eskimo home but instead for the manufacturer of Igloo coolers. The company's manufacturing plant is at the end of it. This product is so popular that surveys show three out of every four American homes own at least one Igloo cooler. [1]

IMPERIAL: The Imperial Sugar Company (not its original name) has operated in the same location since 1843. In 1906 Isaac Kempner and William Eldridge began acquiring sugar plantations near what today is Sugar Land, Texas. By 1908 they had amassed considerable acreage, sugar mills and refineries and gave the business its present name. In the beginning Sugar Land was the classic company town with Imperial owning it lock, stock and barrel. (See **Eldridge** and **Kempner.**) [2]

INCH: Old hands at Planning and Development still laugh about how this street was named. The developer came in to file his plat. All of the streets except one were named. Since a plat must be complete to be recorded, the land developer measured the street with a handy ruler. Since it was an inch in length and was a cross street that would have no addresses (buyers get testy if the street they live on has a funny name) it was christened Inch. [3]

INGOLD: Southside Place developer Edward Crain originally called this street Ingram, honoring his favorite Hill Country town. It was probably misspelled on the plat. [4]

INKS LAKE: See sidebar **The Most Scenic Spots in Texas,** page 310.

INSTITUTE: Rice University was initially named Rice Institute. This shady lane recalls this venerable institution of higher learning's name as given it by the estate of the founder, William Marsh Rice. (See **Rice.**)

» INTERURBAN: The "Interurban" going to Galveston

INTERURBAN: On December 5, 1911 the Galveston-Houston Electric Railway commenced operations. This electric train offered commuter service between these two cities. Called the "Interurban," passengers paid $1.25 for the one hour and forty minute ride. The line was very popular due to its fast and frequent service. Unfortunately, the train's owner fell on hard times during the Great Depression and filed for bankruptcy. The Interurban made its last run in 1936. [5]

INVERNESS: The Inverness Golf Club is located in the Scottish Highlands. This old course is famous for its extremely difficult 475-yard dogleg 14th hole. There is another possibility for this street. According to information from Robin Elverson Realtors, it was named for the Toledo, Ohio country club made famous for first allowing professional golfers to enter the front door of the facility, use the locker rooms and eat at the restaurants during the 1920 U.S. Open Golf Tournament. [6]

INWOOD: The Inwood Country Club is located on Jamaica Bay in the New York town of Inwood. The course here hosted the 1921 PGA championship and the 1923 U.S. Open. The 10th hole, a 106-yard 3 par, is the shortest hole ever played in U.S. Open history. [7]

IOWA SCHOOL: This road once led to the Iowa Colony School. Iowa Colony was founded in 1908 by the Immigration Land Company of Des Moines, Iowa. Two officers, G. I. Hoffman and Robert Beard, named the town. Originally it was rice farming country but by the 1970s developers turned it into a bedroom community of Houston. [8]

IRON LIEGE: This long-shot winner of the 1957 Kentucky Derby (he paid $18.80) was the beneficiary of one of the greatest mistakes in the history of the Run for the

Roses. Gallant Man was in the lead when jockey Billy Shoemaker misjudged the finish line and stood up in the irons. That was all the time needed for rival Bill Hartack on Iron Liege to win by a nose. [9]

IRONCLAD: This is an 18th century warship whose wooden infrastructure is covered with armored metal plates. A number of these ships fought in the War Between the States. The most famous were the Monitor and the Merrimack. (See **Merrimack.**) [10]

ISAACKS: Samuel – Born in Tennessee in 1804 he may be the first Jewish settler in Texas, arriving before Stephen F. Austin. He settled somewhere along the Brazos River. When Austin met Isaacks he was short of the full 300 families he promised would colonize Texas. Thus he talked Isaacks into joining the Old 300. In 1824 Austin awarded him a land grant across the Brazos from present day Rosenberg. Isaacks fought in the Texas Revolution. In 1855 he moved to Houston and finally to Seabrook where he died in 1878. [11]

ISAACKS: This Humble, Texas street recalls a family who settled in the area in the late 1880s. [12]

ISABELLA: Frank J. DeMeritt was a real estate developer in Houston in the 1920s. Most of his projects were in what we call Midtown today, i.e. between downtown and Rice University. He named this street for his wife Isabella MacGregor DeMeritt. One of our city's architectural jewels, Isabella Court (W. D. Bordeaux, 1929), is located on the northwest corner of Isabella and Main. [13]

ISETTA: Italian motorcycle designer Renzo Rivolta of Iso Rivolta began manufacturing this tiny vehicle in 1952. Meaning "Little Iso" this car was truth in advertising as it measured only 90" by 54" and had a top speed of 53 MPH. BMW obtained a license to manufacture them in Germany and produced 160,000 between 1955 and 1962. (See **Corvette.**) [14]

» **ISETTA: They really were small**

ISOLDE: Named for the heroine of a medieval love story, Isolde the Fair is the lover of Sir Tristram. Following an estrangement, Tristram is wounded in battle. He sends for Isolde but dies of despair when he believes she is not coming. Of course Isolde arrives, finds Tristram dead and dies of a broken heart. [15]

IVANHOE: He is a knight in Sir Walter Scott's romantic novel of the same name set in 12th century England.

IWO JIMA: This is a volcanic island in the western Pacific Ocean. During WW II there was a large Japanese air base here. The battle was one of the bloodiest of the Pacific campaign. The United States Marine Corps captured the island following a two-month (February-March, 1945) siege. Five marines placed an American flag on its highest point, Mount Suribachi, following the victory. Photographer Joe Rosenthal captured the moment on film. This Pulitzer Prize winning photograph is one of the most famous images of the War. [16]

"BOULEVARD OF HUNDREDS OF BENEFITS"

During the 1990s as Houston's Asian population increased dramatically, City Council voted to allow street signs in Chinese and Vietnamese to be placed on poles underneath the street's English name. (For unknown reasons a 2001 proposal to allow Koreatown to do the same was denied.) The purpose was to assist this influx of immigrants to find their way around. The rule was the Asian word had to be close to either the meaning of the existing street name or phonetically sound like the English street. So if you are driving in Chinatown or Little Saigon look for these signs:

- **Bellaire** – *Bai Li* – Boulevard of Hundreds of Benefits
- **Harwin** – *Hao Yun* – Good Luck
- **Clarewood** – *Wu De* – Martial Arts
- **Wilcrest** – *Wei Dao* – Traditional Moral Principles
- **Milam** - *Nguyen Hue* – Vietnamese king symbolizing patriotism
- **West Gray** – *Hai Ba Trung* – Vietnamese queens, Trung sisters, who defeated the Chinese in the 1st century A. D.
- **Anita** – *An Loc* – Battlefield site during Viet Nam War
- **Elgin** – *Yen Do* – Academic Excellence
- **Holman** – *Hung Vuong* – First King of Viet Nam
- **Travis** – *Tu Do* – Freedom [29]

J

J. B. LEFEVRE: He held the positions of City Manager and Finance Director of Baytown. [1]

J. R. TOWLES: Justin Richard Towles was born in Crosby, Texas, a small community east of Lake Houston. A talented baseball player he was drafted by the Houston Astros in 2004. He worked his was up through the Houston farm system and made his major league debut as a catcher on September 5, 2007. Fifteen days later he chalked up 8 runs batted in, a new Astro record. The street, Sunnyview Way, that ran in front of his childhood home, was renamed in his honor in 2007. [2]

JACINTOPORT: At the end of this street is a 62-acre terminal facility fronting on the Houston Ship Channel and operating under the Port of Houston Authority. It is a cargo handling and stevedoring firm.

JACK JOHNSON: Arthur John "Jack" Johnson was the best heavyweight boxer of his generation and the first black heavyweight champion. His record was 73-13-9-9 (wins, losses, draws and no decisions). Born in Galveston in 1878, he entered the ring as a young man and by 1902 had won 50 fights. He won the heavyweight belt in 1908, knocking out Tommy Burns, a white man, in a 14 round fight in Australia. To say the least this did not sit well with the white population in the pre-civil rights era. Like many athletes today his flamboyant lifestyle got him in trouble with the law. In his case, violating the Mann Act (transporting women across state lines for immoral purposed). He served a prison term for this. Johnson lost his title in a bout with white challenger, Jess Willard, in 1915. He was killed in a car wreck in 1946. [3]

JACK LONDON: He was an American who wrote novels and short stories whose main theme was the 1849 Yukon gold rush. His real name was John Griffith. Among his greatest and most readable works are *Call of the Wild* and *White Fang.* [4]

JACK: Baytown developer W. E Defee named three streets for his children: **Jack, James** and **Murrill.** (See **Defee.**) [5]

JACKSON BAYOU: This street and the 3.5 mile watercourse that meanders through Crosby, Texas are named for Humphrey Jackson. An Irish lawyer, he came to America in 1808 and settled on a sugar plantation in Louisiana. He fought at the Battle of New Orleans. Jackson moved to Texas in 1823 to join Stephen F. Austin's colony. Because of his legal background he became active in local government. He was killed by a falling tree while clearing his land in 1833. [6,7]

JACKSON: Abner – This Virginian and his business partner, James Hamilton, a former governor of Virginia, came to Texas in 1838 after suffering some business reversals in their home state. In 1844 the partners started Retrieve Plantation in Brazoria County. Jackson built Darrington Plantation nearby and founded the town of Lake Jackson. Things were going well until the War Between the States brought disaster to the plantation economy. He died in 1861 a broken man. [8]

» JACKSON: Abner Jackson Plantation House

JACKSON: This is one of several area streets we have named for a U.S. President. Andrew Jackson was the 7th American to hold the nation's highest office. [9]

JACKSON: This road is named for another lumber town in Montgomery County that faded away as the timber industry diminished in that area. Located on the Chicago, Rock Island & Pacific Railroad, Jackson received a post office in 1910 but saw it closed 15 years later. By 1946 it was a ghost town. [10]

JAMES BOWIE: Jim Bowie is revered by Texans for his heroic death at the Battle of the Alamo on March 6, 1836. He is eulogized by the Kingston Trio in their moving 1959 rendition of Texan Jane Bower's song *Remember the Alamo:* "Jim Bowie lay dying but his powder was ready and dry/Flat on his back Bowie killed him a few in reply." He is also remembered for his invention of the famous Bowie Knife. When he first arrived in Texas he searched futilely for lost treasure near the San Saba River, seeking what is known today as the Lost Bowie Mine. [11]

JAMES: (See **Jack.**)

JANE LONG: She is known as the "Mother of Texas" because she bore the first child of Anglo descent on Texas soil. Long was also a member of Stephen F. Austin's Old Three Hundred. [12]

JARDIN: One of developer Edward Crain's favorite places in the world was the Tuileries Gardens in Paris, France. They are probably the finest existing example of formal French gardens. Landscape architect Andre Le Notre designed them in the 1600s as part of the grounds of a palace for Catherine de Medici. Crain used the French word for garden to name this Southside Place street to remind him of this beautiful place. [13]

JARRARD: Ed J. – This gentleman was a real estate developer in West University Place in the 1920s. His partner was Preston R. Plumb. (See **Plumb.**) [14]

JEAN LAFITTE: Called everything from a bloody buccaneer to a gentleman privateer, Lafitte is one of Texas' more colorful characters. In fact no one knew the truth about the man called the "Prince of Pirates." His early life is a mystery but we do know he led a group of smugglers stationed at his stronghold in Barataria, south of New Orleans, from 1810 until 1814. In 1814 he and his men joined with General Andrew Jackson to defeat the British army at the Battle of New Orleans, allowing the Americans to win the War of 1812. For his valorous actions President James Madison pardoned him and his sailors of all crimes they had been accused of committing. In 1817 Lafitte moved his operations to Galveston Island. Unfortunately, some of his subordinates attacked American ships and the government put a price on his head. Not

» **JEAN LAFITTE: Sketch of the swashbuckling pirate Jean Lafitte**

wanting a confrontation with the U. S. Navy, Lafitte enlisted his best men and sailed off in his flagship the *Pride*, never to be heard from again. (See **Maison Rouge.**) [15]

JEANETTA: In 1886 the San Antonio & Aransas Pass Railroad completed its track into the Houston area. Management named a station, in what is now southwest Houston, Jeanetta. [16]

JEB STUART: James Ewell Brown Stuart was a cavalry commander in the Confederate Army during the War Between the States. He performed heroically at the two Battles of Bull Run, Antietam, Fredericksburg, Chancellorsville and Brandy Station. He was killed at Yellow Tavern on May 11, 1864. His death ranks with that of Thomas "Stonewall" Jackson as a major blow to the Confederate cause. [17]

JEBBIA: James – This gentleman operated a general store in Stafford in the early 1900s. (See **Stafford.**) [18]

JEFF DAVIS: Jefferson Finis Davis was an American politician born in 1808. A West Point graduate, he fought in the Mexican-American War (1846-8). While serving as a U. S. senator from Mississippi that state seceded from the Union and Davis was elected president of the Confederate States of America. He was captured after the war in 1865 and charged with treason. However, he was never tried. Davis died in 1889. [19]

JEFFERS: Leroy – This man was an early resident and landowner in Piney Point Village. [20, 21]

JEFFERSON: See sidebar **America the Beautiful,** page 176.

JEFFERSON: While there is a remote probability that this street was named for President Thomas Jefferson, Planning and Development feels it is more likely named for Jefferson Davis, President of the Confederate States of America, as an act of retribution against the oppressive Reconstructionist government. In 1870 these radical forces greatly expanded Houston's city limits to include much rural farmland. This allowed the military government to extract tithes of agricultural goods from the farmers. In 1874 when the Reconstruction government was overthrown, City Council pulled the city limits back dramatically. However, those boundaries would have included the area around Jefferson Street. Just to tweak the noses of the Yankees it is possible city officials decided to honor the fallen president of the CSA. [22]

JENSEN: Lawrence C. – See sidebar: **Houston Streets Named for Men Killed During WW1,** page 22.

JERSEY: This is the main street of the bedroom community of Jersey Village located west of town on the Hempstead Highway. Developed in 1953 on Jersey Lake by real estate promoters Clark W. Henry and N. E. Kennedy, the story goes that the latter gentleman once operated a dairy in the area and named the neighborhood after his Jersey cows. [23]

JESSICA: (See **Bhandara.**)

JETERO PLAZA: In the mid-1960s Houston began to outgrow William P. Hobby Airport, a facility constructed in 1937. A new airfield was planned north of the city. The original name was to be "Jetera Intercontinental Airport." However, a transcription error occurred and the name in the contract officially became "Jetero." Eventually "Houston" was substituted. Today we know the facility as the "George Bush Intercontinental Airport." [24]

JEWETT: This small central Texas town was an important railway center in the early 1900s. It was a station on the Houston & Texas Central Railroad. It is named for Henry J. Jewett, an early settler and attorney in Leon County. [25]

JIM HOGG: James Stephen Hogg was born near Rusk, Texas in 1851. While living in Quitman and assisting the sheriff, Hogg was shot in the back by a band of outlaws. Surviving the ambush, he earned a law degree. He ran for Attorney General of Texas in 1886 and won. In 1891 Hogg was elected governor of the state. An important law he passed was creation of the Railroad Commission. In 1895 Hogg returned to private practice and was able to build a substantial fortune from his profession and sage investments in real estate and oil and gas. He died in 1906. [26]

JIM WEST: This real estate developer named a number of streets in Bellaire including this one for himself. He is responsible for all of the female street names there such as Edith and Vivian to mention two. (See sidebar **The Bellaire Streets Named for Women,** page 20.) [27]

JOAN OF ARC: She was a French peasant girl who was instructed by mysterious voices to take up arms and liberate France from the English during the Hundred Years War. Although victorious at Orleans, she failed to take Paris. Joan was captured, tried for treason and burned at the stake in 1431. She was canonized in 1920. [28]

JOE LOUIS: He was one of the greatest heavyweight champions in the history of boxing. Called the "Brown Bomber" by his fans, Louis became heavyweight champion in 1937 with a knockout of James Braddock, the only fighter to have beaten Louis up until then. Louis held the title from 1937 until 1949. Of his 66 victories, 49 were by knockout (10 of those in round one). Unfortunately, he tried a comeback in 1951 but was annihilated by Rocky Marciano in the aging champ's last fight. Because of his service in the U. S. Army during World War II Louis is buried in Arlington National Cemetery. [29]

JOERGER: F. X. – He was a judge in Fort Bend in the 1920s who was very interested in improving the road system there. At that time there were no paved roads connecting Rosenberg, Needville and Guy. Joerger was instrumental in correcting this situation. He also paved the road to Powell Point and assisted on the construction of FM 1093 linking Houston, Clodine, Fulshear and Simonton. [30]

JOHLKE: These German immigrants arrived in the area northwest of Houston in the

1800s. Like many of their European neighbors they acquired acreage here and probably operated a farm. They were members of the Salem Lutheran Church and many of these early settlers are buried in the Salem Lutheran Cemetery just south of where this street is located. (See **Lutheran Cemetery.**) [31]

JOHN A.: His surname was Old and he was a chemist employed by the Humble Oil & Refining Company's huge facility in Baytown. He must have been a talented fellow as he blew glass into items used in the laboratory and built an organ for his church. [32]

JOHN COOPER: This Woodlands street leads to the 40-acre wooded campus of John Cooper School, a well regarded college preparatory academy. Founded in 1988 it is a co-ed institution with just under 1,000 students. [33]

JOHN DAVIS: See sidebar **Pirates of the Caribbean,** page 280.

JOHN F. KENNEDY: When Intercontinental Airport was being built, City Council decided to change the name of its major thoroughfare to honor the 35th President of the United States. However there was a minor problem. The road was named for the Drummett family who were large landowners in the area. They were perfectly happy with the name and prevented the city from changing it. So Council named the street on airport property JFK. Not long after, a developer to the south of Intercontinental named a street that connected to Drummett and JFK for the President. After Mr. Drummett passed away, the middle section was renamed. [34]

JOHN FREEMAN: A founding partner, along with John Crooker and R. C. Fulbright, of the law firm that today is called Fulbright & Jaworski, Freeman was a major force in the building of the Texas Medical Center. As a trustee of the M. D. Anderson Foundation, his vision and determination carried on after Anderson's death. (See **M.D. Anderson.**) [35]

JOHN HANCOCK: American patriot, merchant, delegate to the second Continental Congress and first governor of Massachusetts he is best remembered for his prominent signature on the Declaration of Independence. He was the first delegate to sign this historic American document. Because of his grand signature we today use the expression "John Hancock" to indicate anyone's signature. [36]

JOHN MARTIN: This Baytown resident was a Harris County Commissioner. Dr. Harvey Whiting was a famous forefather of Martin. (See **Whiting.**) [37]

JOHN SILVER: See sidebar **Pirates of the Caribbean,** page 280.

JOHNSON: G. E. – He was the first railroad station agent in Tomball (then called Peck). He worked for the Trinity & Brazos Valley Railway. The station was a depot, telegraph office, water station and a five stall round house for the locomotives. (See **Tomball.**) [38]

JOHNSON: Ralph A. – See sidebar **Houston Streets Named for Men Killed During**

World War I, page 22.

JOHNSON: Richard J. V. – The Texas Medical Center honored this well-known Houstonian with a street. In addition to serving as Chairman of the Board of that august organization, he was also Chairman of the Houston Chronicle Publishing Company. Born in San Luis Potosi, Mexico, Johnson attended the University of Texas. Following World War II he entered the newspaper business. He joined the *Chronicle* in 1957 as a copywriter. He spent the next 45 years of his career serving in numerous executive positions with that newspaper, being named Chairman and Publisher in 1990. Well known for his civic and charitable endeavors one colleague recalled, "Dick has probably attended more rubber chicken dinners than anyone else in Houston, but he always does it with a smile and a conviction to support worthwhile causes." [39]

JOHNSON: William – This Pasadena street is named for one of the area's earliest settlers. [40]

JOHNSON'S LANDING: This Galena Park street recalls a long gone dock on the Houston Ship Channel. In the late 1800s a merchant named H.H. Graff, who would later become the first mayor of that city, opened a grocery store here. [41]

» **JESSE JONES: Tombstone in Forest Park Lawndale cemetery**

JOLLY ROGER: See sidebar **Pirates of the Caribbean,** page 280.

JONES: Charles – (See **Porter.**)

JONES: Henry – One of Stephan F. Austin's Old 300, he was born in Virginia in 1798 and came to Texas in 1822. Jones settled on a league of land in what would become Fort Bend County. He was a farmer and rancher. He died in 1861 and is buried in the Jones Family Cemetery on the historic George Ranch. (See **Booth** and **A. P. George Ranch.**) [42]

JONES: Jesse H. – Very few Houstonians did so much for our great city as Jesse Holman Jones. Yet until the completion of the Jesse Jones Memorial Bridge on Beltway 8 over the Houston Ship Channel there was no road, street or alley named for this modest giant. It is impossible to list his accomplishments in a paragraph (read *Jesse H. Jones: The Man and the Statesman*

» **JESSE JONES: Builder of Old Texas Company Building**

by Bascom N. Timmons). He was an entrepreneur, visionary, real estate developer, banker, businessman and politician. He helped us get the Ship Channel, built the Texas Company building, was chairman of the National Bank of Commerce, owned the *Houston Chronicle* and was an early stockholder in Humble Oil & Refining (now Exxon Mobil). He and his wife, Mary, started Houston Endowment. During the Great Depression he was chairman of the Reconstruction Finance Corporation and Federal Loan Agency. He served as Secretary of Commerce during President Roosevelt's third term. Jones died in 1956 and is buried in Forest Park Lawndale Cemetery. [31]

JONES: L. D. – (See **Porter.**)

JONES: William J. – See sidebar **Houston Streets Named for Men Killed During World War I,** page 22.

JONES: Y. U. – This street is named for a man who settled in Thompsons about 1910. [43]

JUAREZ: Benito – This Zapotec Indian from Oaxaca became Mexico's greatest president. He was born in 1806. An excellent student, Juarez eventually attained a law degree. He served as a councilman in Oaxaca, a civil judge, federal deputy, governor of Oaxaca, minister of the interior and Supreme Court justice. In 1861 he was elected President of Mexico. From 1863 until 1867 he fought the puppet regime of Maximilian who had been installed by the French. When Maximilian was deposed in 1867, Juarez reassumed control of the government. He is remembered as the leader who returned his country to the Mexican people. [44]

JUBAL EARLY: See sidebar the **Antebellum Streets of River Plantation,** page 122.

JUERGEN: Edward F. – This German immigrant settled in the Cypress Creek area in the late 1800s. He built Juergen's General Store in 1898. Five years later he constructed a second location in the town of Cypress. That village has long been the "dance capital" of the area due to the dance-loving pioneers who lived there. Juergen built a dance hall on Hempstead Road in 1911 that operated until the Great Depression. (See **Siedel Cemetery.**) [33, 45]

JULIET: Named for one of the star-crossed lovers in William Shakespeare's 1597 play *Romeo and Juliet*, it is only appropriate that it intersects Romeo in this Pasadena neighborhood.

JULIFF-MANVEL: Once part of the antebellum Arcola Plantation, the town was named by John J. Juliff, an early pioneer, in the 1850s. It was a quiet little place until a dance hall and saloon opened in 1933. Before long Juliff was known for its gambling, drinking and prostitution. A local pundit gave it a nickname via a short poem – "Ditty Wa Ditty, ain't no town, ain't no city." By the 1960s police has closed most of the joints and Juliff faded into obscurity. (See **Manvel.**) [46]

JUNIOR COLLEGE: This street fronts on Wharton County Junior College. This state supported institution opened in 1946. [47]

JUNKER: Julius – This Rosenberg resident was a founder of KFRD, the first radio station in Fort Bend County, in 1948. This 1,000 watt station reached 22 surrounding counties. Visiting movie star Jack Palance once stopped by the station after hearing it play some Eastern European polka music. He was of Ukrainian origin. (See **Radio.**) [48]

ALL THINGS ENGLISH

Larry Nierth was a real estate developer in Houston in the 1940s and 1950s. He had a passion for all things English and named many streets in his projects for people and places associated with the British Isles. Prior to opening Afton Village, he developed Afton Oaks in what is now the Galleria area. Streets there with an English flare include: **Devon** and **Suffolk,** counties in England; **Banbury** and **Newcastle,** English towns; **Shetland,** islands off Scotland; **Staunton,** a British Shakespearian scholar and **Ivanhoe,** the hero of an 1819 Sir Walter Scott novel. He often added the suffix "shire" to names he liked (**Aftonshire** and **Oakshire**). Shire is a term once used to describe an administrative district in the United Kingdom.

His Anglican passion carried over to the streets of **Afton** Village. While Afton has no meaning, I believe Nierth thought it sounded English. **Alderney** is the northernmost of the larger Channel Islands. It is located in the English Channel between Britain and France and it has been inhabited since prehistoric times. The Romans settled there. The Germans captured Alderney during World War II but the population had been evacuated to England before the invasion. **Blandford** is a tiny borough in Dorsetshire, England. It is mainly remembered for a fire in 1731 that destroyed all but six of the town's homes. The predominant use of thatch and wood as constructions materials in that era often resulted in severe incendiary damage. **Coldstream** is a small burgh in Scotland. It was here in 1659 that General George Monk, 1st Duke of Albemarle, raised the famous Coldstream Guards. These soldiers are the personal bodyguards of the English monarch. They are easily recognized by their bright scarlet and blue uniforms topped with those impressive bearskin caps. **Hartland** may recall Hartland Point, a promontory near the entrance to Bristol Channel on the north coast of Devonshire, England. Islands off the point became hiding places for French privateers in the 17th century. **Northampton,** a country town in central England, has seen more than its share of British history. Battles occurred here during King John's fight against his barons, the War of the Roses and the Civil Wars of the 17th century. It was at nearby Fotheringhay Castle that Mary Queen of Scots was beheaded on February 8, 1587.

Finally, just north of Afton Village is Afton Woods. It seems Mr. Nierth carried his Anglican theme into this development as well. **Muirfield** Place recalls the great Scottish golf course. Jack Nicklaus was a British Open winner here. He was so impressed with the course he decided to name his own course in Ohio 'Muirfield Village'. **Turnbury** Oak is named after another great United Kingdom course. The British Open has been played there three times. In 1977 Mark Hayes shot the lowest round in tournament history, a 63, at Turnbury. [30]

JUTLAND: Off this North European peninsula the only major World War I naval battle between the British and Germans took place on May 31, 1916. While the English navy was the victor, the cost was high in tonnage and lives. [49]

AMERICA THE BEAUTIFUL

Mount Vernon (named for George and Martha Washington's Virginia plantation home) is a quiet little neighborhood in Pasadena built in the 1960s. The theme is patriotic from the old-fashioned white metal arched gateway scripted with *Mount Vernon* under which homeowners pass to enter their subdivision to the street names. On a visit here one will discover:

- **Dandridge,** Martha – Martha Washington, wife of President George Washington, maiden name was Dandridge.

- **Hancock,** John – His large and stylish signature on the Declaration of Independence made his name a synonym for "signature."

- **Jefferson,** Thomas – He was the third president of the United States and author of the Declaration of Independence.

- **Lafayette,** Marie-Joseph – Hero of the Revolutionary War, this French military officer served under George Washington.

- **Potomac** – Legend says General George Washington tossed a silver dollar across this Washington D. C. river. If that is true the Washington Nationals could sure use him in center field.

- **Revere,** Paul – "Listen my children and you shall hear
        Of the midnight ride of Paul Revere."

- **Shenandoah** – "Oh Shenandoah,
        I long to hear you.
        Away you rolling river.
        Oh Shenandoah,
        I long to hear you.
        Away, I'm bound away
        'Cross the wide Missouri.

- **Williamsburg** – This colonial town was ground zero for events in Virginia leading to the American Revolution.

- **Valley Forge** – This Pennsylvania village was the site of the Continental Army's encampment over the winter of 1777-8 during the Revolutionary War. [31]

K

KAISER: See sidebar **Fairbanks Could Have Its Own Concours d' Elegance and Road Rally,** page 140.

KANE: This near downtown street may be named for R. T. Kane who owned a stagecoach line that operated between Houston and Washington-on-the-Brazos in the 1840s. [1]

KARANKAWAS: This tribe of Indians lived along the Texas coast. Some linguists say the name translates to "dog lovers." They were nomadic and reported by the Spanish to be cannibalistic. The French explorer La Salle was most likely the first Caucasian to encounter these people in the mid-1600s. Battlefield casualties in encounters with the pirate Jean Lafitte and Stephen F. Austin's colonists lead to their demise. A few members were rumored to have escaped into Mexico in the 1840s. [2]

KAREN SWITCH: Postmaster John H. Bauer named this sawmill town after his youngest daughter, Karen in 1909. Like other communities in Montgomery County that arose because of the lumber boom in east Texas it also disappeared when the bonanza ran out. [3]

KARNES: See sidebar **Texas Heroes' Names for Houston Streets Urged in 72 Proposed Changes,** page 96.

KASSARINE PASS: This region of western Tunisia was the site of a battle in the North African campaign of World War II. The Axis forces captured the railway station at Kasserine on February 17, 1943. The Allies took it back 10 days later. (Once again a developer misspelled a Houston street name. In this case it is the fourth in the same neighborhood. (See **Remegan, Guadalcannal** and **Mount Batten**) [4]

KATEX: Located west of Houston this street is the combination of two words: Katy and Texas.

KATY MILLS: About 25 miles west of downtown Houston this street leads to a 1.3 million square foot retail and entertainment complex named Katy Mills. It is basically an outlet mall on steroids with huge stores like Bass Pro Shops Outdoor World where you can buy anything for the outdoorsman. [5]

KATY-FULSHEAR: Churchill Fulshear Jr. was one of Stephen F. Austin's Old 300 and a scout for the Texas Army during the fight for independence. He arrived in the area before 1824 and lived on the family plantation on the Brazos River near where the town of Fulshear is today. From 1850 until 1870 he operated a horse race track named Churchill Downs on the plantation. He died in 1892. (Do yourself a favor some weekend and drive to this quiet country village and enjoy some truly great brisket and sausage at Dozier's Barbeque & Market.) [6]

KATY: This freeway (I-10) as well as the Old Katy Road lead to the town of that name that lies directly west of Houston. Originally called Cane Island there are two stories about how it came to be called Katy. First is that since it was a station on the Missouri, Kansas & Texas Railway, nicknamed "the Katy," the name was chosen for the railroad. Second and more colorful is the name honors the beautiful wife of a local saloon owner. You choose. [7]

KEATS: John – He was a 19th century romantic English poet. He is best known for four odes he wrote in 1819 – *Ode on a Nightingale, Ode on a Grecian Urn, Ode on Melancholy* and *Ode on Indolence.* [8]

KEEGAN: This western Harris County road and bayou are named for James Kegans, Jr., an early settler of the area. Why the spelling is different is not known. The bayou itself is rather short, running only 11 miles from its headwaters near Clodine to its mouth at Braes Bayou close to Brae Burn Country Club. [9]

KEENAN: Established in 1906 as a shipping point for timber on the Gulf, Colorado & Santa Fe Railroad, Keenan's economy was dependent upon the logging industry. It was named for W. S. Keenan, a railroad agent for the G, C & SF RR. After the sawmill closed in the early 1930s Keenan faded into history. [10]

KELLEY: A. K. – He was born a slave on a plantation in Brazoria County in 1846. Following Emancipation he went to work for the Southern Pacific Railroad. He invested in real estate and at one time owned between 21 and 42 rent houses. In addition he was the owner of a laundry and Evergreen Negro Cemetery, where he is buried. Kelley was also a founder of Mr. Zion Baptist Church, one of the oldest places of worship in Houston. Not only does a street remember him but also Kelly Courts, a housing project for over 300 families, was named in his honor in 1942, 14 years after his death. Why that facility is misspelled is not known. (See **Kelly Courts.**) [11]

KELLNER: John G. – He plated Brookshire in 1893. It was the first town in the area. Kellner donated land for a train station on the Missouri, Kansas & Santa Fe Railroad.

He owned a farm that produced rice, cattle, peanuts and pecans. [12]

KELLY COURTS: This near eastside street leads to a public housing project named Kelly Courts. In 1942 it was named for A. K. Kelley although the powers that be at that time misspelled his name. (See **Kelley.**) [13]

KELTON: See sidebar **Texas Heroes' Names for Houston Streets Urged in 72 Proposed Changes,** page 96.

KEMAH: This southern boundary of the small beach town of the same name is an Indian word meaning "facing the winds" as the town fronts on Galveston Bay. From its founding in 1898 as a station on the Texas & New Orleans Railroad, Kemah was first known as Evergreen and later as Shell Siding because of the large amounts of oyster shells that were dredged from the bay and shipped around the area for paving materials. Once primarily a fishing village the city still celebrates its heritage with the Blessing of the Shrimp Fleet each summer. [14]

» KEMPNER: Grave marker in Galveston

KEMPNER: Isaac Herbert – Born in Cincinnati, his family moved to Galveston, where as a young man, he entered the cotton warehousing business. His connection with the cotton trade continued for more than 50 years. He invested in real estate and once served as mayor of Galveston. In 1906 he partnered with William Eldridge in establishing what eventually became the Imperial Sugar Company. He died a very wealthy man at the ripe old age of 94 and is buried in Galveston's Hebrew Benevolent Cemetery. (See **Eldridge** and **Imperial**) [15]

K–L

KEN HALL: He played football for Sugar Land High School from 1950 to 1954 and became the state's most prolific rusher of all time. He amassed a staggering 11,232 yards. Second best on the list is Midland Lee High School former star, Cedric Benson, with 8,423 yards. In 1953 Hall averaged 32.9 points and scored an average of 4.8 touchdowns per game during a 12 game season. During Hall's senior year alone, the man dubbed the "Sugar Land Express" rushed for 4,045 yards. Now 65 - "I've joined the society of Medicare and Social Security," he says - Hall has remade his name as part of another great Texas pastime: eating barbecue. Fifteen years ago he moved to the hill country town of Fredericksburg, where he opened Ken Hall's Barbecue Place. His specialty: "If you can't do brisket in Texas," he says, "you should close the doors. And we do brisket well." Until recently, he also announced local high school football games. [16]

KENDALL: W. E. – This gentleman was a sizable landowner on the east side of Houston prior to the turn of the 20th century. [17]

KENNEDY RANCH: Developers of Ranch Country in western Harris County used famous Texas ranches to name the neighborhood's streets. However, in this case they misspelled it. The correct spelling is Kenedy Ranch. John G. Kenedy founded this huge south Texas spread. The closest town is Sarita that is named for his daughter. [18]

KENNESAW MOUNTAIN: Around 900 A.D the inhabitants of this mountainous area northwest of Atlanta were known as the Mound Builders. Their descendents became the Creek Indians. On June 27, 1864, 100,000 Union troops under the command of Major General William T. Sherman faced off against 65,000 Confederates under General Joseph E. Johnson in what historians call the Battle of Kennesaw Mountain. Sherman suffered over 2,000 casualties compared to Johnson's 270. Although Sherman failed to defeat Johnson, this skirmish did little to slow the Union army's march to Atlanta. [19, 20]

KENNY: (See **Bhandara.**)

KENTUCKY DERBY: This is America's premier horse race. Always run on the first Saturday in May, the Derby is often called the "most exciting two minutes in sport." The race is modeled after the Derby at Epsom Downs in England that was the creation of the 12th Lord Derby. The 17th Lord Derby attended the 56th Run for the Roses in 1930 and saw Gallant Fox win the first leg of the Triple Crown that he went on to capture. (See other Derby winners throughout the text.) [21]

KESSLER: George – Houston's first clover leaf intersection opened at Memorial Drive at Waugh in the summer of 1955. It cost the city and Harris County $750,000 to construct. Kessler was a city councilman who was instrumental in getting this interchange built in his district. When the yellow ribbon was cut he drove the first car on it. [22]

KESSLER: Henry – He arrived in Texas in 1836 and was operating a general store called Kessler's Arcade a year later. Kessler was very active in civic affairs. He was treasurer of the Buffalo Bayou Company that sought to make that waterway navigable. Kessler served on the City Council and was a member of the Chamber of Commerce. He was also secretary of the Houston Post Oak Jockey Club. Originally called Susana Street and later Susan it was finally named Kessler in 1900. [23]

KEY: J. E. – It is possible this Heights area street is named for this gentleman who was an officer of the Stude Holding Company, a real estate developer that owned considerable acreage in this area. (See **Stude.**) [24]

KIBER: Faustino – (See **Angleton.**)

KICKAPOO: Located in northwest Harris County is this road as well as Kickapoo Creek for which the street is named. That stream runs three miles and empties into Spring Creek. [25]

KICKERILLO: Vincent D. – In 1957 this gentleman founded the Kickerillo Companies, a builder of custom homes around the Houston area. His homes may be found in more than 28 neighborhoods including Nottingham, Thornwood and Ponderosa Forest. It is not unusual for real estate developers to name streets after themselves. (See **Mott.**) [26]

KIDS R KIDS: This Conroe street leads to a child education business of the same name that focuses on intellectual development for pre-school age children. It was established in 1985. [27]

KILGORE: Constantine Buckley - This lawyer came to Texas in 1846 from Georgia. Although he was opposed to Secession he volunteered for the 10th Confederate Cavalry, eventually reaching the rank of adjutant general. He fought at Corinth and in the Kentucky Campaign. Kilgore was seriously wounded and captured at the Battle of Chickamauga. After the War he came to Texas and resumed his law practice. Entering politics he became a Texas State Senator, U. S. Congressman and a United States Judge in the Indian Territory. [28]

KILGORE: John M. – This Baytown citizen survived the Great Galveston Storm of 1900. Unfortunately his brother was drowned. Kilgore operated a brickyard from the 1930s until the 1950s. In addition he was a boat builder and Grand Master of the Cedar Bayou Lodge. [29]

KINCHELOE: William – This Wharton resident donated the land where this city's magnificent courthouse, designed by Houston architect Eugene Heiner, sits today. (See **Heiner.**)

KING ARTHUR: He is the mythical King of England who presided over the Knights of the Roundtable in the Arthurian legends.

KING RANCH: This is probably the most famous ranch in the world. Just its size, 825,000 acres, makes this south Texas spread memorable. However, there is much more to the story. In 1852 Richard King, a steamboat captain on the Rio Grande River, purchased a 75,000-acre Spanish land grant on Santa Gertrudis Creek. The ranch would eventually total more than 1.25 million acres. Its famous running W brand was introduced in 1860. Santa Gertrudis cattle, a crossbred of Shorthorns and Brahman, were developed here. Humble Oil & Refining Company discovered oil on the ranch in 1939. In 1946, Assault, a thoroughbred from the ranch won the Kentucky Derby by eight lengths and went on to capture the Triple Crown. That trophy is proudly displayed on the breakfast room table in the main ranch house. (See **Kentucky Derby, Triple Crown** and **Kleberg.**) (See photograph on page 182.) [30, 31]

KING RICHARD: King Richard I of England also know as Richard the Lionhearted is remembered for leading the 3rd Crusade (1189-1192) to the Holy Land. Richard failed to liberate Jerusalem from the Moslems but did reach an agreement to allow unarmed

» KINGWOOD: King Ranch headquarters near Kingsville, Texas

Christians to make pilgrimages. On his return he was captured, turned over to the Austrians and held for ransom. His freedom was purchased by raising taxes on the English commoners. [32]

KING: Wilburn Hill - This Georgian attorney paid a short visit to Texas in 1856, liking it so much he returned permanently in 1860. He joined the 18th Texas Infantry as a private. However, his soldiering skills soon propelled him to the rank of major general. He served in the Texas House of Representatives from 1878 until 1881. [33]

KINGWOOD MEDICAL: This north Harris County street leads to the Kingwood Medical Center. This 155-bed acute care hospital has been offering Kingwood residents inpatient, outpatient, surgical and specialty services since 1991. [34]

KINGWOOD: This north Houston street derives its name from the joint venture partners who developed the neighborhood of Kingwood. The "King" is from the King Ranch while "Wood" represents Friendswood Development Company, the real estate division of Exxon Mobil. [35]

KINKAID: Margaret Hunter – This Piney Point street is one of the few in Houston that honors a woman. The city had some odd laws in days of yore including one that prohibited married women from teaching in the public school system. Not to be denied, Kinkaid opened a private school in her home in 1904. By 1924 a new building was necessary so a school was built on Richmond Avenue. In 1957 the school was again moved, this time to the Memorial Villages area. It remains one of the city's premier college preparatory educational institutions. [36]

KIPLING: Rudyard – An English author born in Bombay, India, he wrote such famous novels as *Gunga Din, The Jungle Book, Captains Courageous* and his famous poem *If.* [37]

KIPP: Founded in Houston in 1994, KIPP Academy (Knowledge is Power Program) offers education to children from underserved communities of Houston. The curriculum offers academic and character skills from pre-kindergarten thru 12th grade. Today it is a nationwide movement with more than 50 schools. [38]

KIPP: J. H. – This family, along with the Bradfords, were the largest landowners in the Kemah area at the end of the 19th century. Kipp was chosen to establish a post office here. He applied under the name of "Evergreen" but there was already another Texas town with that moniker. So he asked the residents to pick a name. They chose Kemah, an Indian word meaning "facing the winds." (See **Kemah** and **Bradford.**) [39]

KIRBY CHAPEL: Barely a speck on the road map, this tiny village and its chapel were named by Jared and Helen Kirby in 1858. At first services were held in their home . Later the couple donated land for the chapel, school and cemetery. The building was torn down in 1969. The cemetery is all that remains. [40]

K–L

KIRBY: John Henry – He was called the "father of industrial Texas." Kirby owned the two largest lumber companies in east Texas. In 1895 the Houston Baseball Association was chartered with capital of $3,000 and Kirby as its president. In 1922 Kirby and Joseph Cullinan formed the American Anti-Klan Association to force the Ku Klux Klan to disband. He completed construction of his luxurious mansion at 2006 Smith in 1928. The Kirby Mansion had one of the city's most beautiful gardens. It contained baroque water parterres, conservatory, pergola, natatorium and a lake with a rustic bridge. He owned Camp Killcare on Armand Bayou where he and influential friends partied on weekends, swam, fished and hunted alligators. Kirby and Howard Hughes

» **KIRBY: John Henry Kirby**

Sr. were among the first Houstonians to own automobiles. The Great Depression took its toll on Houstonians including Kirby who filed for bankruptcy in 1933. [41]

KIRWIN: James Martin – This Galveston priest and civic leader was born in Ohio in 1872. While attending Mount St. Mary's Seminary he was incardinated in the Diocese of Galveston in 1892. Ordained in 1895 Kirwin arrived on the Island in 1896 and was appointed rector of St. Mary's Cathedral. He served as a chaplain in Cuba during the Spanish-American War. Kerwin is remembered as a hero of the Great Storm of 1900. He helped restore order, enforced martial law, disposed of the dead and aided hurricane victims. He conducted a study to improve fire protection in Galveston. Kirwin stared down the Ku Klux Klan who had threatened to tar and feather him. Sadly, the good Father died at age 56. [42]

KITTY HAWK: This small town on the Atlantic coast of North Carolina was the site of the Wright brother's first successful airplane flight on December 17, 1903.

KLEB: This pioneer family came to the Klein area from Germany. They were partners in the Kleb & Theiss Lumber Company, a firm that operated a sawmill off of Spring-Cypress Road. It was the last mill in Montgomery County to close due to depletion of the virgin timber in the area. Kleb Intermediate School is also named for this family. Early family members are buried in Roberts Cemetery. (See **Roberts Cemetery.**) [43, 44]

KLEBERG PLACE: Robert Justus Kleberg was a Corpus Christi lawyer who represented King Ranch owner Richard King. Upon King's death in 1885 his widow hired Kleberg to manage the ranch. He later married the King's youngest daughter Alice. Under his stewardship the ranch was expanded considerably. Among his major contributions to Texas were his battle to eradicate the cattle tick and the ceding of acreage for the creation of the township of Kingsville, Texas. (See **King Ranch.**) [45]

KLEE: Paul – This abstract Swiss artist is known for his fanciful use of color and lines on his modernistic canvases. [46]

KLEIN CEMETERY: This road leads to the Trinity Lutheran Cemetery. A number of early settlers who lived in this area are buried here. Many area streets are named for some of the prominent families interred here. (See **Klein, Theiss, Doerre, Mueller, Benfer, Mittlestedt** and **Strack.**) [30]

KLEIN CHURCH: This northwest Harris County road leads to the Trinity Lutheran Church. In 1874 a group of early settlers formed this house of worship. It became the religious, social and educational center of the area. Many of the founding families have area streets named for them. (See **Klein, Klein Cemetery, Benfer, Brill, Lemm, Theiss** and **Wunderlich.**) [31]

KLEIN: Adam – German immigrants pioneered this area in the 1840s. They were farmers and found the land here to be inexpensive and fertile. One of the more interesting of the Kleins was Adam, who left Germany in the 1850s and came to Texas. He went to California to make his fortune in the Gold Rush. Returning to the Houston area he invested his money in land, a cotton gin and gristmill. The town of Klein as well as numerous roads in the area are named after this early settler. The town's original name was Big Cypress for the huge stands of that tree that lined Cypress Creek. [47]

» KLEIN: Adam Klein tombstone

KLOECKER: Henry – In the 1880s this German immigrant settled near Cedar Creek and opened a cotton gin. The family sold the business in 1902-3 to a businessman in Navasota. (See **Cedar Creek.**) [48]

KLUGE: This family of German immigrants settled northwest of downtown near Cypress Creek, an area popular with people from Europe. Some of the family members are buried in Borgestedt Cemetery off Huffmeister Road including Hedwig, Herman, Edward and Clara. (See **Borgestedt Cemetery.**) [49]

KNEITZ: Louis – This early Fairchilds settler arrived from Czechoslovakia. (See **Fairchilds.**)

KNIGGE CEMETERY: This small burying ground contains the remains of several members of the Knigge family including Gottlieb (1862-1936), Minna (1857-1901), Saul (1825-1894) and Johanna (unreadable dates). The cemetery remains in use today with graves as recent as 2003. [50]

KNIGHT'S COURT: This Fort Bend County street runs in front of Elkins High School. The school's mascot is a medieval knight. [51]

KNOLLWOOD: The Knollwood Country Club of Elmsford, NY was established in 1894. Augustus T. Gillender, a New York attorney, purchased 75 acres upon which to construct this Westchester County club. The *crème de la crème* of New York society flocked to join the organization. The 19th Hole at most country clubs is the bar where golfers retire after a round to enjoy a round. However, a unique feature of Knollwood is that there is actually a 3-par 19th hole used for tiebreakers. [52]

KNOWLTON: Charles – This Englishman arrived in Baytown in 1873 to work for his father-in-law Thomas Wright's brickyard. (See **Wright.**) [53]

KNOX: Knox Briscoe Howe was a real estate developer here in the 1940s. He was a descendant of Harrisburg founder John R. Harris, and first Chief Justice of Houston Andrew Briscoe. [54]

KOBAYASHI: Mitsutaro – This Japanese rice farmer arrived in Webster, Texas in 1906. He was very successful in his agricultural ventures. In 1913 he asked his family in Japan to send him a bride. Moto Shigeta, daughter of a prominent whale oil dealer, arrived and the couple was married. She was renowned for her skills in flower arranging, calligraphy and poetry. Moto also had a reputation as an excellent cook. [44]

KOBS: Fertile land and plenty of fresh water were among the reasons so many German immigrants settled in the area surrounding Tomball, Texas. Among these were the Kobs. Friedericke Kobs (1863-1926) is interred in the Salem Lutheran Cemetery. (See **Lutheran Cemetery.**) [55]

KOBS: William – A German immigrant, he arrived in the Tomball area in the 1840s. The

K–L

family owned a large tract of land and in 1933 oil was discovered on their farm creating a rush of drilling in the area and a boomtown atmosphere. Kobs Road remembers this family. [56]

KOCH: John or Ludwig – Many German immigrants settled in the area near what is today Addicks Dam & Reservoir. I don't know when John arrived here but he was buried in the Koch-Schmidt Cemetery, the earliest in the area, in 1854. Other streets here named for early settlers, many of whom were related, include **Brandt** (Frederick and Katherine), **Quade** (Emil and Amelia) and **Matzke**. Sophie Addicks Eggling was the sister of Henry Addicks while her sister Dorothea was married to Frederick **Kobs**. (See **Addicks, Eggling** and **Kobs**.) [57]

KODES: Jan – This Czech tennis pro won the French Open in 1970 and 1971 and Wimbledon in 1973. [58]

KOHRVILLE: This small community southeast of Tomball was begun by a group of free slaves from Alabama who acquired property here and worked in the sawmills in nearby Louetta. **Hufsmith-Kohrville** road is named for Paul Kohrmann. As is often the case this German immigrant was the town's first postmaster. At times in the past the town was named Korville and Pilotville. [59]

KOINM: This immigrant family owned land in the Aldine area where this street is located today. Many people of Swedish and German heritage found this area to their liking. [60]

KOLBE: Carl – This gentleman was a German immigrant who moved into the Memorial/Spring Branch area in the 1830s. He is considered the first resident of Spring Branch. (See **Spring Branch**.) [61]

KOVAR: J. M. – This gentleman was an early resident of Fairchilds. (See **Fairchilds**.) [62]

KRAHN: This family was among the many German immigrants who settled in the Cypress area in the mid-to-late 1800s. [63]

KRASNA CEMETERY: Far western Fort Bend County was settled in the mid-1800s by immigrants from Slovakia. Krasna means "beautiful" in Hungarian and recalls a neighborhood in Kosice, Slovakia. Most of the persons buried here have Slovakian surnames including Dujka, Krnicko, Jecmenek, Vaclau and Zotyka. [64]

KRESS: Samuel H. – He founded the S. H. Kress 5 & 10 store chain in 1897. It became one of the foremost retailing operations in America in the early to mid 20th century. The storefronts are remembered for the use of architecture that fit into the context of the streetscape. As an example, the San Antonio, Texas store built in 1939 resembled a Spanish mission while a 1938 store in Miami features the Art Deco style of Miami's South Beach area. [65]

KRUEGER: Much of the land around Hockley, Texas was settled by German immigrants in the 1800s. The Krueger family was among them and owned land in northwest Harris County. Some of the early family members are interred in nearby Roberts Cemetery. (See **Roberts Cemetery.**) [57]

KRUEGER: Walter – He was the consummate soldier and the only man to rise from private to general in U. S. military history. He fought in the Spanish-American War (1898), Philippines-American War (1898), Pancho Villa (1916) and World War I (1917-18). During World War II he commanded the 6th Army and saw action at New Britain, Admiralty Islands, New Guinea, Layet and Luzon. Krueger was awarded the Distinguished Service Cross, Legion of Merit and Army Distinguished Service Medal. He retired from military service, settled in San Antonio and wrote *From Down Under to Nippon: the Story of the 6th Army in WW II.* [66]

KRUG: The Krug families were land owners in the area west of Tomball, Texas. They, like many of their neighbors, emigrated from Germany during the mid-1800s. Many of them are interred in Salem Lutheran Cemetery just east of where this street is located. The tombstones of Heinrich (1861-1911) and Eva (1881-1910) are inscribed in German. (See **Lutheran Cemetery.**) [67]

KRUGER: William – The 1850 U. S. Census of north Harris County lists a 44-year-old farmer by this name living in the area. A German immigrant, like many of his neighbors, it is likely this street is named for him. [68]

KUHLMANN: Johann F. and Theo H. – In the 1880s these brothers and their families operated a dairy farm in the area we now know as Riverside Terrace, east of Hermann Park. [69]

KUSTOM KASTLES: This 40-year old residential construction company has built more than 1,000 homes in the Houston area since 1962. In 1997 Webster-based Tribble & Perry, Inc. acquired Kustom. [70]

KUYKENDAHL: Henry A. – This early German immigrant was the founder of the German Society of Texas in 1840. The Kuykendahl family lived along Cypress Creek. [71]

KWIK KOPY: The headquarters of this Houston retail office machine rental and Xeroxing store is on this street. [72]

KYLA: (See **Bhandara.**)

KYLE: W. J. – He along with his business partner, Benjamin F. Terry, purchased the Oaklawn Plantation from Samuel May Williams in 1853. They changed the name to Sugarland Plantation. It was located where the town of that name is today. (See **Oaklawn** and **Williams.**) [73]

K-L

LAISSEZ LES BON TEMPS ROULEZ
(LET THE GOOD TIMES ROLL)

Why go all the way to New Orleans when the "Big Easy" can be found in Clear Creek Village off the Gulf Freeway on the way to Galveston? Developed in the 1960s this neighborhood's streets are all named for famous places in and around New Orleans. **Acadia** is a region in Canada where, during the French-Indian War, many Acadians immigrated to Louisiana. Our word "Cajun" is derived from Acadian. **Audubon** is the toniest Uptown street as well as the name of the city's most beautiful park. **Burgundy** is a street in the French Quarter. It is pronounced "bur-gun-de" not like the French wine region of Burgundy. **Chalmette**, a town down river, is where the Battle of New Orleans was fought. **Claiborne** is one of the city's major thoroughfares. **Lafayette** was a French soldier who fought with George Washington as well as a town in Louisiana. **La Salle** claimed Louisiana for the French in 1682. **Metairie** is an upscale bedroom community that abuts New Orleans. **Ponchartrain** recalls the lake. **Rampart** street is the downtown, lakeside border of the French Quarter. **Royal** is the Quarter's major shopping street. Just one question, how did **Aggie** get in this neighborhood? [32]

LA PORTE: Real estate developers, I. R. Holmes, T. W. Lee and brothers A. M. and J. H. York named this Houston Ship Channel town in 1892. In French it means "the door," possibly a reflection on its location at the head of the waterway. St. Mary's Seminary, the oldest Catholic theology school in Texas, started here in 1900. In 1954 this institution of religious schooling moved to Houston where its campus is on Memorial Drive. [1]

LA SALLE: Rene Robert Cavelier Sieur de – Born in Rouen, France in 1643, he became one of the greatest explorers of the North American continent. In 1682 he completed a trip down the Mississippi River and claimed all of the lands in its watershed as property of King Louis, naming the area "Louisiana" for his regent. In 1684 he attempted a return voyage but missed that great river's mouth and was wrecked in Matagorda Bay on the Texas coast. He tried to lead the survivors overland to Canada but was murdered near Navasota, Texas by his own men. [2]

LABRANCH: As the last official act of his administration, President Andrew Jackson appointed Alcee Louis LaBranche as *charge d'affaires* from the United States to the Republic of Texas. LaBranche served in this position from 1837 to 1840. He was the first foreign minister to recognize the Republic of Texas. He returned to his native New Orleans and was elected to Congress. During the campaign he was challenged to a duel (the only one of his career) and killed his opponent, a Whig from Baton Rouge. LaBranch Street (misspelled since being placed on our city map in 1839) was formerly known as Milton Street after John Milton, the author of *Paradise Lost*. (See **Milton.**) [3]

LACOSTE LOVE: Jean Rene "Crocodile" Lacoste, a Frenchman, is better remembered as the inventor of the short-sleeved cotton tennis shirt with the crocodile logo than for his tennis accomplishments. However, he won the French Open three times (1925, 1927, 1929), the U.S. Open twice (1926, 1927) and Wimbledon twice (1925, 1927). [4]

LAFAYETTE: It is named for the hero of the French Revolution, Marquis de Lafayette. He had been touring the eastern United States and impressed the citizens of Easton Pennsylvania who founded a college in 1824 in his honor. It opened its doors in 1832 and in 1866 became the first American institution of higher learning to offer a degree in civil engineering. [5]

LAFAYETTE: See sidebar **America the Beautiful,** page 176.

LAFAYETTE: See sidebar *Laissez les bon temps roulez* (Let the good times roll), page 188.

LAIRD: D. C. – This soldier was the Captain of Company G of the 14th Texas Volunteer Infantry. He saw action with Walker's Texas Brigade during the War Between the States. [6]

LAKE CONROE: About one hour north of Houston is Lake Conroe. This 21 mile long, 21,000 acre body of water acts as a backup water supply for our city as well as a beautiful recreation area. This lake is also known as Honea Reservoir. [7]

LAKE HOUSTON: This parkway is named for Lake Houston, a man-made lake owned and operated by the City of Houston. Construction of the 62-foot high earth-fill San Jacinto Dam began in November 1951. The project was completed in December 1953. The lake covers an area of 12,240 acres. [8]

LAKESHORE: Located in the small community of El Lago (Spanish for "the lake") near Galveston Bay, this street recalls the village's location – abutting Clear Lake and Taylor Lake. [9]

LAKEWOOD: Lakewood Yacht Club is one of the oldest yacht clubs in the Houston/ Galveston Bay area. It was founded in 1955. Since 1995 the club has sponsored Keels & Wheels *Concours d' Elegance,* the largest gathering of classic cars and wooden boats in the U. S. Occurring the first weekend of May, the event is open to the public. Thousands of enthusiasts and collectors walk the beautiful grounds admiring Duesenbergs, Stutz Bearcats, Shelby Cobras and Chris Crafts. [10]

LAMAR FLEMING: He was one of three original partners and the eventual president of the Houston based cotton-trading firm of Anderson, Clayton & Company. Through his association with Monroe D. Anderson, Fleming was actively involved in the creation of the Texas Medical Center. In his honor a street in that world-class complex was named for this civic leader. [11]

LAMAR: Mirabeau Buonaparte – He arrived in Texas in 1835. Lamar volunteered for the Texas army and was a hero at the Battle of San Jacinto because his cavalry charge saved the lives of Thomas Rusk and Walter Lane. He was elected President of the Republic of Texas in 1838. (See **Collinsworth.**) (See photograph on page 191.) [12]

LANAI: See sidebar **Bali Hai May Call You,** page 322.

LANCELOT & SIR LANCELOT: He was the most famous and bravest of King Arthur's Knights of the Roundtable. He became Queen Guinevere's lover, precipitating the downfall of Arthur's kingdom.

LANDRUM: John – He was an early settler near Plantersville and one of the planters the town was named for. [13]

LANGHAM CREEK: This creek rises in northern Harris County and flows 15 miles to its mouth on Bear Creek in Bear Creek Park. (See **Bear Creek.**) [14]

» **LAMAR:** Mirabeau B. Lamar's grave in Richmond, Texas

LANGTRY: See **Roy Bean**.

LARCHMONT: Because so many streets in River Oaks are named for famous country clubs, it is likely that this lovely lane is also for a well-known golf course. Information at the River Oaks Property Association tends to back this claim. However, I cannot find any country club with this name that still exists and was founded before 1923 (when River Oaks was platted). The same problem exists for **Meadowlake, Overbrook** and **Wickersham.** [15]

LARUE: A tragic tale, possibly apocryphal, involves a young Houston girl, her grandfather and the City of Houston. According to the *Houston Post,* in 1904 LaRue Sachs was a resident of the 4th Ward. One day she was run over and killed by a streetcar. The city settled with her grandfather, paying him $2,000. He used the funds to buy a farm just west of the Ward boundary. He developed the property and in 1919 added a north-south street that intersected West Dallas. He named this street for his dearly departed granddaughter and donated the right of way to the city. The story goes that city officials gladly accepted the gift and immediately raised his taxes because of the improved status of the property. So much for appreciating the civic minded! [16]

LATEXO: This drive recalls a small town between Crockett and Palestine that was located on the International-Great Northern Railroad that extended to Houston. It was a major shipping point in East Texas. Latexo's odd name is a contraction of Louisiana & Texas Orchard Company. [17]

LATHAM: Ludowick Justin – This ship captain arrived in Houston in 1839. In 1873 after retiring from sea life he opened a furniture store on Main Street that eventually became the dominant company in that business. Latham was the first merchant to install paved cement sidewalks in front of his store. [18]

K-L

LAUDER: This family owned land in the Aldine area. [19]

LAURA KOPPE: This is one of the mystery street names in our city. It has been on the plat maps since 1940. Most likely it was named for a long-time Houston resident. An obituary in the *El Paso Times* on June 18, 1928 reports the passing of a woman with this name. It states she lived in Houston and was visiting her daughter in El Paso when she died. The *Times* also reports she was a member of the First United Methodist Church and Eastern Star although neither organization has any record of her. So the question is, what did she do to merit a major street named in her honor? [20]

LAUTREC: Henri de Toulouse – One of France's greatest modern artists, he is re- membered for his paintings of the nightlife of Gay Paree. He loved Montmartre and painted the people of that Paris neighborhood – dancers, singers and prostitutes. Lautrec often traded his paintings for sexual favors from the latter group, a practice that eventually resulted in his death from syphilis combined with alcoholism. [21]

LAVER LOVE: Rod Laver was one of the world's greatest tennis players. This redhead- ed Australian is the only player to win the Grand Slam (U. S., Australian and French Opens plus Wimbledon in the same year) twice (1962, 1969). He claimed 11 Grand Slam titles and was the first tennis professional to win $1,000,000 in prize money. Today the Australian Open is played in the Rod Laver Tennis Center in Melbourne. Your au- thor once had the pleasure of meeting this great champion at the River Oaks Tennis Tournament. Laver won the River Oaks tournament four times (1961, 1962, 1972, 1974). The tennis term "love" means one player has a score of zero in the game being played such as "40 love." [22]

LAWRENCE MARSHALL: Located just north of Hempstead, this road is named for the late car dealer of the same name. The dealership was the home of the famous "Clobberthon" phone that pitchman and later owner, Ray Childress, would use to say "We clobber big city prices." When Marshall opened, Hempstead had no large businesses. He employed over 250 people and had revenues of $85 million. The eco- nomic collapse of 2008-9 forced the company out of business and had severe eco- nomic repercussions on the town.

LAWRENCE: Oscar Martin Carter was the developer of the Houston Heights. He raised a considerable amount of his capital from investors in and around Boston. Randy Pace, Historical Preservation Officer of the City of Houston and expert on the Heights, told me that Carter named this street for Lawrence, Massachusetts. (See **Heights** and **Carter.**) [23]

LAZY LANE: This is probably the most beautiful street in River Oaks as well as its most prestigious address. Mike Hogg, one of the three developers of that subdivi- sion, named it. He and his sister Ima lived on Lazy Lane. Miss Hogg later donated her home to the Museum of Fine Arts, Houston, and today it houses the Bayou Bend Collection of American furniture. [24]

LEAFTEX: See sidebar **Howdy Tex,** page 263.

LEAGUE: J. C. – In 1893 this gentleman purchased the land where League City is located today. He laid the town out on the Galveston, Houston & Henderson rail line and named it for himself. It was an agricultural center in its early years. [25]

LEE: Paul U. – Lee street is named for this early Baytown funeral home director. [26]

LEE: T. W. – In 1892 a group of investors founded the seaside resort town of La Porte. This gentleman was among them. Others include I. R. Holmes for whom North and South **Holmes** are named and A. M. and J. H. York who failed to have a street in their honor. (See **La Porte.**) [27]

LEEK: George W. – This man is another veteran of the Battle of San Jacinto. He was under the command of Captain William Fisher. [28]

LEELAND: W. W. – It is possible this street is named for an early Houston resident who lived in the Sixth Ward. W. R. Baker developed that area in 1858. Mr. Leeland acquired two blocks of land there from Baker on January 31, 1859. The street name first appears on the 1866 map spelled as "Lealand." By 1873 it was corrected to read "Leeland." [29]

LEGGETT: (See **Zuber.**)

LEHAVRE: This French port was almost totally destroyed during World War II in fighting between German and English armies. Over 5,000 citizens died and 12,000 homes were leveled. Despite this devastation, LeHavre became one of the largest replacement depots in the European Theater with thousands of American troops arriving on their way to the front. [30]

LEHIGH: In 1865 industrialist Asa Packer, builder of the Lehigh Valley Railroad and owner of a coal-mining empire, founded this university in Bethlehem, Pennsylvania. [31]

LEMAC: For some reason developers like to name streets for words that are spelled backwards. Lemac, camel spelled backwards, is one of several thoroughfares that are a result of this odd habit. (See **Saxet** and **Remlap.**) [32]

LEMKE: Colin G. – See sidebar **Houston Streets Named for Men Killed During World War I,** page 22. [33]

LEMM: The Lemm and Schmidt families have owned this Cypress Creek area ranch since 1861. It is registered with the Texas Department of Agriculture under the Family Land Heritage Program, an honor reserved for farms and ranches with a continuous family ownership of more than 100 years. William Lemm Sr. owned 160 acres of land where the Goodyear blimp base was located. He was a founder of Trinity Lutheran

Church in Klein and is buried in the Budde Cemetery. (See **Lutheran Church** and **Bulde Cemetery.**) [34]

LENTE: See sidebar **Learn a Foreign Language on Your Morning Walk,** page 125.

LEONIDAS: The Trinity River Lumber Company owned this sawmill town and employed most of the residents until the mill closed in 1924. Like other Montgomery County villages tied to the logging industry it faded away and is a ghost town today. [35]

LEVERIDGE: John G. – This East Bernard resident owned a general store there in the early 1900s. He also operated a bank at the same location. [36]

LEVERKUHN: This old Houston family arrived here in the 1840s from Germany. They owned property south of Washington Avenue and north of Buffalo Bayou where this street is today. [37]

LIBBEY: Frank Sharp named this street in Oak Forest Addition for his daughter, Elizabeth. (See **Frank Sharp.**) [38]

LIBERTY: This road was once the main artery to the town of Liberty in east Texas. Americans settled this area as early as 1818. Sam Houston practiced law here from 1830 until 1850. In the early years Liberty was a port on the Trinity River as well as a stop on the Texas & New Orleans Railroad. In 1925 oil was discovered nearby and Liberty became a boomtown. During World War II German prisoners were incarcerated here at the fairgrounds. [39]

» LIGHT COMPANY: Deep Water Power Plant in the 1920s

LIEDER: Most likely this street remembers a landowner in the Spring Cypress area who sold 100 acres for $75 per acre to Cypress-Fairbanks ISD in 1940 to build a school. An article in the *Houston Chronicle* in 1942 called it "one of the most modern equipped and largest school buildings in Harris County." [40]

LIENDO PLANTATION: Early settler Leonard W. Groce named this Waller County plantation for its original owner Jose Justo Liendo in 1853. During the War Between the States it served as a prisoner-of-war camp for Union soldiers captured at the Battle of Galveston. Following the conflict General George Armstrong Custer camped here from September until December 1865. It is one of the few plantation homes in Texas that has been restored and may be visited today. [41]

LIGHT COMPANY: At the end of this industrial street, fronting on the Houston Ship Channel at the confluence of Buffalo and Vince Bayous stands the Deep Water Power Station. Opened in 1924, it is one of the oldest in the city. It is currently mothballed. Officials at Houston Lighting & Power (now Reliant Energy) named the street. (See photograph on page 194.) [42]

LILLJA: S. E. – Lillja was a Swedish immigrant who came to Texas via Chicago. He was a blacksmith who settled in the Aldine area. By the time he arrived Aldine had a number of Swedish and German settlers. The family owned land there and operated a poultry farm. (See **Aldine.**) [43]

LINA: She was the wife of Houston merchant and landowner Herman Eberhard Detering. (See **Detering** and **Eberhard.**) [44]

LINDLEY: Samuel and Joseph – See **Old Danville.**

LINDSEY: Reverend M. L. – This gentleman was the original pastor of the First United Methodist Church of Katy. This place of worship was established about 1900. Lindsey also served other Methodist churches in the area. [45]

LIPSCOMB: Abner Smith – He was Secretary of State in Mirabeau B. Lamar's Presidency of the Republic. He was also appointed associate justice of the Supreme Court of Texas in 1846 and re-elected again in 1851 and 1856. [46]

LITTLE BIGHORN: See **Crazy Horse, Custer** and **Sitting Bull.**

LITTLE CYPRESS: This tributary of Cypress Creek rises in Hockley, Texas and flows 14 miles to its mouth on Cypress Creek. It travels through stretches of coastal plain interspersed with forested areas of oak and pine. [47]

LITTLE JOHN: He was one of Robin Hood's merry men in Sherwood Forest.

LITTLE YORK: Now a suburb of Houston, Little York was once a small village on the

K-L

banks of Hall's Bayou north of downtown and east of the Eastex Freeway. [48]

LITTLE: See sidebar **Neighborhoods with Interesting Street Names,** page 104.

LIVELY: Located in a Sugar Land neighborhood with streets named Frontier, Old Fort, Settlers Way and Colony this street most likely is named for the schooner *Lively* that Stephen F. Austin and his band of colonists sailed from New Orleans to the mouth of the Brazos River in 1821. [49]

LIVERPOOL-HOSKINS MOUND: Liverpool was founded in 1837 in what became Brazoria County. It was named by a local character named Commodore Nelson for the seaport in England. For a time it was an important port on Chocolate Bayou for transshipment of goods to the Gulf of Mexico. Warren D. C. Hall became the first postmaster in 1846. The post office and Liverpool Cemetery (established 1837) have earned Texas Historical Markers. Hoskins Mound was a sulfur dome discovered in 1920. There was a small community here until the mine played out. The memory of Hoskins has faded into the mists of time. [50]

LOCHRIDGE: Thomas – He platted the townsite of Rosharon. Lochridge moved a cotton gin there from Houston to increase employment in the area. An ancillary benefit was the capability of the gin to generate electricity for Rosharon's first power plant. In addition he operated the first telephone exchange there. (See **Rosharon.**) [51]

LOCKE: This lane is named for Robert E. Locke, an early Houston settler. [52]

LOCKETT: Reese - (See **Salt Grass Trail.**)

» LOGAN: Camp Logan during World War 1

LOCKHART: Robert – He owned several large tracts of land in the 2nd Ward in the 1880s. [53]

LOCKHEED: On the property of William P. Hobby Airport, this short street honors one of America's greatest aircraft manufacturers. Some of their most famous airplanes include the WW II speed demon fighter, the P-38 Lightning, the commercial Constellation, the ill-fated Electra and the workhorse C-130 cargo carrier. [54]

LOFTING WEDGE: See sidebar **A Neighborhood for Linksters,** page 318.

LOGAN: Situated near Memorial Park, this street is named for General John A. Logan, a veteran of the Civil and Mexican Wars. He was also elected a U. S. senator from Illinois. Logan is credited with establishing Memorial Day as a national holiday honoring those men and women who died in the service of our county. The U. S. Army constructed an emergency training center here in 1917 and called it Camp Logan. Virtually nothing remains today of this fort. Most of the structures stood where Memorial Park is located. (See photograph on page 196.) [55]

LOMAX SCHOOL: (See **Lomax.**)

LOMAX: This town and street are named for R. A. Lomax from Illinois who arrived in this area northwest of La Porte in 1895. He donated land for the school in the small community. [56]

LONGBOW: This was a favored weapon of medieval times. It revolutionized warfare by extending the range of firepower over the crossbow allowing archers to strike an enemy from a much farther distance.

LONGENBAUGH: This west Harris County road is named for a couple that owned approximately 8,000 acres in this area. The property was initially used for rice farming but its value increased greatly when oil and gas were discovered there. In their will the family established the Longenbaugh Foundation. The income generated from the assets is used for cancer research. [57]

LONGFELLOW: Henry Wadsworth - He is one of the most famous American poets of the 19th century. Among his works are *The Song of Hiawatha, Evangeline* and *The Wreck of the Hesperus.* J. S. Cullinan named this Shadyside neighborhood street for Longfellow, his favorite poet. [58]

LONGHORN: This street in western Harris County recalls the famous Texas bovine of the Old West. It is located on the former site of the LH-7 Ranch. Emil Marks, known as the Longhorn King of Texas, owned that spread. (See **Marks.**) [59]

LONGHORN CAVERN: See sidebar **The Most Scenic Spots in Texas,** page 310.

K-L

LONGMONT: Mary Catherine Farrington Miller, daughter of Tanglewood developer William G. Farrington, says their family had a summer home in Estes Park, Colorado. They would pass through Longmont on the way to the house. Her father liked the name and since he wanted street names that were easy to spell and remember, he chose it over Estes Park. [60]

LOOSCAN: Michael – This Welshman was a Houston City Attorney. He was a close friend of James S. Hogg and was the campaign manager of Hogg's successful run for governor in 1890. Because of his help in that election, the governor's son, Mike Hogg, named this River Oaks street in Looscan's honor. It is likely that Mike Hogg was named after Looscan. Houston does not have many streets named for women but this one should have been. Adele Briscoe Looscan, his wife, is just too important to ignore. Born in 1848, she was a member of the Ladies Reading Club and a founder of the Houston Public Library. A historian and author, Mrs. Looscan was president of the Texas Historical Association. Looscan Library was named in her honor. [18]

» **LOOSCAN:** Adele Briscoe Looscan

» **LORD NELSON:** Statue in Gibralter near Trafalgar

LORD NELSON: Admiral Lord Horatio Nelson is England's greatest naval hero. By age 20 he was in command of his own ship. He fought in the Battles of Cape St. Vincent, Santa Cruz de Tenerife, Nile, Copenhagen and Cadiz. However, Lord Nelson will always be remembered for his great victory at the Battle of Trafalgar. On October 21, 1805 Nelson engaged the navies of France and Spain off Cape Trafalgar. By nightfall his 27 ships had sunk 22 of his enemies 33 vessels and captured their admirals. Not one British ship went down. Unfortunately, he was killed during the engagement but not before knowing victory was his. Nelson's body was placed in a keg of rum and sent home to England for burial. His statue stands atop a column in Trafalgar Square in the heart of London. [61]

LORRIE LAKE: In the Memorial neighborhood of Sandalwood there are two lakes. In the 1950s the developer named them and the streets for female family members Lorrie and Robin (**Robin Lake.**) **Patti Lynn** is also named for a family member. [62]

LOST MAPLES: See sidebar **The Most Scenic Spots in Texas,** page 310.

LOTUS: See sidebar **Bali Hai May Call You,** page 322.

LOU-AL: Sources say this horseshoe shaped Hedwig Village street was named by combining the names of two residents, Louise and Alfred Riedel. [63]

LOUETTA: This north Harris County street reminds residents of Louetta Station located on the Burlington Rock Island rail line that passed through this Spring-Cypress area in the early 1900s. The main industries were sawmills and cotton gins. Today it is a ghost town. [64]

LOUIE WELCH: He was mayor of Houston from 1964-1974. An auto parts storeowner and real estate speculator, Welch was one of the more colorful of our mayors. His greatest accomplishment was insuring the city had ample water supplies to assure its continued growth. The signing of agreements with the Trinity River Authority in 1964 and the Lake Livingston project in 1973 achieved this goal. [65]

LOUIS: (See **Kneitz.**)

LOUISIANA: Although we have streets named for 48 of our 50 states (no South Carolina or Maine), this one was named to honor a state toward which Texans felt a strong debt of gratitude. Louisiana Street remembers the four men from that state who died at the Alamo, including Jim Bowie. (See **Caroline.**) [66]

LOURDES: Near the Fort Bend County village of Frydek is St. Mary's Catholic Church. Like many Catholic churches it has quite a beautiful grotto. The street leading to it is named for one of the most famous grottos in the world, Lourdes. This small French town in the foothills of the Pyrenees is famous for the Marian apparitions of our Lady of Lourdes that appeared to Bernadette Soubirous in 1858. As a result the grotto there developed into a major Christian place of pilgrimage. Annually it is visited by some 5 million people. (See **Frydek.**) [67]

LOVE: See sidebar **Tennis or Golf, Anyone?,** page 348.

LOVETT: Robert S. – Many people believe this street is named for Dr. Edgar Odell Lovett, the Princeton University mathematician and astronomer who became the first president of Rice Institute (now University) in 1908. However, it actually recalls this early Houston attorney who resided at the corner of Main Street and Gray. He was a founding partner of the law firm we call today Baker & Botts. [68]

LUBBOCK: Francis Richard – He was an early Houston resident who acquired a 400-acre ranch south of town for $0.75 per acre in 1846. Lubbock served as the chief clerk of the Texas House of Representatives during the Second Congress. Sam Houston appointed him comptroller of the Republic. He was a founder of the Democratic Party in Texas. Lubbock became governor of the State in 1861, winning the election by only 124 votes. He stepped down as governor to serve on General Jeb Magruder's staff during the War Between the States. Eventually he became aide-de-camp to Confederate States of America President Jefferson Davis. Following the War he opened a mercantile business in the city. In 1878 he won election as State Treasurer and served five terms in that position. Lubbock retired from public service at the ripe old age of 80. [69]

LUCAS: James S. – This Englishman arrived in Houston in 1873. He owned James S. Lucas & Son, a construction company as well as a brick and cement manufacturing plant. His firm was the general contractor on the original Cotton Exchange building on Market Square. His residence on Chartres was unusual as it was built of bricks when most homes in Houston were wooden. [70]

LUCKEL: L. C. – He was one of three surveyors who platted Katy, Texas. [71]

LUCKENBACH: Jacob and August - German settlers arrived here in the 1840s. In 1886 postmaster August Engel named the place for these two brothers. The tiny town became known for its dance hall in the late 1800s. By the 1960s it was owned by one of August's descendants, Benno Engel. He sold it in 1971 to the man who would put Luckenbach on the map, John Russell "Hondo" Couch. This colorful character was a friend of Texas redneck rock musician, Jerry Jeff Walker. In 1973 Walker recorded his album, *Viva Terlingua,* here. Waylon Jennings turned a cut, *Luckenbach, Texas (Back to the Basics of Love)* into a huge hit song in 1977. Willie Nelson held his Fourth of July picnic here from 1995 until 1999. The dance hall remains a favorite honky-tonk hangout for musicians and their fans. [72]

LUELLA: Deer Park founder, S. H. West, named most of the early streets in this Ship Channel town. In this case the street recalls his youngest daughter. It is one of only three still on the map that he named. The other two are **P** and **X** Streets. Center was originally named West but changed later. The Shell Oil complex covers the majority of the early Deer Park streets. [73]

LUTHE: O.– This gentleman was a dairy farmer in Aldine in the early 1900s. [74]

LUTHERAN CEMETERY: This northwest Harris County road leads to the historic St. John Lutheran Cemetery. Founded in 1853 by settlers from Posen and Pomerania, Germany, it is still in use today. Other early area residents interred here include members of the following families: Kendig, Quade, Teske, Froehlich, Adam, Schuenmann and Zahn. A number of the gravestones here are written in German. Many contain the word *mutter* (mother) and the abbreviations *geb.* and *gest.* (born and died) followed by the respective dates. In 2002 the Texas Historical Commission placed a Historic Texas Cemetery marker here. (See **Lutheran Church** and **Lutheran School.**) [27]

LUTHERAN CHURCH: This road will take you to Salem Lutheran Church. In 1852 German settlers in this area founded this church. The congregation initially met in members homes. In 1857 they erected a wooden church. Later they built a larger framed building. That structure burned to the ground in 1964 and was replaced by the current facility. As late as 1930 services were conducted in German and the men sat on the left side of the nave with the women on the right. (See **Lutheran Cemetery** and **Lutheran School**.) [62]

LUTHERAN SCHOOL: In about 1870 members of the Salem Lutheran Church established a parochial school in this area near the Salem Lutheran Church. (See **Lutheran Church** and **Lutheran Cemetery**.) [73]

LYNBROOK: (See **Chimney Rock**.) [75]

» LYNCHBURG: Early photograph of the Lynchburg Ferry crossing

LYNCHBURG: Nathaniel Lynch was the first American settler in the Houston area in 1822. His land was at the confluence of Buffalo Bayou and the San Jacinto River. A town sprang up that was called Lynchburg and his ferry service plied the waters of the bays, bayous and rivers. Originally called "Lynch's Ferry" today we know it as the Lynchburg Ferry, as in rush hour parlance, "There is a two car wait at the Lynchburg Ferry." [76]

LYONS: Michael Cusick – John and Michael Lyons were Irish immigrants who arrived in Houston at the end of the 19th century. John opened a saloon on the street whose name change in 1894 honored his brother. It is possible that Michael's political connections, he was married to Mayor John Browne's daughter Elizabeth, facilitated the name change. The street was previously known as Odin, for the first Catholic Bishop of the diocese of Galveston named John Mary Odin. It is possible the name may change again if the Fifth Ward Civic Association has its way. They are lobbying to call the thoroughfare Barbara Jordan Avenue. [77]

ODD AND INTERESTING FACTS ABOUT OUR STREETS

⊛ There are over 40,000 streets in the Houston area with more added almost every day that the Planning & Development office is open for developers to file plats.

⊛ All of the streets in Southside Place Addition are in alphabetical order when read from south to north: **Carlon, Darcus, Elmora, Farber, Garnet, Harper, Ingold** and **Jardin.**

⊛ The Houston Chronicle says the name of our city, and therefore **Houston** Avenue, dates back to 1066. According to this legend, a Scottish knight named Sir Hugh fought valiantly at the side of William the Conquer at the Battle of Hastings, the most significant battle ever fought on English soil, on October 14, 1066. For his bravery Sir Hugh was given some land that he christened "Hugh's Town." Over the years the name became "Hughstown" and finally Houston. To what lengths we will go in an attempt to establish our blueblood pedigree.

⊛ Originally Houston streets running north and south were called "streets" while those going east and west were all "avenues."

⊛ We no longer name streets for living people using their first and last names. We could have "unsinkable" Molly Brown street but not Mayor Bill White avenue. However, Planning & Development will allow the use of either the Christian or surname, in this case Bill or White, by themselves or in combination with another word, such as Mayorwhite.

⊛ You can give a street any name, no matter how dopey, as long as that name is not already taken.

⊛ One of the most difficult tasks to undertake is to persuade City Council to change the name of an existing street. It happens but rarely.

⊛ On July 15, 1853 an ordinance was passed prohibiting the discharge of "guns, rifles and pistols" in an area commencing at Lamar and Live Oak, over to Brazos, up to Buffalo Bayou, along the Bayou and back to Live Oak.

⊛ Five of the principal roads that led out of Houston in the 1800s still exist today: San Felipe (to Stephen F. Austin's capitol), Washington (to Hempstead, Brenham and Austin), Montgomery (to Montgomery County), Liberty (to Liberty, Texas and eastward) and Richmond (to Fort Bend County).

⊛ Franklin was the first street to be paved with asphalt. This occurred in 1897.

⊛ While we name streets after many trees, Oak is the most common.

⊛ Houston's first speeding ticket was issued to T. Brady for "fast driving" down Main Street on April 1, 1903. He was fined $10 for exceeding the 6-mile per hour limit.

⊛ According to the Houston Chronicle (2/17/1986), Mary Blazey was elected mayor of the smallest community in the Houston area in 1986. The area was confined to the one block long **Chowning** Road. [33]

M. D. ANDERSON: In 1904 Monroe D. Anderson, his brother Frank and William L. Clayton incorporated Anderson, Clayton & Company. That firm became the largest cotton broker in the world and was the basis of Anderson's wealth. In 1936 he founded the M. D. Anderson Foundation. Being a bachelor, his $20 million estate went to the foundation upon his death in 1939. The bulk of the funds went to establish the Texas Medical Center. One of the finest hospitals in the complex is named in his honor as well as this street. [1]

» M.D. ANDERSON: M.D. Anderson in his cotton warehouse

M.A.S.: Named for real estate developer Melvin A. Silverman, this little street near the intersection of South MacGregor and State Highway 288 dead ends into H.M.C., named for another developer, H. M. Cohen. [2]

MacARTHUR: Douglas – He was unquestionably one of America's greatest military leaders. MacArthur was a very complex person: a military genius, highly intelligent (graduating 1st in his class from West Point), headstrong, flamboyant, fearless and controversial. There was a good reason he was known as the "American Caesar." During World War I he was highly decorated for bravery, winning the Distinguished Service Medal, Distinguished Service Cross and seven Silver Stars. In World War II he commanded the U. S. Army forces in the Far East. President Harry Truman relieved MacArthur of his command in the Korean War in a dispute over policy. He will be remembered for two of his more famous quotes: "I shall return" on retreating from the Philippines in 1942 and "Old soldiers never die; they just fade away" from his farewell speech to the U. S. Congress. [3]

MACBETH: In the east side neighborhood of Highland Estates there are several street names relating to Scotland. This Scottish king (1040-1057), who ascended the throne after killing his cousin Duncan, is most remembered as the focal point of William Shakespeare's tragedy *Macbeth*. [4]

MACEDONIA SCHOOL: (See **Macedonia**.)

MACEDONIA: This Waller County road remembers Macedonia Community that was located west of Tomball. It was established by German immigrants in 1878. A farmer and rancher, Heinrich Konrad Karl Leverkuhn, first named it Foresouth Prairie but later changed it to Macedonia Community. It once had a cotton gin, syrup mill, blacksmith shop, school, Methodist church and cemetery. The latter is all that remains. [5]

MacGREGOR: Henry F. – He was a major influence at the *Houston Post* for many years. MacGregor, along with John Kirby, put up the land for St. Agnes Academy. He was one of the organizers of the Houston Symphony Association. He gave the city a park with a fountain, pool and sculpture on the corner of Main and Richmond. Little of the park remains today, but the statue of his wife Elizabeth Stevens MacGregor, nicknamed Peggy, has been restored and is located in MacGregor Park. Gutzon Borglum who later became famous for his monumental presidential busts on Mt. Rushmore did the sculpture in 1927. (See tombstone on page 205.) [6]

» MACGREGOR: Borglum's sculpture of Peggy

MACONDA: This tree-lined little lane in Royden Oaks is named for one of the three daughters of George R. and Alice Pratt Brown. In *Joy Unconfined* by Ann Hitchcock

Holmes, Houston society portrait painter Robert Joy tells about a painting he did of young Maconda at the request of her parents. "The first attempt was abandoned. The second canvas was stretched over the first and a new portrait was completed, the first one forgotten. I was very surprised to learn it (the forgotten one) was hanging in the Ralph O'Connor residence (Maconda became Mrs. O'Connor). I was only paid for one portrait!" [7]

MACGREGOR

HENRY F. MACGREGOR
LONDONDERRY N.H.
APR. 25, 1855 — SEPT. 3, 1923
CAME TO TEXAS 1873 — TO HOUSTON 1883
ELIZABETH S. MACGREGOR
HOUSTON, TEXAS
FEB. 3, 1864 — MAY 23, 1949

» MACGREGOR: Henry and Peggy's tombstone in Glenwood Cemetery

MACZALI: Years ago the Houston Fire Department asked Planning and Development to use this Hungarian surname to name a street in the southwest part of town. They wanted to use an uncommon name so they searched the phone book and found no other last names with only one listing. Later a firefighter named George J. Maczali saw the street on the map and searched out its provenance. He had a photograph of himself taken in front of the sign. On a trip to Hungary to visit relatives he took the picture along to show them. [8]

MADISON: James – The 4th President of the United States, Madison is remembered as the "Father of the Constitution" for his skillful structuring of that document at the Federal Constitutional Convention of 1787. He was an author of the *Federalist Papers* and strong advocate of the Bill of Rights. The War of 1812 and the burning of the White House by British troops hurt his popularity but an improving economic climate revitalized his presidency. [9]

MAGELLAN: Ferdinand – Located in the maritime themed neighborhood of Newport, this street honors one of the greatest seaman and navigators in history. Among his many accomplishments: he initiated the first circumnavigation of the world, discovered the Straits of Magellan, named the southern tip of South America *Tierra del Fuego* (because of the many fires he saw there) and named the Pacific Ocean. Magellan was born in Portugal in 1480. At 15 he joined the Portuguese navy where he excelled. In 1513 he had a falling out with King Manuel, renounced his citizenship and became a Spaniard. Charles V of Spain knew a good thing when he saw it and commissioned Magellan to sail around the world. His fleet of five ships departed August 10, 1519. It was a difficult expedition. Magellan was killed by islanders in the Philippines on April 27, 1521 but one ship limped home with a crew of 18 to complete the voyage. [10]

MAGNOLIA: This town was settled in the 1840s and named Mink's Prairie for an early settler, Colonel Joseph Mink. Soon it was shortened to Mink. In 1902 the International-Great Northern Railroad built a line through the town and changed the name to Melton. Jim Melton was a large land owner in the county. The post office felt it might be confused with Milton, Texas so it was renamed Magnolia for the thick stands of magnolia trees that lined the banks of Mill Creek. (See **Melton.**) [11]

MAHAFFEY: Amos – This Scotch-Irish settler arrived in the north Harris County area from Mississippi following the War Between the States. He purchased part of the original Elizabeth Smith league and settled down with his wife and eight children. [12]

MAHAFFEY: R. O. – He was a merchant who opened the first general store in Tomball in 1908. Located in a two story building, the store was on the ground floor and the family lived upstairs. His daughter, Hazel, was the first baby born in Tomball. [13]

MAID MARIAN: She was the lover of the mythical Robin Hood, the English hero/ bandit who was known to rob from the rich and give to the poor.

MAIN: In the minds of Houston founders John and Augustus Allen as well as chief surveyors Gail and Thomas Borden this was to be our city's most important thoroughfare. As a result it was platted at 90-feet wide versus 80-feet for the other 16 streets on the first map of Houston in 1836. For many years it was the king of our streets. The best merchants built their stores on it. The leading banks, hotels, entertainment palaces and restaurants were here. At the south end the city's leading citizens built their palatial homes. The changing demographics of our city resulted in a slow process of decay for Main that began in the late 1970s and continues today. Hopefully the new Metro light rail project and other plans can restore it to something of its former glory. [14]

MAIN STREET, HOUSTON, TEX.

» MAIN: Palatial homes on Main

MAISON ROUGE: Upon his arrival in Galveston, Jean Lafitte, the famous pirate, built a home and called it *Maison Rouge* (Red House) as that was the color he painted it. It was part residence and part fort with cannons. Legend says it was beautifully furnished with booty he captured. When the United States government demanded he depart the county, Lafitte burned *Maison Rouge* and sailed off into history. The ruins of this house can be seen in Galveston today. (See **Lafitte.**) [15]

MAJESTIC PRINCE: Legendary jockey Bill Hartack (who rode five winners in 12 rides at the Kentucky Derby) won the 1969 Derby on Majestic Prince. It was the only overwhelming favorite Hartack mounted in the "Run for the Roses," going off at 6-5. The race was close but the Prince won by a neck. [16]

» MAJESTIC: Program cover

MAJESTIC: This Denver Harbor street recalls the magnificent Majestic Theater at the corner of Texas and Milam. Jesse H. Jones built it in 1910 at a cost of $300,000. "Actors praised it, for every comfort has been provided for them, both in the modern dressing room and the large and fully equipped stage. The public appreciates it because in the whole house there is no angle, no obstructing pillar nor column and no seat that does not furnish a good view of the stage" according to an early newspaper review. [17]

MAJURO: See sidebar **Bali Hai May Call You,** page 322.

MAKATEA: See sidebar **Bali Hai May Call You,** page 322.

MALMEDY: The Malmedy Massacre occurred on December 17, 1944 during the Battle of the Bulge. An American truck convoy was intercepted by a German Panzer tank division. The outgunned Americans surrendered. The Germans herded the 81 POWs into a nearby field and mowed them down with machine guns. Survivors were shot in the head where they fell. It was the worst atrocity against American troops in Europe. Following the war 74 Germans were tried and convicted of these war crimes. [18]

MALONE: William – This Houston real estate promoter bought 3,000 acres in north Harris County in 1907. Malone paid approximately $9,100 for this acreage. A small town named Peck was located on his property. He replatted the land and changed the name to Tomball. (See **Tomball.**) [19]

MALTBY: W. J. – Another member of Walker's Texas Division, he was the Captain of Company G of the 17th Texas Volunteer Infantry. [20]

MAN O' WAR: This street is named for arguably the best racehorse that ever lived. Known as "Big Red" he raced 21 times and posted 20 wins during his two-year career (1919-1920). His only loss was in Saratoga where he was second to Upset, thus prompting the use of that word for a victory by an underdog. He did not run in the Kentucky Derby, as his owner did not believe it wise to run a three-year-old horse 1-1/4 miles so early in the year. He did win the Preakness, Belmont and set five world records. He went on to sire another champion for which we have a street name - War Admiral. (See **War Admiral.**) [21]

MANASSAS: Also known as Bull Run, this small Virginia town had two battles fought over it. The first on July 21, 1861 saw the Confederates under General Pierre Beauregard rout the Union army under the command of General Irvin McDowell. Almost a year later on August 30, 1862 the result was the same with General Thomas "Stonewall" Jackson's Southerners defeating General John Pope's Federals. [22]

MANCHESTER: This Houston Ship Channel community was a stop on the Texas & New Orleans Railroad in the 1860s. Since the 1920s the Manchester Corporation has operated a large freight terminal on the south bank of the Channel near Brady Island. [23]

MANGUM: Eugene – This gentleman owned Mangum Development Company. He was asked to attend a meeting at the Houston Planning & Development Department. When he arrived the committee informed him they were naming a road in his honor. [24]

MANSVELT: See sidebar **Pirates of the Caribbean,** page 280.

MANVEL: Originally named Pomona, the name was changed to Manvel when it was discovered that a west Texas town was already know as Pomona. It was named for the president of the Atchison, Topeka & Santa Fe Railroad. The first settlers arrived here in 1857 but the town did not develop until 1890. In 1931 oil was discovered here and Manvel became a very prosperous place. Today it is known as a large rice producing area. [25]

MAPLE VALLEY: This street, along with **Shady River** and **Stones Throw,** were named for streets where Mary Catherine Farrington's classmates at Randolph-Macon Women's College lived, according to her book, *Tanglewood, The Story of William Giddings Farrington.* [26]

MAPLETON: This Iowa town was the home of Q. A. Wooster, Baytown area pioneer, prior to moving to Texas. (See **Wooster.**) [27]

MARC ANTHONY: One of ancient Rome's famous citizens, he is most remembered for his "friends, Romans, countrymen lend me your ears..." speech after the assassination of Julius Caesar. He was given the eastern third of the Roman Empire to govern but, following his torrid affair with Cleopatra, the Queen of Egypt, and a falling out with Octavian, he committed suicide after a major military defeat by other Roman forces.

(See **Brutus, Cassius** and **Caeser.**)

MARCELLA: Marcella Perry was the daughter of James G. Donovan, the City Attorney of Houston Heights. She is remembered as the founder of Heights Savings & Loan as well as for her "Econo-casts" that were heard for years on radio and television. A beloved citizen of the Heights she earned the nickname of "Mrs. Heights." (See **Donovan.**) [28]

MAREK: This family was among the first people to settle in the small town of Guy. (See **Old Guy.**) [29]

MARIACHI: See sidebar **Learn a Foreign Language on Your Morning Walk,** page 125.

MARJORIE: This lady was the daughter of David C. Bintliff. Developer Frank Sharp name it for her and named **Beverly** for her sister. (See **Bintliff** and **Sharpstown.**) [30]

MARKS: Emil Henry – Much to my re-gret this Addicks area road is not named for the author of this opus. However, it does remember one of the county's more interesting men. Born October 26, 1881 in Addicks, he was the son of a German immigrant who arrived in Texas

» MARKS: Street sign near location of E. H. Marks ranch

in 1833. He went to work on a ranch following the death of his father. Marks was only 10 years old. In 1898 he went out on his own and bought his first Longhorn steer. By 1913 he was leading trail drives into Houston every week. In 1917 he bought a section of land and opened the LH-7 Ranch. By the 1950s he owned the largest private herd of Longhorn cattle in the world and was known as the "Longhorn King of Texas." [31]

MARLOWE: Christopher – This 16th century English dramatist's writings had a pro-found influence on William Shakespeare. His works include *Dr. Faustus, The Jew of Malta* and *Hero and Leander.* Marlow died in a tavern fight, stabbed to death by another patron. [32]

MARQUETTE: Opened in 1881 in Milwaukee, Wisconsin, this co-educational university is operated by the Jesuit Fathers. [33]

MARTEN: Rosehill's Salem Lutheran Church is the oldest Lutheran congregation in Texas, founded in 1852. In the 1870's another wave of German settlers arrived in north Harris County. Many of these new immigrants joined Salem including the Marten family. [34]

MARTENS: The Martens were early settlers in the Tomball area. William Martens was the first justice of the peace. Family members are interred in the Seidel (Rosehill) Cemetery. (See **Siedel Cemetery.**) [35]

M-N

MARTIN LUTHER KING: This street is named in honor of the African-American clergyman and civil rights leader. King won the Nobel Peace Prize in 1964. Under his leadership the civil rights movement employed non-violent tactics to achieve racial equality. One of his greatest successes was in 1963 with 250,000 people in the Washington March. This event brought about the Civil Rights and Voting Rights Acts in 1965. He was assassinated in Memphis, Tennessee in 1968. [36]

MARTIN: Daniel W. – A La Grange native this black student arrived at Prairie View A & M University in 1911 to study agriculture. He changed his degree to mechanical arts and graduated in 1918. The following year Martin was hired by the school as a Refrigeration Engineer. He became a instructor after earning his B. S. in Electricity in 1924. His five children also graduated from this university. [37]

» MARTIN: Street sign on Prairie View A & M Campus

MARTIN: Wyly – He was born in Georgia in 1776. Under the command of General Andrew Jackson, Martin fought in the War of 1812. He arrived in Texas in the 1820s and received a league of land. He was a captain in the Texas Army during the fight for independence. Martin settled near Richmond and was elected Chief Justice of Fort Bend County. He died in 1842. [38]

MARTINA: See sidebar **Tennis or Golf, Anyone?,** page 348.

MARY BATES: This Sharpstown area thoroughfare is named for the wife of W. B. Bates, a real estate developer. [39]

MARY LOU: Mary Lou Henry of Vernon G. Henry and Associates Planning Consultants worked for the Planning & Development Department of Houston in the 1960s. A developer brought in a plat with a duplicate street name on it. Since duplication is prohibited, a senior officer, whom everyone called Miss Mack, decided to rename the street Mary Lou. Mrs. Henry's expertise on our city's street names was of great value to your author in writing this book. [40]

MARY MOODY NORTHEN: Born in Galveston in 1892 she was the granddaughter of financier William L. Moody. She was very active in business and philanthropy. Northen was president of American National Insurance Company, Moody Bank, *Galveston News* and W. L. Moody Cotton Company to mention some of her interests. She chaired the Moody Foundation, commissioned the outdoor historical drama, *Lone Star,* established the Railroad Museum and helped to found Texas A& M Maritime Academy. Moody was so critical in the Galveston Historical Society's acquisition of the *Elissa* that the figurehead on the vessel has her face on it. (See **Moody** and **Elissa.**) [41]

MARY'S CREEK: Also known as Mary's Bayou, the two forks of this stream join near Pearland and flow 12 miles to its mouth on Clear Creek. (See **Clear Creek.**) [42]

MASONIC PARK: This Brazoria street recalls a March 1835 day when six Masons met under a large oak tree, since known as the "Masonic Oak," and founded the first Masonic Lodge in Texas. [43]

MASSEY: Charles D. – He was a Harris County Precinct 2 Commissioner from 1927 until 1935. Among his accomplishments during this eight year term were: opening Market Street to Houston Street and completing the Hog Island Causeway to the Morgan's Point Ferry. He also had a ferry named for him that could carry 20 cars from Hog Island to Morgan's Point. [44]

MASTERS: This most prestigious golf tournament in the world was originally named the Augusta National Invitational Tournament by founder Robert "Bobby" Trent Jones in 1934. Five years later it was changed to The Masters. Many of golf's greatest players have triumphed here including Gene Sarazen, Byron Nelson, Ben Hogan, Arnold Palmer, Jack Nicklaus and Tiger Woods. [45]

MATCH POINT: See sidebar **Tennis or Golf, Anyone?,** page 348.

MATHIS: This road runs south from Waller, Texas into Fort Bend County. The Mathis family were early settlers in this area. Many of the family members are interred in the Burton-Mathis-Canon Cemetery at the corner of Burton Cemetery and Mathis roads. (See **Burton Cemetery.**) [46]

MATISSE: Henri – The Memorial area neighborhood of Gaywood is filled with streets associated with artists, composers and operas. One of the most famous French painters of the 19th century, Matisse was greatly influenced by the Impressionists. He was an important member of the *"les fauves"* group. He is renown for his unique treatment of light in his paintings. [47]

MATZKE: (See **Koch.**)

MAUI: See sidebar **Bali Hai May Call You,** page 322.

MAXEY: The Maxey Lumber Company named this road in the 1930s. [48]

MAY: Pam, Holli and Sandy – These three women own May Airport, a private landing strip in northwest Harris County. The elevation here is 166 feet and the runway is 3,440 feet long. [49, 50]

MAYDE CREEK: South Mayde Creek is a 16-mile watercourse with headwaters north of Katy, Texas that meanders southeast, emptying into Buffalo Bayou. [51]

McASHAN: Samuel Maurice – This Virginian came to Texas in 1844. He moved to Houston in 1863 where he was hired as the cashier of Thomas W. House's private bank. David Bintliff, one of the city's well-known financiers and philanthropists, was a young man when he went to work for McAshan. Bintliff says, "I was the flunky auditor. When he heard I was engaged to be married, he called me into his office and gave me a big raise, I mean a whopper: a five-dollar a month raise." McAshan was a founder of the Houston Cotton Exchange & Board of Trade. [52, 53]

McCABE: This family were early settlers in the La Porte area. [54]

McCALL: Andrew - See sidebar **Houston Streets Named for Men Killed During World War I,** page 22.

McCALL: Screven Aaron – This attorney was born in Georgia in 1861. He moved to Texas in 1876 and opened a law office in Willis. McCall served as District Attorney for Montgomery County from 1899 until 1906. He was appointed a District Judge in 1929. His office was eventually moved to Montgomery where it is now open to the public. [55]

McCARTY: J. C. – This gentleman was a railroad surveyor in the late 1800s. The proximity of this road to the huge Englewood Rail Yard south of U. S. 90 leads me to believe McCarty is named for him. In 1904 he gave up surveying and partnered with James B. Earthman Sr. to found Earthman & McCarty Undertaking Company. Upon his death the firm's name was changed to J. B. Earthman Company. This long time Houston family still operates Earthman Funeral Directors and Cemeteries today. [56]

McCORMICK: See sidebar **Brazoria County's Old Plantation Streets and Roads,** page 258.

McCRARY: The McCrary's owned a considerable amount of acreage where this Fort Bend County road is located. They were farmers and ranchers. [57]

McDONALD: Allen J. – See sidebar **Houston Streets Named for Men Killed During World War I,** page 22.

McDONALD: R. D. – He was a land developer in Sweeny during the early 20th century who was president of Bernard River Land Development Company. McDonald donated a plot of land to every church denomination in Sweeny. The town was named for John Sweeny, a plantation owner in the area. [58]

McENROE MATCH: John McEnroe was one of America's greatest professional tennis players. He won the U. S. Open in 1979, 1980, 1981 and 1984. McEnroe added the men's singles crown at Wimbledon to his trophy case in 1982, 1983 and 1984. He was also a great doubles player winning three of those championships at the U.S. Open and four more at Wimbledon. McEnroe is also remembered for his bad temper and penchant for screaming at referees and linesmen. [59]

McGOWEN: Andrew – McGowen was a tinsmith. He also owned a general store that sold copperware, cooking stoves and hardware, much of which he manufactured. Elected mayor in 1867, the election was remarkable, according to a newspaper account, because it was "unmarred by a single fight." During his term, enough wooden rails were laid on McKinney Avenue to operate the city's first mule-drawn streetcar in 1868. The fares were a dime for adults and a nickel for children. [60]

McHARD: This family were early settlers of Fort Bend County. [61]

» McILHENNY: The McIlhenny home was known as "The Gables"

McILHENNY: Samuel K. – Named for an early Houston merchant, McIlhenny Company's offices were at Franklin and Fannin. He was also a director and organizer of the Houston Cotton Exchange and Board of Trade in 1874. He served as president of the Exchange on several occasions. (See **Anita.**) [62]

McINTOSH: John McK. – See sidebar **Houston Streets Named for Men Killed During World War I,** page 22.

McKEE: Frostown expert Kirk Ferris believes McKee was a freed slave who owned property in this historic area following Emancipation. The McKee Street Bridge is one of Houston's architectural jewels. Built in 1932 under the direction of City Bridge Engineer James G. McKenzie, this colorful, undulating span's beams demonstrate how the design carries the weight of the bridge and its traffic. Ferris was responsible for the renovation and painting of the bridge in 1985. (See photograph on page 214.) [63]

M-N

» McKEE: McKee Street Bridge

McKINNEY: Collin – This gentleman was a signatory of the Texas Declaration of Independence in 1836. His grandsons, who owned the Milam Brothers Brickyard in Baytown, named the street for him. [64]

McKINNEY: Thomas F. – As one of Stephen F. Austin's Old Three Hundred colonists, McKinney was given a league of land in what is today Brazos County. He became wealthy through trading, lumber and agriculture. In 1834 he partnered with Samuel M. Williams and established the largest commission-merchant firm in Texas. That company helped finance the Texas Revolution by advancing the Republic $150,000 and issuing notes that circulated as legal tender. McKinney became a famous thoroughbred breeder. He was opposed to Secession but reluctantly accepted it. Employed as an agent for Simeon Hart, the Confederate quartermaster for Texas, McKinney sold cotton to Mexico to purchase arms, ammunition and other necessary war supplies. The Civil War and a disastrous speculation in cotton ruined McKinney and he died broke. [65]

McKINNEY FALLS: See sidebar **The Most Scenic Spots in Texas,** page 310.

McKNIGHT: L. W. – I believe this street, south of Tetter Cemetery where he is buried, is named for this early settler. He was born in 1862 and died in 1937. (See **Tetter Cemetery.**) [66]

McMASTER: Clyde: He was a mayor of Pasadena, Texas who moved to this Ship Channel city in 1909. [67]

McNAIR STATION: This small principally black community was once a stop on the Beaumont, Sour Lake & Western Railroad. The town and street recalled by this name have been on area highway maps since the 1930s although the community started 10 years earlier. [68]

McNEIL: H. Lee – See sidebar **Houston Streets Named for Men Killed During World War I,** page 22.

MEADE: George Gordon – Not many Houston streets remember Union generals from the War Between the States. However, Meade was one of President Abraham Lincoln's top commanders. He saw action at numerous battles including Mechanicsville, Glendale (where he was severely wounded), Bull Run II, Antietam and Chancellorsville. But Meade is most remembered for his defeat of General Robert E. Lee at Gettysburg. As commander of the Army of the Potomac, only Ulysses S. Grant outranked him. [69]

MEADOWLAKE: (See **Larchmont**.) [70]

» MECOM: Fountains on South Main at Hermann Park are named for John Mecom

MECOM: John Whitfield Sr. – Born in 1911 this Texas oilman made his initial fortune acquiring abandoned fields and finding large additional reserves others had missed. He also made major discoveries in Louisiana and Saudi Arabia. He purchased a large tract of land in Hitchcock that was once a naval blimp base. His plan to develop it never materialized. Mecom once owned the Warwick Hotel (now Hotel ZaZa). The fountains in the photo front that property. (See **Blimp Base**.) [71]

MEDICAL COMPLEX: This street leads to the Tomball Regional Hospital and the Texas Sports Medicine Center. The former was founded in 1976 and now serves the citizens of Tomball, Magnolia, Waller and Cypress. The latter is a division of the hospital and was the first hospital-based sports medicine center on the Texas Gulf Coast. It opened for business in 1982. [72]

MEDICAL PLAZA: This street leads to Memorial Hermann Hospital in the Woodlands. [73]

MEEK: Chester A. – See sidebar **Houston Streets Named for Men Killed During World**

M-N

War I, page 22.

MELANIE: See sidebar **Gone With the Wind Too Far,** page 303.

MELLOW BREW: The developer and residents of this unincorporated neighborhood of trailer homes must really enjoy a cold beer periodically (or possibly more often) as almost every street is related in some way to the brewing process. Other streets include South & North **Lite, Longneck, Cooter** (as in "drunk as Cooter Brown") as well as two platted but yet unpaved lanes to be called **Six Pack** and **Strohs.** [74]

MELLUS: See sidebar **Texas Heroes' Names for Houston Streets Urged in 72 Proposed Changes,** page 96.

MELODY: See sidebar **It's Music to My Ears,** page 218.

MELTON: Jim – This gentleman was a large land owner near Magnolia in Montgomery County in the early 1900s. (See **Magnolia.**) [75]

MEMORIAL BEND: In 1955 two real estate developers, Howard Edmunds and Robert Puig, formed the Memorial Bend Development Company, so called because the property was where Memorial Drive takes a sharp bend northward. The neighborhood was given the same name and many of the streets there are named for famous operas. (See **Butterfly, Faust, Figaro, Hansel & Gretel, Isolde, Mignon, Tosca** and **Traviata.**) [76]

MEMORIAL CITY: This is one of many huge shopping malls in the Houston area with the entry way street named for the project. [77]

MEMORIAL HERMANN: This Pearland street leads to the Memorial Hermann Hospital in that community. [78]

MEMORIAL: At the end of this road is the Galveston Memorial Park Cemetery in Hitchcock. [79]

MENARD: Michel Branamour – Born near Montreal, Canada in 1805 he came to Texas to trade with the Indian tribes. He later added cattle and horse trading with Mexicans. Menard built a saw and grist mill on Menard Creek in 1833. He signed the Texas Declaration of Independence in 1836. Menard and his partners Samuel May Williams and Thomas F. McKinney formed the Galveston City Company for the purpose of developing a town on the eastern end of Galveston Island. (See **McKinney.**) [43]

MERCEDES: This street runs behind the Mercedes-Binz Center on I-45 North. This fine German motorcar began life as a bus. Karl Binz began manufacturing busses in Manheim, Germany in 1895. He later turned his attention to the production of luxury automobiles. [80]

MERCER: This University was founded in 1833 by Jessie Mercer as an institution to provide students with a classical and theological education. Today it is the second largest Baptist institution in the world. As an aside, one of our city's most eccentric citizens Jeff McKissack, creator of the whimsical folk art environment, The Orange Show, was a Mercer graduate (1925). [81]

MERCURY: See sidebar **Space City U.S.A. or "Houston the Eagle Has Landed",** page 106.

MERKEL: Joseph R. & Caroline – In August 1860 this German immigrant couple paid $3,000 for 101 acres of land where this street is today. Many German families settled in this area, later called Merkel's Grove, in the 1840s and after including the Blau, Schrimpf and Freund families. The family sponsored competitive target shooting contests on the farm. In 1885 Merkel opened the area for public recreation, 14 years before the city constructed its first park. (See **Engelke** and **Canal.**) [35]

MERLIN: In Arthurian legends he is a famous magician and counselor to King Arthur.

MERRIMACK: When the Union forces abandoned the Norfolk Naval Yard early in the Civil War, they scuttled this steam frigate. Raised by the Confederates it was converted into an ironclad and renamed *Virginia*. On March 9, 1862 she squared off against the *Monitor* in the first battle of ironclads. The four-hour, close-range battle was a draw. Although they never fought each other again, both met their fates at the bottom of the sea. The Rebels destroyed the *Virginia* (nee *Merrimack*) in May 1862 to prevent her capture by advancing Union armies. The Monitor sank in rough seas off Cape Hatteras in December of the same year. [82]

METAIRIE: See sidebar *Laissez les bon temps roulez* (Let the good times roll), page 188.

METCALF: W. – A captain of Company F of the 34th Regular Texas Cavalry Dismounted, he fought under Walker's Texas Division during the War Between the States. [83]

METZLER CREEK: There are a number of members of the Metzler family buried in the Salem Lutheran Cemetery west of where this street is located. It is possible it is named for German immigrants who arrived in the Tomball, Texas area in the 1800s. (See **Lutheran Cemetery.**) [84]

MEYER PARK: This street and park are named for Elizabeth Kaiser Meyer. [72, 85]

MEYER: (See **Stavinoha.**)

MICHAUX: Located in developer William A. Wilson's Woodland Heights neighborhood, this street is named for Mr. Michaux, a close friend of Wilson's. A long time resident told me this civic-minded man was president of the Chamber of Commerce as well as the YMCA. [86]

IT'S MUSIC TO MY EARS

Woodwind Lakes in northwest Houston has to be our most musical neighborhood. Visit here and you can drive on **Adagio** (a slow tempo); **Andante** (moderately slow tempo); **Allegro** (a lively tempo); **Brahms** (classical German composer); **Cadenza** (melodic flourish in an aria); **Cantata** (musical piece composed of choruses, solos and recitatives); **Chorale** (Protestant hymn melody); **Clarion** (shrill, Medieval trumpet); **Concerto** (three movement orchestral composition); **Crescendo** (gradually increasing musical volume); **Cymbal** (brass percussion instrument); **Ensemble** (work for two or more musicians); **Golden Chord; Melody; Musical; Opus** (creative musical body of work); **Oratorio** (sacred story composition); **Percussion; Prelude** (short piece for piano); **Rhapsody** (improvisational composition); **Rondo** (triple musical theme between contrasting themes); **Rhythm; Scherzo** (¾ time movement); **Serenade** (musical performance professing love); **Sinfonia** (overture to an opera); **Sonata** (composition for four instruments); **Symphonic; Toccata** (free style piece for organ); **Whistling** and **Woodwind** (wind instrument with a reed). [34]

MICHELANGELO: See sidebar **Neighborhoods with Interesting Street Names,** page 104.

MIDLINE: This town was established in the 1830s and grew when the Houston, East and West Texas Railway passed through it. It got its name due to its location near the Montgomery-Liberty County line. Like many towns in the area it benefited from the lumber boom of 1900. By 1930 the lumber business had declined. Midline began its slide into obscurity and very little remains. [87]

MIDWAY: This small community was established in 1822 but no longer exists. It was located where Baytown is today. [88]

MIDWAY: This street is named for a decisive WW II battle that occurred on and around this South Pacific island on June 3-6, 1942. Fought on sea and in the air, the defeat of the Japanese navy here was the turning point in the momentum of the War in the Pacific. During the action American forces sank four Japanese aircraft carriers, severely impacting that country's ability to deliver offensive blows. [89]

MIGNON: In 1866 the French composer Ambroise Thomas wrote this opera. It is the story of Lothario, an elderly wandering minstrel, in search of his lost daughter, Mignon, who has been kidnapped by gypsies. The plot thickens with heroics, love, rejection, the other woman, attempted murder and finally redemption. During his career Thomas penned cantatas, ballets and 19 other operas. [90]

MIKE GAIDO: In 1911 San Jacinto Gaido opened Gaido's Seafood Restaurant in Galveston. Its first location was atop Murdoch's Bath House that extended on a pier into the Gulf of Mexico. In 1934 it moved to its present location at the intersection of Seawall and 39th Street (now renamed Mike Gaido Boulevard.) Mike was S. J. Gaido's son. The fourth generation of the family operates this excellent eatery now. Treat yourself to a visit here and order the Snapper Sapparito. It might just be the greatest seafood dish in the world. [91]

MILAM: Benjamin Rush – A Kentuckian born in 1788, his first taste of battle was in the War of 1812. His fame came at the Siege of Bexar (December 5-9, 1835) during the Texas Revolution. Despite his diminished forces because of a retreat by Edward Burleson's troops, he said to the remaining soldiers "Who will go with old Ben Milam into San Antonio?" Three hundred men volunteered. Milam was killed in action on December 7 but the Texans captured San Antonio and held it until the Battle of the Alamo. [92]

MILBY: Charles H. – Milby arrived in Harrisburg in 1872. During his life he ran a general store, founded a bank, manufactured bricks and was elected Harris County Commissioner. He was a civic-minded Houstonian, financier and owner of the Milby Hotel (1910). Milby led a drive to construct a new county courthouse. As a landowner in Harrisburg he contributed land, money and time to encourage Congress to deepen and improve the Houston Ship Channel. The Milby home, built in 1885-88, was at 614 Broadway at Elm in Harrisburg. His wife, Maggie Tod Milby, lived in the home until her death in 1942. The house stood vacant for many years and was demolished in 1959. [93]

MILFORD: See **Southampton's English Streets,** page 255.

MILL CREEK: This estuary has two forks that rise in Washington County and flow approximately 30 miles southeast before uniting. From there it continues fourteen more miles to its mouth on the Brazos River near Stephen F. Austin State Park. Early settlers called this creek Palmetto. The current name was adopted between 1820 and 1845. [94]

MILLENNIUM FOREST: (See **Alderon Woods.**)

MILLER: Arthur O. – Following its incorporation in 1945, this man was elected to Katy, Texas' first city council. [95]

MILLER: Charles E. or James E. – See sidebar **Houston Streets Named for Men Killed During World War I,** page 22.

MILLER: Hermann – This German immigrant settled in Bellville in the 1850s and opened a general store on the main square. [96]

MILLET: C. F. – He was a 1st Lieutenant in Company G of the 16th Texas Volunteer Infantry. Millet fought under Major General John George Walker during the War Between the States (1861-65.) [97]

MILLHEIM CEMETERY: (See **Millheim.**)

MILLHEIM: German immigrants founded this community on Clear Creek near Bellville in about 1845. At a meeting at the Engelking & Noltke General Store, a resident, Wilhelm Schneider, suggested the name Mulheim (it was later anglicized) in honor of the German city on the Rhine River. In the 1850s a school, cemetery, chapel and singing society were formed. [98]

MILLIE BUSH: To the best of my knowledge this street is the only one in the Houston area named for a dog. Millie Bush (who is also remembered by the 13-acre Millie Bush Bark Park in Barker Reservoir) was "First Dog" during the administration of President George H. W. Bush. First Lady Barbara Bush chronicled this Springer Spaniel's life in the White House in *Millie's Book* in 1990. In 2005 this dog park was named the best in America by *Dog Fancy* magazine that rated over 700 of this type of facility. [76]

MILLS: Ollie – See sidebar **Houston Streets Named for Men Killed During World War I,** page 22.

MILO HAMILTON: On April 9, 2009 a short stretch of Hamilton Avenue near Minute Maid Park was renamed in honor of long time Houston Astros broadcaster Milo Hamilton. Born in Iowa in 1927, he began his broadcasting career announcing football and basketball games for the Iowa Hawkeyes. His first major league baseball job was with the St. Louis Browns. In the next six decades he would announce games for the St. Louis Cardinals, Chicago Cubs, Chicago White Sox, Atlanta Braves (where he announced Hank Aaron's 715th home run), Pittsburg Pirates and Houston Astros (for 20 years). He will be remembered for his catch phrase, "Holy Toledo, what a play." (See **Hamilton.**) [99]

MILTON: John – This English poet's *Paradise Lost* (1667), a blank verse poem about Satan's revolt against God and Adam and Eve's fall from grace, is one of the greatest literary works of the English language. It was Milton's attempt to explain why there is evil in the world and how God deals with it. He later published *Paradise Regained* (1671), another poem detailing how Christ resisted the Devil's temptation. This is the city's second street called Milton. The first was on the original map of Houston drawn in 1836. Three years later that street name was changed to LaBranch. (See **LaBranch.**) [100]

MIMS: This small town and road are located on the San Bernard River in southwestern Brazoria County. It is named for Joseph Mims, one of Stephen F. Austin's Old 300, who owned the Fannin-Mims Plantation there along with his partner James W. Fannin. All that remains is the Mims Cemetery at the end of this lonely road. (See **Fannin.**) [101]

MINERAL WELLS: See sidebar **The Most Scenic Spots in Texas,** page 310.

MINK LAKE: This Montgomery County street leads to a small lake of the same name. Minks are semi-aquatic carnivores that were in evidence when the first settlers arrived in this area in the mid-1850s. They were hunted for their luxurious pelts that were subsequently turned into coats and hats. [102]

MINK: The Mink family settled here in about 1845. Following the War Between the States an influx of settlers arrived, building a Grange hall, interdenominational church, school, general store and municipal buildings. In 1902 the International-Great Northern Railroad bypassed Mink. Most citizens then moved to nearby Magnolia, turning Mink into another Montgomery County ghost town. [103]

» MINOR: Street sign on Prairie View Campus

MINOR: L. W. – This black Mississippi educator was hired as the first principal of Prairie View A & M University. [104]

MINTER: S. A. – Minter was the captain of Company K of the 19th Texas Volunteer Infantry of Walker's Texas Division during the War Between the States. [105]

MISSIONARY RIDGE: A skirmish here in Tennessee occurred during the Battle of Chattanooga on November 25, 1863. Union General U. S. Grant's men captured this ridge despite orders not to risk it. [106]

MISSOURI CITY: Two real estate promoters, R. M. Cash and L. E. Luckle, purchased a sizable plot of land out South Main Street in Fort Bend County in 1890. They elected to market their development in St. Louis. Three years later another investor, W. R. McElroy, acquired some acreage in the same area and began promoting it under the name of Missouri City. [107]

MISSOURI PACIFIC: On Independence Day 1851 ground was broken for the construction of this railroad, the first "iron horse" west of the Mississippi River. Its advertising motto was "We extend from St. Louis to the Pacific Ocean." [108]

MITTELSTAEDT: This pioneering German family immigrated to the Klein-Spring area in the late 1800s. Many family members are buried in the historic Budde Cemetery off Louetta Road. (See **Budde Cemetery.**) [109]

MOBY DICK: This 1851 novel by Herman Melville follows the tale of a sailor named Ishmael's voyage aboard the whaling ship *Pequod*. The ship's insane Captain Ahab is chasing a huge white whale that had previously ripped off the captain's leg. Ahab's voyage of revenge does not turn out well. This fictional tale is based on a true story about Owen Chase, a sailor aboard the *Essex* that was rammed and sunk by a whale in the Pacific Ocean in 1820. Read about this adventure in *Stove by a Whale* by Thomas Heffernan. [110]

» MOBY DICK: Owen Chase's grave on Nantucket Island

MONET: Claude – This French artist was the heart

and soul of the Impressionist movement during the late 19th and early 20th centuries. It was his painting, *Impression: Sunrise*, that gave the movement its name. He is best remembered for his paintings of water lilies, Paris scenes and the Rouen cathedral. [111]

MONITOR: (See **Merrimack.**)

MONROE: Although we might fantasize that this avenue is named for the glamorous movie star Marilyn, nee Norma Jean Baker, it is actually honoring the 5th President of the United States, James Monroe (1817-25). His greatest accomplishment was the formulation of the Monroe Doctrine, the *ne plus ultra* statement of American foreign policy of the times. [112]

MONTEZUMA: Montezuma Xocoyotl or Montezuma II was the last Aztec emperor of Mexico. He is one of the most tragic figures in Mexican prehistory. His religious superstition allowed the Spanish conquistador Hernando Cortez to seize control of the Aztec empire virtually without a fight. Montezuma believed the conqueror to be Quetzalcoatl, the light-skinned god of Aztec mythology who would one day return to earth. By the time he discovered otherwise it was too late. Cortez imprisoned and humiliated this once proud leader. In 1520 his own people killed Montezuma. [113]

MONTGOMERY: This Conroe street recalls old Texas towns that existed at one time or another in the area. Today they are remembered by names on a map: **Bays Chapel, Beach, Bethel, Brantley, Butlersburg, Honea, Lake Creek, Longstreet, McRae, Peach Creek** and **Pools.** [114]

MONTGOMERY: Andrew J. – This northern Harris County road leads to the town of the same name. Montgomery set up a trading post there in 1823. He later fought in the Texas Revolution. [115]

» **MONTROSE: Southern terminus of Montrose at Hermann Park**

MONTROSE: Sir Walter Scott, Scotland's famous poet and the foremost romantic novelist in the English language, created the historic town of Montrose for use in his stories. J. W. Link, who in 1910 acquired 165 acres west of Courtlandt Place and laid out the neighborhood of Montrose, named the boulevard. He built the first of many mansions that were to grace the subdivision. His home on the southwest corner of Montrose at West Alabama cost $60,000 to build in 1912 and was famous for its large gold doorknobs. Today it is the administration building of the University of St. Thomas. (See photograph on page 222.) [116]

MOODY: William Lewis – He was born in Virginia in 1828. After graduating from law school he moved to Texas to practice his trade. In 1855 he and his brothers formed a mercantile and cotton business. He fought valiantly for the South in the War Between the States. Moody was wounded several times, captured and honored for bravery during the campaign. After the War he moved to Galveston and opened a cotton and banking firm that became known as W. L. Moody & Company. He was a founder of the Galveston Cotton Exchange and became very active in politics. The Moody family remains very prominent in Galveston. (See **Mary Moody Northen**.) [117]

MOON ROCK: See sidebar **Space City U.S.A. or "Houston the Eagle Has Landed",** page 106.

MOONSHINE HILL: This Humble area road conjures up visions of stills brewing up white lightning and revenuers chasing good old boys with 3,000-gallon tanks of moonshine in their stock cars through the back hills of Appalachia. But the truth be known it is named for the Moonshine Oil Company and the tent city of roughnecks, drillers and tool pushers who prospected for black gold here following the discovery of the Humble oilfield in 1904. Founders of the oil company included Walter Sharp and Howard Hughes Sr. It was reported in 1909 that Moonshine Hill had eight saloons but only one church. (See **Sharp** and **Humble**.) [118]

MOORE RANCH: In September 2004 this dusty Ft. Bend County lane was renamed for the Moore family who has owned land here for several generations. Located in the town of Orchard, it is shown on the original plat as Moore Road but for a reason no one can remember it was changed to Jap Road in about 1940. [46]

MOORE: Francis – He came to Texas in 1836 to help in the fight for independence from Mexico. Moore served as an assistant surgeon. Following the war he purchased the *Telegraph and Texas Register*, a newspaper, from Thomas H. Borden. He held the position of editor for 17 years before selling the company to Edward H. Cushing. Moore was elected mayor of Houston for four terms between 1838 and 1853. (See **Cushing**.) [119]

MOORE: Frank M. or Thomas W. – See sidebar **Houston Streets Named for Men Killed During World War I,** page 22.

MOOREA: See sidebar **Bali Hai May Call You,** page 322.

MOPAC: This word is an acronym for Missouri Pacific. This Spring area road leads to the Missouri Pacific Railroad Yard where trains are assembled for shipping goods from Houston around the nation.

MORELAND: Isaac N. – He joined the Texas Army in 1835 and saw action in numerous campaigns including the Siege of Bexar. As the Captain of Artillery at the Battle of San Jacinto he was in command of the famous cannons called the "Twin Sisters." Later he practiced law in Houston along with his partner, the former Texas President David G. Burnet. In 1840 he was elected a Chief Justice of Harris County, a position he held until his death in 1842. (See **Twin Sisters.**) [120]

MORELOS: Jose Maria – This priest/soldier was one of the heroes of the Mexican War of Independence from Spain. In 1813 following the capture and subsequent execution and beheadings of Father Miguel Hidalgo and General Ingacio Allende (the loyalists hung the heads in cages from the walls of the granary in Guanajuato as a warning to other would-be insurgents) Morelos assumed command of the rag tag army of mestizos. He was captured in late 1815 and was also put to death. (See **Hidalgo.**) [10]

MORGAN CEMETERY: The Morgan family of Montgomery County donated the land for this cemetery in 1887. The first burial here was Louis Collins baby daughter, Page, who died while the Collins family was traveling through the area. [79]

MORGAN: Alvin – (See **Alvin-Sugar Land.**)

MORITZ: One of three Spring Branch streets in a row (along with Hillendahl and Pech), Moritz is the Christian name of one of the early members of the Pech family. [121]

MORRIS: Joseph Robert – This tinsmith arrived in Texas in the 1840s. He set up shop in Houston in 1847. Due to his support of the Union he was named mayor of Houston during Reconstruction in 1868. The next year he joined other influential investors in starting the Houston Direct Navigation Company and the Buffalo Bayou Ship Channel Company. Morris is rumored to have built our first skyscraper, a four story building downtown. [122]

MORRIS: Roscoe W. – See sidebar **Houston Streets Named for Men Killed During World War I,** page 22.

MORRISON: Most likely this Katy street is named for that city's second postmaster, W. P. Morrison, a grocer in the 1890s. (See **Thomas.**) [123, 124]

MORSE: A. T. – A subdivision map of the Allen C. Reynolds league indicates Morse owned 1,963 acres of land in what is now Montrose where this street is located. [125]

MORTON CEMETERY: This cemetery road remembers William Morton of Richmond who drowned in 1833. Ironically, he is not burried here as his body was never recovered from the Brazos River. Some of the notable Texans interred here include Mirabeau B. Lamar and Jane Long. (See **Lamar, Jane Long** and **Morton: William.**) [126]

MORTON: E. M. – An early settler in Katy, Texas he was also a founding member of the First United Methodist Church in that community. I was told he operated a rice farm. [127, 128]

MORTON: William – Little is known about this early Fort Bend County resident. He was one of Stephen F. Austin's Old 300. The schooner the Morton family was on wrecked on Galveston Island in 1822. In 1824 he settled near what is today Richmond. The 1826 census lists him as a farmer and stock raiser of unknown age. He opened the city's first burying ground naming it Morton Cemetery. Morton drowned in a Brazos River flood in 1833. (See **Morton Cemetery.**) [102]

MOTT: In the 1920s the name Mott Homes was as recognizable to Houstonians as Perry, David Weekley or Kickerillo Homes are today. Harry Mott was the premier builder of his day. During the Great Depression he was a sales representative for the River Oaks Corporation. Late in his career he constructed some homes in the Memorial Villages area where this street recalls his contribution to the architecture of our city. He and his wife Katherine B. Mott resided at 11527 Memorial Drive, not far from this short lane. [129]

MOUNT BATTEN: Here is another example of a developer misspelling a street name. Louis Francis Albert Victor Nicholas Mountbatten was the great grandson of Queen Victoria and a British war hero in both WW I and WW II. He was the last Viceroy of India (1947) and the first Earl of Burma (1947). The Irish Republican Army assassinated Mountbatten in 1979. [130]

MOUNT EVEREST: Our fair city has an elevation of 43 feet above sea level and the 18th green at River Oaks Country Club may be the closest geological feature resembling a mountain. Nonetheless, it is possible to visit the highest mountain in the world, Mount Everest, in west Houston. Named for English surveyor Sir George Everest, this Himalayan peak on the Tibet-Nepal border tops out at 29,035 feet. It was first climbed in 1953 by Sir Edmund Hillary and Tenzing Norgay. (See photograph on page 226.) [131]

MOUNT HOUSTON: This road once lead to Mount Houston, Texas in north central Harris County. This little community was a stop on the Houston, East & West Texas Railroad in the early 1900s. Houston engulfed it in the 1920s. [132]

MOURSUND: Walter H. – Dr. Moursund joined Baylor Medical School in 1911. From 1923 until his retirement he was Dean of Baylor's medical branch in Houston. This Texas Medical Center street is named in his honor. [133]

MT. CARMEL: This southeast side high school was founded by the Order of Carmelites

» **MOUNT EVEREST: World's tallest mountain**

in 1956. Since its creation over 5,000 students have graduated from this institution. In 1986 the Diocese of Galveston-Houston assumed ownership of the school. It has an interesting Latin motto – *non licet nobis esse mediocribus* or "it is not permitted to be mediocre." Your author competed against students from Mt. Carmel in football and track from 1957 to 1960. [84]

MUELLER CEMETERY: Founded in 1896, this cemetery contains the remains of several early German settlers including the Muellers. The earliest grave stone here is that of Emilie Mueller who was born in Prussia in 1838 and died in Harris County in 1896. Her husband, Johan Friedrich Mueller (born 1832), who is also interred here, lived to the ripe old age of 88 years. [50]

» **MUELLER CEMETERY: Entrance gate to the graveyard**

MUELLER: Members of this family were more than likely German immigrants who arrived in the area northwest of Houston in the 1800s. A number of these early settlers are buried in the nearby Trinity Lutheran (also known as Klein) Cemetery. (See **Klein Cemetery.**) [134]

MUESCHKE CEMETERY: Located near Westfield, this street leads to this small cemetery. Like other burial grounds in this area many of the people emigrated from Germany. Names like Hildebrandt, Kaiser, Krimmel, Mittlestedt and Tautenhahn abound. The final resting places of two members of the Mueschke family (Olga and Paul) are here as well as John S. D. Armstrong, a Confederate soldier. The earliest burial I could find was Maria B. Meyers (March 20, 1891). [134]

MULCAHY: R. T. – Known as the "Father of Rosenberg" Mulcahy is remembered for his civic minded nature. Among other projects he raised the funds for Rosenberg's first school. [135]

MULLINS: This family moved to Texas in 1910 from Kansas. They knew the soil near Simonton was rich and well suited for growing new and red potatoes. Unfortunately, they over planted the fields. The quality of the soil declined leading to an epidemic of potato blight. As a result the business failed. For a time however Simonton and nearby Fulshear were called the "potato capitol of the world." James Simonton arrived in Texas in the 1850s and established a plantation here. [136]

MUNGER: Charles R. – (See **Foster.**)

MUNSON RANCH: Mordello Stephen Munson was born in Liberty County in 1825. By the 1850s he was living on this ranch. He founded Munson Cemetery on the property for burials of family and friends in 1850s. The graveyard is located in Bailey's Prairie. (See **Bailey.**) [137]

MURPHY ROAD MOBILE HOME: Located in Stafford, Texas this road leads to a mobile home park. [66]

MURRILL: (See **Jack.**)

MUSICAL: See sidebar **It's Music to My Ears,** page 218.

MUSTANG CROSSING: This street parallels Mustang Bayou in Missouri City. The bayou starts in that city, flows 45 miles, passes southwest of Pearland, north of Alvin to its mouth on New Bayou in southwest Brazoria County. [138]

MUSTANG: Located in front of Lamar Consolidated High School in Rosenberg, this street is named for the school's mascot.

MUSTANG: The Friendswood High School Mustangs play at a stadium on this street. [77]

MUSTANG: This Alvin street recalls the original name of that town, Mustang Station. It was a stop on the Santa Fe Railroad between Galveston and Richmond. (See **Alvin-Sugar Land.**) [139]

MUSTANG ISLAND: See sidebar **The Most Scenic Spots in Texas,** page 310.

MYKAWA: Shinpei - He was born in Aichi, Japan on December 1, 1874. Mykawa came to the U.S. as a naval officer representing his country at the 1903 World's Fair in

M-N

St. Louis. He returned to Japan via Houston and noted how the countryside seemed prefect for rice growing. Immigrating to America he bought land near Erin Station, 10 miles south of Houston, for a rice farm. Unfortunately he was killed on April 24, 1906 when he fell under a piece of agricultural equipment and was crushed. He is buried in Hollywood Cemetery. Mykawa was very popular with his neighbors. In his honor they changed Erin Station to Mykawa, Texas. When the city cut a road along the railroad tracks to that town it was named Mykawa Road. [140]

» MYKAWA: Shinpei Mykawa's tombstone in Hollywood Cemetery. The writing on the sides of this stone is in Japanese.

NAGLE: John Marion – He came to Houston in 1930 as the City Engineer. Nagle eventually was named the Director of the Public Works Department, a position he held until his retirement in 1958. Mayor Oscar Holcombe called him a "man of great vision." In 1957 he was named Engineer of the Year by the San Jacinto Chapter of the Texas Society of Professional Engineers and cited for "the greatest contribution to the City." (See sidebar **Mayor Oscar Holcombe's Revenge**, page 97.) [1]

NAPLAVA: Claud - See sidebar **Houston Streets Named for Men Killed During World War I,** page 22.

NAPOLEON: (See **Bonaparte.**)

NASA ROAD 1: On October 4, 1957 the United States was shocked by the successful launch of Sputnik 1, the first artificial earth satellite, by the USSR. In 1958 President Dwight D. Eisenhower signed the bill creating the National Aeronautics & Space Administration (known by its more common acronym of NASA). The "Space Race" was on in earnest. Initially operating at Cape Canaveral, Florida, NASA announced plans in 1961 for the construction of the Manned Spacecraft Center on 1,000-acres near Clear Lake in southeast Harris County. In 1963 the facility was opened. In America's heyday of space exploration the Gemini, Apollo (the flights to the Moon) and Skylab missions were controlled from here. [2]

NASH-DAMON-RYCADE: Everette Lee DeGolyer was a geophysicist and petroleum engineer born in Kansas in 1886. He was hired in 1918 by Lord Cowdray of Royal Dutch Shell Petroleum Company to explore the salt domes of the Texas Gulf Coast for oil and gas. He formed a firm and called it Rycade Oil Company. DeGolyer was vice president and manager (1923-26) and president and general manager (1926-41). In 1924 using the first geophysical survey he discovered a major oilfield at Nash, Texas. Nash has long since vanished from the maps. DeGolyer was called the "Father of American

Geophysics" and for many years was considered the world's leading oil consultant. (See **Beasley-Damon.**) [3]

NASHUA: This pedigreed colt was the favorite to win the 1955 Kentucky Derby. His jockey was the fabled Eddie Arcaro. But a California thoroughbred named Swaps, ridden by archrival Bill Shoemaker, bested him. Swaps took control of the race early and was never headed. However, Nashua did go on to victory in the Preakness and the Belmont Stakes. [4]

NATCHEZ TRACE: Humans have used this ancient 450-mile trail from Natchez, Mississippi to Nashville, Tennessee since the dawn of time. It was very important to the American Indians of the area and is today a National Parkway. It is also one of the few places where a speeding ticket (exceeding 55 MPH on this scenic two lane road) is a Federal offense. It virtually requires a Presidential pardon to avoid paying the steep fine. [5]

» **NATCHEZ TRACE: The ancient trail**

NATIONAL FOREST: Sam Houston National Forest is a recreational area totaling 161,508 acres in Montgomery, San Jacinto and Walker Counties. The State of Texas authorized the purchase of land for national forests in 1933. [6]

NATURAL BRIDGE: See sidebar **The Most Scenic Spots in Texas,** page 310.

NAVIGATION: Because of its proximity to the Houston Ship Channel and all the waterborne commerce that takes place in the area, this street was named to reflect the port related activity. [7]

NAZRO: Underwood – This man was a vice president at the Gulf Oil Corporation in Baytown. [8]

NEEDVILLE: August Schendel first named this town Schendelville in 1891. When he applied for a post office he filed under the name of Needmore as a joke. He said he did it because the place needed more of everything. Strangely enough the name was already taken so it was changed to Needville. He operated a general store, cotton gin and a blacksmith shop. [9]

NEIDIGK: Fred – This German immigrant arrived in the Houston area in 1902. He built a sawmill near Decker's Prairie. In the early 1900s Neidigk Station was a stop on the International-Great Northern Railroad. Neidigk Lake on Spring Creek is also named for him. [10]

NETTLETON: Robert E. – See sidebar **Houston Streets Named for Men Killed During**

World War I, page 22.

NEUENS: August – This German immigrant arrived in the Spring Branch area in the mid-1870s. Like many of his industrious neighbors from the Old World he amassed considerable land holdings. His property was where this road is today. Members of this family are buried in the St. Peter's United Church graveyard. [11]

NEVELSON: Louise – This seems to be the only street in Houston named for a female artist. This Russian-born American citizen is famous for her free-standing as well as hanging wooden sculpture. One of her finest works, *Frozen Laces-One*, may be seen in downtown Houston at 1400 Smith. [12]

NEW CANEY: (See **Huffman.**) [13]

NEWCASTLE: See sidebar **All Things English,** page 175.

NEW KENTUCKY: Only a historic marker and a street recall this early trading center that was once located in northern Harris County. Abram Roberts who was from Kentucky established it. The town had a short lifespan, lasting from only 1831 until about 1840. [14]

NEWGULF ACCESS: Newgulf was founded by Texas Gulf Sulfur Company atop the Boling Dome in 1928. Under the dome was the largest known inland sulfur deposit in the world. It was a company town and got its name after management sponsored a naming contest for employees. Mary Ertz won. She based her choice on the fact that Texas Gulf's first town was Gulf. This company town had over 400 homes, shops, hospital, pharmacy, barber shop, library, school, post office, movie theater, tailor, cleaner, four churches, clubhouse and a nine-hole golf course. By 1940 almost 1,600 people lived here. In the 1960s the world sulfur market crashed. The company had located cheaper-to-extract deposits elsewhere so the town was closed. Today it is an interesting ghost town to visit because of its post-apocalyptic, *Mad Max* ruins. Street signs remain named **Texasgulf, Newgulf, Reservoir** and **Burning Stone.** [15]

NGPL: This road leads to Natural Gas Pipeline Compression Station 301 west of Hungerford and north of Wharton. [16]

NIBLICK: Old time golfers know this is a golf club. Before irons were numbered they all had names such as mashie, mashie niblick, etc. The niblick equates to a nine iron today.

MY HOW WE HAVE GROWN

When Houston was founded in 1836 there were only 6.5 miles of streets in the city and none were paved. Paving began in the early 1890s and by 1892 we had 12.5 miles of paved roads. By 1911 that total increased to 90 miles. In 1939 we reached 1,000 miles. Today that number is a staggering 6,000 miles of concrete and asphalt just within the city limits. [35, 36]

M-N

NICHOLAS BRAVO: During the Texas Revolution 21 Texas Army prisoners were held for 11 months in Matamoros, Mexico. Following Santa Anna's defeat at San Jacinto they were supposed to be released. However, the soldiers remained in prison until this gentleman was named commanding officer in Matamoros. He released them in January, 1837. This street is located in the historic town of San Felipe. [17]

NICHOLS: A prominent Dickinson, Texas family, the Nichols first arrived here in 1857. Ebenezer B. Nichols, a director of the Galveston, Houston & Henderson Railroad, had a summer home here. He was a partner with William Marsh Rice in a commission and freight forwarding business. Fred M. Nichols and his partners organized the Dickinson Land and Improvement Company to sell real estate in the town. These civic-minded citizens gave the city the land for the Dickinson Picnic Grounds, a popular gathering place. (See **Dickinson.**) [18]

NICHOLS: This gentleman was granted a league of land in the 1820s where Bellville is today. [19]

NICHOLSON: Claud – See sidebar **Houston Streets Named for Men Killed During World War I,** page 22.

NICHOLSON: E. S. – He was a real estate promoter in the Galveston bayside town of Seabrook in the early 1900s. (See **Sydnor.**) [20]

NIMITZ: Chester W. – A graduate of the Naval Academy in 1905, he was a career officer in the U.S. Navy. A submariner in WW I, Nimitz was most famous for his naval successes in the Pacific Theater during WW II. His forces racked up decisive victories at Guadalcanal, Midway, the Solomons, the Gilberts, the Marshalls, the Marianas, the Philippines, Iwo Jima and Okinawa. Nimitz accepted the Japanese surrender documents on the deck of his flagship, the battleship *Missouri,* in Tokyo Bay on September 2, 1945. [21]

NINA LEE: This lady was the wife of Harold P. Hill, office manager of Oak Forest Addition. Frank Sharp, the developer, named it for her. (See **Chantilly** and **Frank Sharp.**) [22]

NO NAME: This three block long lane runs through a concentration of townhouses. It is not marked in any manner and has no addresses, thus the name and in this case the lack of even street signs. [23]

» **NINA LEE: On her wedding day to Harold Hill**

NOBLE: This 5th Ward street is named for the Noble family. Grace Noble married Elbert E. Adkins. Her grandfather, Stephen Noble, is associated with the Kellum-Noble house located in Sam Houston Park. (See **Adkins.**) [24]

NOGALUS: See sidebar **Learn a Foreign Language on Your Morning Walk,** page 125.

NOLAN RYAN: It is only proper that this high-speed expressway is named for one of the greatest pitchers in baseball history. His record setting career of 324 wins, 7 no hitters, 383 strike outs in a season and 5,714 strike outs in his 26 years (1967-1993) in the majors are the stuff of baseball lore. We were lucky that he sported a Houston Astro uniform for a portion of his career. [25]

NORHILL: Now one of the city's historic districts, Norhill was developed in the 1920s by the Stude family and one of the creators of River Oaks, Will Hogg. It was a nice working-class neighborhood not dissimilar to Houston Heights to its west or Studemont to the east. Its name was probably chosen because it was north of downtown and on a higher elevation. However, Sherrie Chisholm, a resident involved with the historic district, says that years ago a man named Norbert Hill lived in the area and it's possible the street remembers him. (See **Stude.**) [26]

NORMANDY: This region of northwest France on the English Channel was the sight of the D-Day landing on June 6, 1944. Code-named "Operation Overlord," it was led by the Allies' Supreme Commander, General Dwight D. Eisenhower. Remembered as "the Longest Day," the success of the Allied troops here spelled the beginning of the end of the War for Nazi Germany. (See **Eisenhower.**) [27]

M-N

NORRIS: Earnest Mishael – He was born in Normangee in 1903. This black student earned his B. S. (1927) and M. S, (1931) from Prairie View A & M University and Ph.D from University of Ithaca in 1934. He was hired by Prairie View in 1937 to serve as a professor in the Agriculture Department. Norris taught here until he retired in 1968. [28]

» NORRIS: Paririe View A & M street marker

NORTHAMPTON: See sidebar **All Things English,** page 175.

NORTH HOUSTON: This small community grew up on the Trinity & Brazos Railway beginning in 1907. Once known as Tomball and later as Scoville it finally received its present name in 1910. Today little remains of the small oil town. (See **Tomball.**) [29]

NORTH MAIN: Originally know as East Montgomery Road, City of Houston Water Commissioner David Fitzgerald, who lived on this street, got the name changed in 1913. [30]

NORTH: (See **Parkway.**)

NORTHAMPTON: See **Southampton's English Streets,** page 255.

NORTHWESTERN: Opened by the Methodists in 1855, this Evanston, Illinois university is one of the finest centers of higher learning in the country. [31]

MAYOR BOB AND HIS BELOVED ROSES

Long before serving as mayor of Houston, Bob Lanier was a real estate developer with a passion for growing roses. His home featured some of the finest rose gardens in the city. To honor this, the most beautiful of flowers, Lanier decided to name the streets in one of his developments, Twin Lakes, for a variety of roses. Today you can drive on **American Beauty, Summer Snow, Tropicana, Gold Medal, King's Ransom, Pristine, Carrousel, Honor, Oregold, China Doll, Sweet Surrender, Peace** and **Spartan.** [37]

O

OAHU: See sidebar **Bali Hai May Call You,** page 322.

OAK RIDGE: In 1964 an Arkansas land developer, Spring Pines Corporation, named this thoroughfare and the neighborhood of Oak Ridge North. The tract was originally owned by early Texas pioneer, Charles Eisterwall. [1]

OAKLAND: Since this street is in a Sugar Land neighborhood with streets referencing other historical names I believe this one is named for a plantation of the same name that was near here. It was owned by Nathaniel F. and Mathew R. Williams. These brothers built the plantation in the 1840s and began raising sugar cane thus starting the industry for which the town is now named. [2]

OAKLAWN PARK: This Hot Springs, Arkansas horse race track is the site of the Arkansas Derby, one of the prep races for three year old thoroughbreds with hopes of going on to the Kentucky Derby in Louisville, Kentucky on the first Saturday in May to "Run for the Roses." [3]

OAKLAWN: This plantation was owned by Samuel May Williams. He gave it the name because there were five varieties of oak trees there. In 1828 he received this league in Fort Bend County on Oyster Creek from Stephen F. Austin. (See **Williams.**) [4]

OAKSHIRE: See sidebar **All Things English,** page 175.

OATES: James Wyatt – Oates Road is just north of Jacinto City. This settler arrived in the area in the early 1860s. Nearby is a cemetery variously referred to as Oates Prairie, Oates-Singleton and Hart-Singleton cemetery. Members from all three families are interred there. In Trevia Wooster Beverly's fascinating book, *At Rest: A Historical Directory of Harris County, Texas Cemeteries (1822-1992)*, she mentions that D. R., Patton, a Houston police officer killed during the 1917 Camp Logan riot, is also buried here. (See **Logan**) [5]

OBERLIN: This street is named for a liberal arts college in the Ohio town of the same name that opened in 1833. Oberlin was one of the first centers of higher learning to have co-educational classes. [6]

OCTAVIAN: Caius – He was the son of Julius Caesar's sister. The first and one of the greatest Roman emperors, Octavian was given the honorific title of Augustus by the Roman Senate in 27 B.C. He is remembered for his political skills, support of road building throughout the empire, fair taxation, construction of the Forum in Rome and his support of the arts. (See **Forum.**) [7]

ODIN: John Mary – A minister ordained in 1823, he was sent to Texas in 1840. Odin was greatly responsible for the rapid growth of the Catholic faith in early Texas. By 1847 he was named Bishop of the Diocese of Galveston (that included Houston then). The original street named for him was later changed to Lyons in honor of a famous local saloonkeeper. Possibly a fit of guilt or fear of heavenly recrimination resulted in another street in this Third Ward neighborhood remembering the Bishop. (See **Lyons.**) [8]

OIL CENTER: This north Harris County street leads into the Houston Intercontinental Oil Center, a commercial development for companies in the energy industry. It this case most of the tenets are oilfield service firms. [9]

OILER: The Pearland High School teams are the Oilers. [10]

OJEMAN: This is one of many streets in the Spring Branch area named for German immigrants. The Ojeman family came from Frankfurt. It is possible that the first to arrive were brothers Carl, Willie and Robert. Some family members are buried in the St. Peter's United Church cemetery on Long Point. In the Borgestedt Cemetery off Huffmeister Road there are a number of persons interred with the sir name of Ojemann. It was not unusual for immigrants to alter the spelling of their names after arriving in America. I believe this is the case here since the street and cemetery are not far apart. Family members buried here include Fred (born 1884), Emma (born 1884), Edna (born 1913) and Marie (born 1914). [11, 12]

OKINAWA: This is the largest of the Ryukyu Islands. It is located about 500 miles southwest of Japan. It was the site of the last amphibious battle of the Pacific War. Casualties were enormous on both sides. The Japanese lost 103,000 of 120,000 troops stationed on the island. U.S. casualties totaled 48,000 with 25% of those killed in action. [13]

OLD ARCADIA: Established on Hall's Bayou in Galveston County, Arcadia was first named Hall's Station in 1889. A year later Henry Runge, an early resident, renamed it Arcadia for a town in Louisiana. Dairy farms became the backbone of the local economy. In the 1920s Arcadia Creamery was established to produce milk, cream, butter and cheese. (See **Santa Fe.**) [14]

OLD CANEY: Caney Creek is a historic estuary. Originally called Canebrake Creek be-

» OLD CANEY: Caney Creek with Hinton/Treichler pier in 1960

cause of the thick stands of cane that grew along its banks, it meanders 155 miles from its source in Colorado County to its mouth on the Gulf Intercoastal Waterway near Sargent. During the War Between the States Confederate General Jeb Magruder fortified the mouth to halt the Union advance up the coast toward Galveston. The fortress at Caney Creek was shelled by Union gunboats in January and February of 1864. Today it is known as a great place to catch speckled trout, drum, sheep head and red fish. [15]

OLD DANVILLE: Samuel and Joseph Lindley moved to this area in 1830. They named it for their hometown of Danville, Illinois. On September 11, 1858 the town hosted a barbeque for Sam Houston. It remains a small, quiet, rural community near Willis today. [16]

OLD DOBBIN-PLANTERSVILLE: The area around Plantersville was settled in the 1830s. Alabaman Isaac Baker operated a 2,850 acre plantation here beginning in 1840. When the post office was established in 1856 Mrs. J. L. Greene suggested the name to honor the many planters like Baker who lived around here. (See **Dobbin-Hufsmith.**) [17]

OLD GUY: No, this street is not named for your author. Orr Rowland was the first postmaster of Guy, Texas. He named the town for his crippled daughter Una Guy Rowland in 1898. When the Galveston, Harrisburg & San Antonio Railroad bypassed Guy most of the townspeople moved near the tracks, called that new town Guy and the few remaining citizens renamed their town Old Guy. This was a popular place to visit because of its rocking dance hall. It was closed in 1980 and the building was

O-P

moved to the George Ranch Historical Park. (See **A. P. George Ranch.**) [18]

OLD HICKORY: See sidebar the **Antebellum Streets of River Plantation,** page 122.

OLD NELSONVILLE: Named for D. D. Nelson, a shopkeeper, who lived in this Austin County village after the War Between the States, it was settled by German immigrants from Bohemia in the late 1860s and 1870s. Most of the citizens were cotton farmers. [19]

OLD RICHMOND: This road once lead to Richmond, Texas, the seat of Fort Bend County. Brothers Henry and Randal Jones settled the area in 1822. These early settlers' hometown was Richmond, Virginia. [20]

OLD RIVER: This street and river are named for the old riverbed of the San Jacinto River. This four-mile watercourse, to the east of that river, separates Channelview and Lynchburg. During World War II the U. S. Army operated the 5,000-acre San Jacinto Ordinance Depot along the banks of Old River. Originally the land here was owned by Texas Revolution hero Lorenzo de Zavala. (See **de Zavala.**) [21]

OLD SAN FELIPE: (See **Peters-San Felipe.**)

OLD SPANISH TRAIL: This thoroughfare is named in honor of one of Texas' earliest highways. However, the actual route of the Old San Antonio Road, the King's Highway or *El Camino Real,* its original names, is nowhere near Houston. It started on the Sabine River near what is today the Toledo Bend Reservoir, went southwest to San Antonio and ended on the Rio Grande River in Maverick County near Eagle Pass. Initially traversed in 1691, it was ordered surveyed by the Texas Legislature in 1915 and named a state highway worth preserving in 1929. [22]

OLD TEXACO CAMP: On December 13, 1931 George W. Strake, a Houston wildcatter, discovered oil southeast of Conroe. Soon the Texas Company (now Texaco) and Humble Oil & Refining (now Exxon Mobil) began developing the field. Your author's father, C. M. Hinton Sr., went to work for the Texas Company in the mid 1930s as a field foreman. In 1940 he and my mother, Mocco Dunn Hinton, were transferred to this oilfield company camp. On the morning of June 23, 1942 my mother went into labor

» **OLD TEXACO CAMP: Childhood home of your author**

and was rushed to Houston's St. Joseph Hospital where your author arrived at 10:15 AM weighing in at 8 lbs. and 7 oz. On July 7 we were taken by ambulance to our home at Texaco Camp where I would live until age two. Except for this road sign nothing remains of the camp. [23]

OLYMPIA: The Olympia Country and Golf Club is in the Washington State city of the same name. This scenic course, founded in 1926, is located on beautiful Puget Sound. [24]

OMAR: Karla Cisneros, a Houston Heights resident who lives on this street, was told years ago that the name Omar was chosen since it means "the highest" in Persian. The street has the highest elevation in the area north of White Oak Bayou before the land begins to slope downward again. [25]

OPELOUSAS: The old Fifth Ward has several streets named for locations in Louisiana. Examples are **New Orleans** and **Conti.** This one is named for the town of Opelousas, also the name of an Indian tribe that inhabited the area. It became a bayou trading post for the French and Indians in 1720. It is famous for its Zydeco music and is the birthplace of "Zydeco King" Clifton Chenier. [26]

> ## THE GREAT TEXAS DEPARTMENT OF TRANSPORTATION MILEAGE GAP MYSTERY
>
> Have you ever wondered why when you are approaching a metropolitan area like Houston the Texas Department of Transportation mileage markers telling how far it is to Houston do not match up with how far you know it is to the city? Well there is a good reason. TXDOT does not measure from city limit to city limit because cities expand and communities may incorporate. That would require constant changing of the mileage markers. Instead they measure from the closest state exit to one city's center to another. For example, if you were traveling from Dallas or Katy to Houston TXDOT would use I-10 Houston exit 768 because that is the closest exit to the center of Houston. Yet the city limit sign may be 10 miles ahead but downtown is 20 miles further. Thus the mileage marker would say Houston 30 miles. [38]

OPUS: See sidebar **It's Music to My Ears,** page 218.

ORATORIO: See sidebar **It's Music to My Ears,** page 218.

ORION: See sidebar **Starry Night,** page 111.

OROZIMBO: James Aeneas Phelps received a land grant northwest of what is today Angleton in 1824. Legend says he named his plantation after a local Indian chief. Phelps was one of Austin's Old 300 and surgeon for the Texas Army at the Battle of San Jacinto. Following his capture, General Santa Anna was held prisoner at the Phelps plantation where the Mexican *commandante,* suffering severe depression, was diagnosed as suicidal. The good doctor talked Santa Anna out of killing himself. Six years later Phelps' son, Orlando, was captured by the Mexican army while on the Mier Expedition. In a show of gratitude Santa Anna saved the doctor's son from facing the firing squad. Orlando lived to the ripe old age of 75. [27]

OSCEOLA PLANTATION: William Green Hill was born in North Carolina in 1801. He

O-P

moved to Texas in 1830 and settled in what is Brazoria County today. In 1835 he joined the Texas Army and saw action at the Battle of Concepcion, Grass Fight and Siege of Bexar. In 1836 William Barrett Travis ordered him to recruit soldiers for the upcoming fight with Mexico. After Texas Independence he was given land between East Columbia and Orozimbo Plantation. On this property he built Osceola Plantation. Hill prospered and died a wealthy man in 1860. (See **Travis, Texas Army** and **Orozimbo.**) [28]

OVERBROOK: (See **Larchmont.**)

OXFORD: It is named for the English University that was founded in the 12th century. [29]

OYSTER CREEK: Named for the creek that runs from north of Richmond, Texas to the Gulf of Mexico, this area was a favorite of some of Stephen F. Austin's Old 300. Many of these families owned plantations along its banks. It was named for the large number of oyster beds it contained. [30]

» O'BANION: Street marker remembers this educator

O'BANION: Elmer E. – This black educator was Chairman of the Natural Sciences Department at Prairie View A & M University. He was hired in 1937 after earning his B. S., M. S. and Ph.D from University of Indiana. O'Banion was a member of the first graduating class in Atomic Energy at Oak Ridge Institute in Oak Ridge, Tennessee. The first atomic bomb was built there. [31]

O'HARA: Scarlett – She was the heroine of Margaret Mitchell's Pulitzer Prize winning novel (1937) and blockbuster motion picture (1939), *Gone With the Wind,* staring Vivien Leigh as Scarlett and Clark Gable as Rhett Butler. The street to the west is **Scarlett.**

O'REILLY: W. M. – See sidebar **Houston Streets Named for Men Killed During World War I,** page 22.

P

P: (See **Luella.**)

PABLO PICASSO: This Spanish artist was the father of Cubism, a style of painting and sculpture that developed in Paris in the early 20th century. Its principal characteristic is the reduction and fragmentation of natural forms into abstract geometric structures rendered in different planes. His most famous and powerful painting, *Guernica* (1937), depicts the horrors of the Spanish Civil War. Today it hangs in the Reina Sophia, Spain's national museum of modern art, in Madrid.[1]

PACKARD: See sidebar **Fairbanks Could Have Its Own Concours d' Elegance and Road Rally,** page 140.

PAIGE: David H. – This early Houston businessman was co-owner of the Houston & Texas Central Railroad that he and his partner Cornelius Ennis bought for $10,000 out of bankruptcy. The street to the immediate east is Ennis. (See **Ennis.**)[2]

PALM AIRE: See sidebar **Tennis or Golf, Anyone?,** page 348.

PALMER: Arnold - See sidebar **Tennis or Golf, Anyone?,** page 348.

PALMER: This early Houston family amassed significant land holdings east of downtown Houston in the 1880s and 1890s.[3]

PALMETTO: See sidebar **Bali Hai May Call You,** page 322.

PALOMINO: (See **Appaloosa.**)

PANDORA: This mythical Greek goddess was Zeus' creation as retribution for Prometheus stealing fire from the gods. She was given a jar (Pandora's Box) and told

O-P

not to open it. However, Pandora's curiosity got the better of her. When she took a look, all manner of evil poured out into the mortal world. Only hope remained in the jar as she slammed the box closed before it could escape. [4]

PANORAMA: This small (1.1 square mile in area), unincorporated jurisdiction called Panorama Village is just north of Conroe. It was begun in the 1960s. [5]

PANTHER CREEK: This Woodlands street is named for a watercourse called Panther Branch. It flows southeast from its headwaters in Montgomery County to where it empties into Spring Creek on the Harris County line. [6]

PAPEETE: See sidebar **Bali Hai May Call You,** page 322.

PAR ONE: Had the developers of Roman Forest Country Club ever played golf before naming this street? In a neighborhood full of winding lanes with golf associated names (**Eagle, Putters Green, Fairway** and **Pebble Beach**) how could you not know there is no such hole as a one par. Even in miniature golf the lowest is a par two.

PARK PLACE: This southeast side neighborhood was developed in the 1930s by Park Place Company who named this main thoroughfare for the corporation. [7]

PARK TEN: The location of this west side drive produces its name. It is situated between I-10 and Bear Creek Park. [8]

PARKVIEW: In 1903 Houston Electric Company, a firm that operated a number of the city's electric streetcar lines, constructed a private park east of Houston Avenue and north of White Oak Bayou. It was called Highland Park. The street on the north side of this green space was named Parkview. In 1911 the park was sold to the city and renamed Woodland Park. [9]

PARKWAY: James A. Baker, Jr., father of the former Secretary of Treasury and State James III, was the developer of Broadacres. He and architect William Ward Watkin named the U-shaped pattern of streets **North, West** and **South** Boulevards and since there was a small private park on the east side, that street became Parkway rather than East. [10]

PARTHENON: Developers of Roman Forest got their geography a bit muddled when they named this street. This famous Greek temple to the goddess Athena sits on the hilltop called the Acropolis in Athens. [11]

PASADENA: This is the Chippewa Indian word for "Crown of the Valley." A detailed study of this ship channel city fails to produce any noticeably beautiful valleys. Rather Charles Munger named the street and town in honor of the California city of the same name. [12]

PASCHALL: Samuel – Early in Houston's history it was suggested to city officials that they name a street for each of Austin's Old 300 plus every soldier that fought at the Battle Of San Jacinto. Although this did not come to pass we do have a number of streets honoring veterans of that battle. Paschall was born in Tennessee in 1815 and came to Texas to help with the fight for independence. There is a historical marker honoring him in St. Vincent's Cemetery on Navigation. [13]

PATRICIA: Land developer Herman E. Detering named this street for a female friend when he was building an office park off of the Gulf Freeway. [14]

PATRICK HENRY: This American patriot, lawyer, orator and Governor of Virginia during the American Revolution is best remembered for his speech before the Virginia Provisional Convention in 1775. At that gathering he uttered the famous words, "Give me liberty or give me death." [15]

PATTERSON: Charles H. – See sidebar **Houston Streets Named for Men Killed During World War I,** page 22.

PATTI LYNN: (See **Lorrie Lake.**)

PATTON: George Smith, Jr. – He was a brilliant tank commander in WW I and WW II and earned the nickname "Old Blood and Guts." During the Second World War his tactical genius was displayed with victories in North Africa, Sicily and the charge of Allied troops from Normandy, across France and through Germany to ultimate victory. The only blemish on his outstanding military career was a highly publicized incident in which he slapped a soldier he thought was a coward. The man was actually suffering from battle fatigue. Patton died in an automobile accident shortly after the close of the War. [16]

PATTON: See sidebar **Brazoria County's Old Plantation Streets and Roads,** page 258.

PAUL QUINN: William Paul Quinn was the fourth bishop of the African Methodist Episcopal Church. Paul Quinn College, the oldest black liberal arts college in Texas, was also named in his honor. It was founded in Austin in 1872 for the purpose of educating former slaves in industrial skills such as blacksmithing and carpentry. In 1990 the school moved to Dallas taking over the former campus of Bishop College. [17]

PAUL REVERE: This American patriot was a participant in the Boston Tea Party, a Revolutionary War hero and is known by every school child who reads Longfellow's poem about his midnight ride on April 18, 1775 from Charlestown to Lexington to warn Bostonians that "the British are coming!" [18]

PAYNE: Houston Lighting & Power (now Reliant Energy) once owned some acreage in Woodland Heights. They developed an amusement park near what today is Woodland Park. This street that dead-ends into that park is named for Mr. Payne who was president of the Light Company at that time. [19]

O–P

PEACH CREEK: An Anglo-American settlement started in this area of Montgomery County in the mid-1830s. Early pioneers named this 37-mile spring-fed creek. One of the longer creeks in the area its banks are lined with loblolly and short leaf pine; sweet and blackgum; water, post and willow oak; elm; pecan and black hickory trees. Oddly there are no peach trees. [20]

PEACH POINT: (See **Chocolate Bayou.**)

PEACHTEX: See sidebar **Howdy Tex,** page 263.

PEARCE: Louis, J. E., Lafayette and Oscar – These men worked at Texas Iron Works in Baytown. As far as I know this is the only area street named for four brothers. [21]

PEARLAND SCHOOL: This road leads to Pearland High School and its nearby football stadium. [22]

PEARLAND: This northern Brazoria County town began life in 1882 as Mark Belt, a siding on the Gulf, Colorado & Santa Fe Railroad. In 1893 the name was changed to Pearland because of the large number of pear tree orchards in the area. The city was once grandly promoted as an "agricultural Eden." [23]

PEARSON: Edward Adolphus – His father, P. E. Pearson, came to Texas in 1867 and settled in Fort Bend County. Edward was born in Matagorda in 1867. Later he was elected Sheriff of the county. [24]

PEARTEX: See sidebar **Howdy Tex,** page 263.

PEASE: Elisha Marshall – This Connecticut Yankee arrived in Stephen F. Austin's court of Texas in 1835. A strong advocate of Texas independence, Pease fought in the first battle of the revolution at Gonzales. This Texas patriot served as chief clerk of the Texas Navy, Secretary of the Treasury, legislator and senator in the Texas Legislature and two-term Governor (1853 and 1855). He opposed secession from the Union and did not participate in the War Between the States. His influence with the Union occupation government benefited Texas greatly during the period of Reconstruction. [25]

PECANTEX: See sidebar **Howdy Tex,** page 263.

PECH: Here is another Spring Branch street named for one of the pioneer German families who immigrated to America. Moritz Pech was one of the first immigrant children born in the area in 1860. His son, Albert "Boots" Pech, was a founding member of the Spring Branch Volunteer Fire Department. [26]

PECORE: R. C. – See sidebar **Houston Streets Named for Men Killed During World War I,** page 22. [27]

PEDEN: Edward Andrew – In 1902 he founded Peden Iron and Steel Company, a supply house for hardware, iron, steel, rails and oilfield equipment. He was a very important man holding directorships with the Harris County Navigation and Canal Company, First National Bank, Goose Creek Oil Company, Houston Lighting & Power, to mention a few. He was a trustee of the Houston Art League (now the Museum of Fine Arts, Houston). It is possible that since this Montrose area street is not far from that venerable old arts organization that it was named for Peden. [28]

PEDERNALES FALLS: See sidebar **The Most Scenic Spots in Texas,** page 310.

PELICAN ISLAND: This is a small island north of Galveston Harbor. It was named for the huge number of pelicans that nested there. During the War Between the States Confederates tried to fool the Union Navy by installing "quakers" or fake cannons at the small fort there. The trick failed and Union forces captured Pelican Island. When the South recaptured Galveston six real casement guns were brought and secured the island. Since then it has been used by the fishing and oyster industries, as an immigration station, shipyard and by Texas A & M University. [29]

PELLY: Fred T. – This native of Great Britain was a large landowner on Galveston Bay. The place was first called Old Town, then Middle Town and finally Pelly in 1920. He was the town's first mayor. Pelly remained independent until its incorporation into Baytown in 1947. So while the town no longer exists, the street name remembers this early settler. (See **Tri-Cities.**) [30]

PEMBERTON: Incorporated in 1927, The Pemberton Company was a land developer in West University Place where this street is located. The firm paid $86,000 for 40 acres of raw land. A shareholder of the company was H. B. Schlesinger, the first mayor of West University (1925-33). [31]

PENN CITY: Years ago this was a small town on the banks of Buffalo Bayou near where the Houston Ship Channel is today. Eventually the town was absorbed into Cloverleaf. (See **Cloverleaf.**) [32]

PENN: William – This English citizen was drawn toward the principles of Quakerism after he graduated from Oxford in 1662. However, he is most remembered as the colonizer of what would come to be known as Pennsylvania, a place where the Society of Friends could practice religious freedom. (See **Friendswood** and **Quaker.**) [33]

PERCUSSION: See sidebar **It's Music to My Ears,** page 218.

PERKINS: The Perkins Development Company developed Trinity Gardens where this east side street is located. Among their other projects were Bonita Gardens, Burbank Gardens, Colonial Gardens and Kashmere Gardens. [34]

PERRY LANDING: This boat landing was on the Brazos River south of Angleton. It was owned by James F. Perry who had established Peach Point Plantation there in 1832. (See **Chocolate Bayou**.) [35]

PERRY: Fred – This English tennis professional was one of the great players of the 1930s. He won the Australian Championship (1934), French Open (1935), Wimbledon (1934-36) and U. S. Open (1933, 1934, 1936). Perry is the last British player to win all four major singles titles. He was also quite a ladies man having relationships with movie stars Marlene Dietrich, Helen Vinson and Sandra Breaux before entering a 40 year marriage to Barbara Riese. [36]

PERSHING: John J. - He was one of the greatest generals in American military history. Never one to dodge a fight, "Blackjack" Pershing fought in the Indian, Spanish-American and Philippine Wars as well as WW I. Texans remember him for leading the punitive force that chased Pancho Villa in 1916 following Villa's attack on Columbus, New Mexico. [37]

PETERS-SAN FELIPE: This Austin County road connects these two small towns. The area around Peters was settled in the mid 1820s. The town was established in 1880 as a station on the Bellville-Sealy spur of the Gulf, Colorado & Santa Fe Railroad. Albert Peters was an early resident. San Felipe was founded by Stephen F. Austin as the unofficial capitol of his colony. It was the first urban center in what would become Texas. The whole name was San Felipe de Austin. Felipe de Garza, the governor of the Eastern Interior Provinces of Mexico, named it to honor Stephen F. Austin and his own patron saint. History buffs should pay a visit to the Stephen F. Austin State Historical Park here. (See **Railspur**.) [38]

PETERSBURG: See sidebar **Antebellum Streets of River Plantation**, page 122.

PETRICH: Wilhelm F. – This German settler arrived in northwest Harris County in the mid-1800s. The Petrich farm was where this road is located. His grave in the historic St. John Lutheran Cemetery is the oldest dated tombstone there. (See **Lutheran Cemetery**.) [7]

PEVETO: Michael, Jr. – He was a soldier in the Texas Army who fought at the Battle of San Jacinto under the command of Captain William M. Logan. For unknown reasons he died of poor health shortly after the battle. [39]

PHAIR CEMETERY: This Brazoria County community has been called Ranch Prairie, Phair and Stratton Ridge. Reverend George H. Phair was a Methodist circuit rider who served churches in Velasco in 1875-1885. Two parishioners, E. B. and Mollie Thomas, donated the land for this cemetery in 1853. Today it is a ghost town. [40]

PHILLIPS COMPANY: Both Phillips Petroleum and Phillips Chemical have an industrial district here on the Houston Ship Channel. Phillips Petroleum was founded in 1917. In 1921 they branded their famous "Phillips 66" gasoline. It got its name for two reasons.

First, an executive was riding back to Bartlesville, Oklahoma, the corporate head-quarters, and commented on the speed of the automobile saying: "This car goes like 60 on our new gas." To which the driver responded: "Sixty nothing. We are going 66!" Second, this event took place on the "Mother Road," U.S. Highway 66, often remembered as Route 66. The decision was made and the rest is history. In 1951 chemists at Phillips invented polyethylene plastic. One of the more famous products made from this material was "hula hoops" during that 1950s craze. [41]

PICCADILLY CIRCUS: This world famous traffic circle in western London is remembered for its quaint name and the statue or Eros, the Greek god of love, who towers above it. [42]

PICKENS: See sidebar **Texas Heroes' Names for Houston Streets Urged in 72 Proposed Changes,** page 96.

PICKETT: George Edward – This gentleman was an able general for the Confederates during the War Between the States. He served admirably at the battles of Williamsburg, Seven Pines, Gaines Mill, Fredericksburg, Petersburg and Cold Harbor. Unfortunately, he is remembered for leading the disastrous attack on Cemetery Hill during the Battle of Gettysburg on July 3, 1863. Known as "Pickett's Charge," of the 4,500 men who entered the fray, 3,393 were killed. This unmitigated defeat was certainly the turning point of this battle and possibly of the entire war. [43]

PICNIC: Located in Memorial Park, the largest urban park in Texas at 1,466-acres, this loop has been popular with Houstonians as a place for family outings since the park opened in 1925. (See **Memorial** and **Logan.**) [44]

PIERCE: Franklin - As the 14th President of the United States he tried to govern during the tumultuous time just prior to the Civil War. Because he opposed President Lincoln during the War for what he believed was exceeding constitutional authority, Texans could identify with him. [45]

PIERRE SCHLUMBERGER: This gentleman is a member of the founding family of oil-field service giant Schlumberger. (See **Schlumberger.**)

PIFER: Claude and Hilda – This couple donated the land for this tiny Hunter's Creek Village street. [46]

PIGEON: (See **Shooting Center.**)

PILLOT: Eugene – Located near the Houston Ship Channel, this street recalls a man who was involved early on in the development of that great project. Pillot was born in France, learned carpentry in New York and came to Texas in 1837. He made his money in the building business and invested in a number of ventures including the Houston, East & West Texas Railway, Texas Western Railway and Houston Direct

Navigation Company. Chartered in 1866 this firm dramatically improved navigation and transportation along Buffalo Bayou. His son, Camille, became a partner of Henry Henke in the Henke & Pillot grocers. [47]

PIMLICO: The Maryland Jockey Club owns this Baltimore horse race course. Every May it is the site of the Preakness Stakes, the second leg of racing's Triple Crown. (See **Preakness** and **Triple Crown.**)

PIN OAK: This Galleria area street was named for the Pin Oak Stables that once were on the site. The Abercrombie family owned the land and built the facility for their only daughter, Josephine. She began riding horses at four years of age and became an accomplished horsewoman. Annually the Pin Oak Charity Horse Show was held at the arena there. It was one of the premier social events of the season in the 1950s. [48]

PINE GULLY: This street is named for a short stream that starts south of Gulfgate Mall, runs northeast and empties into Sims Bayou. [49]

PINE ISLAND: This small town is southeast of Hempstead. It was founded when settlers erected the Pine Island Baptist Church in the 1880s. This street, named for the church, is one of the main thoroughfares here. [50]

PINE VALLEY: Information from the real estate firm of Robin Elverson says this street is named for the Clementon, New Jersey country club. For his first round here, a young and not-yet-so-famous or wealthy Arnold Palmer broke par, won enough money to buy an engagement ring and eloped with his bride. [51]

PINEHURST: This small Montgomery County village was founded in 1860 under the name of "Prairie Home." In 1871 it was rechristened as "Hunters Retreat." With the arrival of the International-Great Northern Railroad it was renamed again to its present name. This short loop recalls the town. [52]

PINETEX: See sidebar **Howdy Tex,** page 263.

PINEVIEW: In 1923 Edward L. Crane purchased this east side tract of land. Due to its proximity to the Missouri, Kansas & Texas Railroad tracks, Crane needed all of his creative talents to make the neighborhood attractive to prospective buyers. Many trees were planted to wall off the unsightly tracks. In another marketing ploy Crane called the neighborhood "Pineview Place - The Rose Garden of Houston." The houses here were prefabricated and were made in the Crane Ready Cut House Company plant. (See **Edloe.**) [53]

PINEY POINT: Records indicate that in 1824 Stephen F. Austin issued a one league land grant to John D. Taylor. The property was centered on "Pine Point" at the southernmost turn of Buffalo Bayou. Taylor called his plantation home "Piney Point." [54]

PINO: See sidebar **Learn a Foreign Language on Your Morning Walk,** page 125.

PINTO: (See **Appaloosa.**)

PIPER: It makes sense that a road adjacent to an airport would be named for an airplane. William Thomas Piper developed this light aircraft in 1937. The Piper Cub was originally designed for flight training but the USAF bought 5,677 for observation planes during World War II. After the war it became very popular with civilian pilots. [55]

PIPING ROCK: The Piping Rock Club, founded in 1912, is located in Locust Valley, New York. Unlike our street, that golf course is built on rolling terrain with numerous water hazards. [56]

» **PIPING ROCK: One of the old tile street markers**

PIPPINS: Oscar – A black lawman, he joined the faculty of Prairie View A & M University in 1937. Pippins worked in the Men's Department. In addition to his 20 years of service to the university as a law enforcement officer, he was a night watchman and deputy sheriff in Waller County. [57]

PIRTLE: Jess R. – Government officials have the power to name streets for themselves and can't resist the desire to do so. This Sugar Land alderman (1959) did just that. [58]

PITCHING WEDGE: This is a golf club. This wedge is characterized by a high loft (typically 45-60 degrees) to increase trajectory and significant sole weighting to help on grass. It is also heavier than the typical iron. [59]

PITTS: B. H. – The City of Pasadena was incorporated in 1928. This gentleman was the first city marshal. [60]

PITTS: This Katy area road is named for one of the earlier settlers in that area. The family arrived here in 1894. [61]

PITTSBURGH: The University of Pittsburgh was founded in 1787. Initially a private school known as Pittsburgh Academy, it

OUR HISTORIC CURBSIDE CERAMIC TILE STREET MARKERS

In River Oaks, Houston Heights and Montrose, to mention a few older neighborhoods, some streets still have their name and block number in tile on the curb at the end of each block. The city began using this form of identification in the 1920s and carried the practice into the early 1950s. It was cheap, attractive, durable and easy to read. Unfortunately, the growing popularity of the automobile brought an end to this naming practice. Drivers were going faster and found that street signs on poles were easier to read at higher speeds. Today while a number of these relics remain in pristine condition, most are in various states of deterioration. Age, contact with automobiles and trucks, repaving, recurbing, name changes and destruction for handicapped access at corners have all taken their toll on this pleasant reminder of Houston's more slower paced past. But the next time you are out for a Sunday drive (also a practice that has waned in modern times) look for these beautiful pieces of artwork and craftsmanship. [39]

O-P

became a state school in 1966. The school is renown for its scientific research. In 1932 the chemical structure of Vitamin C was established here. Twenty-three years later in 1955, Dr. Jonas Salk produced his famous polio vaccine. [62]

PIZNER: Nathan L. – See sidebar **Houston Streets Named for Men Killed During World War I,** page 22.

PIÑATA: See sidebar **Learn a Foreign Language on Your Morning Walk,** page 125.

PLEAK: This small village south of Richmond developed as a result of an oil discovery in the Pleak Oil Field in the 1920s. A cotton gin built by Wilber Krenek in 1934 was still in operation in the 1990s. [63]

PLEASANTVILLE: This black Houston neighborhood was developed by Judson Robinson Sr. in the early 1950s. His son later became a Houston city council member. [64]

PLEDGER: Stephen F. Austin's colonists began settling near what would become Pledger between 1824 and 1827. John Walton Brown, the town's first postmaster, named it for the family of his deceased wife, Narcissa Pledger, in 1880. Pledger became a boom town in the 1920s and 30s with the discovery of sulfur at Newgulf. The area has always been used for agriculture. Today the main crops are turf grass and pecans. (See **Newgulf Access.**) [65]

PLUM GROVE: This is the main street of the small (population 480) Liberty County town of the same name. Unlike many villages in this area Plum Grove is a relative newcomer, being incorporated in 1968. [66, 67]

PLUMB: Preston R. – This gentleman was a real estate developer in Houston. He began building homes in West University Place in 1925. Preston Place Addition in that area is named for him also. Plumb, along with Manuel Meyerhoff and Charles Coskey, began developing the Rice Village shopping center in 1932. Plumb was also a city commissioner. [68]

PLUMTEX: See sidebar **Howdy Tex,** page 263.

POCAHONTAS: She was the daughter of American Indian chief Powhatan. Legend has it that when her father was about to kill Captain John Smith, leader of the Jamestown settlers, she saved Smith's life by placing her head on his chest and begging for mercy. Pocahontas married settler John Rolfe in 1614. In her native tongue her name translates as "playful one." [69]

POINT CLEAR: See sidebar **Tennis or Golf, Anyone?,** page 348.

POLARIS: See sidebar **Starry Night,** page 111.

POLK: James K. – James Polk was president of the United States during the annexation controversy. In 1837 the Van Buren administration had opposed Texas joining the Union. By 1841 President Tyler was worried about British intentions concerning the state. These fears reached a fever pitch during the presidential campaign of 1844. Polk won the election. Because of his support for Texas annexation Houston honored him with a street. [70]

POLLEY: Joseph H. – This veteran of the War of 1812 was born in 1795. He accompanied Stephen F. Austin on his first trip to Mexico. Polley was awarded a land grant in 1824 and named a member of the Old 300. He established a ranch near Richmond and raised a herd totaling 150,000 head of cattle. [71]

» POLO PONY

POLO PONY: Located on the property of the Houston Polo Club this street is named for the hardy equines that are critical to that game. Polo ponies are of no special breed. Most are thoroughbreds or three-quarter thoroughbreds. These brave animals must be able to stop on a dime, accelerate rapidly, turn quickly and have no fear of colliding with other fast moving animals. [72]

POMEROY: This family settled in Pasadena, Texas, in 1901. Payson Pomeroy has the distinction of being the first person interred in Crown Hill Cemetery, an old burying ground on the banks of Vince Bayou. C. David Pomeroy Jr. is the author of *Pasadena: The Early Years*, the definitive text on the city's history from 1890 until 1937. [73]

PONCHARTRAIN: See sidebar *Laissez les bon temps roulez* (Let the good times roll), page 188.

PONCE DE LEON: Born in Spain in 1460, this sailor joined Christopher Columbus on his second voyage to the New World in 1493. As a reward for his service to the Spanish crown De Leon was given the right to search for Bimini, an island in the Bahamas chain, rumored to be the location of the Fountain of Youth. Legend said if you drank its waters you would never grow old. In 1513 his expedition set out. He completely missed the Bahamas and landed on the east coast of what he would name Florida, from the Spanish word for flower, *flora*, because of its tropical beauty. In 1521 de Leon set sail again. Unfortunately, upon arriving in Florida the landing party was attacked by Indians and the great explorer died of his wounds. [74]

POOR FARM: This road ran south of the town of Wharton to the Wharton County Poor Farm. For many years most counties in Texas established communities where indigents could live. In Houston there is a ditch that runs through the posh neighborhood of West University that is still called Poor Farm Ditch which was on Harris County's farm. [75]

PORT ROYAL: See sidebar **Tennis or Golf, Anyone?,** page 348.

O–P

PORTER: This rural Montgomery County road intersects FM 1314 that leads to the small town of Porter (sometimes referred to as Porters). Founded in the late 1800s Porter was the county seat from 1896 until 1915. The town's most famous resident was astronaut Robert L. Crippen who piloted the space shuttle Columbia in 1981. [76]

PORTER: William – He was an attorney in the Nathaniel H. Davis law firm in the town of Montgomery beginning in 1849. L. D. Jones (1861) and Charles Jones (1855) were also lawyers in that firm. [77]

POST OAK: The post oak (also known as the cross or iron oak) occurs in all areas of Texas except the High Plains and the Trans-Pecos. It can reach 75 feet high with a dense, rounded canopy. The leaves have a distinctive cross shape while the bark is thick with plate-like scales thus the other two names for this deciduous tree. [78]

POTOMAC: See sidebar **America the Beautiful,** page 176.

POWELL POINT CEMETERY: (See **Powell Point School.**)

POWELL POINT SCHOOL: In the 1890s Powell Point, the school and the cemetery were named for Elizabeth Powell. She was given a land grant here by Stephen F. Austin in the early 1830s. In 1869 William E. Kendle purchased thousands of acres of farm land here to sell to Freedmen following the War Between the States. He subdivided the plots into 100 acre sections and sold these for $0.50-$1.50 per acre exclusively to the freed slaves. Telly B. Richardson, a native of Kendleton, established the two-room schoolhouse in 1904. Kendleton remains principally a black community. (See **Braxton.**) [79]

POWER: James – An Irish merchant and adventurer, Power came to Texas in 1826. He was very active politically and was a signer of the Texas Declaration of Independence. Power served as a representative in the 2nd Congress of the Republic. [80]

PRAIRIE VIEW-WALLER: This road recalls these two Waller County towns. Prairie View was originally named Alta Vista, for the plantation owned by Jared E. and Helen M. Kirby. It was one of four owned by that family in the area in the 1860s. Kirby died in 1867, leaving his wife in debt. To make ends meet, Mrs. Kirby opened a boarding school for young women in the plantation's mansion house. Nine years later she moved to Austin and sold the school to the State of Texas. In 1876 the state legislature established the first institution of higher learning for black Texans in the Alta Vista mansion. It opened with eight students. In 1879 the name was changed to Prairie View Normal and Industrial Training School. Today we know it as Prairie View A & M University. (See **Waller.**) [81]

PRAIRIE: On the original plan of the City of Houston, as surveyed by Gail and Thomas Borden in 1836, this southern-most street was named because beyond it, there was nothing but open grassland or prairie. [82]

PREAKNESS: The second jewel in the horse racing's Triple Crown is the Preakness Stakes. Sponsored by the Maryland Jockey Club, this race is held at Pimlico Race Track in Baltimore, Maryland two weeks after the Kentucky Derby. The first Preakness Stakes was held on May 23, 1873, two years before the inaugural Kentucky Derby was run at Churchill Downs. (See **Pimlico** and **Triple Crown.**) [83]

PRELUDE: See sidebar **It's Music to My Ears,** page 218.

PRENTISS: Henry Bowdoin – This businessman and land speculator was born in Massachusetts in 1792. He sailed to Texas in 1831 to trade in real estate. As an early settler he received a land grant (where this street is located) from Stephen F. Austin in 1833. He then went to New York where he sold the property in 1834. He returned to Texas once more but his health declined rapidly and he died in 1836. [32]

PRESIDIO: Although the developer of Mission Estates misspelled this word (*Presedio*), correctly spelled it means a garrison fortress similar to those erected in the southwestern United States by the Spanish to protect their land holdings and missions when they still controlled this region. [34]

PRESSLER: Herman P. – Located in the Texas Medical Center, the street is named for this great Houstonian. Mr. Pressler was a founding board member of the Texas Children's Hospital. He was chairman of the board from 1976-1982. During his tenure, Texas Children's grew from a small regional health facility to the nation's largest pediatric hospital. The west tower lobby of the hospital was named for him in 1995. His philanthropic efforts also extended to the Salvation Army, Sheltering Arms and the United Way. A highly respected attorney, he served as president of the Houston Bar Association. [84]

PRESSWOOD: Austin and Sarah - This couple settled in the New Caney area in 1862. This agricultural community became a major shipping point for livestock. Originally the town was called Presswood but the name was changed to Caney Station in the late 1870s (as it was on the Houston & East Texas Railroad) and changed again to New Caney in 1882. The Caney name refers to the large number of canebrakes on the nearby Caney Creek. (See **Caney Creek.**) [85, 86]

PRESTON: Anne C. – Born in Petersburg, Virginia, this black professor earned two bachelors degrees from Virginia State University and a Masters at Columbia University. Preston began teaching at Prairie View A & M University in 1937. She was supervisor of the campus laboratories, taught elementary education and was director of student teaching. Preston retired in 1967. [87]

» **ANNE PRESTON: She was a professor at Prairie View A & M University**

PRESTON: W. C. – In our early history we were very good at remembering our friends by naming streets in their honor. Preston was a U.S. Senator from South Carolina who was one of the major supporters of Texas annexation. Since there was significant opposition in Washington D. C. to adding our state to the Union, it took strong leadership in Congress to win approval. [88]

PRICE: (See **Pruett.**)

PRINCETON: One of the greatest universities in America, Princeton opened in 1746 in the New Jersey town of the same name. The campus was occupied by both American and British troops during the Revolution and a number of its buildings suffered damage as a result of the fighting. [89]

PRISON: This private road runs through the former site of the Jester State Prison Farm. Established in 1885 this 5,005-acre facility was operated by convict labor and produced sugarcane and bricks for the Texas Prison System. The farm's original name was Harlem Prison Farm but it was changed in the 1950s to honor Texas governor Beauford H. Jester. (See **Harlem.**) [90]

PRODUCE ROW: At the end of this street is the Houston Produce Center where many grocers in the area buy their fresh fruits and vegetables. [91]

PRUETT: Price – This early Baytown pioneer laid out the original site of Goose Creek, Texas. He was a major land owner in the area. [92, 93]

PRUETT: Rolland "Red" H. – Under his watch as Baytown mayor the Baytown-La Porte Tunnel under the Houston Ship Channel was constructed. Started in 1950, this 4,110 foot tunnel cost $10.2 million. It was officially opened September 22, 1953. It has since been closed, removed and replaced by the Fred Hartman Bridge. (See **Hartman.**) [94]

PUGH: Located just north of Clinton Drive and East of Loop 610 North is Pugh Street. These early settlers were land owners in the area. Their family cemetery was nearby and contained 16 graves. (See **Zuber.**) [95]

PULTAR: Vaclav – Born in Russia in 1896, he moved to Rosenberg in 1912. Pultar was a large landowner in Fort Bend County including land on the Brazos River near Rocky Falls. As a boy he remembered hearing the riverboats firing cannons at the rocks. In 1961 he sold 200 acres of land to the George Foundation on which to build the Richmond State School. Pultar donated the $100,000 purchase price to his church. (See **Rocky Falls, A. P. George Ranch** and **Richmond State School.**) [96]

PURDUE: Opened in 1874, Purdue University is a land grant college in West Lafayette, Indiana. It is famous for its engineering school. [97]

SOUTHAMPTON'S ENGLISH STREETS

Houstonians have always loved English things. Some of us might be described as "English-Lite." We adore English muffins, English bulldogs, English tea, English saddles, English walnuts and English sheepdogs to mention a few. This fascination with our friends across the great pond has never been lost on our real estate developers. Southampton was one of our city's earliest neighborhoods to pay homage to "Jolly Olde England." In 1922 real estate developer E. H. Fleming teamed up with the great Houston architect William Ward Watkin to create this residential area to the north of Rice Institute. The target market for this 160-acre tract was middle-income families, many of whom were on the faculty at Rice. Watkin developed the plan and Fleming named the streets. In my opinion, the provenance of the neighborhood street names is as follows:

⊛ **Albans** – St. Alban was England's first martyr. He was a prominent citizen of the village now called St. Albans in Hertfordshire. During the persecution of Diocletian, Alban hid a Christian priest in his home. He was so impressed by the priest he converted to Christianity. Diocletian's forces did not appreciate this change of faith and tortured and beheaded Alban in 304 A. D.

⊛ **Ashby** – This village plays a large role in Sir Walter Scott's oh so medieval English novel, *Ivanhoe*. One of the country's finest horse markets started there in 1219. Mary, Queen of Scots, was held prisoner in Ashby Castle in 1569.

⊛ **Banks** – Sir Joseph Banks was one of England's greatest naturalists. A very wealthy man, he financed and sailed with Captain James Cook on his first voyage aboard the famous sailing ship, *Endeavor*. Upon his death in 1820 the British Museum was the bequeathee of Banks' huge collection of botanical specimens and books.

⊛ **Bartlett** – Although John Bartlett was an American and is best remembered as the creator of *Bartlett's Familiar Quotations* (first published in 1855), his *New and Complete Concordance* of *Shakespeare* surpasses all other collections of citations of the Bard's writings.

⊛ **Bolsover** – This charming village grew up around a castle that existed prior to 1099. This area of England has produced some of the earliest traces of civilization in the Isles. Ice age sites here have been carbon dated to 45,000 to 12,000 B. C.

⊛ **Dunstan** – St. Dunstan is one of the main English saints. Born in 909 near Glastonbury, he was named abbot of the famous monastic school there when he was just 34 years old. His high principles often placed him in conflict with the ruling powers but somehow he always prevailed. In 959 he was elected Archbishop of Canterbury.

⊛ **Hazard** – John Warren Hazard was one of the developers of Southampton. Coincidently, in the United Kingdom, hazard was a popular dice game played for very high stakes in the parlors along St. James and Pall Mall. It later became popular in the United States and we know it here today as craps.

⊛ **Milford** – Once a small hamlet in the midst of a deer forest, its ample water supply allowed Jedediah Strutt to erect a water-powered cotton mill here in the 1700s and the town boomed. Eventually the mill closed and was torn down in the 1960s. Milford once again became a quiet little village.

⊛ **Northampton** – This country town has been famous since the 17th century for high quality boots and shoes produced here. The Norman castle has been the site of many battles as well as the meeting place of the English Parliament during the 12th to 14th centuries.

O–P

CONTINUED ON THE NEXT PAGE

SOUTHAMPTON'S ENGLISH STREETS (CONTINUED)

⊛ **Quenby** – This High Jacobean country house in Leicestershire is one of England's finest. George Ashby built it in 1627. It is most famous for its kitchen as it was there that Stilton cheese was first produced making the culinary world a much better place. After all what did we have to eat with port wine before Stilton?

⊛ **Robinhood** – (See Robin Hood)

⊛ **Southampton** – It was from this English Channel seaport that the great White Star Line ocean liner *RMS Titanic* departed on her fateful voyage on April 10, 1912. On Sunday April 14 at 11:40 PM the ship collided with a massive iceberg. The *Titanic* was mortally wounded. At 2:20 AM on Monday she broke in two and slipped beneath the icy waters of the North Atlantic carrying 1,500 souls to their deaths.

⊛ **Wilton** – There are two possibilities for this street name. First is that it recalls an English bone china pattern of the same name manufactured by several top-of-the-line producers including Haviland and Royal Doulton. Or it could be named after the famous Wilton carpets that are manufactured in the market town of Wilton in Wiltshire.

⊛ **Wroxton** – This Oxfordshire village is located in the county where the greatest of England's institutions of higher learning have held sway since the 1100s. The most famous of these is Oxford University. Its earliest colleges can be traced back to 1163. [40]

QUADE: This family came to Texas in the late 1870s from Germany and settled in Cypress. (See **Koch.**) [1]

QUAIL VALLEY: This large subdivision was the first of this type of mega project in Missouri City. Development began in 1969. [2]

QUAKER: Located in Friendswood, a community founded by the Society of Friends in the 1890s, this street is named for members of that religious sect. The term Quaker is derived from an early leader's admonishment to "tremble at the word of the Lord." [3]

QUEEN VICTORIA: Arguably one of the greatest rulers to grace the English throne, she ruled the British Empire from 1837 to 1901. A very strong-willed woman she stood up against Lord Palmerston and his aggressive foreign policy, despised liberal Prime Minister William Gladstone and adored PM Benjamin Disraeli, one of Britain's most capable statesmen. [4]

QUEEN'S CLUB: This private sporting club in West Kensington, London was founded in 1886. It was the world's first multipurpose sports complex. It is named for Queen Victoria, its first patron. It hosts the prestigious grass court Queen's Club Tennis Championships each year. [5]

QUENBY: See **Southampton's English Streets,** page 255.

QUINN: T. H. – See sidebar **Houston Streets Named for Men Killed During World War I,** page 22.

QUINTANA: Named for Mexican General Andres Quintana, it became an important seaport for early Texas. Its strategic location on the Gulf of Mexico earned it bombardment by Union ships during the War Between the States. Up until the war it was

Q–R

the only shipyard west of New Orleans. Quintana was destroyed by the Great Storm of 1900. Rebuilt, it is now a quiet resort and fishing center. [6]

QUITMAN: John A. – It is possible that Houston Mayor Andrew Briscoe may have named this north side street in honor of his mentor. General Quitman was a Mississippi attorney who allowed Briscoe to study law in his Jackson office. [7]

BRAZORIA COUNTY'S OLD PLANTATION STREETS AND ROADS

Brazoria County is one of the oldest and most historic in Texas. Anglo settlement began here as early as 1820. Stephen F. Austin gave land grants in 1824. Many communities (Velasco, East & West Columbia, Brazoria, Quintana and Liverpool) were thriving by 1832. The rich soil, plentiful water supply and long growing season made the area an ideal location for plantations. These historic plantations are long gone but not forgotten because of the streets and roads named for them. [41]

- **Bryan** – Moses Austin Bryan, a nephew of Stephen F. Austin, owned this cotton plantation. It was near Velasco. Bryan fought in the Battle of San Jacinto. He acted as General Sam Houston's interpreter when Santa Anna was captured.

- **Duranzo** – This plantation was the home of W. Joel Bryan, a nephew of Stephen F. Austin. The principal crops here were cotton and sugarcane.

- **McCormick** – J. M. McCormick owned this cotton plantation. It was located on a beautiful bend in the San Bernard River. McCormick fought in Captain William H. Patton's Company during the Battle of San Jacinto. The family was active in Texas affairs for many years.

- **Patton** – William H. Patton came from Mississippi and started this sugar plantation. He was Captain of a company and an aide-de-camp at San Jacinto Battleground. It was his duty to guard General Santa Anna while he was held captive at the Phelps Plantation. Governor James Stephan Hogg bought the place from Patton and told his heirs to hold it 20 years because oil would be discovered here. He was correct and the Hogg family became very wealthy.

- **Phelps** – This cotton plantation was owned by Dr. J. A. E. Phelps. It is most famous as being the place where General Santa Anna was held captive after the Battle of San Jacinto. The doctor treated Santa Anna well. The General never forgot that and when Phelps son, Orlando, was captured in Mexico after the ill founded Mier Expedition, Santa Anna saved the young man from the firing squad.

- **Spencer** – A gentleman known as Captain Spencer raised cotton on this plantation that was just outside of Brazoria.

- **Waldeck** – Morgan L. Smith came to Texas from Massachusetts. Stories say this was one of the finest of the sugar plantations and the first to have a sugar refinery. Prince Waldeck, a cousin of Queen Victoria of England, was visiting Smith and was so impressed with the property he purchased it. Smith returned to Boston and later committed suicide.

R

R. W. J.: The R. W. Johnson Construction Company owns the RWJ Airpark where this street is located. The facility serves private aircraft in the Baytown and Chambers County area. [1]

RABB RIDGE: This deep seated salt dome is in the Thompson Oilfield near Rosenberg. In 1931 Hugh Cullen and his partner Jim West of the Cullen & West Oil Company discovered oil at 9,314 feet along the flanks of the dome. They eventually sold their interest to Humble Oil & Refining Company for a gigantic profit. (See **Cullen** and **Jim West.**) [2]

RABB: John – This Indian fighter was given a league of land in what would become Fort Bend County in 1824. [3]

RADIO: KFRD Radio was originally located on Avenue H in Rosenberg. When it outgrew that space and moved the new street leading to it was named Radio. (See **Junker.**) [4]

RAILHEAD: This northwest Harris County street leads to the Burlington Northern Santa Fe Railroad yard where locomotives are matched with trains cars and dispatched on their routes. [5]

RAILROAD: The Union Pacific rail line in Baytown parallels this street. [6]

RAILROAD: This street runs along the Southern Pacific Railroad line that parallels the La Porte Highway. [7]

RAILSPUR: This short branch of rail line leads to the main Union Pacific track in east Harris County. [8]

RAINS: See sidebar **Texas Heroes' Names for Houston Streets Urged in 72 Proposed Changes,** page 96.

Q-R

RAMPART: See sidebar *Laissez les bon temps roulez* (Let the good times roll), page 188.

RANCHO BAUER: Located in Montgomery County, this road is named for descendents of early pioneer Carl Siegsmund Bauer. (See **Bauer.**) [9]

RANDON SCHOOL: John and David Randon were members of Stephen F. Austin's Old 300. The town was built in 1898 with the arrival of the Texas & New Orleans Railroad. In 1921 the rural Randon School had one teacher and 21 students. It closed in the 1930s. [10]

RANKIN: George Clark – An ordained Methodist minister, Rankin was transferred to the Shearn Church in Houston in 1892. Known for his "hell, fire and brimstone" sermons, he toured the saloons, fleshpots and gambling halls of the city in disguise. Then on Sunday evenings he would call down damnation on customers and the establishments. It was said the church was packed from "the vestibule to amen corner" with the faithful, anxious to hear of the gambling, drinking, womanizing and other unspeakable obscenities committed by fellow Houstonians. He claimed over 500 prostitutes were in the city and many lived near Shearn Church. In the end, despite his harangues, little changed. In 1896 Rankin was called by the First Methodist Church of Dallas. Houston was left to wallow in its sodomic practices. [11]

RANSOM: R. J. or Henry Lee – R. J. was born in Mississippi in 1835 and arrived in Texas in 1859. He managed a plantation for Colonel B. F. Terry. Following the War Between the States, R. J. was in charge of the Harlem Plantation. At that time the State of Texas leased convicts to plantation owners to work the fields. In 1886 the State bought Harlem and turned it into the first prison farm and the leasing of convicts ended. Henry was a native of Brenham, he was born in 1870. He came to Fort Bend County in 1889. Ransom joined the army during the Spanish-American War (1898) and was the only person in the county to serve in that brief engagement. His military records state he was of "good character" and "honest and faithful." After the war he joined the sheriff's department. (See **B. F. Terry.**) [12]

RAOUL WALLENBERG: He was a Swedish diplomat during the middle of the 20th century. Wallenberg is best remembered for his work in Hungary following World War II. The Raoul Wallenberg Institute of Human Rights and Humanitarian Law at Lund University in Sweden was founded and named in his honor in 1984. [13]

RAPIDAN: See sidebar the **Antebellum Streets of River Plantation,** page 122.

RAPIDO: In this bloody World War II river crossing, hubris won out over reason and the result was a slaughter of American troops. In Italy's Liri Valley in January 1944 the Texas 36th Infantry Division was ordered to cross the freezing Rapido river at night in rubber boats under withering German fire. The result was a slaughter with 2,877 casualties including 1,681 killed. One soldier said, "If you didn't get wounded, if you didn't get killed, if you didn't get captured, you weren't at the river." [14]

RAYBURN: L. N. – This man was the commander of Company E of Terry's Texas Rangers during the War Between the States. Wounded at the Battle of Shiloh, he recovered and saw action at Murfreesboro. [15]

RAYFORD: In the early 1900s this road led to the small town of Rayford, which no longer exists. It was a stop on the International-Great Northern Railroad. The Rayford Forest and Spring Hill North neighborhoods now sit on the former town site. [16]

REAGAN: John Henninger – He was born in rural Tennessee in 1818. Like many of our ancestors Reagan's talents seem unlimited. He was a lawyer, postmaster general and treasurer of the Confederate States of America, U. S. Representative, U. S. Senator (1887-91) where he earned the nickname "the Old Roman" and first chairman of the Texas Railroad Commission. He died in Palestine, Texas in 1905 and is buried there in East Hill Cemetery. In addition to this Houston Heights area street, Reagan County and John H. Reagan Senior High School (1927 - William Ward Watkin, Architect) are also named in his honor. [17]

REBA: River Oaks developer Will Hogg named this street for his friend Rebecca Meyer who lived in the area. The park in the middle of the 3200 block is named for her also. [18]

REBECCA BURWELL: Located in Williamsburg Settlement, a west Houston neighborhood with many early American street names, she was the first great love of Thomas Jefferson. It is believed he proposed to her in 1764 when Rebecca was 17 but she must have said no. She later married Jacquelin Ambler with whom she had six children. [19]

RED BLUFF: – This small Galveston Bay town was founded in about 1880. It has since been absorbed into Seabrook. [20]

RED-N-GOLD: The powers that be took the opportunity to name the streets around the Stafford Municipal School District property for things relating to the schools. The school's colors are red and gold. **Spartan** is named for the team mascot. The third street is **Stafford Pride.** (See **Stafford.**) [21]

REHAB: So named because it leads to the Harris County Prison Center where hopefully some rehabilitation occurs. This could be a street with two different names depending on the direction of the traveler. For those going north or out it is Rehab but for the miscreants who are returning or going south it could be Recidivism Road. [22]

REID: W. R. – When this gentleman developed Lindale Park in the 1930s it was outside of the city limits but did have all the city conveniences. It would eventually contain over 1,800 homes. [23]

REIDEL: Otto – This early Spring Valley resident was a farmer. [24]

Q-R

REID'S PRAIRIE: This village was organized in the 1800s west of Houston. The Reid's Prairie Baptist Church was established in 1890. The congregation erected a sanctuary in 1895. [25]

REINERMAN: John – It is not unusual for streets in Houston to be named after the surveyor who surveyed the plat. In this case the street is the surname of the man chosen, in 1847, to record this property that today would be bounded by Loop 610 on the west, Crestwood on the east, I-10 on the north and Buffalo Bayou to the south. Much of this land was occupied by Camp Logan during the early 1900s and is Memorial Park today. (See **Logan.**) [26]

REINICKE: Ben – He was County Commissioner Precinct 4. Reinicke was credited with much of the city's street construction. He once stated his goal as, "I want the most up to date system of roads in the county for my precinct." [27]

REMEGAN: This is another of our misspelled street names. The correct spelling is Remagen. It is a town in Germany on the Rhine River. As the Allied forces were closing the noose on Nazi Germany, Adolph Hitler ordered all the bridges crossing that estuary to be demolished to slow the advancing armies. In May 1945 the 9th Armored Division of the 1st U.S. Army captured the Ludendorff railroad bridge at Remagen, minutes before the German demolition team was to blow it up. Troops and supplies poured into the Rhineland over this span in their drive toward Berlin. Hitler was so infuriated with the team's failure he had all of them executed by firing squad. [28]

REMINGTON: Frederic – This American painter and sculptor is famous for his Old West subjects such as cowboys, Indians, buffalos, the U.S. Cavalry, cattle drives, etc. He was the favorite artist of the developer of Shadyside, J. S. Cullinan. [29]

REMLAP: This is Palmer spelled backwards. (See **Lemac.**) [30]

RENNER: Joseph – He was a landowner in the Sixth Ward prior to the War Between the States. [31]

RENOIR: Pierre – He was one of the most influential of the French Impressionists of the late 19th century. Although an excellent painter of landscapes, still life and flowers, he excelled at nudes such as his famous *Bathers.* [32]

RENSHAW: A. D. – This soldier fought with Walker's Texas Division during the Civil War. He was captain of Company E of the 22nd Texas Volunteer Infantry. [33]

RENTAL CAR: This short street leads to the automobile rental companies (Hertz, Avis, Budget, etc.) at George Bush Intercontinental Airport.

REO: See sidebar **Fairbanks Could Have Its Own Concours d' Elegance and Road Rally,** page 140.

REPUBLIC: This Baytown street recalls the old Republic Oil Company that operated in the numerous fields around Baytown. [34]

RESEARCH POINT: The Shell Westhollow Research facility is at the end of this lane. The staff here is involved in research, process and product development, manufacturing support and technical support. Fields of study include chemistry, physics, mechanical and electrical engineering, materials science engineering, polymer science and engineering, environmental engineering and metallurgy. [35]

HOWDY TEX

In 1956 Eastex Oaks was platted near the newly constructed Eastex Freeway. The developer decided to combine an arboreal theme with the suffix "tex." As a result the neighborhood has such oddly named streets as **Elmtex, Pinetex, Willowtex, Hickorytex, Leaftex, Plumtex, Peartex, Peachtex, Mosstex, Pecantex** and **Ashtex.** Why **Sweet Gum** did not get a "tex" added is a mystery. [42]

RESERVE: On the original plat of the Freeland Addition this street was named Reserved. It is possible that developers Prentiss Granberry and Walter and Mary Freeland had plans to call it something else but failed to do so. When it was recorded at the Houston Planning and Development Department is was mistranslated and has remained so ever since. (See **Granberry** and **Frasier.**) [36]

RETRIEVE: Retrieve Plantation was located on Oyster Creek north of Lake Jackson. It was established by Abner Jackson in 1839. Three years later he sold a half interest to James Hamilton, a former governor of South Carolina and an emissary to the Republic of Texas. By the 1850s they were two of the largest sugar cane growers in the state. Following the deaths of Jackson and Hamilton the property passed through many hands. Finally in 1918, the Texas Department of Corrections purchased Retrieve and converted it into a prison farm unit of the same name. (See **Jackson.**) [37]

RETTON: Mary Lou – We have streets named for baseball players (Nolan Ryan), football players (Ken Hall), boxers (Joe Louis), tennis champions (Rod Laver) and golfers (Lee Trevino) however, this is our only street honoring a gymnast. Mary Lou Retton became America's sweetheart during the 1984 Olympic Games in Los Angeles. During that Olympiad she won a gold medal in the Women's All-Around, silver medal in the Vault, bronze medals in Uneven Bars and Floor Exercises and a silver Team medal, the most won by any athlete at those games. Her athletic prowess, marvelous personality and radiant smile earned her the Sports Illustrated "Sportswoman of the Year." Retton is a member of the International Gymnastics Hall of Fame. [38]

REVERSE: This Westview Terrace street connects Saxet (Texas in reverse) and Remlap (the reverse spelling of Palmer). (See **Remlap** and **Palmer.**) [39]

RHAPSODY: See sidebar **It's Music to My Ears,** page 218.

RHEMAN: Casper John – He was a plantation manager for Houstonian T. W. House

Q-R

in the mid 1800s. The plantation was between where Brookshire and Fulshear are today. [40]

RHETT BUTLER: See sidebar **Gone with the Wind Too Far,** page 303.

RHODE ISLAND: In the 1800s this short rail line went from Cumberland, Rhode Island to the Massachusetts state line. [41]

RHYTHM: See sidebar **It's Music to My Ears,** page 218.

RICE DRYER: This short Pearland road leads to an old American Rice, Inc. rice dryer. This company produces approximately 10% of the rice grown in the U. S. Some of their better known brand names are Comet, Blue Ribbon and Adolphus. [19]

RICE FIELD: The counties west of Houston were some of the largest rice farming areas in America. This Sealy road recalls this fact. Rice growing began here at the start of the 20th Century. Decade by decade it expanded. With the advancements in agriculture, rice production grew tremendously in the 1950s and 1960s. However, with urban sprawl rapidly moving west land used to grow rice began falling. In Waller County rice fields declined 59% from 1980 until 1992. [42]

» RICE: A portrait of William Marsh Rice

RICE: William Marsh – Rice gave an endowment of $200,000 in 1891 "for the foundation of an institute for the advancement of literature, science and art," now Rice University. Rice died in New York City under mysterious circumstances on September 24, 1900. It was actually a case of the "butler did it." On April 23, 1901 Charles Jones, Rice's manservant, was indicted for his murder. He was tried and convicted. Rice was cremated and his ashes are kept under his statue in the quadrangle at the university he founded, making the campus the largest private cemetery in the city. Rice Institute opened September 23, 1912. [43]

RICEVILLE SCHOOL: Leonard Rice founded the small southwest Harris County town of Riceville in 1850 as a black farming community. In addition to the school, the community centered around the Mount Olive Baptist Church and the Riceville Cemetery. Like Bordersville and other black neighborhoods, it was annexed by the City of

Houston in the 1960s. However, as late as 1982 Riceville had no city services, public water facilities nor sanitary sewer lines. [44]

RICHEY: Calvin – He was an early resident of Westfield. Richey was known for his agricultural skills and his farm raised everything from produce and cotton to cattle and chickens. [45]

RICHEY: John – This Texas pioneer settled in the area near Pasadena. He bought 20 acres of land along Vince's Bayou for $500 in January 1893. This was the first land sale recorded in Pasadena. He later doubled the size of his land holdings. [46]

RICHMOND STATE SCHOOL: The Richmond State School for the Mentally Retarded opened in April 1968. The 242-acre campus is operated by the Texas Department of Mental Health. Plans called for a capacity of 1,500 patients but it never housed more than 1,023 (1980.) With a change in thinking as to the best way to treat mental health problems the school has become the focal point of a controversy. [47]

RICHMOND: As one of Houston's oldest streets, it was the road to Richmond, Texas, county seat of Fort Bend County. In 1822 a group of men led by William W. Little set up camp here. Soon they were joined by colonists with Stephen F. Austin. Together they built a fort on a bend in the Brazos River that was the nucleus of the settlement they called Fort Bend. In 1837 the town of Richmond was established by Robert E. Handy and William Lusk. It was named for Richmond, England. Some of Texas' most famous citizens have lived here including Erastus "Deaf" Smith, Mirabeau B. Lamar and Jane Long. (See **Deaf Smith, Lamar** and **Jane Long.**) [48]

RICHWOOD: This street is in Richwood Village, a suburban community north of Brazosport that was established in 1944. It was originally part of Stephen F. Austin's league. [49]

RIEDEL: The Riedel family arrived in the Spring Branch area in 1903. They bought 50 acres of land and started a farm. [50]

RIESNER: Edmund L. – The son of a German immigrant, B. A. Riesner came to Houston in 1866 when he was 10 years of age. Starting as a blacksmith he soon founded a structural steel company. In addition he owned a carriage manufacturing company. Riesner made a fortune in real estate and owned the land where the street is today. In honor of his son Edmund (79th Company, 6th Regiment, United States Marines) who was killed in action on June 14, 1916 at Chateau Thierry in WW I, the elder Riesner changed the name of the street from Young's Alley. (See photograph on page 266.) [51]

RIETTA: (See **Antha.**)

RIGEL: See sidebar **Starry Night**, page 111.

Q–R

» RIESNER: E.L. Riesner's tombstone in Glenwood Cemetery

RILEY FUZZEL: The Riley Fuzzel Farm is a wholesale nursery near Spring. It commenced operations in 1996. In 2002 a second location was opened in Leon County and operates as a tree farm. [8]

RIP VAN WINKLE: This ne'er-do-well character appeared in Washington Irving's 1820 story collection, *The Sketch Book of Geoffrey Crayon, Gent.* He was famous as the man who fell asleep in the Catskill Mountains and did not awaken for 20 years. [52]

RIVA RIDGE: This colt won the 98th Kentucky Derby in 1972. After being bumped at the start he assumed command and cruised to a 3-3/4-length victory. He fell short in the Preakness, losing his chance for the Triple Crown. However, Ron Turcotte guided him to victory two weeks later at the Belmont. [53]

RIVER OAKS: Although now named for the abundance of oak trees that lined the banks of Buffalo Bayou, this is not the street's original name. It was the first street in the neighborhood on which ground was broken and it was christened Ball Boulevard after Houston Port Commissioner Thomas Ball. (See 1924 plat map on page 267.) However, it was quickly renamed River Oaks Boulevard. There are several stories as to why this change occurred. Some say it better reflected the lush environment of the neighborhood. Others claim there was a skeleton in Mr. Ball's closet that concerned the developers. Whatever the reason it remains one of that neighborhood's more interesting mysteries. To find out more on Mr. Ball visit the River Oaks Home Owners Association and see if they will let you review their archives. You might just find something very interesting. [54]

RIVER PLANTATION: Located on the West Fork of the San Jacinto River in Montgomery

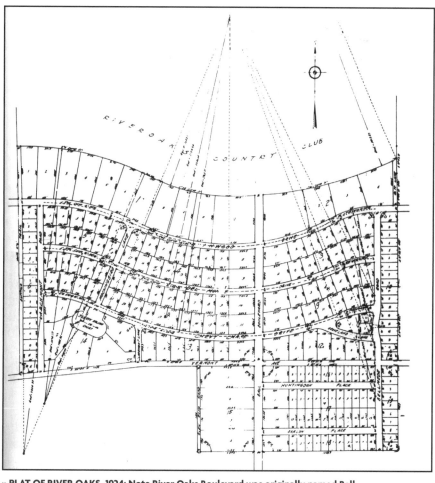

» PLAT OF RIVER OAKS, 1924: Note River Oaks Boulevard was originally named Ball

» RIVER OAKS: The Boulevard and original Country Club

Q-R

County, this unincorporated community is home to more than 1,300 families. Homes are situated around a 27-hole golf course. Streets in the neighborhood have a War Between the States theme. (See **Jeb Stuart, Gettysburg, Bull Run, Shiloh, Vicksburg** and **Jeff Davis.**) [55]

ROARK: Elijah Andrew – He came to Texas from Illinois in 1824 as one of Stephen F. Austin's Old Three Hundred colonists receiving a league of land in what was to become Fort Bend County. He was a farmer and rancher. Roark was killed by Indians while transporting produce to San Antonio on December 24, 1829. His son, Leo Elijah Roark, survived the attack. He later joined the Texas Army and fought at the Siege of Bexar, Grass Fight and Conception. He may have served at the Battle of San Jacinto but is not listed on the official muster records. [56, 57]

ROBECK: This pioneer family owned land in northwest Harris County. If you pay a visit to the Siedel (Rosehill) Cemetery you can pay your respects to them. (See **Siedel Cemetery.**) [45]

ROBERT E. LEE: This soldier who was born in 1807 in Virginia became one of the most celebrated generals in American History. He graduated first in his class from West Point. He had a distinguished career in the U. S. Army for 32 years. He is best remembered for commanding the Confederate Army of Northern Virginia during the War Between the States. Washington & Lee University was named after him. Lee died in 1870. [58]

ROBERTS CEMETERY: Abram Roberts arrived in Texas in 1827 from Georgia. He was a member of Stephen F. Austin's Colony. He established a town called New Kentucky in 1831 that attracted many German immigrants. It was abandoned in 1840. This road leads to the Roberts Cemetery where many of these early settlers are buried. A 1997 count lists 258 marked and 15 unmarked graves. Robert's (1773-1850) unmarked grave is here. His son, George (1811-1874) is also interred here. The cemetery remains in use today. (See **New Kentucky.**) [59]

ROBERTS: Abraham – In 1831 this gentleman was given a land grant along Spring Creek. He was in the second group of colonists that Stephen F. Austin brought to Texas. [60]

BUON GIORNO, LET'S VISIT ITALIA

In this small neighborhood north of U. S. Highway 290 everything is *molto bene* because everywhere you look you are reminded of one of the world's most beautiful countries – Italy. Here we have **Via Torre de Pisa** (Tower of Pisa), **Via Ponte Vecchio** (Florence's old bridge over the Arno River), **Via Barolo** (Italy's finest red wine), **Via Chianti** (Italy's most popular red wine), **Via Da Vinci** (Leonardo), **Via Siena** (a beautiful medieval city), **Via Firenze** (Florence), **Via Michelangelo** (painter of the Sistine Chapel), **San Rocco** (St. Roch, healer of black plague victims), **Via Toscano** (Tuscany), **Via Vina** (wine but it is misspelled) and **Via Palazzo** (palace). [43]

ROBERTS: T. G. – He was an early settler in Katy, Texas. Roberts along with Reverend M. L. Lindsey, W.P. Bowers, J. E. Cabiness and E. M. Morton were founding members of the First United Methodist Church there in 1900. [61]

ROBERTS: The Roberts family were some of our earliest settlers. Abram arrived in 1827. He founded New Kentucky, a short lived community in 1831. On April 16, 1836 the Texas Army with General Sam Houston in command arrived at Roberts home and asked for directions to Harrisburg. Houston led his army there where five days later he defeated the Mexican Army at the Battle of San Jacinto and earned Texas her independence. [17]

ROBIN HOOD: This legendary 12th century hero/outlaw lived in Sherwood Forest outside of Nottingham, England with his "merry band" that included Little John, Friar Tuck and Maid Marion. They robbed from the rich and gave to the poor much to the chagrin of the infamous Sheriff of Nottingham.

ROBIN LAKE: (See **Lorrie Lake**.)

ROBINDELL: Developer Robert Kuldell named this street from a combination of his daughter's name, Robin, with the last four letters of his surname. Other streets in the neighborhood have avian related names such as **Bob White, Sandpiper** and **Birdwood.** [62]

ROBINOWITZ: Cecil and Abe – This Russian family immigrated to the United States in waves between 1898 and 1910 to begin a new life in Texas. They were initially peddlers but built up enough capital to establish a mercantile business. They opened stores in Richmond, Rosenberg and Beasley. [63]

ROBINSON: Emerson T. – Born in Arlington, Texas in 1876, Robinson moved his family to Missouri City in 1894. He owned a dry goods store, was postmaster and a member of the school board. [64]

ROBINSON: This family was prominent in the New Caney area. An early pioneer was John Wesley Robinson who in addition to ranching and farming owned a general store, a cotton gin and a mill. James B. Robinson was the first postmaster of New Caney. (See **Presswood**.) [65]

ROBINSON: W. Allen – This man and his family acquired 80 acres of land in 1894 where Missouri City is today. They lived in a spacious two story house with a large barn, smoke house, chicken coop and some farm outbuildings. [66]

ROCHEN: Not all immigrants who settled in the Houston area were German. In the 1890s Czechs arrived and bought farm land near Waller. In 1891 they founded St. Mary's Catholic Church and Cemetery just north of where this road is located. Joe Rochen (1830-1911) is interred in the burial ground. The Great Hurricane of 1900

Q-R

seriously impacted the community and by 1947 the church closed. Today the cemetery is known as St. Martin de Porres. [102]

ROCK ISLAND: Barbara Groce Clark named her plantation Rock Island. Located on the Brazos River, it was north of her grandfather's Bernardo Plantation and northwest of his Liendo Plantation. Amos Gates, an early settler in the area, named the place for a small rock island in the Brazos River. Little is left to see here. When Hempstead was established most of the citizens of Rock Island moved there. [67]

» **ROCK OF CASHEL: One of Ireland's most beautiful structures**

ROCK OF CASHEL: This historic castle is in Cashel, County Tipperary, Ireland. Local lore says it was once part of Devil Bit Mountain, 18 miles north of Cashel. But when St. Patrick banished Satan from a cave there the rock flew off and landed in Cashel. It was the seat of the Munster kings for centuries before the Norman invasion. The oldest part of the castle today is the round tower, dating from 1100. [68]

ROCKY FALLS: A waterfall caused by large boulders in the Brazos River was located at Richmond. Early on the steamboats attempting to navigate from the mouth of the river to Waco would blast away at them in order to widen the passage between the rocks. They have long since been removed to ease navigation. (See **Pultar.**) [69]

ROHM & HASS: With operations on the Houston Ship Channel, this company is one of the world's leading producers of specialty chemicals such as adhesives, sealants, coatings and additives. They own the world's largest salt company, Morton's. Originally called Onondaga Salt Company, Joy Morton purchased that firm in 1886 and renamed the company after himself. This division traces it roots back to 1848 and is famous for its slogan, "When it rains, it pours." [70]

ROMAN FOREST: This 1.48 square mile unincorporated village is in southeast Montgomery County. The streets have a Roman theme and include Caesar, Mark Anthony (misspelled), Brutus, Cassius, Octavian, Chariot, Coliseum and Gladiator. However, the developer's historic acumen broke down when Athens and Parthenon (the most famous Greek monument) were added to the plat. (See **Caesar, Marc Anthony, Brutus, Cassius, Octavian** and **Coliseum.**) [71]

ROMAN: Richard – This soldier was one of General Sam Houston's company commanders at the Battle of San Jacinto. [72]

ROMEO: (See **Juliet.**)

RONDO: See sidebar **It's Music to My Ears,** page 218.

ROOS: Simon – This Houston merchant owned a department store on Preston Street in downtown. Old timers may remember he had brass boot prints implanted in the sidewalk that led to the front door of the store. Employees shined the prints so they glistened like gold on sunny days. [73]

ROOSEVELT: Franklin Delano – The 32nd President of the United States, Roosevelt served his country during arguably some of the most difficult times a president ever faced including the Great Depression and WW II. As the only person to serve four consecutive terms in office some of the most important legislation in American history was passed under his administrations: Works Progress Administration, Securities & Exchange Commission, Social Security Administration and the Tennessee Valley Authority, just to mention a few. Do yourself a favor and read Hugh G. Gallagher's *FDR's Splendid Deception.* It is probably the best book ever written on this amazing and controversial man. [74]

ROSALIE: (See **Anita** and **McIlhenny.**) [75]

ROSE: P. W. – The subdivision map of the A. C. Reynolds league indicates this gentleman owned a league of land near what is today the Texas Medical Center. This short court may recall this early landowner. [76]

ROSEHILL CHURCH: Follow this road and you will arrive at the historic Rosehill United Methodist Church in the old town of Rosehill. (See **Rosehill.**) [77]

ROSEHILL: Located near Spring Creek, Rosehill was a rural community west of Tomball. There are three stories about the naming of this road and village. The first says it is named after P. W. Rose, an early resident of the now ghost town of New Kentucky. He arrived in the area in 1836. Sources indicate he was one of the first citizens to serve on

Q-R

a grand jury in Harris County. Second says the area was covered in wild roses. And finally, there was a very important slave there named Rose who ran the Duer Plantation. [78]

» ROSENBERG: This statue is made from melted pennies gathered by Galveston children

ROSENBERG-KATY: Some of Stephen F. Austin's Old 300 settled in what would become Rosenberg in 1823. The town owes its birth to its neighbor, Richmond, who refused to allow a right-of-way to the Gulf, Colorado & Santa Fe Railroad (GCSFRR). So the line was laid three miles to the west and Rosenberg was established. The town is named for Henry Rosenberg, a Swiss immigrant, who settled in Galveston. From 1874 until 1877 Rosenberg was president of the GCSF Railroad. (See **Katy**.) [79]

ROSENBERG: Henry – He was born in Switzerland in 1824. In 1843 he followed a Swiss friend, John Hessly, to Galveston where he went to work in Hessly's dry goods store. He eventually bought his partner out and built it into Texas leading mercantile establishment. Rosenberg invested wisely in banking, real estate and transportation, making himself a sizable fortune. Being civic minded he served as an alderman in Galveston for many years. He is remembered for his philanthropy. He donated generously to the Orphan's Home, Grace Episcopal Church, YMCA, erected the Texas Heroes Monument at Broadway and 25th streets and created the first free library in Texas, the Rosenberg Library. [80]

ROSHARON: Settlers arrived in northern Brazoria County in the 1850s. In 1859 George Wetmore Colles, a major landowner, named the town Rose of Sharon Garden Ranch after the Cherokee roses that grew in the area. He also named his plantation the same. Colles also designed the community water system. When the post office opened in 1912 the name was shortened to Rosharon. This community has been the rice bowl of coastal Texas for decades. [81]

ROSILLE: Rosille Myers was the wife of a Baytown mayor. [82]

ROSS STERLING: He was a classic Houston entrepreneur. Sterling got into the oil business in 1903. In 1910 he bought two oil wells that became the Humble Oil and Refining Company (Exxon Mobil today). He sold out in 1925 and bought the *Houston*

Post (former morning newspaper) in 1926. In 1930 he was named chairman of the Texas Highway Commission. A year later he was elected governor of Texas. [83]

ROSSLYN: This early German settlement was located on Houston's outskirts near White Oak Bayou. Some early settlers referred to the village as White Oak due to its proximity to the Bayou. Rosslyn was a station on the Trinity & Brazos Railroad. It was still listed on Texas highway maps in the 1930s but has long since been swallowed by Houston. [84]

ROTHKO: Mark – He is one of the greatest abstract expressionists in the history of American painting. His use of color is amazing. You can track his downward emotional spiral and eventual suicide through the use of darker and darker colors. Visit the Rothko Chapel, 1409 Sul Ross at Yupon, to see some of his finest works displayed in Philip Johnson's marvelous sacred space. [85]

» **ROTHKO: Rothko Chapel with Barnett Newman's** *Broken Obelisk* **in reflecting pool**

ROUGHNECK: This is the name of a person who works on a drilling rig. Other positions on the rig include driller, tool pusher, roustabout and company man.

ROY BEAN: Known as the "Law West of the Pecos," Judge Bean administered justice from the front porch of his saloon in Langtry, Texas. He was a real character. While some of the stories about the judge are likely mythical, they remain amusing. He claims to have named his town after the English actress Lily Langtry. He once fined a dead man $40 for carrying a concealed weapon and staged a heavyweight-boxing match on a sand bar in the Rio Grande River because Texas, Arizona and New Mexico prohibited the bout. [86]

ROY HARRIS: Born in 1933, this boxer from Cut and Shoot, Texas, fought Floyd Patterson for the heavyweight championship in 1958. He lost the bout on a TKO in round 13. Later he was KOed by Sonny Liston. He retired from the ring with a 31-5 record and went to law school, thus becoming the first heavyweight to practice law. Harris served as a county clerk of Montgomery for 28 years. His hometown got its name from a dispute over who could preach in the town's only church. An argument turned ugly between the Baptists and an apostolic minister. A fight seemed inevitable. A young boy said "I am scared! I am going to "cut" around the corner and "shoot" through the bushes." And the town was born. Locals say Cut and Shoot is

Q-R

where the "men are tough, the horses are swift, the women are soft and we take a bath every Saturday night whether we need one or not." [87]

ROY: Eliza – John Reinermann was an active surveyor in this area near Memorial Park between 1857 and 1888. He had been awarded a land grant here in 1847. In 1881 and again in 1886 Roy purchased land in the area. Since this street parallels Reinermann I suspect it was named for Roy. [88]

ROYAL: See sidebar *Laissez les bon temps roulez* (Let the good times roll), page 188.

RUDEL: Christian – Originally from Wittenberg, Germany, this blacksmith set up shop near Tomball in 1865. The Rudel family were early members of the Salem Lutheran Church in Rosehill, Texas' earliest Lutheran congregation. [89]

RUEBEN WHITE: This early settler was born in Louisiana in 1795. White was a U. S. Army captain and fought in the War of 1812. He and his family moved to Texas in 1824 as one of Stephen F. Austin's Old Three Hundred. He received a league of land on the east bank of the San Jacinto River where this street is today. The Atascosito Census of 1826 lists him as a farmer and stock raiser. [90]

RUFFIAN: She may have been the greatest thoroughbred mare to ever set foot on a track. In 1974 and 1975 she ran off ten wins in ten starts. Then on July 6, 1975 she was matched against Kentucky Derby winner Foolish Pleasure. During the race she shattered her ankle and despite great efforts to save her she was put down at about 2 AM the next morning. Ruffian is buried at Belmont Park with her head pointed toward the finish line. (See **Belmont.**) [91]

RUMMEL CREEK: – (See **Rummel.**)

RUMMEL: Wilhelm – He was one of the earlier settlers in the Spring Branch area. He named Rummel Creek, a stream that ran through his property. Rummel was also a founding member of St. Peter's Evangelical Lutheran Church (now St. Peter's United Church of Christ) in 1850. [92]

RUNAWAY SCRAPE: This event was one of the most ignominious events in Texas history and makes one wonder why a developer would name a street after it. In April 1836, Santa Anna was advancing unchecked across Texas toward Harrisburg following his victory at the Alamo. Government officials of the Republic of Texas took flight. The Secretary of State went to the United States. The Navy Secretary fled to Galveston. Civilians took note and began to retreat as well. This mass exodus continued until word of Santa Anna's defeat at the Battle of San Jacinto reached them in Louisiana. At that point the refugees began the trek back to their hometowns. This road recalls the trail that led down Buffalo Bayou to Lynch's Ferry at the San Jacinto River, northeast to Liberty, Texas and finally to Opelousas, Louisiana. [93]

RUNNELS: Hiram George – Indian fighter and one-term governor of Mississippi, he moved to Texas in 1842 and started a cotton plantation on the Brazos River. Runnels was a significant landowner in what later became Houston's 2nd Ward. He died in Houston in 1857. Runnels County is named in his honor. [94]

RUNNY MEADE: In this meadow on the Thames River on June 19, 1215 King John was forced to sign the Magna Carta, a document guarantying the political and civil liberties of the English people. It represents one of the greatest moments in Western Civilization. It's too bad the developer of the Meyerland area neighborhood spelled the name incorrectly. It's Runnymede. [95]

RUSK: Thomas Jefferson – He arrived in Texas in 1832 in hot pursuit of a gang of con artists who absconded with some of his money. It is not known if he found them and recouped his investment. However, Rusk liked Texas and stayed. He signed the Declaration of Independence from Mexico. Elected Secretary of War in 1836, he fought with Sam Houston at the Battle of San Jacinto. In 1838 he was a founder and second vice-president of the Houston Jockey Club. Rusk County was named for him in 1843 and the town of Rusk in 1846. After Texas annexation by the United States he and Sam Houston were elected our first U.S. Senators in 1846. Rusk served in that august body until his death. He and General Sam Houston often made public addresses from the pulpit of one of the three churches in Houston at that time (Methodist, Presbyterian, Roman Catholic). Depressed over the death of his wife, Rusk committed suicide in Nacogdoches in July 1857. [96]

RUSKIN: John – This English writer and critic was born in London in 1819. In his early years Ruskin was a lost intellectual soul trying his hand at poetry, art and architecture before discovering his true talent – social commentary. He spent the last 40 years of his life writing about social and industrial problems, education, morality and religion. Much of his philosophy is summarized in an 1862 publication *Unto This Last*. [97]

RUSSELL: Charles E. – See sidebar **Houston Streets Named for Men Killed During World War I,** page 22.

RUSSET: (See **Chimney Rock.**) [98]

RUTGERS: This was the eighth college in colonial America, receiving its charter from King George III. It was renamed in 1825 after Col. Henry Rutgers, a major benefactor. It became the state university of New Jersey in 1946. [99]

RUTHVEN: A. S. – He was an early railroad man. Ruthven was involved in the founding of the Houston & Texas Central Railroad. This Houstonian made his fortune in the insurance business. As president of the Southern Mutual Life Insurance Company he was the first in his field to sell insurance policies to slaves. This was unheard of in 1850. The *Democratic Telegraph & Texas Register* called him "distinguished for accurate business habits, strict integrity and great discernment." [100]

RUTLAND: This village is the geographic center of Massachusetts and the hometown of some of the original investors in Houston Heights. The land was purchased from natives in 1686 but not settled until 1719. Rutland suffered from Indian attacks until 1724 when a peace pact was signed. Today the only buffalo herd in the Boston area is located here. [101]

» **RUTLAND:** This Houston Heights house was originally owned by that community's blacksmith

WEDDING BELLS IN THE WOODLANDS

Susan Vreeland-Wendt, Director of Marketing for The Woodlands Development Company, has named over 1,600 streets in her 25 year career in real estate development. When she needed to name the streets in the Carlton Woods area of The Woodlands she must have been thinking of new brides who would be choosing their sterling silverware patterns. As a result almost every street in this neighborhood recalls a famous silverware. Included are: **Silver Iris** Way, **Angelique** Way, **Frontenac** Way, **Grand Regency** Circle, **Eloquence** Way, **Hepplewhite** Way, **Damask Rose** Way, **Baronial** Circle, **Fleury** Way, **Grand Colonial** Way, **Carlton** Woods Drive, **Golden Scroll** Circle, **Lamerie** Way, **Margaux** Way and **Provence** Circle. (See **Chantilly** and **Nina Lee**.) [44]

S

SABINE: This street is named to remember Dick Dowling's victory over the Union Navy at Sabine Pass on the Sabine River on September 8, 1863. In this 45 minute engagement the Confederates, with only six cannons and 42 men, captured 2 steamers and 315 Northern troops. Union General William B. Franklin ordered the 18 other vessels and 4,500 soldiers to retreat to New Orleans. This ignominious defeat earned Franklin the dubious honor "of being the first American general … who managed to lose a fleet in a contest with land batteries alone." (See **Dowling** and **Colorado**.) [1]

SADDLEBROOK: The Detering families were large landowners in Harris County. Among the properties they held was a horse farm on the Harris-Fort Bend County line in west Houston. When they decided to develop this piece of acreage Carl Detering Sr. named many of the streets to start with the word "saddle." Thus we have **Saddle Spur** and **Saddle Horn Trail** as well as **Saddlebrook** combined with **North, South, Court** and **Way**. (See **Detering**.) [2]

SAGE: Charles – This Tanglewood area street is located in a former land grant given to Sage by Republic of Texas President Anson Jones in 1845. [3]

SAKOWITZ: Simon and Tobias Sakowitz opened a dry goods store in Galveston in 1902. Because of the ever-present danger of hurricanes in the island city they moved to Houston and opened a store in the Kiam Building. A son, Bernard, who had worked at Macy's in New York City returned home and took over the family business in the 1930s. Bernard's son Bobby, nicknamed the "Merchant Prince," ran the department store chain during the oil boom and bust of the 1970s and 80s. [4]

SALT GRASS TRAIL: This is the oldest of the trail rides that come into Houston just before the start of the Houston Livestock Show and Rodeo each February. Founded in 1953 by Pat Flaherty, Reese Lockett, Emil Marks and John Warnasch, the first ride had less than 100 participants versus thousands now. The 7-day, 70-mile ride goes

S–T

from Brenham, Texas to downtown Houston where it forms the start of the Rodeo Parade. (See **Marks.**) [5]

SAM HOUSTON: (See **Houston.**)

SAM RAYBURN: Samuel Taliaferro Rayburn was born in Tennessee in 1882. Five years later the family moved to a 40-acre farm in Fannin County near Bonham, a town that he would call home for the rest of his life. In 1906 he won a seat in the Texas House of Representatives thus launching his long political career. Rayburn was reelected twice. In 1912 he was elected to the U. S. House of Representatives. His tenure of 48 years of continuous service is unprecedented in American history. Rayburn held the Speaker of the House title under every Democratic controlled Congress until his death in 1961. [6]

SAMPRAS ACE: Pete Sampras is one of, if not the best American to ever pick up a tennis racquet. He was the youngest man to win the U.S. Open. He has won 14 Grand Slam titles including the U. S. Open (1990, 1993, 1995, 1996, 2002), Wimbledon (1993, 1994, 1995, 1997, 1998, 1999, 2002) and the Australian Open (1994, 1997). [7]

SAMPSON: Henry – Most likely this street is named for an early settler who operated as a general commission merchant. He lived at 1104 Preston, across from Courthouse Square where the Harris County Courthouse is today. The Sampsons were quite prominent socially and the exclusive ZZ Social Club was founded in their home in 1868. [8]

SAMUEL ADAMS: An American patriot, Adams was involved in the Boston Tea Party, signed the Declaration of Independence and fought in the Revolutionary War. He served in the Continental Congress and was eventually elected governor of Massachusetts. [9]

SAN BERNARD: This river rises near New Ulm in Austin County and flows 120 miles to its mouth at the Gulf of Mexico. In 1929 the Texas Gulf Sulfur Company erected a dam on the river to form the Newgulf Reservoir, a 2,150 acre-feet lake used by the company for municipal water and irrigation of their company town at Newgulf. Legend says for over 100 years people near the river have heard a violin playing, earning the San Bernard the nickname of "Singing River." (See **Newgulf Access.**) [10]

SAN FELIPE ROAD: This was the route from Harrisburg in eastern Harris County to Stephen F. Austin's colony at the town of San Felipe on the Brazos River. Listed on early maps as Route Number 6 by Prince Carl of Solms-Braunfels, commissioner of the Association for the Protection of German Immigrants in Texas, the Prince set the distance at 49 miles and noted the lack of water between Houston and Piney Point (now one of the Memorial Villages) 10 miles to the west. [11]

SAN JACINTO: Named for the final battle of the Texas Revolution on April 21 of 1836, it was here that Sam Houston defeated Santa Anna in an 18-minuite skirmish that won Texas her independence from Mexico. [12]

SAN LEON: Located on a 5,000 acre peninsula surrounded by Galveston, Trinity and Dickinson Bays, this fishing and shrimping community began as Edward's Point in the late 1800s. The name was changed to North Galveston when the North Galveston, Houston & Kansas City Railroad began here. In 1912 a real estate speculator named Thomas B. Brian bought the town. As a marketing ploy he threw in a free grave site with each lot purchased. Joe Vega was the town's next owner and he held a contest to rename it. San Leon won. This peninsula has been a historically interesting site for centuries. Karankawa Indians had a campsite here and the pirate Jean Lafitte used it as a base. Unfortunately in 2008 San Leon suffered devastating damage from Hurricane Ike. (See **Jean Lafitte** and **Karankawas.**) [13]

» SAN LEON: Hurricane Ike destroyed much of this Galveston Bay village in 2008

SAN LUIS PASS: (See **Termini-San Luis Pass.**)

SAN ROCCO: See sidebar **Neighborhoods with Interesting Street Names,** page 104.

SAN SABA: In Texas we have a town, a river and a county with this name. Yet there is very little of historic significance that has happened in this agricultural area. This may be why this street, at just one block long with no addresses on it, merited its name. [14]

SAN SOUCI: This means "carefree" in French.

SANDERS: William L. — See sidebar **Houston Streets Named for Men Killed During**

S-T

PIRATES OF THE CARIBBEAN

The Galveston Island city of Jamaica Beach was founded in 1956 and incorporated in 1975. Developers named the streets for some of the bloodiest pirates in the history of the high seas, the great pirates of literature as well as **Buccaneer** and **Jolly Roger.** Residents here live on **Edward Teach,** also known as **Blackbeard, Captain Kidd, Captain Hook, Jean Lafitte, John Davis** (the alias of Robert Searle), **Henry Morgan,** (Edward) **Mansvelt, Francis Drake** and **John Silver.** And the famous mutineer **Fletcher Christian** of HMS *Bounty* fame is thrown in for good measure. I imagine **Captain Blight** references William Bligh who was captain of that ill fated ship. We only lack the most famous pirates of the Caribbean in this day in age – Captain Jack Sparrow of the *Black Pearl* and Jimmy Buffet (*A Pirate Looks at 40*). Maybe Jamaica Beach Public Works will cut new streets in their honor. [45]

World War I, page 22.

SANDPIT: Sand is an important ingredient in construction materials. It is often mined along the bank of a watercourse. In this case this road leads toward a sandpit adjacent to Willow Creek near Tomball, Texas. I doubt the pit I found is the original one this road led to as sandpits like any other type of mining operation tend to play out over time. I expect the original site was west of the current location. (See **Willow Creek.**) [5]

SANDRINGHAM: This English village is home to the 19,500 acre royal estate of the same name. Acquired in 1861 for the Prince of Wales it has been used mostly by the royal family and their guests for partridge hunting. [15]

SANDY POINT: This small farming community is near the entrance to the Darrington Prison Farm. Founded in 1854 the cemetery has graves of soldiers from the Texas War of Independence, Mier Expedition and the War Between the States. Originally the area was used for cotton and sugar cane production as it was dotted with plantations. Those crops eventually gave way to cattle ranches and rice fields. It is thinly populated today. (See **Darrington.**) [16]

SANTA ANITA: This is the premier horse race track in California. It is the home of one of the top prep races prior to the Kentucky Derby. Run in early April the Santa Anita Derby has sent a number of horses to Louisville who "won the roses" including Majestic Prince, Affirmed and Sunday Silence. (See **Affirmed** and **Majestic Prince.**) [17]

SANTA FE: Located 16 miles northwest of Galveston, this town was named for the Gulf, Colorado & Santa Fe Railroad that was laid here in 1877. Santa Fe incorporated in 1978 and began to grow. By the 1980s the town had absorbed Arcadia and Alta Loma. (See **Old Arcadia.**) [18]

SANTA FE: This rail line was chartered in 1867 as the Atchison, Topeka & Santa Fe. By the early 1890s, its 9,000 miles of track and connections extending from Chicago to Los Angeles ranked it as one of the world's longest railroads. In 1995 it merged with the Burlington Northern RR and is know today as the Burlington Northern Santa Fe Railroad. "On the Atchison, Topeka and the Santa Fe" became a popular song recorded by swing artist Johnny Mercer. In 1946 it won an Oscar for "best song in a movie," *The Harvey Girls*. [19]

SARATOGA TRAIL: Named for the famous horse racing track in Saratoga, New York, it is the oldest organized sporting venue of any kind in America, opening August 3, 1863. Since 1864 it has been the site of the Travers Stakes, the oldest major thorough-bred horse race in the U. S. Saratoga's nickname is "Graveyard of the Favorites." Man o' War suffered his only defeat in 21 starts. Secretariat, a Triple Crown winner, was upset by Onion. And Kentucky Derby winner Gallant Fox was beaten by 100-1 long shot Jim Dandy in 1930. (See **Secretariat, Gallant Fox, Man o' War** and **Triple Crown.**) [20]

SARTARTIA: Now a ghost town located south of Sugar Land, Texas, in 1907 it was the location of the corporate offices of the Imperial Valley Railway. This rail line was created to serve the needs of the Imperial Sugar Company. Although the plans for this railroad were grandiose, only five miles of track were ever laid. There was also a plantation here of the same name. Today the site is a real estate development named New Territory. [21]

SASQUATCH: In pseudo-scientific language this beast is known as a crypto-bipedal primate. To the rest of us it is an unclassified two-legged mammal usually called Bigfoot or Yeti. The first sightings of this mysterious ape-like creature came from American Indians in the northwest hundreds of years ago. It is usually described as covered with hair, standing 6 to 9 feet in height and weighing 300 to 1,000 pounds. The Sasquatch seems to prefer remote areas and shuns human contact. This street is located near Montgomery County, a rural, less populated area. There have been eight reported sightings in that county with the latest being on February 28, 2005. We do not know if alcohol was involved in any of these reports. [22]

SATCHMO: Louis Daniel Armstrong was born in New Orleans August 1, 1904. He has been described as "perhaps the most important American musician of the 20th century." He came to prominence in the 1920s with his innovative playing of the cornet and trumpet as well as his famous gravelly singing voice. His genres included Jazz, Dixieland, Swing and Pop. Satchmo was also a master of scat singing or wordless vocalizing. He passed away in 1971. [23]

SATURN: See sidebar **Space City U.S.A. or "Houston the Eagle Has Landed"**, page 106.

SAUER: Reinhold – Some evidence indicates this street is named for an early Dutch settler who owned property north of Brays Bayou west of where Herman Park is today. It is more likely that it is named for Private Herman Sauer who was killed in action in France during World War I. He was also Conrad Sauer's youngest brother. (See **Conrad Sauer** and sidebar **Houston Streets Named for Men Killed During World War I.** page 22.) [24]

SAXET: This is one more of our streets that is a word spelled in reverse. It is Texas

S-T

backwards. (See **Lemac** and **Remlap.**) [25]

SAYERS: This street lies northeast of downtown and recalls a family of early Houston settlers. [182]

SCANLIN: (See **Scarcella.**)

SCANLOCK: D. – He was a 2nd lieutenant in Company D of the 11th Texas Volunteer Infantry under Walker's Texas division during the War Between the States. [26]

SCARBOROUGH FAIR: Located on a sandy peninsula on the east coast of England near Yorkshire, Scarborough was given the right to hold an annual fair by King Henry III in 1253. For centuries it was held on the beach there. It was made famous by the 1970s rock stars Simon and Garfunkle. [27]

SCARCELLA: In the early 1900s Stafford was a booming place and many families were moving there as were these people. Others joining them were Scanlin and Vaccaro families. (See **Stafford.**) [28]

SCARLETT: (See **O'Hara** and sidebar **Gone with the Wind Too Far,** page 303.)

SCARSDALE: The Farm & Home Savings Association of Nevada, Missouri developed this southeast side neighborhood in 1969. They opted to use a New York theme in naming the streets including the main street, **Scarsdale,** that is a suburb of New York City. Others follow the score including **Gotham, Flushing Meadows, Nyack, Algonquin, Teaneck, Barbizon, Astoria, Amsterdam, New Rochelle** and **White Plains.** [29]

SCHAUER: Stephen and Elizabeth – This couple, like so many in the Tomball area, emigrated via the port of Galveston in 1854. Their home had been in Brandenburg, Germany. [30]

SCHENDEL: August – (See **Needville.**)

SCHERER: George – He arrived in Rosehill in the 1850s. In 1852 he was a founding member of the Salem Lutheran Church. The Scherer family donated land to the church for a burial ground. Many of the tombstones are written in German. By the 1880s Scherer was a very successful cotton gin operator. [31]

SCHERZO: See sidebar **It's Music to My Ears,** page 218.

SCHIEL: Numerous families from Germany arrived in the Houston area during the 1800s. Among them were the Schiels. Many of them are interred in St. John's Lutheran Cemetery, a burial ground established in 1878. Another early resident, Henry Raatz, donated the land to St. John's Lutheran Church for this graveyard. Other Schiels are interred in the Fritsche Cemetery. (See **Lutheran Cemetery** and **Fritsche Cemetery.**) [32, 33]

SCHILLING: Nicholas – He was a doctor who immigrated to the Baytown area from Bavaria. Schilling originally built a lean-to on the bank of Cedar Bayou where he practiced medicine. If a patient had no cash the good doctor would accept produce in exchange for treatment. He later built an office/house that may be seen today in a state park in Anahuac. [34]

SCHLUMBERGER: This street was named by company management as it formed the western boundary of the property owned by this oilfield service company's North American Wireline Division in east Houston. [35]

SCHOLL: Ignatius – The first wave of German immigrants arrived in Texas in the 1840s. A second group came here 20 years later. Scholl arrived in 1869 from Fulda, Germany. Hundreds of German immigrants left for Texas in the 1800s. Many settled west of Tomball, Texas. The Scholl family members are buried in the nearby Siedel Cemetery (often called Rosehill Cemetery). (See **Siedel Cemetery.**) [36, 37]

SCHOOL ROAD: This street leads to Missouri City Middle School and E. A. Jones Elementary School in Missouri City. [38]

SCHOOL: Tomball Intermediate School is on this street. [39]

SCHULER: Marion – See sidebar **Houston Streets Named for Men Killed During World War I,** page 22.

SCHWARTZ: These early German immigrants settled in the Rosehill area where they were members of the Rosehill United Methodist Church. Services in this sanctuary were held in German until World War II. [183]

SCOTT: Henry – This Rosenberg street is most likely named for this gentleman who received a league of land here from Stephen F. Austin in the early 1830s. [40]

SCOTT: William – This Baytown street is named for one of Stephen F. Austin's Old Three Hundred. In 1824 Scott received a land grant covering in excess of 9,000 acres where the city is today. He operated a sawmill, gristmill, cotton gin, general store and wharf. Rumor has it that Scott contributed the blue silk to make one of the first State flags in 1835. Scott is credited with naming the area Baytown. (See **Baytown.**) [41]

SEA BISCUIT: If this street were spelled Seabiscuit, residents could point to a thoroughbred that won Horse of the Year honors in 1938. In 2003 Universal Pictures released a wonderful film about the "never say die" thoroughbred. The movie was based upon the book *Seabiscuit: An American Legend* by Laura Hillenbrand. However, as it is designated on the city map, sea biscuit is another name for hard tack, a tough bread made from flour and water. [42]

SEA-LAND: This company operates container vessels used in international marine

S–T

trade. With about 70 ships and over 200,000 containers, Sea-Land's business is world-wide. Containers are protective steel boxes 20' or 40' long into which cargo is placed. They are loaded and shipped on ocean going vessels. Upon arrival the containers are offloaded onto trailers or railroad flat cars for delivery. [43]

SEABROOK SHIPYARDS: This large facility is the oldest of the Houston, Clear Lake and Galveston Bay area full service marinas. It was founded in 1939. (See **Sydnor.**) [44]

SEABROOK: (See **Sydnor.**)

SEALY: Anglo-Americans began arriving here in the 1820s. Soon, nearby San Felipe would become the capitol of Stephen F. Austin's colony. In 1875 the Gulf, Colorado & Santa Fe Railroad (GCSFRR) bought land and laid a track. Sealy was established in 1880. It was named for George Sealy, a director of the GCSFRR. The town rapidly developed into a market and manufacturing center because of its good access to the railroads in the area. The most famous business started here was the Sealy Mattress Company. [45]

SEALY: John Hutchings – Born in Galveston in 1870 he was the son of John Sealy who co-founded Hutchins-Sealy Bank. When his father died he became a full partner in that financial institution. This civic minded Galvestonian was instrumental in the Seawall construction as well as the grade raising. Sealy was president of the Gulf, Colorado & Santa Fe Railroad and the Galveston Wharf Company. He founded Magnolia Petroleum Company and sold it to Standard Oil Company of New York for a small fortune. He was greatly involved in philanthropic efforts and is most remembered for giving the

» **SEALY:** Sealy-Hutchins Building on the Strand in Galveston

city the John Sealy Hospital that he named for his father. When Sealy died in 1926 he was reportedly the wealthiest man in Texas. [46]

SEATTLE SLEW: Another Triple Crown champion, this rough and tumble thorough-bred had the mentality of a bone-crushing fullback combined with the destructive-ness of a middle linebacker. In the 1977 Kentucky Derby he got off to a slow start. Forced to come from behind he banged Get the Axe out of the way, sideswiped Sir Sir and shoved three more horses toward the outside rail. Spying the leader, For the Moment (literally), Slew took up chase. He captured the lead at the head of the stretch and won by 1 1/2 lengths. (See **Triple Crown.**) [47]

» SEAWALL: It was pre-cast and assembled in sections

» SEAWALL: As it looks today

SEAWALL: The citizens of Galveston knew they had to do something radical to protect the city following the destruction caused by the Great Storm of 1900. In 1902 they decided to erect a seawall to separate the city from the Gulf of Mexico. It was to be 17 feet high, 3 miles long and made of solid concrete. Construction began in October 1902. The work was done by J. M. O'Rourke & Company who built the wall in 60 foot sections. The job took one year and four months to complete. The wall started at the South Jetty on the Island's east end, followed 6th Street to Broadway and then paralleled the beach to 39th Street. To protect Fort Crocket the U. S. Government added a one mile section in 1905. Over the years it was extended several more times, finally reaching its current length of 10.4 miles in 1960. Since Hurricane Ike blasted Galveston in 2008 there has been talk of extending it to protect the beach houses on the West End. [48]

SEAWOLF: Located on Pelican Island in Galveston, this street honors the *USS Seawolf*, a submarine that was sunk by friendly fire on December 28, 1944 while on her 15th combat patrol. A Japanese submarine had fired on the 7th Fleet task force. While seeking to find and sink the ship the U. S. destroyer *Richard M. Rowell* unknowingly mistook the *Seawolf* for the Japanese submarine and sank it with depth charges. This road leads to Seawolf Park where visitors can tour the *USS Cavala*, a submarine built in 1943, and the *USS Stewart*, a destroyer escort that went into service in 1942. [49]

SECRETARIAT: This Triple Crown winner is the stuff of sports legends like Babe Ruth, Michael Jordan, Joe DiMaggio and Jack Nicklas. His 2 1/2-length victory in the 1973 Kentucky Derby in 1:59 2/5 is one of only two times under 2 minutes and a record that stands until this day. In both the Run for the Roses and the Preakness he came from last to first to win in record time. In the Belmont he annihilated the field with a 31-length margin of victory. Secretariat was virtually a unanimous choice for Horse of the Year in 1972 and 1973. (See **Triple Crown.**) [50]

SECURITY CEMETERY: Originally known as Pocahontas, the name was changed to Bennette in honor of J.O.H. Bennette in 1902. Bennette sold his acreage to Security Land Company and the name was changed again. Security suffered the fate of many small Montgomery County towns — the timber supply dwindled and SH 105

RULES CONCERNING PUBLIC STREET NAMES

The process of naming our streets is governed by a strict but not lengthy law. You can find the regulations in Chapter 42, Section 133 of the Houston City Code of Ordinances. That ordinance is reproduced below:

1) The name of a new street that is not an extension of an existing street shall not duplicate the name of any existing street located within the city or the city's extraterritorial jurisdiction.
2) The name of a new street that is a direct extension of an existing street shall be the name of the existing street, except in those instances where the existing street name is a duplicate street name.
3) Street name prefixes such as "North," "South," "East" and "West" may be used to clarify the general location of the street, provided that these prefixes must be consistent with the existing and established street naming and numbering system of the general area in which the street is located.
4) Street name endings shall be used as follows:
    a "Court," "Circle" and "Loop" shall be limited to streets that terminate at a cul-de-sac or are configured as a loop street.
    b. "Boulevard," "Speedway," "Parkway" and "Expressway" shall be limited to major thoroughfares or other streets designed to handle traffic volumes in excess of normal neighborhood traffic generation or that are divided streets with at least two lanes of traffic in each direction separated by a median.
    c. "Highway" and "Freeway" shall be used only to designate highways or freeways falling under the jurisdiction of the state department of transportation.
5) Alphabetical and numerical street names must not be used to name any new street on any subdivision plat except in those instances where the street is a direct extension of an existing street with an alphabetical or numerical name that is not a duplicate street name." [46]

bypassed it. These events caused most of the population to move elsewhere. The historic cemetery remains, however. [51]

SEGUIN: Juan Nepomuceno – This hero of the Texas Revolution fought with James Bowie at the Battle of Concepcion, participated in the Siege of Bexar, was sent from the Alamo to request reinforcements, fought a rear guard against Santa Anna during the retreat to San Jacinto and joined Sam Houston there to participate in the battle that gained Texas her independence. In addition he was elected to the Republic of Texas Senate, fought Comanches during Senate recesses and served as mayor of San Antonio in 1841-1842. He died in 1889 at the age of 83 while living in Nuevo Laredo. (See **James Bowie.**) [52]

SEIDEL CEMETERY: At the end of this short road is the Seidel Rosehill Cemetery. Most of the people interred here were German immigrants and their descendents including members of the Juergen family. (See **Juergen.**) [53]

SEIDEL: The Rosehill area of north Harris County was appealing to many German immigrants who came to Texas. This family settled there in the 1800s and became members of the Salem Lutheran Church in that community. [54]

SEILER: (See **Stavinoha.**)

SEMINARY RIDGE: Much fighting occurred here during the massive and bloody Battle of Gettysburg on July 1-3, 1863. Seminary is just one of several ridges including Herr and McPherson's, from which the Confederates launched their attack on this Pennsylvania town. (See **Gettysburg.**) [55]

SEMINOLE CANYON: See sidebar **The Most Scenic Spots in Texas,** page 310.

SEMMES: Raphael – This Mobile, Alabama native was an admiral in the Confederate navy. [56]

SENATOR LLOYD BENTSEN: The 270 miles of this highway (also known as U. S. 59) from Laredo to Houston were renamed in honor of this Texas senator. Bentsen was born in Hidalgo, Texas in 1921. He served in the U. S. Army Air Corps during World War II. He flew 35 combat missions over Europe and won the Distinguished Flying Cross and Air Medal with three oak leaf clusters. From 1949 until 1955 he was a U. S. Representative. Then he went to work in the financial sector and had a very successful business career. Bentsen was elected U. S. Senator in 1971 and served until 1993. President Bill Clinton made him Secretary of the Treasury in 1993. He died in 2006. [57]

SERENADE: See sidebar **It's Music to My Ears,** page 218.

SETTEGAST: Empirical evidence leads me to believe this street is named for the Settegasts, an old line Houston family. (Many family members are buried in the historic Glenwood Cemetery off Washington Avenue.) They were large land owners in this area. It is likely the large (375-acre) eastside railroad yard named Settegast Yard (opened by the Missouri Pacific Railroad in 1950) is also named for them. The family is still prominent in the city today and operates Settegast-Kopf Funeral Home. [58]

SETTLERS VILLAGE: This northwest Harris County street recalls the old town of Settlers Village that was once located along the banks of Dinner Creek. (See **Dinner Creek.**) [59]

SEWANEE: This is the nickname for the University of the South, an arts and sciences college and theology school in Sewanee, Tennessee. It opened in 1868. [60]

SEYMOUR: The original plan of Pasadena was platted on the Vince & Seymour surveys, land named for two early settlers. (See **Vince.**) [61]

SHADDER WAY: This peaceful little street looms large in the urban legendry of River Oaks. My mother swore this story was true. It seems that a lady wanted to buy

S-T

an oversized lot on this street. The developer refused to sell her so much property so she filed suit. She won in court and neighbors suggested naming the street Shadder Way because "she had her way." True, part true or apocryphal? Who knows? Of course it could have been named by Mrs. H. A. Kip, the wife of the River Oaks Corporation vice president, for the street in London. But that's nowhere near as good a tale. [62]

SHADOW CREEK: This parkway leads into the 3,500 acre lake-themed master-planned community south of downtown in Pearland. It is named for the famous Tom Fazio golf course of the same name in Las Vegas. That property was the ultra-exclusive retreat of casino magnate Steve Wynn (Bellagio, Treasure Island, Wynn, etc.). Wynn owned the name and guarded it jealously. Fortunately, an investor in the Pearland development was an old pal of Wynn. After hearing that the development was to be first class, Wynn allowed his friend to use the Shadow Creek name. [63]

SHADOW LAWN: This small garden subdivision was developed by Houston attorney and judge, John Henry Crooker, a founder of Fulbright, Crooker, Freeman and Bates. As it was near prestigious Shadyside, it was marketed to upscale builders who were able to sell essentially prairie land at the edge of town in the 1920s. It was named after the Shadowlawn mansion in West Branch, New Jersey that was used as the summer "white house" by President Woodrow Wilson. The main street bears the neighborhood's name. [64]

SHADY RIVER: (See **Maple Valley.**) [65]

SHAFT: When Ravensway was being platted all of the streets had an avian connection such as **Raven's Claw, Raven Roost, Raven Flight, Nevermore** (a genuflection to Edgar Allen Poe) or **Birdcall** to mention a few. Developers believed the lots would sell faster if the neighborhood had a school. They gave the Cy-Fair Independent School District land for Millsap Elementary. Unfortunately, the school's location did

» SHAFT: Street sign in front of Milsap Elementary School

not have adequate access for emergency vehicles. So city officials required another street run in front of the campus. The developer asked CFISD to return some of the donated land to the company so they could build the necessary road. The school district said they would be happy to sell the land back but were unwilling to donate it. The furious developer purchased the property and went to Planning and Development to name the new street. He requested the name "Screwed" but officials said no. Since he did "get the shaft," he was allowed to select that moniker. [66]

SHAKESPEARE: William – He was the "Bard of Avon." Need we say more?

SHAMROCK: This tiny street is all that remains of one of our city's greatest legends. The Shamrock Hotel wasn't just a building. Newspaper society columnist Bill Roberts said, "the opening of the Shamrock changed Houston forever." It was built at a cost of $21 million by Glenn "King of the Wildcatters" McCarthy, a legend in his own right. Opening night, March 17, 1949 (St. Patrick's Day), the Shamrock hosted the greatest party in Houston's history. McCarthy had private trains bring the biggest movie stars of the day from California to attend. It was "a cast of thousands" including Dorothy Lamour, Maureen O'Hara, Ginger Rogers, Walter Brennan, Robert Stack and Edgar Bergen among them. An estimated 50,000 people lined South Main Street to see the stars roll by in yellow convertibles. It was such a scene that Texas-bashing author Edna Ferber modeled the character Jett Rink after McCarthy and called the hotel the "Conquistador" in her novel *Giant*. This 18-story, 1,110-room structure was the largest hotel built in America in the 1940s. The pool was so massive (165'x142') that water skiing exhibitions were held in it. McCarthy experienced huge financial reversals in the 1950s and lost control of the property in 1952. Hilton acquired the hotel in 1954 but it just was not the same anymore. The Shamrock fell to the wrecking ball in 1987 while more than 20,000 Houstonians attended a "grand Irish wake" to celebrate the life of this greatest of legends. (See **Glenhaven.**) [67]

» **SHAMROCK: The fabulous Shamrock Hotel**

S-T

SHANGRI LA: This mythical place name is from James Hilton's novel *Lost Horizon*. Released in 1939 it was the first paperback novel ever published by Ian Ballantine, a pioneer in that field. It was also made into a successful motion picture by the great director Frank Capra. Hidden the Kuen-Lun mountains, the Valley of Shangri La with its lamasery is a peaceful place. It is a good read filled with adventure, mystery, religion and philosophy. [68]

SHARMAN: (See **Eichwurzel**.)

SHARP: Walter Benona Sharp was an oilman and a partner of Howard R. Hughes Sr. Their drilling rigs found it impossible to drill through hard rock. Sharp knew Hughes had an inventive mind and put him to work to improve the technology of oil drilling. Hughes developed the rock bit with its movable cone-shaped cutters with steel teeth. In 1909 they founded the Sharp-Hughes Tool Company to mass-produce these revolutionary bits. Unfortunately Sharp died in 1912 and Hughes derived a massive fortune from this patented product that changed the petroleum industry forever. [69]

» SHARPSTOWN: Developer Frank Sharp

SHARPSTOWN: In 1936 Frank W. Sharp started a construction company with capital of $150. Ten years later, sensing the pent-up demand for housing in Houston following World War II, Sharp said, "See all that land? I'm going to build $32 million dollars worth of homes there. It'll be a city with 25,000 people living in it." And he made good on this bodacious promise. Sharp developed Oak Forest, Brookhaven, Jacinto City, Royden Oaks and Lamar-Wesleyan before building his crown jewel, Sharpstown. In 1954 Sharp unveiled plans for this mega-project. To assure its success Sharp and others donated land for the Southwest Freeway. The thoroughfare makes a leftward bend at Westpark so it goes through the middle of his development. In 1961 Sharpstown Center opened as the city's first totally air-conditioned shopping mall. [70]

SHARTLE: Thomas – The Shartle family were landowners and early residents of Hunters Creek Village. [71]

SHEARN: Charles – The third church in the city was a Methodist congregation in

1837. Shearn, was a member in good standing so it was called Shearn Church, later renamed First Methodist. He was called "a most earnest and devout Christian and he devoted his life to the advancement of the Church." [72]

SHEKEL: The developers of the Woodforest Addition must have had some interest in old coinage. A shekel is an ancient Hebrew coin of gold or silver weighing approximately half an ounce. That neighborhood also contains a street called **Two Penny,** an Americanized spelling of the English "two pence," a very small coin of low value. [184]

SHELDON: Henry K. – Located on the old Texas & New Orleans Railroad route, this village and the street are named for a New York investor in that railroad. The Sheldon Reservoir and Wildlife Management Area, on the east side of town, have the same provenance. [73]

SHELL COMPANY: The Shell Oil Company's Houston operations and docks are located on the Ship Channel in Deer Park. This huge corporation began as a small antique, curio and seashell shop in London. The owner, Marcus Samuel, began exporting oil for lamps and cooking under the name Shell Transport & Trading Company in 1897. In 1904 he chose a pecten shell as the firm's logo – still used today. The company expanded into oil and gas production and chemicals as the years went by. Today it is one of the world's biggest energy companies. [74]

SHENANDOAH: See sidebar **America the Beautiful,** page 176.

SHENANDOAH: This bedroom community was developed in the 1960s as Shenandoah Valley. It was made popular by its large lots and low land costs as well as lower tax and insurance rates. [75]

SHEPHERD: Benjamin A. – Shepherd was a Virginian who came to Houston in 1844. In 1847 his Commercial and Agricultural Bank became the first chartered bank in Texas. Although he was not invited in 1866 to be a founder of the city's first national bank, he was elected to the board of directors a year later. In 1867 he was named president of the First National Bank when it encountered financial difficulties following the Civil War. Shepherd managed the bank with an iron hand for the next 25 years. He was one of the incorporators of the Buffalo Bayou, Brazos & Colorado Railroad as well as one of the founders of the Cotton Exchange and Board of Trade in 1874. The town of Shepherd in San Jacinto County was named for him following

» **SHEPHERD: Benjamin A. - Tombstone in Glenwood Cemetery**

S-T

his laying out of the route of the Houston, East & West Texas Railroad in 1875. The family, now six generations old, gave the city land for Shepherd Drive and funded the Shepherd School of Music at Rice University. [76]

SHEPHERD: Thomas – An Englishman, Shepherd arrived in Texas in the 1840s. He bought 1,000 acres fronting on the east bank of Cedar Bayou and built Willesden Plantation. This farmer, sailor and boat builder died in 1881. [77]

SHERIDAN: Philip Henry – Although Sheridan was not a brilliant tactician, he was a leader and one of the better cavalry officers in the Union army during the Civil War. He saw action at the battles of Murfreesboro, Chickamauga and the Wilderness to name a few. His scorched earth strategy in the Shenandoah Campaign was so successful it was said "a crow flying over the place would have to take his rations with him." [78]

SHERMAN: Sidney – Although Yankees might think this street is named for William Tecumseh "War is Hell" Sherman, one of the greatest of the Union generals in the Civil War, it actually honors Sidney Sherman, a hero of the battle of San Jacinto. He commanded the left wing of the Texas Army in that decisive engagement. Sherman launched the attack with the now famous battle cry "Remember the Alamo." The city and county of Sherman are named for him as well. [79]

SHERWOOD FOREST: This ancient English forest north of Nottingham is best remembered as the refuge of Robin Hood and his band of Merry Men.

SHETLAND: See sidebar **All Things English,** page 175.

SHILOH: One of the bloodiest battles of the War between the States took place on April 6-7, 1862 at Shiloh Church near Pittsburg Landing, Tennessee. General Ulysses S. Grant squared off against General Albert Sidney Johnson. Each army experienced losses exceeding 10,000 men. The South won the first day but lost General Johnson. The Rebels withdrew as reinforcements poured in for Grant. This battle was a key to the Union's later successful campaigns in the West. [80]

» SHILOH: Texas Memorial at the Shiloh National Military Park

SHOOTING CENTER: A short drive on this street into the Barker Reservoir Flood Control Pool leads to the North American Hunting Club's American Shooting Center. This club is America's largest association of hunting enthusiasts. Intersecting streets include Skeet and Trap as well as Pigeon. (See **Skeet and Trap** and **Pigeon.**) [81]

SHOREACRES: This boulevard and small community on Galveston Bay were incorporated in 1949. It was originally called Bay Oaks. That community is honored by a street but it is just outside the Shoreacres city limit in La Porte and named for the spacious waterfront lots on the northwestern edge of Galveston Bay, Shoreacres suffered catastrophic damage from Hurricane Ike in 2008 when a 15-20 foot storm surge rendered 88% of its homes unlivable. [82, 83]

» **SHOREACRES: Hurricane Ike damaged hundreds of homes here in 2008**

SHORT SHELL: Although this Independence Heights street is officially called 31 1/2 Street on city maps, everyone in the neighborhood knows it as "Short Shell." When it was graded between 31st and 32nd streets, it was only two blocks long (extending from Courtland to Yale) and paved with oyster shells, thus the nickname. [84]

SHORTHORN: This street is located near Jersey Village, a town with a long history of cattle production. Shorthorns are one of the oldest recognized breeds of cattle in the world. They came from northeastern England near Northumberland and York. In 1783 they arrived in the U. S. Shorthorns were prized for the quality of their milk and meat. And of course here in Texas this street intersects **Longhorn** Circle. [85]

SIBELIUS: Jean – This Finnish composer of romantic, nationalistic works died in 1957. He is best remembered for his symphonic poem, *Finlandia*, written in 1899. [86]

SIDNEY: The area known as the Brady Place Addition contains the names of many members of the Brady clan. General Sidney Sherman was John Brady's father-in-law. (See **Brady** and **Sherman.**) [79]

S–T

SIEDEL CEMETERY: Also known as the Rosehill Cemetery, this burying ground is the final resting place of a number of German immigrant families for whom we have streets named. Interred here are members of the Siedel, Scholl, Burkhardt, Mueller, Juergen, Martens, Hirsch and Robeck families. (See **Siedel.**) [185]

SIEDEL: This family of German immigrants settled east of Tomball, Texas in the 1800s. A number of these early residents are buried in the Siedel Cemetery that is just south of this lane including Gustave (1849-1924), Mary (1848-1934) and Fridericke Siedel (1815-1879). (See **Siedel Cemetery.**) [87]

SILBER: H. F. – This Spring Branch road is named after a gentleman who was a major landowner and farmer in the area and granted the city the right of way through his property. [88]

SILLS: (See **Stockdick School.**)

SILVER: Located in a Stafford neighborhood with streets named for Kentucky Derby winners is this street named for an even more famous horse owned by the Lone Ranger, Hi-Ho Silver. It's a mystery why Tonto's Scout was left out. [89]

SIMMONS: Claude C. or William L. – See sidebar **Houston Streets Named for Men Killed During World War I,** page 22.

SIMS: Bartlett – Evidence indicates this street as well as the bayou it parallels is named for this early area resident and member of Stephen F. Austin's Old 300. He arrived in Texas in the 1820s. Sims was an Indian fighter and later a surveyor for Austin. He married in 1825 and became a rancher and farmer. Sims died in 1862. Sims Bayou is a meandering estuary that rises just inside the southern city limit of Houston, flows 28 miles through town and empties into the Houston Ship Channel. [90, 91]

SINCLAIR: Today Sinclair Oil & Refining Company is a subsidiary of ARCO. However, the firm was started in 1916 by one of the more colorful characters in the history of the petroleum industry. Harry Ford Sinclair was born in Wheeling, W.Va., July 6 1876. He started to become a pharmacist but in 1901, he went into the oil business. He dreamed of becoming bigger than John D. Rockefeller. Harry flew in private aircraft at a time when other oil barons took the train. He went to the new Soviet Union, met Lenin, and promised to raise money via bond issues in exchange for oil rights in Siberia. Sinclair returned to America to find that he was the key participant in the Teapot Oil Dome scandal of 1923. He allegedly bribed the United States Secretary of the Interior, Albert Fall, in return for the rights to the Elk Hills and Teapot Dome U.S. Navy oil reserves. He was acquitted of bribery charges but later was given a 9-month prison sentence for contempt of court and of Congress, a term he served in 1927. He died in Pasadena, California on November 10, 1956. This Pasadena, Texas street recalls this swashbuckling wildcatter and his company that most remember by its famous "Dino the Dinosaur" gasoline advertisements. [92]

SINFONIA: See sidebar **It's Music to My Ears,** page 218.

SINGER: See sidebar **Fairbanks Could Have Its Own Concours d' Elegance and Road Rally,** page 140.

SINGLETON: Drue — See sidebar **Houston Streets Named for Men Killed During World War I,** page 22.

SINGLETON: James W. — He arrived in Texas in 1828. Singleton fought in the Texas Revolution for which he was awarded 1/3 of a league of land near where Baytown is today. Like many soldiers who were paid with land there is no record that he every lived on it. [93]

SIR RALEIGH: Sir Walter Raleigh was an English soldier of fortune, writer, explorer and courtier. He once laid his cape across a mud puddle so Queen Elizabeth I could cross without mussing her shoes and gown. He partiticipated in the colonization of America and led expeditions to find the lost city of gold, El Dorado. Eventually charged with treason he was executed in 1618 for attacking Spanish galleons when under orders from the Crown to not engage them. [94]

SITTING BULL: This Dakota Sioux chief's refusal to return to the reservation in 1876 lead to the campaign that included the Battle at Little Bighorn where General George A. Custer and his troops were wiped out. Fearing retribution he took his people to Canada. Sitting Bull returned to the U.S. where he was killed in 1890. (See **Crazy Horse** and **Custer.**) [95]

SIVLEY: According to Jerry Wood, deputy assistant director of the City of Houston Planning & Development Department, this oddly named street is Elvis spelled backwards with a "y" added. What prompted the developer to come up with this name is not known. [96]

SJOLANDER: John Peter — Born in Sweden in 1851, at 15 he left home for Germany. Sjolander was a prisoner of war during the Franco-Prussian War. When freed in 1871, he went to Wales and boarded a ship bound for Galveston. As a young man he was a brick maker, boat builder, lighter captain, history buff and writer. He farmed for a living but because of the quality of his poetry he was called the "Sage of Cedar Bayou." His works appeared in *Peterson's Magazine, New York Weekly, Galveston News* and *New Orleans Times-Democrat.* His only book, *Salt of the Earth and Sea,* was published in 1928. Sjolander died in 1939 and is buried at Cedar Bayou. (See **Cedar Bayou.**) [97]

SKEET & TRAP: This form of sport shooting was created in Andover, Massachusetts in 1920. It involves clay discs called "pigeons" being thrown from traps. Marksmen use shotguns in an attempt to bring down these simulated birds. The pigeons are fired upon from a series of stations arranged around an arc. (See **Shooting Center.**) [98]

S–T

SKYWALKER: See sidebar **Space City U.S.A. or "Houston the Eagle Has Landed",** page 106.

SLEEPY HOLLOW: This is the secluded glen where Washington Irving set his tale *The Legend of Sleepy Hollow.* (See **Washington Irving, Brom Bones, Crane** and **Tarrytown.**) [99]

SMADA: This is Adams spelled backwards. A. J. Adams owned the Adams Ranch here on Oyster Creek. In addition, **Adams Street** in Missouri City is named for him. (See **Lemac.**) [100, 101]

SMITH: Benjamin F. – His military career started as a member of Andrew Jackson's staff during the Battle of New Orleans. Smith arrived in Texas in 1832. He saw action in the Revolution at the battles of Gonzales, Goliad and Siege of Bexar. He was the inspector-general at the battle of San Jacinto. In 1837 he built the city's first hotel. For unknown reasons he operated it for less than six months before selling it. The next year he was made president of the Board of Land Commissioners of Harrisburg. [102]

SMITH: More than likely this Brazoria street is named for an early settler, Henry Smith. He was the first governor of the independent state of Texas before it became a republic. Smith was ornery. The Congress removed him from office. However, in reply Smith dismissed that legislative body. [103]

SMITHDALE: E. C. Smith, an early resident, owned the land where this road is today. It was originally called Smith Road but was later changed to its present name to prevent confusion at the post office for mail delivery to Smith Street. [104]

SMITHERS LAKE: Houston Lighting and Power Company (now Reliant Energy) began construction of this man made lake on Dry Creek in Fort Bend County in 1956. Work was completed a year later. The company uses the water to cool the steam-electric generating station located on the banks. [105]

SNOVER: Oscar – See sidebar **Houston Streets Named for Men Killed During World War I,** page 22.

SOLOMON: Thomas Ralph – A educator, he was born in Macon, Georgia in 1904. He earned an A. B. (1929) and A. M. (1933) at Wayne State University. Solomon went on to receive a Ph.D from the University of Michigan (1939). He was the second black American to earn that degree in Political Science. Solomon joined the faculty at Prairie View A & M University in 1939. Until his retirement in 1972 he taught history, coached and was Dean of Students. He was elected to the City Council of Prairie View, Texas also. (See photograph on page 297.) [106]

SOLOMON: In the 1870s freed slaves from Alabama moved to northwest Harris County and started a community named Kohrville. Many members of the Solomon family are buried in the Kohrville Cemetery. The Solomon Temple Church of God in Christ still conducts services near the burying ground. (See **Cossey.**) [107]

» SOLOMON: Street marker on Prairie View A & M campus

SONATA: See sidebar **It's Music to My Ears,** page 218.

SORREL: (See **Appaloosa.**)

SOUTH HOUSTON: Named Dumont in 1901 by its founder C. S. Woods of the Western Land Company, it was incorporated in 1913 as South Houston, Texas. In its early years the area was principally truck farming for vegetables and fruits to ship to the farmer's market in Houston via the old Galveston, Houston & Henderson Railroad. (See **Dumont.**) [108]

SOUTH SHORE: This Galveston County road dead-ends at the southern shore of Clear Lake, one of our area's major recreation destinations. It passes by the South Shore Harbour Resort & Conference Center and through an upscale residential area of the same name. [109]

SOUTH: (See **Parkway.**)

SOUTHGATE: E. H. Borden developed this neighborhood and named the boulevard that is its main street. Because of its location just south of Rice University, it likely recalls the southern entrance to the campus. Rice is known for it magnificent gates that front on Main Street. [186]

SOUTHAMPTON: See **Southampton's English Streets,** page 255.

SOUTHWAY: In 1951 when a *Houston Post* reporter asked real estate developer B. F. Sturman how he came up with the name of this drive he replied it sounded good in conjunction with the street to its north, Briefway, that he also named. (See **Briefway.**) [110]

SOUTHWESTERN: This Methodist university opened its doors in Georgetown, Texas in 1873. However, it can trace it roots back to a letter written by Colonel William Barret Travis in 1835 requesting a Methodist presence in the Mexican colony of Texas. In 1840 Rutersville College, a predecessor institution, opened. One of its more famous alums is author J. Frank Dobie (class of 1910.) [111]

SPACE CITY: This street is the northern boundary of NASA's Lyndon B. Johnson Space Center near Webster. [112]

SPANISH CAMP: This area was settled by Stephen F. Austin's colonists in the early 1830s. After 1836 it got its name because General Antonio Lopez de Santa Anna

S-T

camped on Peach Creek near here. Some of the soldiers remained here as the Mexican Army pursued Sam Houston. Legend has it that when they heard of Santa Anna's defeat at San Jacinto they buried a large amount of gold and fled back to Mexico. So far no treasure has turned up. [113]

SPARTAN: Stafford High School's mascot is the Spartan, named for the fearsome ancient Greeks soldiers. [114]

SPELL: Daniel – A native of Louisiana, Spell arrived in the Willow Creek region in 1852. [115]

SPENCER: R. H. – He was a county judge in the 1930s best remembered for creating Sylvan Beach Park. An old Pasadena native told me that one of that city's eccentric characters, George W. "Little Barnum" Christy, a two term mayor as well as circus owner, lent his elephants to the road crews during construction of this highway. (See **Sylvan.**) [116]

» SPENCER: R.H. – Circus elephants working on construction of Spencer Highway

SPENCER: See sidebar **Brazoria County's Old Plantation Streets and Roads,** page 258.

SPENCER: Thomas M. – It is possible this west Houston road is named for this gentleman. He was superintendent of the Cypress-Fairbanks ISD from 1942 until 1947. [117]

SPICA: See sidebar **Starry Night,** page 111.

SPINDLETOP: This Pearland area street recalls the greatest oil discovery in Texas history. On January 10, 1901 on a salt dome south of Beaumont, Anthony F. Lucas hit the jackpot. The drilling rig began to shake as six tons of drill pipe blew out of the hole. That was followed by mud, natural gas and finally oil – lots and lots of oil – 100,000 barrels per day to be exact. It took nine days to cap the blowout. Beaumont's population soared from 10,000 to 50,000 as speculators, land men, drillers and gawkers poured into the city to seek their fortune. Some of today's major energy companies were born during that boom including the Texas Company (now Texaco), Humble (now Exxon Mobil), Gulf (now Chevron), Magnolia (now Exxon Mobil) and Sun (now Sonoco). [118]

» SPINDLETOP: Lucas Gusher blew on January 10, 1901

SPLASHTOWN: This short Spring area street leads to a water-oriented theme park of the same name. It is owned by Six Flags, Inc., the largest regional theme park operator. In Houston, the company once owned Six Flags Astroworld (now demolished). [119]

SPLENDORA: In the late 1800s this town was called Cox Switch for Charles Cox who was instrumental in getting the Houston, East & West Texas Railroad to extend a narrow-gauge spur here. In 1896 Cox requested the postmaster, M. S. King, to rename the town. King chose Splendora because of the "splendor of its floral environment." [120]

SPOONER: This Kansan was one of the developers of Pasadena. [121]

SPORTSPLEX: League City opened this 30-acre athletic complex in March 1998. It contains 10 baseball, 7 soccer, 2 football fields and 6 volleyball courts. It is used by Little League, Youth Football, Girls Softball and Youth Soccer teams. [122]

SPRING BRANCH: This street, suburb and the creek share a common name. Located in west Harris County, the farming community was founded as a German religious community. Karl Kolbe was the first settler here in 1830. In 1848 settlers established St. Peter's United Lutheran Church. (See **Kolbe.**) [123]

SPRING PINES: The Montgomery County town of Oak Ridge North was developed beginning in 1964 by the Spring Pines Corporation. [124]

SPRING-STUEBNER: Stephen F. Austin's colonists first settled the area around Spring Creek in the 1820s. In 1838 William Pierpont established a trading post here. Carl Wunsche, a German immigrant, moved here in the mid-1840s. The Goodyear blimp, *America*, was based in the town of Spring from 1969 until 1992. A major tourist attraction, Old Town Spring, draws antique hunters from all over the region. (See **Wunsche** and **Stuebner.**) [125]

S–T

SPRINGER CEMETERY: Along this Waller County road are two historic German cemeteries – Springer and Macedonia. The tiny community of Springer was also known as Hegar. Early settlers of the area are interred in these small cemeteries. (See **Hegar.**) [126, 127]

SPRITE: See sidebar **Fairbanks Could Have Its Own Concours d' Elegance and Road Rally,** page 140.

ST. ANDREW'S: Named for the Royal & Ancient Golf Club of the same name on Scotland's east coast, pilgrims have been coming here for millennia. Early on worshippers visited the area because the bones of the Saint were rumored to have been brought here from Patras, Greece in 390 A. D. Today the devotees still arrive but for more secular reasons - to try their skills on the oldest surviving golf links in the world. [128]

ST. CLOUD: See sidebar **Tennis or Golf, Anyone?,** page 348.

ST. CYR: When an extensive search of "Saint" sites on the Internet produced no St. Cyr, I could not help but think a developer with a good sense of humor perhaps decided to name this Sharpstown area street for Lili St. Cyr, the "Queen of the Strippers," whose 25 year career started in 1944. Tall (5'6"), curvy (36"-24"-36"), blonde and beautiful she is remembered for her "bubble bath" act where she emerged from the bath totally nude except for the bubbles that covered her "forbidden zones." [129]

ST. JAMES: This English palace in the Westminster borough of London was built as a residence by King Henry VIII. Much of it was destroyed in a fire in 1809. [130]

ST. JOHN: This NASA area street leads to Christus St. John Hospital on the shores of Clear Lake. [187]

ST. JOSEPH PARKWAY: In 1866 two congregations of nuns arrived in Galveston from France. They founded the Congregation of the Sisters of Charity of the Incarnate Word and opened the first Catholic hospital in Texas. In 1887 the congregation moved to Houston and opened St. Joseph Infirmary (now Christus St. Joseph Hospital.) For more than half a century that facility has been a fixture in downtown Houston. This street (once named Crawford) honors that institution's contribution to the health and well being of several generations of Houstonians including your author who was born at St. Joseph in 1942. (See photograph on page 301.) [131]

ST. LO: This was the name of a U. S. Navy Casablanca class escort carrier that fought in the Pacific in World War II. On October 25, 1944 the St. Lo became the first major warship to sink as a result of a kamikaze attack. She went down in the Battle of Layet Gulf. [132]

STADIUM: Follow this street south from Braeswood and it will lead you to Reliant Park – home of several stadiums including Reliant and the "world's eighth wonder," the Astrodome. [133]

» **ST. JOSEPH PARKWAY: The old St. Joseph Infirmary under construction**

STAFFORD: In 1830 William Stafford opened a cotton gin and sugar cane mill here. Both were the first installations of their kind in Austin's colony. General Santa Anna's Mexican army raided Stafford's plantation in April 1836 as they gave chase to General Sam Houston who was retreating to San Jacinto. At various times the town was called Stafford's Point and Staffordville. [134]

STAFFORD'S POINT: (See **Stafford.**)

STAGECOACH: This Montgomery County street actually follows part of a 19th century stagecoach route. The developer purchased this land from a farmer named W. L. Swinley and began development on Stagecoach Farms in 1958. In keeping with the old west history of the area other streets have western names such as **Broken Spoke** and **Boot Hill.** (See **Boot Hill, Tomahawk Trail, Wagon Wheel** and **Westward Ho.**) [135, 136]

STAITTI: I believe this Humble, Texas street is misspelled. H. T. Staiti was a geologist from Marshall, Texas. He formed Staiti Oil Company and drilled his first well in Humble in 1903. This discovery at Moonshine Hill was the beginning of his fortune. Staiti predicted in 1896 that oil would be discovered at Spindletop. His forecast proved correct when Anthony Lucas brought in a gusher on January 10, 1901 that flowed 100,000 barrels per day. Staiti moved to Houston and built a mansion at 400 Westmoreland. You can visit that house in Sam Houston Park where it was moved in 1986. (See **Humble, Moonshine Hill, Spindletop** and **Westmoreland.**) [137]

STALLONES: B. E. – He was an officer for the Harris County Fair when it took place in Tomball. He was principally responsible for the dairy entries. In addition he was a founder of the city's first hospital in 1948. (See **Hospital** and **Tomball.**) [138]

S-T

STANFORD: Opened in 1891 as the Leland Stanford Junior University in Palo Alto California, it has become one of the finest centers of learning in the country. [139]

STANLEY: See sidebar **Fairbanks Could Have Its Own Concours d' Elegance and Road Rally,** page 140.

STANOLIN: This is a misspelling of Stanolind Oil & Gas Company. (See **Hasting Field.**) [140]

STATE HIGHWAY 105: Paralleling this Montgomery County highway is Old Highway 105 and Old-Old Highway 105. If you live on one of these you best be specific when giving directions. [141]

STAUNTON: See sidebar **All Things English,** page 175.

STAVINOHA: In the early 1900s a number of families settled in Needville. This was one. Others include Banker, Fenske, Seiler and Meyer. They operated farms and ranches. (See **Needville.**) [142]

STEINMAN: Steve – This gentleman was the son-in-law of Baytown area pioneer Quincy Adams Wooster. (See **Wooster.**) [143]

STELLA LINK: Contrary to popular opinion this Bellaire area street was not named for Mr. Link's daughter. The street paralleled a railroad line that ran from Bellaire to Stella, Texas, a junction of the International-Great Northern and the Texas & New Orleans Railroads south of Houston. Ergo, it was the link to Stella. [144]

STERRETT: John H. – This old salt was captain of the steamboat *Neptune* during the Battle of Galveston on New Years Day of 1863. He was seriously wounded in the leg during that skirmish resulting in his having a pronounced limp for the rest of his life. Following the War he prospered as a boat captain plying the waters of Galveston Bay and the surrounding bayous. He held the position as commander of the Houston Navigation Company, a firm that regularly operated three steamboats between Houston and Galveston. [145]

STEVENS: James H. – Stevens is another bigger than life Houstonian. He came to the city in 1840 and opened a general store. This was the start of his rather sizable fortune. Interested in politics he served as a representative from the 2nd Ward and was elected Mayor in 1855. He invested in the Buffalo Bayou, Brazos & Colorado Railroad, allowing him to increase his wealth through the transportation of cotton. In his will he bequeathed $5,000 to the city to build a school. Other Houstonians matched his gift and Houston Academy was founded. [146]

STEWART: Amos – This early settler in La Marque donated land for the city's second school in 1895. Originally called Highlands for its location on Highland Creek, the city was renamed by postmistress Madam St. Ambrose when another town had already laid claim to Highlands. It means "the mark" in French. [147]

STEWART: Charles Bellinger – This Montgomery, Texas pioneer was a true Renaissance man. He was born in South Carolina in 1806 and came to Texas in 1830. Stewart was a physician, pharmacist, scientist and horticulturalist. He was the first man to sign the Texas Declaration of Independence, fought in the Texas Revolution, acted as inter-preter for General Sam Houston with the captured Santa Anna, was the first Texas Secretary of State and designed the Lone Star flag to mention just a few of his accom-plishments. He opened a drugstore in Montgomery in 1837. (See **Montgomery.**) [148, 149]

STEWART: J. M. – Doctor Stewart and John. H. Wright opened Katy's first drugstore in 1904. In addition, Wright is credited with certain municipal improvements including the water system and the installation of telephone lines. [150]

STEWART: Maco – Born in Galveston in 1896, Stewart was educated at Culver Military Academy and the University of Texas and its Law School. During World War I he was a captain in the Marine Corps First Aviation Force. Stewart was a very successful businessman. He was president of Stewart Title Company and a director of American National Insurance Company. Stewart was actively involved with the Texas State Historical Society. He passed away in 1950. [151]

STILLWELL: William Shaler – This Texas soldier fought at the battle of San Jacinto. [152]

STOCKDICK SCHOOL: Katy was ringed by one-room school houses named for area families. Adam Henry Stockdick was an early settler here. A school and drive are named for that family who have also been residents of Katy for years. (See **Stockdick.**) [153]

GONE WITH THE WIND TOO FAR

Serious *Gone With the Wind* junkies will fall in love with this neighborhood the second they hear the name – Twelve Oaks. Everything about this tiny community is related to Margaret Mitchell's epic novel and Hollywood's 1939 blockbuster motion picture *Gone With the Wind*. Twelve Oaks is the plantation of Ashley **Wilkes.** He is a southern gentle-man who although married to his cousin, **Melanie** Hamilton Wilkes, still has amorous feel-ings about the book's heroine, **Scarlett** O'Hara. She lives on her plantation, **Tara.** Scarlett is enamored with the protagonist **Rhett Butler,** a raconteur and Confederate blockade run-ner. Brent and Stuart **Tarlton** are twin brothers who live on a nearby plantation and with whom Scarlett periodically flirts. **Belle** Watling owns a brothel in Atlanta and is Rhett's mistress. Also remembered here is one real life character associated with *Gone with the Wind*, David O. **Selznick,** the motion pictures' producer.

The title is often erroneously thought to come from a line of Scarlett's when she wonders if Tara is still standing or has "also gone with the wind which had swept through Georgia." It actually is from the third stanza of Earnest Dowson's poem *Non Sum Qualis Eram Bonae Sub Regno Cynarae:* "I have forgot much, Cynara! gone with the wind." [47]

STOCKDICK: Adam – This gentleman was in the real estate business in Katy, Texas. [154]

STONE MOUNTAIN: See sidebar the **Antebellum Streets of River Plantation,** page 122.

STONEHENGE: There are five Houston area streets named in honor of this most famous and mystical ancient place. One of the most important archeological sites in Britain, this circle of huge standing stones is located on the plains near Salisbury. Construction was started around 3,000-2,500 B. C. Clearly the ancient people who built this phenomenal henge had excellent engineering skills as well as a solid knowledge of astronomy. A "henge" is a circular earthwork ditch or bank. Often these embankments contain circles of standing stones or timbers. [155]

STONES THROW: (See **Maple Valley.**) [156]

STONEWALL JACKSON: See sidebar the **Antebellum Streets of River Plantation,** page 122.

STRACK: E. F. – This man owned a farm near Cypress Creek in 1875. In 1974 the Texas Department of Agriculture started a program of registering farms and ranches that had been in continuous operation for 100 years or more. Strack Farm is one of a handful of Harris County properties so registered. It is likely this family arrived in the area from Germany prior to 1850. Land records show two brothers, Henry and Herman, who were blacksmiths, were included in the 1850 U. S. Census. [157]

STRAKE: George William – This oilman and philanthropist was born in St. Louis, Missouri in 1894. He served in the U. S. Army Air Corps in World War I. In 1927 Strake moved to Houston and began drilling for oil near Conroe. In 1931 he hit the mother lode. The Conroe Field became the third largest reserve of oil in America. He donated much of his estimated $200 million fortune to educational institutions, civic organizations and charities. Strake was a huge backer of the Boy Scouts of America, donating thousands of wooded acres near Conroe for a camp. (See **Camp Strake.**) [158]

STRAND: This is Galveston's most historic and famous street. It was named for a street of the same name in London. The five block area from 20th to 25th earned it the nickname of "Wall Street of the South" for the numerous banks and brokerage houses located there prior to 1900. Architect Nicholas Clayton designed 15 buildings on the Strand, 8 of which still exist. Like much of Galveston following the Great Storm of 1900, the street fell on hard times as business and commerce moved north to Houston. However, a restoration by the Galveston Historical Society in the 1970s revived the area and now it is listed in the National Register of Historic Places. [159]

STRATFORD: (See **Avondale.**)

STRATTON: See sidebar **Texas Heroes' Names for Houston Streets Urged in 72 Proposed Changes,** page 96.

STRATTON RIDGE: Previously called Phair, this ghost town was named for a nearby sulfur dome. Most likely it was named by a resident, Carrie Stratton Brock in honor of her father, J. T. Stratton. (See **Phair.**) [160]

STRAWBERRY: While we have other area streets named for fruits, this one certainly has the most interesting story concerning its christening. The killer hurricane that hit Galveston Island in September 1900 caused massive damage in the coastal areas near Pasadena as well. Farmers' crops were particularly hard hit. An economic disaster was in the making. However, Clara Barton, the founder of the American Red Cross, had 1.5 million strawberry plants shipped to the devastated city knowing they would produce a cash crop quickly. The plan worked and Pasadena became the "Strawberry Capital of the South." In 1974 the city held the first Pasadena Strawberry Festival. Although the strawberry fields long ago yielded to refineries, the festival is held each May. [161]

STRINGFELLOW: Robert Edward Lee – He was born in Old Brazoria in 1866. His first job was on a cattle ranch at age 14. Soon he acquired his own herd and began buying land. Stringfellow created a 20,000 acre ranch in southern Brazoria County. He opened a large meat market in Velasco in 1890. He was severely injured in the 1932 hurricane and his wife Nannie assumed management of their operations. [162]

STUDE: The Stude family owned land on the north bank of White Oak Bayou where Stude Park is today. They gave the city approximately 22 acres there for the development of a park system, a concept that would eventually spread to include other waterways such as Buffalo, Braes and Sims Bayous lateral parks. Studewood is named in honor of the same family. [163]

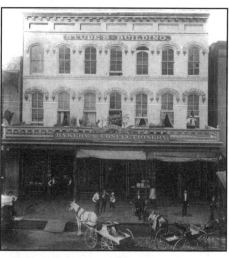

» STUDE: The original Stude Bakery

STUDEMONT: This street name was created when the city paved a section of road to connect Studewood with Montrose and took part of the name from each connecting street. [164]

STUEBNER: This was a prominent pioneering German immigrant family in the area west of Houston. Adolph Stuebner was an early Houston merchant who operated a general store on this road. Christian Frederick August Stuebner founded the town of Stuebner, Texas in the mid-1800s. However, the railroad chose to go through Huffsmith and the post office was established there effectively turning Stuebner into a ghost town. [165]

STYERS: James L. – See sidebar **Houston Streets Named for Men Killed During World War I,** page 22.

SUE BARNETT: When Garden Oaks real estate developer Edward Lillo Crane, Sr. turned his plat in to the Planning and Development Department of the City of Houston for approval there was a problem about intersecting numbered streets. As often happens in these meetings a quick solution is usually worked out. Sue Barnett was the planning director's secretary and a wonderful lady (your author lived across the street from her on E. Cowen in the early 1940s). So those in attendance voted to add Sue's name to our street map. [166]

SUFFOLK: See sidebar **All Things English,** page 175.

SUGAR CREEK: A real estate development company owned by Jake Kamin bought 3,500 acres from Sugar Land Industries to build this master planned community. The five stone columns at the neighborhood's entrance came from the old Galveston County Courthouse. Kamin had previously developed Nassau Bay on Clear Creek for employees of NASA. [167]

SUGAR HILL: (See **Chimney Rock.**) [168]

SUGAR LAND: (See **Howell-Sugar Land.**)

SULPHOR COUNTRY: Although there is no such word as "sulphor" the citizens of Damon want to remind passers through that they truly are in what was once the largest sulfur producing area in the world. [169]

SUL ROSS: The Lawrence Sullivan Ross family moved to Texas in 1839 when he was just one year old. He became an Indian fighter, captain in the Texas Rangers and organized and led Ross' Cavalry Brigade in the War Between the States. Entering politics he was eventually elected governor of Texas in 1887. On leaving office in 1891 he was named president of Texas A & M University. [170]

SUN OIL COMPANY: This Mont Belvieu road recalls an early player in the Spindletop field, at the time (1901) the greatest petroleum discovery in history. Founded in 1886, it was named Sun Oil in 1890. Over the years the corporation was involved in numerous ventures including ship building, gasoline stations, mercury mining, oil and gas production and oilfield equipment manufacturing. Today Sunoco as it is called, engages in refining and marketing of petroleum products and chemical production. [171]

SUNNY SIDE: This virtual ghost town was settled in 1866. It was named in 1877 when it got a post office. An early resident, James Rainwater, said he believed sun would always shine on the post office building that was located on the prairie land above the river bottoms. At its peak Sunny Side had two general stores, four grist mills, cotton gin, blacksmith shop, school, doctor and Methodist church. Today a handful of those structures stand unoccupied at the end of this rural road. One of which is the post office. So Rainwater remains partially correct in his prediction. [172]

SUNSET: I think this story is probably apocryphal but it is still a good tale. This boulevard was named because of the beautiful sunsets that reflected off the newly constructed buildings of Rice Institute in the 1920s. The developer of Southampton supposedly used this line in his marketing pitches to prospective homebuyers. [173]

SUPERIOR: Baytown is proud of its oilfield boomtown heritage and has a number of streets named in honor of petroleum companies that operated facilities there over the years. William M. Keck was born in Bradford, Pennsylvania in 1879. Forced to go to work at a young age, he only completed six grades of school. However, he retained a strong interest in education. He moved to California where he struck oil in 1922 and founded the Superior Oil Company. Keck remained chairman of the board of this very successful oil giant until his retirement at age 83. He used his great wealth for philanthropic purposes and gave millions to a number of California institutions of higher learning including Stanford University. He died in 1964. [174]

SURF: This near beachfront street recalls the small community of Surfside at the mouth of the Brazos River. Originally known as Follett's Island it occupies the site of old Velasco. It has been a popular beach resort since before 1875. (See **Velasco**.) [175]

SUTTON MILL: Alex Sutton is an executive with The Woodlands Operating Company. [176]

SWARTHMORE: The Society of Friends founded this co-educational college in 1864 in the Pennsylvania town of the same name. [177]

SWIFT: Jonathan – Swift was the greatest satirist of the 18th century. In his *pièce de rèsistance* tale, *Gulliver's Travels* (1726), he frames a brilliant political and social satire within what appears to be a child's story about a man who visits the imaginary lands of Lilliput, Brobdingnag, Laputa and Houyhnhnms. [178]

SYDNOR: John - In 1901 he worked for the Clear Creek Development Company that platted and promoted the town of Seabrook, Texas. Named for his son, Seabrook Sydnor, the town was initially a beach resort on Galveston Bay. Weekenders reached the village via the commuter train called the Interurban that ran from Houston twice a day. (See **Interurban**.) [179]

» SYLVAN: Houston architect Alfred C. Finn's plans for Sylvan Beach Park

S-T

SYLVAN: Sylvan Beach Amusement Park on Galveston Bay at La Porte was the hottest spot in the area during the 1920s and 1930s. As it gained national attention all of the big stars in America wanted to play there. Records indicate Rudy Vallee, Phil Harris and Benny Goodman were regulars. In addition it was very popular for its bathing beauty contests. The Houston Launch Club held its annual regatta in the bay waters off Sylvan Beach. Old timers recall it as the grandest event of its kind anywhere on the Gulf Coast. (See **Spencer.**) (See photograph on page 307.) [180]

SYMPHONIC: See sidebar **It's Music to My Ears**, page 218.

SYRACUSE: Opened in 1891 this co-educational university in New York is famed for its instruction in technological subjects, communications and computer applications. [181]

T

T. C. JESTER: This gentleman was the pastor at the Baptist Temple on the corner of 20th Street and Rutland in the Houston Heights. He was appointed to the position in 1927 and remained in the job until his death in 1950. Every business in the Heights closed for his funeral. He began a program of tithing by the members in 1938. Some of the older parishioners still tithe to the Baptist Temple. He was very active in the community and served on the Houston City Planning Commission and the board of Baptist Hospital. [1]

TAFT: William Howard – The 27th President (1909-13), had the misfortune of following the popular and flamboyant Teddy Roosevelt. Despite his lack of political skills, Taft was able to pass important legislation. The highlight of his career was being appointed Chief Justice of the Supreme Court, the only American to hold both positions. [2]

TAGGART: Harry – See sidebar **Houston Streets Named for Men Killed During World War I,** page 22.

TAHITI: See sidebar **Bali Hai May Call You,** page 322.

TALCOTT: Patching – Nathanial Lynch owned a league of land where this street is to-day just south of the Sheldon Reservoir. Talcott and his wife Clarrisa purchased some land that was part of this piece of property in the late 1800s. [3]

TAM-O-SHANTER: This is a Scottish cap usually with a pompom on the top. It is named for the hero of Robert Burn's 1790 poem of the same name. [4]

TAMANA: See sidebar **Bali Hai May Call You,** page 322.

TAMINA: Located near The Woodlands, this street was named by James H. Berry. This real estate promoter seemed to admire Tammany Hall in New York City. When he

THE MOST SCENIC SPOTS IN TEXAS

In a Fort Bend neighborhood just north of the Sugar Land Municipal Airport the developer chose place names of some of the most beautiful places in our fair state for the street names. Among those locations are: **Lost Maples** (a Hill Country stand of bigtooth maple trees), **Inks Lake** (a beautiful body of water on the Colorado River near Austin), **Natural Bridge** (the largest cave in the state located in Comal County), **Longhorn Cavern** (a cave between Burnet and Marble Falls), **Matagorda** (a major coastal bay), **Pedernales Falls** (a waterfall and state park near Johnson City known for its flora and fauna), **Davis Mountains** (this west Texas range is the second highest in the State), **Hueco Tanks** (giant granite rock formations known for its prehistoric petroglyphs near El Paso), **Mineral Wells** (the old "crazy waters" spa west of Ft. Worth), **Caprock Canyon** (rugged cliffs in the Panhandle), **Copano Bay** (a small coastal bay near Rockport), **Mustang Island** (a rugged barrier island off of Corpus Christi), **McKinney Falls** (a swimming hole southeast of Austin), **Copperas Creek** (a tributary of the North Llano River), **Possum Kingdom** (a recreational area and lake near Graham), **Seminole Canyon** (a park northwest of Del Rio known for its ancient petroglyphs), **Garner Park** (a recreation area in Uvalde County renown for flora and fauna) and **Choke Canyon** (over 20,000 acres of untouched South Texas scrub brush filled with deer, turkeys and javelinas). [48]

requested the name from the postal service he obviously did not know how to spell the name of this powerful political organization, thus the odd spelling. However, locals still call the road "Tammany." [5]

TANG CITY: In 1985 real estate developer Calvin Leung began construction on Tang City, a $200 million multi-use project in Missouri City. It was the first master-planned Chinese community in the United States. It was to include an oriental supermarket,

» TANGLEWOOD: The gate sign

Asian restaurants and retail shops in a 120,000 square foot mall. Leung envisioned a beautiful tourist attraction. However, Houston's fickle real estate market put an end to the dream and the property was taken over by the Resolution Trust Corporation in 1990. For more than a decade the property was a graffiti covered, weed choked eyesore. In 1999 former Houston Rocket's star Hakeem Olajuwon purchased the property with plans to build a mosque on the site. To date, little progress has been made. [6]

TANGLEWOOD: Mary Catherine Farrington Miller, daughter of Tanglewood developer William G. Farrington, named this street. She cited several reasons for her choice: it was easy to pronounce and remember, she had enjoyed reading Nathaniel Hawthorn's *Tanglewood Tales* in junior high school and was also familiar with the Boston Symphony's 210-acre formal gardens in Lennox, Massachusetts. (See photograph on page 310.) [7]

TANGLEY: This was a very swampy and overgrown part of West University. Early residents recall their house pets wondering into this fenced off area catching crawfish. When it was eventually paved the name of the street was chosen to remember the jumble of vines that were previously here. [8]

TANNER: G. H. – In the early 1900s this man offered his farmhouse to Fairbanks, Texas for a school. His generosity earned him a street name. [9]

TARA: See sidebar **Gone with the Wind Too Far,** page 303.

TARA: This Bunker Hill Village street is named for the famed plantation in Margaret Mitchell's epic novel about the South during the War Between the States, *Gone with the Wind.* One street to the north is **Rhett,** named for the dashing Rhett Butler, Scarlett O'Hara's love interest in the novel. (See **O'Hara.**)

TARAWA: In a bloody four-day battle from November 20 - 23, 1943, the U.S. Marines captured this island in the South Pacific Ocean. The Japanese had heavily fortified the atoll in the Gilbert Islands. The fighting was fierce and casualties heavy on both sides. When it ended the Americans reported almost 1,000 Marines dead and over 2,300 wounded. The approximately 4,800 Japanese defenders were killed. [10]

TARLTON: See sidebar **Gone with the Wind Too Far,** page 303.

TARPLEY: William P. – When Texas City incorporated and chose the commission form of government in 1901 this state representative from Galveston County was elected mayor. [11]

TARRYTOWN: Washington Irving set his story *The Legend of Sleep Hollow* in Tarrytown, New York. (See **Washington Irving, Sleepy Hollow, Crane** and **Brom Bones.**) [12]

TAUTENHAHN: Herman – This German immigrant built a general store in Westfield in

S–T

1864. When the International-Great Northern Railroad laid its rail line from Houston to Spring, Tautenhahn moved his operation to a trackside location near the Bammel and Hardy Road intersection. Business boomed and in 1911 he built a fancy two story brick building from which to offer his goods. It was the precursor to the supermarket of the 20th century. [13]

TAYLOR: E. W or Horace Dickinson – There are two possibilities for the provenance of this street. First is E. W. Taylor. This gentleman was an official of the Texas Central Railroad and a friend of William Baker who developed the Sixth Ward where this street is located. The second is Horace D. Taylor. In 1838 this pioneer and his brother moved from Massachusetts to Independence, Texas. Ten years later the brothers came to Houston and established a cotton business. The cotton brokerage firm operated out of a warehouse on Buffalo Bayou. Taylor was a founder of the Cotton Exchange & Board of Trade. He married and built a home on 3.5 acres of land northwest of downtown where this street is located. Taylor was an alderman (1861-2) and served as mayor in 1866. [14, 15]

TAYLORCREST: It is possible this Memorial Villages street recalls John D. Taylor who owned a league of land in this area. [16]

TEAS NURSERY: (See **Teas**.)

TEAS: Edward T. Sr. – The son of horticulturist John C. Teas, Edward arrived in Houston in the early 1900s. Bellaire developer William W. Baldwin hired him in 1909 to mastermind the landscaping of that new city. In 1910 he opened Teas Nursery, a family business that existed until 2009. Over the next few years, Teas took on projects including the landscaping of Rice Institute (now University) and River Oaks. [17]

TEETSHORN: Ray G. – Originally this Houston Heights street was named Reichman. However, after World War I it was renamed to honor a Heights resident who died of disease in Europe during the war. [18]

TEJAS: Texas got its name from the Hasnai Caddo Indians who used the word *tayshas* (friend or ally) that the Spaniards translated as *tejas*. [19]

TELEPHONE: When this route was named many years ago Houston children thought it was called Telephone because every house on the street had one. In those days that would have been real news. However, like most urban legends there was no truth in the story. Instead, its name came from the fact that it followed the route of the first long-distance telephone line in Texas. [20]

TELGE: This family owned land in the area around Cypress Creek. They emigrated from Hanover, Germany in the late 1800s. A number of family members are buried in the Knigge Cemetery off Huffmeister Road in northwestern Harris County. Among these persons are Chester, Alma, Louis and Geborne Telge. (See **Knigge Cemetery**.) [21, 22]

TELLEPSEN: Howard T. – He was president of the Chamber of Commerce when on July 3, 1954, the one-millionth resident of Houston was honored. That date was chosen Houston's "M Day." The winner received thousands of dollars in gifts and toured other metropolitan areas with populations of one million or more and brought greetings to the mayors and Chamber of Commerce presidents from the citizens of Houston. Tellepsen also was president of a major construction company responsible for many huge projects in the Houston area. Tellepsen Construction celebrated its 100th birthday in 2009. [23]

TEMPLE TRAIL: Located in Todd Mission the street recalls the days when a Mormon colony lived here and worshiped in their temple. [24]

TENNECO: This road leads into the Tenneco Industrial District and Dock on the Houston Ship Channel. The company was founded in 1943 as Tennessee Gas Transmission Company (renamed Tenneco in 1966) to deliver natural gas by pipeline to defense plants in Appalachia during WW II. In later years Tenneco expanded into oil and gas exploration, chemical production, insurance and foodstuffs. [25]

TENNYSON: Alfred – He was among the most famous English poets of the Victorian age. Some of his best remembered poetry includes *The Lotus Eaters, Morte d'Arthur* and *The Charge of the Light Brigade.* [26]

TERLINGUA: This small village arose on the banks of Terlingua Creek in far West Texas. In the 1880s it became a booming mining town with the discovery of quicksilver in the area. By 1922 over 40% of the quicksilver mined in America came from here. The mines began playing out in the 1930s and production ceased following World War II. Terlingua rapidly became a ghost town. It was rediscovered in the 1960s and soon became famous for its chili cook off. In 1967 Terlingua was named "Chili Capitol of the World." [27]

TERMINI-SAN LUIS PASS: The Termini family are third generation Galvestonians. D. J. Termini owned a pharmacy or grocery store on the island years ago. His son Joe managed the Broadway Funeral Home. Today the grandson, also named D. J., owns the J. Levy & Termini Funeral Home. San Luis Pass, the body of water between the Gulf of Mexico and West Bay, lies between Galveston Island and the Texas mainland at Treasure Island. It is about two miles wide and ranges from 10 to 40 feet deep. [28]

TERRY: Benjamin Franklin – Located just northeast of downtown in an area where many streets are named for famous Texans, it is likely that this one honors a Fort Bend planter and hero of the War Between the States.

» **TERRY: Tombstone and historic marker in Glenwood Cemetery**

S-T

Colonel Terry saw action at the first battle of Manassas. He subsequently returned to Houston and organized a cavalry unit that became know as Terry's Texas Rangers. Terry was killed at the battle of Woodsonville on December 17, 1861 while leading the unit's first charge. [29]

TESORO: See sidebar **Learn a Foreign Language on Your Morning Walk,** page 125.

TETTER CEMETERY: This pioneer burying ground is in Pine Grove just north of Bush Intercontinental Airport. There is a brass plaque on one grave indicating it is the last resting place of Caldonia Tetter (1785-1800) and stating she was the first person buried here and the cemetery is named for her. I have discussed this with other Houston historians and we think this information is at best odd and at worst incorrect (at least as to the dates). Moses Austin did not arrive in Texas until 1820 and Stephen F. Austin did not begin the colonization process until 1825. So what would a 15 year old girl be doing here twenty years earlier? [30]

TEXACO: This east side street leads to the Texaco Golf Club. This facility opened in 1924. It was one of the first clubs to become involved with the Houston Golf Association when that organization was responsible for the Houston Open PGA Golf Tournament in 1967. [31]

» TEXACO: This street leads to a private golf club

TEXAS ARMY: Our army was of great importance to the Republic of Texas. We needed strong defenses against Mexico and Indian tribes. The size of the army put great strains on the Republic's treasury and manpower. During much of the time from 1836 until 1845 more than 10% of the Anglo population was in the army causing the Republic to continually face fiscal crisises. [32]

TEXAS CITY DIKE: This levee extends five miles out into Galveston Bay from its start in Texas City. Construction was approved by the Texas Legislature in 1935. It was designed to reduce the impact of sediment accumulating along the lower Bay. Since then its purpose has changed. Today it protects the city from hurricane storm surge. It was worth its weight in gold when Hurricane Ike blasted into the Texas Gulf Coast in 2008. Despite structural damage to the Dike itself, Texas City reported minor damage compared to the catastrophic destruction seen at almost every other coastal town in the area. Repairs are now completed. Once again what the locals call the "world's longest man-made fishing pier" will hopefully be back in action with its bait shops, restaurants and beer joints. [33]

TEXAS INDEPENDENCE: This freeway also known as State Highway 225 runs through some of the most historic and sacred ground in Texas. It recalls the framing, approval and issuance of the Texas Declaration of Independence at the Convention of 1836 convened at Washington-on-the-Brazos. Signed by the 59 delegates on March 2, 1836, five copies were sent to the towns of Bexar, Goliad, Nacogdoches, Brazoria and San Felipe. The highway also passes just south of the San Jacinto Battleground where our independence was won on April 21, 1836. [34]

TEXAS: This is one of the main streets in the industrial Galveston Bay town of Texas City. First known as Shoal Point, three Brothers from Minnesota, Jacob, Henry and Benjamin Myers, visited the area in the late 1890s and saw great potential as a port city. They bought 10,000 acres here and created the Texas City Improvement Company and changed the town's name. Dredging a ship channel began in 1893. Soon railroads began arriving and Texas City was on its way. Industries poured in as well including smelting, pipe bending, refining and chemicals to mention a few. In 1947 Texas City was literally almost blown off the map when the *Grandecamp*, a freighter loaded with ammonium nitrate fertilizer, blew up setting off a chain reaction of explosions that killed 576 people and injured over 4,000 more. In excess of 1,000 structures were destroyed. The 10,640 pound anchor of the *Grandecamp* was found half a mile from the harbor. You can visit where it landed and has remained since that fateful day. Many excellent books have been written about the "Texas City Disaster." [35]

TEXIAN: This term was used to describe citizens of the Anglo-American province of Coahuila and Texas and later citizens of the Republic of Texas. After annexation by the United States the name changed to Texan. [36]

TEXMATTI: The prairie lands west of Houston are among the most prolific rice pro-ducing areas in the world. This unusual street name is a rice. The most flavorful of the world's rice is the Indian basmati, a short grain rice. When bred with Texas long grain rice it is called Texmati. Here is another of our misspelled names.

THE BEAST: Houstonians like to give their freeways names. So we call I-45 South the Gulf Freeway because it leads to the Gulf of Mexico, U. S. 59 is the Southwest Freeway as it runs that direction to Richmond, U. S. 59 North is the Eastex Freeway since it will take you to East Texas and I-10 West we call the Katy Freeway because it goes to the town of Katy. Unfortunately, I-10 East earned the nickname "The Beast" due to it con-tinually wretched construction condition and bumper-to-bumper traffic. [37]

THEISS: Johann Henrich Theis, his wife, Katherina and four children were early German settlers in the Tomball/Rosehill area, arriving in 1846. They were among the families who founded Salem Lutheran Church. Their oldest son, Jacob, was a carpen-ter who went on to establish Trinity Lutheran Church in Klein. In the 1890s there was confusion at the post office about mail delivery to family members in Rosehill and Klein. So the Rosehill group continued spelling their name with one "s" and the Klein clan added an "s." [38]

THIN LIZZY: According to Jerry Wood at Planning & Development, this lane is in hon-or of the 1970s rock band of the same name. [39]

S-T

THIS WAY & THAT WAY: Nothing historic here, your author just got a kick out of the fact these two Lake Jackson streets intersect. [40]

THOMAS: Oscar John – This black educator was born in Trawick, Texas. He earned a B. S. and M. S. in Agriculture from Prairie View A & M University. After serving as a high school principal he joined the staff at Prairie View in about 1931. Thomas earned many honors in his life including President of the Colored Teachers Association of Texas (1937) and President of the National Chapter of the Prairie View Alumni Association. [41]

» THOMAS: Oscar John Thomas, an educator at Prairie View A & M University

THOMAS: J. O. – Katy's first postmaster was named Thomas. He was also a grocer and partner of W. P. Morrison, also a grocer and the second man to captain the city's post office. It's possible this street honors him. (See **Morrison.**) [42]

» THOMPSONS: Old general store

THOMPSON FERRY: This ferry carried early Texas settlers across the Brazos River at Richmond. The ferry and this road are named for Jessie Thompson who operated the ferry from 1830 until 1847. Sam Houston's retreating Texas Army used this ferry to cross the Brazos River. Santa Anna and his army crossed the river on this craft one week before his disastrous defeat at San Jacinto. [43]

THOMPSON OILFIELD: (See **Rabb Ridge.**)

THOMPSONS: Hiram – Robert A. Bohannan moved to Texas from Alabama and received a land grant in 1836 south of where Sugar Land is today. When he died his widow married Hiram Thompsons. She named the town of Thompsons for him. (See photograph pge 314.) [44]

THOMPSON'S CHAPEL: Thompson's Chapel Baptist Church is in Sugar Land. It is an independent fundamentalist KJV (King James Version) church. This sect believes the King James version of the Bible is the complete and final revelation of the will of God to mankind. [45]

THOR: See sidebar **Space City U.S.A. or "Houston the Eagle Has Landed",** page 106.

TIEL: This curvy River Oaks lane was given its name by developer Hugh Potter. It is the nickname of his wife. This area was the second-to-last part of this neighborhood to be opened for development in 1946. [46]

TIERWESTER: This gentleman was a Houston surveyor at the end of the 19th century. He surveyed the area where this street is today in 1890 according to an old city map. As was often the case, the surveyor would name a street for himself when filing the plat. By 1912 Tierwester appeared on Houston maps. [47]

TIFCO: This short northwest side road leads to the headquarters of TIFCO Industries. Founded in 1961, TIFCO is a single source stocking distributor of over 45,000 quality, expendable maintenance and repair products for industrial, fleet and heavy duty equipment. [48]

TIGRIS: One of the two principal rivers of ancient Mesopotamia (now Iraq), it, along with the Euphrates, is considered the cradle of civilization.

TIMBERLANE: Herbert A. Kip was a vice-president of the River Oaks Corporation and the landscape and consulting engineer. Prior to the River Oaks project he worked on the development of Shadyside and Southampton. He named this street. It is interesting that it is spelled four ways in just nine blocks (Timberlane, Timber Lane, Timber Ln. and Timber). Planning and Development says that most likely when the street signs were ordered the correct name was misunderstood by the sign makers. [49]

TIN HALL: On a street of the same name this country and western honky-tonk opened in Cypress in 1889 and has operated continuously since. It claims to be the oldest reception venue in Texas. (See **Glen Cheek.**) [50]

TITAN: See sidebar **Space City U.S.A. or "Houston the Eagle Has Landed",** page 106.

TOBRUK: A Libyan port city on the Mediterranean Sea, it was captured by the British

S-T

on January 22, 1941, was recaptured in a counter attack by German General Edwin Rommel, the "Desert Fox," in March and April of 1942 and retaken by British forces on November 30 of that year. [51]

TOCCATA: See sidebar **It's Music to My Ears,** page 218.

TODD MISSION: This Montgomery County village was established in 1900 when a Mr. Todd, who owned a saw mill nearby, erected a station on the International-Great Northern Railroad. In 1919 a congregation of Mormons arrived and built a school and called it Todd Mission. At that time the town name was changed from Todd. In 1957 the congregation moved to Navasota. For more than 25 years the Texas Renaissance Festival has been held in Todd Mission. This is eight fun filled weekends where you can go mingle with kings, queens, magicians, court jesters, dragons and knights and their ladies. [52]

A NEIGHBORHOOD FOR LINKSTERS

If golf is your passion you might consider buying property near the old line Pearland golf links course called Golfcrest Country Club. Here you can live on **Augusta** (as in Augusta National), **Birdie, Lofting Wedge, Five Iron** or **Pitching Wedge.** [49]

TODD: (See **Todd Mission.**)

TODVILLE: Paralleling the western rim of Galveston Bay and passing through the towns of Pasadena and Seabrook is a road named for the former beach town of Tod or Todville. John G. Tod, Jr established it in 1900. Prior to that date it was called Morristown in honor of Ritson Morris, the owner of the original land grant. [53]

TOMBALL: Originally called Peck, Texas, when it was founded in 1906 as a station on the Trinity & Brazos Valley Railroad, a year later it was renamed to honor Thomas H. Ball. Tom Ball was a lawyer and congressman from Harris County. He is also remembered for his support of the Houston Ship Channel project. According to *The Heritage of North Harris County,* Ball lost his run for governor in 1914 on the Prohibitionist ticket when photographs of saloons he owned were made public by his opponent (see **River Oaks.**). [54]

TOP GALLANT: Not all of our thoroughfares named for racehorses are in honor of Kentucky Derby winners, Triple Crown champions or world record holders. This nag barely earned enough purses to pay for his oats. His one claim to fame is he was the son of 1957 Derby loser, Gallant Man (see **Iron Liege.**) [55]

TORREY PINES: This beautiful golf course is located in San Diego, California and is home to the PGA's Buick Open every January. Known for its dramatic ocean views the links derives its name from the many Torrey Pine trees that line the course. These trees are the rarest of pines only existing here and Santa Rosa Island off Santa Barbara, California. [56]

TOSCA: This is another Gaywood street named for a famous opera. Composer

Giacomo Puccini premiered this three-act classic at Rome in 1900. [57]

TOWER BRIDGE: Located on the Thames River next to the Tower of London, it is often confused with the less impressive London Bridge that was eventually moved to Lake Havasu, Arizona, in the 1960s to grace a man-made lake in a retirement community. [58]

TOWN & COUNTRY: This upscale shopping center was built in the 1960s and anchored by major department stores that are no longer with us like Sakowitz and Joske's. Real estate developer Moody Rambin did a major renovation of the property in the 1990s. [59]

TOWNE CENTER: This street leads into Pearland Towne Center, a 718,000 square foot shopping center with approximately 100 retail outlets. The owner is CBL & Associates Properties, a company that operates malls around the U. S. It is architecturally interesting because the mall is designed like the center of a small Texas town. Each store front is different. But instead of the stores being a local café, antique shop, hardware store, etc. they are Ann Taylor, Brooks Brothers, Eddie Bauer and the like. [60]

TRACK: In the 1890s the Missouri, Kansas & Texas Railroad laid a line through the middle of Cat Spring. Thus the main street was named Track. Although the M K & T line is now the Union Pacific Railroad the street name remains the same. [61]

TRAMMEL-FRESNO: This highway ran between the small agricultural towns of Trammels (somehow the "s" was lost when the road was named) and Fresno (see **Fresno.**) [62]

TRAVIATA: This three-act Italian opera by Giuseppe Verdi premiered in Venice in 1853. [63]

TRAVIS: William Barret – He arrived in Texas in the early 1830s following the failure of his marriage. He was a leader of the Anahuac Disturbances of 1832 for which he was arrested. At that time the Mexican authorities did not look favorably on the Texans' grievances. In February 1836 he was sent to reinforce the garrison at the Alamo. It is for his stand there and ultimate death for which he is remembered as one of Texas' greatest heroes. Songwriter Jane Bowers sings his praises in *Remember the Alamo:* "One hundred and eighty were challenged by Travis to die, with a line that he drew with his sword when the battle was nigh, the man who will fight to the death cross over but him that would live better fly, and over the line came one hundred and seventy nine." The line in the sand may be mythical, but what a great story. [64]

TRAWEEK: Phillip B. and/or M. B. – These men were land developers in Spring Valley. Phillip's wife was named Bonnie. He named a subdivision, Bonnie Oaks, for her. [65]

TREICHEL: In the mid-1800s many German immigrant families settled around what is now the Tomball, Texas area. The Treichel's were among them. A number of family members are buried in the historic St. John Lutheran Cemetery off of Mueschke Road. (See **Lutheran Cemetery.**) [79]

S-T

TREMONT: Henry Greenwall, a German immigrant, arrived in Galveston following the War Between the States. He and his brother Morris opened a stock brokerage firm. In 1867 a client and actress of note, Augusta L. Dargon, owed the Greenwall brothers money. In exchange they took over management of her career. Henry became a theater manager. He convinced Willard Richardson, owner of the *Galveston Daily News*, to build the Tremont Opera House which Greenwall immediately leased. What happened to the distressed damsel Augusta is shrouded in the mists of time. Henry went on to own opera houses all over America. When he died in 1913 he was the oldest active theater manager in the country. [66]

TREVINO: Lee – Located on the grounds of the Friendswood Golf Club, this street recalls one of the most talented and colorful golfers to pick up a set of clubs. This El Paso native was born in 1939 and took to the links as a young man. He won the U.S. Open (1968, 1971), British Open (1971, 1972) and the PGA (1974, 1984). He was named Player of the Year on the PGA tour in 1971 and the Senior tour in 1990, 1992 and 1994. Remembered for his quick humor Trevino was once struck by lightening. Asked how to avoid such an unfortunate accident again he said "I'll carry a one iron from now on." When the writer asked why, Trevino quipped "Even God can't hit a one iron." [80]

TRI-CITIES: This road recalls when Baytown, Goose Creek and Pelly, Texas were three separate towns on Galveston Bay. In 1947 citizens of the latter two voted to merge into one town and call it Baytown. [67]

TRINITY: (See **Colorado.**) [68]

TRIPLE CROWN: The three-year-old thoroughbred that wins the Kentucky Derby, the Preakness Stakes and the Belmont Stakes is known as the Triple Crown winner. Only 11 horses have achieved this lofty goal in the last 135 years of competition. Winners such as Affirmed (1978), Secretariat (1973), Whirlaway (1941) and War Admiral (1937) earn legendary status in the pantheon of thoroughbred racing. It was Gallant Fox's victories in 1930 that resulted in the name. (See **Affirmed, Secretariat, Whirlaway, War Admiral** and **Gallant Fox.**) [69]

TROON: The Troon Golf Club (Royal Troon) is one of the most well known of the Scottish links. It traces its history back to 1878. It is most famous for its 3 par 8th hole, called the Postage Stamp. [70]

TRUETT: William – See sidebar **Houston Streets Named for Men Killed During World War I,** page 22.

TRUXILLO: According to Bart Truxillo, a Houston architect specializing in historical preservation, this street was named for a member of his family who immigrated to America from Spain. The Truxillo family arrived in New Orleans and one of them came to Houston. He lived in the area where the street is today. Being very popular with his neighbors they petitioned to have a street named for Mr. Truxillo. When

Bart and his family moved to Houston in the early 1950s there were no Truxillos living here. However, in the taxi on the way to their new house they kept hearing the name Truxillo on the cab's radio. It turned out that the dispatcher had a fare on that street that needed a ride. William Sidney Porter, who would become famous under the *nom de plume* of O. Henry, lived at 1310 Truxillo when he worked as a reporter for the *Houston Post* in 1895-96. [71]

TUAM: This street is named for the Irish hometown of Civil War hero Dick Dowling (see **Dowling.**) [72]

TUCK: Robert E. – See sidebar **Houston Streets Named for Men Killed During World War I,** page 22.

TUCKERTON: The Tucker family were landowners and rice farmers in this area of northwestern Harris County. [73]

TULANE: This Heights avenue is named for Tulane University in New Orleans. On the original plat of the Houston Heights it is named Portland. The name was changed by a city ordinance. [74]

TULLY: Darrell – This street is located next to a football stadium of the same name. It honors Coach Tully, the head football coach and athletic director of Spring Branch High School from 1957 until 1964 and athletic director of the Spring Branch ISD from 1964 until he retired in 1978. Seating 15,000 fans it opened in 1969. The first game was between Memorial High and Dallas Kimball. [81]

» TURNING BASIN: Houston Ship Channel Turning Basin in the early 1900's

S-T

TUPPER LAKE: Named for a village in upstate New York, William Farrington, developer of Tanglewood among many other Houston projects, just liked the sound of the words. It also met his criteria of being easy to spell and not difficult for a telephone information operator to understand. [75]

TURNING BASIN: In order for Houston to build a port on Buffalo Bayou it was necessary to have a location for ocean going vessels to turn around and head back out to sea. In 1906 the Atlantic, Gulf & Pacific Company of New York began dredging this basin. The project took two years to complete. (See photograph on page 321.) [76]

TUSKEGEE: This predominately black university is located in the Alabama town of the same name. Booker T. Washington was the founder and the first teacher. The inaugural class had 30 students. Dr. Washington was principal of the institution from 1881 until his death in 1915. The all-black Tuskegee Airmen flight training program was conducted here during WW II. Many of those pilots were highly decorated during that war. [77]

TWIN SISTERS: These are the two most famous pieces of artillery in Texas history. Originally they were a gift from the citizens of Cincinnati, Ohio to the Texas revolutionaries. The cannons were instrumental in winning the Battle of San Jacinto. The Confederates used them during the War Between the States. In November 1863 to prevent them from being captured by the Union, some soldiers buried them near Harrisburg on Buffalo Bayou and they haven't been seen since despite more than 140 years of intense searching. They may have been named for the twin daughters of C. C. Rice. The girls accompanied the cannons on their initial trip to Texas in 1836. [78]

TWO PENNY: (See **Shekel**.)

BALI HAI MAY CALL YOU

Tiki Island, Texas is perched on a tiny peninsula in Jones Bay just north of Galveston Island. Development began at this resort community in the 1960s. The master plan called for all of the streets to have a South Sea connection. So if you collect Tiki mugs, Trader Vic's memorabilia or just fondly remember sipping rum laced fruit drinks from large ceramic bamboo bowls with floating gardenias this community is right up your coconut palm. You can own a home on Polynesia (**Tahiti, Papeete, Moorea, Bora Bora**), Hawaii (**Hawaii, Maui, Oahu, Lanai, Diamond Head**), Kiribati (**Tamana**), Marshall Islands (**Majuro**), Cook Islands (**Makatea**) of something more generic: **Leilani** (heavenly flower in Hawaiian), **Tiki, Coconut, Lotus, Bamboo, Mango, Wahini** (Hawaiian for woman), **Outrigger, Palmetto, Copra, Castaway, Port O' Call** or how about **Paradise.** [50]

U

U. H. UNIVERSITY: This east side institution of higher learning celebrated its 83rd birthday during the 2009-10 academic year. From humble beginnings as Houston Junior College, established in 1927, the University of Houston expanded into a four-year institution in 1934 and was admitted into the Texas public higher education system in 1963. Its founders, Hugh Roy Cullen, considered by many as the "father of the university," and his wife Lillie Cranz Cullen were among the school's many early supporters. Its TV station, KUHT-TV, began broadcasting in 1953. It was the nation's first public educational television station. (See **Cullen.**) [1]

U. S. STEEL: This company is the largest producer of integrated steel products in America. Founded in 1901 by financiers Andrew Carnegie, J. P. Morgan, Charles Schwab and Elbert Gary, it was the greatest financial enterprise launched up until that time. U. S. Steel was initially capitalized at $1.4 billion, an enormous sum in the early 20th century. In its first year of operation the company supplied 67% of the steel utilized in the country. [2]

ULRICH: Minnie – Elected as one of Sugar Land's first aldermen in 1959, she had a street named for her. Not all of her colleagues were so lucky. (See **Pirtle.**) [3]

ULTRA LIGHT: This lane leads to the location of a former ultra light airport when that craze hit America in the 1980s. [4]

UNCLE BEN'S: This gentleman was a black rice grower famous for the yield and quality of his rice crops. His product was so good that other growers would brag that their rice "was as good as Uncle Ben's." Many years later the Converted Rice Company chose Uncle Ben to symbolize the high quality of its product. [5]

UNITY: This west Houston street leads to Unity Church of Christianity. The non-denominational group is often incorrectly associated with the Unitarian or Unification church. Housed in a gold anodized aluminum pyramid designed by Rapp, Tackett, Fash in 1975, it is quite striking architecturally. And one must remember that Houston and Cairo, home of the great Egyptian pyramids at Giza, are both located on the 30th parallel of latitude. [6]

UNIVERSITY OAKS: See sidebar **Neighborhoods with Interesting Stories,** page 104.

UNIVERSITY: This Galveston street is on the campus of the University of Texas Medical Branch, better known as UTMB. This facility has been a

» **UNITY: Cairo on the Bayou, Unity Church's golden pyramid**

major part of Galveston's community since its founding in 1891. It operates numerous facilities including John Sealy Hospital, Shriners Burn Institute and the well respected Medical School. Hurricane Ike dealt a devastating blow to the complex in 2008 with damages totaling over $700 million. For a time the University of Texas planned to close UTMB but has since elected to rebuild it. (See **Sealy.**) [7]

UNIVERSITY: This road leads to the Sugar Land campus of the University of Houston. A street of the same name will take you to the U of H Clear Lake campus. [8]

UPTOWN PARK: This Galleria area street bounds Uptown Park, an upscale retail center of restaurants, shops, banks and spas. It was built by Interfin, a Houston-based real estate developer. Other Houston projects by this firm include the high rise condominiums Four Leaf Towers, Villa d' Este and Montebello. [9]

URBAN: E. E. – He was a businessman in Hempstead in the early 1900s. [10]

URSULINE: The Ursuline Sisters began construction on Ursuline Academy in Galveston in 1847. It was the city's first parochial school and was attended by girls of all faiths. The main building, convent and chapel were designed by Nicholas Clayton. More than 1,000 residents took shelter here during the Great Storm of 1900. In 1968 the school was consolidated with Kerwin Catholic High School and Dominican Girl's School and renamed O'Connell High School. Unfortunately the Clayton buildings were demolished in 1960s and 70s. [11]

USENER: The Usener family arrived in Galveston from Germany on Christmas Day 1839 aboard the brig *North.* They moved to Houston and finally settled in the Heights. John Daniel Usener owned one of the seven saloons in Houston (along with Dick Dowling) in the 1840s until the 1860s. Both barkeeps gave away free whiskey during the yellow fever epidemics. He was also a well-known sportsman and a founder of the Redfish Boating, Fishing and Hunting Club in 1865. [12]

VACCARO: (See **Scarcella.**)

VALENTINE: Most likely this 3rd Ward street is named for the Valentine family who were early residents of Houston. [1]

VALKA: Oswald – In the early 1900s he owned the city café and meat market in Needville. (See **Needville.**) [2]

VALLEY FORGE: See sidebar **America the Beautiful,** page 176.

VAN BUREN: Martin – America's 8th President (1837-41) had a difficult time in office. Just after his election a financial panic broke out. He failed to be nominated by the Democrats for a 2nd term as he opposed the annexation of Texas. Based on that last fact one wonders why a developer would consider naming a street after such an anti-Texan. [3]

VAN FLEET: James Alward – This soldier graduated from West Point in 1915. His classmates included Dwight Eisenhower and Omar Bradley. He was a battalion commander in World War I and fought with John J. Pershing's American Expeditionary Force chasing Pancho Villa. In World War II he participated in the D-day landing on Utah Beach in June 1944. He took command of the U. S. 8th Army and United Nations forces in Korea in 1951. Van Fleet was highly decorated, winning three Distinguished Service Crosses, four Distinguished Service Medals, three Silver Stars and three Bronze Stars. He died in 1992 and is buried in Arlington National Cemetery. [4]

VANDERBILT: This Nashville, Tennessee university opened its doors in 1875 as a result of a gift from the tycoon Cornelius Vanderbilt. [5]

VANWALL: See sidebar **Fairbanks Could Have Its Own Concours d' Elegance and Road Rally,** page 140.

U–V

VAQUERO: This is a Spanish word for cowboy. It is derived from the word *vaca* or cow. [6]

VARNER: Martin Varner was the original owner of this plantation and a member of Austin's Old 300. He arrived in what became Brazoria County in 1824. Varner was a rancher and farmer. Varner sold the place in 1834 to the Patton family. Former Texas governor James Hogg acquired the property in 1901 and the name changed to Varner-Hogg. Miss Ima Hogg donated the property to the State in 1958 to make into a state park. Today visitors see a refurbished Greek revival plantation house, outbuildings, grounds and learn about plantation life. [7]

VARSITY: See sidebar **Neighborhoods with Interesting Stories,** page 104.

VELASCO: This street recalls the town of Old Velasco near the mouth of the Brazos River. It was founded in 1831 but 10 years earlier the first 38 of Stephen F. Austin's Old 300 landed here. Following the Battle of San Jacinto President David G. Burnet named it the temporary capitol of the Republic of Texas. It was destroyed in the hurricane of 1875 and again by the Great Storm of 1900. With the arrival of the pet-rochemical industry after World War II it began growing again and was annexed by Freeport in 1957. (See **Surf.**) [8]

VASSAR: Opened in 1865 in Poughkeepsie, New York as an institution of higher learning for women, it was a pioneer in the fields of music and physical education. Vassar became co-educational in 1969. [9]

VERA CRUZ: See sidebar **Learn a Foreign Language on Your Morning Walk,** page 125.

VETERANS MEMORIAL: This road passes the Veterans Administration's Houston National Cemetery. This 400-acre place of rest is for those who fought defending our country. There are more that 15,000 graves of veterans of wars from the Spanish-American War forward. Several Congressional Medal of Honor winners are interred here including Staff Sergeant Macario Garcia. (See **Garcia.**) [10]

VIA BAROLO: See sidebar **Neighborhoods with Interesting Stories,** page 104.

VIA CHIANTI: See sidebar **Neighborhoods with Interesting Stories,** page 104.

VIA DAVINCI: See sidebar **Neighborhoods with Interesting Stories,** page 104.

VIA FIRENZE: See sidebar **Neighborhoods with Interesting Stories,** page 104.

VIA MICHELANGELO: See sidebar **Neighborhoods with Interesting Stories,** page 104.

VIA PALAZZO: See sidebar **Neighborhoods with Interesting Stories,** page 104.

VIA PONTE VECCHIO: See sidebar **Neighborhoods with Interesting Stories,** page 104.

VIA SIENNA: See sidebar **Neighborhoods with Interesting Stories,** page 104.

VIA TORRE DE PISA: See sidebar **Neighborhoods with Interesting Stories,** page 104.

VIA TOSCANO: See sidebar **Neighborhoods with Interesting Street Names,** page 104.

VIA VINA: See sidebar **Neighborhoods with Interesting Street Names,** page 104.

VICK: Charles – See sidebar **Houston Streets Named for Men Killed During World War I,** page 22.

VICKSBURG: This riverfront town was the last stronghold of the Confederate States of America on the Mississippi River. From November 1862 until July 1863 a series of battles raged for control of the river. New Orleans and Memphis had fallen to Union armies in early 1862 but Vicksburg stubbornly held out. General Ulysses S. Grant launched two unsuccessful attacks on the city before laying siege to Vicksburg. Unable to attain supplies or reinforcements the Southerners were forced to surrender after holding out for six weeks. [11]

VIEUX CARRE: Better known as New Orleans's French Quarter, the original name was *Vieux Carre* or "Old Square" in French. It is the site of the first settlement in Louisiana in 1718. Later the town was called *Nouvelle Orleans.* [12]

VIKING: Historically the Vikings were Scandinavian seafarers who plundered England and northern Europe between the 8th and 10th centuries. In the case of this street, John Foster Dulles High School in Fort Bend County chose these fierce marauders as the school's mascot. [6]

» VILLA DE MATEL: The Conventional Chapel of the Sisters of Charity of the Incarnate Word

VILLA DE MATEL: This East End street honors the motherhouse, novitiate and conventional chapel of the Sisters of Charity of the Incarnate Word. The congregation arrived in Texas in 1866 to serve as nurses during a yellow fever epidemic. In 1920 the sisters purchased a 72-acre plot of swampland on the far outskirts of town. They hired Houston architect Maurice J. Sullivan to design the project. It was his first major commission and it remained his favorite. It is one of the most spectacular sacred spaces in our city. [13]

U–V

VILLANOVA: This university is located in a Pennsylvania town of the same name. It was established as a Roman Catholic men's college in 1842. It became co-ed in 1967. [14]

VINCE: William – This early pioneer and one of Stephen F. Austin's Old 300 was given a league of land in July 1824 in what today is the city of Pasadena. For many years he and his brothers, Allen, Richard and Robert, ran a plantation on their land. The estuary that ran through his property into Buffalo Bayou was named Vince's Bayou. [15]

VINCE'S BRIDGE: Allen Vince built a bridge near San Jacinto that Erastus "Deaf" Smith burned down during the Texas Revolution to impair Santa Anna's arrival at the battlefield. Vince was a farmer and rancher who purchased land on Oyster Creek in 1840. Today the town of Arcola occupies the property. [16]

VIRGIE COMMUNITY: W. M. Donnley bought Fred Neidigk's sawmill in 1906 and changed the name of the rail station to Virgie Switch in honor of his daughter. (A switch is a device consisting of two sections of railroad track used to transfer rolling stock from one track to another.) A few years later a real estate con artist started marketing lots in a place called Virgie Town, Texas, to out-of-staters. When those poor souls came to claim their property they discovered he had taken the money and disappeared without ever paying Donnley for the land. (See **Neidigk.**) [17]

VIRGINIA POINT: This point of land on the Texas mainland is where the Galveston Causeway connects the island to the coast. It was a part of Stephen F. Austin's original colony. By 1840 there was a small town here. Virginia Point was fortified during the War Between the States. The town was destroyed by the Great Storm of 1900 and again in the 1915 hurricane. Today it is mostly marshland. [18]

VOGT: Fred – This immigrant arrived in the Tomball area from Stutchberg, Germany in 1863. [19]

VOLLMER: Henry and Kate – These German immigrants came to Houston in the 1850s. They owned a farm in the Spring Branch neighborhood where this road is today. [20]

VOSS: Records lead us to believe this thoroughfare is named for a landowner in the area named C. H. Voss. Among his holdings were 12 acres at the intersection of Westheimer and Post Oak where the Galleria is today. According to *Tanglewood*, William Farrington wanted to build the first regional shopping center at that location. In 1951 the only building on the property was a tavern and pool hall owned by Voss and his wife Ella. While cold beer may have been a drawing card for clients, many came to use the pay phone, as it was the only telephone within miles. Voss was not interested in selling his land but after repeated offers he decided to lease his property to Farrington for 99 years. [21]

W

W. E. "BILL" CROWLEY PARK: This gentleman was a long time Harris County employee. Crowley was General Superintendent for Roads and Bridges for Harris County Precinct 4. In 1977 former County Commissioner E. A. "Squatty" Lyons had this road and park named in Crowley's honor. (See **Fern** and **Gessner.**) [1]

W. W. THORNE: This gentleman was a former superintendent of the Aldine Independent School District and a civic leader in that community. Upon his retirement he won the Star Award from the Aldine Scholarship Foundation for his years of service. [2]

WADDELL: C. H. – It is likely that this Rosenberg street was named for this man who established the Fort Bend Telephone Company. [3]

WAFER: John F. – This early Pasadena settler came to Texas from Kansas. Active in city affairs, he served on the first school board. [4]

WAGNER: Leland J. – See sidebar **Houston Streets Named for Men Killed During World War I,** page 22.

WAHINI: See sidebar **Bali Hai May Call You,** page 322.

WAKE FOREST: This Winston-Salem, North Carolina university was chartered in 1833. [5]

WALDECK: See sidebar **Brazoria County's Old Plantation Streets and Roads,** page 258.

WALKER SCHOOL: This street leads to Walker Station Elementary School. The Fort Bend ISD opened this facility in 1993. This institution has received a Great School Rating of 10 out of 10. [6]

W-X

WALKER: Robert J. and/or Samuel Hamilton – The provenance of this street makes for a great tale. In 1845 Robert J. Walker, a Mississippi congressman, introduced legislation in the U.S. Congress to annex Texas. Because of his support of this controversial law Texas honored him by naming a county after him. It is likely that Houston followed suit as the area around Walker Street was annexed by the city in 1840. However he turned out to favor the Union in the War Between the States. As a result the Texas Legislature renamed the county in 1863 for Samuel H. Walker. He was a legendary fighter who "distinguished himself for courage and coolness." Walker's introduction to combat came in the Indian Wars. He became a Texas Ranger in the 1830s. Captured during the Mier Expedition near Saltillo, Mexico in 1842, he escaped to join General Zachary Taylor as a scout during the Mexican-American war in 1846. Walker saw action in the battles of Palo Alto, Monterrey and the mountainous jungles between Vera Cruz and Mexico City. He was killed leading a charge at Huamantla on October 9, 1847. The mystery is: Does Houston now honor the second Walker? No one knows. [7]

WALLER-SPRING CREEK: This road goes from Waller to a bend on Spring Creek. That estuary, also known as *Arroyo de Santa Rosa*, rises near Field Store. It flows 64 miles southeastward to its mouth on the San Jacinto River near Lake Houston. On April 15, 1836 Sam Houston's Army camped at McCurley's Plantation on the creek near Waller. (See **Field Store** and **Waller**.) [8]

WALLER: Edwin – K. H. Faulkner, the man who platted this small village northeast of Houston named it after this early Texas patriot. Waller fought at the battle of Velasco, signed the Texas Declaration of Independence, served as postmaster general of the Republic of Texas, commanded Confederate troops in the Civil War battles of Mansfield and Pleasant Hill in 1864 and was the first mayor of Austin. Waller County and Waller Creek also recall this Texan. One unusual story about the town according to the *Handbook of Texas* concerns a general store called "God's Mercy Store." Owner A. D. Purvis priced all the merchandise at cost and allowed the customer to add whatever markup seemed fair. [9, 10]

WALLISVILLE: Prior to the construction of Interstate 10 this was the road to Wallisville, Texas in Chambers County. The town was founded in 1825 by Elisha Henry Roberts Wallis who held Santa Anna prisoner in his home in 1836 following his capture at the Battle of San Jacinto. Up until the late 1870s Wallisville served as a major steamboat port on the Trinity River. Today it is on the National Register of Historic Places. [11]

WALNUT CREEK: This creek was first discovered by Rene Robert Cavelier, Sieur de La Salle on February 13, 1687 on one of his many expeditions searching for the Mississippi River. Settlement of this area began in 1829. It rises southeast of Navasota, flows 24 miles through Waller and Montgomery Counties before emptying into Spring Creek. [12, 13]

WALNUT CREEK: This Fort Bend County plantation was established on the banks of Oyster Creek in 1835 by Thomas W. Nibbs. He died at a young age and his widow married a lawyer, Constantine W. Buckley. In the following years the plantation prospered. By 1860 their net worth was estimated at $325,000, a tremendous amount of money in those days. Unfortunately, Walnut Creek suffered severely during the War Between the States resulting in its demise shortly thereafter. [14]

WAR ADMIRAL: This colt won the 63rd running of the Kentucky Derby in 1937. He took the lead after a quarter of a mile and extended the distance over the field as the race progressed, winning by 1-3/4 lengths. He went on to become a Triple Crown winner with first place finishes in the Preakness and the Belmont. (See **Triple Crown.**) [15]

WARD: William L. – This Baytown resident was a Harris County Judge. [16]

WARNASCH: John - (See **Salt Grass Trail.**)

WARREN RANCH: This 6,478 acre spread near Hockley has been a working ranch since its founding in the 1850s by the Warren family. At that time the family operated a boarding house and restaurant (where they served meals from local game shot on the property). In 2004 the Katy Prairie Conservancy purchased the ranch to keep it out of the hands of real estate developers and assure it will remain a wildlife area. It offers some of the best nature viewing in the area with birds, deer, jackrabbits and coyotes to mention a few that are often spotted. [105]

WARREN: In 1955 the Warren Petroleum Company built an underground salt dome storage terminal beneath the town of Mont Belvieu, Texas where this road is located. The facility contains 26 caverns, can store 43 million barrels of natural gas and natural gas liquids and is the largest terminal of its kind in North America. [18]

WASHBURN TUNNEL: This Houston Ship Channel tunnel is named for longtime Harris County auditor Harry Washburn. He first ran for auditor in 1905 but failed to get one single vote. However, eight years later he won the job and served the county for the next 41 years. County Commissioner E. A. "Squatty" Lyons once called him "an almost irreplaceable official." The tunnel connects Pasadena with the north side of the Ship Channel. Opened in May 1950, this $9 million project was built using a prefabricated tunnel that was placed into a trench dug in the channel. [19]

WASHINGTON IRVING: This early American author was born in 1783 in New York City. He is famous for his humorous stories and satirical essays, which poked fun at New York City's fashionable society. Irving's best-known works are the short stories, *Rip Van Winkle* and *The Legend of Sleepy Hollow*. In *Rip Van Winkle*, the title character falls asleep for 20 years and awakens to find everything different. *The Legend of Sleepy Hollow* tells about Ichabod Crane, a poor schoolmaster, and his encounter with a headless horseman. Other streets in this Pearland neighborhood are **Crane, Rip Van Winkle** and **Sleepy Hollow.** [20]

WASHINGTON: This avenue is not named for the first president of the United States,

W-X

HISTORIC HOUSTON STREETS

George Washington, but rather for a small town about 70 miles west of Houston called Washington-on-the-Brazos. Here between March 1 and 17 of 1836 the Texas Declaration of Independence was written and signed. Although revered by Texans as the "Cradle of Independence" few recall it was a rough and tumble town. In 1837 Captain John W. Hall constructed a horse race track here that resulted in a building boom of saloons and gambling halls. Furloughed Texas Army veterans poured into town and things became disorderly. It took a confederacy of town ministers to restore law and order. [21]

WATERBURY: Forest John – This young soldier was killed in Iraq by a sniper on March 14, 2008. He was raised in Richmond and graduated from Terry High School. The City Council decided to honor this fallen hero by naming a street for him. [22]

WATERGATE: This yachting center was established on 45 acres along the shore of Clear Lake in 1965. It has over 1,100 boat slips and has won "Marina of the Year" from the Marina Association of Texas. [23]

WATERLOO: At this small Belgian town Napoleon Bonaparte met his final crushing defeat at the hands of the Duke of Wellington on June 18, 1815, thus prompting the expression to "meet one's Waterloo." Four days later Napoleon abdicated and was exiled to the island of Elba and later to St. Helena where he died in 1821. [24]

WATSON: Wiley – This gentleman was the secretary of William A. Wilson's real estate development company. It is located in Woodland Heights, a subdivision developed by Wilson. [25]

WAUGH: Thomas Terrell – When we were a smaller city and people believed we knew each other better it was not unusual for the City Council to name streets for the young men who gave their lives in defense of our country. (See sidebar **Houston Streets Named for Men Killed During World War I,** page 22.) Tom Waugh was killed in WW I. His father, T. L. Waugh, was Houston's Street & Bridge Commissioner. He had the street named for his son in 1922. [26]

WAUKEGAN: Like many other Montgomery County towns, Waukegan, named for the Illinois city of the same name, rose and fell with the timber industry. When the last sawmill closed in the mid-1920s and state Highway 105 by-passed the town it disappeared from the Texas map.. All that remains is this road. [27]

WEAVER: James Baird – He was born in Dayton, Ohio in 1833. Weaver became active in politics. He was a U. S. Representative of the Greenback Party, a group that opposed the gold standard and national banks. Twice he unsuccessfully ran for president on that ticket. Q. A. Wooster of Baytown supported his efforts and named a street for him. (See **Wooster.**) [28]

WEBER: Joseph C. – See sidebar **Houston Streets Named for Men Killed During**

World War I, page 22.

WEBSTER RANCH: This community in southeast Harris county was established where James W. Webster had his ranch. Originally it was called Gardenland in 1879 as it was founded by English colonists who enjoyed gardening. It was renamed Websterville in 1882 and Webster in 1893. [29]

WEBSTER: George – He was a printer who worked for the *Houston Informer*, a newspaper owned by C. F. Richardson. Webster lived on Elgin Street. [30]

WEINGARTEN: From 1901 until 1980 when it was sold, the J. Weingarten Inc. grocery chain was Randall's, Central Market and Whole Foods Market rolled into one. It was the city's premier purveyor of foodstuffs. Harris Weingarten arrived in Texas from Germany in the 1880s. He moved from the Richmond-Rosenberg area to Houston in 1895 and opened a general store. In 1901 his son, Joe, opened a grocery on Congress. By 1914 Joe was joined by his brothers, Sol and Abe, and the expansion began. This southeast side street runs beside a former Weingarten store that was at 4431 Griggs. [31]

» **WEINGARTEN:** Interior of one of the early Weingarten grocery stores

WELCH: Both City of Houston Historic Preservation Officer Randle Pace and sources at the Robert A. Welch Foundation believe this Montrose area street is named for either Professor Chris W. Welch and/or his brother Robert Alonzo Welch. The brothers founded Welch Academy for Boys in 1896. Many of Houston's distinguished citizens were graduates. Robert worked for James Bute Paint Company before making his fortune in oil and real estate. In addition he established the Welch Foundation to encourage chemical research. Robert died in 1952, leaving $25 million in his will to that organization. [32]

W–X

WELLS FARGO: This north Harris County street recalls the image of six-horse stage-coaches thundering across the great American West. In 1852 Henry Wells and William Fargo founded Wells, Fargo & Co. The business plan called for the firm to deliver mail, gold, currency and negotiable instruments across America as fast as possible. Over the years the company used stagecoaches, ships, railroads, telegraph and the Pony Express. [33]

WERLEIN: Ewing – He was the secretary of the Belle Court Land Company, a firm that was active in real estate development in West University Place in the 1920s. [34]

WESLAYAN: This street first appears on a city map in 1935. Since it is in West University, where a number of streets are named for institutions of higher learning, it could be a misspelling of Wesleyan. That university was founded in 1831 and named for an Englishman named John Wesley. He went on to found the Methodist church. [35]

WESSENDORFF: Anton – In 1854 this immigrant from Hamburg, Germany arrived in Fort Bend County. He acquired 565 acres of land to live on. Wessendorff served under Confederate General John B. Hood during the War Between the States. He was severely wounded during the Battle of Chickamauga but did recover. Returning to Richmond he opened a lumber yard. Wessendorff became so famous for his beautiful wooden caskets he became an undertaker. Then he began building hearses. One of these may still be seen today at Arroyo Seco Park in Richmond. [36]

» **WEST COLUMBIA: Photograph of the First Capitol of the Republic of Texas prior to its destruction in the Great Storm of 1900**

WEST 11TH: This little street was referred to as "oddly named" since "there are no other numbered streets for miles" in Doug Milburn's classic guide book *Houston, The Last American City*. However, early maps of Houston as well as Southampton Place indicate that Bissonnet, the street West 11th intersects just west of Montrose, was called Eleventh Street and started west of Main. [37]

WEST COLUMBIA: This Brazoria County town was founded by Josiah Hughes Bell in 1836 and named Columbia. It was still known by that name when it served as the first capitol of the Republic of Texas from September until December 1836. When the capitol was moved to Houston the name was changed to West Columbia. Its economy is driven by cotton, rice, sulfur and oil and gas. There are many historic sites to visit here including the Varner-Hogg Plantation, a replica of the first capitol and sister city East Columbia. That whole community is on the National Register of Historic Places. (See photograph on page 334 and **Bell's Landing** and **Varner.**) [38]

WEST POINT: Located on the west bank of the Hudson River is the United States Military Academy at West Point, New York. President Thomas Jefferson established the Academy in 1802. Many of America's greatest military leaders are graduates of West Point including **Lee, Grant, Sherman, Jackson, MacArthur, Eisenhower** and **Patton** to mention just a few. (See individual streets named for these soldiers.) [39]

WEST RANCH: This is a 766 acre real estate development near Friendswood. It is bordered by Clear and Chigger Creeks. When built out it should contain about 1,300 homes. (See **Pearland.**) [40]

WEST: (See **Parkway.**)

WEST: Simeon – This gentleman platted the town of Deer Park. It is possible this street in the neighboring town of Pasadena recalls this surveyor. The town's name is derived from the fact that prior to its incorporation a privately owned game park that contained deer occupied the site. This area is known as the "Birthplace of Texas" since it was here that the treaty between Sam Houston and Santa Anna was signed following the Battle of San Jacinto. [41]

WESTCOTT: The Westcott family were large landowners in the area east of what is now Memorial Park. The street also honors Charles H. Westcott, a U. S. Army soldier who died of disease in Europe during World War I. [42]

WESTFIELD VILLAGE: This northern Harris County road recalls the oil town of Westfield. It was founded in 1870 and named after Gate F. West by officials of the International-Great Northern Railroad. The railroad track passed through property owned by West. (See **Bammel.**) [43]

WESTHEIMER: Michael Louis – An immigrant from Germany, Westheimer came to Houston in 1859. He was quite an entrepreneur. Westheimer owned a flourmill, a

W-X

» WESTHEIMER: An early Westheimer moving van

livery stable on the corner of Milam and Congress, was a hay merchant and laid the city's first streetcar tracks. At auction he bought a 640-acre farm for $2.50 an acre west of town where St John's School is today. He started a school on the property for his 16 children as well as nieces and nephews who migrated from Germany. The shell lane that led to the schoolhouse became known as "the road to Westheimer's place." Out of the family livery business came the Westheimer Transfer and Storage Company. They once owned the Westheimer Undertaking and Embalming Company. The family remains prominent in the city today. [44]

WESTLANE: This street was named by H.A. Kip, as it was the westernmost extension of River Oaks. (See **Timberlane.**) [45]

WESTMINSTER: This London borough is the home of the British government including the Prime Minister's residence at 10 Downing Street, the Houses of Parliament and Buckingham Palace. Located on the Thames River it also contains the most famous place of worship in England, Westminster Abbey. [46]

WESTMORELAND: In 1902, William W. Baldwin, an officer of the Missouri-Kansas & Texas Railroad, incorporated the South End Land Company to create a classy neighborhood at the edge of downtown. Baldwin knew St. Louis, Missouri well, as the MK & T was headquartered there. He hired the architect, Julius Pitzman, who had platted the beautiful Westmoreland Place in St. Louis to recreate that masterpiece in Houston. Westmoreland was the first neighborhood in the city to have deed restrictions, most of which are still in effect today. (See photograph on page 337 and **Bellaire.**) [47]

Entrance to Westmoreland, Houston, Tex.

» WESTMORELAND: Early photograph of the Westmoreland entrance and gates

WHARTON WEEMS: This gentleman was an early resident of La Porte, Texas where this street is located. [48]

WHARTON-BOLING-PLEDGER: Located on the east bank of the Colorado River in the county of the same name, the town was named for John and William Wharton, leaders in the struggle for Texas Independence who arrived in Texas in 1827 from Virginia. The brothers settled in Wharton in 1846. Wharton began to expand with the arrival of the New York, Texas & Mexican and the Gulf, Colorado & Santa Fe Railroads in 1881 and 1889, respectively. Texas President Sam Houston appointed William Wharton the first minister to the United States. He died when a pistol accidentally fired while he was dismounting from his horse on March 14, 1839. Wharton nearly burned to the ground in 1902 so city fathers decreed downtown be rebuilt using brick. Among its famous citizens were Academy Award winning author and screenwriter Horton Foote (*To Kill a Mockingbird*) and television newsman Dan Rather. (See **Boling** and **Pledger.**) [49, 50]

WHEATLEY: Phillis – Located in a predominately African-American neighborhood, I believe this street honors this well-regarded black poet. Born in Africa in 1753 she was kidnapped and sent to America at the age of seven. Too young to be sold as a slave, she was purchased by John Wheatley of Boston as an attendant for his wife. She was a very intelligent girl and a quick learner. She published her first poem at the age of 14. In 1773, 39 of her poems were published in London. *Poems on Various Subjects, Religious and Moral* was her only book and the first book of poetry published by an Africa-American. Wheatley Senior High School (established in 1927) also recalls this amazing woman. [51]

WHEELER: Rebecca Wheeler named this street in honor of her family. In 1873 she

W-X

married Benjamin C. Simpson, a New Yorker who came to Houston in 1859 and later fought in Hood's Texas Brigade on the Confederate side in the War. Her father, Daniel G., was an owner of Phoenix Iron Works. The Wheeler's lived in a family compound on the block bounded by **Main, Rusk, Travis** and **Capitol.** [52]

WHIDBEY ISLAND: Dwight Dawson speculates that someone based at the naval air station on this Washington State island may have named this street. [53]

WHIRLAWAY: In 1941 this thoroughbred won the 67th running of the Kentucky Derby by eight lengths. His trip around the track was done in record time (2:01 2/5), a mark that stood for 21 years. Legendary jockey Eddie Arcaro was in the irons. This thoroughbred went on to win the Triple Crown with victories at the Preakness and Belmont with Arcaro aboard. This difficult colt was the first winner for the legendary Calumet Farm, an organization that went on to breed eight more Derby champions. (See **Triple Crown.**) [54]

WHISTLING WOODWIND: See sidebar **It's Music to My Ears,** page 218.

WHITE: Francis Menefee – He fought in the Texas Revolution, seeing action at the Siege of Bexar and the Grass Fight. White entered politics and held a number of elected positions, the most important being commissioner of the General Land Office (1857-1862). Sixth Ward developer William Baker named this street for him. [55, 56]

WHITING: Harvey – He arrived in Texas from Connecticut in 1833. Whiting was a jack-of-all-trades. He practiced medicine, operated a farm and ranch on Oyster Creek and ran a boot and shoe manufacturing plant in the Baytown area. Whiting treated both Texas and Mexican soldiers who were wounded at the Battle of San Jacinto. He died in 1852. (See **John Martin.**) [57]

WICKED WICKET: In the classically English game of cricket the action centers around two wickets, three wooden stumps topped by two sticks called bails. A bowler (pitcher) delivers a ball toward a batsman (hitter) whose job is to keep the wicket from being knocked over by the ball. If he fails and the wicket falls, the batsman is out. A wicked wicket is British slang for a wicket that is particularly difficult to knock over. [58]

WICKERSHAM: (See **Larchmont.**) [59]

WIGGINSVILLE: This rural community south east of Conroe was started in the early 1900s. In 1931 the Conroe Oilfield was discovered nearby. When oil production ceased so did Wigginsville. [60]

WILDER: Joseph – This man came to Texas in 1836 and enlisted to serve with Captain John Hart's Company at Velasco. At San Jacinto he fought under the command of Captain Richard Roman. During the Texas Revolution soldiers were paid in land for their services. The men were given a certificate to exchange for 640 acres. Since

Wilder did not cash in his voucher and they were non-transferable we must assume he died shortly after the Battle of San Jacinto or left the state. [61]

WILDING: Anthony "Tony" Frederick – This New Zeeland native was a champion tennis player. Wilding was ranked number one in the world in 1913. He won singles titles at Wimbledon (4), Australia (2) and a bronze medal in the 1912 Olympics. He enlisted in the Royal Marines during World War I and was killed in action at the Battle of Aubers Ridge in France on May 9, 1915. [62]

WILKES: See sidebar **Gone With the Wind Too Far,** page 303.

WILKINS: Horace M. – He was the president of the State National Bank of Houston. Following the death of Monroe D. Anderson, Wilkins was named successor trustee of the M. D. Anderson Foundation in 1940. Colonel Bates acknowledged Wilkins work in creating the Texas Medical Center saying, "He was a wise trustee with farsighted vision, judgment and discretion. He deserves a full share of credit for the worthwhile things the Foundation has done." (See **Bates.**) [63]

WILL CLAYTON: As one of the founders of the hugely successful cotton brokerage company, Anderson, Clayton & Company, William L. Clayton established the base for his fortune. Clayton and his wife Susan lived at 5300 Caroline Street (today the Clayton Geological Library). He would walk to his office in the Old Cotton Exchange Building at 202 Travis, a distance one way of about 2.5 miles. A philanthropist and civic-minded citizen he served as Undersecretary of State in the Truman administration in the 1940s. [64]

WILLIAM TELL: This 14th century Swiss hero was forced to shoot an apple off of his son's head with a bow and arrow for refusing to acknowledge Austrian supremacy over Switzerland.

» **WILL CLAYTON:** William Lockhart Clayton

WILLIAMS: Amanda, Daisy, J. W and Marion – This family filed the plat for Mont Belvieu in 1922. (See **Barbers Hill.**) [65]

WILLIAMS: Austin M. – This gentleman was a farmer and grandson of pioneer William Scott. His home on Pleasant Point, near Baytown today, was known as Point Comfort. (See **Scott.**) [66]

W-X

WILLIAMS: Samuel May – Born in Rhode Island in 1795, Williams arrived in Texas in 1822. The following year Stephen F. Austin hired him as a translator and secretary. He became postmaster at San Felipe and a tax collector as well. For his service he received eleven leagues (almost 50,000 acres of land) between Oyster Creek and Buffalo Bayou. Following the Texas Revolution he and Thomas F. McKinley formed a commission house that dominated the cotton trade in the Republic. Williams was an investor in the Galveston City Company that founded that city. He moved there, became interested in banking and lived there until his death in 1858. (See **McKinney** and **Oaklawn.**) [67]

WILLIAMSBURG: See sidebar **America the Beautiful,** page 176.

WILLIAMSON: Jerome – There is a good possibility that this street is named for this early Houston area resident (1860-1928). He is buried in Tetter Cemetery located north of this road. (See **Tetter Cemetery.**) [68]

WILLIS-OLD WAVERLY: Waverly was founded in the mid-1800s. When the citizens refused the Houston & Great Northern Railroad a right-of-way in 1870 the tracks were laid 10 miles away at a town they named Waverley Station. As that town began to prosper many people move there and the name was changed to New Waverly while the population losing Waverly added Old to its name. Today little remains of Old Waverly. (See **Willis-Waukegan.**) [69]

WILLIS-WAUKEGAN: Galveston merchants Peter J. and Richard S. Willis donated this Montgomery County land for a town site along the Houston & Great Northern Railroad in 1870. Early on it was an agricultural and lumber market town. Unlike many towns in this area that depended on lumber, Willis survived and had a population of 3,985 persons in the 2000 census. (See **Waukegan.**) [70]

WILLOW CREEK CEMETERY: This Tomball area road leads to the old Willow Creek Cemetery. During the mid-1800s the village of Willow Creek, named for the nearby watercourse, was located here. In 1837 Claude Nicholas Pillot established a farm in the area and is buried in the nearby Pillot Cemetery. (See **Pillot.**) [71]

WILLOW CREEK: This 18 mile watercourse runs through northeast Harris County, emptying into Spring Creek. Early settlers named it for the plethora of willow trees that lined its banks. The small community of Willow derives its name from the creek. Settlers arrived in the 1830s. An unusual fact about this area is while most of the early pioneers were German immigrants this spot was first settled by the French. Claude Nicholas Pillot, a farmer, arrived in 1837. For a time the area was called French Settlement. (See **Pillot.**) [72,73]

WILLOWICK: The Santa Anna, California Willowick Golf Course was built in 1928. Although this is a beautiful street, the links for which it is named are not visually exciting. [74]

WILLOWTEX: See sidebar **Howdy Tex,** page 263.

WILMA-LOIS: Pasadena real estate developer Herbert Tatar named this street for his daughter-in-law (Lois) combined with the name of his partner's daughter (Wilma). [75]

WILSON: Emma – Churchill Fulshear, Jr. hired this lady in the 1860s as a housekeeper and children's nurse. Wilson was such a faithful employee and adopted member of the Fulshear family that when he died in 1892 Fulshear left the bulk of his estate to her. She also operated the first dairy in Fort Bend County. (See **Katy-Fulshear.**) [76]

WILSON: James Theodore Dudley – This Missouri native arrived in Texas in 1835. He served as a private in the Republic of Texas Army, participating in the capture of the Mexican sloop, *Correo Mexicano*. In 1837 Wilson came to Houston and became one of our city's first real estate developers. He served as mayor from 1877 until 1879. [77]

WILSON: Woodrow – This tragic figure was the 28th President of the United States (1913-1921). Although significant legislation was passed on his watch including creation of the Federal Reserve System and the Federal Trade Commission as well as the graduated income tax and the Clayton Anti-Trust Bill, his failure to make Congress enroll the U.S. in the League of Nations left him a broken man. The pressure of this shortfall resulted in Wilson suffering a stroke and becoming incapacitated, unable to exercise the duties of President. However, he was awarded the Nobel Peace Prize in 1920. [78]

WILTON: See **Southampton's English Streets,** page 255.

WIMBLEDON: See sidebar **Tennis or Golf, Anyone?,** page 348.

WIMBLEDON: This peaceful London suburb becomes the focus of the world of major tournament tennis each June when the best players match their talents in the All-England Tennis Championship. A win in this tournament assures the victor tennis immortality. (See **Agassi Ace, Borg Breakpoint, Laver Love, McEnroe Match** and **Sampras Ace.**) [79]

WINDSOR CASTLE: This magnificent structure has been the residence of English monarchs since William the Conqueror erected a stone enclosure to replace a wooden one. Built on a large mound that fronts on the Thames River this castle is located 22 miles west of London. The site was selected because mythology said this high ground was used by King Arthur who would hold fourth with his Knights of the Round Table. [80]

WINDWOOD: See sidebar **Tennis or Golf, Anyone?,** page 348.

WINFREE: Z. T. – Mont Belvieu opened its post office in 1890 with this man as the first postmaster. (See **Barbers Hill.**) [81]

W-X

WINGATE: See sidebar **Texas Heroes' Names for Houston Streets Urged in 72 Proposed Changes,** page 96.

WINKLER: Henry F. – He was a member of Local Union No. 84 of the International Association of Bridge, Structural and Ornamental Ironworkers. In addition Winkler was president of the Houston Labor Council (1931-34) and first vice president of the Texas State Federation of Labor. The street was named for him on September, 6, 1936. [82]

WINKLER: Milton J. – See sidebar **Houston Streets Named for Men Killed During World War I,** page 22. [83]

WINROCK: – Arkansas investor Winthrop Rockefeller III calls his investment company Winrock. Through that corporation he was involved in real estate development in the area around Westheimer and Voss. [84]

WIRT: Roy David – This gentleman was a Spring Branch area sheriff for more than 20 years. As one of the city's best lawmen, citizens wanted to honor him with a street. [85]

WISTER: The original street sign for this Timbergrove Manor street was Wisteria. However, during a storm the "ia" broke off resulting in Wister. It was never corrected when a new sign was made. [86]

WITTE: The Wittes were a prominent Spring Branch family. [87]

WITTER: Pasadena founder Charles Munger's wife's maiden name was Alvida Witter. (See **Munger** and **Pasadena.**) [88]

WOLVIN: Captain Augustus B. – A founder of Texas City, he persuaded the U. S. Government to finance the dredging of a ship channel in that town in 1900. (See **Texas** and **Texas City Dike.**) [89]

WOOD: Charles H. or Thomas W. - See sidebar **Houston Streets Named for Men Killed During World War I,** page 22.

WOODHEAD: John – This gentleman was an early settler from England. He was reported to be "a great church worker who left many descendants" in the Houston area. In 1935 pupils from Lanier Junior High School appeared before City Council to request the street name be changed to Higginbotham in honor of the school principal, Miss Blanche Higginbotham. But they also had one other motive besides just "polishing an apple" for the principal. It seems students at another school had begun calling the Lanier kids "woodheads" implying they were not very smart. After hearing testimony as to the high character of Mr. Woodhead, Council decided to retain the street name. The students wrote a letter of apology to E. S. Woodhead, John's brother and a Houstonian. In that letter they said "If we have offended members of your family by this petition, we offer our sincere apology; and yet we cannot regret the opportunity that has come to us to learn more about the distinguished gentleman for whom this street is named." [90]

WOODLANDS: This parkway is the main entrance to the huge master-planned community known as The Woodlands. Located on approximately 25,000 acres in southern Montgomery County, this town was developed by Mitchell Energy & Development Corporation beginning in 1972. [91]

WOODLOCH: This tiny town (.01 square miles) near Montgomery only has four streets making it the smallest in the county. Woodloch is a bedroom community of Houston that was established in 1974. [92]

WOODRIDGE: Carl Detering Sr., a real estate developer and son of Herman E. Detering, owned the land around an office complex he built on the Gulf Freeway. He called the street Woodridge after a company he owned of the same name. (See **Detering.**) [93]

WOODRUFF: See sidebar **Texas Heroes' Names for Houston Streets Urged in 72 Proposed Changes,** page 96.

WOODWAY: On the original plat of Tanglewood this thoroughfare was called Park Drive. However, the city felt it would be confused with Parkway in Broadacres and asked developer William Farrington to rename it. His daughter says he chose Woodway because it sounded like a nice and pretty place. [94]

WOOLWORTH: This is another Denver Harbor Addition street recalling one of the city's early retail establishments, Woolworth's 5 & 10. In 1878 Frank Winfield Woolworth developed the concept of displaying a large number of products all of which sold for either five or ten cents. He opened a store in Lancaster, Pennsylvania in 1880. The idea caught on and by his death in 1919 there was more than 1,000 outlets around the country. In 1913 he paid for the company's New York headquarters building, at that time the tallest skyscraper in the world, with cash. [95]

WOOSTER: Quincy Adams – This gentleman arrived in the Baytown area in 1891. He purchased over 1,000 acres of land with the intention of starting a town. Although a community formed, it was never incorporated and was absorbed by Baytown in the mid-20th century. The street, however, remains. A prisoner of war camp holding captured German soldiers was located here in World War II. His great-granddaughter, Trevia Wooster Beverly, a Houstonian, wrote *At Rest: A Historical Directory of Harris County, Texas, Cemeteries (1822-1992)*. This is an excellent book on the area's burying grounds. [96]

WORDSWORTH: William – Alphabetically, Wordsworth is the last of the great English authors, poets, essayists and playwrights that Houston developers used to emphasize the superior intellect of their neighborhood. A poet with an affinity for writing about his beloved Lake District and its natural beauty, he was named Poet Laureate of England in 1843. [97]

W-X

WORTHINGTON: R. H. – He was born in North Carolina in 1826 and moved to Fort Bend County in 1849. He is remembered for the nursing care he gave to citizens of Richmond during the great yellow fever epidemic of 1853. Miraculously, Worthington did not catch the disease which was one of the most deadly plagues that swept through Texas in the 1800s. [98]

WRIGHT: John H. – (See **Stewart.**) [99]

WRIGHT: Thomas, Jr. – Baytown land developer W. E. Defee named this street for his friend Wright. [100]

WROXTON: See **Southampton's English Streets,** page 255.

WUNDERLICH: Peter – Over 100 years ago this north Harris County farm was founded by this German immigrant. Today it is listed in the Family Land Heritage Program by the State Department of Agriculture. It has been under the same family ownership since 1861. (See **Strack.**) [101]

WUNSCHE: Carl – An early settler in Spring, Texas, Wunsche arrived in the 1840s. A German immigrant and farmer he took advantage of the Texas Homesteading Law. That statute stated the people could settle on public property and if the person added improvements the land could not be taken away by the courts to settle debts. The family operated Wunsche Bros. Saloon and Hotel in the early years. (See **Spring-Stuebner.**) [102]

WYATT EARP: Born in Illinois in 1848, Wyatt Berry Stapp Earp would become a legend in his own time. During his life he was a farmer, teamster, buffalo hunter, gunfighter, boxer, gambler, saloon owner and lawman. He is best remembered for the famous "Gun Fight at the O. K. Corral." In Tombstone, Arizona on October 26, 1881 Earp, his brothers, Virgil and Ike, and Doc Holliday shot it out with Ike and Billy Clanton and Tom and Frank McLaury. The McLaurys and Billy Clanton were killed. Virgil, Morgan and Doc had minor wounds. Wyatt was unscathed. He gave up gun fighting, moved to California, ran a saloon and gambling parlor, became a newspaper sports reporter and died of old age at 80. [103]

WYETH: Andrew – He was one of America's best known realist painters of the middle 20th century. Wyeth's favorite subjects were the land and people around his homes in Chadds Ford, Pennsylvania and Cushing, Maine. *Christina's World* is one of the 20th century's most recognizable images. He is also remembered for the 247 studies of his neighbor Helga Testorf, done between 1971 and 1985. [104]

X: (See **Luella.**)

XENOPHON: This Greek historian and philosopher was born in Athens about 430 B.C. He is best remembered for his writings about having Athens use its influence to maintain peace in the Greek world and for using the Temple of Delphi to settle questions of diplomacy. [1]

TYPICAL STREET CLASSIFICATIONS

Street classifications define the function of each of our many highways and byways. The Houston Planning and Development Department considers many factors when determining a street's classification including: travel demand, street right-of-way width, maintenance cost, needs for access to adjacent property, safety, preservation of neighborhood character, distance between major streets known as arterials, adjacent land uses and connections to the regional transportation system and to major destinations. The following table details the characteristics of each type of street. [51]

Classification	Local Access	No. of Lanes	Ave. Daily Traffic	Typical Speed Limit	Signal of Block Length
Regional Freeway	restricted	4 – 12	30,000+	55 mph	No standard
Principal Arterial	limited	2 – 6	5,000 – 40,000	30 – 45 mph	1 mile
Minor Arterial	somewhat limited	2 – 4	3,000 – 15, 000	30 mph	½ mile intervals
Collector	unlimited	2	1,000 – 15,000	30 mph	¼ mile intervals
Commercial Street	unlimited	2 – 4	low	25 mph	1-block intervals
Residential Street	unlimited	2	under 1,500	25 mph	500 feet intervals

W–X

WHY HISTORIC GALVESTON HAS SO FEW STREETS NAMED FOR FAMOUS CITIZENS

As one our most historic towns it seemed odd that only a handful of streets in Galveston recall the people who made it what was once called the "Wall Street of the South." Well there is a very simple reason. It was laid out using a gridiron pattern copied from eastern cities like New York City and Philadelphia by an eccentric surveyor named Gail Borden. He rode his pet bull around town, tried to make jelly from oxen hoofs and horns, invented condensed milk and founded the Borden Company. The plan was simple. Avenues that paralleled the Gulf of Mexico and Galveston Bay were labeled alphabetically. Streets that intersected the avenues were named numerically. As Galveston grew the city officials just continued to expand Borden's grid. Over the years half of the alphabetical avenues and 13 of the numerical streets were renamed as follows:

- Avenue A – Port Industrial (now Harborside)
- Avenue B – Strand
- Avenue C – Ship's Mechanic
- Avenue D – Market
- Avenue E – Post Office
- Avenue F – Church
- Avenue G – Winnie
- Avenue H – Ball
- Avenue I – Sealy
- Avenue J – Broadway
- Avenue P – Bernardo de Galvez
- Avenue P ½ - Heard's Lane
- Avenue S – Stewart
- 2nd Street – Ferry
- 4th Street – Holiday
- 6th Street – University
- 14th Street – Christopher Columbus
- 21st Street – Moody
- 22nd Street – Kempner
- 23rd Street – Tremont
- 25th Street – Rosenberg
- 29th Street – Martin Luther King
- 39th Street – Mike Gaido
- 41st Street – Jack Johnson
- 53rd Street – Mary Moody Northen
- 61st Street – Central City

And finally, where did the ½ streets come from. Legend says the Galveston City Company felt Borden had made the lots too big so they halved some of them by placing a street between say O Street and P Street and calling it O ½. More likely as the town grew toward the Gulf they had run out of letters so they back filled with the use of the ½. [52]

YALE: This Houston Heights Street is named for Yale University in New Haven, Connecticut. Elihu Yale was a successful merchant who made a large donation to the school that then changed its name to honor their patron. [1]

YEARLING: In thoroughbred racing this is a one-year old horse whose age is measured from January 1 of the year in which it was foaled. [2]

YELL CEMETERY: This private family cemetery is on the Raleigh Rogers league in Montgomery County. It contains the remains of the Yell and Rogers families. The earliest burial, Raleigh Rogers, was 1854. He was an early settler who was born in Tennessee in 1792. Pleasant Yell died in 1894. [3]

YMCA: This short Pearland street leads to the Vic Coppinger Family YMCA. Born in Missouri City in 1918 his parents moved to Pearland when Coppinger was an infant and except for a stint as a radar bombardier/navigator on a B-29 in the Pacific during World War II, he never left his beloved hometown. He was a banker, two time winner of Citizen of the Year (1987 and 1994) and a two term mayor of the city. He died in 1995 at the age of 76. [4]

YMCA: Baytown also named a street for their YMCA, the Baytown Family YMCA. [5]

YOAKUM: Benjamin Franklin – Although his parents wanted him to be a minister, Yoakum was taken with railroad fever. His first job was on a survey gang laying the route of the International-Great Northern Railroad into Palestine, Texas. Working his way up the corporate ladder at several rail lines, Yoakum joined the St. Louis & San Francisco Railway Company (Frisco). Under his tutelage this railroad grew from 1,200 to 6,000 miles of track. In 1905 the Frisco and the Rock Island Line merged to form a 17,000-mile system, the largest in America at the time. As one of Texas' leading agrarians he is credited with creating the great agricultural counties of the Rio Grande

Y-Z

Valley and South Texas. In 1907 he moved to New York and became a financier, activist agrarian and prizewinning cattle raiser. Yoakum died in 1929 and is buried in New York City. [6]

YOUNG: Houston – This early Humble area resident was a veteran of the War Between the States. [7]

TENNIS OR GOLF, ANYONE?

River Oaks was the first Houston neighborhood to name streets after famous golf courses. Since then other developments have used sporting themes for streets. However, few have exhibited the fervor demonstrated by the streets surrounding Friendswood Golf Club. **Belmont** most likely recalls the golf links at Lake Macquarie, Australia. Opened in 1952 it is famous for its annual amateur tournament. Such famous golfers as Bruce Devlin, Mark O'Meara and Vijay Singh won here before turning pro. Colorado Springs' **Broadmoor** Hotel, better known as the "grande dame of the Rockies," was opened in 1891 as a gambling casino. Today it is a world renowned facility sporting three golf courses by designers Donald Ross (1918), Robert Trent Jones (1965) and Arnold Palmer (1976). **Castle Harbour** is a 6,440 yard course located on the island of Bermuda. It was designed by Charles Henry Banks. **Dawn Hill** is a golf and racquet club in the foothills of the Ozark Mountains in Siloam Springs, Arkansas. **Desert Aire** may refer to the Ted Robinson (1960) links in Palmdale, California. **Everett** may be a misspelling of Evert, as in Chris. She ranks as one of America's greatest female tennis players, winner of 18 Grand Slam tournaments (6 U. S. Opens, 7 French Opens, 2 Australian Opens and 3 Wimbledons) in the 1970s and 80s. A **Fairway** is the stretch of land on a golf course that is covered in short grass and extends from the tee to the green. **Love** is a score of zero in tennis. **Martina** probably recalls the great Czech tennis pro Martina Navratilova who won 18 Grand Slam single titles (including a record 9 at Wimbledon) and 40 Grand Slam doubles championships. **Match Point** is the final point needed to win a tennis match. **Palm Aire** Country Club is in Sarasota, Florida. It has two excellent links – one designed by Joe Lee and the other by Dick Wilson. **Palmer** is for the legendary Arnold. "Arnie," as he was known by his army of fans, won 92 golf championships including 4 Masters, 2 British Opens and 1 U. S. Open. The Grand Hotel at **Point Clear,** Alabama has two Robert Trent Jones golf courses. The 6,561 yard **Port Royal** Golf Course opened in 1970 on the Island of Bermuda. It is another Jones designed links. There are numerous possibilities for **St. Cloud.** I would like to think it is named for the St. Cloud, Minnesota American Legion memorial course honoring the veterans of World War II. The All-England Lawn Tennis Championships have been played at **Wimbledon** since 1877. And finally, **Windwood** may refer to a golf course in Middleton, Wisconsin. [53]

Z

ZAHN: Among the many German immigrants to our area were the Zahns. They were farmers in northwest Harris County where this street is located. This family was among the first settlers in Cypress along Little Cypress Creek in the 1840s. The Zahns arrived in the area after landing at Galveston. Like hundreds of their neighbors, family members were laid to rest in St. John Lutheran Cemetery. (See **Lutheran Cemetery.**) [1]

ZAMBEZI: This river flows from the mountains of the south central African country of Zambia to the Mozambique Channel in the India Ocean.

ZARAGOZA: Ignacio Seguin – This Mexican general was the hero of the famous battle known as *Cinco de Mayo* (Fifth of May). Born near what is today Goliad, Texas in 1829, Zaragoza initially trained as a priest but deciding he lacked the calling, he joined the military. He saw action at the battles of Saltillo and Monterrey, fought with Benito Juarez in the War of Reform and was named Minister of War and the Navy in 1861. However, it is for his defeat of the French army at Puebla on May 5, 1862 that he will always be remembered. Four months later he died of typhoid fever. Three days after his death President Juarez renamed the city Puebla de Zaragoza and declared *Cinco de Mayo* a national holiday in memory of this hero. [2]

ZAREEN: (See **Bhandara.**)

ZINDLER: Benjamin – In 1888 he founded a men and boys clothing store called Zindler's. For many years it was located at the corner of Fannin and Congress. Today it operates under the name of Zindler's Big and Tall Store. His grandson was Marvin "Eyewitness News" Zindler of Channel 13 and the Chicken Ranch fame. Three other streets in this Denver Harbor neighborhood are the names of famous retail establishments. (See **Kress, Woolworth** and **Gazin.**) [3]

ZION LUTHERAN CEMETERY: Located in western Harris County this cemetery began as the Mueller family plot in 1873. In 1907 Henry and Mary Mueller deeded the three acre property to the trustees of the Evangelical Lutheran Zion Church of Hufsmith. Many members of that church rest here. [4]

ZOE: Like its neighboring street to the west, **Majestic,** this one is also named for an early Houston movie palace. Built in the Foster Building in 1915, the Zoe was architecturally interesting because of its large screen, organ, orchestra pit and barrel-vaulted roof. [5]

» **ZOO CIRCLE:** African elephant sculpture (1982) by Texas native Bob Fowler

ZOO CIRCLE: Houston's first zoological garden was located downtown in Sam Houston Park and featured rabbits, raccoons, an owl, a black bear, prairie dogs and an alligator. In 1920 the U. S. Government gave the zoo a buffalo named Earl. In 1922 the zoo moved to Hermann Park. Between 1925 and 1938 lions and elephants were added to the collection. Later additions include Reptile House (1950s), Children's Zoo (1960s) and World of Primates (1993). [6]

ZUBER: Abe and Philip — In the 1950s these two brothers and two partners bought some land in Galena Park and began a development. The Zubers named this street for themselves and the adjoining streets **Leggett** and **Pugh** for their associates. [7]

ZUBIN: (See **Bhandara.**)

HOUSTON STREET PROJECT SIDEBAR NOTES

1 Teas Nursery, Interview 2000
2 Miller, Mary Catherine Farrington, Interview 2001
3 Field trip 2001, Sam Houston Park Memorial & Wood, Jerry, Interview 2001 & Baines, Mrs. W. M., *Houston's Part in the World War* (1919), 25-9
4 *Houston Chronicle*, 1952
5 Various old Houston city maps – 1836 – 2003
6 *Key Map: Houston Harris County Atlas* – 44th Edition – (Key Maps 2003) – Numerous pages
7 *Key Map: Houston Harris County Atlas* – 44th Edition – (Key Maps 2003) – Numerous pages
8 *Key Map: Houston Harris County Atlas* – 44th Edition – (Key Maps 2003) – Numerous pages
9 *Key Map: Houston Harris County Atlas* – 44th Edition – (Key Maps 2003) – Numerous pages
10 Delaney, John J., *Dictionary of Saints* (Doubleday 1980), numerous pages
11 *Houston Chronicle*, Undated
12 Anonymous, Interview 2002
13 "MAGNOLIA POINT, TX." *The Handbook of Texas Online*. <http://www.tsha.utexas.edu/handbook/online/articles/view/MM/hrmfz.html>
14 *Key Map: Houston Harris County Atlas* – 44th Edition – (Key Maps 2003) – Numerous pages
15 *Key Map: Houston Harris County Atlas* – 44th Edition – (Key Maps 2003) – Numerous pages
16 *Houston Chronicle*, May 8, 1929
17 *Houston Press*, Undated
18 Interviews 2007-8 and field trips
19 http://www.nasa.gov
20 Field Trip 2007
21 Begeman, June A., *Stepping Back in Time: History of West University Place* (D. Armstrong 1999), 50
22 *Encyclopedia Britannica* 2005 Ultimate Reference Suite CD-ROM
23 *Key Map: Houston Harris County Atlas* – 44th Edition – (Key Maps 2003) – Numerous pages
24 *Houston Chronicle*, undated
25 *Key Map: Houston Harris County Atlas* – 44th Edition – (Key Maps 2003) – Numerous pages
26 http://www.referencecenter.com
27 Senor Marks Hinton se habla Espanol
28 http://en.wikipedia.org
29 *Houston Chronicle*, July 1998
30 *Encyclopedia Britannica* (1952), Volumes 1, 3,5, 7,11, 12, 16, 20, 21
31 www.ushistory.org
32 Field trip 2001
33 Wood, Jerry and Raia, John, Interviews 2000, 2001
34 *The American Heritage Dictionary of the English Language:* Third Edition (Houghton Mifflin Company, 1992)
35 *Houston Chronicle & Harris County Facts*, 1937, page 548
36 Raia, John B., e-mail 2005
37 *Key Map: Houston Harris County Atlas* – 44th Edition – (Key Maps 2003) – Numerous pages
38 *Houston Chronicle*, September 16, 2007
39 Field trip 2002
40 *Houston Chronicle*, March 7, 2001 and Wood, Jerry interview 2001
41 Rogers, Mary Nixon, *A History of Brazoria County: The Old Plantations & Their Owners* (T. L. smith, Jr. 1958), 21-62
42 *Houston Chronicle*, April 4, 2004
43 Field trip 2009
44 Vreeland-Wendt, Susan, interview 2009
45 Field trip, 2008
46 Houston City Code Ordinances, Chap. 42 Sec.133
47 http://en.eikipedia.org
48 Native Texas knowledge
49 *Key Map*, 46th Edition, 2005
50 Field trip 2008 and Rau, J. M., *Key Map: Galveston/Brazoria Atlas* 4th Edition (Key Maps 2000), 772
51 Papademetriou, Peter C., Transportation and Urban Development of Houston 1830-1980 (Metropolitan Transit Authority 1982)
52 Field trip 2008 and Rau, J. M., *Key Map: Galveston/Brazoria Atlas* 4th Edition (Key Maps 2000), 774-5
53 http://www.broadmoor.com; http://www.belmont-golf.com.au; http://www.golf-travel.com; http://www.golfreview.com/cat; http://www.thegolfcourses.net; http://en.wikipedia.org; http://www.palmaire.net; http://www.sandhillsonline.com; http://www.marriottgrand.com; http://www.bermudashorts.bm; http://www.stcloudcountryclub.com; http://www.wimbledon.org; http://www.madisongolf.com

Y-Z

NOTES

A

1 www.foytracing.com

2 *Handbook of Texas Online*, s.v. "," http://www.tsha-online.org/handbook/online/articles/GG/vrg2.html

3 Denison, Lynne W. & Pugh, L.L., *Houston Public School Buildings: Their History & Location* (L. L. Pugh 1936), 1-2

4 *Houston Business Journal*, July 1, 1985

5 *The American Heritage Dictionary of the English Language:* Third Edition (Houghton Mifflin Company 1992), 9

6 Garraty, John A. Editor, *Encyclopedia of American Biography* (Harper & Row 1974), 12

7 *Handbook of Texas Online*, s.v. "," http://www.tsha-online.org/handbook/online/articles/AA/roa3.html

8 Texas Historical Marker, State Highway 146, Baytown, erected 1984

9 "ADDICKS, TX." *The Handbook of Texas Online.* <http://www.tsha.utexas.edu/handbook/online/articles/view/AA/hla4.html>

10 *Encyclopedia Britannica* (1952), Volume 1, 160-2

11 Adkins, John, e-mail 2008

12 Doolittle, Bill, *The Kentucky Derby: Run for the Roses* (Time Life Books 1998), 144-45

13 www.espn.com

14 *Handbook of Texas Online*, s.v. "PEARLAND, TX," http://www.tsha.utexas.edu/handbook/online/articles/view/PP/hep3.html

15 *Baytown Sun*, May 13, 1996

16 *Houston Chronicle*, May 22, 1929

17 http://www.pollyranch.com

18 Fieldtrip 2002

19 *Houston Chronicle*, January 2, 2008

20 www.starwars.com

21 Texas Historical Marker, 905 FM 525, Houston, erected 1999

22 *Baytown Sun*, May 13, 1996

23 "OLD RIVER-WINFREE, TX." *The Handbook of Texas Online.* <http://www.tsha.utexas.edu/handbook/online/articles/view/OO/hjo10.html>

24 *Handbook of Texas Online*, s.v. "," http://www.tsha-online.org/handbook/online/articles/AA/hla11.html

25 Texas Historical Marker, Bellaire Boulevard at Dairy-Ashford Road, Houston, erected 1984

26 "CLODINE, TX." *The Handbook of Texas Online.* <http://www.tsha.utexas.edu/handbook/online/articles/view/CC/hnc77.html>

27 Houston City Maps

28 Webb, Walter Prescott, *The Hand Book of Texas* (Texas State Historical Assn. 1952), Vol. 1, 29-30

29 *Handbook of Texas Online*, s.v. "," http://www.tsha-online.org/handbook/online/articles/NN/hjn4.html

30 *Handbook of Texas Online*, s.v. "PEARLAND, TX," http://www.tsha.utexas.edu/handbook/online/articles/view/PP/hep3.html

31 Houston District Designation Report, HPO file no. 07HD11, 2007

32 *Key Map*, 50the Edition 2009

33 "ALMEDA, TX." *The Handbook of Texas Online.* <http://www.tsha.utexas.edu/handbook/online/articles/view/AA/hra27.html>

34 "GENOA, TX." *The Handbook of Texas Online.* <http://www.tsha.utexas.edu/handbook/online/articles/view/GG/htg5.html>

35 Baines, Mrs. W. M., *Houston's Part in the World War* (1919)

36 Field trip, 2009

37 "ALVIN, TX." *The Handbook of Texas Online.* <http://www.tsha.utexas.edu/handbook/online/articles/view/AA/hea2.html>

38 "SUGAR LAND, TX." *The Handbook of Texas Online.* ttp://www.tsha.utexas.edu/handbook/online/articles/view/SS/hfs10.html>

39 Doolittle, Bill, *The Kentucky Derby: Run for the Roses* (Time Life Books 1998), 144-45

40 Ibid., 146

41 Field trip 2009

42 Begeman, June A., *Stepping Back In Time: History of West University Place*, (D. Armstrong 1999), 11

43 Ibid., 11

44 www.amherst.edu

45 *Handbook of Texas Online*, s.v. "," http://www.tsha-online.org/handbook/online/articles/AA/hla11.html

46 *Handbook of Texas Online*, s.v. "," http://www.tsha-online.org/handbook/online/articles/AA/hra39.html

47 *Houston Chronicle*, December 20, 1998

48 Johnston, Marguerite, *Houston: the Unknown City, 1836-1946* (Texas A & M 1991), 22

49 http://www.accessgenealogy.com

50 *Handbook of Texas Online*, s.v. "," http://www.tsha-online.org/handbook/online/articles/AA/hla11.html

51 Raia, John B., Interview 2001 & Glenwood Cemetery records

52 *Encyclopedia Britannica* (1952), Volume 1, 981-2

53 *Who's Who in the Bible* (Reader's Digest Assn. 1994), 117

54 Adkins, John, e-mail 2009

55 Laffin, John, *Brassey's Dictionary of Battles: 3,500 Years Of Conflict, Campaigns and Wars* (Barnes & Noble Books 1986), 47.

56 Ibid., 49.

57 *The American Heritage Dictionary of the English Language:* Third Edition (Houghton Mifflin Company 1992), 87, 1340, 158, 1720, 1377

58 *Encyclopedia Britannica* (1952), Volume 2, 137

59 *The American Heritage Dictionary of the English Language:* Third Edition (Houghton Mifflin Company 1992), 89.

60 Old Houston Maps

61 http://www.freepages.family.rootsweb.ancestry.com

62 Laffin, John, *Brassey's Dictionary of Battles: 3,500 Years Of Conflict, Campaigns and Wars* (Barnes & Noble Books 1986), 51-2.

63 Houston District Designation Report, HPO file no. 07HD10, 2007
64 www.dialcorp.com/
65 Begeman, June A., *Stepping Back In Time: History of West University Place*, (D. Armstrong 1999), 11
66 *Sanford Maps* – 1951
67 Texas Historical Marker, 2714 Ferry Road, Baytown, erected 1984
68 Houghton, Dorothy Knox Howe, et al, *Houston's Forgotten Heritage: Landscape, Houses, Interiors, 1824-1914* (Rice University Press 1991), 41
69 Webb, Walter Prescott, *The Hand Book of Texas* (Texas State Historical Assn. 1952), Vol. 1, 75
70 www.auburn.edu
71 *West University Magazine*, 1993
72 Bering, August C. III, letter and family tree, December 20, 2002
73 www.augusta.com/
74 *Handbook of Texas Online*, s.v. ".", http://www.tsha-online.org/handbook/online/articles/BB/hgb10.html
75 Webb, Walter Prescott, *The Hand Book of Texas* (Texas State Historical Assn. 1952), Vol. 1, 1-4
76 *Encyclopedia Britannica* (1952), Volume 2, 792
77 Wood, Jerry, Interview 2001
78 Wallingford, Sharon, *Fort Bend County Texas: A Pictorial History* (Fort Bend Publishing Group 1996), 151
79 *Houston Business Journal*, July 5-11, 2002
80 Fieldtrip 2001

B

1 *Handbook of Texas Online*, s.v. ".", http://www.tsha-online.org/handbook/online/articles/TT/fte28.html
2 Anderson, Jesse and Strain, Harvey, interview 2009
3 www.bp.com
4 *The American Heritage Dictionary of the English Language:* Third Edition (Houghton Mifflin Company 1992), 525
5 *City of Spring Valley, Texas: Fifty Years 1955-2005,* First Draft 10-22-2005, 17
6 "BACLIFF, TX." *The Handbook of Texas Online.* <http://www.tsha.utexas.edu/handbook/online/articles/view/BB/hjbur.html>
7 Houghton, Dorothy Knox Howe, et al, *Houston's Forgotten Heritage: Landscape, Houses, Interiors, 1824-1914* (Rice University Press 1991), 3
8 Texas Historical Marker, Angleton, erected 1970
9 *Works Projects Administration, Houston: A History & Guide* (Anson Jones Press 1942), 62
10 "KATY, TX." *The Handbook of Texas Online.* <http://www.tsha.utexas.edu/handbook/online/articles/view/KK/hfk1.html>
11 Upchurch, Lessie, *Welcome to Tomball: A History of Tomball, Texas* (D. Armstrong Co. 1995), 32
12 Texas Historical Marker, 2714 Ferry Road, Baytown, erected 1984
13 http://www.accessgenealogy.com
14 Special Collections/Archives, John B. Coleman Library, Prairie View A & M University, Prairie View, Texas
15 www.portofhouston.com

16 Beverly, Trevia W., *At Rest: A Historical Directory of Harris County, Texas, Cemeteries (1822-1992),* (Self published 1992), 16
17 Johnston, Marguerite, *Houston: the Unknown City, 1836-1946* (Texas A & M 1991), 69
18 Ibid., 30-1
19 Webb, Walter Prescott, *The Hand Book of Texas* (Texas Historical Assn. 1952), Vol. 1, 103
20 *The American Heritage Dictionary of the English Language:* Third Edition (Houghton Mifflin Company 1992), 142
21 www.skyways.lib.ks.us
22 "BAMMEL, TX." *The Handbook of Texas Online.* <http://www.tsha.utexas.edu/handbook/online/articles/view/BB/hrb4.html>
23 Begeman, June A., *Stepping Back In Time: History of West University Place*, (D. Armstrong 1999), 74
24 "BARBER, AMOS." *The Handbook of Texas Online.* <http://www.tsha.utexas.edu/handbook/online/articles/view/BB/fbabe.html>
25 Jamison, Jimmy, e-mail 2002
26 Wallingford, Sharon, *Fort Bend County Texas: A Pictorial History* (Fort Bend Publishing Group 1996), 104
27 "BARKER, TX." *The Handbook of Texas Online.* <http://www.tsha.utexas.edu/handbook/online/articles/view/BB/hlb8.html>
28 Christensen, Roberta, *Historic-Romantic Richmond* (Nortex Press, 1982), 75
29 Cohen, Anne Nathan, *The Centenary History of Congregation of Beth Israel of Houston, Texas, 1854-1954*, 58-9
30 "BARRETT, TX." *The Handbook of Texas Online.* <http://www.tsha.utexas.edu/handbook/online/articles/view/BB/hgb3.html>
31 Texas Historical Marker, 110 W. Main, Humble, erected 1972
32 Kimball, Mary Holt, et al, *The Heritage of North Harris County* (American Association of University Women 1977), 30
33 Baines, Mrs. W. M., *Houston's Part in the World War* (1919)
34 Anderson, Thomas, Interview 2002
35 Field Trip with George Donehoo, 2005
36 Simpson, Col. Harold B., *Hood's Texas Brigade: A Compendium* (Hill Junior College Press 1977), 38
37 Christensen, Roberta, *Historic-Romantic Richmond* (Nortex Press, 1982), 105-6
38 Laffin, John, *Brassey's Dictionary of Battles: 3,500 Years Of Conflict, Campaigns and Wars* (Barnes & Noble Books 1986), 71
39 Webb, Walter Prescott, *The Hand Book of Texas* (Texas State Historical Assn. 1952), Vol. 1, 120
40 Laffin, John, *Brassey's Dictionary of Battles: 3,500 Years Of Conflict, Campaigns and Wars* (Barnes & Noble Books 1986), 71
41 Macon, N. Don, *Mr. John H. Freeman and Friends: A Story of the Texas Medical Center and How It Began* (Texas Medical Center 1973), 57-63
42 Texas Historical Marker, Galena Park, erected 1969

[43] Wharton, Charles R., *History of Fort Bend County* (Naylor & Co. 1939), 40

[44] Webb, Walter Prescott, *The Hand Book of Texas* (Texas State Historical Assn. 1952), Vol. 2, 554

[45] McAshan, Marie Phelps, *A Houston Legacy* (Gulf Publishing 1985), 47

[46] *Houston Chronicle*, April 19, 2004

[47] *Key Map*, 617-18

[48] Field trip, 2009

[49] Texas Historical Marker, Baytown, erected 1964

[50] www.baylor.edu

[51] www.novachem.com

[52] Texas Historical Marker, 514 Bayridge Rd., Morgan's Point, erected 1997

[53] http://www.hertiagemuseum.us

[54] "BAYTOWN, TX." *The Handbook of Texas Online.* <http://www.tsha.utexas.edu/handbook/online/articles/view/BB/hdb1.html>

[55] http://www.hertiagemuseum.us

[56] *Handbook of Texas Online*, s.v. "," http://www.tsha-online.org/handbook/online/articles/BB/rbb59.html

[57] www.aliefisd.net/

[58] *Handbook of Texas Online*, s.v. "," http://www.tshaon-line.org/handbook/online/articles/BB/hlb15.html & *Handbook of Texas Online*, s.v. "," http://www.tshaon-line.org/handbook/online/articles/DD/hld5.html

[59] *Handbook of Texas Online*, s.v. "," http://www.tsha-online.org/handbook/online/articles/TT/hnt8.html

[60] *The American Heritage Dictionary of the English Language: Third Edition* (Houghton Mifflin Company 1992), 162

[61] "BEAUCHAMPS SPRINGS, TX." *The Handbook of Texas Online.* <http://www.tsha.utexas.edu/hand-book/online/articles/view/BB/hvbce.html>

[62] http://www.referencecenter.com

[63] Webb, Walter Prescott, *The Hand Book of Texas* (Texas State Historical Assn. 1952), Vol. 1, 132

[64] Garraty, John A. Editor, *Encyclopedia of American Biography* (Harper & Row 1974), 69-70

[65] Beverly, Trevia W., *At Rest: A Historical Directory of Harris County, Texas, Cemeteries (1822-1992)*, (Self published 1992), 19

[66] ad.doubleclick.net

[67] *Encyclopedia Britannica* (1952), Volume 9, 525

[68] *Houston Chronicle*, July 12, 2002

[69] www.ansi.okstate.com

[70] Herridge, Karen, *Spring Branch Heritage* (Wakebrook Press 1998), –22

[71] "BELKNAP, CHARLES." *The Handbook of Texas Online.* <http://www.tsha.utexas.edu/handbook/online/articles/view/BB/fbe32.html>

[72] Wallingford, Sharon, *Fort Bend County Texas: A Pictorial History* (Fort Bend Publishing Group 1996), 157

[73] *Handbook of Texas Online*, s.v. "," http://www.tsha-online.org/handbook/online/articles/BB/hgb5.html

[74] Webb, Walter Prescott, *The Hand Book of Texas* (Texas State Historical Assn. 1952), Vol. 1, 141-2

[75] Gay, Mrs. Robert N. Jr. and Hawks, Mrs. J. W. Editors, *Bellaire's Own Historical Cookbook* (Steck-Warlick 1969) 9

[76] Dunn, Jeff, *Bellaire: An Attractive Garden City*, Historical Feature 1991

[77] River Oaks Property Owners Association, Interview & Records

[78] Dedication of George & Ann Bellows Drive, June 9, 2000

[79] Texas Historical Marker, East Columbia, erected 1965

[80] www1.nyra.com

[81] Garraty, John A. Editor, *Encyclopedia of American Biography* (Harper & Row 1974), 1144-45

[82] "TAUB, BEN." *The Handbook of Texas Online.* <http://www.tsha.utexas.edu/handbook/online/articles/view/TT/fta43.html>

[83] Texas Historical Marker, 110 W. Main, Humble, erected 1972

[84] Texas Historical Marker, 16715 Stuebner-Airline Road, Klein, erected 1977

[85] Johnston, Marguerite, *Houston: the Unknown City, 1836-1946* (Texas A & M 1991), 35

[86] Webb, Walter Prescott, *The Hand Book of Texas* (Texas Historical Assn. 1952), Vol. 1, 668

[87] Macon, N. Don, *Mr. John H. Freeman and Friends: A Story of the Texas Medical Center and How It Began* (Texas Medical Center 1973), 57-63

[88] Baines, Mrs. W. M., *Houston's Part in the World War* (1919), 25-9

[89] Houston Metropolitan Research Center Files, Houston Public Library.

[90] www.bettyboop.com/

[91] http://www.springvalleytx.com

[92] "BEXAR." *The Handbook of Texas Online.* <http://www.tsha.utexas.edu/handbook/online/articles/view/BB/uqb1.html>

[93] Wood, Jerry, Interview 2001 & Fieldtrip 2001

[94] Bhandara, Fred, interview 2009

[95] http://www.visitleaguecity.com

[96] "HOUSTON AND BRAZOS RAIL ROAD." *The Handbook of Texas Online.* <http://www.tsha.utexas.edu/handbook/online/articles/view/HH/eqhet.html>

[97] http://www.raytheonaircraft.com

[98] Adkins, John, e-mail 2008

[99] McAshan, Marie Phelps, *A Houston Legacy* (Gulf Publishing 1985), 105

[100] Houghton, Dorothy Knox Howe, Interview 2002

[101] Sam Houston Park Memorial & Wood, Jerry, Interview 2001

[102] Field Trip with George Donehoo, 2005

[103] Upchurch, Lessie, *Welcome to Tomball: A History of Tomball, Texas* (D. Armstrong 1976), 47

[104] *Encyclopedia Britannica* 2005 Ultimate Reference Suite CD/ROM

[105] "BLAIR, JOHN." *The Handbook of Texas Online.* <http://www.tsha.utexas.edu/handbook/online/articles/view/BB/fbl65.html>

[106] *Handbook of Texas Online*, s.v. "," http://www.tsha-online.org/handbook/online/articles/HH/qch4.html

[107] Raia, John B., Interview 2001

108 "BLOUNT, STEPHEN WILLIAM." *The Handbook of Texas Online*. <http://www.tsha.utexas.edu/handbook/online/articles/view/BB/fbl31.html>

109 *Handbook of Texas Online*, s.v. ".," http://www.tshaonline.org/handbook/online/articles/MM/hem6.html

110 Field trip 2008

111 Field trip 2009

112 *Handbook of Texas Online*, s.v. ".," http://www.tshaonline.org/handbook/online/articles/BB/htb15.html

113 Field trip, 2001

114 Texas Historical Marker, Hufsmith

115 Barrus, Thu Nhi, Interview 2002

116 www.horse-races.net

117 *Handbook of Texas Online*, s.v. ".," http://www.tshaonline.org/handbook/online/articles/BB/hlb43.html

118 http://www.crystalbeach.com

119 *Encyclopedia Britannica* (1952), Volume 3, 836-41

120 "BONHAM, JAMES BUTLER." *The Handbook of Texas Online*. <http://www.tsha.utexas.edu/handbook/online/articles/view/BB/fbo14.html>

121 http://www.artcyclopedia.com

122 *Houston Chronicle*, June 1, 2006

123 Fieldtrip, 1998

124 *Handbook of Texas Online*, s.v. ".," http://www.tshaonline.org/handbook/online/articles/BB/hnb62.html

125 *Handbook of Texas Online*, s.v. ".," http://www.tshaonline.org/handbook/online/articles/DD/hjd2.html

126 "BORDERSVILLE, TX." *The Handbook of Texas Online*. <http://www.tsha.utexas.edu/handbook/online/articles/view/BB/hrb81.html>

127 Miller, Mary Catherine Farrington, *Tanglewood: The Story of William Giddings Farrington* (Gulf Publishing Company 1989), 43

128 www.espn.com

129 Kimball, Mary Holt, et al, *The Heritage of North Harris County* (American Association of University Women 1977), 40

130 Henry, Mary Lou, Interview 2002

131 Fieldtrip 2001

132 www.bowlinggreen.edu

133 "BOYCE, ALBERT GALLATIN." *The Handbook of Texas Online*. <http://www.tsha.utexas.edu/handbook/online/articles/view/BB/fbo97.html>

134 http://boysandgirlscountry.org

135 Hinton, Marks, visit to the Boyt family compound on Bolivar Peninsula in 1970

136 www.kemah.net

137 Webb, Walter Prescott, *The Hand Book of Texas* (Texas State Historical Assn. 1952), Vol. 1, 204-5

138 http://braeburncc.com

139 *The American Heritage Dictionary of the English Language:* Third Edition (Houghton Mifflin Company 1992), 228

140 www.txrmref@hpl.lib.tx.us, May 24, 2000

141 www.txrmref@hpl.lib.tx.us, May 24, 2000

142 McAshan, Marie Phelps, *A Houston Legacy* (Gulf Publishing 1985), 109

143 Upchurch, Lessie, *Welcome to Tomball: A History of Tomball, Texas* (D. Armstrong Co. 1995), 31

144 *Fort Bend County Sesquicentennial 1822-1972* (Commemorative Booklet Committee 1972), 67

145 Houston Metropolitan Research Center Files, Houston Public Library.

146 *Handbook of Texas Online*, s.v. ".," http://www.tshaonline.org/handbook/online/articles/BB/hjb18.html

147 Webb, Walter Prescott, *The Handbook of Texas* (Texas Historical Assn 1952), Vol. 1, 211

148 Webb, Walter Prescott, *The Hand Book of Texas* (Texas Historical Assn. 1952), Vol. 1, 212

149 Johnston, Marguerite, *Houston: the Unknown City, 1836-1946* (Texas A & M 1991), 54

150 *River Oaks Times*, September 10, 1948

151 *Houston Post*, undated

152 Raia, John B., Interview 2001

153 http://www.imagi-nation.com

154 Texas Historical Marker, 2503 S. Cherry, Tomball, erected 1985

155 *Houston Post*, March 25,1943

156 Keezel, Roy, interview 2008

157 Henson, Margaret Sweet, *The History of Baytown* (Bay Area Heritage Society 1986), 14-29

158 City Federation of Women's Clubs, *Houston & Harris County Fact-1939*, (Facts Publishing 1939), Pg 341-2

159 www.online-literature.com

160 *Handbook of Texas Online*, s.v. ".," http://www.tshaonline.org/handbook/online/articles/BB/hjb17.html

161 "BROOKSIDE VILLAGE, TX." *The Handbook of Texas Online*. <http://www.tsha.utexas.edu/handbook/online/articles/view/BB/hjb18.html>

162 Special Collections/Archives, John B. Coleman Library, Prairie View A & M University, Prairie View, Texas

163 www.brown.edu

164 Fifth Ward, Houston Texas, circa 1915-1920, September 1982

165 *Encyclopedia Britannica* (1952), Volume 4, 275-9

166 http://www.ourbaytown.com

167 "BRUSHY CREEK." *The Handbook of Texas Online*. <http://www.tsha.utexas.edu/handbook/online/articles/view/BB/rbbkj.html>

168 *The American Heritage Dictionary of the English Language:* Third Edition (Houghton Mifflin Company 1992), 246

169 *Handbook of Texas Online*, s.v. ".," http://www.tshaonline.org/handbook/online/articles/BB/hnbak.html

170 Henson, Margaret Sweet, *The History of Baytown* (Bay Area Heritage Society 1986), 35-55

171 www.brynmar.edu

172 Carroll, Benajah H., *Standard History of Houston, Texas* (no publisher listed – undated), 108

173 Kimball, Mary Holt, et al, *The Heritage of North Harris County* (American Association of University Women 1977), 75

174 Andrews, Patsy Fox, *City of Spring Valley: Fifty Years 1955-2005*, 20

175 www.fortbend.k12.tx.us/campuses/mhs/

176 Anderson, Thomas, Interview 2002

177 Laffin, John, *Brassey's Dictionary of Battles: 3,500 Years of Conflict, Campaigns and Wars* (Barnes & Noble, 1986), 91

[178] Paterson, Melissa M., *The Road to Piney Point* (Piney Point Village Historic Committee 1994), 71

[179] *Houston Chronicle*, April 15, 1931

[180] http://atlas.thc.state.tx.us

[181] http://www.bnsf.com

[182] http://www.sinoam.com/

[183] Webb, Walter Prescott, *The Hand Book of Texas* (Texas State Historical Assn. 1952), Vol. 1, 252-3

[184] Texas Historical Marker, 414 S. Burnet, Baytown, erected 1936

[185] Pomeroy, C. David Jr., *Pasadena: The Early Years* (Pomerosa Press 1993), 21,27

[186] http://rd.yahoo.com/sports/*http://cgi.cnnsi.com/cgi-bin/partners/partner_gol_yahoo.redir?http://www.golfcourse.com/search/course

[187] http:///baileysprairie.org

[188] Texas Historical Marker, 711 William, Houston

[189] "LEAGUE CITY, TX." *The Handbook of Texas Online.* <http://www.tsha.utexas.edu/handbook/online/articles/view/LL/hel6.html>

[190] "STAGECOACH LINES." *The Handbook of Texas Online.* <http://www.tsha.utexas.edu/handbook/online/articles/view/SS/ers1.html>

[191] Barrus, Thu Nhi, Interview 2002

[192] Ibid., Volume 4, 478-84

C

[1] Raia, John B., Interview 2001

[2] Blessington, J. P., *The Campaigns of Walker's Texas Division* (Pemberton Press 1968), 56

[3] http://www.merriam-webster.com

[4] Vreeland-Wendt, Susan, interview 2009

[5] *Encyclopedia Britannica* (1952), Volume 4, 521-6

[6] http://www.sanjacinto-museum.org/veterans

[7] Laffin, John, *Brassey's Dictionary of Battles: 3,500 Years Of Conflict, Campaigns and Wars* (Barnes & Noble Books 1986), 98

[8] Webb, Walter Prescott, *The Hand Book of Texas* (Texas State Historical Assn. 1952), Vol. 1, 270

[9] Wharton, Charles R., *History of Fort Bend County* (Naylor & Co. 1939), 52

[10] *Encyclopedia Britannica* (1952), Volume 4, 652-4

[11] http://www.georgestrakedistrict.org

[12] Webb, Walter Prescott, *The Hand Book of Texas* (Texas Historical Assn. 1952), Vol. 1, 285

[13] www.co.harris.tx.us

[14] Herridge, Karen, *Spring Branch Heritage* (Wakebrook Press 1998), --22

[15] Fieldtrip 1993

[16] http://www.users.hal-pc.org

[17] Raia, John B., Interview 2001

[18] Miller, Mary Catherine Farrington, *Tanglewood: The Story of William Giddings Farrington* (Gulf Publishing Company 1989), 43

[19] "CANEY CREEK." *The Handbook of Texas Online.* <http://www.tsha.utexas.edu/handbook/online/articles/view/CC/rbc72.html>

[2]

[0] Wallingford, Sharon, *Fort Bend County Texas: A Pictorial History* (Fort Bend Publishing Group 1996), 115

[21] www.chef-de-race.com

[22] Doolittle, Bill, *The Kentucky Derby: Run for the Roses* (Time Life Books 1998), 133

[23] Raia, John B., Interview 2001

[24] Andrews, Patsy, e-mail 2009

[25] *Encyclopedia Britannica* 2005 Ultimate Reference Suite CD/ROM

[26] http://www.cmu.edu

[27] Raia, John B., Interview 2001

[28] http://www.dictionary.com

[29] Upchurch, Lessie, *Welcome to Tomball: A History of Tomball, Texas* (D. Armstrong Co. 1995), 187-8

[30] www.houstonheights.org

[31] Wallingford, Sharon, *Fort Bend County Texas: A Pictorial History* (Fort Bend Publishing Group 1996), 90

[32] Garraty, John A. Editor, *Encyclopedia of American Biography* (Harper & Row 1974), 179-80

[33] Henson, Margaret Sweet, *The History of Baytown* (Bay Area Heritage Society 1986), 62

[34] http://ci.katy.tx.us

[35] *Encyclopedia Britannica* (1952), Volume 4, 971

[36] Ibid., Volume 4, 975

[37] www.pantheon.org

[38] Webb, Walter Prescott, *The Hand Book of Texas* (Texas Historical Assn. 1952), Vol. 1, 309

[39] *Houston Chronicle*, January 2, 2008

[40] *Houston Chronicle*, January 2, 2008

[41] "CEDAR BAYOU." *The Handbook of Texas Online.* <http://www.tsha.utexas.edu/handbook/online/articles/view/CC/rhc6.html>

[42] Miller, Mary Catherine Farrington, *Tanglewood: The Story of William Giddings Farrington* (Gulf Publishing Company 1989), 43

[43] *Handbook of Texas Online*, s.v. "," http://www.tsha-online.org/handbook/online/articles/CC/hrcde.html

[44] *Handbook of Texas Online*, s.v. "," http://www.tsha-online.org/handbook/online/articles/CC/hrcnc.html

[45] "CEDAR GROVE, TX." *The Handbook of Texas Online.* <http://www.tsha.utexas.edu/handbook/online/articles/view/CC/hrcjn.html>

[46] http://www.centenary.edu

[47] http://www.lakejackson-tx.gov

[48] *The American Heritage Dictionary of the English Language:* Third Edition (Houghton Mifflin Company 1992), 312

[49] Garraty, John A. Editor, *Encyclopedia of American Biography* (Harper & Row 1974), 193-4

[50] http://cessna.com

[51] http://www.sanjacinto-museum.org/veterans

[52] www.artencyclopedia.com

[53] *Houston Chronicle*, January 28, 1968

[54] Fieldtrip 2000

[55] "GALVESTON, HARRISBURG AND SAN ANTONIO RAILWAY." *The Handbook of Texas Online.* <http://www.tsha.utexas.edu/handbook/online/articles/view/GG/eqg6.html>

56 "CHANNEL, TX." *The Handbook of Texas Online.* <http://www.tsha.utexas.edu/handbook/online/articles/view/CC/hrczz.html>

57 Field trip, 2001

58 Hill, Nina Lee and Nancy, interview 2009

59 Fieldtrip 1996

60 www.zoominfo.com

61 Beverly, Trevia W., *At Rest: A Historical Directory of Harris County, Texas Cemeteries (1822-1992)*, 68

62 *Houston Chronicle,* July 6, 2005

63 Old Houston map

64 Laffin, John, *Brassey's Dictionary of Battles: 3,500 Years of Conflict, Campaigns and Wars* (Barnes & Noble, 1986), 115-16

65 *Encyclopedia Britannica* (1952), Volume 5, 326-30

66 *Key Map,* 46th Edition, 2005

67 Webb, Walter Prescott, *The Hand Book of Texas* (Texas Historical Assn. 1952), Vol. 1, 332

68 Old Houston map

69 www.danford.net

70 Deaca, Marian, *Heritage Society News* (Vol. 1 No. 2, Fall 1974), 12

71 http://www.chevron.com

72 River Oaks Property Owners Association, Interview & Records

73 Carvelli, Lou, Interview 2001

74 Laffin, John, *Brassey's Dictionary of Battles: 3,500 Years of Conflict, Campaigns and Wars* (Barnes & Noble, 1986), 117

75 Robin Elverson Realtors, Sales Brochure

76 Miller, Mary Catherine Farrington, *Tanglewood: The Story of William Giddings Farrington* (Gulf Publishing Company 1989), 43

77 *Handbook of Texas Online,* s.v. "," http://www.tshaonline.org/handbook/online/articles/JJ/fjo32.html

78 Webb, Walter Prescott, *The Hand Book of Texas* (Texas State Historical Assn. 1952), Vol. 1, 341-2

79 "LIVINGSTON, TX." *The Handbook of Texas Online.* <http://www.tsha.utexas.edu/handbook/online/articles/view/LL/hgl8.html>

80 *Handbook of Texas Online,* s.v. "," http://www.tshaonline.org/handbook/online/articles/CC/hnc54.html and *Handbook of Texas Online,* s.v. "," http://www.tshaonline.org/handbook/online/articles/CC/rhc12.html

81 *Encyclopedia Britannica* (1952), Volume 4, 619-20

82 Wharton, Charles R., *History of Fort Bend County* (Naylor & Co. 1939), 60,68

83 www.greatbuildings.com

84 Fieldtrips 1997, 1998, 1999

85 http://www.cincoranch.com

86 Doolittle, Bill, *The Kentucky Derby: Run for the Roses* (Time Life Books 1998), 165

87 www.clubcorp.com

88 *River Oaks Times,* September 10, 1948

89 http://www.springvalleytx.com

90 Herridge, Karen, *Spring Branch Heritage* (Wakebrook Press 1998), –22

91 Raia, John B., Interview 2001

92 "CLEAR CREEK." *The Handbook of Texas Online.* <http://www.tsha.utexas.edu/handbook/online/articles/view/CC/rbcex.html>

93 "CLEAR LAKE CITY, TX." *The Handbook of Texas Online.* <http://www.tsha.utexas.edu/handbook/online/articles/view/CC/hjc23.html>

94 http://en.wikipedia.org

95 Special Collections/Archives, John B. Coleman Library, Prairie View A & M University, Prairie View, Texas

96 *Handbook of Texas Online,* s.v. "," http://www.tsha-online.org/handbook/online/articles/CC/hrc65.html

97 www.clemson.edu

98 *Baytown Sun,* May 13, 1996

99 *Handbook of Texas Online,* s.v. "," http://www.tsha-online.org/handbook/online/articles/CC/hfc8.html

100 "CLEVELAND, TX." *The Handbook of Texas Online.* <http://www.tsha.utexas.edu/handbook/online/articles/view/CC/hfc8.html>

101 *Houston Press,* October 7, 1958

102 Webb, Walter Prescott, *The Handbook of Texas* (Texas Historical Assn 1952), Vol. 2, 234-5

103 "CLOVERLEAF, TX." *The Handbook of Texas Online.* <http://www.tsha.utexas.edu/handbook/online/articles/view/CC/hrchk.html>

104 Webb, Walter Prescott, *The Hand Book of Texas* (Texas Historical Assn. 1952), Vol. 1, 364

105 http://www.britannica.com/

106 Houghton, Dorothy Knox Howe, Interview 2002

107 Morgan, George T. Jr. and King, John O., The Woodlands: New Community Development, 1964-1983 (Texas A & M University 1987), 150

108 Wood, Jerry, e-mail 2002

109 *Encyclopedia Britannica* (1952), Volume 6, 9-11

110 *Encyclopedia Britannica* (1952), Volume 6, 51

111 Texas Historical Marker, Founders Memorial Park, 1217 W. Dallas Ave., Houston, Texas, erected 1936

112 Webb, Walter Prescott, *The Handbook of Texas* (Texas State Historical Association 1952), Vol. 1, 379-80

113 Ibid., Vol. 1, 381

114 http://www.dictionary.reference.com

115 http://education.yahoo.com

116 Agatha, Sister M., *The History of Houston Heights: 1891-1918* (Premier Publishing 1956), 18

117 Wood, Jerry, Interview 2001

118 www.hccs.edu/

119 www.compaq.com/

120 http://www.milleroutdoortheater.com

121 *Handbook of Texas Online,* s.v. "," http://www.tsha-online.org/handbook/online/articles/BB/hgb5.html

122 Fieldtrip 2001

123 Raia, John B., Interview 2001

124 www.infoplease.com

125 *Houston Chronicle,* August 8, 2002

126 Gandy, William H., *A History of Montgomery County,* Texas (Master's thesis 1952), 88

127 *Handbook of Texas Online,* s.v. "," http://www.tsha-online.org/handbook/online/articles/PP/hdp6.html

128 http://members.tripod.com

129 Field trip, 2002

130 http://www.convair880.com

131 Texas Historical Marker, Alief Cemetery, Bellaire at Dairy-Ashford, Houston, erected 1984

132 Garraty, John A. Editor, *Encyclopedia of American Biography* (Harper & Row 1974), 219-21

133 Blessington, J. P., *The Campaigns of Walker's Texas Division* (Pemberton Press 1968), 56

134 Herridge, Karen, *Spring Branch Heritage* (Wakebrook Press 1998), --22

135 "SIXTH WARD, HOUSTON." *The Handbook of Texas Online.* <http://www.tsha.utexas.edu/handbook/online/articles/view/SS/hpsxc.html>

136 Wallingford, Sharon, *Fort Bend County Texas: A Pictorial History* (Fort Bend Publishing Group 1996), 159

137 www.cornell.edu

138 Laffin, John, *Brassey's Dictionary of Battles: 3,500 Years of Conflict, Campaigns and Wars* (Barnes & Noble, 1986), 48

139 *Encyclopedia Britannica* (1952), Volume 6, 457

140 Houston District Designation Report, HPO file no. 07HD11, 2007

141 Field trip with George Donehoo, 2005 and *Handbook of Texas Online*, s.v. "KOHRVILLE, TX," http://www.tsha.utexas.edu/handbook/online/articles/KK/hrk18.html

142 www.uh.edu/

143 http://www.cfisd.net

144 http://www.tomballcountryclub.org

145 Field trip, 2002

146 www.golfcrestcountryclub.com/

147 Field trip, 2009

148 Fox, Stephen, *Houston Architectural Guide* (AIA and Herring Press 1999), 70-1

149 *Handbook of Texas Online*, s.v. "," http://www.tsha-online.org/handbook/online/articles/CC/rbclr.html

150 www.online-literature.com

151 Looscan, Adele B., *Harris County: 1822-1845* (Texas State Historical Association, 1915), 55

152 www.pbs.org

153 Garraty, John A. Editor, *Encyclopedia of American Biography* (Harper & Row 1974), 241-2

154 "CROSBY, TX." *The Handbook of Texas Online.* <http://www.tsha.utexas.edu/handbook/online/articles/view/CC/hgc18.html>

155 Old Houston maps

156 Beverly, Trevia W., *At Rest: A Historical Directory of Harris County, Texas Cemeteries (1822-1992)*, 64

157 http://www.crowncentral.com

158 www.strakejesuit.org

159 http://www.ci.pasadena.tx.us

160 Hinton, Marks, *And Death Came from the Sea* (Archival Press 2009), 36-8

161 Webb, Walter Prescott, *The Handbook of Texas* (Texas Historical Assn 1952), Vol. 1, 443

162 Kilman, Ed & Wright, *Theon, Hugh Roy Cullen: A Story of an American Opportunity* (Prentice-Hall 1954), dust jacket

163 The Houston Place Preservation Association of Houston, The Trailblazer Series, 1993

164 Wallingford, Sharon, *Fort Bend County Texas: A Pictorial History* (Fort Bend Publishing Group 1996), 116-17

165 Houghton, Dorothy Knox Howe, et al, *Houston's Forgotten Heritage: Landscape, Houses, Interiors, 1824-1914* (Rice University Press 1991), 146

166 Webb, Walter Prescott, *The Handbook of Texas* (Texas Historical Assn 1952), Vol. 1, 449

167 Garraty, John A. Editor, *Encyclopedia of American Biography* (Harper & Row 1974), 250

168 Webb, Walter Prescott, *The Hand Book of Texas* (Texas Historical Assn. 1952), Vol. 1, 451

169 *Handbook of Texas Online*, s.v. "," http://www.tsha-online.org/handbook/online/articles/CC/rbcpa.html

170 http://www.cypressgardens.com

171 "CYPRESS, TX." *The Handbook of Texas Online.* <http://www.tsha.utexas.edu/handbook/online/articles/view/CC/hlc66.html>

D

1 Anderson, Jesse and Strain, Harvey, interview 2009

2 *Handbook of Texas Online*, s.v. "," http://www.tsha-online.org/handbook/online/articles/DD/hld2.html

3 Field trip, 2009

4 Field trip, 2004

5 Texas Historical Marker, Houston, erected 1991

6 "SATSUMA, TX." *The Handbook of Texas Online.* <http://www.tsha.utexas.edu/handbook/online/articles/view/SS/hrs18.html>

7 Field trip 2009

8 *Handbook of Texas Online*, s.v. "," http://www.tsha-online.org/handbook/online/articles/DD/hld5.html

9 *Handbook of Texas Online*, s.v. "," http://www.tsha-online.org/handbook/online/articles/DD/hjd2.html

10 *Handbook of Texas Online*, s.v. "," http://www.tsha-online.org/handbook/online/articles/DD/hvd7.html

11 http://www.tdcj.state.tx.us

12 http://www.accessgenealogy.com

13 Christensen, Roberta, *Historic-Romantic Richmond* (Nortex Press, 1982), 103

14 www.dartmouth.edu

15 http://www.en.wikipedia.org

16 Pomeroy, C. David Jr., *Pasadena: The Early Years* (Pomerosa Press 1993), 33, 42

17 www.airfields-freeman.com

18 http://www.fortbendchamber.org

19 http://www.en.wikipedia.or

20 Houston Metropolitan Research Center Files, Houston Public Library.

21 Houston Metropolitan Research Center Files, Houston Public Library.

22 http://translate.google.com

23 *Houston Post*, September 4, 1949

24 Texas Historical Marker, 531 Crockett, Channelview, erected 1968

25 Webb, Walter Prescott, *The Hand Book of Texas* (Texas State Historical Assn. 1952), Vol. 2, 622

26 Detering, Deborah, Interview 2001

27 *The Heritage of North Harris County* (American Association of University Women 1978), 28

28 *Baytown Sun*, May 13, 1996

29 "DEEPWATER, TX." *The Handbook of Texas Online*. <http://www.tsha.utexas.edu/handbook/online/articles/view/DD/hrdwr.html>

30 *Baytown Sun*, May 13, 1996

31 www.jsc.nasa.gov

32 River Oaks Property Owners Association, Interview & Records

33 Delaney, Alissa, e-mail 2008

34 demontrondautogroup.com

35 Gay, Mrs. Robert N. Jr. and Hawks, Mrs. J. W. Editors, *Bellaire's Own Historical Cookbook* (Steck-Warlick 1969) 5

36 *River Oaks Times*, September 10, 1948

37 Carroll, Benajah H., *Standard History of Houston, Texas* (no publisher listed – undated), 165

38 Texas Historical Marker, 2700 Albany, Houston, erected 1984

39 Field trip 2007

40 *Encyclopedia Britannica* (1952), Volume 21, 4

41 Detering, Carl, Interview 2001

42 *Fort Bend County Sesquicentennial 1822-1972* (Commemorative Booklet Committee 1972), 62

43 "NEWPORT, TX." *The Handbook of Texas Online*. <http://www.tsha.utexas.edu/handbook/online/articles/view/NN/hrncn.html>

44 http://www.jsc.nasa.gov

45 River Oaks Property Owners Association, Interview & Records

46 "DICKINSON, TX." *The Handbook of Texas Online*. <http://www.tsha.utexas.edu/handbook/online/articles/view/DD/hfd3.html>

47 Laffin, John, *Brassey's Dictionary of Battles: 3,500 Years 0f Conflict, Campaigns and Wars* (Barnes & Noble Books 1986), 146-7

48 http://www.answers.com

49 *Handbook of Texas Online*, s.v. "," http://www.tsha.utexas.edu/handbook/online/articles/DD/rbd54.html

50 "DOBBIN, TX." *The Handbook of Texas Online*. <http://www.tsha.utexas.edu/handbook/online/articles/view/DD/hld27.html>

51 Miller, Mary Catherine Farrington, *Tanglewood: The Story of William Giddings Farrington* (Gulf Publishing Company 1989), 43

52 Doolittle, Bill, *The Kentucky Derby: Run for the Roses* (Time Life Books 1998), 55

53 Blessington, J. P., *The Campaigns of Walker's Texas Division* (Pemberton Press 1968), 52

54 *Handbook of Texas Online*, s.v. "," http://www.tsha-online.org/handbook/online/articles/BB/hjb17.html

55 Hill, Nina Lee and Nancy, interview 2009

56 Houston Metropolitan Research Center Files, Houston Public Library

57 www.arlingtoncemetery.com

58 http://www.holidaycity.com

59 Taylor, Bryan interview 2000 and *Houston Post*, June 24, 1965

60 http://www.dow.com

61 *The Heritage of North Harris County* (American Association of University Women 1978), 100

62 Texas Historical Marker, 1700 MacGregor, Houston, erected 1998

63 http://www.aframnews.com

64 http://www.drake.edu

65 *Handbook of Texas Online*, s.v. "," http://www.tsha-online.org/handbook/online/articles/DD/rhd5.html

66 *Encyclopedia Britannica* (1952), Volume 7, 686-8

67 www.co.harris.tx.us

68 http://www.duke.edu

69 Garraty, John A. Editor, *Encyclopedia of American Biography* (Harper & Row 1974), 250

70 "SOUTH HOUSTON, TX." *The Handbook of Texas Online*. <http://www.tsha.utexas.edu/handbook/online/articles/view/SS/hes6.html>

71 Tardy, Courtney, Interview 2001

72 Laffin, John, *Brassey's Dictionary of Battles: 3,500 Years of Conflict, Campaigns and Wars* (Barnes & Noble, 1986), 151-2

73 Houston Press, January 15, 1927

74 Texas Historical Marker, Humble Cemetery, S. Houston at Isaacks, Humble, erected 1992

75 Huckabee, Flossie, Interview 2001

76 Webb, Walter Prescott, *The Handbook of Texas* (Texas Historical Assn 1952), Vol. 1, 528-9

77 *Handbook of Texas Online*, s.v. "," http://www.tshaon-line.org/handbook/online/articles/MM/fmo31.html

78 http://www.accessgenealogy.com

E

1 Beverly, Trevia W., *At Rest: A Historical Directory of Harris County, Texas Cemeteries (1822-1992)*, 31

2 Houghton, Dorothy Knox Howe, Interview 2002

3 Webb, Walter Prescott, *The Hand Book of Texas* (Texas Historical Assn. 1952), Vol. 1, 533

4 *Handbook of Texas Online*, s.v. "," http://www.tsha-online.org/handbook/online/articles/EE/rne6.html

5 *Houston Chronicle*, April 4, 2004

6 "EASTGATE, TX." *The Handbook of Texas Online*. <http://www.tsha.utexas.edu/handbook/online/articles/view/EE/hre4.html>

7 http://www.imh.org

8 *Houston Post*, May 30, 1982

9 Detering, Carl, Interview 2001

10 Teten, Paul, Interview 2001

11 River Oaks Property Owners Association, Interview & Records

12 Unsigned and undated letter from a Davis co-worker

13 http://www.sanjacinto-museum.org/veterans

14 Beverly, Trevia W., *At Rest: A Historical Directory of Harris County, Texas Cemeteries (1822-1992)*, 42

15 http://www.hertiagemuseum.us

16 Beverly, Trevia W., *At Rest: A Historical Directory of Harris County, Texas Cemeteries (1822-1992)*,31

17 Garraty, John A. Editor, *Encyclopedia of American Biography* (Harper & Row 1974), 325-8

18 www.worldbookonline.com

19 www.newadvent.org

20 "ELDRIDGE, WILLIAM THOMAS." *The Handbook of Texas Online.* <http://www.tsha.utexas.edu/handbook/online/articles/view/EE/fel33.html>

21 Fieldtrip, 2002

22 Houghton, Dorothy Knox Howe, Interview 2002

23 Galveston Historical Foundation pamphlet

24 *River Oaks Times,* September 10, 1948

25 Houston Public Library, Texas Room vertical files

26 Webb, Walter Prescott, *The Hand Book of Texas* (Texas Historical Assn. 1952), Vol. 1, 556

27 "ELLINGTON FIELD." *The Handbook of Texas Online.* <http://www.tsha.utexas.edu/handbook/online/articles/view/EE/qbe2.html>

28 Wallingford, Sharon, *Fort Bend County Texas: A Pictorial History* (Fort Bend Publishing Group 1996), 117

29 Teten, Paul, Interview 2001

30 Houston Metropolitan Research Center Files, Houston Public Library

31 *The American Heritage Dictionary of the English Language:* Third Edition (Houghton Mifflin Company 1992), 600

32 www.markw.com

33 need note

34 Andrews, Patsy, e-mail 2009

35 http://www.emory.edu

36 http://en.wikipedia.org

37 Old Houston maps

38 Werner, George, e-mail, 2005

39 Webb, Walter Prescott, *The Hand Book of Texas* (Texas State Historical Assn. 1952), Vol. 1, 568

40 *Encyclopedia Britannica* (1952), Volume 8, 664

41 1994 Calendar, Bob Bailey Studio

42 *Handbook of Texas Online,* s.v. ".," http://www.tsha-online.org/handbook/online/articles/EE/hre33.html

43 www.ethyl.com/about/htm

44 *Encyclopedia Britannica* (1952), Volume 8, 783

45 "KATY, TX." *The Handbook of Texas Online.* <http://www.tsha.utexas.edu/handbook/online/articles/view/KK/hfk1.html>

46 *Handbook of Texas Online,* s.v. ".," http://www.tsha-online.org/handbook/online/articles/EE/hrekm.html

47 *Houston Chronicle,* June 8, 2003

48 Special Collections/Archives, John B. Coleman Library, Prairie View A & M University, Prairie View, Texas

49 *Houston and Harris County Facts* – Houston Public Library – Texas Room

50 "EVERGREEN PLANTATION." *The Handbook of Texas Online.* <http://www.tsha.utexas.edu/handbook/online/articles/view/EE/ace3.html>

51 Houghton, Dorothy Knox Howe, et al, *Houston's Forgotten Heritage: Landscape, Houses, Interiors, 1824-1914* (Rice University Press 1991), 411

52 www2.exxonmobil.com

53 http://www.hickoksports.com

F

1 Field trip 2008

2 "FAIRBANKS, TX." *The Handbook of Texas Online.* <http://www.tsha.utexas.edu/handbook/online/articles/view/FF/hvf3.html>

3 Christensen, Roberta, *Historic-Romantic Richmond* (Nortex Press, 1982), 91-2

4 *Handbook of Texas Online,* s.v. ".," http://www.tsha-online.org/handbook/online/articles/FF/hnf2.html

5 Field trip 2009

6 Deaca, Marian, *Heritage Society News* (Vol. 1 No. 2, Fall 1974), 12 & 1880 Houston city map

7 *Handbook of Texas Online,* s.v. ".," http://www.tsha-online.org/handbook/online/articles/FF/ffa2.html

8 Houston Chamber of Commerce records

9 *Handbook of Texas Online,* s.v. "FARISH, WILLIAM STAMPS," http://www.tsha.utexas.edu/handbook/online/articles/view/FF/ffa7.html

10 http://hfrc.org

11 Garraty, John A. Editor, *Encyclopedia of American Biography* (Harper & Row 1974), 341-2

12 Pulleine, Imogene, e-mail 2002

13 "FAULKEY GULLY." *The Handbook of Texas Online.* <http://www.tsha.utexas.edu/handbook/online/articles/view/FF/rbf16.html>

14 *Handbook of Texas Online,* s.v. ".," http://www.tsha-online.org/handbook/online/articles/FF/hrfft.html

15 *Encyclopedia Britannica* (1952), Volume 9, 120-2

16 Henson, Margaret Sweet, *The History of Baytown* (Bay Area Heritage Society 1986), 43-69

17 Baines, Mrs. W. M., *Houston's Part in the World War* (1919)

18 http://www.accessgenealogy.com

19 Kimball, Mary Holt, et al, *The Heritage of North Harris County* (American Association of University Women 1977), 58

20 *Houston Chronicle,* April 16, 1997

21 http://www.galveston.com

22 *Handbook of Texas Online,* s.v. ".," http://www.tsha-online.org/handbook/online/articles/FF/hrf49.html

23 http://www.accessgenealogy.com

24 Barrus, Thu Nhi, Houston Grand Opera volunteer, Interview 2002

25 "FINNIGAN, ANNETTE." *The Handbook of Texas Online.* <http://www.tsha.utexas.edu/handbook/online/articles/view/FF/ffi35.html>

26 Wallingford, Sharon, *Fort Bend County Texas: A Pictorial History* (Fort Bend Publishing Group 1996), 170-1

27 Henson, Margaret Sweet, *The History of Baytown* (Bay Area Heritage Society 1986), 43

28 http://co.chambers.tx.us

29 "FLEWELLEN, TX." *The Handbook of Texas Online.* <http://www.tsha.utexas.edu/handbook/online/articles/view/FF/htf4.html>

30 Gibson, Jan, interview 2001

31 *Houston Business Journal,* undated

32 Webb, Walter Prescott, *The Hand Book of Texas* (Texas Historical Assn. 1952), Vol. 1, 614

[33] Texas Historical Marker, 3410 Montrose, Houston, erected 1989

[34] www.humbleisd.net

[35] www.nytimes.com

[36] Webb, Walter Prescott, *The Handbook of Texas* (Texas Historical Assn 1952), Vol. 1, 616

[37] www.fordham.edu

[38] Garraty, John A. Editor, *Encyclopedia of American Biography* (Harper & Row 1974), 374-5

[39] "FORT BEND." *The Handbook of Texas Online.* <http://www.tsha.utexas.edu/handbook/online/articles/view/FF/uef1.html>

[40] Webb, Walter Prescott, *The Hand Book of Texas* (Texas Historical Assn. 1952), Vol. 1, 623

[41] Ibid., Vol. 1, 623-4

[42] *Handbook of Texas Online*, s.v. "," http://www.tsha-online.org/handbook/online/articles/FF/hcf7.html

[43] http://www.electricscotland.com/history/america/civilwar

[44] *Baytown Sun*, May 13, 1996

[45] Field trip, 1959

[46] *Fort Bend County Sesquicentennial 1822-1972* (Commemorative Booklet Committee 1972), 63

[47] Pomeroy, C. David Jr., *Pasadena: The Early Years* (Pomerosa Press 1993), 39-43

[48] Webb, Walter Prescott, *The Hand Book of Texas* (Texas Historical Assn. 1952), Vol. 1, 636

[49] Upchurch, Lessie, *Welcome to Tomball: A History of Tomball, Texas* (D. Armstrong Co. 1995), 69

[50] *Handbook of Texas Online*, s.v. "," http://www.tsha-online.org/handbook/online/articles/FF/hrf20.html

[51] *Handbook of Texas Online*, s.v. "," http://www.tsha-online.org/handbook/online/articles/FF/apf1.html

[52] *West U Magazine*, Decembe r, 1993

[53] Webb, Walter Prescott, *The Handbook of Texas* (Texas Historical Assn 1952), Vol. 1, 640-1

[54] Katy Heritage Society interview, 2009

[55] http://www.tennisfame.com/

[56] Houston District Designation Report, HPO file no. 08hd12, 2008

[57] Laffin, John, *Brassey's Dictionary of Battles: 3,500 Years Of Conflict, Campaigns and Wars* (Barnes & Noble Books 1986), 174

[58] http://www.katytexas.com

[59] Macon, N. Don, *Mr. John H. Freeman and Friends: A Story of the Texas Medical Center and How It Began* (Texas Medical Center 1973), 57-63

[60] *Handbook of Texas Online*, s.v. "," http://www.tsha-online.org/handbook/online/articles/FF/hef3.html

[61] "FRESNO, TX." *The Handbook of Texas Online.* <http://www.tsha.utexas.edu/handbook/online/articles/view/FF/hlf29.html>

[62] "FRIENDSWOOD, TX." *The Handbook of Texas Online.* <http://www.tsha.utexas.edu/handbook/online/articles/view/FF/hef4.html>

[63] http://www.springvalleytx.com

[64] Field Trip with George Donehoo, 2005

[65] Wallingford, Sharon, *Fort Bend County Texas: A Pictorial History* (Fort Bend Publishing Group 1996), 147

[66] Webb, Walter Prescott, *The Hand Book of Texas* (Texas Historical Assn. 1952), Vol. 1, 654

[67] Field trip 2009

[68] Houghton, Dorothy Knox Howe, Interview 2002

[69] *The American Heritage Dictionary of the English Language:* Third Edition (Houghton Mifflin Company 1992), 736

G

[1] "GOOSE CREEK OILFIELD." *The Handbook of Texas Online.* <http://www.tsha.utexas.edu/handbook/online/articles/view/GG/dog1.html>

[2] http://www.lib.rochester.edu/camelot

[3] "GALENA PARK, TX." *The Handbook of Texas Online.* <http://www.tsha.utexas.edu/handbook/online/articles/view/GG/hfg1.html>

[4] Doolittle, Bill, *The Kentucky Derby: Run for the Roses* (Time Life Books 1998), 156

[5] Webb, Walter Prescott, *The Hand Book of Texas* (Texas State Historical Assn. 1952), Vol. 1, 662

[6] *Houston and Harris County Facts* – Houston Public Library – Texas Room

[7] *Houston Chronicle*, June 27, 1981

[8] Teten, Paul, Interview 2001

[9] Teten, Paul, Interview 2001

[10] www.txrmref@hpl.lib.tx.us, May 24, 2000

[11] Texas Historical Marker, 19 Courtlandt Place, erected 1997

[12] "GASTON, TX." *The Handbook of Texas Online.* <http://www.tsha.utexas.edu/handbook/online/articles/view/GG/htg2.html>

[13] *Encyclopedia Britannica* (1952), Volume 10, 70-1

[14] *Encyclopedia Britannica* (1952), Volume 10, 73-4

[15] Wood, Jerry, Deputy Assistant Director City of Houston Planning & Development Department, Interview 2002

[16] Beverly, Trevia W., *At Rest: A Historical Directory of Harris County, Texas Cemeteries (1822-1992)*, 37

[17] Montgomery County Parks Department, interview 2009

[18] Johnson, Liz, Port of Houston, e-mail, 2005

[19] *Houston and Harris County Facts* – Houston Public Library - Texas Room

[20] www.georgetown.edu

[21] Garraty, John A. Editor, *Encyclopedia of American Biography* (Harper & Row 1974), 414

[22] *Parade*, May 3, 1981

[23] Laffin, John, *Brassey's Dictionary of Battles: 3,500 Years Of Conflict, Campaigns and Wars* (Barnes & Noble Books 1986), 181

[24] http://www.accessgenealogy.com

[25] http://www.hansonpipeandproducts.com

[26] Webb, Walter Prescott, *The Hand Book of Texas* (Texas State Historical Assn. 1952), Vol. 1, 691

[27] Field trip with George Donehoo, 2009

[28] Ferris, Kirk, Interview 2001

[29] http://www.tomahawkdistrict.org

[30] *Encyclopedia Britannica* (1952), Volume 10, 421-3

[31] *Houston Chronicle*, September 28, 2008

32 www.gleneagles.com

33 Teich, Len & Susan, interview 2008

34 http://www.referencecenter.com

35 http://www.imh.org

36 http://ww.ftp.rootsweb.com

37 http://www.sfmuseum.org/

38 Handbook of Texas Online, s.v. "," http://www.tsha-online.org/handbook/online/articles/GG/hrgzj.html

39 Handbook of Texas Online, s.v. "," http://www.tsha-online.org/handbook/online/articles/GG/hjg5.html

40 Webb, Walter Prescott, The Hand Book of Texas (Texas State Historical Assn. 1952), Vol. 1, 699-703

41 West U Magazine, December, 1993

42 Webb, Walter Prescott, The Handbook of Texas (Texas Historical Assn 1952), Vol. 1, 709

43 Kimball, Mary Holt, et al, The Heritage of North Harris County (American Association of University Women 1977), 67

44 Fieldtrip 2001

45 "GOOSE CREEK, TX." The Handbook of Texas Online. <http://www.tsha.utexas.edu/handbook/online/articles/view/GG/hvg32.html>

46 en.wikipedia.org

47 http://www.hertiagemuseum.us

48 Houston District Designation Report, HPO file no. 08hd12, 2008

49 Blessington, J. P., The Campaigns of Walker's Texas Division (Pemberton Press 1968), 54

50 ad.doubleclick.net

51 "MOONSHINE HILL, TX." The Handbook of Texas Online. <http://www.tsha.utexas.edu/handbook/online/articles/view/MM/hrmnl.html>

52 Houston District Designation Report, HPO file no. 08hd12, 2008

53 Handbook of Texas Online, s.v. "," http://www.tsha-online.org/handbook/online/articles/GG/hrg81.html

54 Old Houston maps

55 Johnston, Marguerite, Houston: the Unknown City, 1836-1946 (Texas A & M 1991), 21, 57, 88

56 http://www.mahalo.com/

57 "GREENS BAYOU." The Handbook of Texas Online. <http://www.tsha.utexas.edu/handbook/online/articles/view/GG/rhg3.html>

58 Prather, Patricia Smith, Interview 2002

59 "GRIMES, ALFRED CALVIN." The Handbook of Texas Online. <http://www.tsha.utexas.edu/handbook/online/articles/view/GG/fgram.html>

60 http://www.hq.nasa.gov

61 Houston Chronicle, undated

62 "MAGNOLIA, TX." The Handbook of Texas Online. <http://www.tsha.utexas.edu/handbook/online/articles/view/MM/hlm23.html>

63 Wallingford, Sharon, Fort Bend County Texas: A Pictorial History (Fort Bend Publishing Group 1996), 143

64 Laffin, John, Brassey's Dictionary of Battles: 3,500 Years of Conflict, Campaigns and Wars (Barnes & Noble, 1986), 187-8

65 Handbook of Texas Online, s.v. "," http://www.tsha-online.org/handbook/online/articles/VV/hdv1.html

66 Houston Post, August 3, 1951

67 Field trip, 2009

68 Field trip, 2008

69 www.gulfoil.com

70 "GUM GULLY." The Handbook of Texas Online. <http://www.tsha.utexas.edu/handbook/online/articles/view/GG/rbg93.html>

71 Field trip, 2003

H

1 Raia, John B., Interview 2001

2 Houston Post, January 2, 1938

3 Field trip, 2001

4 Handbook of Texas Online, s.v. "," http://www.tsha-online.org/handbook/online/articles/HH/rbh23.html

5 www.wardocuments.com

6 Webb, Walter Prescott, The Hand Book of Texas (Texas State Historical Assn. 1952), Vol. 1, 760

7 Garraty, John A. Editor, Encyclopedia of American Biography (Harper & Row 1974), 476-7

8 Webb, Walter Prescott, The Handbook of Texas (Texas Historical Assn 1952), Vol. 1, 765

9 Field trip 2008

10 Garraty, John A. Editor, Encyclopedia of American Biography (Harper & Row 1974), 483-5

11 Beverly, Trevia W., At Rest: A Historical Directory of Harris County, Texas Cemeteries (1822-1992), 40

12 Handbook of Texas Online, s.v. "JESTER STATE PRISON FARM," http://www.tsha.utexas.edu/handbook/online/articles/view

13 Andrew, P., interview 2009

14 Encyclopedia Britannica (1952), Volume 11, 214-15

15 Handbook of Texas Online, s.v. "," http://www.tsha-online.org/handbook/online/articles/HH/hch7.html

16 Handbook of Texas Online, s.v. "," http://www.tsha-online.org/handbook/online/articles/HH/rohms.html

17 Fort Bend County Sesquicentennial 1822-1972 (Commemorative Booklet Committee 1972),, 65

18 Texas Historical Marker, El Jardine del Mar Park, Palm at Park streets, Seabrook, erected 1981

19 Works Projects Administration, Houston: A History & Guide (Anson Jones Press 1942), 295-7

20 Garraty, John A. Editor, Encyclopedia of American Biography (Harper & Row 1974), 495-6

21 Houston Metropolitan Research Center Files, Houston Public Library

22 Hinton, C. Marks Sr., Interview 1960

23 Webb, Walter Prescott, The Handbook of Texas (Texas Historical Assn 1952), Vol. 1, 783

24 Webb, Walter Prescott, The Hand Book of Texas (Texas Historical Assn. 1952), Vol. 1, 784

25 Kimball, Mary Holt, et al, The Heritage of North Harris County (American Association of University Women 1977), 75

26 Garraty, John A. Editor, Encyclopedia of American Biography (Harper & Row 1974), 500-2

27 "HEDWIG VILLAGE, TX." The Handbook of Texas Online. <http://www.tsha.utexas.edu/handbook/online/articles/view/HH/hgh6.html>

28 Kimball, Mary Holt, et al, *The Heritage of North Harris County* (American Association of University Women 1977), 54

29 Houston Metropolotian Research Center Files, Houston Public Library

30 *Houston Business Journal,* August 6-12, 2004

31 Inner-View, March 1982

32 Texas Historical Marker, 2525 Washington Ave., Houston, erected 2000

33 "HEMPHILL, JOHN." *The Handbook of Texas Online.* <http://www.tsha.utexas.edu/handbook/online/articles/view/HH/fhe13.html>

34 *Old Sixth Ward Reporter,* December, 1979, 2

35 Henson, Margaret Sweet, *The History of Baytown* (Bay Area Heritage Society 1986), 137

36 "HEMPSTEAD, TX." *The Handbook of Texas Online.* <http://www.tsha.utexas.edu/handbook/online/articles/view/HH/hgh7.html>

37 *Old Sixth Ward Reporter,* December, 1979, 2

38 Writers' Program of the Work Projects Administration, *Houston: A History and Guide* (Anson Jones Press 1942), 156

39 http://www.ci.shreveport.la.us

40 *Houston Chronicle,* June 20, 1980(?)

41 www.ansi.okstate.edu

42 Writers' Program of the Work Projects Administration, *Houston: A History and Guide* (Anson Jones Press 1942), 278

43 Christensen, Roberta, *Historic-Romantic Richmond* (Nortex Press, 1982), 101

44 *Houston and Harris County Facts* – Houston Public Library – Texas Room

45 Hill, Nina Lee and Nancy, interview 2009

46 http://www.horse-races.net

47 Http://en.wikipedia.org

48 www.mexconnect.com

49 "MOONSHINE HILL, TX." *The Handbook of Texas Online.* <http://www.tsha.utexas.edu/handbook/online/articles/view/MM/hrmnl.html>

50 Webb, Walter Prescott, *The Hand Book of Texas* (Texas Historical Assn. 1952), Vol. 1, 808

51 Witt, Dorothy, interview 2002

52 "HIGHLANDS, TX." *The Handbook of Texas Online.* <http://www.tsha.utexas.edu/handbook/online/articles/view/HH/hfh4.html>

53 Fieldtrip 2001

54 *Houston Chronicle,* August 29, 2001

55 Houston Press, August 7, 1930

56 Webb, Walter Prescott, *The Hand Book of Texas* (Texas Historical Assn. 1952), Vol. 1, 346

57 *Hinton Family History,* unpublished

58 www.hbu.edu

59 Fieldtrip 2001

60 Houston Metropolitan Research Center Files, Houston Public Library

61 *Encyclopedia Britannica* 2005 Ultimate Reference Suite CD/ROM

62 *Handbook of Texas Online,* s.v. "," http://www.tsha-online.org/handbook/online/articles/HH/hfh6.html

63 ad.doubleclick.net

64 "BLUE RIDGE, TX." *The Handbook of Texas Online.* <http://www.tsha.utexas.edu/handbook/online/articles/view/BB/hnb51.html>

65 "HOCKLEY, TX." *The Handbook of Texas Online.* <http://www.tsha.utexas.edu/handbook/online/articles/view/HH/hlh49.html>

66 http://tsr.4101.org

67 Kimball, Mary Holt, et al, *The Heritage of North Harris County* (American Association of University Women 1977), 61, 64

68 Pomeroy, C. David Jr., Pasadena: The Early Years (Pomerosa Press 1993), 34

69 Gurasich, Marj, *History of Harris County Sheriff's Department: 1837-1983,* 11-13

70 www.referencecenter.com

71 Johnston, Marguerite, *Houston: the Unknown City, 1836-1946* (Texas A & M 1991), 219-21

72 Texas Historical Marker, Hufsmith

73 Field trip 1980

74 Field trip, 2004

75 Writers' Program of the Work Projects Administration, *Houston: A History and Guide* (Anson Jones Press 1942), 47

76 *Houston Chronicle,* August 16, 2004

77 www.vatican.va

78 http://ww.ftp.rootsweb.com

79 Hinton, C. Marks, Sr., Interview 1999

80 *Encyclopedia Britannica* (1952), Volume 11, 688-99

81 Garraty, John A. Editor, *Encyclopedia of American Biography* (Harper & Row 1974), 534-6

82 http://www.referencecenter.com

83 *Handbook of Texas Online,* s.v. "," http://www.tsha-online.org/handbook/online/articles/WW/hfw1.html

84 Wallingford, Sharon, *Fort Bend County Texas: A Pictorial History* (Fort Bend Publishing Group 1996), 104

85 *City of Spring Valley, Texas: Fifty Years 1955-2005,* First Draft 10-22-2005, 9-10

86 *Handbook of Texas Online,* s.v. "," http://www.tsha-online.org/handbook/online/articles/SS/dks4.html

87 Upchurch, Lessie, *Welcome to Tomball: A History of Tomball, Texas* (D. Armstrong Co. 1995), 188

88 Field trip 2009

89 Henry, Mary Lou, Interview 2002

90 Kimball, Mary Holt, et al, *The Heritage of North Harris County* (American Association of University Women 1977), 17-20

91 Field trip, 2002

92 "HOUSTON CHRONICLE." *The Handbook of Texas Online.* <http://www.tsha.utexas.edu/handbook/online/articles/view/HH/eeh2.html>

93 Field trip, 2000

94 Houghton, Dorothy Knox Howe, Interview 2002

95 *Handbook of Texas Online,* s.v. "," http://www.tsha-online.org/handbook/online/articles/SS/hfs10.html

96 Miller, Mary Catherine Farrington, *Tanglewood: The Story of William Giddings Farrington* (Gulf Publishing Company 1989), 43

[97] "HUFFMAN, TX." *The Handbook of Texas Online.* <http://www.tsha.utexas.edu/handbook/online/articles/view/HH/hnh49.html>

[98] Houston Metropolitan Research Center Files, Houston Public Library

[99] Upchurch, Lessie, *Welcome to Tomball: A History of Tomball, Texas* (D. Armstrong 1976), 37

[100] *Baytown Sun,* May 13, 1996

[101] *Fort Bend County Sesquicentennial 1822-1972* (Commemorative Booklet Committee 1972), 65

[102] *Handbook of Texas Online,* s.v. "HUGHES, HOWARD ROBARD, SR," http://www.tsha.utexas.edu/handbook/online/articles/view/HH/fhu16.html

[103] www.glossary.oilfield.slb.com/

[104] "HUMBLE, TX." *The Handbook of Texas Online.* <http://www.tsha.utexas.edu/handbook/online/articles/view/HH/hfh8.html>

[105] Webb, Walter Prescott, *The Hand Book of Texas* (Texas State Historical Assn. 1952), Vol. 1, 863

[106] Field Trip, 2001

[107] *River Oaks Times,* September 10, 1948

[108] Laffin, John, *Brassey's Dictionary of Battles: 3,500 Years Of Conflict, Campaigns and Wars* (Barnes & Noble Books 1986), 200

[109] *Handbook of Texas Online,* s.v. "," http://www.tshaonline.org/handbook/online/articles/WW/kcw5.html

[110] Houghton, Dorothy Knox Howe, et al, *Houston's Forgotten Heritage: Landscape, Houses, Interiors, 1824-1914* (Rice University Press 1991), 37, 132

[111] Webb, Walter Prescott, *The Hand Book of Texas* (Texas Historical Assn. 1952), Vol. 1, 870

[112] Writers' Program of the Work Projects Administration, *Houston: A History and Guide* (Anson Jones Press 1942), 96

[113] http://www.royalparks.org.uk

[114] Fieldtrip 2001

I

[1] http://www.igloocoolers.com and field trip 2007

[2] "IMPERIAL SUGAR COMPANY." *The Handbook of Texas Online.* <http://www.tsha.utexas.edu/handbook/online/articles/view/II/diicy.html>

[3] Raia, John B., Interview 2001

[4] Teten, Paul, Interview 2001

[5] Baron, Steven M., *Electric Houston: The Street Railways of Houston, Texas* (Steven M. Baron 1996), 184-8

[6] Robin Elverson Realtors, Sales Brochure

[7] River Oaks Property Owners Association, Interview & Records

[8] *Handbook of Texas Online,* s.v. "," http://www.tshaonline.org/handbook/online/articles/II/hli8.html

[9] www.drf.com

[10] Allen, Thomas B., *The Blue and the Gray* (National Geographic 1992), 120-1

[11] Wharton, Charles R., *History of Fort Bend County* (Naylor & Co. 1939), 15, 26

[12] Texas Historical Marker, 110 W. Main, Humble, erected 1972

[13] Peterson, Martha, Comment 2003

[14] www.mindspring.com

[15] Barrus, Thu Nhi, Interview 2002

[16] Laffin, John, *Brassey's Dictionary of Battles: 3,500 Years Of Conflict, Campaigns and Wars* (Barnes & Noble Books 1986), 210

J

[1] *Baytown Sun,* May 13, 1996

[2] *Houston Chronicle,* September 28, 2008

[3] http://www.virtualtourist.com

[4] Garraty, John A. Editor, *Encyclopedia of American Biography* (Harper & Row 1974), 683-4

[5] Henson, Margaret Sweet, *The History of Baytown* (Bay Area Heritage Society 1986), NEED PAGE NUMBER

[6] Texas Historical Marker, Old U. S. 90 near Crosby-Lynchburg Road, Crosby, erected 1982

[7] *Handbook of Texas Online,* s.v. "," http://www.tshaonline.org/handbook/online/articles/JJ/rhj1.html

[8] *Handbook of Texas Online,* s.v. "," http://www.tshaonline.org/handbook/online/articles/JJ/fja29.html

[9] *Encyclopedia Britannica* (1952), Volume 12, 851-3

[10] *Handbook of Texas Online,* s.v. "," http://www.tshaonline.org/handbook/online/articles/JJ/hvj1.html

[11] Webb, Walter Prescott, *The Hand Book of Texas* (Texas State Historical Assn. 1952), Vol. 1, 197

[12] Webb, Walter Prescott, *The Handbook of Texas* (Texas Historical Assn 1952), Vol. 2, 76

[13] Teten, Paul, Interview 2001

[14] Begeman, June A., *Stepping Back In Time: History of West University Place,* (D. Armstrong 1999), 11

[15] *Encyclopedia Britannica* (1952), Volume 13, 589

[16] Paterson, Melissa M., *The Road to Piney Point* (Piney Point Village Historic Committee 1994), 61

[17] www.jebstuart.org

[18] Wallingford, Sharon, *Fort Bend County Texas: A Pictorial History* (Fort Bend Publishing Group 1996), 115

[19] http://www.en.wikipedia.org

[20] Houston Metropolitan Research Center Files, Houston Public Library

[21] Adkins, John, e-mail 2008

[22] Raia, John B., Interview 2001

[23] "JERSEY VILLAGE, TX." *The Handbook of Texas Online.* <http://www.tsha.utexas.edu/handbook/online/articles/view/JJ/hgj6.html>

[24] http://www.houstonairportsystem.org

[25] Webb, Walter Prescott, *The Handbook of Texas* (Texas Historical Assn 1952), Vol. 1, 911-12

[26] www.lib.utexas.edu/taro/tslac

[27] Miller, Mary Catherine Farrington, Interview 2001

[28] *Encyclopedia Britannica* (1952), Volume 13, 72-5

[29] www.worldbookonline.com/

[30] Wallingford, Sharon, *Fort Bend County Texas: A Pictorial History* (Fort Bend Publishing Group 1996), 132

[31] http://www.findagrave.com

[32] http://www.ourbaytown.com

[33] http://www.johncooper.org/

[34] Raia, John B., Interview 2001

35 Macon, N. Don, *Mr. John H. Freeman and Friends: A Story of the Texas Medical Center and How It Began* (Texas Medical Center 1973), 57-63
36 www.colonialhall.com
37 *Baytown Sun*, May 13, 1996
38 Upchurch, Lessie, *Welcome to Tomball: A History of Tomball, Texas* (D. Armstrong Co. 1995), 65
39 *Houston Chronicle*, February 3, 2002
40 Pomeroy, C. David Jr., *Pasadena: The Early Years* (Pomerosa Press 1993), 29, 30
41 North Channel Area Map, North Channel Chamber of Commerce, 1988
42 http://www.accessgenealogy.com
43 Wallingford, Sharon, *Fort Bend County Texas: A Pictorial History* (Fort Bend Publishing Group 1996), 117
44 www.mexconnect.com
45 Kimball, Mary Holt, et al, *The Heritage of North Harris County* (American Association of University Women 1977), 59
46 *Handbook of Texas Online*, s.v. ",", http://www.tsha-online.org/handbook/online/articles/JJ/hlj15.html
47 *Handbook of Texas Online*, s.v. ",", http://www.tsha-online.org/handbook/online/articles/WW/kcw5.html
48 Wallingford, Sharon, *Fort Bend County Texas: A Pictorial History* (Fort Bend Publishing Group 1996), 165
49 Laffin, John, *Brassey's Dictionary of Battles: 3,500 Years Of Conflict, Campaigns and Wars* (Barnes & Noble Books 1986), 215

K

1 Houston Metropolitan Research Center Files, Houston Public Library
2 Webb, Walter Prescott, *The Hand Book of Texas* (Texas State Historical Assn. 1952), Vol. 1, 938
3 *Handbook of Texas Online*, s.v. ",", http://www.tsha-online.org/handbook/online/articles/KK/htk2.html
4 Laffin, John, *Brassey's Dictionary of Battles: 3,500 Years Of Conflict, Campaigns and Wars* (Barnes & Noble Books 1986), 220
5 www.katytexas.com
6 *Handbook of Texas Online*, s.v. ",", http://www.tsha-online.org/handbook/online/articles/FF/hlf34.html
7 "KATY, TX." *The Handbook of Texas Online.* <http://www.tsha.utexas.edu/handbook/online/articles/view/KK/hfk1.html>
8 *Encyclopedia Britannica* (1952), Volume 13, 307-9
9 "KEEGANS BAYOU." *The Handbook of Texas Online.* <http://www.tsha.utexas.edu/handbook/online/articles/view/KK/rhk2.html>
10 *Handbook of Texas Online*, s.v. ",", http://www.tsha-online.org/handbook/online/articles/KK/hvk3.html
11 Prather, Patricia Smith & Lee, Bob, *Texas Trailblazer Series* (Texas Trailblazer Preservation Association, 1992-7)
12 http://www.geocities.com
13 Prather, Patricia Smith & Lee, Bob, *Texas Trailblazer Series* (Texas Trailblazer Preservation Association, 1992-7)

14 "KEMAH, TX." *The Handbook of Texas Online.* <http://www.tsha.utexas.edu/handbook/online/articles/view/KK/hjk1.html>
15 "KEMPNER, ISAAC HERBERT." *The Handbook of Texas Online.* <http://www.tsha.utexas.edu/hand-book/online/articles/view/KK/fke56.html>
16 www.texasmonthly.com
17 Early Houston map
18 *Handbook of Texas Online*, s.v. ",", http://www.tsha-online.org/handbook/online/articles/SS/hls22.html
19 http://www.nps.gov
20 Ibid.
21 Doolittle, Bill, *The Kentucky Derby: Run for the Roses* (Time Life Books 1998), 119
22 *Houston Business Journal*, June 29, 2007
23 "KESSLER, HENRY." *The Handbook of Texas Online.* <http://www.tsha.utexas.edu/handbook/online/articles/view/KK/fke37.html>
24 Houston District Designation Report, HPO file no. 08hd12, 2008
25 "KICKAPOO CREEK." *The Handbook of Texas Online.* <http://www.tsha.utexas.edu/handbook/online/articles/view/KK/rbk16.html>
26 www.kickerillo.com
27 Field trip with George Donehoo, 2009
28 Blessington, J. P., *The Campaigns of Walker's Texas Division* (Pemberton Press 1968), 56
29 Henson, Margaret Sweet, *The History of Baytown* (Bay Area Heritage Society 1986), NEED 62-138
30 Webb, Walter Prescott, The Handbook of Texas (Texas State Historical Association 1952), 961
31 Field trip, 2004 celebrating the 150th anniversary of the King Ranch
32 http://en.wikipedia.org/wiki/Third_Crusade
33 Webb, Walter Prescott, *The Hand Book of Texas* (Texas State Historical Assn. 1952), Vol. 1, 960
34 www.kingwoodmedical.com
35 "KINGWOOD, TX." *The Handbook of Texas Online.* <http://www.tsha.utexas.edu/handbook/online/articles/view/KK/hrk23.html>
36 Texas Historical Marker, 201 Kinkaid Drive, Houston, erected 1981
37 *Encyclopedia Britannica* (1952), Volume 13, 409-10
38 www.kipphouston.org/
39 www.kemah.net
40 *Handbook of Texas Online*, s.v. ",", http://www.tsha-online.org/handbook/online/articles/KK/hrk30.html
41 "KIRBY, JOHN HENRY." *The Handbook of Texas Online.* <http://www.tsha.utexas.edu/handbook/online/articles/view/KK/fki33.html>
42 www.tshaonline.org
43 Kimball, Mary Holt, et al, *The Heritage of North Harris County* (American Association of University Women 1977), 51
44 *Houston Chronicle*, September 29 2004
45 Webb, Walter Prescott, The Handbook of Texas (Texas State Historical Association 1952), 968
46 www.artcyclopedia.com

[47] "KLEIN, TX." *The Handbook of Texas Online.* <http://www.tsha.utexas.edu/handbook/online/articles/view/KK/hrk19.html>

[48] *Handbook of Texas Online,* s.v. "," http://www.tsha-online.org/handbook/online/articles/CC/hrcde.html

[49] Field Trip with George Donehoo, 2005

[50] Field Trip with George Donehoo, 2005

[51] www.fortbendisd.com/

[52] River Oaks Property Owners Association, Interview & Records

[53] Beverly, Trevia Wooster, e-mail 2009

[54] Houghton, Dorothy Knox Howe, Interview 2002

[55] Beverly, Trevia W., *At Rest: A Historical Directory of Harris County, Texas Cemeteries (1822-1992),* 48

[56] Upchurch, Lessie, *Welcome to Tomball: A History of Tomball, Texas* (D. Armstrong 1976), 13

[57] Beverly, Trevia W., *At Rest: A Historical Directory of Harris County, Texas Cemeteries (1822-1992),* 40

[58] www.prague-tribune.cz/

[59] "KOHRVILLE, TX." *The Handbook of Texas Online.* <http://www.tsha.utexas.edu/handbook/online/articles/view/KK/hrk18.html>

[60] *The Leader,* undated

[61] Paterson, Melissa M., *The Road to Piney Point* (Piney Point Village Historic Committee 1994), 36

[62] Wallingford, Sharon, *Fort Bend County Texas: A Pictorial History* (Fort Bend Publishing Group 1996), 100

[63] Kimball, Mary Holt, et al, *The Heritage of North Harris County* (American Association of University Women 1977), 58

[64] Field trip 2009

[65] www.wolfsonian.fiu.edu

[66] http://www.geocities.com

[67] Beverly, Trevia W., *At Rest: A Historical Directory of Harris County, Texas Cemeteries (1822-1992),* 48

[68] *The Heritage of North Harris County* (American Association of University Women 1978), 100

[69] Beverly, Trevia W., *At Rest: A Historical Directory of Harris County, Texas Cemeteries (1822-1992),* 48

[70] Field trip 2001

[71] Raia, John B., Interview 2001

[72] Field trip, 2001

[73] Wallingford, Sharon, *Fort Bend County Texas: A Pictorial History* (Fort Bend Publishing Group 1996), 116

L

[1] "LA PORTE, TX." *The Handbook of Texas Online.* <http://www.tsha.utexas.edu/handbook/online/articles/view/LL/hel2.html>

[2] *Encyclopedia Britannica* (1952), Volume 13, 731

[3] *Bayou City Banner,* July 30, 1971

[4] www.tennisfame.org

[5] http://www.lafayette.edu

[6] Blessington, J. P., *The Campaigns of Walker's Texas Division*

[7] Http://www.lakeconroe.com

[8] "LAKE HOUSTON." *The Handbook of Texas Online.* <http://www.tsha.utexas.edu/handbook/online/articles/view/LL/rol42.html>

[9] Rau, J. M., *Key Maps: Houston Harris County Atlas* 44th Edition (Key Maps 2002), 620

[10] www.lakewoodyachtclub.com/ and www.keels-wheels.com

[11] Macon, N. Don, *Mr. John H. Freeman and Friends: A Story of the Texas Medical Center and How It Began* (Texas Medical Center 1973), 57-63

[12] Webb, Walter Prescott, *The Hand Book of Texas* (Texas State Historical Assn. 1952), Vol. 2, 13-14

[13] *Handbook of Texas Online,* s.v. "," http://www.tsha-online.org/handbook/online/articles/PP/hnp43.html

[14] *Handbook of Texas Online,* s.v. "," http://www.tsha-online.org/handbook/online/articles/LL/rbl24.html

[15] *River Oaks Times,* September 10, 1948

[16] Johnston, Marguerite, *Houston: the Unknown City, 1836-1946* (Texas A & M 1991), 152

[17] Webb, Walter Prescott, *The Hand Book of Texas* (Texas State Historical Association 1952), Vol. 2, 34

[18] Houghton, Dorothy Knox Howe, Interview 2002

[19] *Houston Chronicle,* June 20, 1980

[20] *El Paso Times,* June 18, 1928

[21] www.worldbookonline.com/

[22] www.infoplease.com

[23] Pace, G. Randle "Randy", Interview 2001

[24] *River Oaks Times,* September 10, 1948

[25] "LEAGUE CITY, TX." *The Handbook of Texas Online.* <http://www.tsha.utexas.edu/handbook/online/articles/view/LL/hel6.html>

[26] Henson, Margaret Sweet, *The History of Baytown* (Bay Area Heritage Society 1986)

[27] *Handbook of Texas Online,* s.v. "LA PORTE, TX," http://www.tsha.utexas.edu/handbook/online/articles/view/LL/hel2.html

[28] http://www.sanjacinto-museum.org/veterans

[29] For Preservation, March/April 1991

[30] http://www.wikipedia.org

[31] http://www3.lehigh.edu

[32] Field trip, 2001

[33] Baines, Mrs. W. M., *Houston's Part in the World War* (1919)

[34] www.lib.utexas.edu

[35] *Handbook of Texas Online,* s.v. "," http://www.tsha-online.org/handbook/online/articles/LL/hrl25.html

[36] *Handbook of Texas Online,* s.v. "," http://www.tsha-online.org/handbook/online/articles/EE/hje3.html

[37] *Houston Chronicle,* April 16, 1997

[38] Hill, Nina Lee and Nancy, interview 2009

[39] "LIBERTY, TX." *The Handbook of Texas Online.* <http://www.tsha.utexas.edu/handbook/online/articles/view/LL/hfl4.html>

[40] www.cfisd.net

[41] Webb, Walter Prescott, *The Hand Book of Texas* (Texas Historical Assn. 1952), Vol. 2, 55-6

[42] Fieldtrip 2001

[43] *Houston Chronicle,* June 20, 1980(?)

[44] Detering, Deborah, Interview 2001

45   Texas Historical Marker, Avenue A and Fifth Street, Katy, erected 1984

46   Webb, Walter Prescott, *The Handbook of Texas* (Texas State Historical Association 1952), Vol. 2, 61-2

47   *Handbook of Texas Online*, s.v. ",", http://www.tshaonline.org/handbook/online/articles/LL/rbl69.html

48   "LITTLE YORK, TX." *The Handbook of Texas Online*. <http://www.tsha.utexas.edu/handbook/online/articles/view/LL/hvl60.html>

49   *Handbook of Texas Online*, s.v. ",", http://www.tshaonline.org/handbook/online/articles/LL/etl2.html

50   Texas Historical Markers, Liverpool, erected 1966 and 1998

51   *Handbook of Texas Online*, s.v. ",", http://www.tshaonline.org/handbook/online/articles/RR/hlr42.html

52   River Oaks Property Owners Association, Interview & Records

53   Early Houston map

54   www.lockheedmartin.com

55   Texas Historical Marker, Arnot & Haskell, erected 1992

56   *Handbook of Texas Online*, s.v. ",", http://www.tshaonline.org/handbook/online/articles/LL/hgl10.html

57   Henry, Mary Lou, Interview 2002

58   *Encyclopedia Britannica* (1952), Volume 14, 378-9

59   *Houston Chronicle*, August 8, 1956

60   Miller, Mary Catherine Farrington, Interview 2001

61   Hinton, Marks, *One Ocean and Seven Seas* (Archival Press of Texas 2009), 44-7

62   Zuber, Harry, Interview 2005

63   Herridge, Karen, *Spring Branch Heritage* (Wakebrook Press 1998), 23

64   "LOUETTA, TX." *The Handbook of Texas Online*. <http://www.tsha.utexas.edu/handbook/online/articles/view/LL/htl20.html>

65   Wood, Jerry, Interview 2001

66   Daughters of the Republic of Texas, Interview 2001

67   http:www.sealycvb.org

68   Houghton, Dorothy Knox Howe, Interview 2002

69   Wood, Jerry, Interview 2001

70   Houghton, Dorothy Knox Howe, et al, *Houston's Forgotten Heritage: Landscape, Houses, Interiors, 1824-1914* (Rice University Press 1991), 97, 171

71   http://ci.katy.tx.us

72   Hinton, Marks, long time visitor to Luckenbach

73   Weidig, Barbara Y., *Deer Park: A History of a Texas Town* (Naylor Company 1976), 79-81

74   *Houston Chronicle*, June 20, 1980

75   Miller, Mary Catherine Farrington, *Tanglewood: The Story of William Giddings Farrington* (Gulf Publishing Company 1989), 43

76   Texas Historical Marker, U. S. 90, Houston

77   Fifth Ward, Houston Texas, circa 1915-1920, September 1982

M

1   Macon, N. Don, *Mr. John H. Freeman and Friends: A Story of the Texas Medical Center and How It Began* (Texas Medical Center 1973), 57-63

2   Raia, John B., Interview 2001

3   Garraty, John A. Editor, *Encyclopedia of American Biography* (Harper & Row 1974), 700-703

4   *Encyclopedia Britannica* (1952), Volume 14, 548

5   http://www.geocities.com

6   Webb, Walter Prescott, *The Handbook of Texas* (Texas State Historical Association 1952), Vol. 2, 113

7   Holmes, Ann H., *Joy Unconfined: Robert Joy In Houston* (San Jacinto Museum of History Association 1986), 103-6

8   Maczali, Dorothy L., interview 2009

9   Garraty, John A. Editor, *Encyclopedia of American Biography* (Harper & Row 1974), 719-20

10   *Encyclopedia Britannica* (1952), Volume 14, 623-4

11   http://www.hertiagemuseum.us

12   Kimball, Mary Holt, et al, *The Heritage of North Harris County* (American Association of University Women 1977), 39

13   Upchurch, Lessie, *Welcome to Tomball: A History of Tomball, Texas* (D. Armstrong Co. 1995), 84

14   Old Houston maps

15   Texas State Historical Marker, 1417 Avenue A, Galveston, erected 1965

16   Doolittle, Bill, *The Kentucky Derby: Run for the Roses* (Time Life Books 1998), 152

17   Carroll, Benajah H., *Standard History of Houston, Texas* (no publisher listed – undated), 430, 432

18   http://www.historyplace.com

19   Webb, Walter Prescott, *The Hand Book of Texas* (Texas State Historical Assn. 1952), Vol. 2, 134

20   Blessington, J. P., *The Campaigns of Walker's Texas Division* (Pemberton Press 1968)

21   Rice, Timothy J., Interview 2001

22   Laffin, John, *Brassey's Dictionary of Battles: 3,500 Years Of Conflict, Campaigns and Wars* (Barnes & Noble Books 1986), 91

23   "MANCHESTER, TX." *The Handbook of Texas Online*. <http://www.tsha.utexas.edu/handbook/online/articles/view/MM/hvm20.html>

24   Mangum, Michael, interview 2009

25   *Handbook of Texas Online*, s.v. ",", http://www.tshaonline.org/handbook/online/articles/MM/hgm2.html

26   Miller, Mary Catherine Farrington, *Tanglewood: The Story of William Giddings Farrington* (Gulf Publishing Company 1989), 43

27   Beverly, Trevia Wooster and Holland, Wybra Wooster, e-mail 2009

28   Field trip, 2002

29   Wallingford, Sharon, *Fort Bend County Texas: A Pictorial History* (Fort Bend Publishing Group 1996), 104

30   Adkins, John, e-mail 2008

31   *Houston Chronicle*, August 12, 1956

32   *Encyclopedia Britannica* (1952), Volume 14, 924-6

33   www.marquette.edu

[34] Kimball, Mary Holt, et al, *The Heritage of North Harris County* (American Association of University Women 1977), 62

[35] Greater Houston Preservation Alliance, *Historic Neighborhoods Council e-Newsletter*, May, 2004, 4

[36] Garraty, John A. Editor, *Encyclopedia of American Biography* (Harper & Row 1974), 620-22

[37] Special Collections/Archives, John B. Coleman Library, Prairie View A & M University, Prairie View, Texas

[38] Christensen, Roberta, *Historic-Romantic Richmond* (Nortex Press, 1982), iii

[39] Raia, John B., Interview 2001

[40] Henry, Mary Lou, Interview 2002

[41] *Handbook of Texas Online*, s.v. "," http://www.tsha-online.org/handbook/online/articles/NN/fno15.html

[42] *Handbook of Texas Online*, s.v. "," http://www.tsha-online.org/handbook/online/articles/MM/rhm1.html

[43] Field trip 2009

[44] Henson, Margaret Sweet, *The History of Baytown* (Bay Area Heritage Society 1986), 42

[45] http://www.masters.org

[46] *Houston Chronicle*, September 29 2004

[47] *Encyclopedia Britannica* (1952), Volume 15, 91

[48] Maxey, Mary and Bryan, interview 2009

[49] http://www.ohwy.com

[50] http://images.trafficmp.com

[51] "SOUTH MAYDE CREEK." *The Handbook of Texas Online*. <http://www.tsha.utexas.edu/handbook/online/articles/view/SS/rbsdv.html>

[52] Houghton, Dorothy Knox Howe, Interview 2002

[53] Johnston, Marguerite, *Houston: the Unknown City, 1836-1946* (Texas A & M 1991), 262

[54] Pulleine, Imogene, e-mail 2002

[55] http://www.mctxbar.com

[56] www.earthmanfunerals.com & Earthman, Jim, interview 2005

[57] Whitley, Jack, interview 2009

[58] *Handbook of Texas Online*, s.v. "," http://www.tsha-online.org/handbook/online/articles/SS/hgs17.html

[59] www.top-biography.com

[60] *Works Projects Administration, Houston: A History & Guide* (Anson Jones Press 1942), 83

[61] Eisemann, Elaine, e-mail

[62] Raia, John B., Interview 2001 & Glenwood Cemetery Records

[63] Ferris, Kirk, Interview 2001

[64] http://www.ourbaytown.com

[65] *Bayou City Banner*, July 30, 1971

[66] Field trip 2004

[67] Pomeroy, C. David Jr., *Pasadena: The Early Years* (Pomerosa Press 1993), 106,112

[68] "MCNAIR, TX." *The Handbook of Texas Online*. <http://www.tsha.utexas.edu/handbook/online/articles/view/MM/hjm11.html>

[69] Garraty, John A. Editor, *Encyclopedia of American Biography* (Harper & Row 1974), 746-7

[70] *River Oaks Times*, September 10, 1948

[71] http://en.wikipedia.org

[72] *Key Map*, 46th Edition, 2005

[73] *Key Map*, 252

[74] Field trip, 2001

[75] http://www.hertiagemuseum.us

[76] http://www.houstondogpark.org

[77] http://www.memorialcitymall.com

[78] Field trip, 2009

[79] www.celinea.com

[80] www.mercedes-benz.com

[81] www.mercer.edu

[82] www.library.thinkquest.org/

[83] Blessington, J. P., *The Campaigns of Walker's Texas Division* (Pemberton Press 1968), 294

[84] Houston Metropolitan Research Center Files, Houston Public Library

[85] *Houston Post*, April 17, 1953

[86] Dupont, Ivon, Interview 2002

[87] *Handbook of Texas Online*, s.v. "," http://www.tshaon-line.org/handbook/online/articles/MM/hvm76.html

[88] http://www.ourbaytown.com/

[89] Laffin, John, *Brassey's Dictionary of Battles: 3,500 Years of Conflict, Campaigns and Wars* (Barnes & Noble, 1986), 279

[90] Barrus, Thu Nhi, Interview 2002

[91] Field trips for decades

[92] Webb, Walter Prescott, *The Hand Book of Texas* (Texas State Historical Assn. 1952), Vol. 2, 191

[93] Denison, Lynne W. & Pugh, L.L., *Houston Public School Buildings: Their History & Location* (L. L. Pugh 1936), 52-3

[94] *Handbook of Texas Online*, s.v. "," http://www.tshaon-line.org/handbook/online/articles/MM/rbmac.html

[95] "KATY, TX." *The Handbook of Texas Online*. <http://www.tsha.utexas.edu/handbook/online/articles/view/KK/hfk1.html>

[96] *Handbook of Texas Online*, s.v. "," http://www.tsha-online.org/handbook/online/articles/BB/hgb5.html

[97] Blessington, J. P., *The Campaigns of Walker's Texas Division* (Pemberton Press 1968), 20

[98] Webb, Walter Prescott, *The Hand Book of Texas* (Texas Historical Assn. 1952), Vol. 2, 198

[99] *Houston Chronicle*, April 9, 2009

[100] www.luminarium.org

[101] Webb, Walter Prescott, *The Hand Book of Texas* (Texas Historical Assn. 1952), Vol. 2, 203

[102] *Key Map*, 46th Edition, 2005

[103] *Handbook of Texas Online*, s.v. "," http://www.tshaon-line.org/handbook/online/articles/MM/hvm89.html

[104] Special Collections/Archives, John B. Coleman Library, Prairie View A & M University, Prairie View, Texas

[105] Blessington, J. P., *The Campaigns of Walker's Texas Division* (Pemberton Press 1968), 58

[106] Blessington, J. P., *The Campaigns of Walker's Texas Division* (Pemberton Press 1968), 281

[107] "MISSOURI CITY, TX." *The Handbook of Texas Online*. <http://www.tsha.utexas.edu/handbook/online/articles/view/MM/hem6.html>

[108] www.mopac.org/history

[109] Kimball, Mary Holt, et al, *The Heritage of North Harris County* (American Association of University Women 1977), 75

[110] http://en.wikipedia.org
[111] www.ibiblio.org
[112] www.whitehouse.gov
[113] www.mexconnect.com
[114] Gandy, William H., *A History of Montgomery County, Texas* (An Abstract Thesis 1952), 63-4
[115] Gandy, William H., *A History of Montgomery County, Texas* (Master's thesis 1952), 64-7
[116] *Progressive Houston*, July, 1911
[117] *Handbook of Texas Online*, s.v. ".," http://www.tshaonline.org/handbook/online/articles/MM/fmo21.html
[118] Texas Historical Marker, 2735 FM 1960 E, Humble, erected 1986
[119] "MOORE, FRANCIS, JR." *The Handbook of Texas Online.* <http://www.tsha.utexas.edu/handbook/online/articles/view/MM/fmo26.html>
[120] http://www.sanjacinto-museum.org/veterans
[121] *Houston Chronicle*, April 16, 1997
[122] "MORRIS, JOSEPH ROBERT." *The Handbook of Texas Online.* <http://www.tsha.utexas.edu/handbook/online/articles/MM/fmo60.html>
[123] Houston Metropolitan Research Center Files, Houston Public Library
[124] "KATY, TX." *The Handbook of Texas Online.* <http://www.tsha.utexas.edu/handbook/online/articles/view/KK/hfk1.html>
[125] Map of the Subdivision of the A. C. Reynolds League
[126] *Handbook of Texas Online*, s.v. ".," http://www.tshaonline.org/handbook/online/articles/MM/htmnq.html
[127] Texas Historical Marker, Avenue A and Fifth Street, Katy, erected 1984
[128] Katy Heritage Society interview, 2009
[129] Highsmith, Carol M. & Landphair, Ted, *Houston: Deep in the Heart* (Archetype Press 2000), 72
[130] www.cyber-north.com
[131] http://www.referencecenter.com
[132] "MOUNT HOUSTON, TX." *The Handbook of Texas Online.* <http://www.tsha.utexas.edu/handbook/online/articles/view/MM/hrmuq.html>
[133] *Houston Chronicle*, March 16, 1951
[134] http://www.interment.net
[135] *Handbook of Texas Online*, s.v. ".," http://www.tshaonline.org/handbook/online/articles/RR/her2.html
[136] *Fort Bend County Sesquicentennial 1822-1972* (Commemorative Booklet Committee 1972), 69
[137] Texas Historical Markers, Bailey's Prairie, erected 1966
[138] *Handbook of Texas Online*, s.v. ".," http://www.tshaonline.org/handbook/online/articles/MM/rhm5.html
[139] *Brazoria County*, 1999-2000, 3-4
[140] *Houston Post*, undated

N

[1] *Houston Post*, February 17, 1957
[2] "LYNDON B JOHNSON SPACE CENTER." *The Handbook of Texas Online.* <http://www.tsha.utexas.edu/handbook/online/articles/view/LL/sql1.html>
[3] *Handbook of Texas Online*, s.v. ".," http://www.tshaonline.org/handbook/online/articles/DD/fde29.html

[4] Doolittle, Bill, *The Kentucky Derby: Run for the Roses* (Time Life Books 1998), 160
[5] Crutchfield, James A., The Natchez Trace: A Pictorial History (Rutledge Hill Press, 1985), 16-18
[6] http://www.tpwd.state.tx.us
[7] Field trip, 2001
[8] *Baytown Sun*, May 13, 1996
[9] *Handbook of Texas Online*, s.v. ".," http://www.tshaonline.org/handbook/online/articles/NN/hjn4.html
[10] Upchurch, Lessie, *Welcome to Tomball: A History of Tomball, Texas* (D. Armstrong 1976), 32
[11] Herridge, Karen, *Spring Branch Heritage* (Wakebrook Press 1998), --23
[12] Garraty, John A. Editor, *Encyclopedia of American Biography* (Harper & Row 1974), 805-6
[13] "NEW CANEY, TX." *The Handbook of Texas Online.* <http://www.tsha.utexas.edu/handbook/online/articles/view/NN/hgn2.html>
[14] Charlton, Magdalena, New Kentucky and the Great Decision (Spring Creek County Historical Assn. 1962), 1,3
[15] *Handbook of Texas Online*, s.v. ".," http://www.tshaonline.org/handbook/online/articles/NN/hln18.html
[16] Field trip 2009
[17] *Handbook of Texas Online*, s.v. ".," http://www.tshaonline.org/handbook/online/articles/MM/qum1.html
[18] Houghton, Dorothy Knox Howe, Interview 2002
[19] *Handbook of Texas Online*, s.v. ".," http://www.tshaonline.org/handbook/online/articles/BB/hgb5.html
[20] Beverly, Trevia W., *At Rest: A Historical Directory of Harris County, Texas Cemeteries (1822-1992)*, 62
[21] Garraty, John A. Editor, *Encyclopedia of American Biography* (Harper & Row 1974), 810-11
[22] Hill, Nina Lee and Nancy, interview 2009
[23] Field trip 2001
[24] Adkins, John, e-mail 2008
[25] www.nolanryan.net
[26] Chisholm, Sherrie, Interview 2001
[27] Laffin, John, *Brassey's Dictionary of Battles: 3,500 Years Of Conflict, Campaigns and Wars* (Barnes & Noble Books 1986), 141-3
[28] Special Collections/Archives, John B. Coleman Library, Prairie View A & M University, Prairie View, Texas
[29] "NORTH HOUSTON, TX." *The Handbook of Texas Online.* <http://www.tsha.utexas.edu/handbook/online/articles/view/NN/hrn27.html>
[30] Houston Press, January 26, 1932
[31] www.northwestern.edu

O

[1] "OAK RIDGE NORTH, TX." *The Handbook of Texas Online.* <http://www.tsha.utexas.edu/handbook/online/articles/view/OO/hgozw.html>
[2] *Handbook of Texas Online*, s.v. ".," http://www.tshaonline.org/handbook/online/articles/II/diicy.html
[3] www.oaklawn.com
[4] Wallingford, Sharon, *Fort Bend County Texas: A Pictorial History* (Fort Bend Publishing Group 1996), 115

[5] Beverly, Trevia W., *At Rest: A Historical Directory of Harris County, Texas Cemeteries (1822-1992)*, 41

[6] www.oberlin.edu

[7] Field trip, 2002

[8] Fifth Ward, Houston Texas, circa 1915-1920, September 1982

[9] Field trip with George Donohoo, 2005

[10] http://www.pearland school.net

[11] Field Trip with George Donohoo, 2005

[12] Herridge, Karen, *Spring Branch Heritage* (Wakebrook Press 1998), 19, 25

[13] Laffin, John, *Brassey's Dictionary of Battles: 3,500 Years Of Conflict, Campaigns and Wars* (Barnes & Noble Books 1986), 315

[14] *Handbook of Texas Online*, s.v. ",", http://www.tsha-online.org/handbook/online/articles/AA/hla24.html

[15] *Handbook of Texas Online*, s.v. ",", http://www.tsha-online.org/handbook/online/articles/CC/rbc47.html

[16] *Handbook of Texas Online*, s.v. ",", http://www.tsha-online.org/handbook/online/articles/DD/hvd7.html

[17] *Handbook of Texas Online*, s.v. ",", http://www.tsha-online.org/handbook/online/articles/PP/hnp43.html

[18] *Handbook of Texas Online*, s.v. ",", http://www.tsha-online.org/handbook/online/articles/GG/hng41.html

[19] Webb, Walter Prescott, *The Hand Book of Texas* (Texas Historical Assn. 1952), Vol. 2, 269-70

[20] Metz, Leon C., *Roadside History of Texas* (Mountain Press Publishing 1994), 207

[21] Webb, Walter Prescott, *The Hand Book of Texas* (Texas State Historical Assn. 1952), Vol. 2, 309

[22] Webb, Walter Prescott, *The Handbook of Texas* (Texas Historical Assn 1952), Vol. 2, 309-10

[23] *Hinton family history*

[24] www.olygolf.com

[25] Cisneros, Karla, e-mail 2002

[26] http://www.cityofopelousas.com/

[27] *Handbook of Texas Online*, s.v. ",", http://www.tshaonline.org/handbook/online/articles

[28] Field trip 2009

[29] Agatha, Sister M., *The History of Houston Heights: 1891-1918* (Premier Publishing 1956), 18

[30] "OYSTER CREEK." *The Handbook of Texas Online.* <http://www.tsha.utexas.edu/handbook/online/articles/view/OO/rbo37.html>

[31] Special Collections/Archives, John B. Coleman Library, Prairie View A & M University, Prairie View, Texas

P

[1] www.artmag.com

[2] Writers' Program of the Work Projects Administration, *Houston: A History and Guide* (Anson Jones Press 1942), 143

[3] Old Houston Maps

[4] *The American Heritage Dictionary of the English Language:* Third Edition (Houghton Mifflin Company 1992), 1307

[5] http://texashometownlocater.com

[6] "PANTHER BRANCH." *The Handbook of Texas Online.* <http://www.tsha.utexas.edu/handbook/online/articles/view/PP/rbp26.html>

[7] *Houston and Harris County Facts* – Houston Public Library - Texas Room *Houston and Harris County Facts* – Houston Public Library - Texas Room

[8] Field trip, 2001

[9] Baron, Steven M., *Electric Houston: The Street Railways of Houston, Texas* (Steven M. Baron 1996), 125

[10] Houston Metropolitan Research Center Files, Houston Public Library

[11] www.greatbuildings.com

[12] Pomeroy, C. David Jr., *Pasadena: The Early Years* (Pomerosa Press 1993), 30

[13] Texas Historical Marker, St. Vincent's Cemetery Navigation at St. Charles, erected 1956

[14] Detering, Deborah, Interview 2001

[15] Garraty, John A. Editor, *Encyclopedia of American Biography* (Harper & Row 1974), 517-19

[16] Garraty, John A. Editor, *Encyclopedia of American Biography* (Harper & Row 1974), 838-9

[17] *Handbook of Texas Online*, s.v. "PAUL QUINN COLLEGE," http://www.tsha.utexas.edu/handbook/online/articles/view/PP/kbp8.html

[18] Garraty, John A. Editor, *Encyclopedia of American Biography* (Harper & Row 1974), 903-4

[19] Dupont, Ivon, Interview 2002

[20] "PEACH CREEK." *The Handbook of Texas Online.* <http://www.tsha.utexas.edu/handbook/online/articles/view/PP/rbp48.html>

[21] *Baytown Sun*, May 13, 1996

[22] *Key Map*, 615

[23] "PEARLAND, TX." *The Handbook of Texas Online.* <http://www.tsha.utexas.edu/handbook/online/articles/view/PP/hep3.html>

[24] http://www.accessgenealogy.com

[25] Webb, Walter Prescott, *The Hand Book of Texas* (Texas State Historical Assn. 1952), Vol. 2, 351-2

[26] *Houston Chronicle*, April 16, 1997

[27] Sam Houston Park Memorial & Wood, Jerry, Interview 2001

[28] "PEDEN, EDWARD ANDREW." *The Handbook of Texas Online.* <http://www.tsha.utexas.edu/handbook/online/articles/view/PP/fpe14.html>

[29] *Handbook of Texas Online*, s.v. ",", http://www.tsha-online.org/handbook/online/articles/PP/rrp12.html

[30] "PELLY, TX." *The Handbook of Texas Online.* <http://www.tsha.utexas.edu/handbook/online/articles/view/PP/hdp3.html>

[31] Begeman, June A., *Stepping Back In Time: History of West University Place,* (D. Armstrong 1999), 13

[32] Houston Metropolitan Research Center Files, Houston Public Library

[33] Garraty, John A. Editor, *Encyclopedia of American Biography* (Harper & Row 1974), 845-7

[34] Houston Metropolitan Research Center Files, Houston Public Library

[35] *Handbook of Texas Online*, s.v. ",", http://www.tsha-online.org/handbook/online/articles/PP/hvpcw.html

[36] http://www.wikipedia.org

37 Garraty, John A. Editor, *Encyclopedia of American Biography* (Harper & Row 1974), 852-5

38 *Handbook of Texas Online*, s.v. "," http://www.tshaonline.org/handbook/online/articles/PP/hnp20.html and *Handbook of Texas Online*, s.v. "," http://www.tshaonline.org/handbook/online/articles/SS/hls10.html

39 Houston Metropolitan Research Center Files, Houston Public Library

40 Texas Historical Marker, Oyster Creek, erected 1966

41 http://www.phillips66.com/about/history.html & e-mail Brown, Jenny L., 2003

42 Field trip, 1984

43 *Encyclopedia Britannica* (1952), Volume 17, 912

44 Field trip with George Donehoo, 2005

45 Garraty, John A. Editor, *Encyclopedia of American Biography* (Harper & Row 1974), 857-8

46 Herridge, Karen, *Spring Branch Heritage* (Wakebrook Press 1998), --23

47 Johnston, Marguerite, *Houston: the Unknown City, 1836-1946* (Texas A & M 1991), 95, 141

48 Houghton, Dorothy Knox Howe, et al, *Houston's Forgotten Heritage: Landscape, Houses, Interiors, 1824-1914* (Rice University Press 1991), 319, 360

49 "PINE GULLY." *The Handbook of Texas Online.* <http://www.tsha.utexas.edu/handbook/online/articles/view/PP/rbp86.html>

50 *Handbook of Texas Online*, s.v. "," http://www.tshaonline.org/handbook/online/articles/PP/hrpad.html

51 Robin Elverson Realtors, Sales Brochure

52 "PINEHURST, TX." *The Handbook of Texas Online.* <http://www.tsha.utexas.edu/handbook/online/articles/view/PP/hlp28.html>

53 Teten, Paul, Interview 2001

54 Paterson, Melissa M., *The Road to Piney Point* (Piney Point Village Historic Committee 1994), 8-10

55 http://www.museumofflight.org

56 River Oaks Property Owners Association, Interview & Records

57 Special Collections/Archives, John B. Coleman Library, Prairie View A & M University, Prairie View, Texas

58 Wallingford, Sharon, *Fort Bend County Texas: A Pictorial History* (Fort Bend Publishing Group 1996), 159

59 http://www.texashiker.com

60 http://www.ci.pasadena.tx.us

61 "KATY, TX." *The Handbook of Texas Online.* <http://www.tsha.utexas.edu/handbook/online/articles/view/KK/hfk1.html>

62 http://www.pitt.edu

63 *Handbook of Texas Online*, s.v. "," http://www.tshaonline.org/handbook/online/articles/PP/hlpyl.html

64 Anderson, Jesse and Strain, Harvey, interview 2009

65 *Handbook of Texas Online*, s.v. "," http://www.tshaonline.org/handbook/online/articles/PP/hlp32.html

66 "PLUM GROVE, TX." *The Handbook of Texas Online.* <http://www.tsha.utexas.edu/handbook/online/articles/view/PP/hlp62.html>

67 *Handbook of Texas Online*, s.v. "," http://www.tshaonline.org/handbook/online/articles/PP/hlp62.html

68 Miller, Mary Catherine Farrington, Interview 2001

69 Garraty, John A. Editor, *Encyclopedia of American Biography* (Harper & Row 1974), 863-4

70 Wood, Jerry, Interview 2001

71 Wharton, Charles R., *History of Fort Bend County* (Naylor & Co. 1939), 53-5

72 Rice, Timothy J., Interview 2001

73 Pomeroy, C. David Jr., *Pasadena: The Early Years* (Pomerosa Press 1993), 129-135

74 *Encyclopedia Britannica* (1952), Volume 18, 205

75 Field trip 2008

76 "PORTER, TX." *The Handbook of Texas Online.* <http://www.tsha.utexas.edu/handbook/online/articles/view/PP/hdp6.html>

77 http://www.mctxbar.com

78 forestry.about.com

79 *Handbook of Texas Online*, s.v. "," http://www.tshaonline.org/handbook/online/articles/PP/hrp81.html

80 "POWER, JAMES." *The Handbook of Texas Online.* <http://www.tsha.utexas.edu/handbook/online/articles/view/PP/fpo36.html>

81 "PRAIRIE VIEW, TX." *The Handbook of Texas Online.* <http://www.tsha.utexas.edu/handbook/online/articles/view/PP/hgp12.html>

82 *Houston Post*, April 11, 1937

83 www.marylandracing.com

84 *Texas Medical Center News*, May 1, 1995

85 "NEW CANEY, TX." *The Handbook of Texas Online.* <http://www.tsha.utexas.edu/handbook/online/articles/view/NN/hgn2.html>

86 *Handbook of Texas Online*, s.v. "," http://www.tshaonline.org/handbook/online/articles/NN/hgn2.html

87 Special Collections/Archives, John B. Coleman Library, Prairie View A & M University, Prairie View, Texas

88 Looscan, Adele B., *Harris County: 1822-1845* (Texas State Historical Association, 1915), 54

89 www.princeton.edu

90 *Handbook of Texas Online*, s.v. "JESTER STATE PRISON FARM," http://www.tsha.utexas.edu/handbook/online/articles/view

91 Field Trip, 2002

92 *Baytown Sun*, May 13, 1996

93 Houston Metropolitan Research Center Files, Houston Public Library

94 Henson, Margaret Sweet, *The History of Baytown* (Bay Area Heritage Society 1986), 136

95 Zuber, Harry, Interview 2006

96 Wallingford, Sharon, *Fort Bend County Texas: A Pictorial History* (Fort Bend Publishing Group 1996), 163

97 www.purdue.edu

Q

1 Kimball, Mary Holt, et al, *The Heritage of North Harris County* (American Association of University Women 1977), 58

2 Field trip 2008

3 *The American Heritage Dictionary of the English Language:* Third Edition (Houghton Mifflin Company 1992), 1,479.

4 www.britannia.com

[5] http://www.queensclub.co.uk/
[6] Texas Historical Marker, Quintana, erected 1964
[7] Webb, Walter Prescott, *The Hand Book of Texas* (Texas State Historical Assn. 1952), Vol. 2, 425

R

[1] www.ohwy.com
[2] Christensen, Roberta, *Historic-Romantic Richmond* (Nortex Press, 1982), 83
[3] Christensen, Roberta, *Historic-Romantic Richmond* (Nortex Press, 1982), 82-3
[4] Wallingford, Sharon, *Fort Bend County Texas: A Pictorial History* (Fort Bend Publishing Group 1996), 166
[5] Field trip, 2009
[6] Field trip, 2009
[7] Field trip, 2001
[8] Field trip, 2009
[9] Andrews, Patsy, e-mail 2009
[10] *Handbook of Texas Online*, s.v. ",", http://www.tsha-online.org/handbook/online/articles/RR/hvr11.html
[11] *Houston Post*, June 16, 1991
[12] http://www.accessgenealogy.com and Christensen, Roberta, *Historic-Romantic Richmond* (Nortex Press, 1982), 94
[13] http://www.rwi.lu.se
[14] http://texasmilitaryforcesmuseum.yuku.com
[15] Houston Metropolitan Research Center Files, Houston Public Library
[16] "RAYFORD, TX." *The Handbook of Texas Online.* <http://www.tsha.utexas.edu/handbook/online/articles/view/RR/hvr16.html>
[17] http://politicalgraveyard.com
[18] River Oaks Property Owners Association, Interview & Records
[19] http://www.ishipress.com
[20] Pomeroy, C. David Jr., *Pasadena: The Early Years* (Pomerosa Press 1993), 23
[21] http://www.stafford.msd
[22] Fieldtrip 2001
[23] *Houston and Harris County Facts* – Houston Public Library - Texas Room
[24] Andrews, Patsy Fox, *City of Spring Valley: Fifty Years 1955-2005*, 21
[25] http://www.geocities.com
[26] Old Houston map
[27] Houston Metropolitan Research Center Files, Houston Public Library
[28] Laffin, John, *Brassey's Dictionary of Battles: 3,500 Years Of Conflict, Campaigns and Wars* (Barnes & Noble Books 1986), 357
[29] Garraty, John A. Editor, *Encyclopedia of American Biography* (Harper & Row 1974), 901-2
[30] Fieldtrip 2001
[31] *Old Sixth Ward Reporter*, (XXX)
[32] Richard Shiff, "Renoir, Pierre Auguste," *World Book Online* Americas Edition, http://www.aolsvc.world-book.aol.com

[33] Blessington, J. P., *The Campaigns of Walker's Texas Division* (Pemberton Press 1968), 50
[34] *Baytown Sun*, May 13, 1996
[35] http://www.shell.com
[36] Houston District Designation Report, HPO file no. 08hd12, 2008
[37] Webb, Walter Prescott, *The Hand Book of Texas* (Texas Historical Assn. 1952), Vol. 2, 465
[38] McDonough, Ranney, interview 2005 & http://www.ighof.com
[39] Donehoo, George, Interview 2005
[40] Rheman, Kathleen, e-mail 2008
[41] www.skyways.lib.ks.us
[42] http://dewberryfarm.com
[43] McAshan, Marie Phelps, *A Houston Legacy* (Gulf Publishing 1985), 125-6
[44] "RICEVILLE, TX." *The Handbook of Texas Online.* <http://www.tsha.utexas.edu/handbook/online/articles/view/RR/hrrsm.html>
[45] Kimball, Mary H. et. al., *The Heritage of North Harris County* (North Harris County Branch American Association of University Women 1977), 79
[46] Pomeroy, C. David Jr., *Pasadena: The Early Years* (Pomerosa Press 1993), 34, 37
[47] *Handbook of Texas Online*, s.v. ",", http://www.tsha-online.org/handbook/online/articles/RR/sbr1.html
[48] http://www.roserichchamber.org
[49] *Handbook of Texas Online*, s.v. ",", http://www.tsha-online.org/handbook/online/articles/RR/hgr4.html
[50] Herridge, Karen, *Spring Branch Heritage* (Wakebrook Press 1998),
[51] Baines, Mrs. W. M., *Houston's Part in the World War* (1919)
[52] www.cwrl.utexas.edu/
[53] Doolittle, Bill, *The Kentucky Derby: Run for the Roses* (Time Life Books 1998), 142, 173
[54] River Oaks Property Owners Association, Interview & Records
[55] Field trip, 2009
[56] *Handbook of Texas Online*, s.v. "ROARK, ELIJAH ANDREW," http://www.tsha.utexas.edu/handbook/online/articles/RR/fro2.html
[57] *Handbook of Texas Online*, s.v. "ROARK, LEO A ELIJAH," http://www.tsha.utexas.edu/handbook/online/articles/RR/fro3.html
[58] http://www.wikipedia.org
[59] http://www.historictexas.net
[60] Kimball, Mary Holt, et al, *The Heritage of North Harris County* (American Association of University Women 1977), 20
[61] Texas Historical Marker, Avenue A and Fifth Street, Katy, erected 1984
[62] Houston Metropolitan Research Center Files, Houston Public Library
[63] Texas Historical Marker, Rosenberg, erected 1988
[64] Texas Historical Marker, Missouri City, erected 1985
[65] "NEW CANEY, TX." *The Handbook of Texas Online.* <http://www.tsha.utexas.edu/handbook/online/articles/view/NN/hgn2.html>
[66] http://www.missouricitytx.gov

67 Webb, Walter Prescott, *The Hand Book of Texas* (Texas Historical Assn. 1952), Vol. 2, 493

68 http://www.cashel.ie/

69 Wallingford, Sharon, *Fort Bend County Texas: A Pictorial History* (Fort Bend Publishing Group 1996), 163

70 www.rohmhaas.com/

71 Field trip, 2009

72 Webb, Walter Prescott, *The Hand Book of Texas* (Texas State Historical Assn. 1952), Vol. 2, 500

73 Houston City Directories

74 Garraty, John A. Editor, *Encyclopedia of American Biography* (Harper & Row 1974), 926-29

75 Raia, John B., Interview 2001 & Glenwood Cemetery Records

76 Map of the Subdivision of the A. C. Reynolds League

77 Field trip, 2009

78 Upchurch, Lessie, *Welcome to Tomball: A History of Tomball, Texas* (D. Armstrong 1976), 11-12

79 *Handbook of Texas Online*, s.v. ".," http://www.tsha-online.org/handbook/online/articles/RR/her2.html

80 Webb, Walter Prescott, *The Hand Book of Texas* (Texas Historical Assn. 1952), Vol. 2, 504-5

81 *Handbook of Texas Online*, s.v. ".," http://www.tsha-online.org/handbook/online/articles/RR/hlr42.html

82 http://www.ourbaytown.com

83 Webb, Walter Prescott, *The Hand Book of Texas* (Texas State Historical Assn. 1952), Vol. 2, 669

84 "ROSSLYN, TX." *The Handbook of Texas Online.* <http://www.tsha.utexas.edu/handbook/online/articles/view/RR/hrrxj.html>

85 Garraty, John A. Editor, *Encyclopedia of American Biography* (Harper & Row 1974), 939-40

86 Webb, Walter Prescott, *The Handbook of Texas* (Texas State Historical Association 1952), Vol. 1, 129-30

87 http://www.eastsideboxing.com

88 http://www.rice.edu/fondren/woodson

89 Upchurch, Lessie, *Welcome to Tomball: A History of Tomball, Texas* (D. Armstrong Co. 1995), 14

90 *Handbook of Texas Online*, s.v. "WHITE, REUBEN," http://www.tsha.utexas.edu/handbook/online/articles/view/WW/fwh28.html

91 members.aol.com

92 *Works Projects Administration, Houston: A History & Guide* (Anson Jones Press 1942), 188

93 Webb, Walter Prescott, *The Handbook of Texas* (Texas State Historical Association 1952), Vol. 2, 514-15

94 "RUNNELS, HIRAM GEORGE." *The Handbook of Texas Online.* <http://www.tsha.utexas.edu/handbook/online/articles/view/RR/fru14.html>

95 *The American Heritage Dictionary of the English Language:* Third Edition (Houghton Mifflin Company 1992), 1579

96 *Bayou City Banner*, July 30, 1971

97 *Encyclopedia Britannica* (1952), Volume 19, 674-7

98 Miller, Mary Catherine Farrington, *Tanglewood: The Story of William Giddings Farrington* (Gulf Publishing Company 1989), 43

99 www.rutgers.edu

100 Carroll, Benajah H., *Standard History of Houston, Texas* (no publisher listed – undated), 237

101 Houston District Designation Report, HPO file no. 07HD11, 2007

102 Field trip with George Donehoo, 2007

S

1 Webb, Walter Prescott, *The Hand Book of Texas* (Texas State Historical Assn. 1952), Vol. 2, 523, 525

2 Detering, Carl, Interview 2001

3 Miller, Mary Catherine Farrington, *Tanglewood: The Story of William Giddings Farrington* (Gulf Publishing Company 1989), 48

4 Johnston, Marguerite, *Houston: the Unknown City, 1836-1946* (Texas A & M 1991), 140, 304

5 Field trip with George Donehoo, 2008

6 *Handbook of Texas Online*, s.v. ".," http://www.tsha-online.org/handbook/online/articles/RR/fra49.html

7 *Houston Chronicle*, September 9, 2002

8 Houghton, Dorothy Knox Howe, et al, *Houston's Forgotten Heritage: Landscape, Houses, Interiors, 1824-1914* (Rice University Press 1991), 76, 118, 310

9 Garraty, John A. Editor, *Encyclopedia of American Biography* (Harper & Row 1974), 16-17

10 *Handbook of Texas Online*, s.v. ".," http://www.tsha-online.org/handbook/online/articles/SS/rns7.html

11 Ibid., Vol. 2, 550

12 Texas Historical Marker, Houston, erected 1936

13 Webb, Walter Prescott, *The Hand Book of Texas* (Texas Historical Assn. 1952), Vol. 2, 557

14 Webb, Walter Prescott, *The Handbook of Texas* (Texas State Historical Association 1952), Vol. 2, 560-1

15 *Encyclopedia Britannica* 2005 Ultimate Reference Suite CD/ROM

16 *Handbook of Texas Online*, s.v. ".," http://www.tsha-online.org/handbook/online/articles/SS/hns16.html

17 www.santaanita.com

18 *Handbook of Texas Online*, s.v. ".," http://www.tsha-online.org/handbook/online/articles/SS/hfsdk.html

19 www.bnsf.com

20 www.saratogaracetrack.com/

21 "IMPERIAL VALLEY RAILWAY." *The Handbook of Texas Online.* <http://www.tsha.utexas.edu/handbook/online/articles/view/II/eqi1.html>

22 www.bfro.net

23 www.satchmo.com/

24 *Houston Chronicle*, August 8, 2002

25 Fieldtrip 2001

26 Blessington, J. P., *The Campaigns of Walker's Texas Division* (Pemberton Press 1968), 52

27 Field trip, 1959

28 Wallingford, Sharon, *Fort Bend County Texas: A Pictorial History* (Fort Bend Publishing Group 1996), 115

29 Wood, Jerry, Interview 2002

30 Upchurch, Lessie, *Welcome to Tomball: A History of Tomball, Texas* (D. Armstrong 1976), 13

31 Kimball, Mary Holt, et al, *The Heritage of North Harris County* (American Association of University Women 1977), 61-2

32 Field Trip with George Donehoo, 2005

33 Houston Metropolitan Research Center Files, Houston Public Library

34 Henson, Margaret Sweet, *The History of Baytown* (Bay Area Heritage Society 1986), 73

35 Field trip, 1984

36 http://www.tomball.com

37 Houston Metropolitan Research Center Files, Houston Public Library

38 *Key Map*, 50the Edition 2009

39 Field trip, 2009

40 *Handbook of Texas Online*, s.v. ",", http://www.tsha-online.org/handbook/online/articles/RR/her2.html

41 "BAYTOWN, TX." *The Handbook of Texas Online*. <http://www.tsha.utexas.edu/handbook/online/articles/view/BB/hdb1.html>

42 www.horse-racing.net

43 www.maersksealand.com/

44 http://ww.seabrookshipyard.com/

45 *Handbook of Texas Online*, s.v. ",", http://www.tsha-online.org/handbook/online/articles/SS/hgs6.html

46 *Handbook of Texas Online*, s.v. ",", http://www.tsha-online.org/handbook/online/articles/SS/fsekh.html

47 Doolittle, Bill, *The Kentucky Derby: Run for the Roses* (Time Life Books 1998), 151

48 Cartwright, Gary, *Galveston: A History of the Island* (Atheneum 1991), 187-94

49 http://www.oldsubsplace.com

50 www.horse-racing.net

51 *Handbook of Texas Online*, s.v. ",", http://www.tsha-online.org/handbook/online/articles/SS/hns28.html

52 Webb, Walter Prescott, *The Handbook of Texas* (Texas State Historical Association 1952), Vol. 2, 590

53 Field trip, 2009

54 Kimball, Mary Holt, et al, *The Heritage of North Harris County* (American Association of University Women 1977), 62

55 Laffin, John, *Brassey's Dictionary of Battles: 3,500 Years Of Conflict, Campaigns and Wars* (Barnes & Noble Books 1986), 181

56 Houston Metropolitan Research Center Files, Houston Public Library

57 http://www.wikipedia.org

58 Werner, George, e-mail, 2005

59 www.infoplease.com

60 www.sewanee.edu

61 Pomeroy, C. David Jr., *Pasadena: The Early Years* (Pomerosa Press 1993), 35, 39

62 Hinton, Mocco Dunn, Interview 1955 & Robin Elverson Realtors, Sales Brochure

63 http://www.shadow-creek.net/

64 Houston District Designation Report, HPO file no. 08hd13, 2008

65 Miller, Mary Catherine Farrington, *Tanglewood: The Story of William Giddings Farrington* (Gulf Publishing Company 1989), 43

66 Mickelis, Leslie, Interview 2002

67 McAshan, Marie Phelps, *A Houston Legacy* (Gulf Publishing 1985), 205-6

68 www.sfsite.com

69 Robin Elverson Realtors, Sales Brochure

70 http://www.texasfreeway.com/houston

71 Houghton, Dorothy Knox Howe, Interview 2002

72 Carroll, Benajah H., *Standard History of Houston, Texas* (no publisher listed – undated), 61, 63, 148, 150, 176

73 "SHELDON, TX." *The Handbook of Texas Online*. <http://www.tsha.utexas.edu/handbook/online/articles/view/SS/hjs13.html>

74 www.shell.com/

75 "SHENANDOAH, TX." *The Handbook of Texas Online*. <http://www.tsha.utexas.edu/handbook/online/articles/view/SS/hjsrd.html>

76 *Houston Post*, January 9, 1938

77 Henson, Margaret Sweet, *The History of Baytown* (Bay Area Heritage Society 1986), 35-6

78 Garraty, John A. Editor, *Encyclopedia of American Biography* (Harper & Row 1974), 990-1

79 Webb, Walter Prescott, *The Hand Book of Texas* (Texas State Historical Assn. 1952), Vol. 2, 506-7

80 Laffin, John, *Brassey's Dictionary of Battles: 3,500 Years of Conflict, Campaigns and Wars* (Barnes & Noble, 1986), 389

81 www.huntingclub.org

82 Field trip with Barbara Hinton, 2008

83 "SHOREACRES, TX." *The Handbook of Texas Online*. <http://www.tsha.utexas.edu/handbook/online/articles/view/SS/hjs16.html>

84 Seals, Vivian Hubbard, Interview 2003

85 www.ansi.okstate.com

86 www.helsinki.fi

87 *Houston and Harris County Facts* – Houston Public Library - Texas Room

88 Herridge, Karen, *Spring Branch Heritage* (Wakebrook Press 1998), 24

89 *Key Map*, 50the Edition 2009

90 *Handbook of Texas Online*, s.v. ",", http://www.tsha-online.org/handbook/online/articles/SS/rhs1.html

91 Hancock, Virginia E., Interview 2002

92 http://sinclair2.quarterman.org

93 Henson, Margaret Sweet, *The History of Baytown* (Bay Area Heritage Society 1986), 19-20

94 www.luminarium.org

95 Garraty, John A. Editor, *Encyclopedia of American Biography* (Harper & Row 1974), 1002-3

96 Wood, Jerry, Interview 2001

97 Texas Historical Marker, 6330 Sjolander Rd., Baytown, erected 1967

98 http://www.nssa-nsca.com

99 www.online-literature.com

100 Fieldtrip 2001

101 Carter, Robert F., *A History of Missouri City, Texas* (D. Armstrong 1986), 1

102 *Houston Chronicle*, March 7, 1981

103 *Brazoria County*, 1999-2000, 13

104 Paterson, Melissa M., *The Road to Piney Point* (Piney Point Village Historic Committee 1994), 71

105 *Handbook of Texas Online*, s.v. ",", http://www.tsha-online.org/handbook/online/articles/SS/ros12.html

106 Special Collections/Archives, John B. Coleman Library, Prairie View A & M University, Prairie View, Texas

107 Beverly, Trevia W., *At Rest: A Historical Directory of Harris County, Texas Cemeteries (1822-1992)*, 66

108 "SOUTH HOUSTON, TX." *The Handbook of Texas Online.* <http://www.tsha.utexas.edu/handbook/online/articles/view/SS/hes6.html>

109 http://reservations.houstonareahotels.com

110 *Houston Post*, 1951

111 http://www.southwestern.edu

112 Field trip, 2001

113 *Handbook of Texas Online*, s.v. "," http://www.tsha-online.org/handbook/online/articles/SS/hrs55.html

114 http://www.stafford.msd.esc4.net/

115 Upchurch, Lessie, *Welcome to Tomball: A History of Tomball, Texas* (D. Armstrong Co. 1995), 46

116 *Houston Post*, June 21, 1931

117 www.cfisd.net

118 http://www.tsha.utexas.edu/handbook/online/articles/view/SS/dos3.html

119 http://www.sixflags.com/parks/splashtown

120 http://www.hertiagemuseum.us

121 Pomeroy, C. David Jr., *Pasadena: The Early Years* (Pomerosa Press 1993), 29

122 http://www.rainbird.com

123 "SPRING BRANCH, TX." *The Handbook of Texas Online.* <http://www.tsha.utexas.edu/handbook/online/articles/view/SS/hrsrj.html>

124 "OAK RIDGE NORTH, TX." *The Handbook of Texas Online.* <http://www.tsha.utexas.edu/handbook/online/articles/view/OO/hgozw.html>

125 "SPRING, TX." *The Handbook of Texas Online.* <http://www.tsha.utexas.edu/handbook/online/articles/view/SS/hls74.html>

126 Field trip, 2009

127 "HEGAR, TX." *The Handbook of Texas Online.* <http://www.tsha.utexas.edu/handbook/online/articles/view/HH/hrh25.html>

128 www.randa.org

129 www.joebates.com

130 Field trip, 1959

131 www.christushealth.org

132 http://www.wikipedia.org

133 Fieldtrip, 2005

134 "STAFFORD, TX." *The Handbook of Texas Online.* <http://www.tsha.utexas.edu/handbook/online/articles/view/SS/hgs15.html>

135 "STAGECOACH, TX." *The Handbook of Texas Online.* <http://www.tsha.utexas.edu/handbook/online/articles/view/SS/hlsmy.html>

136 http://www.hertiagemuseum.us

137 Johnston, Marguerite, *Houston: the Unknown City, 1836-1946* (Texas A & M 1991), 126

138 Upchurch, Lessie, *Welcome to Tomball: A History of Tomball, Texas* (D. Armstrong Co. 1995), 171, 187

139 www.stanford.edu

140 energy.ihs.com

141 *Key Map Montgomery County*, 151

142 Wallingford, Sharon, *Fort Bend County Texas: A Pictorial History* (Fort Bend Publishing Group 1996), 106

143 Beverly, Trevia Wooster and Holland, Wybra Wooster, e-mail 2009

144 *West U Magazine*, December 1993

145 Carroll, Benajah H., *Standard History of Houston, Texas* (no publisher listed – undated), 246

146 "STEVENS, JAMES H." *The Handbook of Texas Online.* <http://www.tsha.utexas.edu/handbook/online/articles/view/SS/fstbb.html>

147 Webb, Walter Prescott, *The Hand Book of Texas* (Texas Historical Assn. 1952), Vol. 2, 15

148 http://www.prweb.com

149 "STEWART, CHARLES BELLINGER TATE." *The Handbook of Texas Online.* <http://www.tsha.utexas.edu/handbook/online/articles/view/SS/fst53.html

150 "KATY, TX." *The Handbook of Texas Online.* <http://www.tsha.utexas.edu/handbook/online/articles/view/KK/hfk1.html>

151 Webb, Walter Prescott, *The Hand Book of Texas* (Texas Historical Assn. 1952), Vol. 2, 672

152 Houston Metropolitan Research Center Files, Houston Public Library

153 Katy Heritage Society interview, 2009

154 "KATY, TX." *The Handbook of Texas Online.* <http://www.tsha.utexas.edu/handbook/online/articles/view/KK/hfk1.html>

155 Field trip, 1995

156 Miller, Mary Catherine Farrington, *Tanglewood: The Story of William Giddings Farrington* (Gulf Publishing Company 1989), 43

157 Houghton, Dorothy Knox Howe, et al, *Houston's Forgotten Heritage: Landscape, Houses, Interiors, 1824-1914* (Rice University Press 1991), 324

158 *Handbook of Texas Online*, s.v. "," http://www.tsha-online.org/handbook/online/articles/SS/fst70.html

159 *Handbook of Texas Online*, s.v. "," http://www.tsha-online.org/handbook/online/articles/SS/ghs1.html

160 *Handbook of Texas Online*, s.v. "," http://www.tsha-online.org/handbook/online/articles/SS/hvscj.html

161 www.pasadenatexas.com

162 Texas Historical Marker, Freeport, erected 1980

163 Stude, Mike, Interview 2002

164 Stude, Mike, Interview 2002

165 Raia, John B., Interview 2001

166 Kostelecky, Susan & Gardner, Pam interview 2008

167 Wallingford, Sharon, *Fort Bend County Texas: A Pictorial History* (Fort Bend Publishing Group 1996), 170

168 Miller, Mary Catherine Farrington, *Tanglewood: The Story of William Giddings Farrington* (Gulf Publishing Company 1989), 43

169 Field trip 2003

170 Webb, Walter Prescott, *The Hand Book of Texas* (Texas State Historical Assn. 1952), Vol. 2, 506-7

171 http://www.sunoil.com

172 *Handbook of Texas Online*, s.v. "," http://www.tsha-online.org/handbook/online/articles/SS/hls85.html

173 Urban myth

174 http://:pangea.stanford.edu

175 Webb, Walter Prescott, *The Hand Book of Texas* (Texas Historical Assn. 1952), Vol. 2, 690

176 *Houston Chronicle*, January 2, 2008

177 www.swarthmore.edu

178 www.genealogy.org

179 "SEABROOK, TX." *The Handbook of Texas Online.* <http://www.tsha.utexas.edu/handbook/online/articles/view/SS/hgs4.html>

180 "LA PORTE, TX." *The Handbook of Texas Online.* <http://www.tsha.utexas.edu/handbook/online/articles/view/LL/hel2.html>

181 www.syracuse.edu

182 Houston Metropolitan Research Center Files, Houston Public Library

183 Field trip with George Donehoo, 2008

184 *The American Heritage Dictionary,* page 353

185 Field trip with George Donehoo, 2006

186 Houston Metropolitan Research Center Files, Houston Public Library, page 155 and field trip with Barbara Hinton, 2001

187 http://www.christusstjohn.org

· ·

T

1 Huckabee, Flossie, Interview 2001

2 Garraty, John A. Editor, *Encyclopedia of American Biography* (Harper & Row 1974), 1074-6

3 Beverly, Trevia W., *At Rest: A Historical Directory of Harris County, Texas Cemeteries (1822-1992),* 56

4 http://www.robertburns.org/

5 "TAMINA, TX." *The Handbook of Texas Online.* <http://www.tsha.utexas.edu/handbook/online/articles/view/TT/hrt3.html>

6 *Houston Chronicle,* April 29, 1986, June 7, 2000

7 Miller, Mary Catherine Farrington, *Tanglewood: The Story of William Giddings Farrington* (Gulf Publishing Company 1989), 43

8 *Directory & History of West University Place, Harris County, Texas, U.S.A.* (The Civic Club 1975), 57

9 www.cfisd.net

10 Laffin, John, *Brassey's Dictionary of Battles: 3,500 Years Of Conflict, Campaigns and Wars* (Barnes & Noble Books 1986), 419

11 *Handbook of Texas Online,* s.v. "," http://www.tsha-online.org/handbook/online/articles/TT/hdt3.html

12 www.online-literature.com

13 Kimball, Mary Holt, et al, *The Heritage of North Harris County* (American Association of University Women 1977), 78-9

14 *Old Sixth Ward Reporter,* December, 1979, 2

15 Texas Historical Marker, 500 block of Preston, Houston, erected 1993

16 Old Texas maps

17 Texas Historical Marker, 4400 Bellaire Blvd., Houston, erected 1993

18 Center, Catherine, Interview 2001

19 http://www.aks.reference.com

20 *Houston Chronicle,* January 24, 1961

21 Field Trip with George Donehoo, 2005

22 Old Houston maps

23 Houghton, Dorothy Knox Howe, et al, *Houston's Forgotten Heritage: Landscape, Houses, Interiors, 1824-1914* (Rice University Press 1991), 243

24 *Handbook of Texas Online,* s.v. "," http://www.tsha-online.org/handbook/online/articles/TT/hvt38.html

25 http://www.infoplease.com

26 65.107.211.206/victorian/tennyson/tennybio

27 *Handbook of Texas Online,* s.v. "," http://www.tsha-online.org/handbook/online/articles/TT/hnt13.html

28 Termini, D.J., interview and Webb, Walter Prescott, *The Hand Book of Texas* (Texas Historical Assn. 1952), Vol. 2, 558

29 Texas Historical Marker, Mayglen Lane and Fernbluff Drive, Tomball, erected 1983

30 Field trip with George Donehoo, 2008

31 Field trip with George Donehoo, 2005

32 *Handbook of Texas Online,* s.v. "," http://www.tsha-online.org/handbook/online/articles/AA/qja3.html

33 Texas City Dike brochure and field trip 2008

34 *Handbook of Texas Online,* s.v. "," http://www.tsha-online.org/handbook/online/articles/TT/mjtce.html

35 *Fort Bend County Sesquicentennial 1822-1972* (Commemorative Booklet Committee 1972), 69-70

36 *Handbook of Texas Online,* s.v. "," http://www.tsha-online.org/handbook/online/articles/TT/pft5.html

37 Webb, Walter Prescott, *The Hand Book of Texas* (Texas Historical Assn. 1952), Vol. 2, 735 and field trip 2008

38 Texas Historical Marker, Mayglen Lane and Fernbluff Drive, Tomball, erected 1983

39 Wood, Jerry, Interview 2001

40 Field trip 2009

41 Special Collections/Archives, John B. Coleman Library, Prairie View A & M University, Prairie View, Texas

42 "KATY, TX." *The Handbook of Texas Online.* <http://www.tsha.utexas.edu/handbook/online/articles/view/KK/hfk1.html>

43 "THOMPSON'S FERRY." *The Handbook of Texas Online.* <http://www.tsha.utexas.edu/handbook/online/articles/view/TT/rtt1.html>

44 *Handbook of Texas Online,* s.v. "," http://www.tsha-online.org/handbook/online/articles/TT/hvt38.html

45 http://ww.wholesomewords.org

46 River Oaks Property Owners Association, Interview & Records

47 Old Houston map

48 http://www.tifco.com

49 *River Oaks Times,* September 10, 1948

50 *Houston Chronicle,* September 28, 2008

51 Laffin, John, *Brassey's Dictionary of Battles: 3,500 Years of Conflict, Campaigns and Wars* (Barnes & Noble, 1986), 426

52 www.teyrenfest.com

53 "TODVILLE, TX." *The Handbook of Texas Online.* <http://www.tsha.utexas.edu/handbook/online/articles/view/TT/hvt40.html>

54 "TOMBALL, TX." *The Handbook of Texas Online.* <http://www.tsha.utexas.edu/handbook/online/articles/view/TT/hgt6.html>

55 Rice, J. Timothy, Interview 2001

56 http://ww.sandiegogolf.com

57 Barrus, Thu Nhi, Interview 2002

58 Field trip, 2010

59 http://www.en.wikipedia.org
60 http://www.pearlandtowncenter.com/
61 Field trip 2008
62 "TRAMMELS, TX." The Handbook of Texas Online. <http://www.tsha.utexas.edu/handbook/online/articles/view/TT/hrt31.html>
63 Barrus, Thu Nhi, Interview 2002
64 Webb, Walter Prescott, The Hand Book of Texas (Texas State Historical Assn. 1952), Vol. 2, 795
65 Andrews, Patsy, e-mail 2009
66 Handbook of Texas Online, s.v. "," http://www.tsha-online.org/handbook/online/articles/GG/fgr40.html
67 "GOOSE CREEK, TX." The Handbook of Texas Online. <http://www.tsha.utexas.edu/handbook/online/articles/view/GG/hvg32.html>
68 Webb, Walter Prescott, The Hand Book of Texas (Texas State Historical Assn. 1952), Vol. 2, 802
69 cbssportsline.com
70 Robin Elverson Realtors, Sales Brochure
71 Truxillo, Bart, Interview 2001
72 Houston Chronicle, September 11, 1967
73 Henry, Mary Lou, Interview 2002
74 Agatha, Sister M., The History of Houston Heights: 1891-1918 (Premier Publishing 1956), 18
75 Miller, Mary Catherine Farrington, Interview 2001
76 Sibley, Marilyn McAdams, The Port of Houston: A History (University of Texas 1968), 129
77 http://wwww.tuskegee.edu
78 Webb, Walter Prescott, The Hand Book of Texas (Texas State Historical Assn. 1952), Vol. 2, 813-14
79 Field trip with George Donehoo, 2008
80 www.pgatour.com
81 www.springbranchisd.org

U
1 www.uh.edu
2 www.usx.com/
3 Wallingford, Sharon, Fort Bend County Texas: A Pictorial History (Fort Bend Publishing Group 1996), 159
4 Fieldtrip, 2001
5 www.unclebens.com
6 http://www.unityhouston.org
7 Handbook of Texas Online, s.v. "," http://www.tsha-online.org/handbook/online/articles/UU/kcu29.html
8 Field trip, 2009
9 http://www.interfin.com
10 http://www.geocities.com
11 Webb, Walter Prescott, The Hand Book of Texas (Texas Historical Assn. 1952), Vol. 2, 826
12 von der Mehden, Fred R., The Ethnic Groups of Houston (Rice University Studies 1984), 167

V
1 Houston Public Library, Texas Room vertical files
2 Wallingford, Sharon, Fort Bend County Texas: A Pictorial History (Fort Bend Publishing Group 1996), 107
3 Garraty, John A. Editor, Encyclopedia of American Biography (Harper & Row 1974), 1120-2
4 www.arlingtoncemetery.net/

5 www.vanderbult.edu
6 The American Heritage Dictionary of the English Language: Third Edition (Houghton Mifflin Company 1992)
7 Handbook of Texas Online, s.v. "," http://www.tsha-online.org/handbook/online/articles/VV/ghv1.html
8 Handbook of Texas Online, s.v. "VELASCO, TX," http://www.tsha.utexas.edu/handbook/online/articles/VV/hvv7.html
9 www.vassar.edu
10 Field trip, 2001
11 Laffin, John, Brassey's Dictionary of Battles: 3,500 Years Of Conflict, Campaigns and Wars (Barnes & Noble Books 1986), 448-9
12 http://www.new-orleans.la.us
13 Shorten, Sister Wilfred, Interview 2000
14 www.villanova.edu
15 Webb, Walter Prescott, The Hand Book of Texas (Texas State Historical Assn. 1952), Vol. 2, 844
16 Handbook of Texas Online, s.v. "VELASCO, TX," http://www.tsha.utexas.edu/handbook/online/articles/VV/rtv1.html
17 Upchurch, Lessie, Welcome to Tomball: A History of Tomball, Texas (D. Armstrong 1976), 32-3
18 Webb, Walter Prescott, The Hand Book of Texas (Texas Historical Assn. 1952), Vol. 2, 845
19 Upchurch, Lessie, Welcome to Tomball: A History of Tomball, Texas (D. Armstrong Co. 1995), 36
20 Houston Metropolitan Research Center Files, Houston Public Library
21 Miller, Mary Catherine Farrington, Interview 2001

W
1 www.co.harristx.us/comm_lwe/pcrowley/index.html
2 www.aldine.k12.tx.us
3 Handbook of Texas Online, s.v. "," http://www.tsha-online.org/handbook/online/articles/RR/her2.html
4 Pomeroy, C. David Jr., Pasadena: The Early Years (Pomerosa Press 1993), 41, 43, 46
5 www.wakeforest.edu
6 http://www.fortbendisd.com
7 Wood, Jerry, Interview 2001
8 Handbook of Texas Online, s.v. "," http://www.tsha-online.org/handbook/online/articles/SS/rbsfr.html
9 "WALLER, TX." The Handbook of Texas Online. <http://www.tsha.utexas.edu/handbook/online/articles/view/WW/hjw1.html>
10 "WALLER, EDWIN, JR." The Handbook of Texas Online. <http://www.tsha.utexas.edu/handbook/online/articles/view/WW/fwaas.html>
11 Webb, Walter Prescott, The Hand Book of Texas (Texas State Historical Assn. 1952), Vol. 2, 858
12 Handbook of Texas Online, s.v. "," http://www.tshaon-line.org/handbook/online/articles/WW/rbw23.html
13 "WALNUT CREEK." The Handbook of Texas Online. <http://www.tsha.utexas.edu/handbook/online/articles/view/WW/rbw23.html>
14 Wallingford, Sharon, Fort Bend County Texas: A Pictorial History (Fort Bend Publishing Group 1996), 52

15 www.horse-racing.net

16 *Baytown Sun*, May 13, 1996

17 Kimball, Mary Holt, et al, *The Heritage of North Harris County* (American Association of University Women 1977), 54

18 http://co.chambers.tx.us

19 *Houston Post*, January 4, 1954

20 Sargent Bush, Jr., "Irving, Washington," *World Book Online* Americas Edition, http://www.aolsvc.worldbook.aol.com

21 "WASHINGTON-ON-THE-BRAZOS, TX." *The Handbook of Texas Online*. <http://www.tsha.utexas.edu/handbook/online/articles/view/WW/hvw10.html>

22 *Houston Chronicle*, January 30, 2009

23 http://www.watergatemarina.com

24 Laffin, John, *Brassey's Dictionary of Battles: 3,500 Years 0f Conflict, Campaigns and Wars* (Barnes & Noble Books 1986), 459-61

25 Dupont, Ivon, Interview 2002

26 Sam Houston Park Memorial & Wood, Jerry, Interview 2001

27 *Handbook of Texas Online*, s.v. "," http://www.tshaonline.org/handbook/online/articles/WW/hvw22.html

28 Beverly, Trevia Wooster and Holland, Wybra Wooster, e-mail 2009

29 Webb, Walter Prescott, *The Hand Book of Texas* (Texas Historical Assn. 1952), Vol. 2, 875

30 *Houston and Harris County Facts* – Houston Public Library - Texas Room

31 Fieldtrip, 2001 & City Directory 1955

32 Pace, Randle, interview 2001 and Robert A. Welch Foundation, interview 2001

33 http://www.wellsfargohistory.com

34 Begeman, June A., *Stepping Back In Time: History of West University Place*, (D. Armstrong 1999), 74

35 www.wesleyan.edu and 1935 city map

36 http://www.accessgenealogy.com

37 Old Houston maps

38 *Handbook of Texas Online*, s.v. "," http://www.tshaonline.org/handbook/online/articles/WW/hgw3.html

39 http://www.usma.edu

40 http://ww.visitwestranch.com

41 http://www.deerpark.org

42 Houghton, Dorothy Knox Howe, Interview 2002

43 "WESTFIELD, TX." *The Handbook of Texas Online*. <http://www.tsha.utexas.edu/handbook/online/articles/WW/htw6.html>

44 *Houston Chronicle*, February 23, 1949 & July 8, 1951

45 River Oaks Property Owners Association, Interview & Records

46 Field trip, 1959

47 Pace, Randy, Interview 2001

48 Pulleine, Imogene, e-mail 2002

49 *Handbook of Texas Online*, s.v. "," http://www.tshaonline.org/handbook/online/articles/WW/hfw1.html

50 "WHARTON, WILLIAM HARRIS." *The Handbook of Texas Online*. <http://www.tsha.utexas.edu/handbook/online/articles/view/WW/fwh8.html>

51 http://www.lib.udel.edu

52 Houghton, Dorothy Knox Howe, et al, *Houston's Forgotten Heritage: Landscape, Houses, Interiors, 1824-1914* (Rice University Press 1991), 32

53 Dawson, Dwight, e-mail 2008

54 Doolittle, Bill, *The Kentucky Derby: Run for the Roses* (Time Life Books 1998), 163

55 Webb, Walter Prescott, *The Hand Book of Texas* (Texas State Historical Assn. 1952), Vol. 2, 894

56 *Old Sixth Ward Reporter*, December, 1979, 2

57 Henson, Margaret Sweet, *The History of Baytown* (Bay Area Heritage Society 1986), 15-116

58 Field trip, 1959

59 *River Oaks Times*, September 10, 1948

60 *Handbook of Texas Online*, s.v. "," http://www.tshaonline.org/handbook/online/articles/WW/hrw83.html

61 http://www.sanjacinto-museum.org/veterans

62 www.annawilding.com/tennis/

63 Macon, N. Don, *Mr. John H. Freeman and Friends: A Story of the Texas Medical Center and How It Began* (Texas Medical Center 1973), 57-63

64 *Houston Chronicle*, December 24, 1983

65 "MONT BELVIEU, TX." *The Handbook of Texas Online*. <http://www.tsha.utexas.edu/handbook/online/articles/MM/hjm15.html>

66 Henson, Margaret Sweet, *The History of Baytown* (Bay Area Heritage Society 1986), 46-7

67 Webb, Walter Prescott, *The Hand Book of Texas* (Texas Historical Assn. 1952), Vol. 2, 915

68 http://www.co.harris.tx.us

69 *Handbook of Texas Online*, s.v. "," http://www.tshaonline.org/handbook/online/articles/NN/hln14.html

70 *Handbook of Texas Online*, s.v. "," http://www.tshaonline.org/handbook/online/articles/WW/hjw12.html

71 *Handbook of Texas Online*, s.v. "WILLOW, TX," http://www.tsha.utexas.edu/handbook/online/articles/WW/hvw56.html

72 "WILLOW, TX." *The Handbook of Texas Online*. <http://www.tsha.utexas.edu/handbook/online/articles/view/WW/hvw56.html>

73 "WILLOW CREEK." *The Handbook of Texas Online*. <http://www.tsha.utexas.edu/handbook/online/articles/view/WW/rbwas.html>

74 River Oaks Property Owners Association, Interview & Records

75 *Houston Chronicle*, June 8, 2003

76 Wallingford, Sharon, *Fort Bend County Texas: A Pictorial History* (Fort Bend Publishing Group 1996), 101-2

77 "WILSON, JAMES THEODORE DUDLEY." *The Handbook of Texas Online*. <http://www.tsha.utexas.edu/handbook/online/articles/view/WW/fwi54.html>

78 Garraty, John A. Editor, *Encyclopedia of American Biography* (Harper & Row 1974), 1214-7

79 Field trip, 1984

80 Field trip, 1959

81 "MONT BELVIEU, TX." *The Handbook of Texas Online*. <http://www.tsha.utexas.edu/handbook/online/articles/view/MM/hjm15.html>

82 Jard, Michael J., photograph of a sign at Winkler and Galveston Road, 2009

83 Baines, Mrs. W. M., *Houston's Part in the World War* (1919)

84 Field trip, 1973

85 Herridge, Karen, *Spring Branch Heritage* (Wakebrook Press 1998), 24

86 Daigle, Chris, e-mail 2006

87 Herridge, Karen, *Spring Branch Heritage* (Wakebrook Press 1998), 24

88 Pomeroy, C. David Jr., *Pasadena: The Early Years* (Pomerosa Press 1993), 30, 38

89 *Handbook of Texas Online*, s.v. "," http://www.tsha-online.org/handbook/online/articles/TT/hdt3.html

90 *Houston Post*, March 2, 1935

91 "THE WOODLANDS, TX." *The Handbook of Texas Online.* <http://www.tsha.utexas.edu/handbook/online/articles/view/TT/hltgl.html>

92 http://en.wikipedia.com

93 Detering, Deborah, Interview 2001

94 Miller, Mary Catherine Farrington, Interview 2001

95 www.skyscraper.org

96 "WOOSTER, TX." *The Handbook of Texas Online.* <http://www.tsha.utexas.edu/handbook/online/articles/view/WW/hvw68.html>

97 eclecticesoterica.com

98 http://www.accessgenealogy.com

99 "KATY, TX." *The Handbook of Texas Online.* <http://www.tsha.utexas.edu/handbook/online/articles/view/KK/hfk1.html>

100 Henson, Margaret Sweet, *The History of Baytown* (Bay Area Heritage Society 1986), 70

101 Houghton, Dorothy Knox Howe, et al, *Houston's Forgotten Heritage: Landscape, Houses, Interiors, 1824-1914* (Rice University Press 1991), 324

102 Texas Historical Marker, 103 Midway, Spring

103 http://www.wyattearp.net

104 www.andrewwyeth.com

105 http://www.katyprairie.org

X

1 *Encyclopedia Britannica* (1952), Volume 13, 837-8

Y

1 Agatha, Sister M., *The History of Houston Heights: 1891-1918* (Premier Publishing 1956), 18

2 *The American Heritage Dictionary of the English Language:* Third Edition (Houghton Mifflin Company 1992), 2,069.

3 Http://www.texgenweb2.org

4 http://www.ymcahouston.org/vic-coppinger/

5 Field trip, 2009

6 *Houston Post*, April 7, 1951

7 Texas Historical Marker, Humble Cemetery, S. Houston at Isaacks, Humble, erected 1992

Z

1 Kimball, Mary Holt, et al, *The Heritage of North Harris County* (American Association of University Women 1977), 58

2 *Handbook of Texas Online*, s.v. "," http://www.tshaonline.org/handbook/online/articles/fza04

3 Zindler, Marvin, e-mail 2001

4 http://www.ziontomball.org

5 *Houston Chronicle*, July 24, 1980

6 http://www.houstonzoo.org

7 Zuber, Harry, Interview 2005

SIDEBAR INDEX

LIST OF ILLUSTRATIONS & CREDITS